<u>Worlds Apart</u>
<u>Author: Jordan Simpson</u>

Worlds Apart

A World So Cold Universe, Volume 1

Jordan Simpson

Published by Jordan Simpson, 2024.

WORLDS APART

First edition. December 13, 2024.

ISBN: 979-8230871569

Written by Jordan Simpson.

To my Grandmother and Grandfather, thank you for believing in me.

Prologue – The Beginning – World So Cold

The roads that night was slick, the rain covering the ground like a wet blanket. Drake Miller, the man of the house, sat behind the wheel of his sleek black Toyota Corolla. Its once glossy exterior now obscured by the downpour, mirroring the darkness that seemed to envelop Drake's soul. His heart beat a hollow rhythm, shriveled like a cancerous tumor, pumping cold, coagulated blood through his veins. To Drake, family was nothing more than a disposable accessory, a steppingstone on his path to success. Raised on the belief that work and appearance were the keys to prosperity, he viewed his loved ones as expendable obstacles in his pursuit of wealth. That's not of course to say that he didn't love them. Of course he adored his family, Drake however was always taught that work was a priority. Anyone can be a husband, a loving father – but a real man always provided and to provide you need to succeed.

Beside him, his wife Linda Miller slept, her face illuminated by the soft glow of streetlights filtering through the rain-streaked windshield. Despite the turmoil within their relationship, there was a hint of compassion in Drake's heart towards her, buried beneath layers of indifference and neglect.

In the back seat, their son Harrison Miller lay asleep, exhausted from the warmth of the meal they had just shared. Drake glanced at him through the rear-view mirror, a flicker of hope igniting within him at the sight of his slumbering child.

As they navigated Cape Turn Road, a treacherous stretch known for its sharp bends and lack of guardrails along the coast of Bridgewater, Maine, Drake's thoughts drifted to the countless accidents that had occurred along its winding path. His own law firm had profited handsomely from the resulting lawsuits, a fact he conveniently chose to overlook in his pursuit of profit.

Suddenly, the tranquility of the night was shattered by the blare of a horn behind them. Drake glanced in his side mirror to see a car speeding towards them, its headlights piercing through the darkness like twin daggers.

"What the hell is this asshole doing?" Drake muttered under his breath, his grip tightening on the steering wheel.

The driver continued to tailgate them, laying on the horn and flashing their high beams in a display of reckless aggression. Drake rolled down his window and gestured for them to go around, but the driver showed no signs of backing off.

With a sickening jolt, the car slammed into the back of Drake's Corolla, sending it swerving out of control. Panic surged through Drake's veins as he fought to regain control of the vehicle, his wife stirring awake beside him.

"What's happening? What's going on?" Linda's voice was laced with fear as she looked around in confusion.

Before Drake could respond, the car behind them struck them again, sending them careening off the road and into the darkness below. The world spun in a dizzying blur as the car tumbled down the embankment, glass shattering and metal crunching with each impact.

Time seemed to slow to a crawl as Drake's mind raced with a thousand thoughts. His family's terrified screams echoed in his ears as the cold embrace of the river below loomed closer with each passing second.

Finally, with a bone-jarring thud, the car came to a rest, submerged in the murky waters below. Drake's head spun as he struggled to orient himself, shards of glass raining down around him.

With trembling hands, he reached for his seatbelt, his heart pounding in his chest. But before he could free himself, the airbag exploded into his face, dazing him with its force.

For a moment, he teetered on the brink of consciousness, his mind a whirlwind of confusion and fear. Then darkness descended, swallowing him whole as the icy waters of the river closed in around him.

Drake's consciousness ebbed and flowed in the darkness, his mind adrift in a sea of pain and confusion. He struggled to piece together the events that had led him to this moment, his thoughts fragmented and disjointed. He could have sworn the car that hit them stopped, the driver having gone out to observe the wreckage. There was something uncanny about the appearance of the watcher, if only he could remember the face. Was it male or was it female? Age? Race? All he could remember was that white robe. Before he lost total consciousness, he could have sworn he say Jesus standing on the embankment. But this was no savior.

Somewhere in the depths of his subconscious, he heard the faint sound of voices, distant and muffled as if coming from another world. Slowly, agonizingly, he clawed his way back to awareness, his senses gradually coming back into focus.

The steady beep of monitors filled the air, mingling with the hushed whispers of medical staff bustling around him. Drake's eyelids fluttered open, his vision blurred and unfocused as he tried to make sense of his surroundings.

He was lying in a hospital bed, surrounded by sterile white walls and the faint scent of antiseptic. Tubes snaked from his arms, connecting him to various machines that hummed softly in the background.

A figure approached him, their features obscured by the harsh glare of overhead lights. Drake squinted against the brightness, trying to discern their identity.

"Mr. Miller, can you hear me?" The voice was calm and measured, tinged with a hint of concern.

Drake nodded weakly, his throat raw and parched. "What... happened?" His words came out as a hoarse whisper, barely audible above the din of the room.

"You were in a car accident," the figure explained, their tone gentle yet firm. "You've been in a coma for three weeks."

The words hit Drake like a physical blow, sending a surge of panic coursing through his veins. Memories of the crash flooded back to him in a torrent of pain and fear, each detail etched into his mind like a searing brand.

"My family..." Drake's voice trailed off, his heart constricting with a sudden, overwhelming sense of dread. Suddenly that was all that mattered most. His family. But was he more concerned about there safety or his own image? Surely he wouldn't be the husband to a murdered son, or become the widow of the town.

The figure hesitated, their expression somber. "I'm sorry, Mr. Miller. Your wife... she didn't make it."

Drake felt as if the world had been ripped out from beneath him, leaving him adrift in a sea of grief and despair. His chest tightened with a suffocating sense of loss, tears stinging his eyes as he struggled to come to terms with the enormity of his pain.

"And... my son?" Drake's voice cracked, his words barely more than a whispered plea.

The figure hesitated once more, their gaze dropping to the floor. "I'm afraid he didn't survive the accident either."

A strangled cry tore from Drake's throat, raw and primal in its intensity. He felt as if he were being consumed by a black void, the weight of his grief crushing him beneath its merciless weight.

For days, Drake drifted in and out of consciousness, his mind consumed by visions of his lost loved ones. In his dreams, he saw them alive and whole, their laughter echoing through the corridors of his mind like a bittersweet melody.

But with each waking moment, the reality of his loss came crashing down upon him like a tidal wave, leaving him gasping for breath in its wake. He struggled to reconcile the fractured pieces of his shattered existence, clinging to the faint hope that somehow, someway, he might find a way to make sense of the senseless.

As the days turned into weeks, Drake's physical wounds began to heal, but the scars left by his ordeal ran far deeper than the surface of his skin. He sought solace in therapy and support groups, grappling with the enormity of his grief in the company of others who shared his pain.

Yet try as he might, Drake could not escape the specter of his past, the haunting memories of that fateful night forever etched into his soul. He would never forget the sound of tires screeching on wet pavement, the sickening crunch of metal on metal, the anguished cries of his family as their world came crashing down around them.

And as he lay in his hospital bed, surrounded by the sterile confines of the world he now inhabited, Drake knew that he would carry the weight of his loss with him for the rest of his days. But in the depths of his despair, he also found a flicker of hope, a glimmer of light amidst the darkness that threatened to consume him.

For even in his darkest hour, Drake knew that he was not alone. He had loved and been loved in return, and though his heart may be battered and bruised, it still beat with the rhythm of life, a testament to the resilience of the human spirit in the face of unimaginable tragedy.

As Drake lay in his hospital bed, grappling with the devastating loss of his wife and son, he found himself caught in a whirlwind of confusion and despair. Memories of the accident flooded his mind, each detail etched into his consciousness like shards of broken glass.

He remembered the sound of tires screeching on wet pavement, the sickening crunch of metal, the anguished cries of his family as their world came crashing down around them. And then, the suffocating darkness of unconsciousness, swallowing him whole as the icy waters of the river closed in around him.

But as he struggled to make sense of the chaos swirling within him, a nagging sense of unease gnawed at the edges of his consciousness. There was something missing, something he couldn't quite put his finger on—a void that echoed with the absence of his loved ones. But suddenly he could no longer keep his eyes – amazing, after three weeks he could still be so tired. He decided it was best to rest, maybe when he woke up, he would be in a better world, and leave this one long dead and buried.

When he finally awoke he pressed the call button to ring a nurse. Upon seeing he was awake the nurse went ahead and grabbed the attending doctor. This time Drake could see that the doctors' name tag read Dr. Lee. He was a hefty looking Asian man, late 40s same age as Drake he imagined.

"Good morning! I see we are finally awake again. Hopefully you'll be awake long enough to actually get some solids into your stomach today," chuckled Lee.

Drake had a sudden impulse. Was last night a nightmare. He had to ask, although he feared he knew the answer.

"My family... What about my family?" Drake's voice cracked with desperation, his heart pounding in his chest as he searched for answers.

"We will wheel your wife in to visit you momentarily," the doctor said, his voice tinged with sympathy.

But Drake's thoughts were consumed by a single, all-encompassing question. "What about my son? Where is he? Is he alright?"

The doctor's expression faltered, a shadow passing over his features. "I need you to try and relax, Mr. Miller. Any induced stress could cause harm to your body."

But Drake refused to be placated. "Tell me where my son is!" he demanded, his voice rising with desperation as he struggled against the IV tubes restraining him.

In response, the doctor motioned to the nurse, a silent signal to administer another dose of sedative. As the drug flowed into his veins, Drake felt his consciousness slipping away, his thoughts clouded by a haze of confusion and fear.

But even in his semi-conscious state, Drake clung to a glimmer of awareness, reaching out with trembling hands to grasp the fleeting tendrils of reality.

"What... happened to... my... son?" he slurred, his words slurred and disjointed as the sedative took hold.

The doctor's gaze softened, a flicker of sympathy passing through his eyes. "I'm sorry, but your son did not survive the accident."

A single tear slipped from Drake's eye, tracing a path down his cheek as darkness closed in around him once more, swallowing him whole.

When he awoke again, the monitors were beeping frantically, their shrill cries piercing the silence of the room. Panic surged through Drake's veins as he struggled to orient himself, his mind clouded by the fog of medication.

He begins to choke, and his hand reaches up to follow a tube along up to his mouth. They have him placed on life support again; he is panicking franticly trying to pull the tube out. The nurses and doctors come to his aid, removing it without tearing at his throat. He begins coughing, gasping for fresh air. "What happened? Did something happen to me last night?" He asks confused, just the other day he had awoken to find himself lying in a hospital bed and the news of his son's death had been the last thing he heard before he was induced back into a sleeping state.

The nurse exchanged a worried glance with the doctor, their expressions mirroring the concern etched into Drake's features. "You were in an accident," she said softly. "You've been in a coma for three weeks."

Drake's heart skipped a beat, the gravity of her words sinking in with a sickening sense of dread. "But... what about my family? Where is my wife?"

The nurse hesitated, her gaze faltering as she struggled to find the right words. " Calm Down. You're at Saint Montague Hospital. I'm sorry, Mr. Miller. Your wife... she didn't make it."

A wave of grief washed over Drake, threatening to engulf him in its relentless embrace. "And... my son?" he whispered, his voice barely more than a hoarse whisper.

As Drake lay in his hospital bed, the weight of his grief pressing down on him like a leaden blanket, he struggled to make sense of the bewildering reality unfolding around him.

The nurse's words echoed in his mind, each syllable laden with a profound sense of disbelief. "You were in an accident. You have been in a coma for three weeks. Your wife... she didn't make it."

But Drake couldn't reconcile her explanation with the vivid memories that haunted his dreams—memories of waking up, of speaking with doctors and nurses, of grappling with the devastating news of his family's fate. But surely they told him earlier that his wife was alive, or was that a dream. He needed to know.

The nurses look around confused, calling for Dr. Harmon. The doctor comes in and they address him of the situation. "Where is Dr. Lee? I need to speak to Dr. Lee."

The doctor tries to calm him down. "There is no Doctor Lee at this hospital. You must be confused about you whereabouts. You're at the Saint..."

"I know I'm at the Saint Montague Hospital. I know where I'm at. I was told yesterday when I awoke that I had been in an accident, and I demand to know what happened." He interrupts the doctor before he can finish what he has to say.

"You never awoke yesterday because today was your first day waking up. You are lucky to even be here today. That was quite an accident you had."

"Where is Linda? I want to speak with my wife." He begins to scream and shout. The doctor gives him a somber look and places his hand on his shoulder.

"I'm sorry, but your wife never survived the accident."

Drake begins to break down and cry, screaming as his son is wheeled around the corner and into his room. He stares at his son in disbelief; he is looking at a ghost.

"No, you are not supposed to be here! You died; it was supposed to be you who died."

Days pass as Drake lies in his hospital bed resting from his injuries. He spends most of his time receiving cat scans for additional brain injuries. For days he has been between two worlds, one he cannot explain. He spends the day trying to rebuild his relationship with his son, explaining that it was a terrible dream he had, that he never meant to hurt him. But when he sleeps, he awakes within a similar world, yet entirely different. Instead of his son being alive it is now his wife, everyday he wakes up and must deal with the loss of a loved one. He can never have them in his arms at the same time. The doctors assure him that there is nothing wrong; this could be a result of Post Traumatic Stress Disorder and anxiety. He is informed to come back in for multiple checkups and to receive additional medical treatment if his visions and memory loss become too severe. He signs his medical charts and release forms, and leaves. Once he arrives home, he admires the family portrait on the wall. It is the one time they were all happy together.

"First thing tomorrow I'm having the petition signed and sent in. Nobody else needs to be hurt on that road." He tries to embrace his wife, but she pulls away.

"What is the point, it won't bring back our son." She says walking away leaving him standing all by himself, his hands shaking.

"He's not dead. He's still alive." She turns toward him, eyes red, but she has no more tears to cry.

"Please do not rip this family apart anymore then what it already is. Let him go."

Within the next two weeks Drake attends two funerals, a parent should never have to outlive their spouse and child. The emotional strain takes a toll on him. He seeks grieving counselling with his wife. He learns to move on with his losses, in his mind his wife and son are separate, but still very much alive and well to him. This is what his father and mother were always smiling about; it was not the money that mattered, but family. Someone to care for and love, because love is all a person will ever need. Drake may not know what his condition is, but he knows he must live with it for the rest of his life. He can never have his family back together in his arms. This is what he deserves for being a greedy businessman, and it cost him his family. There is no heaven awaiting men like him, only the depths of hell that would drive a man to insanity.

Crash and Awakening

1 - 2

The acrid stench of burnt rubber assaulted Drake's nostrils as he blinked awake, disoriented. Raindrops pelted the shattered windshield, each impact like a hammer blow to his throbbing skull. He tried to move but found himself pinned, the steering wheel crushing his chest.

"Linda? Harrison?" Drake's voice came out as a raspy whisper. No response.

Panic clawed at his throat as he turned his head, ignoring the searing pain in his neck. In the passenger seat, Linda's golden hair was matted with blood, her face deathly pale in the dim light. Harrison lay slumped in the back, unnaturally still.

God, no. Not them. Please, not them.

Drake's mind raced, the relentless lawyer in him already cataloging details, searching for a solution. The car had flipped, ending up on its side. The smell of gasoline hung heavy in the air.

We need to get out. Now.

"Linda, honey, wake up," Drake pleaded, reaching out with a trembling hand to touch her face. "Harrison, buddy, can you hear me?"

Silence answered him, broken only by the steady patter of rain and the distant wail of sirens.

Drake's breath came in ragged gasps as he fought against the crushing weight of the steering column. "Come on, come on," he muttered through gritted teeth, channeling every ounce of his determination into freeing himself.

A sudden spark of pain shot through his leg as he shifted, eliciting a strangled cry. Drake glanced down, his stomach churning at the sight of a jagged piece of metal protruding from his thigh.

I can't let them down. Not now. Not like this.

With a primal roar, Drake pushed against the steering wheel, ignoring the agony that threatened to overwhelm him. Inch by excruciating inch, he managed to create enough space to slip free.

"Hold on, Linda. Hold on, Harrison," he gasped, reaching for his wife's seatbelt with trembling fingers. "I'm getting us out of here. I promise."

As Drake worked frantically to free his family, a grim realization settled over him. This moment, this crucible of twisted metal and shattered glass, would define him far more than any courtroom victory ever could.

3 - 4

Dr. Lee's voice drifted through the haze of Drake's memory, soft yet penetrating. "So, tell me how it works."

Drake blinked, his mind reeling as he tried to reconcile the vivid crash scene with the present moment. He ran a hand through his disheveled hair, wincing as his fingers brushed against a tender spot on his scalp.

"I... I don't know," he stammered, his voice hoarse. "One moment I'm there, in the car, and the next..." Drake trailed off, his eyes darting around the room as if searching for an anchor in reality.

As he struggled to form coherent thoughts, a flood of images cascaded through his mind. The gleaming brass nameplate on his office door at Miller & Co. The endless nights poring over case files, fueled by ambition and black coffee. The fierce satisfaction of winning a high-stakes trial, followed by the hollow ache of missed family dinners.

"I see the firm," Drake continued, his words tumbling out faster now. "God, I worked so hard to build it. Every waking moment was about the next big case, the next client."

He leaned forward, elbows on his knees, head in his hands. "I remember the day we landed the Hartley account. It was huge, career-defining. But I also remember..."

Drake's voice caught in his throat. "I remember the look on Linda's face when I missed Harrison's school play. Again."

Dr. Lee's pen scratched softly against his notepad. "And how does that make you feel now, Drake?"

Drake looked up, his eyes haunted. "Like I've been chasing the wrong things all along. But doc, how can I fix it if I can't even tell what's real anymore?"

5 - 6

Drake's words hung in the air, heavy with regret and uncertainty. As if in response to his troubled state, the scene around him shifted, melting away into a new setting.

The harsh fluorescent lights of his memories faded, replaced by a soft, welcoming glow. Drake found himself standing at the entrance of Dr. Lee's office, the warm atmosphere a stark contrast to the cold, competitive world of his law firm.

He blinked, taking in the soothing neutral tones of the walls and the carefully curated artwork. A painting of a single-horned creature – a xiezhi, he recalled from his studies of Eastern mythology – caught his eye. Its piercing gaze seemed to look right through him, as if judging his very soul.

"Mr. Miller?" a gentle voice called out, snapping Drake back to the present moment.

He turned to see a friendly receptionist smiling at him from behind a polished wooden desk. "Dr. Lee will be with you shortly," she said, her voice harmonizing with the soft instrumental music playing in the background.

Drake nodded; his throat tight. "Thank you," he managed, his voice barely above a whisper.

As he approached the desk, he couldn't help but notice the stark organization – neat stacks of files, a pristine computer monitor. It was a far cry from the controlled chaos of his own office.

"This is real," Drake thought to himself, running his hand along the smooth surface of the desk. "Or is it? God, I can't even tell anymore."

He glanced at the receptionist, who was now busily typing away. "Excuse me," he said, his voice stronger now. "Can I ask you something?"

She looked up, her smile unwavering. "Of course, Mr. Miller. What can I help you with?"

Drake hesitated, then asked, "How long have I been coming here? To see Dr. Lee, I mean."

The receptionist's brow furrowed slightly, a flicker of concern crossing her face. "I'm sorry, Mr. Miller, but I'm not at liberty to discuss patient information. Perhaps that's a question best addressed with Dr. Lee during your session?"

Drake nodded, feeling a chill run down his spine despite the warmth of the office. "Right, of course. I'll do that. Thank you."

As he turned away, his mind raced. "Even here, in this place of calm, I can't escape the uncertainty," he thought. "What if this is just another layer of illusion? What if Dr. Lee isn't real either?"

The soft music continued to play, a soothing counterpoint to the turmoil in Drake's mind as he waited for his session to begin.

7 - 8

Drake sank into one of the plush chairs lining the waiting area, the soft fabric enveloping him like a comforting embrace. He ran his fingers over the sleek coffee table, stacked neatly with an array of magazines and informational brochures. His eyes darted to the large windows, where sunlight streamed in, illuminating the serene garden outside.

"It's beautiful, isn't it?" Linda's gentle voice startled him. She had settled into the chair beside him, her long wavy hair catching the light.

Drake nodded, his voice heavy with emotion. "Yeah, it is. Almost too perfect."

He glanced at his wife, noting the mix of warmth and sorrow in her eyes. "Linda, do you ever feel like... like this isn't quite real?"

She reached out, squeezing his hand. "Drake, honey, we're here to help you work through these feelings. Remember what Dr. Lee said about grounding yourself in the present?"

Drake's gaze drifted to the small nook near the reception desk, where a water dispenser stood next to a vibrant potted plant. "I know, I know. It's just..." He trailed off, lost in thought.

"What is it?" Linda prompted gently.

He leaned in, lowering his voice. "Sometimes I close my eyes here, and when I open them, I'm back in that mangled car, or in my office with Vega, talking about conspiracies. How do I know which reality is true?"

Linda's eyes glistened with unshed tears. "Oh, Drake. We're here, now. This is real. Focus on that."

As Drake nodded, trying to take comfort in her words, he couldn't shake the nagging feeling that something was off. The peaceful atmosphere of the waiting room seemed to mock his internal turmoil, a stark contrast to the chaos of his fractured memories.

9 - 10

Drake's fingers brushed against the cold metal handle of the examination room door; his reflection distorted in its polished surface. He paused, taking a deep breath before pushing it open.

The hallway stretched before him, a sterile expanse of gleaming tiles and fluorescent lights. Each step echoed softly as he moved forward, his eyes scanning the nameplates on the doors. "Dr. Charles Lee, Psychiatrist," one read, causing a flutter of anxiety in his stomach.

"You okay?" Linda's voice came from behind him, her hand gently touching his back.

Drake nodded, not trusting his voice. His mind raced, trying to reconcile the pristine corridor with flashes of twisted metal and screeching tires. He shook his head, attempting to dispel the intrusive memories.

"It's just up ahead," Linda said, guiding him towards the last door on the right.

As they entered Dr. Lee's examination room, Drake was struck by the contrast between its professional atmosphere and the turmoil in his mind. Soft, warm lighting bathed the space in a comforting glow, while plush chairs invited relaxation. Medical charts and diagrams adorned the walls, their complex illustrations a stark reminder of the intricacies of the human mind.

"This equipment," Drake murmured, eyeing the state-of-the-art computer terminal and diagnostic tools. "It's so advanced. Almost like..."

"Like what, honey?" Linda asked, settling into one of the chairs.

Drake swallowed hard. "Like something from another world. Or timeline. I can't shake the feeling that this isn't where I'm supposed to be."

Linda's face fell, a mixture of concern and frustration crossing her features. "Drake, we've talked about this. Dr. Lee is here to help you sort through these feelings."

"I know, I know," Drake sighed, running a hand through his hair. "But what if he can't? What if I'm right, and there's more to this than just... mental health?"

The door opened, and Dr. Lee entered with a warm smile. "Good afternoon, Mr. and Mrs. Miller. How are we feeling today?"

Drake met the doctor's kind gaze, his own eyes filled with a desperate plea for understanding. "Doctor, I need to know. How can I tell which reality is real?"

11 - 12

Dr. Lee sits across from Drake, his fingers hovering over the keyboard of his sleek computer. The soft tapping of keys fills the room as he takes notes, his eyes flicking between the screen and Drake's face. The gentle hum of medical equipment in the background seems to amplify the tension in the air.

Drake shifts uncomfortably in the plush white chair, the leather creaking beneath him. His gaze darts around the room, taking in the medical charts and diagrams that suddenly feel alien and threatening. He clenches and unclenches his fists, trying to ground himself in this reality that feels increasingly tenuous.

"I don't know," Drake finally blurts out, his voice strained. "I close my eyes. I open them. Just like you." He pauses, his mind racing. Is this really happening? Or am I still trapped in that mangled car, dreaming all of this?

Dr. Lee's fingers pause over the keyboard, his expression softening with empathy. "Can you elaborate on that, Drake? What do you mean by 'just like you'?"

Drake leans forward, elbows on his knees, hands clasped tightly. "I mean, it's supposed to be simple, right? We all do it. Close our eyes, open them. But for me, it's like flipping a switch between two different worlds. Two different lives. And I can't tell which one is real anymore."

The weight of his words hangs heavy in the air, and Drake can feel his heart pounding in his chest. He desperately searches Dr. Lee's face for any sign of understanding, any indication that he's not losing his mind.

"Sometimes," Drake continues, his voice barely above a whisper, "I wonder if I ever really woke up from that crash at all."

13 - 14

Dr. Lee's eyes lift from the computer screen, his gaze meeting Drake's with a mixture of concern and professional curiosity. The soft click of keys falls silent as he focuses his full attention on his patient.

"Very well. You're back to work?" Dr. Lee asks, his voice gentle yet probing.

Drake's stomach tightens at the question. He runs a hand through his disheveled hair, buying time as memories of his law firm's sleek offices and bustling corridors flash through his mind. The familiar weight of his briefcase, the scent of leather and coffee, the constant hum of phones and printers – it all feels so tangible, yet so impossibly distant.

"Yes," Drake finally responds, his voice barely above a whisper. "Though it feels like a lifetime ago."

He shifts in the chair, the plush upholstery suddenly feeling too soft, too unreal. Is this a dream, or is the office? Drake's thoughts race, trying to reconcile the two realities competing for dominance in his mind.

"It's strange," he continues, more to himself than to Dr. Lee. "I can remember every detail of my office, every case file on my desk. But when I'm there, it's like I'm watching myself from the outside. Like I'm playing a role in someone else's life."

Dr. Lee nods slowly, his expression unreadable. "And how does that make you feel, Drake?"

Drake's hands clench involuntarily. "Terrified," he admits. "Because I don't know which version of me is real anymore."

15 - 16

The acrid smell of burnt rubber assaults Drake's nostrils as he pushes through the throng of onlookers. Flashing red and blue lights paint the scene in an eerie, pulsating glow. His eyes dart between the mangled wreckage and the faces of the crowd, searching for... what? Answers? Absolution?

"Excuse me," he mutters, shouldering past a gawking couple. His mind races, juggling thoughts of depositions and client meetings with the gnawing fear that this crash scene is more than just a random accident.

Suddenly, a firm hand grips his shoulder. Drake whirls around, coming face to face with Richard Vega, his new partner. Vega's usually immaculate appearance is disheveled, his tie askew and a sheen of sweat on his brow.

"Drake," Vega says, his voice low and urgent. "We need to talk. There's more to this accident than meets the eye."

Drake's stomach churns. His thoughts back to the wreckage, then to Vega's intense gaze. "What do you mean?" he asks, fighting to keep his voice steady.

Vega leans in closer, his breath hot on Drake's ear. "Not here. Too many eyes and ears. But trust me, this isn't just about a car losing control. It's got to be about the Parker case."

Drake's blood runs cold. The Parker case – their biggest yet, with stakes higher than he'd ever dared to imagine. Could it really be connected to this chaos?

"How can you be sure?" Drake whispers, his mind reeling.

Vega's eyes dart around nervously. "Just watch your back."

As Vega melts back into the crowd, Drake stands frozen, the cacophony of sirens and murmuring spectators fading to a dull roar in his ears. He stares at the twisted metal of the crash, a chill running down his spine as he wonders: is this the price of success, or something far more sinister?

17 - 18

Dr. Lee's voice fades in, pulling Drake from the vivid memory. "And they've got you working with a partner?"

The question hangs in the air, heavy with implication. Drake shifts in his chair, the plush upholstery suddenly feeling too soft, too comfortable for the weight of his thoughts. He looks up at Dr. Lee, taking in the psychiatrist's calm demeanor, his kind eyes behind wire-rimmed glasses.

"Yes, Vega," Drake responds, his voice tight. "He's new, but he's eager to prove himself." He pauses, considering his next words carefully. "Maybe a little too eager."

Dr. Lee leans forward slightly, his pen poised over his notepad. "How so?"

Drake's mind races, flashing back to Vega's intensity at the crash site. "He's... intense. Always pushing, always digging." His fingers drum nervously on the armrest. "Sometimes I wonder if he's digging too deep."

"And how does that make you feel?" Dr. Lee's voice is gentle, probing.

Drake lets out a mirthless chuckle. "Honestly? Paranoid. Like I'm constantly looking over my shoulder." He runs a hand through his hair, disheveling it. "Is this normal, Doc? To feel this way about a partner?"

Dr. Lee's expression remains neutral, but his eyes soften with understanding. "In high-stress professions, it's not uncommon to experience heightened anxiety, especially when working closely with new individuals." He pauses, allowing his words to sink in. "Perhaps we should explore why Vega's eagerness unsettles you so much."

Drake nods slowly, his gaze drifting to the window. Outside, the trees of Henderson sway gently in the breeze, a stark contrast to the turmoil in his mind. He takes a deep breath, steeling himself for the uncomfortable introspection ahead.

19 - 20

Drake's eyes flick open, the sterile white of Dr. Lee's office fading away as he finds himself back at his desk in Miller & Co. The bustling sounds of the law firm filter through his closed office door - phones ringing, muffled conversations, the rhythmic tapping of keyboards. He glances down at the mountain of paperwork before him, each document a potential landmine of legal intricacies.

His gaze drifts to the framed accolades lining the walls, testaments to his professional triumphs. A bitter smile tugs at his lips. "What good are you now?" he mutters under his breath, the weight of his fractured reality pressing down on him.

Drake's fingers tap an anxious rhythm on his mahogany desk as he contemplates the duality of his existence. In one world, Linda's absence leaves an aching void; in the other, Harrison's loss is a constant, gnawing pain. He closes his eyes, trying to center himself.

"Get it together, Miller," he whispers harshly, running a hand through his disheveled hair. The polished exterior of success feels like a thin veneer, barely concealing the chaos beneath.

A soft knock at the door jolts him from his thoughts. "Come in," he calls, straightening his tie and adopting a mask of composure.

His secretary, Sarah, pokes her head in. "Mr. Miller, your 3 o'clock's here. And Mr. Vega left another message about those files."

Drake nods, his jaw tightening at the mention of Vega. "Thank you, Sarah. I'll be right out."

As Sarah closes the door, Dr. Lee's voice echoes in his mind: "And are you okay?"

Drake pauses, his hand on the doorknob. Am I okay? he wonders, the question reverberating through his conflicted psyche. With a deep breath, he squares his shoulders and steps out into the office, ready to face another day of navigating the treacherous waters of his dual existence.

21 - 21

Drake's eyes scan the bustling office, the familiarity of it all suddenly feeling alien. He turns to Dr. Lee, his gaze unfocused, as if looking through the psychiatrist rather than at him.

"I'm fine," Drake says, his voice low and gravelly. He pauses, weighing his next words carefully. The memory of his gleaming office fades, replaced by the sterile walls of Dr. Lee's room. "But this world... is not what it seems."

His fingers grip the armrests of the white upholstered chair, knuckles turning white. The scent of Linda's perfume, a phantom from another reality, drifts through his consciousness.

"Every day, I wake up not knowing which life I'll be living," Drake continues, his words tinged with a mix of frustration and bewilderment. "In one, I'm grieving Linda. In the other, it's Harrison. How can both be real?"

He leans forward, eyes now laser-focused on Dr. Lee. "I was so caught up in winning cases, in being the best. Now, I'm caught between two lives, and I can't seem to win in either."

Drake's mind races, recalling the piles of paperwork on his desk, the accolades that once meant everything. Now, they feel hollow, meaningless in the face of his fractured reality.

"Doctor," he says, his voice barely above a whisper, "what if this isn't just grief or trauma? What if there's something more... something we're all missing?"

Fractured Shadows

The sunlight filtering through the venetian blinds' casts striped shadows across Dr. Lee's office, the alternating bands of light and dark mirroring Drake Miller's fractured existence. He shifts uncomfortably in the plush leather chair, his fingers tracing the worn armrests as he avoids meeting the doctor's compassionate gaze.

Dr. Lee leans forward, his kind eyes searching Drake's face. "So, tell me how this works," he prompts gently, his voice carrying a soothing timbre that seems to fill the room.

Drake's throat constricts, the weight of his dual realities pressing down on him. He swallows hard, buying time as he struggles to find the right words. How can he explain something he barely understands himself?

"I don't know," Drake finally admits, his voice barely above a whisper. He runs a hand through his disheveled hair, acutely aware of how unkempt he must appear. The grief and confusion of the past weeks had taken their toll, etching new lines around his tired eyes.

As the silence stretches between them, Drake's mind wanders. One moment, he's a lawyer mourning his son. The next, he's a cop grieving his wife. Both realities feel equally vivid, equally painful. Which one is real? Or are they both fabrications of a fractured psyche?

Dr. Lee's calm voice breaks through his spiraling thoughts. "It's okay not to have all the answers, Drake. This process takes time."

Drake nods, grateful for the doctor's patience. He takes a deep breath, steeling himself to share more. "It's like... living two lives simultaneously. In one, I've lost Harrison. In the other, Linda's gone. And I can't... I can't tell which one is real."

As he speaks, Drake's hands clench into fists, his knuckles turning white with the effort of maintaining composure. He wants desperately to make sense of it all, to find an anchor in the storm of his conflicting realities.

Drake leans back in his chair, the leather creaking softly beneath him. His gaze drifts to the window, where the late afternoon sun casts long shadows across the city skyline. He feels the weight of Dr. Lee's expectant silence, waiting for him to continue.

"I close my eyes," Drake says, his voice low and strained. As he speaks, he does just that, shutting out the world around him. In the darkness behind his eyelids, he sees flashes of both realities - Linda's smile, Harrison's laugh. The memories blur together, a kaleidoscope of joy and pain.

His breath catches in his throat as he forces himself to continue. "I open them. Same as you." Drake's eyes snap open, meeting Dr. Lee's steady gaze. "But when I do, I never know which world I'll be in. Which loved one I'll have lost."

The confession hangs heavy in the air between them. Drake's hands tremble slightly as he grips the armrests of his chair, anchoring himself to this moment, this reality.

"It's exhausting," he admits, his voice barely above a whisper. "Living with this constant uncertainty. Never knowing if I'm grieving the right person, if I'm living the right life."

Dr. Lee leans forward, his brow furrowed in concentration. "And how does that make you feel, Drake? This constant shifting between realities?"

Drake lets out a bitter laugh. "How does it make me feel? Torn apart. Guilty. Like I'm betraying one of them every time I wake up in the other world." He pauses, swallowing hard against the lump in his throat. "And terrified. Terrified that one day, I'll open my eyes and they'll both be gone."

The solemn tolling of St. Michael's Cathedral bells pierces the air, each resonant peal a mournful reminder of why they've gathered. Drake Miller stands rigid among the sea of black-clad mourners, his gaze fixed on the ornate wooden casket at the front of the church. White roses drape the polished surface, their pristine petals a stark contrast to the darkness consuming his heart.

Sunlight filters through stained glass windows, casting vibrant hues across the marble floor. The kaleidoscope of colors feels like a cruel mockery of the life extinguished too soon. Drake's eyes trace the patterns, desperate for any distraction from the reality before him.

"He was so young," Linda whispers beside him, her voice cracking with emotion. "Our beautiful boy."

Drake's throat constricts, words failing him. He reaches for Linda's hand, intertwining their fingers. The warmth of her touch grounds him, a lifeline in the tumultuous sea of grief.

"I keep thinking this is just another nightmare," he finally manages, his voice low and rough. "That I'll wake up and he'll be..."

He trails off, unable to finish the thought. The weight of Harrison's absence crushes down on him, threatening to steal the very air from his lungs.

As the minister begins to speak, Drake's mind drifts. He sees Harrison's mischievous grin, hears the echo of his laughter. The memories are so vivid, so real, that for a moment, he questions which reality is true.

Is this the world where I've lost my son? Or will I blink and find myself in a universe where Linda is gone instead?

The uncertainty gnaws at him, a constant companion in his fractured existence. Drake closes his eyes, willing the conflicting realities to merge, to make sense. But when he opens them again, the harsh truth remains unchanged. Harrison's casket looms before him, a testament to the cruel finality of death in this world.

7 - 8

The minister's solemn voice cuts through Drake's tumultuous thoughts. "Ashes to ashes, dust to dust."

Drake feels his heart constrict, each word a dagger piercing his soul. He stares at the casket, its polished surface gleaming under the cathedral's lights. The white roses adorning it seem to mock the darkness consuming him.

"We now lay Harrison Miller to rest," the minister continues, "a life extinguished far too soon."

Linda's grip on Drake's hand tightens, her quiet sobs echoing in his ears. He wants to comfort her, but finds himself paralyzed, caught between grief and disbelief.

Is this real? Drake wonders, his mind reeling. Or will I wake up to find Harrison alive and Linda gone?

"He had so much life ahead of him," Drake murmurs, his voice barely audible. "So many dreams..."

Linda turns to him, her blue eyes swimming with tears. "We have to remember the joy he brought us, Drake. It's what he would want."

Drake nods mechanically, but inside, he's screaming. How can I accept this when I've seen him alive in another world? The duality of his existence threatens to tear him apart.

As the congregation begins to move, Drake remains rooted to the spot, his gaze fixed on the casket. In this moment, he silently vows to uncover the truth behind his fractured reality, no matter the cost.

9 - 10

The casket begins its slow descent into the earth, each inch deepening the chasm in Drake's heart. The hollow thud of dirt hitting wood reverberates through the air, a sound so final it makes Drake's stomach lurch.

"This can't be happening," Drake whispers, his voice choked with emotion. He runs a trembling hand through his disheveled hair, his tired eyes never leaving the casket.

Linda squeezes his arm. "We'll get through this together, Drake."

But Drake barely hears her, his mind spiraling. How can I grieve when I'm not sure which reality is true? The weight of his dual existence presses down on him, threatening to crush his sanity.

Suddenly, the cathedral fills with the ethereal voices of the choir. Their haunting melody washes over Drake, and for a moment, he's transported back to the night of the crash. The screeching of tires, the shattering of glass, the sickening crunch of metal – it all comes flooding back with vivid clarity.

"No," Drake mutters, his eyes squeezing shut. "Not now."

But the memories persist, as does the choir's somber hymn. In his mind's eye, Drake sees the twisted wreckage, feels the icy grip of fear as he searches for his family. The conflicting images of Harrison – both alive and lifeless – battle for dominance in his psyche.

"Drake?" Linda's concerned voice breaks through his reverie. "Are you alright?"

He opens his eyes, forcing a weak smile. "Just... remembering," he manages, the words tasting bitter on his tongue.

As the choir's voices swell to a crescendo, Drake finds himself torn between the crushing grief of this moment and the maddening uncertainty of his fractured reality. He clenches his fists, a newfound determination rising within him.

I will find the truth, he vows silently. For Harrison, for Linda, for my sanity. No matter which world is real, I won't rest until I uncover what's really going on.

11 - 12

Drake blinks rapidly, trying to clear the tears that have begun to blur his vision. The choir's voices reach a fever pitch, their harmonies soaring through the cathedral's vaulted ceiling. He feels as though he's drowning in a sea of grief and confusion.

"I can't..." he whispers, his voice breaking. "I can't bear this."

Linda's hand squeezes his shoulder gently. "We're in this together," she murmurs, her voice barely audible above the music.

Drake turns to look at her, struck by the depth of love and sorrow in her blue eyes. For a moment, he's overwhelmed by the conflicting realities warring in his mind. In one, Linda stands beside him, a pillar of strength. In the other...

No, he thinks fiercely. I can't think about that now.

"How do we move forward from this?" he asks, his voice raw with emotion.

Linda's lips curve into a sad smile. "One day at a time," she replies, her fingers intertwining with his. "We'll honor Harrison's memory by living the lives he'd want for us."

As the choir's song begins to fade, Drake feels a strange sense of resolve settling over him. He may not understand the dual realities he's experiencing, but he knows one thing for certain: he won't let his family down again, in this world or any other.

13 - 14

Drake Miller rises from the polished wooden pew, his legs unsteady beneath him. The weight of grief presses down on his shoulders as he joins the solemn procession moving towards the church exit. Linda's hand remains firmly clasped in his, anchoring him to this reality.

As they step out into the fading sunlight, Drake squints, the golden rays casting long shadows across the graveyard. The procession moves silently towards the freshly dug grave where Harrison will be laid to rest.

"This isn't right," Drake mutters, his voice barely above a whisper. "He was so young, so full of life."

Linda squeezes his hand. "I know, darling. I know."

As they approach the grave, Drake's mind reels. Just two weeks ago, he stood in this very spot, watching as Linda's casket was lowered into the ground. Harrison had been by his side then, both of them shattered by the loss. But now...

"How is this possible?" Drake thinks, his brow furrowing. The dual realities he's been experiencing clash violently in his mind.

The minister's voice cuts through his thoughts. "We commit Harrison Miller's body to the ground, earth to earth, ashes to ashes, dust to dust."

Drake watches, numb, as the casket is lowered. The finality of it threatens to overwhelm him.

"Dr. Lee says this is the only reality," he thinks. "But it feels so real when I'm with Harrison in the other world. How can I reconcile this?"

As the first shovelful of earth hits the casket, Drake makes a silent vow. "I'll find out what's happening, son. I promise you that. I'll find justice for you, in this world or any other."

15 - 16

The golden rays of morning sunlight filter through the curtains, casting a warm glow across Drake Miller's bedroom. He stirs, his eyes fluttering open to meet the new day. For a fleeting moment, there's peace. Then reality crashes down, heavy as lead.

Drake sits up slowly, his heart constricting as memories of Harrison flood his mind. The laughter, the mischievous glint in his son's eyes, the dreams left unfulfilled - all gone now. He runs a hand through his disheveled hair, feeling every bit the broken man he's become.

The door creaks open, and Linda enters. Her blonde hair catches the light, and her blue eyes shine with a mix of love and sorrow. She offers Drake a gentle smile, a lifeline in his sea of grief.

"Good morning, darling," she says, her voice soft and comforting. "How did you sleep?"

Drake swallows hard, torn between the urge to cling to Linda's presence and the gnawing doubt about which reality is true. "I... I'm not sure," he admits, his voice rough with emotion. "It's all so confusing, Linda. One moment I'm here with you, and the next..."

He trails off, unable to voice the impossible duality he's experiencing. How could he explain that in another world, it was Linda who was gone, and Harrison who lived?

Linda sits on the edge of the bed, taking Drake's hand in hers. "It's okay, love. We're here together. That's what matters."

Drake nods, but his mind races. "Is this real?" he wonders silently. "Or am I losing my grip on sanity?" The weight of his dual existence presses down on him, threatening to crush his spirit entirely.

17 - 18

Drake forces a smile, his eyes betraying the pain he feels deep inside. "As well as can be expected," he replies, his voice tinged with sadness. He squeezes Linda's hand, drawing strength from her touch.

As the day unfolds, Drake moves through familiar routines with a sense of detachment. He showers, dresses for work, and sips coffee in the kitchen, all while his mind drifts back to the accident. The screeching tires, shattering glass, and Harrison's final cry echo in his thoughts.

"I should have been there," he thinks, guilt gnawing at him. "If I hadn't been working late that night..."

Linda's voice cuts through his reverie. "Don't forget your briefcase, dear."

Drake nods, grateful for her steady presence. "Thanks, darling. I don't know what I'd do without you."

As he drives to his law office, the streets of Bridgewater blur past. Students hurry to class, the scent of coffee wafts from cafes, but Drake barely notices. His mind replays memories of Harrison – his laugh, his mischievous grin, the way his curls would never stay tamed.

At a stoplight, Drake closes his eyes. "Is this my punishment?" he wonders. "For always choosing work over family?"

The honk of a car behind him jolts Drake back to reality. He drives on, the weight of grief threatening to overwhelm him.

19 - 20

As night falls, Drake wearily climbs into bed, his body heavy with exhaustion. He closes his eyes, willing sleep to come, but instead feels a strange shift in the air around him. When he opens his eyes again, the world has changed.

The bedroom is different - darker, colder. Drake's heart races as he realizes Linda's side of the bed is empty, the sheets untouched. Panic rises in his throat as he stumbles out of bed, calling out, "Linda? Linda, where are you?"

Suddenly, a familiar voice cuts through the darkness. "Dad? What's wrong?"

Drake whirls around to see Harrison standing in the doorway, his curly hair tousled from sleep, eyes wide with concern. The sight of his son, alive and well, sends a jolt of both joy and confusion through Drake's body.

"Harrison?" Drake whispers, his voice trembling. "You're... you're here?"

Harrison steps closer, brow furrowed. "Of course I'm here, Dad. Where else would I be?"

Drake's mind reels as he tries to make sense of this new reality. He reaches out, touching Harrison's shoulder, feeling the solid warmth beneath his fingers. "I... I had a dream. A nightmare. You were..."

"Dad, it's okay," Harrison interrupts, his tone unexpectedly mature. "I'm here. But... Mom isn't."

The words hit Drake like a physical blow. He staggers back, memories flooding in - a different accident, a different loss. Linda's absence suddenly feels painfully real, a gaping void in his heart.

"How can this be happening?" Drake thinks, his chest tight with anguish. "How can I lose them both, yet have them both?"

Aloud, he manages to say, "I'm sorry, Harrison. I didn't mean to wake you. Go back to bed, son."

As Harrison retreats, Drake sinks to the floor, his back against the bed. He buries his face in his hands, torn between relief at seeing his son and devastating grief for Linda.

"What's happening to me?" he whispers into the darkness, feeling utterly lost between two realities, each painfully real, each missing a crucial piece of his heart.

21 - 22

Drake rises slowly, his legs unsteady as he makes his way to the living room. The soft glow of early morning light filters through the curtains, casting long shadows across the floor. He pauses at the mantel, his eyes drawn to a framed photograph of Linda in her white wedding dress, her smile radiant and full of life.

"I miss you," he whispers, his fingers tracing the outline of her face. A bittersweet warmth spreads through his chest as he recalls their last anniversary dinner, her laughter echoing in his memory.

Harrison's voice breaks through his reverie. "Dad, you okay?"

Drake turns to see his son leaning against the doorframe, concern etched on his young face. For a moment, the sight of Harrison alive and well overwhelms him with joy.

"Yeah, buddy. I'm okay," Drake manages, his voice thick with emotion. "Just... remembering your mom."

Harrison moves closer, his eyes reflecting a wisdom beyond his years. "Tell me about her? Something I might not remember?"

Drake hesitates, then smiles softly. "Did I ever tell you about the time she tried to bake me a birthday cake? It was a disaster, but we laughed so hard..."

As Drake recounts the story, he feels a flicker of happiness amidst the sorrow. Harrison's laughter, so similar to Linda's, fills the room, and for a brief moment, the weight on Drake's shoulders lifts.

But even as he cherishes this moment with his son, a nagging thought persists in the back of his mind. "This can't last," he thinks, his smile fading. "I have to figure out what's real, what really happened that night. But how can I choose between them?"

Drake swallows hard, pushing the thought aside for now. He focuses on Harrison's smile, determined to savor this precious time with his son, real or not.

23 - 24

Dr. Lee's gentle voice cuts through Drake's tumultuous thoughts. "You do realize that the other reality isn't real, don't you, Drake?"

Drake blinks, suddenly aware of his surroundings. He's back in Dr. Lee's office, the familiar scent of leather and old books grounding him in this version of reality. He runs a hand through his disheveled hair, his tired eyes meeting Dr. Lee's compassionate gaze.

"I... I know you keep saying that, Dr. Lee," Drake responds, his voice tinged with frustration and confusion. "But it feels so real. How can I be a lawyer here, living the life I've always known, minus Harrison... and then in the other world, everything's so vivid, so surreal? My son's alive, but Linda..." His voice breaks, unable to finish the sentence.

Dr. Lee leans forward, his kind eyes reflecting understanding. "What you're experiencing is often referred to as 'dual reality' or 'dual consciousness.' It's a complex psychological phenomenon where an individual experiences two distinct realities, each with its own set of circumstances and outcomes."

Drake nods slowly, having heard this explanation before. He glances out the window, watching the old oak trees sway in the eastern breeze of Bridgewater. The familiar sight both comforts and unsettles him.

"But how do I know which one is real?" Drake asks, his voice barely above a whisper. "They both feel so..."

Suddenly, a memory flashes in Drake's mind. He sees another office, starkly different from Dr. Lee's warm, inviting space. In it sits a stoic young man with piercing eyes.

"Dr. Harmon," Drake mutters, his brow furrowing.

"I'm sorry?" Dr. Lee inquires, tilting his head.

Drake looks back at Dr. Lee, a chill running down his spine. "I just remembered... in the other reality, there's another doctor. Dr. Harmon. He's younger, Caucasian, mid-thirties. And he... he tells me the exact same things you do. Word for word."

Dr. Lee's expression remains neutral, but Drake notices a flicker of something—concern? Surprise?—in his eyes.

"That's... interesting," Dr. Lee says carefully. "What do you make of that, Drake?"

Drake leans back in his chair, his mind racing. "I don't know. It's like... it's like you're both reading from the same script. But how is that possible?"

As he grapples with this realization, Drake can't shake the feeling that he's on the verge of uncovering something crucial. But what? And at what cost?

25 - 26

The crisp smell of freshly pressed uniforms and gun oil fills Drake's nostrils as he steps into the bustling Bridgewater police station. Fluorescent lights hum overhead, casting harsh shadows across the faces of officers hurrying past. Drake's hand instinctively moves to adjust a tie that isn't there, his body still caught between realities.

"Miller!" A sharp voice cuts through the noise. Holly Keirstead strides towards him, her dark hair pulled back in a tight ponytail, eyes scanning him with a mix of concern and determination. "You're early."

Drake nods, trying to mask his disorientation. "Thought I'd get a head start," he manages, the words feeling foreign on his tongue.

Holly's piercing gaze softens slightly. "Look, I know you're eager to jump back in, but..." She lowers her voice, leaning in closer. "Are you sure you're fit for duty?"

The question hangs in the air, heavy with implication. Drake's mind races, torn between the instincts of a lawyer and the newfound muscle memory of a cop. He swallows hard, fighting back the urge to confess his confusion.

"I'm fine," he asserts, more to convince himself than Holly. "Just need to get back into the swing of things."

As Holly begins to brief him on their current case, Drake's thoughts drift. How can this feel so real when just moments ago he was sitting in Dr. Lee's office? The weight of the badge on his chest, the familiar-yet-unfamiliar faces around him – it all seems tangible, present. Yet a part of him still longs for the courtroom, for the life he once knew.

"Drake?" Holly's voice snaps him back to attention. "You with me?"

He nods, forcing a smile. "Yeah, sorry. Just... processing."

27 - 28

Drake's fingers trace the outline of his badge, the cool metal grounding him in this surreal reality. "I know I'm not at a hundred percent," he admits, his voice low and tinged with conflict. "But if this is real, if I'm really a cop..." He pauses, the weight of his next words heavy on his tongue. "I could use these skills to find out what happened to Linda."

The bustling precinct fades into the background as Drake's mind races with possibilities. He could access police databases, interview witnesses, piece together the puzzle of his fractured existence. But as he contemplates this course of action, doubt creeps in like a shadowy intruder.

"What if this isn't real?" he thinks, his heart rate quickening. "What if I'm jeopardizing my time with Harrison for a wild goose chase?"

Suddenly, the voices of Dr. Harmon and Dr. Lee seem to echo in his mind, overlapping and indistinguishable: "And they've got you working with a partner?"

Drake blinks hard, trying to shake off the disorienting sensation. He focuses on Holly, her presence a lifeline in this sea of uncertainty.

"Yeah," he responds, unsure which doctor he's answering. "They thought it best to ease me back in."

Holly raises an eyebrow, clearly picking up on his distracted state. "Drake, if you need more time—"

"No," he interrupts, perhaps too forcefully. He softens his tone. "No, I need this. I need to be doing something, anything to make sense of... everything."

As he speaks, Drake can't help but wonder if he's trying to convince Holly or himself. The weight of his dual existence presses down on him, a constant reminder of the impossible choice he faces: pursuit of truth or precious moments with loved ones lost and found.

29 - 30

Drake's mind races, struggling to keep the two realities separate yet interconnected. He takes a deep breath, steadying himself before responding to the lingering question about his partner.

"New guy, Vega," he says, his voice carrying a hint of uncertainty. The name feels foreign on his tongue, a detail from a life he's not sure he's lived.

In the same breath, as if speaking to an unseen presence, Drake adds, "New girl Kierstead." His eyes flick to Holly, gauging her reaction. She furrows her brow, clearly noticing the discrepancy.

Drake's heart pounds as he realizes his mistake. He's answered both realities simultaneously, the lines blurring dangerously. Sweat beads on his forehead as he tries to backpedal.

"Sorry, I meant Kierstead. You, Holly," he stammers, forcing a weak smile. "Still getting my bearings, you know?"

Holly's piercing gaze softens slightly, but Drake can see the concern etched in her features. He wonders if she suspects something more than just post-accident confusion.

"Drake," Holly says, her voice low and measured, "are you sure you're ready for this? There's no shame in taking more time."

As she speaks, Drake's mind drifts. He sees flashes of case files, of late nights poring over evidence. But are these memories real, or fabrications of a fractured psyche? The weight of his dual existence presses down on him, threatening to crush him under its impossible burden.

31 - 32

Drake's throat tightens as he processes Holly's concern. He runs a hand through his hair, feeling the weight of both realities pressing down on him. The precinct bustles around them, a cacophony of ringing phones and shuffling papers that only serves to heighten his disorientation.

"They just want someone to hold my hand until they know I'm okay," Drake mutters, his voice tinged with a mixture of frustration and resignation. He leans against his desk, the cool metal grounding him momentarily in this version of reality.

As the words leave his mouth, the scene before him flickers. For a brief, dizzying moment, he's no longer in the police station but in Dr. Lee's office, the psychologist's kind eyes studying him intently. Then, just as quickly, he's back with Holly, her worried expression mirroring the one he'd seen on Dr. Lee's face.

"And are you okay?" The question comes simultaneously from Dr. Lee's gentle, empathetic tone and Dr. Harmon's more direct, probing voice. The dual voices echo in Drake's mind, blending and overlapping until he can't distinguish which reality they're coming from.

Drake blinks hard, trying to focus on Holly's face, to anchor himself in this moment. But the question lingers, unanswered, as he grapples with the impossible task of defining "okay" when his entire existence feels fractured and uncertain.

33 - 33

"Yes," Drake responds, the word falling from his lips with a hollow certainty that fails to convince even himself. He runs his fingers through his disheveled hair, a nervous habit that betrays the turmoil churning beneath his composed exterior.

Holly leans in, her brow furrowed with concern. "You sure about that, Miller? You look like you've seen a ghost."

Drake forces a weak smile, his mind racing to reconcile the overlapping realities. "Just tired," he offers, his voice low and gravelly. "Still adjusting to being back on the job."

As he speaks, his gaze drifts to the bustling bullpen beyond his desk. Officers move with purpose, their actions a stark reminder of the life he's supposed to be living here. Yet, in his mind's eye, he sees the sleek office of a high-powered lawyer – his other self, his other life.

"Maybe I should take you up on that coffee offer," Drake says, hoping the familiar routine might help ground him in this reality. He stands, his movements slightly unsteady, as if his body isn't quite sure which world it belongs to.

Holly nods, relief washing over her face. "Good idea. I know just the place."

As they walk towards the precinct exit, Drake's thoughts wander. *How long can I keep this up?* he wonders silently. *How long before someone realizes I'm living two lives, mourning two losses, being torn apart by grief and confusion?*

The warm Bridgewater sun hits his face as they step outside, momentarily blinding him. For a split second, he's not sure which version of himself will emerge when he opens his eyes again.

Green World

Green World – 2024

1 - 2

The neon glow of the bar sign flickers, casting an eerie red haze over the chaos below. Detective Drake Miller squints against the assault of flashing police lights, his tired eyes struggling to focus on the cab before him. The stale smell of booze with the unmistakable copper tang of blood, turning his stomach.

"Jesus," Drake mutters, running a hand through his disheveled hair. He can't shake the feeling that he's been here before, caught in some twisted déjà vu. The yellow police tape flutters in the night breeze, a stark boundary between the mundane and the macabre.

Beside him, Holly Kierstead's brow furrows as she flips through her notes. The rookie detective's intensity is palpable, her sharp eyes darting between the wreckage and her notepad.

"What've we got, Kierstead?" Drake asks, his voice gravelly from lack of sleep.

Holly's response is crisp and professional. "Male victim, mid-forties. Cab driver. Obvious signs of—"

Her words fade as Drake's mind wanders. He sees himself in his car, hears the screech of tires, feels the struggle. No, that's not right. He wasn't here. Was he?

"Detective Miller?" Holly's voice cuts through the fog. "Are you alright?"

Drake blinks, forcing himself back to the present. "Yeah, just... thinking." He gestures towards the bar. "Any witnesses come forward?"

As Holly briefs him on the witness situation, Drake can't shake the nagging feeling that this case is more than it seems. The cacophony of the crime scene fades to white noise as he stares at the gleaming metal of the cab, a chill running down his spine.

This isn't just another case, he realizes. This is a piece of the puzzle – his puzzle. The key to understanding the fractured reality he's been living in. With renewed focus, Drake turns back to Holly, determined to uncover the truth hidden within this tragic tableau.

3 - 4

Holly Kierstead's eyes narrow as she gestures towards the cab, her voice tinged with a mix of confusion and determination. "So... the driver picked up a fare downtown, registered this address with dispatch." She points to the cab's GPS device, its screen still glowing in the darkness. "Um, he's still got his wallet, and there's a twenty on the seat beside him, so I think not only was it not a robbery, it looks like the fare was actually paid."

Drake Miller's brow furrows as he processes this information. Something doesn't add up, and he can feel the familiar tug of a mystery unraveling in his mind. Why would someone pay for a ride only to...? He shakes his head, pushing away the intrusive thoughts that threaten to cloud his judgment.

"Witnesses?" Drake asks, his voice low and gravelly. He scans the crowd gathered behind the police tape, searching for any signs of someone who might have seen more than they're letting on.

As he waits for Holly's response, Drake can't shake the feeling that this case is somehow connected to his own fractured existence. The pieces are there, just out of reach, like a half-remembered dream. He clenches his fist, frustrated by the gaps in his memory and the nagging sense that he's missing something crucial.

5 - 6

Holly Kierstead nods, her piercing eyes sweeping across the chaotic scene. The flashing lights paint her determined face in alternating hues of red and blue as she spots what she's looking for. With a sharp gesture, she summons an officer who's escorting a witness – a gaunt man wrapped in a knit cap, his face etched with worry.

Drake watches Holly's efficient movements, a mix of admiration and curiosity stirring within him. She's young, eager, but there's a raw talent there that he can't deny. As the witness approaches, Drake finds himself wondering about the story behind Holly's rapid rise through the ranks.

"Okay, so I've interviewed about thirty," Holly reports, her voice crisp and professional. "Basically, everybody came out of the bar when it happened. But this guy lives in the apartment building above it, saw from his window."

Drake's mind races, processing the information. A witness from above – that could change everything. He glances at the looming apartment building, its windows like dark eyes staring down at the crime scene. What secrets did those walls hold?

"Good work, Kierstead," Drake murmurs, his tone gruff but appreciative. He turns his attention to the witness, studying the man's nervous demeanor. Something about the witness's anxious energy reminds Drake of the mythical xiezhi – a creature said to discern truth from lies. If only solving this case were as simple as having a magical beast point out the guilty party.

As Holly prepares to question the witness further, Drake steels himself for what's to come. This case is far from over, and he can feel the weight of it settling on his shoulders like a familiar, if unwelcome, burden.

7 - 8

The witness steps forward, his thin frame trembling slightly as if buffeted by an unseen wind. Drake watches intently, noting the man's fidgeting hands and darting eyes. There's fear there, but also something else - a nervous energy that sets Drake's instincts on edge.

"After I heard the commotion," the witness begins, his voice quavering, "I looked out, saw a man in a mask jump in a car and take off that way?" He points with a shaky finger down the dimly lit street.

Drake's mind races, piecing together the fragmented information. A masked man fleeing the scene - it fits the pattern of other recent crimes, but something feels off. He can't shake the nagging feeling that there's more to this story.

"Did you get a good look at the car?" Drake asks, his voice low and gravelly. "Make, model, color - anything stand out?"

The witness shakes his head, his eyes wide with anxiety. "It all happened so fast. I just... I couldn't..."

Drake nods, understanding the witness's distress. He's seen it countless times before - the shock of witnessing a violent crime often clouds the memory, leaving only fragments behind. But those fragments could be crucial.

As Holly continues questioning the witness, Drake's gaze drifts back to the crime scene. The yellow police tape flutters in the night breeze, a stark reminder of the violence that has shattered the peace of this neighborhood. He can't help but wonder how many more lives will be upended before they catch this killer.

9 - 10

Holly gently touches the witness's arm, her voice soft but firm. "Thank you for your help. We appreciate your cooperation." She watches as the man shuffles away, his shoulders hunched against the weight of what he's seen.

Turning back to Drake, Holly's expression hardens, her eyes glinting with determination in the harsh glare of the crime scene lights. "Detective Miller," she says, her tone clipped and professional, "I've got a rundown of the witness statements."

Drake nods, his attention fully on his partner. He admires Holly's efficiency, the way she hit the ground running on this case. It reminds him of himself, years ago, before the job started to wear him down.

"Go ahead, Kierstead," he prompts, his voice low and gravelly.

Holly takes a deep breath, her brow furrowing as she delivers her report. "Exact same report from the bar witnesses, just a little more chaos on the ground. Guy in a mask running away, but no one close and no one who claims to have seen what happened."

Drake's mind whirs, processing the information. It's frustratingly vague, yet oddly specific. A masked man, chaos, but no direct witnesses. It doesn't add up. He can feel the weight of the case settling on his shoulders, a familiar burden that both exhausts and energizes him.

"No one saw anything specific?" he asks, his tone skeptical. "In a crowded bar area?"

Holly shakes her head, her short dark hair swaying with the movement. "It's like they all saw the same thing, but through a fog. I can't shake the feeling that we're missing something crucial."

Drake nods, understanding her frustration. It mirrors his own. "Keep digging, Kierstead. There's more here than meets the eye. I can feel it."

11 - 12

Drake's eyes scan the crime scene, searching for any detail they might have missed. The neon lights from the nearby bar cast an eerie glow on the wet pavement, creating a surreal atmosphere that only heightens his unease. His gaze settles on a nearby building, its facade illuminated by flickering streetlights.

The gears in his mind start turning, years of experience kicking in. He can almost hear Linda's voice in his head, urging him to look deeper, to find the clues others might miss. It's a bittersweet reminder of the life he's lost - or perhaps the life he's still fighting to save.

"Building looks like it's got a secured front door," Drake muses aloud, his voice a low rumble that cuts through the ambient noise of the crime scene. He turns to Kierstead, a glimmer of hope in his tired eyes. "Let's see if they've got a camera on it. Might have caught something we can use."

As he speaks, Drake can't help but think of Harrison. Would his son be proud of him, piecing together clues like this? Or would he see it as just another example of his father choosing work over family? The thought sends a pang of guilt through his chest, but he pushes it aside. This case could be the key to understanding his fractured reality, to finding a way back to his family - both versions of it.

"Good thinking, sir," Kierstead responds, her eagerness evident in her voice. "I'll get on that right away."

Drake nods, grateful for her enthusiasm. It reminds him of his younger self, before the weight of two realities began to crush him. "Let's move quickly," he adds, his tone urgent. "Every minute counts in a case like this."

13 - 14

Kierstead nods, her sharp eyes gleaming with admiration as she watches Miller take charge. The flickering neon from the nearby bar casts an eerie glow across her face, highlighting the determination etched in her features. She falls into step beside him, her footsteps echoing on the pavement as they approach the building.

"You've got good instincts, Miller," she says, her voice low and respectful. "I can see why they brought you in on this case."

Drake's mind races, cataloging every detail of the scene around them. The acrid smell of burnt rubber from the screeching cars going by, the muffled chatter of witnesses, the oppressive weight of the night pressing down on them. He feels the familiar tug of two realities vying for dominance in his mind, but he pushes it aside, focusing on the task at hand.

"Instincts are just the start," he replies, his voice gruff. "It's the legwork that solves cases. And right now, that camera might be our best lead."

As they reach the building's entrance, Drake's gaze locks onto the security camera mounted above the door. He can't shake the feeling that whatever it captured might be the key to unraveling this mystery – and perhaps his own fractured existence.

Kierstead's expression softens, a mixture of gratitude and resolve evident in her eyes as she absorbs Miller's words. She nods slowly, acknowledging the weight of the situation. "I'm ready to put in the hours, sir. Whatever it takes to crack this case."

Drake feels a surge of appreciation for his young partner's dedication. It reminds him of his own early days on the force, before the lines between realities blurred. He allows himself a small, grim smile. "Good. Because I have a feeling this is just the beginning of a very long night."

15 - 16

Kierstead hesitates, her fingers fidgeting with the edges of her notepad. The flickering neon from the bar casts an eerie glow across her face, accentuating the nervous tension in her eyes.

"Well, I-I-I been meaning to thank you, sir," she stammers, her usual confident demeanor faltering. "I been passed over for detective, twice, before this assignment, so I'm pretty sure I'd still be in uniform if you hadn't requested me."

Drake's brow furrows, a mixture of confusion and irritation crossing his features. He feels a familiar tug at the back of his mind, as if another version of himself is trying to surface. He pushes it down, focusing on the present.

"I didn't request anyone," he says flatly, his tired eyes scanning the crime scene. "If you got promoted, it has nothing to do with me. They probably didn't want to waste anyone else's time baby-sitting me."

As the words leave his mouth, Drake winces inwardly. He hadn't meant to sound so harsh, but the weight of his dual realities and the gruesome scene before them had frayed his nerves. He wonders briefly how his other self would have handled this moment – the version who still had a wife waiting at home. Would he have been kinder, more patient?

Kierstead's face falls slightly, but she quickly composes herself, straightening her shoulders. Drake admires her resilience, recognizing a familiar determination in her eyes. It reminds him of Harrison, always bouncing back from setbacks with unwavering optimism.

"Right," Kierstead nods, her voice steadier now. "Of course, sir. I appreciate the honesty."

Drake sighs, running a hand through his disheveled hair. "Look, Kierstead," he begins, his tone softening slightly, "you're here because you earned it. Don't let anyone, including me, make you think otherwise."

17 - 18

Kierstead's posture shifts, her spine straightening as a newfound resolve settles over her features. Drake observes the transformation, noting how she seems to grow taller, more assured in the flickering neon light of the crime scene. He's reminded of Harrison's determined stance when tackling a challenging homework assignment, and a pang of longing for his son's presence tugs at his heart.

"Now, go check the camera," Drake instructs, his voice gruff but not unkind. He watches as Kierstead nods sharply, her eyes gleaming with purpose.

As she turns to leave, Drake finds himself caught in a moment of introspection. He wonders if this is how he used to mentor young lawyers in his previous life, before the accident that shattered his reality. The thought brings a bitter taste to his mouth, and he swallows hard, pushing the memory aside.

"Kierstead," he calls out suddenly, causing her to pause mid-step. "Remember, details matter. Every frame could be crucial."

She turns back, a hint of a smile playing at the corners of her mouth. "I won't let you down, sir," she assures him before striding purposefully towards the building.

Drake watches her go, his mind racing. 'What would Linda say about this case?' he muses, the ghost of his wife's presence a constant ache in this reality. He shakes his head, refocusing on the task at hand. The night air feels heavy with secrets, and as he surveys the chaotic scene around him, Drake can't shake the feeling that this is just the beginning of something much larger and far more sinister.

19 - 20

The echo of Kierstead's determined footsteps fades into the night, leaving Drake alone with his thoughts amidst the chaotic crime scene. He runs a hand through his disheveled hair, his tired eyes scanning the area one last time. The yellow police tape flutters in the breeze, a stark reminder of the tragedy that unfolded here.

As Drake turns to face the cab once more, a familiar voice reverberates through his mind, clear and analytical.

"And then what?" Dr. Harmon's words slice through the ambient noise of the crime scene, causing Drake to flinch involuntarily.

Drake closes his eyes, his brow furrowing as he grapples with the psychiatrist's probing question. "Then... I keep digging," he mutters under his breath, his voice barely audible. "I follow every lead, no matter how small."

He opens his eyes, his gaze fixed on the cab's rain smeared windshield. The glass reflects the flickering neon lights from the nearby bar, creating a kaleidoscope of colors that dance across like a fractured surface. It reminds Drake of the broken pieces of his own life, each shard a fragment of a reality he's struggling to piece together.

"But what if the truth isn't what you expect, Drake?" Dr. Harmon's voice persists in his mind, challenging and relentless. "Are you prepared for where this path might lead?"

Drake clenches his jaw, his hands balling into fists at his sides. "I have to be," he whispers, his voice thick with determination and a hint of fear. "For Linda... for Harrison... I need to understand what's happening to me, to us."

As he stands there, caught between the physical world of the crime scene and the internal landscape of his fractured psyche, Drake feels the weight of responsibility settle heavily upon his shoulders. He knows that every decision, every clue, could be the key to unlocking the mystery of his existence – or the trigger that sends him spiraling further into the abyss.

21 - 22

Drake's feet carry him away from the crime scene, his mind a whirlwind of conflicting thoughts and emotions. The city streets blur past as he drives home, the case files scattered on the passenger seat a constant reminder of the mystery that now consumes his life.

"I go home," Drake mutters to himself, gripping the steering wheel tighter. "But the case stays with me, haunting my thoughts as I try to make sense of the world I've been thrust into."

As he pulls into his driveway, the modest suburban home looms before him, a silent sentinel in the dim glow of the streetlights. Drake steps out of the car, his eyes scanning the neatly trimmed lawn, a stark contrast to the chaos swirling in his mind.

The porch creaks beneath his feet as he approaches the front door, the familiar sound both comforting and unsettling. It's as if the house itself is speaking to him, whispering secrets of a life he's struggling to remember.

Drake pauses, his hand on the doorknob. "Which version of my family waits for me on the other side?" he wonders, his heart racing. "Linda or Harrison? Which loss am I reliving tonight?"

Taking a deep breath, he pushes the door open, bracing himself for whichever reality greets him. The weight of his dual existence presses down on him, a constant reminder of the fractured world he now inhabits.

23 - 24

As Drake steps inside, the warmth of the house envelops him, a stark contrast to the cool night air. The soft glow of lamps bathes the living room in a gentle light, illuminating the plush sofas and the coffee table adorned with family photos. His eyes linger on a picture of Linda and Harrison, their smiles frozen in time, mocking the uncertainty of his current reality.

"Home sweet home," Drake murmurs, his voice tinged with a mixture of comfort and unease. He moves towards the fireplace, where flames dance and cast flickering shadows across the walls. The crackling wood provides a soothing background noise, yet it does little to quiet the tumultuous thoughts in his mind.

As he sinks into the familiar embrace of his favorite armchair, Drake can't shake the feeling of déjà vu that washes over him. Every trinket, every worn spot on the rug, every scuff on the wall seems to hold a memory he can't quite grasp.

"It's like I'm caught in a loop," he thinks, running a hand through his disheveled hair. "Every night, I come home to this... but which home is real?"

His gaze drifts to the hallway leading to the bedrooms. The silence of the house weighs heavily on him, amplifying the absence of either Linda's soothing presence or Harrison's energetic chatter.

"Linda?" he calls out hesitantly, his voice barely above a whisper. "Harrison?" The lack of response sends a chill down his spine, despite the warmth of the room.

Drake leans forward, elbows on his knees, head in his hands. "What am I missing?" he mutters, frustration evident in his tone. "There has to be a connection, a way to make sense of all this."

As he sits there, surrounded by the comforting familiarity of his home yet feeling utterly lost, Drake can't help but wonder if he'll ever truly find his way back to the life he once knew.

25 - 26

Drake rises from his chair, his muscles aching from the long night at the crime scene. He moves towards the kitchen, drawn by a sliver of light peeking from beneath the door. As he pushes it open, the scene before him tugs at his heart.

Harrison sits hunched over the kitchen table, his curly hair a disheveled mess. The boy's face is illuminated by the soft glow of a desk lamp, casting long shadows across the scattered papers and open textbook before him. Despite the late hour, Harrison's brow is furrowed in intense concentration, his pen tapping rhythmically against the edge of the table.

Drake pauses in the doorway, drinking in the sight of his son. A bittersweet ache fills his chest as he considers the parallel world where this moment doesn't exist.

"Hey there, champ," Drake says softly, his voice rough with fatigue. "Burning the midnight oil, I see?"

As he speaks, Drake can't help but wonder, "Is this real? Or just another fragment of a life I'm desperately trying to piece together?" The weight of his dual existence presses down on him, threatening to overwhelm the warmth of this simple, domestic scene.

27 - 28

Harrison looks up, startled by his father's voice. A tired smile tugs at the corners of his lips as he pushes his glasses up his nose, the gesture so familiar it makes Drake's heart ache.

"Hey, Dad," Harrison says, his voice a mix of exhaustion and typical teenage cockiness. "Yeah, just trying to get through this history assignment. It's due tomorrow."

Drake studies his son's face, noting the dark circles under his eyes and the slight slump of his shoulders. He feels a pang of guilt, wondering how many nights Harrison has stayed up late, struggling alone while he was out chasing ghosts and shadows.

"History, huh?" Drake muses, fighting the urge to ruffle Harrison's unruly hair. "What's the topic?"

As Harrison launches into an explanation, Drake's mind wanders. He thinks about the crime scene he just left, the flickering neon lights of Bridgewater's bustling nightlife contrasting sharply with the quiet domesticity of this moment. He wonders how he can reconcile these two worlds – the gritty reality of his work and the warm, if fragile, sanctuary of his home.

Harrison's voice brings him back to the present. "...and that's why I'm stuck on this part about World War II. It's just so complex, you know?"

Drake nods, realizing that in many ways, his son's struggle with history mirrors his own battle to make sense of his fractured reality.

29 - 30

Drake crosses the room, his footsteps muffled by the worn carpet. He stands behind Harrison, peering over his son's shoulder at the open textbook. The pages are a maze of dense text and grainy black-and-white photos, a stark contrast to the vibrant world outside their window where Oak trees sway in the breeze.

"World War II, huh?" Drake says his voice softening as he studies the familiar yet distant look of concentration on Harrison's face. "That's a tough one. Mind if I give you a hand?"

As he speaks, Drake feels a familiar tug of guilt. How many times had he been too busy, too preoccupied with work to offer help? The weight of missed opportunities presses down on him, mingling with the exhaustion from the night's crime scene.

Harrison shifts in his chair, his pen tapping rhythmically against the edge of the textbook. Drake notices the slight hesitation in his son's posture, a reminder of the distance that's grown between them.

"You sure, Dad?" Harrison asks, his tone a mix of hope and skepticism. "I mean, it's pretty late, and I know you've had a long day."

Drake places a gentle hand on Harrison's shoulder, feeling the warmth of connection seep through his fingers. He pushes away thoughts of the cab driver, the masked suspect, the lingering questions from the crime scene. Right now, in this moment, his son needs him.

"I'm sure," Drake replies, pulling up a chair next to Harrison. "Besides, a little history might be just what I need to clear my head."

As he settles in beside his son, Drake can't help but wonder how many more chances like this he'll have. In the back of his mind, Dr. Harmon's voice echoes, reminding him of the fragility of this reality. But for now, he pushes those thoughts aside, focusing on the present, on being the father he always wanted to be.

31 - 32

Harrison grins, relief washing over his features at the offer of assistance from his father. The tension in his shoulders visibly eases, and his bright eyes light up with a mixture of gratitude and excitement.

"That'd be great, Dad. Thanks," Harrison says, his voice carrying that familiar blend of teenage cockiness and genuine appreciation. He runs a hand through his unruly curls, a habit Drake recognizes as a sign of his son's focus shifting into gear.

Drake feels a warmth spread through his chest, a stark contrast to the chill of the crime scene that still clings to his bones. He leans in, scanning the open textbook, the scent of fresh ink and paper mingling with the lingering aroma of Harrison's favorite snack - microwave popcorn.

*I've missed this, * Drake thinks, a pang of regret twisting in his gut. *How many nights have I let slip by, too caught up in my own demons to be here for him? *

Harrison's pen hovers over his notebook as he asks, "So, what do you know about the Manhattan Project? It's like, this whole secret part of the war that nobody talks about in the movies."

Drake chuckles, the sound feeling foreign in his throat after the grim events of the evening. "Well, champ, that's because it was one of the best-kept secrets of the entire war. But let me tell you, it changed everything..."

As Drake begins to explain, he can't help but marvel at the eager light in Harrison's eyes, the way his son leans in, hanging on every word. For a moment, the horrors of his job fade away, replaced by the simple joy of connecting with his child over the pages of history.

33 - 33

Drake's voice grows animated as he delves into the subject, his earlier weariness momentarily forgotten. "The Manhattan Project was all about developing the atomic bomb. It brought together some of the brightest minds in science, working in complete secrecy."

Harrison nods, scribbling furiously in his notebook. "That's intense. Did they know how destructive it would be?"

A shadow flickers across Drake's face, his mind briefly flashing to the devastation he's witnessed in his line of work. "Not entirely. They were pushing the boundaries of what was possible, Harrison. Sometimes, we don't fully understand the consequences of our actions until it's too late."

*Just like me, * Drake thinks, a familiar guilt gnawing at him. *Always chasing the next case, never realizing what I was losing at home. *

Harrison looks up, his brow furrowed. "Dad? You, okay?"

Drake forces a smile, pushing aside his dark thoughts. "Yeah, just thinking about the weight of history. You know, decisions that change the world."

"Like the ones you make every day?" Harrison asks, a hint of pride in his voice.

Drake's heart swells, even as a part of him aches. *If only you knew, son. If only you knew. *

"My decisions aren't quite that monumental," Drake says softly, ruffling Harrison's hair. "But they matter. Just like your schoolwork matters. Now, let's get back to this assignment, shall we?"

As they bend their heads together over the textbook once more, Drake savors this moment of peace, knowing all too well how fleeting such moments can be in his fractured reality.

What Will Tomorrow Bring

Green World – 2024

1 - 1

Miller's weary body sank into the mattress, the cool sheets a stark contrast to his feverish skin. He pulled the covers up to his chest, his fingers trembling slightly as they clutched the fabric. The bedroom was bathed in shadows, mirroring the darkness that swirled within his mind.

As he teetered on the edge of consciousness, the day's events flickered through his thoughts like a fragmented film reel. The weight of the police badge in his pocket, the unfamiliar weight of the gun at his hip. The lies that spilled from his lips with practiced ease.

"Just another day on the job," he had told his colleagues, forcing a smile that didn't quite reach his eyes.

Miller's heart clenched as he recalled Harrison's laughter echoing through the house earlier that evening. His son's curly hair had been a mess, his bright eyes sparkling with mischief as he recounted his day at school.

"Dad, you won't believe what happened in science class today!" Harrison had exclaimed, his words tumbling out in excited bursts.

Now, lying in the darkness, Miller savored the memory, knowing it was just that – a memory. Tomorrow, Harrison would be gone, replaced by the cold reality of his son's death.

"I can't keep living like this," Miller whispered into the empty room, his voice cracking. "Linda deserves to know the truth."

He imagined Linda's face, her blonde hair framing those expressive blue eyes that seemed to see right through him. How would she react to learning about the dual lives he'd been leading? The thought made his stomach churn.

Miller's eyelids grew heavy, sleep tugging at the edges of his consciousness. "Tomorrow," he murmured, the word both a promise and a prayer. "I'll tell her everything tomorrow."

As he drifted off, Miller's last coherent thought was of the life he'd left behind – the ruthless lawyer who would do anything to win a case. That Drake Miller seemed like a stranger now, a ghost from another lifetime.

The room fell silent, save for the soft sound of Miller's breathing as he succumbed to exhaustion. In sleep, his face relaxed, the lines of worry momentarily smoothed away. For a few precious hours, he would be free from the weight of his fractured existence, suspended between two realities that threatened to tear him apart.

Blue World

Blue World – 2024

1 - 2

Drake Miller's hand trembled as he turned the cold brass doorknob, stepping into a house that was both achingly familiar and jarringly foreign. The manicured lawn outside had mocked him with its pristine appearance, a stark contrast to the wilted roses that drooped lifelessly in the garden beds. Each step on the porch had elicited a mournful creak, as if the very wood beneath his feet shared in his grief.

"Hello?" he called out, his voice echoing in the emptiness. No response came.

Drake's eyes darted around the dimly lit living room, taking in the glaring absences. Where cherished family photos once hung, only vacant frames remained, their emptiness a cruel reminder of what had been lost. The fireplace, once a gathering spot for warm family moments, now sat cold and lifeless.

This can't be real, he thought, his lawyer's mind desperately searching for a rational explanation. *There has to be some mistake.*

He moved further into the room, his fingers trailing along the dusty mantle. "Linda?" he called again, hoping against hope to hear her voice.

The silence that answered was deafening.

Drake's gaze fell upon Harrison's favorite chair, now pushed into a corner as if to hide the pain of its emptiness. A lump formed in his throat as memories of his son's laughter flooded his mind.

"I'm sorry," he whispered to the empty room, his voice breaking. "I should have paid closer attention to the roads. I should have protected you."

The weight of his guilt threatened to crush him. How many times had he chosen work over family? How many moments had he missed, thinking there would always be more time?

Drake sank to his knees, overwhelmed by the emptiness surrounding him. This house, once filled with love and life, now felt like a tomb – a monument to all he had lost.

"Please," he pleaded to no one and everyone, "let this be a nightmare. Let me wake up."

But as the shadows lengthened and the silence persisted, Drake Miller knew that this was his new reality – a world where his son was gone, and he was left to face the consequences of his choices.

3 - 4

Drake forced himself to his feet, his body heavy with grief as he made his way through the silent house. Each step felt like a betrayal, a reminder of the life that once thrived here. He paused at the kitchen doorway, his breath catching in his throat.

There, silhouetted against the fading light streaming through the window, sat Linda. Her back was turned to him, shoulders slumped under an invisible weight. The sight of her alone, so still and fragile, sent a fresh wave of pain through Drake's chest.

He swallowed hard, trying to find the right words. What could he possibly say to ease this unbearable sorrow? Drake's mind raced, recalling countless legal arguments he'd crafted with ease. But here, faced with the raw anguish of his wife, all his eloquence abandoned him.

"Linda..." he finally managed, his voice barely above a whisper. "How are you holding up?"

The words felt hollow as soon as they left his lips. Drake winced internally, wishing he could take them back. How could she possibly be holding up? Their son was gone, their world shattered. He longed to reach out, to pull her into his arms and shield her from this pain. But the distance between them felt vast, an ocean of grief neither knew how to cross.

5 - 6

Linda remained motionless; her gaze fixed on some distant point beyond the window. Her voice, when it came, was barely audible, a fragile thread of sound in the oppressive silence.

"I'm fine, Drake. Just... trying to get through the day."

The words hung in the air, heavy with unspoken pain. Drake's heart clenched, recognizing the lie for what it was – a thin veneer of strength covering a bottomless well of sorrow. He longed to bridge the gap between them, to offer some comfort, but found himself paralyzed by uncertainty.

His mind raced, grasping for something, anything to say. *We should be facing this together,* he thought, the guilt of his divided existence weighing on him. *But how can I be there for her when part of me lives in another world?*

Drake's hand twitched at his side, wanting to reach out but fearing rejection. The kitchen, once a place of warmth and family gatherings, now felt alien and cold. The absence of Harrison's laughter echoed in every corner, a ghostly reminder of what they'd lost.

"Linda, I..." he began, then faltered, the words dying on his lips. What could he possibly say to make this better?

7 - 8

Drake took a hesitant step forward, the floorboard creaking beneath his weight. The sound seemed to reverberate through the room, amplifying the tension that hung between them.

"Linda, I need to tell you something," he said, his voice low and strained. He paused, swallowing hard against the lump in his throat. "Something... strange."

His heart raced, pounding against his ribcage as he struggled to find the right words. How could he explain the inexplicable? The duality of his existence, the parallel worlds that tore at his sanity?

She'll think I've lost my mind, he thought, a cold sweat breaking out on his forehead. *But I can't keep living this lie. She deserves to know.*

Drake's fingers fidgeted at his sides, his lawyer's instincts screaming at him to present a logical argument, to make her understand. But this defied all logic, all reason. This was about faith, about the impossible becoming possible.

He took another step closer, close enough now to see the tension in Linda's shoulders, the slight tremor in her hands as they gripped the edge of the kitchen counter. The air between them was thick with unspoken grief, with the shared pain of losing their son.

"Linda, please," he whispered, his voice cracking with emotion. "I know it sounds crazy, but I need you to listen. I need you to believe me."

9 - 10

Linda finally turned to face him, her blonde hair catching the dim light from the kitchen window. Her blue eyes, once sparkling with joy, now seemed hollow and distant, as if all the life had been drained from them. The weight of their loss was etched into every line of her face, a constant reminder of the void in their lives.

Drake's breath caught in his throat. Even in her grief, Linda's beauty was haunting, a painful echo of happier times. He longed to reach out and touch her, to bridge the chasm that had opened between them, but he held back, afraid of her reaction.

Linda's gaze met his, a mixture of weariness and wariness in her expression. Her voice, when she spoke, was barely above a whisper, rough with unshed tears. "What is it, Drake? What could possibly be stranger than losing our son?"

The words hit Drake like a physical blow. He flinched, his mind racing. *How can I tell her? How can I make her understand when I barely understand it myself?* The weight of his dual existence pressed down on him, threatening to crush him under its impossibility.

He opened his mouth to respond, but the words stuck in his throat. The kitchen suddenly felt too small, too confining. The silence stretched between them, filled with unspoken pain and the ghosts of what might have been.

11 - 12

Drake took a deep breath, his heart hammering against his ribs. The scent of Linda's favorite lavender hand cream lingered in the air, a bittersweet reminder of the life they once shared. He steeled himself, knowing his next words could shatter what little remained of their relationship.

"Linda," he began, his voice low and strained. "In my dreams..." He paused, swallowing hard against the lump in his throat. The ticking of the kitchen clock seemed to grow louder, marking each precious second. "I'm in another world, Harrison is still alive."

The words hung in the air between them, heavy with implication. Drake watched Linda's face, searching for any sign of understanding or belief. His mind raced, replaying countless moments with Harrison in that other reality - his son's laughter, the warmth of his hugs, the pride in his eyes when he mastered a new skill.

Please, Linda, he thought desperately. *Try to understand. I'm not crazy. I'm not running from our loss. I'm trying to find a way back to our boy.*

Drake's hands trembled slightly as he waited for Linda's response, the weight of his confession pressing down on him like a physical force. He longed to reach out to her, to bridge the gulf between them, but he remained still, afraid that any movement might shatter this fragile moment.

13 - 14

Linda's eyes widened, disbelief etching deep lines across her forehead. A flicker of anger flashed across her features, her blue eyes darkening like storm clouds gathering on the horizon. Drake's heart sank as he recognized the familiar mix of pain and frustration that had become all too common in their interactions since Harrison's death.

"Another world?" Linda's voice trembled, a mixture of incredulity and rising anger. "What are you talking about, Drake? This isn't some fantasy; this is our reality." She gripped the edge of the kitchen counter, her knuckles turning white. "Our son is gone, and there's nothing you can say or do to change that."

Drake felt a sharp pang in his chest at her words. He knew how it sounded – crazy, delusional, a desperate attempt to escape their grief. But he couldn't shake the vivid memories of Harrison in that other place, couldn't ignore the undeniable realness of those experiences.

How can I make her understand? he thought frantically. *How can I describe the warmth of Harrison's hand in mine when we high-five after working on an assignment, the sound of his laughter echoing through a house that isn't broken by loss?*

He opened his mouth to speak, to try and explain further, but the words caught in his throat. The kitchen suddenly felt too small, too confining, the air thick with unspoken pain and accusations.

15 - 16

Drake took a tentative step toward Linda, his hand outstretched, fingers trembling slightly. The distance between them felt like a chasm, one he desperately needed to bridge.

"Linda, please," he said, his voice hoarse with emotion. "I know it sounds crazy, but it's true." He swallowed hard, trying to find the right words. "When I go to bed in this world, I wake up in another where Harrison is alive. I see him, I talk to him..." His voice broke slightly. "He's still here, Linda. He's still with us."

As he spoke, Drake's mind raced with vivid images from that other reality – Harrison's mischievous grin as he recounted his latest adventure, the way his curly hair stuck up in all directions after a nap, the sound of his footsteps bounding down the stairs. The memories were so tangible, so real, that it physically hurt to be standing in this kitchen where those sounds were absent.

Linda's expression shifted, a mix of confusion and pain replacing the anger. For a moment, Drake thought he saw a flicker of hope in her eyes, quickly extinguished by the harsh reality surrounding them.

She wants to believe me, Drake realized. *But how can she when everything around us screams of loss?* He glanced at the empty chair where Harrison used to sit for breakfast, the refrigerator devoid of colorful drawings that once adorned its surface. Every corner of their home was a reminder of what they'd lost.

17 - 18

Linda recoiled from his outstretched hand as if his touch might burn her. Her eyes, once filled with warmth and love, now blazed with a mixture of anger and unbearable grief. Drake's heart clenched at the sight, his wife's pain palpable in the air between them.

"How dare you?" Linda's voice was low, trembling with barely contained emotion. "How dare you come in here with your delusions, your lies?" Her words gained strength, fueled by the rage of a mother denied her child. "You think this is some kind of game? Some way to ease your guilt?"

Drake took a step back, overwhelmed by the force of her reaction. He wanted to explain, to make her understand, but the words caught in his throat. The kitchen suddenly felt too small, the air too thick.

Linda's next words cut through him like a knife. "Well, let me tell you something, Drake. Our son is dead, and he's never coming back." Her voice cracked on the word 'dead', and Drake saw tears welling in her eyes. "And if you can't accept that, then maybe you should just leave."

Leave? The thought sent a jolt of panic through Drake. *I can't leave her like this. I can't lose her too.* But as he looked at Linda, her body rigid with anger and sorrow, he realized that his presence might be causing more harm than good.

19 - 19

Tears welled up in Drake's eyes, blurring his vision as he watched Linda crumble before him. Her shoulders sagged, the fight draining out of her as quickly as it had come. The weight of their shared loss hung heavy in the air, crushing them both beneath its unbearable burden.

"Linda, I..." Drake's voice cracked, his words failing him. He reached out instinctively, but his hand hovered in the space between them, afraid to bridge the gap.

Linda's gaze dropped to the floor, her voice barely a whisper. "Just go, Drake. Please."

As he stood there, frozen in indecision, Drake's mind raced. *How can I make her understand? How can I leave her alone in this pain?* The thought of his other world, where Harrison still lived, felt like a cruel taunt now.

"I never meant to hurt you," Drake said softly, his heart breaking anew. "I just... I miss him so much."

Linda's eyes met his, a flicker of shared anguish passing between them. "We both do," she replied, her voice hollow. "But your dreams won't bring him back."

Drake felt the chasm between them widening, a rift born of grief and disbelief. As he stood there, locked in this emotional deadlock, a desperate thought emerged: *Will I ever find my way back? To Harrison, to the family we once were?*

Under Pressure

Blue World – 2024

1 - 2

The acrid smell of stale coffee permeates the air as Drake Miller hunches over his desk, his fingers flying across the keyboard. The rhythmic clacking provides a counterpoint to the bustling sounds of the law firm around him. Phones ring incessantly, papers rustle, and muted conversations blend into a constant hum of activity.

Drake's brow furrows as he types, his mind racing with thoughts of the accident that shattered his world. *I have to make this right. No one else should suffer like we did.* He pauses, rubbing his tired eyes. The weight of his dual existence presses down on him, a constant reminder of what he's lost—and what he still has to lose.

"Hey, Miller!" a colleague calls out. "You joining us for lunch?"

Drake shakes his head, not looking up from his computer. "Can't. Too much to do." *I can't waste a single moment. Linda and Harrison are counting on me.*

He reaches for his coffee mug, grimacing as he takes a sip of the cold, bitter liquid. The taste brings back a flash of memory—Linda's warm smile as she handed him a steaming cup each morning. The image sends a pang through his chest.

Suddenly, the door to his office swings open with a bang. Drake's head snaps up, his heart rate spiking at the unexpected intrusion. His law partner, Vega, strides in, his face a mask of urgency and excitement.

"Drake," Vega says, his voice tight with barely contained emotion. "We need to talk. Now."

Drake leans back in his chair, studying his partner's face. *Something's happened. Something big.* "What is it, Vega? You look like you've seen a ghost."

Vega runs a hand through his hair, his eyes darting around the room as if searching for eavesdroppers. "It's about the accident," he says in a low voice. "There's been a development."

Drake's breath catches in his throat. *The accident. Linda's smile. Harrison's laugh.* His two worlds collide in his mind, a kaleidoscope of joy and pain. "Tell me,"He says, his voice barely above a whisper.

As Vega begins to speak, Drake's mind races. *Could this be it? The key to bringing my family back together?* He listens intently, his heart pounding, knowing that whatever Vega has to say could change everything—in both of his realities.

3 - 4

Vega leans forward, his eyes intense. "Drake, you won't believe what just came in. The police found the car."

The words hit Drake like a physical blow. His heart skips a beat, then begins to race. He looks up from his desk, his eyes locking with Vega's. The world around him seems to fade away, leaving only this moment, this revelation.

The car. They found it. Drake's mind whirls with possibilities. Images flash through his consciousness: the mangled wreckage of his own vehicle, Linda's lifeless body, Harrison's terrified face. He swallows hard, trying to keep his composure.

"Where?" Drake manages to ask, his voice hoarse. He clears his throat, attempting to regain some semblance of control. "How did they find it?"

As Vega begins to explain, Drake's thoughts continue to race. *This could be the breakthrough we've been waiting for. A chance to find the person responsible, to get justice for Linda... and for Harrison.*

He leans forward, hanging on to every word Vega says, knowing that this information could be the key to bridging the gap between his two realities. In the back of his mind, a small voice whispers, *Be careful what you wish for. The truth might be more than you can handle.*

5 - 6

Drake's voice trembles slightly as he asks, "The car? The one that caused the accident?" His fingers grip the edge of his desk, knuckles turning white. The weight of potential answers hangs heavy in the air, suffocating in its intensity.

Vega nods, a solemn look crossing his features as he takes a seat across from Miller. The leather chair creaks under his weight, the sound unnaturally loud in the tense silence of the office.

Drake's mind reels, a kaleidoscope of emotions swirling within him. *This is it. The moment that could change everything.* He can almost hear Linda's gentle voice urging him to stay calm, to approach this rationally. But rationality seems a distant concept when faced with the possibility of answers he's been seeking for so long.

"What did they find?" Drake asks, leaning forward. His heart pounds so loudly he's sure Vega must hear it. "Any evidence of the driver?"

As Vega begins to respond, Drake's gaze drifts to the family photo on his desk. Harrison's smiling face stares back at him, a stark reminder of what's at stake. *I'll find out what happened,* he silently promises his son. *No matter what it takes.*

7 - 8

Vega leans forward, his voice low and intense. "That's right. They found it abandoned on the side of the road, not too far from where the accident happened. And get this... the license plate matches the one you described."

Miller's breath catches in his throat as he processes the news, a surge of adrenaline coursing through his veins. His mind races, images of that fateful night flashing before his eyes - the screeching tires, the shattering glass, the sickening crunch of metal. He can almost smell the acrid scent of burnt rubber and spilled gasoline.

"Abandoned," Drake whispers, more to himself than to Vega. His hands tremble slightly as he reaches for a pen, needing something tangible to ground himself. "How long has it been there?"

As Vega begins to answer, Drake's gaze drifts to the window, where the bustling city outside seems suddenly muted and distant. *This is real,* he thinks, a mixture of hope and dread swirling in his gut. *We're one step closer to the truth. But what if I'm not ready for what we find?*

He forces himself to focus on Vega's words, knowing that every detail could be crucial. Yet part of him wants to run from this office, to find Linda and Harrison, to hold them close and pretend that their family was never torn apart. *No,* he reminds himself sternly. *I owe them the truth. All of us deserve closure.*

"What else can you tell me about the car?" Drake asks, his lawyer's instincts kicking in despite the emotional turmoil. He needs facts, evidence, anything to piece together this maddening puzzle.

9 - 10

Drake leans forward, his eyes searching Vega's face for any hint of what's to come. "Did they find anything else? Any clues as to who was driving?" His voice is steady, but there's an undercurrent of desperation that he can't quite hide.

Vega's expression darkens, the lines around his eyes deepening as he delivers the next piece of information. Drake feels his stomach tighten, bracing himself for whatever his partner is about to reveal.

Please, Drake thinks, his mind racing. *Let there be something, anything that can lead us to the person responsible.* He can almost hear Linda's voice, soft and comforting, telling him not to get his hopes up. But he can't help it. This is the closest they've come to answers in months.

The silence stretches between them, thick with tension. Drake's fingers drum nervously on his desk, the sound echoing in the suddenly too-quiet office. He wants to shake Vega, to force the words out of him, but he restrains himself. Years of courtroom experience have taught him the value of patience, even when every fiber of his being screams for action.

"Vega," Drake finally says, his voice low and intense. "Whatever it is, I need to know. For Linda's sake. For Harrison's."

11 - 12

Vega leans forward, his voice dropping to a near whisper. "They found a white robe in the driver's side of the car. It looks like whoever was behind the wheel might have been involved in some kind of cult or religious group."

Drake's breath catches in his throat, the unexpected revelation hitting him like a physical blow. His mind struggles to process this new information, images flashing through his head in rapid succession. A pristine white robe, stark against the twisted metal of the crash site. Shadowy figures in ceremonial garb, lurking on the fringes of Willow Grove. The tranquil surface of Moose Pond, disturbed by arcane rituals under the cover of darkness.

"A cult?" Drake murmurs more to himself than to Vega. His fingers unconsciously trace the edge of his desk, seeking something solid to anchor him as his thoughts spiral. "Here in Bridgewater?"

He can almost hear Harrison's voice, filled with that teenage mix of fascination and skepticism. "A cult, Dad? Seriously? That's some next-level conspiracy stuff." The imagined conversation brings a fleeting smile to Drake's face, quickly replaced by a renewed sense of urgency.

Leaning back in his chair, Drake closes his eyes for a moment, trying to piece together this new puzzle. "Tell me everything," he says, opening his eyes to fix Vega with an intense gaze. "Every detail about the robe, where exactly they found it, any markings or insignia."

As Vega begins to relay the specifics, Drake's mind races, connecting dots he hadn't even known existed. The pieces are starting to come together, but the picture they're forming is far more complex – and potentially dangerous – than he ever imagined.

13 - 14

Drake's brow furrows as he processes the information, his mind a whirlwind of possibilities and implications. He leans forward, elbows on the desk, fingers steepled under his chin.

"A cult..." he says, his voice low and contemplative. "That's... unexpected. But it might explain why they didn't stop after the accident. They were probably trying to cover their tracks."

As the words leave his mouth, Drake feels a chill run down his spine. The image of Linda's face, etched with grief, flashes before his eyes. He can almost hear her voice, soft and pained, asking, "Why? Why didn't they stop to help?" The memory fuels a surge of determination within him.

Vega nods in agreement, his gaze fixed on Drake with a mixture of concern and determination. The silence between them is heavy with unspoken thoughts and theories.

Drake's mind races, considering the implications. A cult in Bridgewater? It seems almost surreal. Yet, as a lawyer, he knows all too well that the most unassuming places often harbor the darkest secrets. He finds himself wondering what other mysteries might be lurking beneath the surface of their quiet city.

"We need to tread carefully here," Drake says, breaking the silence. "If there's really a cult involved, we could be dealing with something far more dangerous than we initially thought."

15 - 16

Vega's eyes narrow, a glint of steel in his gaze. "Well, whatever their reasons, we're one step closer to getting justice for you and your family. We'll make sure they pay for what they did."

The words hang in the air, charged with promise. Drake feels a surge of gratitude for his partner's unwavering support. He nods, a renewed sense of purpose flooding through him. The weight of grief that's been crushing his chest since the accident seems to lift, if only slightly.

"You're right," Drake says, his voice low but firm. "We can't let them get away with this."

As he turns back to his desk, his mind is already racing ahead. The stack of papers before him blurs as he envisions a future where the dangerous stretch of road that claimed so many lives is finally made safe. He can almost see the new guardrails, the improved lighting, the warning signs that could prevent another family from suffering as his has.

But there's something else nagging at the back of his mind. A possibility he hadn't considered before. In the other world, the one where he's a cop instead of a lawyer, he now has a crucial piece of information: the exact location of the abandoned car.

Drake's heart begins to pound as he realizes the implications. Maybe, just maybe, in that other reality, he could use his newfound police tactics to pursue the one who put him in this ordeal in the first place. The thought is both exhilarating and terrifying.

He looks up at Vega, a mix of determination and uncertainty in his eyes. "We're not just seeking justice here, are we? We're unraveling something much bigger."

17 - 18

Drake leans back in his chair, the leather creaking softly as he processes the new information. His eyes narrow, focusing on the pristine white robe laid out on his desk. The fabric seems to glow under the harsh office lights, its purity a stark contrast to the dark implications it brings.

"A cult," Drake mutters, his voice barely above a whisper. He runs a hand through his disheveled hair, his mind racing. "It's not just a hit-and-run anymore, is it?"

Vega shakes his head, his usually confident demeanor tinged with unease. "This robe... it's not something you'd typically find in a car. And definitely not one abandoned after an accident."

Drake leans forward, his fingers tracing the hem of the garment. The material feels expensive, almost silky to the touch. "It's in pristine condition," he observes, his brow furrowing. "Like it was placed there deliberately."

As he examines the robe, a chill runs down Drake's spine. He can't shake the feeling that this discovery is pulling him deeper into a mystery far more complex than he initially thought. In his mind's eye, he sees Linda and Harrison, their faces etched with worry. He has to solve this, not just for justice, but for their safety.

"What kind of organization would use something like this?" Drake asks, more to himself than to Vega. He looks up at his partner, his eyes dark with determination. "We need to dig deeper. This isn't just about the accident anymore. There's something... sinister at play here."

Vega nods solemnly, reaching for his phone. "I'll get our team on it. We'll need to be careful though, Drake. If we're dealing with a cult, who knows how far their influence reaches?"

Drake's jaw clenches, his resolve hardening. "We have to risk it. For Linda, for Harrison... for everyone who's been affected by that road. We can't let fear stop us from uncovering the truth."

As Vega steps out to make the calls, Drake turns back to the robe, his mind racing with possibilities. What secrets does this seemingly innocent piece of cloth hold? And more importantly, how deep into the darkness will he have to go to find the answers he seeks?

19 - 20

Drake's fingers trembled slightly as he traced the intricate golden threads of the embroidered symbol on the white robe. The serpentine dragon seemed to writhe beneath his touch, its scales shimmering with an otherworldly glow that sent a chill down his spine.

"Vega," he called, his voice barely above a whisper. "Come look at this."

His partner hurried over, leaning in close to examine the symbol. Drake could feel the tension radiating from Vega's body, mirroring his own unease.

"I've never seen anything like it," Vega muttered, his brow furrowed.

Drake nodded, his mind racing. "It's not just the dragon. Look at these runes intertwined with it. They're... ancient. I can't make heads or tails of them."

As he studied the symbol, Drake couldn't shake the image of Harrison from his mind. His son's curious eyes, always eager to unravel mysteries, would have been captivated by this enigma. The thought brought a pang of longing and determination.

"We need to find out what this means," Drake said, straightening up. "This isn't just some random cult symbol. It's too intricate, too... purposeful."

Vega ran a hand through his hair, visibly disturbed. "I'll reach out to some contacts in religious studies. Maybe they can shed some light on this."

Drake nodded; his gaze still fixed on the robe. "Good idea. I'll see if I can find any similar symbols in our database. There has to be a connection somewhere."

As Vega left to make his calls, Drake found himself alone with the robe and its haunting emblem. He couldn't shake the feeling that this discovery was pulling him deeper into a mystery far more complex than he had initially thought. In his mind's eye, he saw Linda and Harrison, their faces etched with worry. He had to solve this, not just for justice, but for their safety.

21 - 22

Drake's fingers traced the air above the golden threads, his mind racing with possibilities. The silence in the room was oppressive, broken only by the soft hum of the office air conditioning. A chill ran down his spine, not from the cool air, but from the ominous aura emanating from the symbol before him.

He glanced up at Vega, catching his partner's uneasy expression. Their eyes met, a silent acknowledgment passing between them. This was no ordinary piece of evidence. It was a gateway to something far more sinister.

"Vega," Drake said, his voice low and gravelly, "I've seen my share of cult symbolism in cases before, but this... this is different."

Vega nodded, leaning in closer to examine the intricate design. "You're right. There's something almost... alive about it. The way the dragon seems to writhe around that tree, it's unsettling."

Drake's mind flashed to Linda, imagining her reaction to this discovery. She'd always had a keen intuition about these things. He could almost hear her cautioning voice, urging him to tread carefully.

"What do you think it means?" Drake asked more to himself than to Vega.

His partner straightened up, his brow furrowed in concentration. "I'm not sure, but I can tell you one thing, Drake," Vega's voice cut through the tense silence, carrying a weight that made Drake's stomach churn. "This isn't just any robe. This symbol... it's emblematic of something deeper, something darker."

Drake exhaled slowly, feeling the weight of Vega's words settle on his shoulders. "You're right," he murmured, his eyes never leaving the haunting symbol. "And whatever it is, I have a feeling it's at the heart of this whole mess."

23 - 24

Drake Miller nodded grimly, his eyes narrowing as he stared at the enigmatic symbol. The golden thread seemed to shimmer under the harsh office lights, mocking him with its arcane secrets. His mind raced, memories of his fractured life colliding with the present mystery.

"We need to dig deeper," he said, his voice thick with determination. "Find out everything we can about this cult, their beliefs, their practices. There's more to this than just a simple accident."

Vega leaned back in his chair, running a hand through his hair. "Where do we even start, Drake? This isn't exactly our usual wheelhouse."

Drake's gaze drifted to the window, taking in the swaying Oak trees of Bridgewater outside. For a moment, he thought of Harrison, wondering what his perceptive son would make of all this. The boy's natural curiosity might have offered a fresh perspective.

"We start with research," Drake replied, turning back to Vega. "Religious symbolism, obscure cults, anything that might give us a lead on this dragon and tree motif."

As he spoke, Drake felt a familiar surge of adrenaline, the kind that used to fuel his relentless pursuit of courtroom victories. But this time, it was different. This wasn't about winning a case; it was about uncovering the truth that might bridge the gap between his two realities.

"I'll reach out to some contacts in the religious studies department at the university," Vega offered, already pulling out his phone.

Drake nodded, his mind churning with possibilities. "Good. I'll start combing through our archives, see if there's any precedent for cult activity in the area."

As they began their respective tasks, Drake couldn't shake the feeling that they were stepping into something far beyond their understanding. The weight of the unknown pressed down on him, mixing with the ever-present grief that haunted both versions of his life.

"Whatever we find," Drake said softly, almost to himself, "we need to be prepared. This could go deeper than we imagine."

Vega looked up, meeting Drake's eyes with a mix of concern and resolve. "We'll figure it out, partner. One step at a time."

With renewed determination, they set out to unravel the mysteries surrounding the enigmatic symbol, knowing that the truth they sought might lie hidden within the shadows of the ancient and arcane. As Drake immersed himself in the research, he couldn't help but wonder how this new development would impact his dual existence, and what dark secrets awaited them in the depths of this emerging conspiracy.

25 - 26

The serpentine symbol from the white robe danced behind Drake Miller's eyelids as he blinked, trying to focus on the piles of documents before him. The office's fluorescent lights cast a harsh glare on the papers, mirroring the intensity of his search for answers. His fingers, slightly trembling from a mix of exhaustion and anticipation, traced the edges of a particularly promising file.

Suddenly, a familiar voice echoed in his mind, cutting through his concentration like a scalpel through flesh.

"The cult, tell me what you learned about the cult."

Dr. Lee's gentle yet probing tone reverberated in Drake's consciousness, bridging the gap between his parallel realities. The question hung in the air, unanswered, as Drake's tired eyes darted to the window. Outside, a breeze had picked up, a stark contrast to the tension coiled within him.

Drake's jaw clenched, his scruffy beard accentuating the weariness etched into his features. He took a deep breath, steadying himself before responding to the phantom inquiry.

"In due time," he muttered, his voice barely above a whisper.

His gaze returned to the documents, but his mind raced. How could he explain to Dr. Lee the depths of this mystery when he himself was still grappling with its implications? The weight of his dual existence pressed down on him, heavier than ever.

"I need more time," Drake thought, his internal dialogue a jumble of frustration and determination. "There's so much we don't know yet. The symbol, the robe, the abandoned car... it's all connected, but how?"

He leaned back in his chair, running a hand through his disheveled dark hair. The quiet hum of the office faded into the background as he wrestled with the complexities of his situation. How could he navigate this investigation while straddling two realities? And more importantly, how could he protect his family from whatever sinister forces were at play

Haunted Sanctuary

Blue World – 2024

1 - 2

The door creaks open, a discordant note in the silence of the house. Drake Miller stands frozen on the threshold, his hand trembling on the doorknob as he stares into the room beyond. Harrison's sanctuary, preserved like a museum exhibit of a life interrupted.

Drake's eyes roam over the walls, taking in the chaotic collage of posters—rock bands with snarling lead singers next to grinning athletes mid-victory pose. A lump forms in his throat as he thinks of Harrison's passionate debates about music and sports, the way his eyes would light up as he defended his latest obsession.

"I should have listened more," Drake murmurs, his voice rough with regret. "I was always too busy with work, always promising 'next time.'"

He steps inside, careful not to disturb the clothes strewn across the floor. Each crumpled t-shirt and inside-out pair of jeans is a painful reminder of the carefree teenager who once inhabited this space.

Drake's gaze is drawn to the desk, where a half-finished model airplane sits in suspended animation. He approaches slowly, as if afraid to break the spell of stillness that hangs over the room.

"Oh, Harrison," he whispers, running a hand over the plane's delicate frame. His fingers trace the intricate details—tiny rivets and precisely painted panels—that his son had so painstakingly crafted. "You always did have an eye for detail, didn't you?"

A memory surfaces: Harrison, tongue poking out in concentration as he carefully applied glue to a minuscule wing strut. "Dad, come look!" he had called excitedly. "I think I've finally got it right!"

Drake closes his eyes, fighting back tears. "I'm sorry I didn't make time to see it then, buddy. I'm looking now. I see you."

He picks up a small paintbrush, still crusted with dried blue paint. The weight of it in his hand is almost unbearable, a tangible link to his lost son.

"I don't know how to do this, Harrison," Drake admits, his voice barely audible. "How do I keep going when half of me is missing?"

The silence of the room offers no answers, only the crushing weight of absence.

3 - 4

As Drake stands frozen, lost in the haunting stillness of Harrison's room, Dr. Lee's gentle voice echoes in his mind.

"How are you feeling, Detective?"

The question hangs in the air, unanswered for a moment as Drake struggles to find the words. His eyes drift from the model airplane to a framed photograph on Harrison's bedside table. In it, his son's vibrant smile beams back at him, frozen in time—a moment of pure joy captured forever.

Drake's throat tightens as he stares at the image. "I..." he begins, his voice barely above a whisper. "I feel like I'm standing on the edge of an abyss, Doc."

He takes a step closer to the photograph, his fingers hovering just above the glass. Harrison's eyes, so full of life and promise, seem to look right through him.

"Every time I look at him," Drake continues, his words heavy with emotion, "I'm reminded of everything we've lost. Everything I failed to protect."

The weight of guilt presses down on Drake's shoulders, threatening to crush him. He can't help but wonder how different things might have been if he'd been a more present father, if he'd prioritized his family over his work.

"I know it's not healthy," he admits, both to Dr. Lee and to himself, "but I can't stop thinking about all the what-ifs. All the moments I missed, thinking there'd always be more time."

5 - 6

Drake's hand trembles as he reaches for the photograph, gently lifting it from the bedside table. His voice is strained, barely above a whisper. "I'm... I'm trying to keep it together."

The cool glass of the frame presses against his calloused fingers, a stark contrast to the warmth of the memories it holds. Drake's eyes trace every detail of Harrison's face—the crooked smile, the mischievous glint in his eyes, the unruly curls that Linda was always trying to tame.

A lump forms in Drake's throat as he remembers the day this photo was taken. It was Harrison's first day of high school, and the boy had been a bundle of nervous energy, masking it with his typical bravado. Drake had been rushing to get to court, his mind already on the case ahead.

"I should've been there more," he thinks, the regret washing over him in waves. "I should've seen how much he needed me."

As he stares at the image of his son, Drake feels a familiar sting behind his eyes. He blinks rapidly, trying to hold back the tears that threaten to spill over. But it's a losing battle, and soon his vision blurs, Harrison's frozen smile becoming a watery smear of color.

"God, I miss him," Drake chokes out, his voice barely audible. A single tear escapes, rolling down his cheek and landing on the glass with a soft plink.

In that moment, Drake feels the full weight of his loss, the enormity of the void Harrison's absence has left in his life. He wants to scream, to rage against the unfairness of it all. But instead, he stands there, silent and still, cradling the photograph as if it were the most precious thing in the world.

7 - 8

Drake's fingers tighten around the frame, his knuckles turning white. He takes a shuddering breath, the air feeling thick and heavy in his lungs.

"But every room in this house... it's like a tomb," he whispers, the words barely audible.

His eyes dart around Harrison's bedroom, taking in the posters, the scattered belongings, the unfinished projects. Each item is a stark reminder of a life cut short, of potential unfulfilled. The silence in the room is deafening, broken only by the soft ticking of a clock on the nightstand.

Drake swallows hard, trying to dislodge the lump in his throat. "I can't... I can't do this," he manages, his voice cracking under the strain of suppressed emotion.

The weight of grief presses down on him like a suffocating blanket, threatening to crush him beneath its unyielding mass. His shoulders slump, and for a moment, he feels as if his legs might give out beneath him.

In his mind, he sees Harrison laughing, playing catch in the backyard, arguing about curfews – all the mundane moments that now seem so precious, so painfully out of reach.

"I'm sorry," Drake thinks, closing his eyes tightly. "I'm so sorry I wasn't the father you deserved."

9 - 10

Dr. Lee's voice, soft yet clear, cuts through Drake's spiraling thoughts. "It's important to allow yourself to grieve, Detective. Your emotions are valid."

The words hit Drake like a gentle wave, washing over him and momentarily easing the tightness in his chest. He inhales deeply, his eyes still fixed on Harrison's photograph.

"Valid," Drake thinks, turning the word over in his mind. "As if feeling this way could ever be invalid."

He nods slowly, a silent acknowledgment of the pain he carries with him every day. His fingers trace the edge of the picture frame, feeling every ridge and imperfection.

"I know," Drake says quietly, his voice rough with emotion. "But knowing that doesn't make it any easier to bear."

He sets the photograph down gently, his gaze lingering on Harrison's frozen smile. The weight of absence presses down on him, a constant, unyielding force.

"How do I move forward?" Drake asks more to himself than to Dr. Lee. "How do I live in a world where he's gone?"

The questions hang in the air, unanswered. Drake's mind races, filled with memories of Harrison – his first steps, his kindergarten graduation, the last conversation they had. Each recollection is both a comfort and a knife to the heart.

11 - 12

Drake's fingers linger on the glass of the photograph, as if touching it could somehow bridge the impossible gap between life and death. He can almost feel the warmth of Harrison's smile beneath his fingertips, a cruel illusion that makes the reality of his loss even more unbearable.

"I know," Drake finally manages, his voice barely above a whisper. "But sometimes it feels like... like I'm drowning in it."

The words hang heavy in the air, each one a testament to the overwhelming grief that threatens to consume him. Drake's eyes remain fixed on the photograph, drinking in every detail of his son's face as if afraid it might fade from his memory.

He carefully sets the frame back on the bedside table, his touch gentle as if handling something infinitely precious. For a moment, his fingers remain on the glass, unwilling to break that final connection.

In his mind, Drake can hear Linda's voice, soft and comforting, telling him it's okay to let go. But the thought of moving on, of living in a world without Harrison, feels like a betrayal of everything they once were.

"How do I keep going?" Drake thinks, his heart aching with each beat. "How do I find my way back to the surface when every memory pulls me deeper?"

13 - 14

Drake's fingers finally slip from the photograph, leaving behind a smudge on the glass—a physical reminder of his desperate need to hold onto Harrison. He turns away, his gaze sweeping across the room, taking in the remnants of a life cut short.

"I just wish I could find some way to bring him back," Drake murmurs, his voice cracking under the weight of impossible longing. The words hang in the air, a futile prayer to an unresponsive universe.

He moves to the window, pushing it open to let in a cool breeze. The familiar scent of the backyard wafts in—freshly cut grass and the faint aroma of Linda's rose garden. It's achingly normal, a stark contrast to the frozen-in-time quality of Harrison's room.

As Drake stares out at the world continuing without his son, a painful realization settles in his chest. His lawyer's mind, once sharp and focused on finding solutions, now grapples with a problem that has no legal remedy, no clever argument to present.

"There's no case to win here," he thinks, his hands gripping the windowsill tightly. "No amount of evidence or persuasion can change this verdict."

The breeze rustles through Harrison's posters, making them flutter like fragile wings. Drake watches, transfixed by the movement, a cruel reminder of the life that once filled this space.

But deep down, beneath the raw ache of grief, a part of Drake knows the truth. Some wounds can never fully heal, no matter how hard we try to mend them. The loss of Harrison has carved out a piece of his heart that will always remain empty, a void that no amount of time or acceptance can completely fill.

15 - 16

Miller takes a deep breath, his chest expanding as he inhales the familiar scent of Harrison's room—a mixture of old sports equipment and the lingering trace of his son's favorite cologne. The air feels heavy, laden with memories and unspoken words. He closes his eyes for a moment, willing the strength to flow through his veins.

When he opens them again, his gaze falls on Linda's reflection in the window. She's standing in the doorway, her blue eyes brimming with unshed tears. The sight of her vulnerability ignites a protective instinct within him.

"Drake," Linda's voice wavers, barely above a whisper. "Are you okay?"

Miller turns to face her, forcing a weak smile. "I'm... I'm managing," he replies, his voice gravelly with emotion. "How about you?"

Linda steps into the room, her fingers trailing along the edge of Harrison's desk. "It's hard," she admits, her blonde hair falling forward to obscure her face. "But we have to keep going, don't we?"

Miller nods, swallowing the lump in his throat. He thinks to himself, "I can't let her see how much this is tearing me apart. She needs me to be strong."

"We do," he says aloud, crossing the room to stand beside her. He gently places a hand on her shoulder, feeling the slight tremor running through her body. "We have to, for Harrison."

Linda looks up at him, her eyes searching his face. "Sometimes I wonder if we're doing the right thing, keeping his room like this."

Miller's mind races, torn between the desire to preserve every trace of Harrison and the need to move forward. He takes another deep breath, steeling himself against the overwhelming tide of emotions threatening to engulf him. He knows he must stay strong, not just for himself, but for Linda too.

"I need to be strong," he whispers to himself, so softly that Linda doesn't hear.

Aloud, he says, "Maybe... maybe we can talk about that later. For now, let's just remember him as he was." He gestures to the room around them, a bittersweet smile tugging at his lips. "Our boy, in all his messy, wonderful glory."

Linda nods, leaning into his embrace. As they stand there, surrounded by the remnants of their son's life, Miller can't help but feel the weight of his dual existence pressing down on him. In this world, he's a grieving father; in another, a detective searching for answers. The contradiction threatens to tear him apart, but he clings to his resolve.

"One day at a time," he thinks, tightening his hold on Linda. "That's all we can do."

17 - 18

Miller's shoulders straighten, a flicker of determination igniting in his eyes as he surveys Harrison's room once more. The chaos of teenage life surrounds him, but now he sees it as a challenge to be tackled, a way to honor his son's memory.

"I think I'll tidy up a bit," he says softly to Linda, his voice rough with emotion. "You okay with that?"

Linda nods, squeezing his hand before leaving him alone with his thoughts. Miller begins the task, carefully picking up discarded clothes and returning them to drawers. As he works, he mutters to himself, "You were always in such a rush, weren't you, buddy? Never time to put things away properly."

His hands tremble as he picks up a faded baseball cap, memories flooding his mind. "Remember when I taught you to ride that bike?" he asks the empty room, a sad smile playing on his lips. "You were so determined, even after you fell and skinned your knees."

Miller's eyes mist over as he recalls Harrison's triumphant grin when he finally mastered the two-wheeler. "You yelled so loud, the whole neighborhood must have heard. 'Dad, look! I'm doing it!'"

He moves to the window, gazing out at the backyard where countless summer evenings were spent playing catch. "We had some good times out there, didn't we?" he muses, his voice barely above a whisper. "You had one hell of an arm, kid. Could've gone pro if..."

Miller's voice trails off, the weight of what might have been settling heavily on his shoulders. He shakes his head, trying to focus on the task at hand. "One thing at a time," he reminds himself, echoing Dr. Lee's advice from his other reality. "Just keep moving forward."

19 - 20

Miller's fingers trace the outline of a framed photograph on Harrison's desk, the glass cool against his skin. The image captures a moment of pure joy - Harrison, gap-toothed and grinning, holding up a trophy from his Little League championship. The sight sends a sharp pang through Miller's chest.

"God, I miss you," he whispers, his voice thick with emotion. "Every single day."

He picks up a discarded t-shirt, carefully folding it as he speaks to the empty room. "You know, sometimes I still expect to hear you stomping down the stairs, complaining about homework or begging for pizza money."

A mirthless chuckle escapes his lips. "It's funny how the little things stick with you."

As he places the folded shirt in a drawer, Dr. Lee's voice echoes in his mind, "You're doing the best you can, Detective. Remember to take things one step at a time."

Miller pauses, his hand resting on the drawer handle. "Detective," he mutters, shaking his head. "Right. Because that's who I am... there."

He resumes his tidying, each item a bittersweet reminder of Harrison's presence. "One step at a time," he repeats softly, clinging to the mantra like a lifeline in the sea of grief that threatens to overwhelm him.

21 - 22

Miller nods, almost imperceptibly, as if responding to Dr. Lee's voice in his head. His eyes drift to a photo of Linda on Harrison's nightstand, her smile radiant and full of love. A flicker of determination sparks in his chest.

"Linda," he whispers, his voice barely audible. "We'll get through this together."

He runs a hand through his disheveled hair, exhaling slowly. The weight of grief still presses down on him, but there's a glimmer of resolve in his tired eyes.

"One step at a time," Miller murmurs, his voice gaining a hint of strength. He picks up a stray baseball from the floor, turning it over in his hands. The stitches are worn, testament to countless hours of catch in the backyard.

As he places the ball on a shelf, Miller's mind wanders to Linda. Her unwavering support, her quiet strength in the face of their shared loss. He realizes that her presence has been his anchor, keeping him tethered to hope even in his darkest moments.

"We've got each other," he says softly to the empty room, as if affirming a promise. "Whatever comes next, we'll face it together."

23 - 24

Miller's hands move methodically, straightening Harrison's belongings with a tenderness that belies his grief. Each item he touches stirs a memory: a soccer trophy from the championship game he'd barely made it to, a dog-eared copy of "To Kill a Mockingbird" they'd discussed over countless dinners. As he works, a faint smile tugs at the corners of his mouth.

"You always did love a good debate, didn't you, buddy?" Miller murmurs, his voice thick with emotion.

He pauses, holding a faded concert ticket stub. The memory of Harrison's infectious excitement floods back, and for a moment, the room seems less empty.

As Miller continues tidying, Dr. Lee's voice echoes in his mind. "Detective, how are you feeling now?"

Miller furrows his brow, a flicker of confusion crossing his face. "Detective?" he repeats aloud, his hands stilling on a stack of comics. "Why do you call me that? I'm not a detective, not in this world at least."

The words hang in the air, heavy with implication. Miller's heart races, a surge of adrenaline coursing through him. He glances around the room, suddenly hyper-aware of his surroundings.

"What did I just say?" he whispers to himself, his mind reeling. "This world? What other world could there be?"

25 - 26

Dr. Lee's soothing voice cuts through Miller's confusion, a gentle anchor in the storm of his thoughts. "Oh, but you've already referred to yourself as a detective in the other world. I find it helps connect with the patient if you bring up key details. Should I stop?"

Miller's hands tremble slightly as he sets down the comic books. He turns, his gaze sweeping across Harrison's room, searching for something familiar yet feeling oddly disoriented. The posters on the wall seem to waver, like mirages in a desert heat.

"I... I don't understand," Miller mutters, more to himself than to Dr. Lee. His mind races, trying to reconcile conflicting memories. "I'm a lawyer. I practice civil allegations in court."

He pauses, rubbing his temples as if to ward off an impending headache. The scent of Harrison's favorite cologne lingers in the air, grounding him momentarily.

"But maybe you're right," Miller continues, his voice gaining strength. "Maybe I am a Detective. Lord knows these past few days I've proved that."

As the words leave his mouth, Miller feels a strange sense of déjà vu. He glances at the model airplane on Harrison's desk, its wings outstretched, frozen mid-flight. For a fleeting moment, he sees himself examining crime scenes, piecing together clues. The image is so vivid, so real, that it takes his breath away.

"Dr. Lee," Miller says, his voice barely above a whisper, "what's happening to me?"

Threshold of Longing

Green World – 2024

1 - 2

The soft morning light filters through the curtains, casting a warm glow on the hallway. Drake Miller stands at the threshold of his son's room, a mixture of longing and uncertainty etched across his scruffy features. His tired eyes, reflecting the weight of internal struggles, roam over the familiar contours of Harrison's space—the rumpled bedsheets, the soccer trophies lining the shelves, the faint scent of his son's cologne lingering in the air.

"I wake up," Drake thinks, the words echoing in his mind with a hollow resonance. He runs a hand through his disheveled dark hair, feeling the stubble on his chin as he exhales slowly.

His gaze falls on a framed photo of Harrison holding up a soccer trophy, triumph radiating from his young face. Drake's fingers twitch, longing to reach out and touch the glass, to somehow bridge the chasm between them.

"Another day, another chance," he murmurs to himself, his voice low and contemplative. "To make things right, to be the father he deserves."

Drake's mind races with possibilities, weighing each potential interaction with his son like a seasoned lawyer preparing his case. But this isn't a courtroom, and the stakes are far higher than any legal battle he's ever fought.

He takes a tentative step into the room, then hesitates. "Harrison?" he calls out softly, his tone tinged with hope and apprehension. "You up, buddy?"

Silence greets him, and Drake's shoulders slump slightly. He moves to the window, pulling back the curtains to let more light flood the room. As he does, he catches a glimpse of his reflection in the glass—a middle-aged man with the weight of two worlds resting on his shoulders.

"I can do this," Drake reassures himself, straightening his posture. "I have to do this. For Harrison. For us."

With renewed determination, he turns back to face the empty room, ready to face another day in this fractured existence, holding onto the hope that someday, somehow, he'll find a way to bridge the gap between father and son.

3 - 4

Drake inhales deeply, his chest rising and falling as he steels himself for the day ahead. The morning light catches the green rubber band encircling his wrist, drawing his attention. He runs his thumb along its smooth surface, a tactile reminder of the tightrope he walks between realities.

"One day at a time," Drake mutters, his voice barely above a whisper. The band stretches slightly under his touch, its elasticity a stark contrast to the rigidity of his circumstances.

As he stands there, lost in thought, a familiar voice cuts through the silence of his mind. Dr. Harmon's measured tones echo in his consciousness, probing and insistent.

"What's the purpose of the rubber bands, Drake?" the psychiatrist's voice inquires, its clarity startling in the quiet room.

Drake's brow furrows, his fingers instinctively tightening around the band. He closes his eyes, grappling with the weight of the question and the implications of his answer.

"They're... they're anchors, Dr. Harmon," he finally responds, his words slow and deliberate. "A physical reminder of where I am, which... which reality I'm inhabiting at any given moment."

The admission hangs in the air, heavy with unspoken fears and uncertainties. Drake opens his eyes, his gaze fixed on the green band, a lifeline in the turbulent sea of his dual existence.

5 - 6

Drake's fingers tighten around the rubber band, the pressure grounding him in the present moment. "Sometimes it gets confusing," he admits, his voice barely above a whisper. "They just help me keep things straight."

The words hang in the air, laden with the weight of his fractured reality. Drake shakes his head, as if to clear away the lingering echoes of Dr. Harmon's voice. He moves towards the coat rack, his movements mechanical, a familiar routine in an unfamiliar world.

As he shrugs on his coat, Drake can't help but wonder which version of himself he's dressing today - the grieving husband or the mourning father. The thought sends a chill down his spine, colder than the morning air seeping through the windows.

Just as he passes his son's door, a soft creaking sound breaks the silence. Drake's heart leaps into his throat, a mix of anticipation and dread coursing through him. The door swings open, revealing Harrison Miller.

Drake's breath catches as he takes in the sight of his son. Harrison stands there, the embodiment of youthful vitality, yet something in his posture, in the set of his shoulders, speaks of a burden far too heavy for his years.

"Harrison," Drake thinks, his chest constricting with a cocktail of love and sorrow. "My boy, what have our fractured lives done to you?"

7 - 8

"Morning," Drake says, his voice soft and tentative, as if afraid to shatter the fragile moment.

He studies Harrison's face, searching for a glimmer of the carefree boy he once knew. The shadows under his son's eyes tell a story of sleepless nights and unspoken worries. Drake's heart aches, longing to reach out and smooth away the lines of tension etched across Harrison's young features.

Harrison responds with a half-hearted grumble, the weight of the world evident in his weary demeanor. The sound, more akin to a wounded animal than a teenage boy, cuts through Drake like a knife.

"God, he looks so tired," Drake thinks, fighting the urge to pull Harrison into his arms. "Is this my fault? Have I failed him in both realities?"

Drake's hand twitches, instinctively reaching for the green rubber band on his wrist. He catches himself, not wanting Harrison to see his moment of weakness. Instead, he forces a smile, hoping it doesn't look as strained as it feels.

"Big day ahead?" Drake asks, trying to inject some normalcy into their stilted interaction. He silently curses himself for the banality of the question, wishing he knew how to bridge the chasm that seems to stretch between them.

9 - 10

The kitchen table stretches between them like a vast, uncharted sea. Drake watches Harrison pour cereal into a bowl, the clink of spoon against ceramic unnaturally loud in the oppressive silence. The television drones on in the background, a lifeline of white noise filling the void where conversation should be.

Drake clears his throat. "So, uh, how's school going?"

Harrison shrugs, his eyes fixed on the soggy flakes drowning in milk. "Fine."

Drake's mind races, searching for something, anything to say. He remembers a time when words flowed easily between them, when laughter echoed through this very kitchen. Now, every sentence feels like navigating a minefield.

"Listen, Harrison, I know things have been... difficult," Drake begins, his voice barely above a whisper. "But I want you to know-"

A car horn blares outside, shattering the fragile moment. Harrison jolts as if electrified, nearly knocking over his cereal bowl as he scrambles to his feet.

"Gotta go," he mutters, grabbing his backpack.

Drake rises, his chair scraping against the floor. "Wait, don't you want to finish your-"

But Harrison is already moving, a whirlwind of teenage urgency. Drake watches helplessly as his son throws on his jacket, fumbling with the zipper.

"Harrison," Drake calls out, desperation creeping into his voice. "I... I love you, son."

Harrison pauses at the door, his hand on the knob. For a fleeting moment, Drake sees a flicker of something in his eyes – pain? Longing? – before it's swallowed by that ever-present weariness.

"Yeah," Harrison says, not quite meeting Drake's gaze. "See you later."

The door closes, leaving Drake alone in the kitchen, the echo of his son's departure ringing in his ears.

11 - 12

Harrison's hand is already on the doorknob when Drake's voice cuts through the air, tinged with a desperate attempt at connection.

"That's Mike. I gotta go," Harrison says, his words clipped and rushed.

Drake's heart clenches. He can feel the distance between them, a chasm that seems to widen with each passing day. He wants to reach out, to bridge that gap, but every attempt feels like grasping at smoke.

"What about the match?" Drake asks, trying to keep his voice steady. He remembers a time when Harrison's soccer matches were a source of shared excitement, a bond between father and son. Now, they feel like just another reminder of what's been lost.

Harrison's shoulders tense, his back still turned to Drake. The silence stretches between them, heavy with unspoken words and buried emotions. Drake watches his son, noting the slight tremor in Harrison's hand as it grips the doorknob. He wants to cross the room, to pull his boy into an embrace, to tell him that everything will be okay. But he remains rooted to the spot, paralyzed by the fear of pushing Harrison further away.

I'm losing him, Drake thinks, a wave of panic washing over him. How do I hold onto someone who's slipping through my fingers?

13 - 14

Harrison pauses, his hand still on the doorknob. He turns slightly, just enough for Drake to catch a glimpse of his profile. The uncertainty flickering in Harrison's eyes is a stark contrast to the cocky teenager he usually portrays. For a moment, Drake sees the little boy who used to run to him with skinned knees and wild stories.

"What about it?" Harrison asks, his voice a mix of defensiveness and genuine confusion. The words hang in the air, loaded with unspoken tension.

Drake's mind races, searching for the right words. He wants to say so much - how proud he is, how much he misses their old relationship, how desperately he wants to be there for his son. But the words stick in his throat, trapped behind years of misunderstandings and growing distance.

I used to know exactly what to say to him, Drake thinks, a pang of regret hitting him. When did we become strangers?

Harrison shifts his weight, clearly impatient to leave but something holding him back. His eyes dart around the room, landing briefly on the Star Wars decorations scattered about - remnants of a shared passion that now feels like it belongs to another lifetime.

"It's just a match," Harrison mumbles, but there's a hint of something else in his voice. Disappointment? Longing? Drake can't quite place it, and the uncertainty gnaws at him.

15 - 16

Drake swallows hard, his heart pounding. He takes a deep breath, steeling himself for the answer he fears.

"Do you want me there?" he asks, his voice softer than intended, betraying his vulnerability.

The question hangs in the air, heavy with the weight of their fractured relationship. Drake watches his son intently, searching for any flicker of emotion beneath the teenage bravado.

Harrison shrugs, a gesture so casual yet so devastating. The indifference radiating from him is palpable, a barrier between them as impenetrable as any physical wall.

God, when did it become so hard to reach him? Drake thinks, a wave of sadness washing over him. He remembers a time when Harrison would beam with pride at having his father in the stands, cheering him on. Now, that eager little boy seems like a distant memory.

"It's whatever," Harrison mutters, his eyes fixed on a point somewhere beyond Drake's shoulder.

Drake feels the sting of rejection, but pushes past it. "I'd like to be there," he says, trying to keep his voice steady. "To support you. Like I used to."

Harrison's eyes flick to meet his father's for a brief moment, and Drake catches a glimpse of something - uncertainty? - before the teenager's guard slams back into place.

"Suit yourself," Harrison says with another shrug, but there's a slight catch in his voice that gives Drake a glimmer of hope.

17 - 18

"Whatever you think," Harrison mumbles, his tone a mixture of forced nonchalance and suppressed emotion.

Drake's heart clenches at the dismissive words, but he refuses to let his disappointment show. He watches as Harrison slings his backpack over his shoulder, turning the doorknob with an air of finality that feels like a physical blow.

As Harrison makes his way out, Drake rises from his seat, his body moving almost of its own accord. His arms lift slightly, reaching out in a silent, desperate plea for connection. The gesture feels awkward, foreign – when was the last time he'd hugged his son?

I can't let him leave like this, Drake thinks, his mind racing. Not again. Not when every moment could be...

He swallows hard, pushing away the thought of the other world, where Harrison is gone forever. The rubber band on his wrist suddenly feels tight, a reminder of the precarious balance he's trying to maintain.

"Harrison," Drake calls out, his voice rough with emotion. "I... I'll be there. Front row."

Harrison pauses at the threshold, his hand on the doorknob. For a moment, he doesn't turn, and Drake holds his breath, hoping for some sign that his words have reached through the wall between them.

19 - 20

"Wait," Drake says, his voice cracking with a desperation he can't fully hide. The single word hangs in the air, heavy with unspoken emotion.

Before Harrison can react, Drake crosses the room in two quick strides. He wraps his arms around his son, pulling him into a tight embrace. Harrison's body stiffens in surprise, but Drake doesn't let go. He holds on as if his son might disappear at any moment, his grip a physical manifestation of his fear and love.

Drake closes his eyes, drinking in the sensation of holding his child. He breathes in deeply, catching the faint scent of Harrison's shampoo, mixed with the lingering aroma of their shared breakfast. This is real, he tells himself. This moment, this world – it's real.

"Dad," Harrison mumbles, his voice muffled against Drake's shoulder. There's a hint of embarrassment in his tone, but he doesn't pull away.

Drake's mind races, awash with conflicting emotions. How many times had he been too busy for moments like this? How many embraces had he missed, prioritizing work over these precious connections? The weight of his past choices threatens to overwhelm him.

"I love you, son," Drake whispers, the words catching in his throat. He wants to say more – to apologize for every missed game, every distracted conversation. But he knows this isn't the time. Not yet.

As he holds his son, Drake can't shake the feeling that he's clinging to a lifeline in a stormy sea. This embrace is his anchor, tethering him to a reality that feels increasingly fragile with each passing day.

21 - 22

Harrison's body remains tense in Drake's arms, his teenage defenses still firmly in place. But Drake doesn't let go, not yet. He holds on, his fingers gripping the fabric of Harrison's jacket, memorizing the feeling of his son's solid presence.

Drake's mind races. In another world, this moment doesn't exist. In another world, his arms are empty, grasping at nothing but grief and regret. The thought makes him tighten his embrace involuntarily.

"Dad, seriously," Harrison mumbles, a hint of exasperation creeping into his voice. "I'm gonna be late."

Drake takes a deep breath, steeling himself to let go. He pulls back slightly, his hands moving to Harrison's shoulders. His eyes roam over his son's face, drinking in every detail – the slight furrow of his brow, the flicker of impatience in his eyes, the way his curls fall across his forehead.

"Take care out there, son," Drake says, his voice thick with emotion. He searches Harrison's face for any sign of understanding, any hint that his son can sense the depth of his feelings.

Harrison's expression remains guarded, but there's a flicker of something – concern? confusion? – in his eyes. For a moment, Drake sees the little boy who used to run to him with scraped knees and fantastic stories, seeking comfort and validation.

As Harrison shifts his weight, ready to break away, Drake feels the weight of unspoken words between them. He wants to say more, to bridge the chasm that's grown between them. But he knows that now isn't the time. He has to let go, has to trust that there will be more moments, more chances to reconnect.

23 - 24

Harrison nods, a flicker of something akin to gratitude crossing his features. "Yeah, okay," he mumbles, his cocky teenage facade momentarily slipping. Then, with a quick glance at his watch, he's gone, slipping out the door and leaving Drake alone in the suddenly quiet kitchen.

The sound of the door closing echoes through the house, and Drake feels the absence of his son like a physical ache. He stands there for a moment, his hand still outstretched, before letting it fall to his side.

"Another day," he murmurs to himself, running a hand through his disheveled hair. The weight of his dual realities settles back onto his shoulders as he moves into the living room.

Sunlight filters through the half-drawn curtains, casting dappled patterns on the walls. Drake's eyes are drawn to the mantle, where a collection of family photos stands in silent testament to happier times.

He approaches slowly, his gaze lingering on each frozen moment of joy. There's Harrison at his first soccer match, Linda beaming with pride at a school event, the three of them laughing on a long-ago beach vacation.

"God, Linda," Drake whispers, his fingers ghosting over her smiling face in one of the photos. "How did we end up here?"

The silence of the house offers no answer, and Drake finds himself drowning in a wave of conflicting memories. In one world, Linda's laughter still fills these rooms. In another, it's Harrison's presence that's achingly absent.

"How do I fix this?" he asks the empty room, his voice barely audible. "How do I save you both?"

25 - 26

Drake's fingers tremble as they reach out, drawn inexorably to a particular frame. It's Harrison, beaming with pride, a gleaming trophy held aloft in his hands. The boy's curly hair is tousled, his eyes alight with the thrill of victory. Drake's throat tightens as he gently traces the edge of the frame, his calloused fingertips grazing the cool glass.

"You were so happy that day," he murmurs, lost in the memory. "I promised I'd be there for your next match, didn't I?"

The weight of that broken promise settles heavily in his chest. Drake closes his eyes, inhaling sharply as he tries to anchor himself in the present moment. When he opens them again, his gaze is filled with a mixture of longing and determination.

"In one world, he's alive, vibrant," Drake whispers, his voice barely audible. "In the other..."

He can't bring himself to finish the thought, the pain too raw, too immediate. Instead, he focuses on the warmth of Harrison's smile in the photograph, trying to draw strength from it.

"I'll find a way to make this right, son," Drake vows, his fingers still resting on the frame. "I don't know how, but I'll find a way to bring our family back together. In both worlds."

As he stands there, caught between grief and hope, Drake can almost hear the echo of Harrison's laughter, a bittersweet reminder of what he's fighting for. The silence of the house presses in around him, but in that moment, looking at his son's triumphant face, Drake feels a flicker of the determination that once made him an unstoppable force in the courtroom.

"No more letting you down," he promises softly. "Whatever it takes, I'll be there. In every world."

27 - 28

Drake's fingers slip from the frame, the cold glass a stark reminder of the reality he faces. He turns away, his shoulders slumping under an invisible weight as he makes his way to the police station.

The precinct buzzes with activity, but Drake barely notices as he slumps into his chair. A mountain of paperwork looms before him, each file a potential lead or dead end in the maze of his fractured existence. He flips through them mechanically, his mind a whirlwind of fragmented memories and unanswered questions.

"Harrison's match," he mutters to himself, rubbing his temples. "I can't miss it. Not again."

His eyes drift to the green rubber band on his wrist, a lifeline in the storm of his dual realities. Drake snaps it gently, the sting grounding him in the present.

"Focus, Miller," he chides himself. "One case at a time. One world at a time."

But as he stares at the files, the words blur together. Images flash through his mind: the white robe, the mysterious symbol, the abandoned car. Each piece of evidence feels like it's just out of reach, taunting him with answers he can't quite grasp.

"What am I missing?" Drake whispers, his voice tinged with frustration. "What's the connection?"

He leans back in his chair, closing his eyes for a moment. In the darkness behind his eyelids, he sees Linda's face, then Harrison's, their features overlapping in a haunting reminder of what he's lost - and what he's desperately trying to save.

29 - 30

The door creaks open, the sound jarring Drake from his introspection. He looks up, his tired eyes meeting the concerned gaze of Holly Kierstead as she steps into the office. Her brow is furrowed, lips pressed into a thin line - a telltale sign that something's amiss.

Drake's heart rate quickens, his mind instantly alert. What now? he thinks, bracing himself for whatever news his partner brings.

Holly's presence fills the small space, her determination palpable. She closes the door behind her with a soft click, then turns to face him.

"Drake, we need to talk," she says, her voice low and urgent.

The gravity in her tone sends a chill down Drake's spine. He straightens in his chair, pushing aside the scattered files. His fingers instinctively find the green rubber band on his wrist, twisting it as he tries to anchor himself in this reality.

"What is it, Holly?" he asks, his voice rough with fatigue and apprehension. "Did something break in the case?"

Drake watches as Holly takes a deep breath, her shoulders squaring as if preparing to deliver a blow. The tension in the room thickens, and he finds himself holding his breath, waiting for the words that might shatter his fragile grip on this world - or bring him one step closer to understanding the mystery that plagues his existence.

31 - 32

Drake's weary gaze meets Holly's intense stare, the lines etched deep around his eyes testament to the weight he carries. His fingers continue to fidget with the green rubber band, a nervous habit that grounds him in this reality.

"What is it, Holly?" he asks, his voice a gravelly whisper. The words hang in the air, heavy with anticipation and dread.

As he waits for her response, Drake's mind races. What could be so urgent? Has she discovered something about the accident? About the other world? The possibility both terrifies and excites him, sending a surge of adrenaline through his exhausted body.

He leans forward slightly, elbows resting on the cluttered desk, his dark eyes searching Holly's face for any clue. The silence stretches between them, thick with unspoken tension and the promise of revelations that could change everything.

33 - 34

Holly's voice cuts through the silence, her words sharp and clear. "The police found the car."

The impact of her statement hits Drake like a physical blow. His heart stutters, then begins to race, pumping adrenaline through his veins. The world around him seems to fade, the bustling police station receding into a muted blur as his focus narrows to this single, earth-shattering piece of information.

"The car," he repeats, his voice barely above a whisper. His mind reels, struggling to process the implications. Is this the breakthrough he's been desperately seeking? The key to unraveling the mystery of his fractured existence?

Drake's hand instinctively moves to the green rubber band on his wrist, snapping it gently. The subtle sting helps anchor him in this reality, even as his thoughts threaten to spiral. He takes a deep breath, trying to steady himself.

"How... when did they find it?" he manages to ask, his eyes locked on Holly's face, searching for any additional clues she might offer.

As he waits for her response, Drake's heart continues to pound, each beat a reminder of the relentless passage of time and the weight of the secrets he carries. The possibility of answers, of finally understanding the connection between his two lives, looms tantalizingly close.

35 - 36

Drake leans forward in his chair, his hands gripping the edge of his desk so tightly his knuckles turn white. "Where?" he asks, his voice hoarse with a mixture of anticipation and dread.

Holly's sharp gaze meets his, her expression a blend of professional detachment and underlying concern for her partner. "Abandoned in an alley downtown," she replies, her tone measured and precise. "License plate matches the one from the accident. The one you described."

Drake's breath catches in his throat. The confirmation sends a jolt through him, a surge of validation mingled with a creeping sense of unease. His mind races, piecing together the implications of this discovery.

'It's real,' he thinks, a wave of relief washing over him. 'I'm not losing my mind. The accident, the car... it all happened.'

But even as this realization settles, new questions arise, crowding his thoughts. Who abandoned the car? Why there? And most importantly, what other evidence might it hold?

Drake's fingers unconsciously find the green rubber band on his wrist, twisting it as he struggles to maintain his composure. He wants to rush out, to see the car for himself, to search for any clue that might bridge the gap between his two realities. But he forces himself to remain seated, to approach this methodically.

"Have they processed it yet?" he asks Holly, striving to keep his voice steady despite the tumult of emotions coursing through him.

37 - 38

Drake's mind whirls with the implications, his fingers still idly twisting the green band on his wrist. Two worlds, one car, but found in different locations. The dichotomy of his fractured reality hits him anew, a dizzying sensation that threatens to overwhelm him.

He takes a deep breath, centering himself. "And the driver?" he asks, his voice tight with barely contained urgency.

As he waits for Holly's response, Drake's thoughts race. In one world, Harrison is alive, a sullen teenager grappling with the loss of his mother. In the other, it's Linda who survives, bearing the weight of their son's absence. The stark differences between these realities suddenly seem more pronounced than ever.

'How can the same car exist in both worlds, yet be found in different places?' he wonders, the paradox gnawing at him. 'What does it mean for the driver? For the truth I'm seeking?'

Drake leans forward, his eyes fixed on Holly, silently willing her to provide some answers, some thread he can follow to unravel this maddening mystery. The weight of his dual existence presses down on him, a constant reminder of what he's lost and what he's desperately trying to hold onto in both realities.

39 - 40

Holly meets Drake's intense gaze, her own eyes reflecting a mix of concern and determination. "The driver was gone," she says, her voice low and steady. "But they found something in the car."

Drake's heart rate quickens, his palms growing clammy. He leans forward, bracing himself for whatever revelation is coming. "What did they find?" he asks, his voice barely above a whisper.

Holly pauses, her expression grave. The silence stretches between them, heavy with unspoken tension. Drake can see the wheels turning in her mind, her analytical nature warring with her instinct to protect him from potentially disturbing information.

'What could be so serious?' Drake wonders, his mind racing through possibilities. 'Evidence of the driver's identity? A clue to their motive? Or something far more sinister?'

He watches Holly closely, noting the slight furrow of her brow, the way her fingers tap lightly on the edge of his desk. Her hesitation only fuels his anxiety, each passing second feeling like an eternity.

"Holly," Drake prompts, unable to bear the suspense any longer. "Whatever it is, I need to know. Please."

41 - 42

Holly takes a deep breath, her eyes locking onto Drake's. "A white robe," she says, her voice low and measured, "embroidered with a symbol."

The words hit Drake like a physical blow. His blood runs cold, a chill creeping up his spine as if icy fingers were tracing his vertebrae. The fluorescent lights of the office suddenly seem too harsh, too bright, as the world around him narrows to a pinpoint.

'A white robe,' he thinks, his mind reeling. 'Why does that feel so... significant?'

Drake's hands clench involuntarily, his knuckles turning white as he grips the edge of his desk. He can feel Holly's eyes on him, watching, assessing his reaction. But he can't bring himself to meet her gaze, too caught up in the storm of emotions and half-formed memories swirling through his mind.

"Drake?" Holly's voice seems to come from far away. "Are you okay?"

He forces himself to take a deep breath, trying to steady his racing heart. "Yeah," he manages, though his voice sounds strained even to his own ears. "I'm fine. It's just... unexpected."

'But why?' he wonders. 'Why does this feel like more than just another piece of evidence? Why does it feel like a key to something I've forgotten?'

Drake looks up at Holly, seeing the concern etched on her face. He knows he should say more, should ask questions, but the words stick in his throat. Instead, he finds himself staring at the space between them, his mind grappling with the implications of this new information and the unsettling feeling that he's on the verge of uncovering something both vital and terrifying.

43 - 44

Drake swallows hard, his throat dry as sandpaper. "What symbol?" he asks, his voice barely above a whisper.

Holly leans in closer, her brow furrowed with concern. "I'm not sure. But it's... unsettling," she says, her eyes searching Drake's face. "I think it's a dragon circling around a tree."

Drake's mind reels, fragments of memory flashing through his consciousness like shards of broken glass. A dragon... a tree... why does this sound so familiar? His heart pounds in his chest, each beat echoing in his ears like a thunderclap.

"A dragon and a tree," he repeats, tasting the words, feeling their weight on his tongue. His fingers unconsciously trace the outline of the green rubber band on his wrist, a lifeline between realities. "That's... specific."

Holly nods, her gaze intense. "It is. Drake, what aren't you telling me?"

He shakes his head, struggling to articulate the storm of emotions and half-formed thoughts swirling within him. "I don't know," he admits, frustration seeping into his voice. "It's like... like I should know what this means, but I can't quite grasp it."

The office seems to shrink around him, the walls closing in. Drake fights the urge to flee, to escape the suffocating weight of this new revelation. Instead, he forces himself to meet Holly's eyes, seeing the determination mirrored there.

"We need to find out more about this symbol," he says, his resolve strengthening with each word. "It could be the key to everything."

45 - 46

Drake leans forward, his palms flat on the desk, eyes blazing with newfound purpose. "This symbol, Holly. It's not just a coincidence. It's the same in both..." he catches himself, realizing he can't fully explain his dual realities. "It's significant."

Holly raises an eyebrow, curiosity piqued. "Both what, Drake?"

He waves off her question, mind racing. "Never mind that. What matters is this symbol connects everything. The car, the robe, the... the accident." His voice catches on the last word, memories of screeching tires and shattering glass threatening to overwhelm him.

Pushing back from the desk, Drake begins to pace, his movements agitated. "We need to cross-reference this symbol with every database we have access to. Religious organizations, cults, secret societies - anything that might use a dragon and tree motif."

"Drake," Holly interjects, concern evident in her tone. "You're getting that look again. The one that says you're about to dive headfirst into something dangerous."

He pauses, a rueful smile tugging at his lips. "Maybe I am. But this is the first real lead we've had. I can feel it, Holly. This is the thread that will unravel everything."

His mind drifts to Harrison, to Linda, to the fractured family he's desperately trying to hold together across two realities. "I have to know what happened that night," he says softly, more to himself than to Holly. "For all our sakes."

47 - 48

Holly nods, her eyes reflecting his determination. The set of her jaw and the slight furrow of her brow speak volumes about her commitment to the case and her loyalty to her partner. She understands the gravity of the situation, the weight it carries for Drake.

"I'm on it," she says, her voice firm and resolute. There's a glint of steel in her gaze, a promise of relentless pursuit. Holly's fingers twitch slightly, already itching to start digging into databases and following leads.

Drake feels a surge of gratitude for his partner's unwavering support. He knows Holly's tenacity, her ability to piece together seemingly unrelated bits of information. If anyone can help him unravel this mystery, it's her.

"Thanks, Holly," he says, his voice thick with emotion. "I don't know what I'd do without you on this."

As Holly turns to leave, Drake's mind races, trying to connect the dots between the two realities he's been navigating. The symbol, the robe, the car - they're constants in both worlds. But what does it all mean? And how deep does this rabbit hole go?

49 - 49

As Holly's footsteps fade down the hallway, Drake's mind drifts back to the image of the white robe, its pristine fabric a stark contrast to the darkness it represents. A chill crawls up his spine, his fingers unconsciously tightening around the edge of his desk.

"A dragon circling a tree," he mutters, his brow furrowing. The symbol tugs at something in his memory, a wisp of recognition that dances just out of reach. He closes his eyes, trying to focus, to grasp that elusive thread of thought.

In his mind's eye, the robe takes shape, the embroidered symbol seeming to writhe and pulse with an otherworldly energy. Drake's breath catches in his throat, a sudden wave of unease washing over him.

"What are you?" he whispers, opening his eyes and staring unseeing at the cluttered surface of his desk. "What's your connection to all of this?"

He reaches for his wrist, fingers brushing against the green rubber band. Its presence grounds him, a touchstone between his fractured realities. Drake takes a deep breath, centering himself.

"I need to dig deeper," he thinks, determination setting his jaw. "There has to be a link between the symbol and the accident. Something I'm missing."

Drake stands, restless energy propelling him to pace the small confines of his office. His mind races, connecting fragments of information, searching for patterns.

"If the robe and symbol are consistent in both worlds," he muses aloud, "then whoever's behind this must exist in both realities too. But how? And why?"

The questions swirl in his mind, each one spawning a dozen more. Drake runs a hand through his disheveled hair, frustration and determination warring within him.

"I have to find answers," he mutters, his voice low and intense. "For Harrison. For Linda. For my own sanity."

He pauses by the window, gazing out at the bustling city below. Somewhere out there, hidden among the crowds and concrete, lurks the truth he so desperately seeks.

"I won't stop until I uncover it," Drake vows, his reflection in the glass staring back at him with haunted, determined eyes. "No matter what it takes."

Solitude and Anxieties

Green World – 2024

1 - 2

The door clicks shut behind Kierstead, leaving Miller alone in the suffocating silence of his office. His fingers drum an anxious rhythm on the polished wood of his desk, each tap echoing like a heartbeat in the empty room. He leans back in his chair, the leather creaking under his weight, and closes his eyes.

Behind his eyelids, the mysterious symbol flashes, burning like a brand on his retinas. Its intricate lines and curves seem to writhe and twist, defying logic and reason. Miller's brow furrows, a bead of sweat trickling down his temple.

"The symbol..." he mutters, his voice barely above a whisper. "It's like something out of a nightmare."

He opens his eyes, blinking rapidly as if to dispel the haunting image. The fluorescent lights overhead flicker, casting strange shadows across the room. For a moment, Miller swears he sees the symbol etched in the play of light and dark on the wall, but it vanishes as quickly as it appeared.

His hand instinctively reaches for the drawer where he keeps his anxiety medication, but he stops himself. No, he needs a clear head for this. He can't afford to dull his senses, not when every instinct screams that he's on the precipice of something monumental.

Miller's gaze drifts to the case files spread across his desk, each one a piece of a puzzle he can't quite solve. The weight of unsolved mysteries presses down on him, a familiar burden that seems heavier than ever before.

He leans forward, elbows on the desk, and buries his face in his hands. The scent of coffee and old paper fills his nostrils, grounding him in the familiar when everything else feels alien and threatening.

"What am I missing?" he asks the empty room, his words muffled against his palms. "What aren't I seeing?"

The silence offers no answers, only the faint hum of the air conditioning and the distant sounds of the city beyond his window. Miller raises his head, his eyes bloodshot and weary, but filled with a determined glint.

"I won't let this beat me," he declares, straightening in his chair. "Whatever this symbol means, whoever's behind it... I'll find them. I have to."

His resolve doesn't quite mask the tremor in his voice, the underlying fear of what he might uncover. But as he reaches for the nearest file, Miller knows he has no choice but to press on. The truth is out there, hidden in the shadows, and he's the only one who can bring it to light.

3 - 4

Drake's hand trembles as he reaches for his phone, the sleek device a stark contrast to the chaos swirling in his mind. His fingers, usually steady and precise, now fumble across the screen, betraying the anxiety gnawing at his core. He pulls up a search engine, his dark eyes reflecting the blue glow of the display.

"Come on," he mutters, typing in a description of the symbol that's been haunting him. "There has to be something."

The phone buzzes softly as results populate the screen. Drake's heart races, hope flickering briefly before being extinguished by disappointment. Page after page yields nothing but unrelated images and irrelevant information.

He tries different combinations of keywords, his frustration mounting with each fruitless search. The symbol, with its intricate lines and haunting symmetry, seems to exist only in his mind and on that fateful piece of evidence.

Drake's thoughts drift to Harrison, wondering if his son's inquisitive nature might have helped unravel this mystery. The pang of longing is sharp and immediate, reminding him of the life he's lost – or perhaps the life he's living in another reality.

"Nothing," he says aloud, his voice a mix of disbelief and resignation. "It's like it doesn't even exist."

The words hang heavy in the air, a verbal manifestation of the dead ends surrounding him. Drake stares at his phone, the screen now dark, reflecting his own tired face back at him. The absence of information feels more oppressive than any lead, leaving him adrift in a sea of questions without answers.

5 - 6

Frustration claws at Drake's insides, his mind a tempest of unanswered questions. The weight of uncertainty presses down on him, threatening to crush his resolve. He runs a trembling hand through his dark hair, disheveling it further.

"I can't let this go," he murmurs, his voice barely audible. The memory of Linda's gentle encouragement echoes in his mind, a stark contrast to the chaos of his current reality. "She'd want me to keep digging, to find the truth."

Drake's eyes dart around the room, searching for something, anything that might offer a clue. The shadows seem to lengthen, closing in on him like the creeping tendrils of doubt.

"There has to be a connection," he thinks, his inner voice tinged with desperation. "Some thread I'm missing."

He leans back in his chair, the leather creaking under his weight. The sound startles him, momentarily breaking his spiral of frustration.

"Damn it," Drake growls, the words escaping through clenched teeth. His fists ball up, knuckles white with tension. "I can't let them win. I can't let my family down again."

The thought of failure, of letting his loved ones slip away in both realities, sends a shudder through his body. He takes a deep breath, trying to center himself, to find that spark of determination that's gotten him through countless trials in the courtroom.

"One step at a time, Miller," he tells himself, echoing the advice he once gave to a young, eager Harrison. "The truth is out there. You just need to find it."

7 - 8

Drake's fist crashes down on the desk, the thunderous impact reverberating through the empty office. Pens rattle in their holder, and a framed photo of Linda and Harrison teeters precariously on the edge. He catches it reflexively, his fingers trembling as they brush across the smiling faces frozen in time.

"I should call the police," he mutters, reaching for his phone. But as his thumb hovers over the keypad, doubt creeps in. What would he even tell them? A mysterious symbol, a vanished cult, and two parallel realities? They'd think he was mad.

Drake's mind races, recalling every procedural hurdle he'd ever thrown up as a defense attorney. "Without concrete evidence, they'd be useless," he realizes, his voice barely above a whisper. "They'd be chasing shadows, just like me."

He slumps back in his chair, the weight of isolation pressing down on him. The office, once a sanctuary of order and control, now feels like a prison of unanswered questions. Drake's gaze drifts to the window, the city lights blurring as he loses focus.

"It's like they vanished into thin air," he says, his words hanging in the stillness. The frustration in his voice is palpable, tinged with a hint of awe at the cult's efficiency. "How does an entire organization just... disappear?"

His thoughts turn to Harrison, imagining his son's inquisitive mind tackling this puzzle. "He'd probably have some wild theory about invisible ink or secret tunnels," Drake muses, a sad smile tugging at his lips. The ache of separation, of loss, threatens to overwhelm him once more.

9 - 10

Drake exhales heavily, his body sinking deeper into the leather chair as the gravity of the situation settles over him. The dim office lights cast long shadows across his face, accentuating the lines of worry etched into his features.

"What kind of game are they playing?" he mutters, his mind churning with possibilities. Each theory seems more outlandish than the last, yet none can be dismissed. The weight of two realities presses on him, making even this singular mystery feel insurmountable.

His eyes flick to the framed photo on his desk – Linda's smile frozen in time, a reminder of what's at stake. "I can't let them win," Drake whispers, his resolve strengthening. "Not when my family's on the line."

He leans forward, elbows on the desk, head in his hands. The silence of the office is broken only by the soft ticking of the clock, each second a reminder of time slipping away.

"Well," Drake says, his voice low and determined, "they won't get away with it. Not if I have anything to say about it." The words hang in the air, a declaration of intent against an unseen enemy.

His jaw sets, a flicker of the old, tenacious lawyer emerging through the haze of confusion and grief. For a moment, he can almost hear Harrison's voice, full of teenage bravado: "Go get 'em, Dad. Show 'em what a Miller can do."

The thought brings a mix of pain and determination. Whatever this cult is, whatever reality-bending power they possess, Drake knows he has to press on. For Linda, for Harrison, for the family he's lost and the one he's fighting to save.

11 - 11

Drake pushes back from his desk, the chair wheels squeaking softly on the worn office carpet. He stands, stretching his tired muscles, and moves to the window. Outside, the streets of Bridgewater are covered in rain, the street lights twinkling against the darkening sky. It's a scene that should bring comfort, but tonight it only serves to remind him of the secrets lurking beneath the town's picturesque facade.

"Time to shake some trees," he mutters, his breath fogging the cold glass.

He turns back to his desk, grabbing his coat and car keys. As he shrugs on his jacket, his mind races through potential leads. Who in town might have information about this mysterious symbol? Who would be willing to talk?

Drake pauses at the door, his hand on the knob. "Linda," he says softly, as if she could hear him across the fractured realities. "I'm doing this for us. For our family."

He steps out into the hallway, locking his office behind him. The building is quiet, most of the other policePolice having gone home hours ago. His footsteps echo as he makes his way to the elevator, each step filled with purpose.

In the parking lot, Drake's breath comes out in white puffs as he hurries to his car. The cold bites at his exposed skin, a sharp reminder of the world beyond his internal struggles. As he slides into the driver's seat, he takes a moment to gather his thoughts.

"Okay, Drake," he says to himself, gripping the steering wheel. "Where do you start when you're looking for answers about a reality-bending cult?" He laughs humorlessly. "God, if Linda could hear me now..."

He starts the engine, the car's heater slowly coming to life. As he pulls out of the parking lot, Drake's mind is already mapping out the seedier parts of Bridgewater. The bars where secrets are traded like currency, the back alleys where whispers carry more weight than shouts.

"Whatever it takes," he promises himself, his eyes fixed on the road ahead. "I'll find the truth, even if I have to turn this whole city upside down."

Crimson Threshold

Green World – 2024

1 - 2

The metallic scent of blood assaulted Drake Miller's nostrils as he stepped over the threshold. His eyes traced the crimson trail across pristine white tiles, leading him inexorably toward the living room. Each step felt heavier than the last, dread building in his chest.

"Oh God," he whispered, bile rising in his throat as he took in the scene before him.

Tom and Irene Johnson lay motionless on their plush beige carpet, limbs splayed at unnatural angles. The violence of their demise stood in stark contrast to the peaceful suburban home surrounding them. Family photos smiled down from the walls, oblivious to the horror below.

Miller's fists clenched at his sides as he fought to maintain his composure. *Focus,* he commanded himself. *You've seen worse.* But even as the thought formed, he knew it wasn't true. This felt personal in a way no other crime scene ever had.

He heard footsteps behind him and turned, expecting to see Keirstead. But his partner breezed past without a word, her gaze fixed on something in the kitchen. Miller followed, puzzled.

"Keirstead?" he ventured.

She didn't respond, seemingly mesmerized by an elaborate coffee maker on the counter. Her fingers traced its sleek chrome surface, lost in thought.

Miller cleared his throat. "What is it? Did you find something?"

Keirstead's eyes remained on the appliance. "It's nothing," she murmured. "Just... thinking."

What the hell? Miller wondered. *Two people are dead, and she's fixated on a coffee maker?* He opened his mouth to press further, but something in Keirstead's expression gave him pause. There was a faraway look in her eyes, tinged with an emotion he couldn't quite place.

Instead, he turned back to survey the crime scene, his mind racing. *Focus on what matters,* he chided himself. *There's a killer out there, and a missing girl who needs to be found.*

The weight of responsibility settled heavily on his shoulders. He thought of Harrison, of the unimaginable pain of losing a child. His resolve hardened.

"We need to start processing the scene," he said firmly, pushing aside his confusion at Keirstead's behavior. "Every second counts."

As if snapping out of a trance, Keirstead nodded. "You're right," she agreed, her usual businesslike demeanor returning. "Let's get to work."

Miller took a deep breath, steeling himself for the grim task ahead. *Whatever happened here,* he vowed silently, *we'll find the truth. No matter what it takes.*

3 - 4

Keirstead's piercing gaze suddenly snapped to the coffee maker. She pointed, her voice taking on an unexpected, almost wistful tone. "You see this thing? My ex always wanted one of these. Told her she wanted a six-hundred-dollar coffee maker, she should've married a CEO. We eventually agreed on that."

Miller blinked, caught off guard by the abrupt shift in conversation. *What the hell?* he thought, struggling to reconcile Keirstead's seemingly casual reminiscence with the gruesome scene surrounding them. He opened his mouth to respond, but Keirstead had already fallen silent.

She paused, her eyes now scanning the crime scene with a mix of weariness and determination. The momentary vulnerability vanished, replaced by the sharp, analytical gaze Miller was more accustomed to. He watched as her keen eyes darted from the blood-stained tiles to the overturned furniture, cataloging every detail.

There's more to her than meets the eye, Miller mused, a newfound respect mingling with his curiosity. He'd always known Keirstead was tough, but this glimpse into her personal life, however brief, hinted at hidden depths.

The air grew heavy with unspoken tension as they both absorbed the full gravity of the situation before them. Miller's heart raced, his mind already piecing together the puzzle of this brutal crime. But Keirstead's unexpected moment of candor lingered, a reminder of the human element in their grim profession.

5 - 6

Keirstead's piercing gaze locked onto Miller, her voice cutting through the eerie silence. "Tell me what you see, Miller. I'll tell you what you miss."

The challenge in her tone was unmistakable, stirring something within Drake. He took a deep breath, pushing aside the lingering thoughts of his fractured reality, and focused on the scene before him. His eyes swept methodically across the room, years of legal training kicking in as he cataloged every detail.

"Jesus," Drake muttered under his breath, his stomach churning as he took in the full extent of the carnage. The living room, once a picture of suburban comfort, now resembled a war zone. An overturned coffee table lay splintered near the fireplace, its contents strewn across the blood-spattered carpet.

As he moved deeper into the room, the coppery scent of blood grew stronger, threatening to overwhelm him. *Focus, dammit,* Drake chided himself. *This isn't about you.*

"The struggle was... intense," he said, his voice rough with emotion. "Whoever did this, they weren't just here to rob the place. This was personal."

Drake's gaze lingered on a family photo hanging askew on the wall, its glass cracked but the image still visible – a moment of joy forever tainted by the horror that had unfolded here. A lump formed in his throat as he thought of his own family, of the parallel lives he led and the loved ones he couldn't protect.

"There's more," he continued, forcing himself to remain professional. "The blood spatter patterns suggest one attacker. And look at the way the furniture is positioned – they were cornered, trapped with nowhere to run."

7 - 8

Drake swallowed hard, his jaw clenching as he forced himself to verbalize the grim reality before him. "Husband and wife. Multiple stab wounds. Signs of a struggle, but they were overpowered."

His words hung in the air, heavy with the weight of lives lost. Drake's mind raced, drawing parallels to his own fractured existence. In one world, he could be investigating Linda's murder; in another, Harrison's. The thought sent a chill down his spine, and he had to remind himself to breathe.

Keirstead nodded grimly, her gaze fixed on the photographs adorning the walls. Drake watched as her eyes scanned the images, lingering on each frozen moment of happiness. He recognized that look – the same one he wore when examining his own family photos, searching for clues to bridge the gap between his two realities.

"What do you see in those pictures, Keirstead?" Drake asked, his voice low and contemplative. He found himself drawn to a particular image – a family vacation photo, all smiles and sunburned noses. It was achingly familiar, reminding him of trips he'd taken with Linda and Harrison... and trips he'd missed due to work.

As Keirstead remained silent, Drake's thoughts drifted. *I can't let this happen to my family – in either world. I have to find a way to protect them, to make things right.* The determination that had driven him as a lawyer surged anew, fueled by a desperate need to safeguard those he loved.

9 - 10

Keirstead's voice cut through Drake's reverie, her tone a mixture of professionalism and underlying concern. "Their daughter's missing. We're reaching out to friends and family, hoping someone saw something."

The words hit Drake like a physical blow, his stomach twisting with a sickening lurch. His eyes darted instinctively to a framed photograph on the nearby side table, capturing a moment of familial bliss. A young girl's radiant smile beamed out at him, frozen in time, her eyes sparkling with an innocence that now felt painfully fragile.

Drake's hand reached out, almost of its own accord, fingertips brushing the cool glass of the frame. *God, she can't be much older than Harrison,* he thought, his throat constricting. The girl's features blurred, momentarily replaced by his son's mischievous grin, then Linda's warm smile. He blinked hard, forcing himself back to the present.

"Any idea how long she's been gone?" Drake asked, his voice rougher than he intended. He cleared his throat, trying to maintain a professional facade even as his heart raced. *Focus, Miller. This isn't about you. This family needs justice... and that little girl needs to be found.*

Keirstead's reply faded into the background as Drake's gaze remained fixed on the photograph. The happy family scene felt like a cruel taunt now, a stark reminder of how quickly everything could change. He thought of his own fragmented reality, of the constant fear of losing those he loved in both worlds.

I have to find her, Drake vowed silently, his jaw clenching with determination. *Whatever it takes. No child should have their world torn apart like this.*

11 - 12

Drake tore his gaze away from the photograph, forcing himself to confront the grim reality of the present. His eyes met Keirstead's, searching for any glimmer of hope.

"Any leads on her whereabouts?" he asked, unable to keep a hint of desperation from creeping into his voice.

Keirstead's shoulders sagged imperceptibly, a flicker of frustration crossing her usually composed features. She shook her head slowly, the gesture heavy with unspoken worry. The weight of their shared concern seemed to settle over the room like a suffocating blanket.

Drake's mind raced, grasping for possibilities. *There has to be something we're missing,* he thought, his fingers drumming restlessly against his thigh. *Some connection, some clue that doesn't fit...*

He found himself scanning the room again, desperate for any detail that might spark a breakthrough. The pristine coffee maker Keirstead had fixated on earlier now seemed to mock them with its mundane presence amidst such horror.

"We need to think outside the box," Drake muttered, more to himself than to Keirstead. "What if this isn't just about the family? What if there's a larger pattern we're not seeing?"

The memory of the symbol from his accident flickered through his mind, sending a chill down his spine. *Could it really be connected?* he wondered, the implications both terrifying and oddly thrilling. *And if it is, what does that mean for this girl?*

13 - 14

Keirstead's voice cut through his spiraling thoughts, her tone a mixture of determination and carefully controlled frustration. "Not yet. But we're working on it. Someone out there knows something, we just have to find them."

Drake nodded, his jaw clenching as he absorbed her words. The weight of responsibility settled heavily on his shoulders, reminding him of countless late nights at the office, prioritizing cases over family dinners. But this time, the stakes were infinitely higher.

I can't let another family be torn apart, he thought, his mind flashing to Linda and Harrison's faces – each one a reminder of what he stood to lose in his fractured realities.

"We need to expand our search," Drake said, his voice low and intense. "Check security cameras in the surrounding blocks, canvas the neighbors again. Hell, even look into any local cults or fringe groups that might use that symbol."

As he spoke, Drake's gaze drifted back to the family photo on the wall. The young girl's frozen smile seemed to plead with him, begging for help. It stirred something primal within him, a fierce protectiveness he'd rediscovered since the accident.

With a resolute nod, Drake's resolve hardened. The familiar fire of determination – the same drive that had once made him a ruthless lawyer – now burned with a new purpose. Justice would be served, no matter the cost.

"Let's get to work," he said, already moving towards the door. "Time isn't on our side, and I'll be damned if we let this bastard slip through our fingers."

15 - 16

Miller's words hung in the air, charged with determination. "We'll find her, Keirstead. And whoever did this, they won't escape justice."

His gaze lingered on the photograph for a moment longer, the smiling faces of the Johnson family etching themselves into his memory. Drake felt a familiar tightness in his chest, a mixture of empathy and resolve that had become all too common since his accident.

As he turned away, a surge of urgency propelled him forward. The ticking of a nearby clock seemed to grow louder, each second a reminder of the precious time slipping away. *Every moment we waste, that little girl could be...* He couldn't bring himself to finish the thought.

Drake's mind raced, piecing together the fragments of information they'd gathered. The blood-stained tiles, the overturned furniture, the missing daughter – it all pointed to something far more sinister than a random home invasion.

"We need to move fast," he said, his voice low and intense. "Let's split up. I'll take another sweep of the house, see if we missed anything. You start coordinating with the team outside."

As Keirstead nodded and moved towards the door, Drake found himself drawn back to the family photos lining the walls. Each happy moment captured felt like a cruel juxtaposition to the horror that had unfolded here.

I won't let this family be torn apart, he thought, his determination fueled by the memories of his own fractured reality. *Not if I can help it.*

17 - 18

Drake Miller stepped into the daughter's bedroom, his senses immediately on high alert. The air felt thick, oppressive, as if the very atmosphere was trying to smother any hope of finding the missing girl. His eyes swept across the room, taking in every detail with the practiced scrutiny of a man accustomed to piecing together fragmented truths.

The bed, neatly made and adorned with an array of stuffed animals, stood in stark contrast to the violence that had unfolded elsewhere in the house. A pink elephant, its trunk curled upwards as if in an eternal embrace, caught Drake's attention. For a fleeting moment, he saw Harrison's favorite toy dinosaur in its place, a bittersweet reminder of the son he'd lost - or hadn't, depending on which reality he was inhabiting.

Focus, Drake. This isn't about you, he chided himself, pushing away the grief that threatened to overwhelm him.

As he approached the bed, his fingers brushed against a colorful blanket draped over its edge. The softness of the fabric felt almost obscene in this context of horror and loss. Drake's throat tightened as he imagined the young girl who should be sleeping here, safe and sound.

"What happened to you, sweetheart?" he whispered, his voice barely audible even in the stillness of the room. "Where are you now?"

His gaze continued to roam, searching for anything out of place, any clue that might lead them to the missing child. It was then that he noticed something in the corner of the room, partially hidden by the shadow cast by a tall bookshelf.

Drake moved closer, his heartbeat quickening as the details came into focus. Etched into the wall was a symbol, intricate and mesmerizing in its design. A dragon, its serpentine body coiled around a tree, seemed to stare back at him with an almost lifelike intensity.

"What the hell?" Drake muttered, leaning in for a closer look. The symbol tugged at something in his memory, a nagging familiarity that he couldn't quite place. "This isn't just random graffiti. It means something."

As he studied the etching, a chill ran down his spine. The dragon's eyes seemed to follow him, and for a moment, Drake could have sworn he saw them glint with a malevolent intelligence.

Am I losing it? he wondered, shaking his head to clear the unsettling thought. *Or is this connected to everything else that's been happening?*

The weight of his dual realities pressed down on him, and Drake found himself questioning which version of events was truly real. Was this symbol a key to understanding the fractured nature of his existence, or just another dead end in a case that seemed to grow more complex by the minute?

19 - 20

As Drake stood transfixed by the symbol, the floorboards creaked behind him. He tensed, his hand instinctively moving towards his holster before he recognized Keirstead's familiar footsteps.

"Miller, what've you got?" Keirstead's voice cut through the heavy silence as she entered the room.

Drake turned, his expression grave. "Take a look at this," he said, gesturing towards the wall.

Keirstead moved closer, her eyes narrowing as she took in the symbol. The lines on her face deepened, a mixture of concern and recognition flashing across her features.

She knows something, Drake thought, studying his partner's reaction. *But how much?*

"Any ideas?" he probed, his tone carefully neutral despite the urgency bubbling beneath the surface.

Keirstead's gaze remained fixed on the etching, her lips pressed into a thin line. "It's... familiar," she admitted after a long pause. "But I can't place it. Not yet."

Drake nodded, his mind racing. The symbol, the missing girl, the brutal murders downstairs - it all had to be connected. But how? And why did he feel like he was missing a crucial piece of the puzzle?

"We need to document this," he said, reaching for his phone to take a picture. "And then we need to find out what it means. Fast."

As the camera flash illuminated the room, Drake couldn't shake the feeling that they were running out of time. Somewhere out there, a young girl's life hung in the balance, and the answers they needed were hidden behind a veil of cryptic symbols and fractured realities.

21 - 22

Keirstead's eyes locked onto Drake's, her gaze piercing and intense. "Recognize it?" she asked, her voice low and tinged with an undercurrent of urgency.

Drake felt a chill run down his spine as he nodded, his mind racing with possibilities. The symbol seemed to pulse with an otherworldly energy, drawing him in and repelling him simultaneously. He couldn't shake the feeling that he'd seen it before, in some half-remembered dream or forgotten memory.

"I've seen something like it," he admitted, his voice barely above a whisper. "But I can't place where or when." He ran a hand through his disheveled hair, frustration evident in the set of his jaw. "It's like trying to grasp smoke."

As he spoke, images flashed through his mind - fractured glimpses of his two realities colliding. In one, Linda's worried face swam before him; in the other, Harrison's mischievous grin. The weight of his dual existence pressed down on him, threatening to overwhelm his senses.

"Whatever it means," Drake continued, forcing himself back to the present, "I have a feeling it's the key to this whole mess. We need to figure it out, and fast."

Keirstead nodded grimly, her eyes never leaving the symbol. "Agreed. Let's get forensics in here to document everything. We can't afford to miss a single detail."

23 - 24

Drake's gaze remained fixed on the intricate symbol, his mind churning with a mixture of dread and determination. The dragon's scales seemed to shimmer in the dim light, its serpentine body winding around the tree in an eternal embrace. He couldn't shake the feeling that it was mocking him, holding secrets just beyond his grasp.

"It's the same symbol from the robe," Drake said, his voice low and gravelly. He turned to Keirstead, his eyes haunted by the weight of the connection. "The one from the accident. It can't be a coincidence."

Keirstead's brow furrowed, her usual composure slipping for a moment as she processed the implications. She stepped closer to the wall, her fingers hovering just above the etched surface.

"Agreed," she replied, her tone matching the gravity of the situation. "We need to find out everything we can about this symbol—what it represents, who might be associated with it."

Drake nodded, his mind already racing ahead. He thought of Harrison, wondering if his son's inquisitive nature might have stumbled upon something in his own reality. Then Linda's face flashed before him, her eyes filled with worry and love. The dichotomy of his existence threatened to overwhelm him, but he pushed it aside, focusing on the task at hand.

"I'll reach out to some contacts," Drake offered, his lawyer instincts kicking in. "There might be someone who specializes in occult symbology. We can't rule out any possibility at this point."

As he spoke, Drake couldn't help but feel a sense of impending doom. Whatever this symbol represented, he knew it was far more than just a simple drawing. It was a gateway to something darker, something that threatened to shatter the fragile balance of his dual lives.

25 - 26

As Keirstead made notes in her small, leather-bound notebook, Drake's gaze remained fixed on the symbol. The intricate lines of the dragon coiling around the tree seemed to writhe and pulse, a trick of the light that sent a chill down his spine. A nagging feeling of unease gnawed at him, reminiscent of the dread he'd felt in the moments before his life-altering accident.

He ran a hand through his disheveled hair, his tired eyes never leaving the etching. In his mind, he could see Harrison's face, curious and bright, asking about the symbol. Then Linda's worried expression, her blue eyes searching his for answers he didn't have. The weight of his dual existence pressed down on him, threatening to crush him under its impossible burden.

"We're dealing with something bigger than a simple home invasion, Keirstead," Drake said somberly, his voice barely above a whisper. He turned to face his partner, his expression grave. "This feels like... something darker. My accident and now this, they are connected."

As he spoke the words, a surge of certainty washed over him. The fractured nature of his reality, the missing girl, this haunting symbol – they were all pieces of a puzzle he was only beginning to comprehend. Drake's jaw clenched, determination replacing the fatigue in his eyes. Whatever force was at play here, he would unravel its mysteries, not just for the sake of this case, but for the family he loved in both of his realities.

27 - 28

Keirstead's eyes met Drake's, her expression mirroring his concern. She nodded gravely, the weight of their shared understanding hanging heavy in the air between them. For a moment, Drake saw a flicker of something else in her gaze – a mix of empathy and determination that reminded him of Linda's unwavering support.

"We'll dig deeper," Keirstead said, her voice low and resolute. She tucked her notepad away, squaring her shoulders. "But first, let's focus on finding the daughter. That's our priority."

Drake's mind raced, torn between the urgency of the missing child and the tantalizing thread connecting his accident to this crime scene. He clenched his fists, willing himself to compartmentalize. 'Focus, Miller,' he chided himself internally. 'One step at a time. Find the girl, then unravel the rest.'

"Agreed," he replied, his tone matching Keirstead's resolve. "Where do we start? Any leads on friends, relatives she might have reached out to?"

As they discussed potential avenues of investigation, Drake couldn't shake the image of Harrison's face from his mind. His son's curiosity would have been piqued by the mystery, his teenage bravado masking the fear Drake knew would lurk beneath. The thought steeled his resolve. Somewhere out there, a young girl was living their worst nightmare. He'd be damned if he let them suffer the way he had.

29 - 29

Drake cast one final glance at the symbol etched into the wall, its intricate lines searing into his memory. As he and Keirstead exited the room, the air seemed to thicken, charged with unspoken tension and the weight of their responsibility.

"We need to move fast," Drake muttered, his voice low and urgent. "Every minute counts in cases like these."

Keirstead nodded, her steps quickening to match his pace. "I've got uniforms canvassing the neighborhood. We'll start with the girl's school friends, then branch out to extended family."

As they descended the stairs, Drake's mind raced, fragmenting between the case at hand and the haunting parallels to his own fractured reality. He could almost hear Harrison's voice, asking the probing questions that always cut to the heart of matters.

"Dad, what if the symbol isn't just a coincidence?" The imagined words echoed in his head, spurring him to voice his thoughts aloud.

"Keirstead," he began, pausing at the foot of the stairs, "we can't ignore the connection to my accident. The symbol, the timing... it's too neat to be coincidental."

She turned to face him, her expression a mix of concern and professional detachment. "I hear you, Miller. But we can't let speculation derail our primary objective. The girl's life could be at stake."

Drake ran a hand through his disheveled hair, frustration and determination warring within him. "I know, I know. It's just... I can't shake this feeling that understanding the symbol might be the key to finding her."

As they stepped out into the crisp night air, the weight of their task settled over them like a shroud. The mysteries they left behind in that child's room loomed large, a haunting reminder of the darkness they were up against and the urgent need to bring light to the shadows that threatened to engulf them all.

Under Pressure in the Doctors Office

Green and Blue World – 2024

1 - 2

The sterile white walls of Dr. Harmon's office seemed to close in around Drake Miller as he sat rigidly in the leather armchair, his fingers unconsciously tracing the green rubber band on his wrist. The faint scent of antiseptic lingered in the air, a constant reminder of the clinical nature of this space where his fractured reality was being dissected.

Drake's gaze fixed on Dr. Harmon, studying the psychologist's impassive features. The weight of unspoken words hung between them, thick and suffocating. Drake's mind raced, trying to discern any hint of judgment or disbelief in the doctor's expression.

Is he seeing through me? Can he tell I'm not even sure if this is real? Drake wondered, his heart rate quickening. He fought the urge to fidget, to betray the turmoil churning within him.

Dr. Harmon leaned forward slightly, his piercing eyes never leaving Drake's face. "Detective Miller," he began, his voice measured and deliberate, "can you describe for me the moment you first realized you were experiencing these... parallel lives?"

Drake's jaw clenched involuntarily. He took a deep breath, buying time as he formulated his response. "It wasn't a sudden realization," he said slowly, each word carefully chosen. "It was more like... waking up from a dream, only to find myself in another one. And then it happened again. And again."

He paused, searching Dr. Harmon's face for any reaction. The psychologist remained unnervingly still, his expression a mask of professional detachment.

What is he thinking? Drake silently implored. *Does he believe me, or am I just another delusional patient to him?*

The silence stretched between them, heavy with unasked questions and unspoken doubts. Drake's fingers unconsciously tightened around the arm of the chair, his knuckles whitening with the pressure.

3 - 4

Drake's unease grew with each passing second of silence. Unable to bear the weight of Dr. Harmon's scrutiny any longer, he broke the tension.

"Is something wrong?" Drake asked, his voice betraying a hint of vulnerability despite his attempt to maintain composure.

Dr. Harmon's eyebrows raised slightly, a flicker of surprise crossing his face before he quickly reined in his expression. He leaned back in his chair, steepling his fingers beneath his chin.

"Nothing," Dr. Harmon replied, his tone measured but tinged with an undercurrent of excitement. "It's fascinating, really."

Drake's heart skipped a beat. *Fascinating? What does he mean by that?* His mind raced, grasping for meaning in the doctor's cryptic response. He watched as Dr. Harmon reached for his notepad, scribbling something quickly before returning his gaze to Drake.

The detective shifted in his seat, acutely aware of every creak of the leather chair beneath him. He fought the urge to glance at the green rubber band on his wrist, the anchor that supposedly tethered him to this reality. Instead, he focused on Dr. Harmon's face, searching for any clue that might reveal the psychiatrist's true thoughts.

Is he seeing something I'm not? Drake wondered, a chill running down his spine. *Or am I just imagining things... again?*

5 - 6

Dr. Harmon cleared his throat, his expression softening as he leaned forward slightly. "Not to be insensitive, it's just... our brain's main function is to protect us. Sometimes that means sensing danger or feeling pain. And sometimes it actually means deceiving ourselves."

Drake's brow furrowed, his mind struggling to process the implications of Dr. Harmon's words. *Deceiving ourselves? Is he suggesting that I'm...* He couldn't bring himself to finish the thought, the possibility too terrifying to contemplate.

The psychiatrist paused, his eyes flickering briefly to his notes before returning to meet Drake's gaze. Drake could see the wheels turning behind those piercing eyes, as if Dr. Harmon was carefully selecting his next words.

What isn't he telling me? Drake wondered, his fingers unconsciously tracing the edge of the armrest. The leather felt cool and smooth beneath his touch, grounding him in the moment even as his thoughts threatened to spiral.

Dr. Harmon took a deep breath, composing himself as he prepared to continue his explanation. Drake tensed, bracing himself for whatever revelation was about to come. The air in the office felt thick with tension, each second stretching into an eternity as he waited for the doctor to speak.

Whatever he's about to say, Drake thought, his heart pounding in his chest, *it's going to change everything.*

7 - 8

Dr. Harmon leaned forward, his voice softening with a mix of clinical detachment and genuine concern. "The loss of a loved one is one of the most emotionally crippling things we face. We come up with all sorts of ways to get through it."

Drake's mind flashed to his son, Harrison, hunched over a chessboard, his small fingers moving pieces with the same deliberate grace his mother once had. The image brought a lump to his throat.

"Like your son taking up his mother's sport to maintain some sense of connection with her," Dr. Harmon continued, as if reading Drake's thoughts. "But your brain... it's created an entire reality where you haven't actually lost your wife at all."

The words hit Drake like a physical blow. He felt the air leave his lungs, his vision blurring at the edges. *No,* he thought desperately. *That can't be right. Linda is real. She has to be.*

As Dr. Harmon's office began to fade around him, Drake's mind suddenly shifted, catapulting him into a memory of a conversation with Dr. Lee. The transition was jarring, leaving him disoriented and struggling to grasp what was real.

He found himself sitting in a different office, the warm tones and gentle lighting a stark contrast to Dr. Harmon's sterile environment. Dr. Lee's compassionate eyes met his, filled with a mixture of fascination and concern.

Which reality is the dream? Drake wondered, his heart racing as he tried to anchor himself in the moment. *And if one is a dream, how do I know which one to believe?*

9 - 10

Dr. Lee leaned forward, his brow furrowed in deep thought. The soft light from the desk lamp cast a warm glow on his face, accentuating the lines of concern etched around his eyes. Drake found himself instinctively mirroring the doctor's posture, drawn in by the man's calm presence.

"An elaborate and ongoing dream in which you haven't lost your son," Dr. Lee said, his voice gentle yet tinged with a hint of awe. "Relieving you of the obligation of dealing with his death. I'm not sure I've ever seen a coping mechanism quite like it."

Drake's stomach churned. The words echoed those of Dr. Harmon, yet here, it was his son's existence being questioned. He clenched his fists, feeling the bite of his nails against his palms. *Harrison is real,* he thought fiercely. *I can still smell the pine scent of his shampoo, hear the excited lilt in his voice when he talks about his latest game.*

"But Doctor," Drake started, his voice hoarse with emotion, "how can you be sure—"

He cut himself off, the question dying on his lips. Asking it felt like a betrayal, an admission that there might be truth to this impossible scenario. Instead, he focused on the warmth of Dr. Lee's office, trying to ground himself in the reality before him.

11 - 12

Drake's gaze locked onto Dr. Lee, searching for any hint of uncertainty in the psychiatrist's expression. The weight of two realities pressed down on him, threatening to suffocate him with their conflicting truths.

"How do you know it's a dream?" Drake finally asked, his voice barely above a whisper. The words felt like a betrayal, but he needed answers. He needed something solid to cling to in this shifting landscape of his life.

As he waited for Dr. Lee's response, Drake's mind raced. He could almost feel the phantom weight of his son's hand in his, hear the echo of Harrison's laughter. But here, in this reality, those memories were supposed to be nothing more than elaborate fabrications of a grieving mind.

Drake's fingers unconsciously traced the outline of the blue rubber band on his wrist. *This is real,* he told himself. *But so is the other world. It has to be.*

The silence stretched between them, heavy with unspoken doubts and fears. Drake leaned forward, his body tense, ready to pounce on whatever explanation Dr. Lee might offer. He needed something, anything, to make sense of the dual lives he was living.

13 - 14

Dr. Lee's brow furrowed, his usually serene expression giving way to a momentary flash of confusion. "I'm sorry?" he asked, his voice tinged with a mix of concern and bewilderment.

The psychiatrist's reaction sent a jolt through Drake's system. He sat up straight, his spine rigid as if bracing for impact. The soft cushions of the armchair suddenly felt like quicksand, threatening to swallow him whole. Drake's heart raced, pounding against his ribcage as if trying to break free from the confines of this reality.

He doesn't understand, Drake thought, a cold sweat breaking out on his forehead. *Or maybe he's testing me. Maybe this is all part of the treatment.*

Drake's eyes darted around the room, taking in the coastal decor and the glimpse of the ocean beyond the window. Everything seemed so real, so tangible. Yet, in his other life, the world felt just as solid, just as true.

"I mean," Drake began, his voice steadier than he felt, "how can you be certain that this world, where my son is gone, is the real one?" He leaned forward, elbows on his knees, hands clasped tightly to stop them from shaking. "What if the dream is this reality, and the world where Harrison is alive is actually real?"

As the words left his mouth, Drake felt a mixture of relief and terror. He'd never voiced these thoughts so explicitly before, and now that they were out in the open, he couldn't take them back.

15 - 16

Dr. Lee's expression shifted, a mix of concern and fascination flickering across his features. The room seemed to close in around Drake, the air growing thick with tension.

"Detective Miller," Dr. Lee began, his voice gentle yet probing, "what you're suggesting is... quite extraordinary." He paused, choosing his words carefully. "But I want you to consider something. In this reality, you have concrete evidence of your son's passing. Medical records, a death certificate, memories shared by others who knew him."

Drake's jaw clenched, his fingers digging into his palms. *He doesn't understand*, he thought desperately. *How can I make him see?*

"But in the other world," Drake countered, his voice barely above a whisper, "I have those same things for Linda. It's all there, just as real, just as painful."

Suddenly, the scene shifted. The coastal view blurred and faded, replaced by the stark white walls of Dr. Harmon's office. The transition was seamless, yet jarring. Drake blinked, momentarily disoriented by the change.

Dr. Harmon leaned forward in his chair, his piercing gaze fixed on Drake. The air in this room felt different – crisper, more clinical. Drake's heart rate picked up again, his mind racing to catch up with the abrupt shift in reality.

Which one is real? he thought, panic rising in his chest. *Am I losing my mind?*

17 - 18

Dr. Harmon's eyes widened, his usual stern composure cracking for a moment. The lines on his forehead deepened as he processed Drake's words, his analytical mind clearly struggling to reconcile this new information.

"Wait," Dr. Harmon said, his voice a mix of disbelief and fascination. "You mean you can't tell them apart?"

Drake's throat tightened as he met Dr. Harmon's intense gaze. The weight of his confession hung in the air between them, heavy and oppressive. He could almost hear the gears turning in the psychiatrist's head, dissecting this revelation with clinical precision.

How can I explain when I don't understand it myself? Drake thought, his fingers absently tracing the green rubber band on his wrist. The tactile sensation grounded him, a small reminder of his current reality – or was it?

"It's... it's like living two lives," Drake finally managed, his voice hoarse. "Every detail, every emotion, it's all there in both worlds. I close my eyes here, and when I open them, I'm with Linda. I sleep there, and I wake up to a world without her but with our son."

Dr. Harmon leaned back in his chair, his eyes never leaving Drake's face. The silence stretched between them, filled with unspoken questions and theories that Drake could almost see forming behind the doctor's piercing gaze.

19 - 20

Drake slowly shook his head, the weight of his confession settling on his shoulders like a heavy cloak. The simple gesture felt monumental, as if he were admitting defeat to an invisible adversary.

Dr. Harmon's eyes widened, a mixture of awe and professional curiosity dancing across his features. "Incredible," he breathed, the word hanging in the air between them.

Drake's jaw clenched, a surge of frustration rising in his chest. *Incredible? Is that all he can say?* He thought bitterly. *This is my life, not some fascinating case study.*

"It's not incredible," Drake muttered, his voice low and strained. "It's... it's hell." He ran a hand through his disheveled hair, feeling the rough texture of his unkempt beard. "Every time I close my eyes, I don't know which world I'll wake up to. Will I see Linda's smile or hear Harrison's laugh? It's like... like living on a knife's edge, never knowing which side I'll fall on."

Dr. Harmon leaned forward, his pen poised over his notepad. "And in both realities, everything feels equally real?" he probed, his tone measured but unable to entirely mask his fascination.

Drake nodded, his gaze drifting to the window. Outside, oak trees swayed in the warm Bridgewater breeze, a cruel reminder of the seemingly normal world that continued on, oblivious to his internal torment.

21 - 22

Dr. Lee's brow furrowed, his usually serene expression giving way to a look of disbelief. The lines around his eyes deepened as he leaned forward in his chair, his gentle demeanor momentarily eclipsed by professional curiosity.

"So you're saying you're not confident whether you're asleep or awake at this very moment?" Dr. Lee asked, his voice a mix of concern and bewilderment.

Drake felt a surge of frustration ripple through him. He clenched his fists, nails digging into his palms. *How many times do I have to explain this?* he thought, struggling to keep his composure.

"That's exactly what I'm saying," Drake replied, his voice taut with tension. He met Dr. Lee's gaze, searching for understanding in those kind eyes. "Every moment, every sensation... it's all equally vivid, equally real. Whether I'm here with you or in the other world with Dr. Harmon, I can't distinguish reality from... whatever this is."

Dr. Lee's expression softened, compassion replacing incredulity. He leaned back, steepling his fingers as he often did when deep in thought. The room fell silent, save for the soft ticking of the clock on the wall, each second punctuating the weight of Drake's confession.

23 - 24

Drake's eyes darted down to his wrist, seeking the one anchor he had between his two realities. The blue rubber band stretched across his skin, a vibrant contrast against his pale flesh. He ran his thumb over it, feeling its elasticity, its tangible presence. *Blue for this world,* he reminded himself. *Green for the other.*

Taking a deep breath, Drake looked back up at Dr. Lee. "Everything feels just as real in one world as it does in the other," he began, his voice low and measured. "I never look down and discover I'm naked, or late for a test. Never suddenly start to fly."

He paused, swallowing hard as images of Linda and Harrison flashed through his mind. His heart ached with a familiar, crushing weight. *How can I choose between them?* he wondered, not for the first time. *How can either of them not be real?*

"Whether I'm with my wife or my son, everything is completely normal," Drake continued, his words tinged with a mixture of wonder and despair. "Then I close my eyes, open them, and the other one is waiting."

As he spoke, Drake could feel the familiar disorientation creeping in at the edges of his consciousness. *Which world will I wake up to next?* The uncertainty gnawed at him, a constant companion in both his realities.

25 - 26

The room fell into a heavy silence. Drake's words hung in the air, almost tangible in their weight. He watched Dr. Lee closely, searching for any hint of reaction in the psychologist's composed features. The gentle ticking of a wall clock seemed to grow louder in the quiet, each second stretching into an eternity.

Dr. Lee's eyes, usually warm and reassuring, now held a glimmer of something Drake couldn't quite place. Fascination? Concern? The doctor's brow furrowed slightly as he reached for his notepad, the soft rustle of paper breaking the stillness.

Drake's heart rate quickened. *What's he writing?* he wondered, fighting the urge to crane his neck and peek at the doctor's notes. *Does he think I'm crazy? Or is he finally starting to believe me?*

As Dr. Lee's pen scratched across the paper, Drake found himself fidgeting with the blue rubber band on his wrist. He snapped it gently against his skin, the small sting a reminder of his current reality. But for how long?

The silence stretched on, becoming almost unbearable. Drake opened his mouth to speak, to ask what Dr. Lee was thinking, but found himself hesitating. What if the answer wasn't one he was prepared to hear?

27 - 28

Dr. Lee finally set his pen down, his eyes meeting Drake's with an intensity that made the detective shift in his seat. The psychologist's voice was soft but firm as he spoke.

"Well, I can assure you, Detective Miller, this is not a dream."

Drake couldn't help but smile, a small, wry twist of his lips that didn't quite reach his eyes. The irony of the situation wasn't lost on him. How many times had he heard those exact words, in both of his realities? The certainty in Dr. Lee's voice was almost comforting in its familiarity.

If only it were that simple, Drake thought, his fingers absently tracing the smooth surface of the blue rubber band. *How can I explain that your assurance means nothing when I've heard it echoed in another world?*

He leaned back in his chair, feeling the weight of his conflicted existence pressing down on him. The office suddenly felt smaller, the walls closing in with the magnitude of his predicament. Drake's smile remained, a shield against the confusion and fear threatening to overwhelm him.

What if there's no way out of this maze? The thought crept in, unwelcome but persistent. *What if I'm doomed to forever question which reality is real, which loved one I've truly lost?*

29 - 30

Dr. Lee's brow furrowed, his calm demeanor momentarily shaken by Drake's unexpected smile. He leaned forward, his elbows resting on his knees as he studied his patient with renewed interest.

"What?" Dr. Lee asked, his voice a mixture of curiosity and concern. The single word hung in the air, heavy with unspoken questions.

Drake's smile widened, though it didn't reach his eyes. He met Dr. Lee's gaze, feeling a strange sense of déjà vu wash over him. How many times had he had this exact conversation, in this world and the other? The parallels were becoming almost comical in their consistency.

"That's exactly what the other Doctor said," Drake replied, his voice tinged with a hint of weary amusement. He ran a hand through his disheveled hair, feeling the weight of his dual existence pressing down on him.

How do I make him understand? Drake wondered, his mind racing. *That every assurance, every certainty offered in one world is mirrored in the other? That I'm caught in an endless loop of reassurances that mean nothing?*

The silence that followed his words was thick with tension, filled with the unspoken complexities of Drake's situation. He watched Dr. Lee's face, searching for any sign of comprehension, any flicker of understanding in the psychologist's eyes.

Parallel Realities

1 - 2

The rain pelted my face as I stood rooted before the Miller house, its cheerful windows mocking the turmoil within me. My leg throbbed, a constant reminder of the accident that had shattered my world into parallel realities. I gritted my teeth against the pain, both physical and emotional.

"Just a few more steps, Gabriel," I muttered to myself, willing my feet to move. "You've come this far."

As I limped closer, the pristine white picket fence came into sharp focus. It was a jarring contrast to the chaos swirling in my mind - one reality where Linda was gone, another where Harrison...

I shook my head, dispelling the thoughts. Focus on the task at hand.

The manicured lawn squelched beneath my feet as I approached, my heartbeat thundering in my ears. Through the curtains, I caught a glimpse of movement - Harrison's gangly form darting past.

The porch steps loomed before me, a final barrier between the man I once was and the broken shell I'd become. I hesitated, my hand hovering over the railing.

What right did I have to disrupt their peace? To drag them into the nightmare that had become my life?

But the determination that had driven me this far surged anew. I had to know the truth, had to find a way to reconcile these splintered realities.

With a deep breath, I climbed the steps, each one an agony for my injured leg. I raised my fist to knock, then paused, struck by a sudden, paralyzing doubt.

3 - 4

Peering through the glass, I caught a glimpse of their world, so ordinary and yet so tantalizingly out of reach. The laughter of a family echoed faintly from within, a cruel reminder of everything I had lost.

Harrison's voice carried through the window, his teenage cockiness evident even from here. "Dad, come on! It's just a party. Everyone's going!"

Drake's gentle reply followed, "Harrison, we've talked about this. I need to know where you are."

I pressed my forehead against the cool glass, drinking in the scene. Harrison, sprawled on the couch, his curly hair a mess. Drake as always so impatient but now so loving.

A pang of jealousy shot through me. In this reality, Drake Miller still had something to hold on to, like everything I'd lost. The perfect family, the semi normal life. Did he even appreciate it?

"You don't deserve them," I muttered, bitterness coating my words. "You'll take them for granted, just like you always do."

But there was no time for sentimentality, no room for remorse in the cold heart of indifference. I had a job to do, a mission to complete.

Drawing a deep breath, I reached into my pocket and retrieved the envelope, its contents a silent testament to the secrets that lay buried beneath the surface. With a steady hand, I slipped the note inside, addressing it to Harrison Miller, the unwitting pawn in a game he could never hope to understand.

"I'm sorry, kid," I whispered, my fingers trembling slightly as I sealed the envelope. "But you're the key to all of this. You have to understand."

5 - 6

The weight of the envelope felt heavy in my hand, a tangible reminder of the choices that had brought me to this moment. I hesitated, my fingers trembling slightly as I considered the consequences of my actions.

"Is this really the only way?" I muttered to myself, my voice barely audible over the patter of rain.

Inside, I could hear Harrison's voice rising again. "Dad, I'm sixteen! I don't need you tracking my every move!"

Drake's response was muffled, but his tone was unmistakably firm. The argument continued, oblivious to the storm brewing both outside and within me.

I clenched my fist around the envelope, feeling the crisp edges dig into my palm. "There's no turning back now," I reminded myself. "No escape from the path I've chosen."

My gaze drifted back to the window, where I caught a glimpse of Drake entering the room. He looked tired, his shoulders slumped under the weight of unseen burdens. For a moment, our eyes seemed to meet across the divide of realities, and I felt a chill run down my spine.

"You don't even know what you have," I whispered, a mix of envy and determination coloring my words. "But you will. Soon."

With a final glance at the Miller house, I turned and walked away into the night. The rain washed over me, cleansing away the last traces of my presence as if I had never been there at all.

As I limped down the street, my bad knee protesting with each step, I couldn't shake the feeling that I was leaving more than just an envelope behind. I was abandoning the last vestiges of who I used to be, embracing the darkness that had become my constant companion.

"It's for the greater good," I muttered, trying to convince myself as much as anyone else. "They'll understand. Eventually."

7 - 8

The driver's eyes narrowed, his posture stiffening as he assessed me. "Can I help you?" he asked, his voice tinged with suspicion.

My heart raced, adrenaline surging through my veins. This was it - the point of no return. I thought of Drake, of Linda and Harrison, of the fractured realities I was trying to mend. There was no room for hesitation.

"I'm so sorry," I whispered, my words lost in the patter of rain.

Before he could react, I lunged forward, driving my fist into his throat with all the force I could muster. The impact sent shockwaves up my arm, but I didn't relent. He stumbled backward, gasping for air, his eyes wide with terror and disbelief.

"Why?" he choked out, but I couldn't answer. I couldn't explain the weight of worlds on my shoulders, the desperate need to set things right.

I rained blow after blow upon him, each strike fueled by a mixture of determination and despair. "I have to do this," I thought, even as guilt threatened to overwhelm me. "For Drake, for his family, for the balance between realms."

The driver's struggles grew weaker, his attempts to fend me off becoming feeble. I could hear someone shouting in the distance, his voice muffled by the rain and the blood rushing in my ears.

Finally, mercifully, the driver crumpled to the ground, unconscious and bleeding. I stood over him, my chest heaving, my hands trembling. "What have I done?" I thought, the reality of my actions crashing down upon me.

9 - 10

The driver's blood mingled with the rain, a crimson river flowing between the cracks in the pavement. I stared at my trembling hands, the weight of my actions settling like lead in my gut.

"Focus, Gabriel," I muttered to myself, pushing aside the guilt. "You can't falter now."

With a deep breath, I grasped the driver's ankles, dragging his limp form towards the rear of the cab. My bad leg protested, sending sharp pains shooting up my thigh, but I gritted my teeth and pressed on.

"This is for the greater good," I reminded myself, hoisting the unconscious man into the sedan I'd prepared earlier. "For Drake, for his family, for the balance between worlds."

As I maneuvered the body into place, my mind raced. "How many more will suffer before this is over?" I wondered, my heart heavy with the burden of knowledge.

Once the driver was hidden, I turned my attention to the cab. With practiced efficiency, I transferred the taxi sign, my fingers working deftly despite the rain.

"Almost there," I murmured, reaching into my pocket for the note. The symbol of the Green Dragon stared back at me from the paper, a reminder of the path I'd chosen.

As I placed the note in the glove box, a wry smile twisted my scarred lips. "They'll never understand," I thought. "But they'll remember. The Green Dragon Killer... all in due time."

With a final glance around, I slammed the sedan's door shut. The sound echoed through the empty street, a punctuation mark on this chapter of my twisted tale.

11 - 12

The rain-slicked leather of the driver's seat felt cool against my damp clothes as I slid behind the wheel. My hands trembled, betraying the adrenaline coursing through my veins. The keys dangled invitingly from the ignition, their soft metallic jingle a siren song of escape.

"Just one turn," I whispered, my fingers hovering over the keys. "One turn and you're free."

But freedom, I knew, was an illusion. The weight of my actions, of the lives I'd altered, pressed down on me like a physical force. I closed my eyes, seeing Drake Miller's face, imagining the grief that awaited him in one reality, the confusion in another.

"Is this really the only way?" I asked the empty cab, my voice barely audible over the patter of rain on the roof.

The silence offered no answers, only the persistent whisper of doubt in the back of my mind. I gripped the steering wheel, my knuckles turning white with the effort of restraining myself from fleeing.

"No," I said firmly, more to convince myself than anyone else. "There's no going back now. The pieces are in motion."

With a deep breath, I turned the key. The engine roared to life, drowning out the last feeble protests of my conscience. The vibrations of the idling cab seemed to sync with my racing heartbeat.

"For Drake," I muttered, shifting into drive. "For the balance. For the greater good."

As I pulled away from the curb, leaving behind the scene of my latest transgression, I couldn't shake the feeling that I was driving not just away from this place, but towards an inescapable destiny of my own making.

13 - 14

The city streets blurred past, a kaleidoscope of neon and shadows. I drove mechanically, my mind racing faster than the taxi ever could.

"Focus," I muttered, tightening my grip on the wheel. "The mission isn't over."

I made a sharp turn, tires squealing on wet asphalt. The tires wail grew louder as I approached, a banshee's cry cutting through the night. Then there he was, Drake Miller and his family, driving ahead of me.

I sped up, pushing almost double the speed limit. I laid on the horn to get his attention, to distract him from the sharp corner up ahead. Then I struck, using the P.I.T maneuver I collided with the read end drivers side of his car. Drake jerked left then right, but his tires were no match for the rain slicked road.

Drake fishtailed and the car rolled and over the embankment it went. Coming to a loud crash at the bottom but the waters edge.

"Christ," I whispered, slowing as I neared the scene.

Chaos reigned. Twisted metal, shattered glass, the acrid smell of burnt rubber. First responders would soon swarm like ants, their voices a cacophony of urgency.

I parked the cab at a distance, my hands trembling as I cut the engine. For a moment, I sat frozen, the weight of what I'd set in motion crushing me.

"You knew this would happen," I reminded myself, fighting the nausea rising in my throat. "It's necessary."

With a deep breath, I stepped out into the rain, my eyes scanning the wreckage. And there, in the center of it all, was the Miller's sedan – a crumpled testament to the fragility of reality itself.

15 - 16

The twisted wreckage of the sedan lay half-submerged in the murky waters of the lake, its mangled frame a testament to the violence of the crash. My breath caught in my throat as I took in the scene, the reality of what I'd orchestrated hitting me like a physical blow.

"Focus," I muttered to myself, fighting the urge to turn and run. "You're too deep in this now."

As I made my way down the embankment, the rain soaked through my clothes, chilling me to the bone. The headlights of the sedan cast an eerie glow on the water's surface, illuminating the scene with an otherworldly light.

My foot slipped on the muddy slope, and I barely caught myself before tumbling into the water. The sound of splashing drew my attention, and I saw a figure moving inside the car.

"Hello?" a voice called out, strained and desperate. "Is someone there? Please, help us!"

It was Drake Miller. My heart raced as I approached, torn between the mission and the human instinct to help.

As I drew closer, I could see Drake's face illuminated by the eerie glow of the headlights. His eyes were wild with panic, darting between me and the submerged vehicle.

"My family," he gasped. "They're trapped. Please, you have to help them!"

I hesitated, the weight of my choices pressing down on me. This was the moment that would shape Drake's reality – and mine. The rain pelted my face as I stood there, frozen in indecision.

"What am I doing?" I thought, horrified at my own detachment. "These are people, not just pawns in some cosmic game."

But even as that thought crossed my mind, I knew it was too late to turn back. The wheels were already in motion, reality itself bending to the will of forces beyond our comprehension.

17 - 18

I inched closer to the car, my shoes sinking into the muddy bank. Through the rain-streaked windows, I could make out Drake's white-knuckled grip on the steering wheel. His eyes, wide with terror, darted frantically between me and the rising water inside the vehicle.

"Please," Drake pleaded, his voice cracking. "My wife... my son... I can't... I can't get them out."

I placed my hand on the cold, wet metal of the car door, feeling the tremors of Drake's desperation vibrating through it. My mind raced, weighing the consequences of my next move against the mission that had brought me here.

"Mr. Miller," I said, trying to keep my voice steady. "Your life is about to change from this moment on."

Drake's eyes locked onto mine, a flicker of hope battling the panic within them. "Yes... yes, I think so. God, what have I done? This is all my fault."

The self-recrimination in his voice was palpable, and I couldn't help but wonder how this moment would reshape the man I knew him to be – the driven lawyer who had prioritized his career over his family for so long.

19 - 20

Linda's voice cut through the sound of rain and panic, her words a soothing balm in the chaos. "Harrison, sweetheart, look at Mommy. It's going to be okay. We're going to be fine."

I watched as she cradled her son, her long blonde hair forming a protective curtain around his face. Harrison, usually so full of teenage bravado, clung to her like a much younger child. His curls were plastered to his forehead, his bright eyes wide with fear.

"Mom, I'm scared," Harrison whispered, his voice cracking. "What's happening?"

Linda stroked his hair, her blue eyes filled with a mixture of love and fear. "Shh, baby. We're just stuck for a moment. Help is coming."

My chest tightened as I observed their intimate moment. The love between them was palpable, a stark contrast to the cold mission that had brought me here. I found myself wondering about the ripple effects of my actions, how this moment would alter the course of their lives across multiple realities.

Drake's voice came back, strained and desperate. "The doors are jammed. Linda, can you reach the emergency hammer?"

As Linda stretched to search for the tool, I caught Harrison's eye. The boy's gaze was piercing, as if he could see right through me. "Who are you?" he asked, his voice steadier than I expected. "Why aren't you helping us?"

I hesitated, the weight of my choices pressing down on me. How could I explain that I was both their savior and their doom? That this moment was just one thread in a tapestry of realities I was weaving?

"I'm just someone who wants his world back," I replied, the truth tasting bitter on my tongue. As I watched the Millers struggle for survival, I knew with crushing certainty that there was no going back. The wheels I had set in motion would continue to turn, carrying us all into an uncertain future.

21 - 22

The wail of distant sirens pierced the night, growing louder with each passing second. My time was running out.

Drake's eyes widened in panic. "Wait! Don't leave us!"

I stared at him for a moment longer, then I left him some parting words as I watched the car sink further into the murky depths of the lake.

I turned, my heart heavy as lead, and limped into the shadows. The darkness enveloped me, a familiar embrace that offered both comfort and condemnation.

As I moved through the trees bordering the road, my mind raced. I had set this plan in motion, called 911 myself, but now the reality of what I'd done crashed over me like a wave.

"You're doing what needs to be done," I muttered to myself, trying to quell the doubt gnawing at my insides. "For the greater good."

The sound of screeching tires and slamming car doors reached my ears. The police had arrived. I quickened my pace, ignoring the burning pain in my leg.

"This is just one version of events," I reminded myself, my breath coming in ragged gasps. "In another reality, they might be safe. They might be happy."

But even as I tried to rationalize my actions, I couldn't shake the image of Harrison's frightened face from my mind. What kind of monster had I become?

I stumbled onward, leaving behind the chaos I had created. The night stretched before me, full of possibilities and horrors yet to unfold. My time in this reality was done, but my work was far from over.

23 - 24

The old cab groaned as I eased it down the overgrown dirt road, branches scraping against its sides like skeletal fingers. I killed the engine and sat for a moment, listening to the tick of cooling metal and the distant wail of sirens.

"This is necessary," I whispered, my voice hoarse. "Drake needs to understand."

With trembling hands, I wiped down the steering wheel, erasing any trace of my presence. The robe, stained with rain and guilt, landed in a crumpled heap on the cab floor.

As I trudged southward, my thoughts turned to Drake Miller. In another life, another reality, he had been a ruthless lawyer, prioritizing winning over everything – even his family. Now, he was about to embark on a journey that would shatter his perception of reality itself.

"I'm giving you a chance, Drake," I muttered. "A chance to be better."

The dilapidated shack loomed before me, a twisted silhouette against the stormy sky. Its weathered boards and sagging roof spoke of years of neglect.

"Perfect," I breathed, a mirthless smile tugging at my lips.

The door creaked open reluctantly, revealing a musty interior that reeked of decay and desperation. As I made my way through the abandoned bordello, I couldn't help but draw parallels between this place and the fractured realities I now navigated.

"How many lost souls found refuge here?" I wondered aloud, my fingers trailing along peeling wallpaper.

In a small back room, I found what I was looking for – a rickety cot, its threadbare blanket a testament to countless nights of fitful sleep.

I sank onto the edge of the cot, wincing as my injured leg protested. "I hope you appreciate this, Drake," I said to the empty room. "The things I've done... the lines I've crossed... all to give you a chance at redemption."

As exhaustion began to overwhelm me, I couldn't shake the image of Harrison's terrified face from my mind. In one reality, that boy was dead. In another, he lived. And in both, Drake Miller's world was about to be turned upside down.

"Good luck, counselor," I murmured as my eyes drifted shut. "You're going to need it."

25 - 26

The floor rushed up to meet me as my knee finally gave out, pain lancing through my leg like a bolt of lightning. I gritted my teeth, tasting copper as I bit the inside of my cheek.

"Damn it," I hissed, rolling onto my back. The gunshot wound throbbed in time with my heartbeat, a constant reminder of the price I'd paid to set this plan in motion.

As I lay there, staring at the cracked ceiling, exhaustion washed over me in relentless waves. My eyelids grew heavy, the weight of my actions pressing down on me like a physical force.

"Just a few minutes," I murmured to myself. "Just need to rest..."

The world faded to black.

When consciousness returned, I found myself disoriented and groggy. The familiar scent of leather and stale cigarettes filled my nostrils. My eyes snapped open, taking in the interior of a taxi cab.

"What the hell?" I muttered, sitting up straighter. The alleyway beyond the windshield was dark and grimy, littered with overflowing dumpsters and discarded trash.

A chill ran down my spine as realization dawned. "It worked," I whispered, a mixture of awe and trepidation in my voice. "I actually broke reality."

I glanced around, half-expecting to see the cab driver's lifeless body. But of course, that was in another timeline, another version of events.

"Get it together," I chided myself, reaching for the door handle. "You've got work to do."

As I stepped out of the cab, I quickly shed the robe I was wearing, tossing it into a nearby dumpster. My mind raced, trying to process the implications of what I'd accomplished.

As I emerged onto the bustling city street, I couldn't shake the feeling that I was being watched. Paranoia, or a side effect of reality-hopping? Either way, I knew one thing for certain – there was no going back now.

27 - 28

The next three weeks passed in a blur of sleepless nights and feverish planning. I paced the worn carpet of my dingy hotel room, my mind racing with possibilities and pitfalls. Saint Montagues Hospital loomed in my thoughts, a beacon of both hope and dread.

"There has to be a way," I muttered, running a hand through my disheveled hair. "A way to make Drake understand, to break through the barriers of reality."

As I gazed out the grimy window at the city below, a sudden realization hit me like a bolt of lightning. My veins tingled, as if the very radiation coursing through them was whispering the answer.

"Of course," I breathed, a manic grin spreading across my face. "It's so simple. To break Miller's reality, I need to..."

My voice trailed off as exhaustion finally claimed me. I collapsed onto the bed, my last conscious thoughts a jumble of fractured realities and desperate plans.

In my dreams, I saw the world as it was before the accident. Drake Miller, the ruthless lawyer, sat at his desk, oblivious to the impending tragedy that would shatter his life. Linda's warm smile and Harrison's infectious laughter echoed through the corridors of memory.

When I awoke, clarity washed over me. I knew exactly which reality I was in and what I needed to do. With purposeful strides, I made my way to Saint Montagues, slipping on the familiar janitor's uniform I'd worn for the past year.

As I pushed my mop bucket down the ICU corridor, I overheard Drake's anguished voice. "Both of them? No, there must be some mistake," he pleaded with a nurse, his words choked with emotion.

I kept my head down, focusing on the task at hand. They wouldn't recognize me – not in this reality, not as the unassuming janitor who'd been silently observing for months.

"I'm sorry, Mr. Miller," the nurse said softly. "Your wife and son... they didn't survive the accident."

Drake's sob pierced the air, a sound of raw, unbearable pain. I gripped my mop handle tighter, fighting the urge to rush to his side and explain everything.

"Not yet," I reminded myself. "The time isn't right. But soon, Drake. Soon, you'll understand the truth about your fractured existence."

29 - 29

Drake's frantic pleas escalated, his voice hoarse with desperation. "No, you don't understand! I need to see them. There must be something you can do!"

The nurse, her face etched with sympathy, placed a gentle hand on Drake's shoulder. "Mr. Miller, please. You need to rest. Doctor, I think we should—"

"Give him a sedative," the doctor interjected, his voice low but firm. "It's for his own good."

I watched from the corner of my eye as they administered the drug, Drake's protests fading into incoherent murmurs. As the medical staff filed out, leaving Drake alone in his grief-induced slumber, I knew my moment had arrived.

Carefully, I approached his bedside, my heart pounding. "I'm sorry, Drake," I whispered, "but this is the only way to save you – to save all of us."

With trembling hands, I prepared the syringe filled with my own blood. The weight of what I was about to do pressed heavily upon me. Was I playing God? Or was I simply setting right what had gone terribly wrong?

As I injected the mixture into his IV, I couldn't help but wonder, "Which world will you wake up in, Drake? Will you see Linda's gentle smile or hear Harrison's laughter?"

The deed done, I quickly gathered my things. It was time to leave this fractured reality behind. As I walked out of the hospital, a strange sense of peace washed over me. "Good luck, Drake," I thought. "May you find the truth – and yourself – in whatever world awaits you."

Shadows of Reflection

Blue World – 2024

1 - 2

The shadows danced across the worn leather spines of the books lining the study walls, their titles barely visible in the dim light of Drake Miller's desk lamp. He ran a calloused hand over his scruffy beard, eyes fixed on the scattered papers before him yet seeing nothing.

"Focus, Drake," he muttered to himself, willing his mind to concentrate on the task at hand. But the weight of his thoughts pressed down on him, each one a piece of the puzzle he'd been trying to solve since that fateful day.

The soft clink of dishes echoed from down the hall, Linda's presence a comforting reminder of the life they still shared. Drake's gaze drifted to the framed photographs on his desk, memories of happier times mocking him from their gilded prisons.

He shook his head, forcing his attention back to the files. "There has to be something here," he whispered, fingers tracing the edges of a police report. "Some clue I've missed..."

The floorboards creaked behind him, and Drake turned to see Linda standing in the doorway, a steaming mug in her hands. Her blue eyes, once so full of light, now held a sadness that mirrored his own.

"Thought you could use some coffee," she said softly, crossing the room to place the mug beside him.

Drake managed a weak smile. "Thanks, Lin. I'm sorry, I know I've been... distant lately."

Linda's hand rested on his shoulder, a gesture so familiar it made his heart ache. "You don't have to apologize, Drake. I understand."

He covered her hand with his own, relishing the warmth of her touch. "I just can't shake the feeling that I'm missing something. That there's more to what happened than we know."

Linda's voice was gentle but firm. "We've been over this, Drake. The police said it was an accident."

"I know, I know," Drake sighed, his free hand running through his dark hair. "But something doesn't add up. I can feel it in my gut."

As Linda opened her mouth to respond, Drake's eyes caught on a detail in one of the reports. His heart began to race, the pieces suddenly shifting into a new configuration.

"Lin," he breathed, barely able to contain the mix of excitement and dread building within him. "I think I found something."

3 - 4

Drake's fingers trembled as he reached for the photograph on his desk. The smiling faces of his family stared back at him, a stark contrast to the turmoil churning inside him. Linda's radiant smile, her hand resting on his shoulder, and Harrison... their son, his bright eyes twinkling with mischief and laughter.

"What is it, Drake?" Linda asked, her voice laced with concern.

He swallowed hard, his eyes fixed on Harrison's face. "Look at this photo, Lin. Remember that day at the beach?"

Linda leaned in, her blonde hair brushing against his cheek. "Of course. It was just a few weeks before..." Her voice trailed off, unable to finish the sentence.

Drake's mind raced, connecting invisible dots. "Harrison's wearing that shell necklace he made. The one he insisted on wearing everywhere."

"Drake, where are you going with this?" Linda's tone was a mixture of curiosity and apprehension.

He turned to face her, his brown eyes intense. "The police report. It doesn't mention the necklace. Not once. How could they miss something so obvious?"

Linda's brow furrowed. "Maybe it fell off during... during the accident?"

Drake shook his head vehemently. "No, Lin. That necklace was Harrison's prized possession. He never took it off. Something's not right here."

As the implications of his realization sank in, Drake felt a chill run down his spine. The accident that had torn their world apart suddenly seemed far more sinister than he'd ever imagined.

5 - 6

Drake's fingers trembled as he set the photograph down, his mind reeling with the implications. He turned back to the stack of files on his desk, a newfound urgency driving his actions.

"What are you looking for?" Linda asked, her voice barely above a whisper.

Drake rifled through the papers, his eyes scanning each document with laser focus. "Anything, everything. There has to be something we missed."

He pulled out a police report, his fingers tracing the edges of the paper as if he could absorb the information through touch alone. "The initial investigation was rushed," he muttered, more to himself than to Linda. "They were too quick to write it off as a simple accident."

Linda leaned in, her presence a comforting warmth at his side. "But why would they do that, Drake? What reason could they have to cover anything up?"

Drake's brow furrowed, his lawyer's mind kicking into high gear. "I don't know, Lin. But I intend to find out."

As he pored over the documents, fragments of information began to coalesce in his mind. The missing necklace, the inconsistencies in witness statements, the peculiar timing of it all – each piece a potential clue to the truth behind the accident that had stolen their son.

"I've been blind," Drake murmured, his voice thick with emotion. "Too caught up in my grief to see what was right in front of me."

Linda squeezed his shoulder gently. "We both were, Drake. But now we have a chance to make it right."

Drake nodded, a newfound determination settling over him like armor. "For Harrison," he said softly, his eyes meeting Linda's. "We owe him the truth."

7 - 8

Drake's eyes widened as they landed on a scribbled note in the margin of the police report. His heart skipped a beat, and he felt a chill run down his spine.

"Gabriel," he whispered, the name barely audible.

Linda leaned in closer, her brow furrowed. "What is it, Drake? What did you find?"

Drake's fingers trembled as he pointed to the hastily written name. "Look here, in the margin. Gabriel. It's... it's him, Linda. The mysterious figure from the accident scene."

His mind raced, memories flooding back of the shadowy silhouette he'd glimpsed that fateful night. The figure who'd vanished before the paramedics arrived, leaving behind only questions and a gnawing sense of unease.

"I don't understand," Linda said, her voice tight with concern. "Who is Gabriel? And what does he have to do with Harrison's accident?"

Drake shook his head, his eyes never leaving the page. "I don't know, but this... this changes everything." He looked up at Linda, his gaze intense. "Remember how I told you about the man I saw at the scene? The one who disappeared?"

Linda nodded slowly, realization dawning on her face.

"I think," Drake continued, his voice low and urgent, "that man was Gabriel. And if he's connected to the accident somehow..."

He trailed off, the implications too overwhelming to voice. In his mind, he saw Harrison's smiling face, heard his laughter echoing through their home. The weight of his failure to protect his son pressed down on him, threatening to crush him beneath its burden.

"We need to find him," Drake said, determination hardening his voice. "Whoever this Gabriel is, he's the key to unraveling this whole mystery."

As he spoke, Drake couldn't shake the feeling that by uttering that name aloud, he'd set in motion events that would change their lives forever. The hunt for Gabriel had begun, and with it, the desperate search for the truth behind their son's death.

9 - 10

Drake's fingers trembled as he traced the name "Gabriel" on the police report. His mind raced, conjuring dark possibilities. Who was this enigmatic figure? What sinister motive could he have had in their son's accident?

"Gabriel," Drake muttered, tasting the bitterness of the name. "What did you want with us?"

A chill crept up his spine as he imagined a shadowy figure lurking at the edges of their lives, pulling strings they couldn't see. The weight of uncertainty pressed down on him, making the dim study feel suffocating.

Drake's thoughts spiraled. Was Gabriel a mere bystander, or something far more malevolent? The creeping fear that had taken root in his gut began to grow, tendrils of dread spreading through his body.

Suddenly, the soft creak of floorboards broke his reverie. Drake's head snapped up, his heart pounding. There, framed in the doorway, stood Linda. Her blue eyes, pools of concern and unspoken questions, searched his face.

"Drake?" she said softly, her voice barely above a whisper. "What is it? What have you found?"

Without waiting for an answer, Linda crossed the room, her footsteps muffled by the thick carpet. She reached for his hand, her touch warm and reassuring against his cold, clammy skin.

Drake swallowed hard, struggling to find the words. "I think... I think I've stumbled onto something big, Linda. Something that might explain everything about Harrison's accident."

11 - 12

Drake squeezed Linda's hand, drawing strength from her presence. He took a deep breath, his eyes meeting hers with fierce determination.

"I promise you, Linda," he said, his voice low and intense, "I will find out what happened to our boy. No matter where this leads, no matter what it costs me, I'll uncover the truth."

Linda's blue eyes shimmered with unshed tears, but her voice remained steady. "We'll do it together, Drake. You're not alone in this."

Drake nodded, his throat tight with emotion. He glanced at the scattered papers on his desk, then back to his wife. "There's so much we don't know. This Gabriel... he's the key to everything. But digging deeper could be dangerous."

Linda's grip on his hand tightened. "Since when has danger ever stopped you, Drake Miller?" She managed a small, sad smile. "You've always fought for what's right, even when it meant long nights at the office. Now it's time to fight for our family."

Drake's mind raced, considering the implications. The quiet of their home suddenly felt oppressive, as if the very walls were closing in around them. He stood, pacing the small confines of his study.

"This could change everything, Linda," he said, his voice barely above a whisper. "Once we start down this path, there's no going back. Our lives, everything we thought we knew... it might all be different."

Linda moved to stand in front of him, placing her hands on his chest. "Drake, look at me," she said softly. "Our lives changed the moment we lost Harrison. If there's even a chance of understanding why, of finding some kind of justice or peace... we have to take it."

Drake gazed into her eyes, seeing the same mix of determination and fear that he felt churning inside himself. He nodded slowly, bracing himself for the unknown journey ahead.

"You're right," he said, his voice growing stronger. "We owe it to Harrison. To ourselves. Whatever comes next, we'll face it together."

As they stood there, wrapped in each other's arms, Drake couldn't shake the feeling that they were standing on the precipice of something monumental. The world as they knew it was about to shift beneath their feet, and there was no telling where they might land.

Return to the Firm

1 - 2

The cacophony of ringing phones and clacking keyboards assaulted Drake's senses as he stepped into the law firm. The familiar chaos of his old workplace felt alien now, a stark reminder of the life he'd left behind. He navigated the labyrinth of cubicles with practiced ease, his tired eyes scanning the sea of faces until they landed on Richard Vega's desk.

Drake's steps faltered for a moment as he approached. *What if Vega can't help? What if this is all for nothing?* He pushed the doubts aside, steeling himself. For his family—for whichever version of them he could save—he had to try.

Vega sat hunched over a mountain of paperwork, his brow furrowed in concentration. Drake cleared his throat, but the young lawyer remained oblivious.

"Vega," Drake said, his voice cutting through the office din. He winced at the roughness in his own tone, a reminder of sleepless nights and relentless worry. "I need to talk to you."

Vega's head snapped up, surprise flickering across his features. "Drake? I didn't expect to see you here."

Drake leaned against the desk, his fingers drumming an anxious rhythm on the polished wood. "Neither did I," he admitted, a humorless chuckle escaping his lips. "But I need your help."

As he spoke, Drake's gaze darted around the office. How many times had he stood in this very spot, prioritizing cases over family dinners and soccer games? The weight of his past choices pressed down on him, threatening to crush what little resolve he had left.

Focus, he chided himself. *This isn't about the past. It's about saving your future—whatever that might be.*

Drake took a deep breath, steadying himself. "I know it's been a while, Vega, but I'm hoping you can do me a favor. It's... it's important."

3 - 4

Vega looked up, a frown creasing his brow. "What's up, Drake?" He set aside his pen, giving Drake his full attention.

Drake's heart raced, the urgency of his quest pulsing through his veins. He leaned in close, lowering his voice to a near whisper. "I need to know everything you can find out about a man named Gabriel. He's connected to the accident, and I need to know who he is and what he wants."

As he spoke, Drake's mind flickered between images of his wife and son, their faces blurring together in a haunting reminder of his fractured reality. He gripped the edge of Vega's desk, steadying himself against the wave of emotion threatening to overwhelm him.

This is it, Drake thought, his jaw clenching with determination. *This Gabriel could be the key to understanding everything—to saving my family.*

He watched Vega's expression carefully, searching for any sign of recognition or hesitation. The young lawyer's eyebrows knitted together, a mix of concern and curiosity etching itself across his features.

"Gabriel," Drake repeated, the name tasting bitter on his tongue. "He's involved somehow, Vega. I can feel it in my bones."

5 - 6

Vega nodded, scribbling a note on a legal pad. His pen scratched against the paper, the sound grating on Drake's already frayed nerves. "I'll get right on it," Vega said, his voice low and cautious. "But I should warn you,

Drake, there might not be much to go on. The police report mentions a Gabriel, but beyond that, it's pretty slim pickings."

Drake's heart sank, a cold dread seeping into his chest. He'd been hoping for more, for some tangible lead to grasp onto. His mind raced, replaying the fractured memories of the accident, searching for any detail he might have overlooked.

No, he thought, *there has to be more. Gabriel is the link between my two realities. He has to be.*

Drake clenched his jaw, frustration boiling inside him. He could feel the weight of his dual existence pressing down on him, threatening to crush him beneath its impossible burden. "I don't care," he growled, his voice rougher than he intended. "I need answers, Vega. Whatever you can find, I want to know."

He leaned in closer, his eyes boring into Vega's. "This isn't just about the case anymore. It's about my family, my life. Everything hinges on finding out who this Gabriel is and what he wants."

As he spoke, Drake could almost see the ghostly outlines of his wife and son, their faces overlapping in a haunting reminder of what he stood to lose—or perhaps had already lost. The thought sent a shiver down his spine, intensifying his desperation.

"I understand, Drake," Vega replied, his voice tinged with sympathy. "I'll do everything I can. But... are you sure you're okay? You seem—"

"I'm fine," Drake cut him off, perhaps too sharply. He took a deep breath, trying to calm the storm raging inside him. "Just... find what you can. Please."

7 - 8

Vega's expression softened, a mix of concern and empathy flickering across his face. He leaned back in his chair, running a hand through his hair before meeting Drake's intense gaze.

"I'll do my best, Drake," Vega said, his voice low and measured. "But in the meantime, I did manage to get some information about that robe you found at the scene." He paused, as if weighing the impact of his next words. "The DNA sample they took from it came back as a match to a janitor at Saint Montague Hospital."

Drake's eyes widened, his mind reeling at this unexpected revelation. The bustling sounds of the law firm faded into the background as he processed this new information. A janitor? It seemed so... mundane, so at odds with the otherworldly nature of his experiences.

"A janitor?" Drake repeated, his voice a mixture of disbelief and confusion. He leaned forward, bracing his hands on Vega's desk. "What would a janitor be doing with a robe like that?"

As he spoke, Drake's mind raced through possibilities. Was this janitor somehow connected to Gabriel? Or was it just another dead end in his increasingly convoluted search for answers?

The weight of his dual realities pressed down on him, threatening to overwhelm him. In one world, his wife's absence left a gaping hole in his life. In the other, the loss of his son haunted his every waking moment. And here, in this bustling law firm, he stood on the precipice between those two impossible existences, grasping at any clue that might make sense of it all.

9 - 10

Vega shrugged, his expression a mix of sympathy and frustration. "Your guess is as good as mine, Drake. But it might be worth looking into." He leaned forward, lowering his voice. "Maybe this janitor knows something about Gabriel."

Drake's jaw clenched, his mind churning with possibilities. The connection seemed tenuous at best, but in this labyrinth of mysteries, even the faintest thread could lead to answers. He could almost hear the echoes of his son's laughter in one world, his wife's gentle touch in another. The weight of his fractured reality pressed down on him, fueling his desperate need for clarity.

"A janitor at Saint Montague," Drake muttered, more to himself than to Vega. His fingers drummed restlessly on the desk, a physical manifestation of his internal turmoil. "It's not much, but it's something. Maybe he saw Gabriel, or..." He trailed off, lost in thought.

After a moment, Drake nodded, his eyes refocusing on Vega with newfound determination. "Thanks, Vega. Keep me posted on anything you find." He paused, weighing his next words carefully. "And I mean anything. No matter how small or insignificant it might seem."

As he spoke, Drake couldn't shake the feeling that he was being watched. He glanced around the busy office, half-expecting to see Gabriel's piercing gaze and disfigured face amongst the sea of lawyers and paralegals. But there was nothing, just the usual bustle of a law firm at work.

11 - 12

Drake turned to leave, his mind already racing with plans to investigate Saint Montague Hospital. Suddenly, a searing pain shot through his head, like a white-hot knife piercing his skull. He gasped, stumbling forward as the world tilted violently around him.

"Drake?" Vega's voice sounded distant, muffled. "You okay, man?"

Drake tried to respond, but the words wouldn't come. His vision blurred, dark spots dancing at the edges. He reached out, desperate for something to steady himself, but his hand met only empty air.

"I'm... I'm fine," he managed to choke out, even as the darkness closed in. The last thing he saw was the concerned face of Vega, distorted and wavering, before everything faded to black.

When Drake came to, he found himself on the bustling sidewalk outside the law firm, with no memory of how he'd gotten there. His head throbbed relentlessly, each pulse sending waves of pain crashing through his skull.

"What the hell?" he muttered, pressing a hand to his forehead. The cool touch offered little relief. People streamed past him, a blur of faces and bodies, as he struggled to regain his bearings.

Drake's mind raced, trying to piece together the missing moments. Had he blacked out? Or was this another shift between his fractured realities? The uncertainty gnawed at him, adding to the cacophony in his head.

"Get it together, Miller," he growled to himself, forcing his feet to move. Each step was a battle against the dizziness that threatened to overwhelm him. "You've got work to do."

13 - 14

The cacophony of the city enveloped Drake as he stumbled forward. Car horns blared, a discordant symphony accompanied by the rhythmic click of hurried footsteps on concrete. The air was thick with exhaust fumes and the scent of street food, but to Drake, it all felt distant, muted.

"Excuse me," he mumbled, narrowly avoiding collision with a harried businesswoman. She shot him a glare but didn't break stride.

Drake's thoughts drifted back to Gabriel, that enigmatic figure who seemed to hold the key to everything. "Who are you?" he whispered, his words lost in the urban din.

A flash of white caught his eye—a figure in a pale robe disappearing around a corner. Drake's heart raced. Could it be? He quickened his pace, weaving through the crowd.

"Wait!" he called out, but the figure was gone.

Drake leaned against a building, catching his breath. "Am I losing my mind?" he wondered aloud.

An elderly man passing by gave him a concerned look. "You alright there, son?"

Drake forced a weak smile. "Just... trying to figure some things out."

As the man moved on, Drake closed his eyes, trying to focus. "There's something I'm missing," he thought. "Something about Gabriel, about the accident. But what?"

The pieces refused to fit, like a jigsaw puzzle with crucial parts missing. Drake pushed off from the wall, determination setting his jaw. He had to keep moving, keep searching. The truth was out there, hidden in the pulsing heart of the city, and he would find it—no matter the cost.

15 - 16

Drake's feet carried him along familiar streets, his mind adrift in a sea of memories and questions. Before he realized it, he found himself at the edge of the embankment, staring down at the dark waters that had nearly claimed his life.

"Jesus," he muttered, his hands trembling as he gripped the guardrail. The lake's surface was deceptively calm, betraying nothing of the chaos that had unfolded here.

He closed his eyes, the events of that night flooding back with startling clarity. "I should have died here," he whispered, his voice barely audible over the distant traffic.

The screeching of tires echoed in his mind, followed by the sickening crunch of metal. Drake's eyes snapped open, his breath coming in short gasps.

"Why?" he demanded of the silent waters below. "Why did I survive when they..." His voice broke, unable to finish the thought.

A jogger passing by slowed, giving Drake a concerned look. "You okay, man?"

Drake straightened, forcing a nod. "Yeah, just... remembering."

As the jogger moved on, Drake's gaze returned to the spot where his car had disappeared beneath the surface. The memory of cold water rushing in, the panic, the struggle to escape—it all felt so vivid, so immediate.

"What am I missing?" he muttered, running a hand through his disheveled hair. "Gabriel, the robe, the accident... how does it all connect?"

A chill ran down his spine, not entirely due to the cool breeze coming off the water. Something about this place, about that night, held the answers he sought. But as he stood there, trapped between memory and mystery, Drake couldn't shake the feeling that uncovering the truth might cost him more than he was prepared to pay.

17 - 18

Drake's gaze drifted to the sedan that had caused the accident, its windows shattered, its metal twisted and mangled. The sight of it ignited a surge of anger in his chest, hot and suffocating.

"You did this," he growled, his fists clenching at his sides. "You tore my world apart."

He approached the wreckage, each step heavy with the weight of his grief and rage. The closer he got, the more vivid the memories became—the screech of tires, the sickening crunch of metal, the terrified screams of his family.

Drake peered through the broken windows, his heart pounding. The interior was dark and empty, the seats stained with dried blood and water. The sight made his stomach churn.

"God," he whispered, his voice trembling. "How did I survive this?"

His mind raced, trying to piece together the fragmented memories of that night. Who was driving? Was it really Gabriel? And if so, why?

"I should have protected them," he thought, guilt gnawing at him. "I was always so focused on winning cases, on being the best lawyer... and now look where it's gotten me."

A sob caught in his throat, threatening to break free. Drake swallowed hard, forcing it down. He couldn't afford to fall apart now, not when he was so close to uncovering the truth.

"I'll find you, Gabriel," he promised, his voice low and determined. "And when I do, you'll pay for what you've done to my family."

19 - 20

Drake's vision blurred suddenly, the world around him seeming to tilt on its axis. He staggered backward, his legs trembling beneath him as a wave of dizziness crashed over his senses.

"What... what's happening?" he gasped, his words slurring as he fought to maintain his balance.

His hand shot out, desperately seeking something to steady himself, but found only empty air.

"No," Drake mumbled, his thoughts growing hazy. "I can't... I need to..."

He stumbled, his knees buckling as the world spun violently around him. As he fell, a fleeting thought crossed his mind: Was this connected to the accident? To Gabriel? Or was it something else entirely?

Drake's eyes fluttered, darkness creeping in at the edges of his vision. He could feel his consciousness slipping away, and with it, the answers he so desperately sought.

"Linda... Harrison..." he whispered, their names a prayer on his lips as he thought of his wife and son – one lost in each of his fractured realities.

As the blackness consumed him, Drake's mind raced with unanswered questions. What other secrets lay buried beneath the surface of this mystery? What truths awaited him in the depths of this twisted enigma?

His last coherent thought before succumbing to the darkness was a grim determination: he would uncover the truth, no matter the cost. For his family, for himself, he would piece together this shattered puzzle and find his way back to wholeness.

Awakening in Chaos

Green World – 2024

1 - 2

Drake's eyes fluttered open, the world a kaleidoscope of blurred shapes and muted colors. The hardwood floor pressed against his cheek, its familiar oak grain a stark contrast to the disorienting fog clouding his mind. He blinked rapidly, willing his vision to clear as the living room of his Green World home slowly came into focus.

"Linda?" he croaked, his voice barely above a whisper. No response came.

Gritting his teeth against the throbbing in his skull, Drake pushed himself up onto his elbows. The room tilted violently, and he squeezed his eyes shut, fighting back a wave of nausea.

What the hell happened? he thought, struggling to piece together his fractured memories. *One minute I was in the firm, and then...*

His train of thought derailed as a sharp, stabbing pain lanced through his head. Drake hissed, instinctively reaching up to touch his temple. His fingers came away wet and sticky, stained a deep crimson.

"Oh God," he muttered, staring at the blood with wide, panicked eyes. His heart began to race, each frantic beat echoing in his ears like a war drum. "Not again. Please, not again."

The words tumbled from his lips unbidden, a desperate prayer to whatever forces might be listening. Drake's mind reeled, grasping for an explanation that didn't involve losing more precious time, more moments with the family he'd already sacrificed so much for.

He tried to stand, his legs trembling beneath him like a newborn colt's. The room spun, and he stumbled, catching himself on the edge of the coffee table.

"Pull it together, Miller," he growled, his tone a mixture of determination and fear. "You can't afford to fall apart now."

But even as he spoke the words, Drake felt the icy tendrils of panic wrapping around his chest, squeezing the air from his lungs. He closed his eyes, forcing himself to take deep, measured breaths.

Focus, he told himself. *You're a lawyer, dammit. Think this through logically.*

Yet logic seemed to have abandoned him, leaving only the raw, primal fear of a man teetering on the edge of an abyss he couldn't begin to comprehend.

3 - 4

"What... what happened?" Drake muttered, his voice hoarse and shaky. He glanced around the room, searching for any clues that might explain his sudden blackout. His eyes darted from the pristine coffee table to the untouched bookshelf, desperately seeking answers in the familiar surroundings.

Where's Linda? The thought hit him like a freight train, his heart rate spiking. She should be here, her calming presence a balm to his frayed nerves.

"Linda?" he called out, his voice cracking. "Linda, are you home?"

Silence answered him, amplifying the emptiness of the room. Drake's gaze swept across the space again, this time noticing the soft, golden light filtering through the windows. The afternoon sun bathed everything in a deceptively peaceful glow, a stark contrast to the turmoil raging within him.

He stumbled towards the kitchen, hoping to find a note, a sign, anything to indicate where Linda might have gone. But the countertops were bare, the refrigerator door devoid of any hastily scribbled messages.

"This doesn't make sense," Drake mumbled to himself, running a shaky hand through his hair. "She wouldn't just leave, not after..." He trailed off, unable to complete the thought.

The house felt oppressively quiet, each tick of the wall clock like a hammer blow to his already aching head. Drake leaned against the kitchen island, closing his eyes as he tried to piece together the fragments of his memory.

Think, dammit. What's the last thing you remember?

But no matter how hard he concentrated, the moments leading up to his collapse remained frustratingly out of reach, locked away in some dark corner of his mind.

5 - 6

Drake's mind raced, conjuring a parade of terrifying possibilities. His heart pounded in his chest, each beat a painful reminder of his fragile mortality.

"Could it have been a seizure?" he whispered, his voice barely audible in the empty kitchen. The thought sent a shiver down his spine. He'd never had epilepsy before, but then again, he'd never lived two parallel lives before either.

His fingers tightened on the edge of the counter, knuckles turning white. "Or a stroke?" The word felt heavy on his tongue, laden with implications he wasn't ready to face. At his age, it wasn't impossible, especially given the stress he'd been under.

But even as these medical explanations flitted through his mind, a darker, more insidious thought took root. Drake's breath caught in his throat as he considered it.

"What if... what if it's something to do with the accident?" he muttered, his brown eyes widening with dawning horror. "Some kind of... aftereffect?"

The car crash that had torn his reality asunder flashed before his eyes. The screeching tires, the shattering glass, the sickening crunch of metal. And then... nothingness. Until he'd woken up to two different worlds, two different tragedies.

Drake shook his head violently, as if he could physically dislodge the terrifying thoughts. "No, no, no," he growled, pushing himself away from the counter. "I can't... I can't think like that. I need... I need..."

He paused, realizing he didn't know what he needed. Answers? Certainly. But how to get them? And from whom?

"Focus, Drake," he told himself sternly, falling back on the authoritative tone he'd used countless times in the courtroom. "You're a lawyer. You solve problems. Think!"

But the fog of confusion persisted, clouding his usually sharp mind. Drake paced the kitchen, each step echoing in the silent house. "I need to figure this out," he muttered. "For Linda. For Harrison. For... for both of them."

The weight of his dual existence pressed down on him, threatening to crush him beneath its impossible burden. But Drake Miller had never been one to give up easily, not even in the face of the unimaginable.

"One step at a time," he said, trying to inject confidence into his voice. "First, I need to understand what happened. Then... then I can decide what to do next."

7 - 7

Drake's trembling fingers hovered over his phone, the device feeling unnaturally heavy in his hand. The screen blurred as he blinked back tears, his vision swimming with the effort of focusing on the numbers.

"Come on," he muttered, his voice rough with emotion. "Pull yourself together, Miller."

He punched in the hospital's number, each digit feeling like a monumental effort. As the phone began to ring, Drake's heart pounded in his chest, a thunderous rhythm that threatened to drown out everything else.

"Saint Montagues, how may I direct your call?" a cheerful voice answered.

Drake swallowed hard; his throat suddenly dry. "I... I need to speak with someone about... about a possible medical emergency."

"Sir, are you experiencing symptoms right now? Do you need an ambulance?" The receptionist's tone sharpened with concern.

"No, no," Drake hastily replied. "I just... I just woke up on the floor. I don't know what happened. I need to know if... if this could be related to my accident."

There was a pause on the other end of the line. "Your accident, sir?"

Drake's mind raced. Which accident? Which world? He squeezed his eyes shut, fighting back a wave of nausea. "I'm sorry, I'm not... I'm not thinking clearly. Can I please speak with a doctor?"

As he waited to be transferred, Drake's gaze wandered around the room, searching for any sign of Linda or Harrison. "Where are you?" he whispered, a knot forming in his stomach. "What's happening to me?"

Aftereffects

Green World – 2024

1 - 2

The world tilted on its axis as Drake blinked, trying to focus on the living room swimming before his eyes. A metallic taste coated his tongue, and he felt a warm trickle down his chin. Blood. His blood.

Footsteps approached, faltering. Drake's gaze lifted to see Harrison frozen in the doorway, his son's eyes wide with shock and fear. The boy's curly hair was mussed from sleep, but his expression was fully alert, taking in the scene before him.

"Dad? What's going on?" Harrison's voice cracked, a mixture of teenage bravado and genuine concern as he rushed forward, dropping to his knees beside Drake.

Drake opened his mouth to respond, but no words came out. His mind raced, trying to piece together how he'd ended up here, on the floor, bleeding. The last thing he remembered was... what? White light? A voice? Vega? The fragments slipped away like sand through his fingers.

Harrison's hand touched his shoulder, grounding him back to reality. "Dad, you're scaring me. Talk to me, please."

Drake swallowed hard, tasting copper. "I'm... I'm not sure, son," he finally managed, his voice hoarse and unfamiliar to his own ears. "I think I might have fallen."

But even as the words left his mouth, Drake knew they weren't true. Something was terribly wrong, and the weight of it pressed down on him like a physical force. He needed answers, needed to understand what was happening to him. But more than that, he needed to protect Harrison from whatever darkness was creeping into their lives.

"We should get you to a hospital," Harrison said, his tone brooking no argument. It was strange, Drake thought, how their roles seemed to have reversed in this moment – his son taking charge while he sat helpless and confused.

"You're right," Drake agreed, wincing as he tried to push himself up. "Just... give me a moment."

As Harrison helped him to his feet, Drake couldn't shake the feeling that this was only the beginning. Whatever force had brought him to this point – be it Vega, the accident, or something he couldn't yet fathom – it wasn't finished with him. And as he leaned on his son's shoulder, Drake silently vowed to uncover the truth, no matter the cost.

3 - 4

Drake blinked up at his son, his vision blurry and unfocused. The room seemed to tilt and shift around him, making his stomach churn. "Harrison? What... what happened?" he mumbled, his voice thick with confusion.

Harrison's brow furrowed; his teenage cockiness replaced by genuine concern. "You tell me," he replied, running a hand through his unruly curls. "I found you like this when I woke up. You've been sleepwalking all night, Dad. You were talking to yourself, but you kept calling out someone's name... Vega, I think."

Drake's mind reeled, struggling to process the information. Sleepwalking? He'd never done that before. And why Vega? The name tickled something in the back of his mind, but he couldn't quite grasp it.

"I don't... I don't remember any of that," Drake admitted, his lawyer's instinct to maintain control warring with his growing fear. He tried to push himself up, but his arms felt like lead. "Are you sure about the name?"

Harrison nodded; his eyes clouded with worry. "Yeah, pretty sure. You kept saying it over and over. Dad, what's going on? Are you okay?"

Drake wanted to reassure his son, to tell him everything was fine. But the words wouldn't come. Instead, he found himself staring at Harrison, drinking in the sight of him. In this moment, the weight of his dual existence pressed down on him more heavily than ever. How could he explain to this version of his son that in another life, he'd lost him?

"I'm not sure," Drake finally said, his voice barely above a whisper. "But we'll figure it out together, okay?" He reached out, squeezing Harrison's hand, anchoring himself in this reality. Whatever was happening, whatever force was at play, Drake knew one thing for certain: he would do anything to protect his family, in this world and any other.

5 - 6

The name "Vega" echoed in Drake's mind, sending an icy chill down his spine. Fragmented memories of his conversation with Vega at the law firm flashed before his eyes - the stern expression, the cryptic words. But how could he have been calling out to Vega in his sleep?

"Vega," Drake murmured, his brow furrowing. "It must have been Vega."

Harrison leaned closer; concern etched on his face. "Who's Vega, Dad?"

Drake opened his mouth to respond, but a wave of dizziness washed over him. The room began to spin, the edges of his vision blurring. He gripped the edge of the couch, his knuckles turning white.

"I need to..." Drake's voice trailed off as he struggled to form coherent thoughts. The dual realities he inhabited seemed to be colliding, leaving him adrift in a sea of confusion. "Hospital," he finally managed to whisper. "I need to go to the hospital."

As he pushed himself to his feet, Drake's legs trembled beneath him. He stumbled, catching himself on the coffee table. The world tilted precariously, and he closed his eyes, fighting against the vertigo.

"What's happening to me?" he thought, fear gripping his heart. "Am I losing my grip on both worlds?"

7 - 8

Harrison nodded, his teenage bravado melting away to reveal genuine concern. "I'll drive you," he offered, moving swiftly to support his father's unsteady frame.

Drake leaned heavily on his son, marveling at how strong Harrison had become. When had his little boy grown into this capable young man? The thought brought a mix of pride and melancholy.

"Thanks, son," Drake mumbled, his words slightly slurred. "I don't know what's wrong with me."

As they made their way towards the door, Drake's gaze fell upon the mail scattered across the side table. Among the usual bills and circulars, a single envelope stood out. It was addressed to Harrison in neat, unfamiliar handwriting.

Drake's mind, foggy as it was, latched onto this anomaly. Who would be writing to Harrison? A friend? A college? Or something more sinister?

"Harrison," he began, his curiosity momentarily overriding his discomfort. "Do you recognize that handwriting?"

Harrison followed his father's gaze, his expression shifting from concern to confusion. "What? That handwriting? Dad, we need to get you to the hospital."

Drake blinked, wondering if the letter was another figment of his fractured reality. He reached out a shaky hand towards the table, determined to prove its existence to himself.

9 - 10

Drake's fingers hovered over the envelope, his moral compass warring with an inexplicable sense of urgency. The room seemed to tilt slightly as he wrestled with his decision.

"Dad?" Harrison's voice cut through the fog. "What are you doing?"

Drake withdrew his hand, guilt washing over him. "Nothing," he muttered. "Just... thought I saw something important."

As Harrison guided him towards the door, Drake's mind raced. The letter nagged at him, a loose thread in the tapestry of his already unraveling world. Before he could second-guess himself, he reached back and snatched the envelope, slipping it into his pocket in one fluid motion.

"Did you forget something?" Harrison asked, his brow furrowing.

Drake shook his head, forcing a weak smile. "No, just... making sure I had my wallet."

As they stepped out into the sunlight, Drake squinted against the sudden brightness. The weight of the letter seemed to burn against his thigh, a constant reminder of his transgression.

"Harrison," Drake said, his voice low. "I'm sorry I've been... not myself lately."

His son's reply was tinged with that uniquely teenage mix of concern and nonchalance. "It's okay, Dad. We'll figure it out."

Drake nodded but couldn't shake the feeling that he was standing on the precipice of something monumental. Whatever answers that letter held, he knew he wouldn't rest until he uncovered the truth.

11 - 12

The world outside the car window pulsed with an unnatural vibrancy, each color so saturated it made Drake's eyes ache. He squinted against the assault, his head throbbing in sync with his racing heartbeat. A warm trickle down his upper lip reminded him of the persistent nosebleed.

"Christ," Drake muttered, pressing a hand to his face. The metallic tang of blood filled his mouth.

Harrison's knuckles were white on the steering wheel, his usual carefree demeanor replaced by tense silence. Drake wanted to reach out, to reassure his son that everything would be fine, but the words felt hollow in his throat.

Instead, he found himself asking, "Harrison, have you... noticed anything strange lately? At school, maybe?"

Harrison's eyes flickered to him briefly. "Strange how?"

Drake hesitated. How could he explain the fractured reality he was experiencing without sounding completely unhinged? "I don't know. Just... anything out of the ordinary."

"Other than you sleepwalking and talking to yourself all night?" Harrison's attempt at levity fell flat, worry evident in his voice.

Drake winced, both from the pain and the reminder of his inexplicable behavior. "Yeah, other than that."

As they drove, the familiar streets of their town seemed alien, shadows stretching in impossible directions. Drake's mind raced, trying to piece together the fragments of memory from his sleepwalking episode. The name 'Vega' echoed in his thoughts, intertwining with his recollection of Vega from the law firm. Were they connected? And how did the letter burning a hole in his pocket fit into all of this?

"Dad?" Harrison's voice pulled him from his reverie. "We're almost there. You hanging in okay?"

Drake nodded, forcing a weak smile. "Yeah, I'm okay. Thanks for doing this, son."

As they approached the hospital, Drake couldn't shake the feeling that this was more than just a medical emergency. Something was fundamentally wrong with the fabric of his reality, and he was determined to unravel the mystery – no matter the cost.

13 - 14

The antiseptic smell assaulted Drake's senses as they entered the emergency room, the cacophony of beeping machines and hurried voices echoing off sterile walls. A nurse with kind eyes and a no-nonsense demeanor ushered him into a small cubicle, the harsh fluorescent lights stabbing at his already throbbing head.

"Mr. Miller, I'm Nurse Chen. Let's take a look at you," she said, her voice a soothing counterpoint to the chaos outside.

Drake winced as she gently dabbed at the dried blood on his face. "How bad is it?" he asked, his voice rougher than he expected.

"Nothing we can't handle," Nurse Chen replied with a reassuring smile. "Now, can you tell me what happened?"

As she worked, checking his vitals and cleaning his wounds, Drake's mind drifted. The letter in his pocket seemed to burn against his skin, a constant reminder of the mystery at hand.

"I... I'm not sure," he admitted, his brow furrowing. "My son found me like this. I've been sleepwalking, apparently."

Nurse Chen's eyebrows rose slightly. "Sleepwalking? That's unusual for adults. Any history of this?"

Drake shook his head, immediately regretting the movement as pain lanced through his skull. "No, never. It's all so... strange."

His hand unconsciously moved to his pocket, fingers brushing against the envelope. What secrets did it hold? And how did it connect to his fractured reality?

"Mr. Miller?" Nurse Chen's voice pulled him back to the present. "Your blood pressure's a bit high. Try to relax, okay? The doctor will be with you soon."

Drake nodded absently, his mind already racing ahead. As he waited, surrounded by the stark white walls and the steady rhythm of medical equipment, he couldn't shake the feeling that he was on the precipice of something monumental. The letter, the sleepwalking, the name 'Vega' – it all had to be connected. But how?

15 - 16

The clock on the wall ticked relentlessly, each second stretching into an eternity as Drake lay on the examination table. His mind, a whirlwind of fragmented thoughts, kept circling back to the letter in his pocket and vega. The fluorescent lights buzzed overhead, their harsh glare intensifying his throbbing headache.

After what felt like hours, the door swung open. A doctor entered, her white coat pristine, her expression unreadable. Drake's heart rate quickened, his detective's instinct kicking in, searching for any tell in her demeanor.

"Mr. Miller," she began, her voice soft yet authoritative, "I'm Dr. Ramirez. We've reviewed your test results."

Drake pushed himself up slightly, wincing at the movement. "And?" he prompted, his voice hoarse with anticipation.

Dr. Ramirez's eyes met his, her gaze steady. "It appears you suffered a minor concussion," she explained, her tone measured. "The nosebleed was likely a result of the trauma. We'll need to keep you here for observation overnight, just to be safe."

Drake's mind raced, processing the information. A concussion could explain the disorientation, but not the sleepwalking, not the voice calling out to 'Vega'. He opened his mouth to protest, to demand more answers, but the words died on his lips.

Instead, he asked, "Doctor, have you ever heard of sleepwalking being associated with concussions?"

Dr. Ramirez tilted her head slightly. "It's not common, but it's not unheard of either. The brain is complex, Mr. Miller. Sometimes, trauma can trigger unusual responses."

Drake nodded slowly, his fingers unconsciously tracing the outline of the letter in his pocket. "And what about... hearing things? Voices that aren't there?"

The doctor's eyebrows rose slightly. "That could be a symptom of the concussion, or it might be related to stress. Have you been under any unusual pressure lately, Mr. Miller?"

Drake almost laughed at the question. If only she knew about the parallel worlds, the constant tug-of-war between two realities. Instead, he simply said, "You could say that."

As Dr. Ramirez continued explaining the treatment plan, Drake's mind drifted. He knew, deep in his bones, that there was more to this than a simple concussion. The answers he sought weren't going to be found in this sterile hospital room. They were out there, waiting to be uncovered, and the letter in his pocket might just be the key to unlocking it all.

17 - 18

Drake nodded, the weight of Dr. Ramirez's words settling heavily on his shoulders. He glanced over at Harrison, who stood by his side, his face etched with concern. Despite everything, Drake couldn't help but feel a surge of gratitude for his son's unwavering support.

"Thanks for being here, Harrison," Drake said, his voice hoarse.

Harrison's bright eyes met his father's, a flicker of his usual mischief breaking through the worry. "Where else would I be, Dad? Someone's got to make sure you don't try to escape and go chasing after imaginary clues."

Drake managed a weak chuckle, wincing as the movement sent a fresh wave of pain through his head. "I'm not that bad, am I?"

"Only on your good days," Harrison quipped, but his hand reached out to squeeze his father's arm, the gesture conveying more than words ever could.

As the hours dragged on, Drake found himself drifting in and out of sleep, his dreams plagued by fragmented memories and half-formed thoughts. In one moment, he was back in the blue world, his wife's voice echoing in his ears.

"Drake, remember..." Her words faded, lost in the swirling mists of his subconscious.

He tried to call out to her, to beg her to finish her sentence, but his voice was swallowed by the oppressive silence of the dreamscape.

Then, with jarring suddenness, he was standing on the embankment, staring into the sedan where Gabriel sat, his face twisted in a sinister grin. The scarred man's piercing eyes bore into Drake, filled with secrets and hidden meanings.

"You're getting closer, Drake," Gabriel's smooth voice slithered through the air. "But are you prepared for what you'll find?"

Drake jerked awake, his heart pounding. The hospital room came into focus around him, the steady beep of monitors a stark contrast to the eerie silence of his dreams. He pressed a hand to his forehead, trying to make sense of the fragments swirling in his mind.

What did it all mean? And how was he supposed to unravel this mystery when he couldn't even trust his own perceptions?

19 - 19

Drake's eyes darted around the dimly lit hospital room, the shadows seeming to shift and dance at the edges of his vision. He blinked hard, trying to clear the fog from his mind.

"Harrison?" he called out, his voice hoarse.

His son stirred in the chair beside the bed, rubbing sleep from his eyes. "I'm here, Dad. You, okay?"

Drake nodded, though he felt far from okay. "Just... trying to make sense of it all."

Harrison leaned forward; concern etched in his features. "Make sense of what?"

Drake hesitated, weighing his words carefully. How could he explain the inexplicable? "These dreams, these... visions. They feel so real, but they can't be. Can they?"

His son's brow furrowed. "What are you seeing?"

"Your mother," Drake whispered, his heart constricting. "And a man named Gabriel. It's like they're trying to tell me something, but I can't quite grasp it."

As he spoke, Drake's mind raced. The blue world, the accident, the mysterious Gabriel – all pieces of a puzzle he couldn't quite solve. But he had to try. For his family, for himself, he had to uncover the truth.

"I need to get out of here," Drake muttered, more to himself than to Harrison. "There are answers out there, and I'm going to find them.

Laying on the Sidewalk

Blue World – 2024

1 - 2

The world spun in a nauseating kaleidoscope of colors and shapes as Drake's eyelids fluttered open. Harsh sunlight stabbed at his retinas, sending shockwaves of pain through his skull with each throb of his pulse. He groaned, slowly pushing himself up on trembling arms, the rough asphalt biting into his palms.

"What... what happened?" Drake mumbled; his voice barely audible over the cacophony of voices surrounding him. Blinking rapidly, he struggled to focus on the sea of concerned faces peering down at him. Panic clawed at his chest as fragmentary memories flashed through his mind—screeching tires, shattering glass, his son's terrified scream. But which world was this? Linda or Harrison?

A wave of nausea threatened to overwhelm him as he fought to make sense of his fractured reality. "I can't... I can't remember," he whispered, more to himself than anyone else.

Suddenly, a familiar voice cut through the din. "Drake! Drake, are you alright?"

Relief washed over him as he turned to see Vega pushing his way through the crowd, concern etched across his features. Drake reached out a shaky hand, desperately grasping for the lifeline of his friend's presence.

"Vega," he croaked, his fingers closing around the other man's forearm. "Thank God you're here. I... I don't know what's happening to me."

As Vega knelt beside him, Drake's mind raced. Which version of his friend was this? The one who knew about Linda's death, or the one who had comforted him after Harrison's accident? He searched Vega's face for any clue, any hint that might anchor him to one reality or the other.

"Easy, Drake," Vega said softly, his steady gaze meeting Drake's wild eyes. "You've had quite a fall. Just take it slow, alright?"

Drake nodded numbly, his throat constricting with unspoken fears and uncertainties. He wanted to pour out everything—the dual worlds, the constant struggle to discern what was real—but the words caught in his throat. How could he explain something he barely understood himself?

Instead, he focused on steadying his breathing, clutching Vega's arm like a drowning man grasping a lifeline. "I'm sorry," he managed finally, his voice hoarse. "I... I don't know how I got here. Everything's so jumbled..."

Vega's expression softened, a mix of concern and something else—pity, perhaps?—flickering across his features. "It's okay, Drake. We'll figure this out together, alright? Let's just focus on getting you checked out first."

As Vega helped him to his feet, Drake's mind whirled with unanswered questions and mounting dread. Which world would he wake up in next? And how long could he continue to navigate this impossible existence before it tore him apart completely?

3 - 4

Drake's fingers tightened around Vega's arm, his knuckles turning white with the intensity of his grip. The cacophony of the street faded to a dull roar in his ears as he struggled to find the right words.

"Vega," Drake said, his voice barely above a whisper, thick with emotion. "I need to talk to you. It's about the accident, and...and everything that's been happening since."

He searched his friend's face, desperately hoping to see a flicker of understanding, some sign that Vega knew about the dual realities he'd been experiencing. But all he saw was concern and confusion.

Vega knelt down beside him, his brow furrowed. "What do you mean, Drake? What's been happening?"

Drake's heart sank. How could he possibly explain the inexplicable? The weight of his dual existence pressed down on him, threatening to crush him beneath its impossible burden.

"I..." Drake began, then faltered. He closed his eyes, fighting against the maelstrom of memories—Linda's smile in one world, Harrison's laughter in another. When he opened them again, Vega was still there, waiting patiently.

"It's like I'm living two lives," Drake thought, the words echoing in his mind but never reaching his lips. "And I don't know which one is real anymore."

Instead, he swallowed hard and said, "Everything's changed, Vega. Nothing makes sense anymore. I feel like I'm losing my mind."

5 - 6

Drake took a deep breath, steadying himself before he began to speak. His hands trembled as he ran them through his disheveled dark hair, his tired brown eyes meeting Vega's concerned gaze.

"It's hard to explain," he said slowly, choosing his words with care. "But since the accident, I've been...living in two different worlds."

The words hung in the air between them, heavy with implication. Drake's heart raced, anticipating Vega's reaction. Would his friend think he'd lost his mind completely?

Vega's brow furrowed in disbelief, his mouth opening then closing as he struggled to formulate a response. Drake pressed on, desperate to make him understand.

"I know how it sounds," Drake continued, his voice low and urgent. "But I swear to you, Vega, this is real. Every time I close my eyes, I wake up in a different reality. Different lives, different consequences..."

He trailed off, lost in thought. How could he convey the gut-wrenching pain of losing his family over and over again? The constant whiplash of shifting between realities?

"What do you mean, different realities?" Vega asked, his tone cautious but not dismissive.

Drake latched onto that sliver of openness, words tumbling out in a rush. "One moment I'm here, the next I'm... somewhere else. Everything's different. The people, the places, even the rules that govern the world. It's like living two parallel lives, and I can't control when I shift between them."

As he spoke, Drake's mind raced through the bizarre occurrences he'd experienced since waking up in the hospital. The conflicting memories, the impossible choices, the constant fear of losing everything he loved – again.

"I don't know if I'm going crazy, Vega," Drake admitted, his voice cracking. "But I need your help to figure this out. I can't do it alone anymore."

7 - 8

Drake's hands trembled as he clenched them in his lap, his knuckles turning white. He took a shaky breath, steeling himself for what he was about to reveal.

"In one world, Linda is alive," Drake explained, his voice trembling with emotion. The image of his wife's radiant smile flashed through his mind, a bittersweet reminder of the life he desperately clung to. "But in the other, it's Harrison." His throat tightened as he thought of his son's mischievous grin and endless curiosity.

Drake's eyes burned with unshed tears as he continued, "And I... I don't know how to make sense of it all. Every time I wake up, I'm terrified of who I might have lost this time."

Vega listened in stunned silence, his expression a mixture of concern and disbelief. Drake could almost see the gears turning in his friend's mind, trying to reconcile the impossible scenario before him.

"I know it sounds insane," Drake added, his voice barely above a whisper. "But I swear, Vega, I'm not making this up. I can't be."

As the weight of Drake's words settled over them, he found himself wondering if he'd made a mistake in confiding in Vega. Would his friend think he'd lost his mind? Would he abandon him when Drake needed him most?

Vega leaned forward; his brow furrowed in deep thought. "I've heard of cases of dissociative identity disorder before, but this... this seems to be something else entirely."

Drake's heart raced at Vega's words. He hadn't expected immediate belief, but the fact that his friend was considering the possibility gave him a glimmer of hope.

9 - 10

Vega's face hardened with resolve, his eyes meeting Drake's with unwavering intensity. "We need to get you to the hospital," he said firmly, his tone brooking no argument. "We need to make sure you're okay before we can figure out what's going on."

Drake felt a surge of panic at the thought of more sterile rooms and probing questions. "I don't know if that's—"

"Drake," Vega cut him off, his voice softening slightly. "This isn't just about your mind. You were unconscious on the street. We need to make sure you're physically alright too."

Swallowing hard, Drake nodded numbly. He knew Vega was right, even if every instinct screamed at him to run, to hide from the harsh light of reality that threatened to shatter his fragile grip on both worlds.

Vega gently helped Drake to his feet, steadying him as a wave of dizziness washed over him. As they made their way through the crowd, Drake couldn't help but notice the concerned whispers and curious stares. He felt exposed, vulnerable, as if everyone could see the fractures in his psyche.

"Easy does it," Vega murmured, guiding him towards the waiting ambulance.

Drake's mind raced as they approached the flashing lights. *What if they lock me up?* he thought, his chest tightening. *What if I wake up and everyone I love is gone?*

"Vega," Drake said suddenly, his voice hoarse with emotion. "I can't— I can't do this alone. I need—"

"I'm not going anywhere," Vega assured him, squeezing his shoulder. "We'll figure this out together, I promise."

As they reached the ambulance, Drake took a shaky breath. He knew his life was spiraling out of control, but with Vega by his side, he felt a flicker of hope. Whatever darkness lay ahead, at least he wouldn't have to face it alone.

11 - 12

The fluorescent lights of the hospital corridor seared Drake's retinas as he was wheeled into the emergency room. The acrid smell of disinfectant assaulted his nostrils, making him grimace.

"Mr. Miller, can you tell me what day it is?" A nurse with piercing blue eyes loomed over him, penlight in hand.

Drake squinted, his mind a jumble of conflicting memories. "I... I'm not sure," he admitted, his voice barely above a whisper.

The nurse exchanged a concerned glance with a nearby doctor. "We're going to run some tests, Mr. Miller. Just try to relax."

Relax? Drake thought bitterly. *How can I relax when I don't even know which reality is real?*

As they wheeled him from one test to another, Drake's anxiety mounted. Each invasive procedure, each probing question from skeptical medical staff, only added to his growing sense of unease.

"Drake," Vega's steady voice cut through his spiraling thoughts. "I'm right here. You're doing great."

Drake latched onto his friend's words like a lifeline. "Vega, what if they think I'm crazy? What if—"

"Don't go there," Vega interrupted gently. "One step at a time, remember?"

Hours seemed to blur together as Drake endured MRIs, blood tests, and psychological evaluations. Finally, mercifully, the barrage of tests came to an end.

Left alone in the sterile confines of a dimly lit hospital room, Drake stared at the ceiling, the rhythmic beeping of the heart monitor his only company. He closed his eyes, desperately trying to make sense of the fractured pieces of his reality.

Linda... Harrison... Their faces swam before him, both achingly real, both impossibly out of reach. *How can I choose? How can I live knowing I've lost one of them?*

The weight of his dual existence pressed down on him, threatening to crush his very soul. As exhaustion finally claimed him, Drake drifted into an uneasy sleep, haunted by the ghosts of two worlds that refused to let him go.

13 - 14

The scrape of chair legs against linoleum jolted Drake from his fitful sleep. He blinked, his eyes adjusting to the dim light as Vega settled into the seat beside his bed. The familiar face of his friend was a welcome sight, but the grave expression etched into Vega's features sent a chill down Drake's spine.

Vega leaned forward, his voice barely above a whisper. "I spoke to the doctors," he said, his eyes never leaving Drake's face. "They think it might be some sort of...psychological trauma. They want to keep you here for observation, at least for tonight."

Drake's heart sank, the weight of those words settling heavily in his chest. He nodded mechanically, unable to find his voice. His mind raced, a whirlwind of questions and fears threatening to overwhelm him.

Psychological trauma? Drake thought, his inner voice tinged with disbelief. *Is that what they're calling it? Two separate realities, two entirely different lives... how can that be explained away so simply?*

"Drake?" Vega's concerned voice cut through his spiraling thoughts. "Talk to me. What's going on in that head of yours?"

Drake swallowed hard; his throat suddenly dry. "It's just..." he began, his voice hoarse. "It feels like there's so much more to this, Vega. Something deeper, darker than just trauma."

He paused, searching for the right words to convey the enormity of what he was experiencing. How could he explain the visceral reality of both worlds? The gut-wrenching grief of losing Linda in one life, the overwhelming love and fear for Harrison in the other?

"I know it sounds crazy," Drake continued, his eyes pleading with Vega to understand. "But these aren't just dreams or hallucinations. They're real, Vega. Both of them are real."

15 - 16

Drake's eyelids grew heavy as the night wore on, the steady beep of hospital monitors lulling him into a fitful sleep. He drifted between consciousness and something else entirely, his mind a maelstrom of conflicting realities.

In one moment, he was back in his empty house, Linda's absence a palpable ache. "I'm sorry," he whispered to the void, his voice cracking. "I should have been there. I should have..."

The scene shifted abruptly, and suddenly Harrison was there, his small hand clutching Drake's. "Dad, I'm scared," the boy whimpered, eyes wide with terror.

Drake's protective instincts flared. "It's okay, buddy," he soothed, scanning the shadows for unseen threats. "I won't let anything happen to you."

He jolted awake, heart racing, to find Vega watching him with concern.

"Another nightmare?" his friend asked softly.

Drake ran a trembling hand through his disheveled hair. "It's more than that," he admitted. "It's like... like I'm living two lives simultaneously. And in both of them, something's terribly wrong."

Vega leaned forward, his expression a mix of worry and skepticism. "What do you mean, Drake?"

"I can't explain it," Drake said, frustration evident in his voice. "But this feeling... this dread... it follows me everywhere. Like a shadow I can't shake."

As he spoke, Drake couldn't help but wonder if he was truly losing his mind. The weight of his dual existence pressed down on him, threatening to crush him beneath its impossible burden.

17 - 18

The first rays of dawn crept through the hospital blinds, casting long shadows across Drake's haggard face. He stared out the window, his reflection a ghostly overlay on the awakening world beyond.

"I can't stay here," Drake muttered, more to himself than to Vega.

His friend leaned forward; brow furrowed. "What are you thinking, Drake?"

Drake turned, his eyes carrying a newfound intensity. "I need answers, Vega. Real answers. Not just medical theories and brain scans."

"But the doctors—" Vega began.

"The doctors can't help me," Drake interrupted, his voice low but firm. "They don't understand what's happening to me. Hell, I barely understand it myself."

He swung his legs over the side of the bed, wincing as the movement pulled at his IV. "In one world, I've lost Linda. In the other, Harrison. But they both feel equally real, equally devastating. How is that possible?"

Vega's expression softened. "I can't imagine what you're going through, man. But rushing out of here isn't the answer."

Drake shook his head, a bitter smile playing at the corners of his mouth. "Maybe not. But staying here, letting them poke and prod me while my family—families—are out there... I can't do it, Vega. I won't."

As he spoke, Drake's mind raced, considering his options. He knew the risks of leaving, of potentially jeopardizing his health further. But the gnawing dread in his gut told him that time was running out. That somewhere, in one of his realities or perhaps in both, disaster loomed on the horizon.

"I have to do something," Drake said, his voice barely above a whisper. "Before it's too late."

19 - 20

Drake watched as Vega's shoulders slumped in resignation. "I need to file some paperwork at the nurse's station," Vega said, his tone weary. "Just... promise me you won't do anything rash while I'm gone."

Drake nodded, not trusting himself to speak. As soon as the door clicked shut behind Vega, he sprang into action. His lawyer's instincts, honed by years of high-stakes litigation, kicked in as he assessed his surroundings. The IV in his arm was the first obstacle. With gritted teeth, Drake carefully removed the needle, pressing a tissue to the small puncture wound.

"Sorry, Linda," he muttered, thinking of how his wife—in one world, at least—would chastise him for this reckless behavior. "Or maybe I should be apologizing to Harrison." The thought of his son sent a fresh wave of determination through him.

Drake swung his legs over the side of the bed, his bare feet touching the cold linoleum floor. He stood slowly, fighting a wave of dizziness. "Come on, Miller," he growled to himself. "You've faced tougher opponents than a hospital floor."

With careful, measured steps, Drake made his way to the door. He peered out into the hallway, his heart pounding in his chest. The corridor stretched before him, sterile and silent, bathed in the harsh glow of fluorescent lights. It reminded him of the endless nights he'd spent in his law office, poring over case files, sacrificing time with his family for the pursuit of justice—or was it just success?

"Not this time," Drake whispered, his voice barely audible over the soft hum of the lights. "This time, I'm fighting for them."

He stepped out into the hallway, every nerve on high alert. The smell of disinfectant filled his nostrils, bringing back memories of the accident, of waking up in two different worlds. Drake pushed the thoughts aside, focusing on the task at hand. He had to find answers, had to understand why his reality had split in two. And he knew, deep in his bones, that those answers wouldn't be found within these hospital walls.

21 - 22

Drake's mind raced as he shuffled down the corridor, his hand trailing along the wall for support. The weight of his dual existence pressed down on him, each step a reminder of the lives he was living—and losing—simultaneously.

"Linda," he murmured, his voice thick with emotion. "Harrison." Their faces flashed before him, overlapping and blurring together. Which world was real? Which life was he meant to save?

He paused at an intersection, his tired eyes scanning the directory on the wall. Emergency exit, radiology, cafeteria—none of these held the answers he sought. But there had to be something, some clue he was overlooking.

"Think, Drake," he urged himself, running a hand through his disheveled hair. "What connects the two worlds? What's the common thread?"

As he stood there, lost in thought, a chill ran down his spine. The accident. It all came back to that fateful night. But what had really happened? The details were fuzzy, like trying to recall a dream upon waking.

"I need to see the police report," Drake realized, his legal instincts kicking in. "There has to be something—"

"Drake?"

The familiar voice cut through his concentration like a knife, and Drake's heart leapt into his throat. He turned slowly, knowing who he'd see even before his eyes confirmed it.

23 - 24

"Drake, what are you doing here?"

Vega's voice echoed in the empty corridor; concern etched across his face. Drake's pulse quickened as he met his friend's gaze, his mind racing to formulate a plausible explanation. The sterile hospital lights cast harsh shadows across Vega's features, accentuating the worry lines creasing his forehead.

Drake turned fully to face him; his legs unsteady beneath him. He gripped the wall for support, feeling the cool surface beneath his fingertips. The contrast between the hospital's clinical atmosphere and the tumultuous storm raging within him was jarring.

"I..." Drake began, his voice hoarse. He swallowed hard, buying time as he searched for the right words. How could he possibly explain the inexplicable? "I was just..."

His voice trailed off as he looked at Vega, really looked at him. In that moment, Drake was struck by a realization. Vega existed in both of his realities—a constant in his fractured world. Does that mean Holly does as well?

25 - 26

"I... I needed some air," Drake finally replied, his voice barely above a whisper. The words felt hollow, inadequate to convey the storm of emotions and fractured memories swirling within him. "I needed to clear my head."

As soon as the words left his mouth, Drake regretted them. They were true, but they were also a deflection – a habit from his old life, when winning cases had been more important than facing hard truths. He swallowed hard, fighting the urge to look away from Vega's piercing gaze.

Vega didn't respond immediately. Instead, he studied Drake with an unwavering focus, as if trying to peel back layers of deception to reach the core of truth beneath. Drake felt exposed, vulnerable – as though every secret, every fragment of his dual realities, was being laid bare for scrutiny.

In that moment of silent examination, Drake's mind raced. He thought of Linda's smile in one world of Harrison's laughter in another. The weight of his choices – both past and present – pressed down on him, threatening to crush him beneath their burden. He wanted to confide in Vega, to pour out the impossible truth of his existence, but fear held him back. What if Vega didn't believe him? What if this reality shattered too?

"Drake," Vega finally spoke, his voice low and measured. "What's really going on?"

27 - 28

Vega's question hung in the air, heavy with concern and expectation. Drake opened his mouth to respond, but the words caught in his throat. Before he could muster a reply, Vega's expression softened.

"Well, let's get you back to your room," Vega said, gesturing down the sterile hallway. "We can talk more there, if you're up for it."

Drake nodded, grateful for the momentary reprieve. As they walked side by side, the fluorescent lights cast harsh shadows across their faces. Drake's footsteps echoed in the quiet corridor, each one a reminder of the distance between his fractured realities.

"I don't know how to explain it, Vega," Drake finally murmured, his voice barely audible. "Sometimes I feel like I'm losing my mind."

Vega placed a comforting hand on Drake's shoulder. "We'll figure this out together, old friend. One step at a time."

As they approached his room, Drake's unease grew. The pit in his stomach deepened, a gnawing sensation that whispered of hidden truths and unresolved mysteries. He paused at the threshold, his hand resting on the cool metal of the doorframe.

"What if..." Drake began, his tired eyes meeting Vega's. "What if there's more to this than we understand? What if I'm only scratching the surface of something... bigger?"

Vega's brow furrowed, concern etching deeper lines in his face. "What do you mean, Drake?"

Drake shook his head, frustrated by his inability to articulate the swirling thoughts and fragmented realities clashing within him. "I can't shake this feeling that the truth is just out of reach," he said, his voice a mix of determination and desperation. "And I need to uncover it, Vega. For Linda. For Harrison. For my sanity."

Intimate Shadows

Green World – 2024

1 - 2

The sterile hospital room seemed to close in around Drake as Dr. Harmon entered, the fluorescent lights casting harsh shadows across the doctor's face. Drake's gaze lingered on the deep creases etched around Dr. Harmon's eyes, a roadmap of countless sleepless nights and difficult cases. The weariness in those eyes mirrored Drake's own exhaustion, a silent acknowledgment of the weight they both carried.

Drake's fingers twisted in the thin hospital sheets, his mind racing with questions he wasn't sure how to voice. The bifurcated reality of his existence—two worlds, two lives, two losses—pressed down on him like a physical force.

Dr. Harmon's voice cut through the silence, calm and steady. "Good morning, Drake. How are you feeling today?"

The simple question carried layers of meaning, and Drake found himself searching for an answer that could possibly encompass the complexity of his situation. How could he explain the disorientation of living two lives, the guilt that gnawed at him in both realities?

"I'm..." Drake began, then paused, weighing his words carefully. His lawyer's instincts, honed over years of crafting precise arguments, warred with the raw, unfiltered emotions threatening to spill out. "I'm here," he finally said, his voice rough with unspoken truths.

Dr. Harmon's piercing gaze seemed to see right through Drake's evasion, probing for the deeper currents beneath the surface. Drake braced himself for the inevitable follow-up questions, the gentle prodding that would force him to confront the fractured pieces of his existence.

As the doctor settled into the chair beside the bed, Drake found himself longing for the simplicity of his old life—before the accident, before the split in reality. But that Drake Miller was gone, replaced by this new version: a man torn between worlds, desperate to save what remained of his family in both realities.

3 - 4

Drake nodded, offering a weak smile that didn't quite reach his tired eyes. "Better, I suppose. But I have some questions." His fingers absently traced the edge of the hospital blanket, a nervous habit he'd developed since waking up in this fractured reality.

"Of course," Dr. Jesse Harmon replied, pulling up a chair beside the bed. The metal legs scraped softly against the linoleum floor, a harsh sound in the sterile room. "What's on your mind?"

Drake's gaze flickered to the window, where morning light filtered through thin curtains. In his mind's eye, he saw flashes of another world—a world where his son lived, but his wife was gone. The duality of his existence weighed heavily on him, like a physical burden pressing down on his chest.

"Dr. Harmon," Drake began, his voice low and measured, "I'm experiencing... things that I can't explain. Things that shouldn't be possible." He paused, searching for the right words to convey the impossible without sounding completely unhinged.

Dr. Harmon leaned forward slightly, his stern features softening with genuine concern. "Go on, Drake. This is a safe space. Whatever you're experiencing, we can work through it together."

Drake took a deep breath, steeling himself. "I'm living two lives, Doctor. Two separate realities, simultaneously. And what happens in one... it affects the other." The words tumbled out, a dam finally breaking after days of internal struggle.

As he spoke, Drake studied Dr. Harmon's face, looking for any sign of disbelief or judgment. But the doctor's expression remained impassive, his eyes sharp and focused. Drake couldn't help but wonder if the psychiatrist had heard stranger things in his long career, or if he was simply masking his true reaction.

5 - 6

Drake's gaze drifted to the corner of the room, where Harrison sat quietly. The teenager's usually vibrant eyes were clouded with worry, his lanky frame hunched forward in the chair. A pang of guilt shot through Drake's chest. He hated seeing his son like this, burdened by adult concerns far beyond his years.

Harrison caught his father's look and attempted a reassuring smile, but it didn't reach his eyes. The cocky bravado that typically colored the boy's demeanor was conspicuously absent, replaced by a vulnerability that made Drake's heart ache.

Swallowing hard, Drake turned back to Dr. Harmon. "Could you give us a moment alone?" he asked, his voice barely above a whisper. The words felt heavy on his tongue, laden with the weight of unspoken truths and looming revelations.

As he waited for the doctor's response, Drake's mind raced. How much should he reveal to Harrison? How could he possibly explain the inexplicable duality of his existence without sounding completely insane? The thought of burdening his son with this knowledge filled him with dread, yet the need for honesty, for connection, burned within him like a fever.

7 - 8

Harrison nodded, his curly hair bouncing slightly with the movement. "Of course," he said, his voice carrying a maturity that belied his years. "I'll be right outside if you need anything." He rose from the chair, his lanky frame unfolding like a jackknife. As he reached the door, he cast one last concerned glance at his father before slipping out of the room.

The soft click of the door closing echoed in the sudden silence. Drake felt the weight of solitude settle upon him, heavy and oppressive. He drew in a deep breath, the sterile hospital air filling his lungs as he steeled himself for what was to come. His fingers absently traced the edge of the blanket, the rough texture grounding him in the present moment.

'This is it,' Drake thought, his heart hammering against his ribs. 'No turning back now.' The weight of his dual existence pressed down on him, threatening to crush him under its impossible reality. He closed his eyes briefly, conjuring the image of his son's worried face, using it as a talisman against the madness threatening to engulf him.

Opening his eyes, Drake fixed his gaze on Dr. Harmon, noting the lines of concern etched into the doctor's face. "There's something I need to tell you," Drake began, his voice low and gravelly. "It's going to sound impossible, maybe even crazy, but I need you to hear me out."

9 - 10

Drake's fingers curled tightly around the edge of the blanket, his knuckles turning white with the effort. He could feel Dr. Harmon's penetrating gaze upon him, patient yet expectant.

"I need to talk to you about something, Doctor," Drake began, his voice serious. The words felt heavy on his tongue, laden with the weight of his fractured reality. "It's about the accident."

Dr. Harmon leaned forward slightly, his silver hair catching the harsh fluorescent light. His brow furrowed in concern, creating deep furrows that spoke of years of listening to troubled patients. "Of course, Drake. What would you like to know?"

Drake's mind raced, grappling with how to explain the inexplicable. How could he convey the duality of his existence without sounding completely unhinged? He moistened his lips, buying himself a moment to gather his thoughts.

'This is the moment of truth,' he thought, his heart pounding so loudly he was sure Dr. Harmon must hear it. 'Everything hinges on how I explain this.'

"It's not so much what I want to know, Doctor," Drake finally said, his voice barely above a whisper. "It's what I need you to understand about what's happening to me since the accident."

11 - 12

Drake hesitated, searching for the right words. The sterile hospital room seemed to close in around him, amplifying the gravity of his confession. He ran a hand through his disheveled hair, his fingers trembling slightly.

"I've been... experiencing some strange things since the accident," he began, his voice low and strained. "In one world, the one where my son is still alive, I've been... sleepwalking."

The words hung in the air, heavy with implication. Drake watched Dr. Harmon's face intently, searching for any sign of disbelief or judgment. To his surprise, the doctor's eyes widened in surprise, but he remained silent, waiting for Drake to continue.

'He's not dismissing me outright,' Drake thought, a flicker of hope igniting in his chest. 'Maybe he can help me make sense of this madness.'

The silence stretched between them, broken only by the soft beeping of nearby medical equipment. Drake's mind raced, grappling with how to explain the inexplicable nature of his dual existence.

"It's more than just sleepwalking," Drake finally continued, his voice gaining strength. "It's like I'm living two separate lives, Doctor. One where my wife survived the crash, and another where..." His voice caught, the pain of loss still raw. "Where my son did."

Dr. Harmon leaned forward, his stern features softening with concern. "Drake," he said gently, "trauma can manifest in many ways. What you're describing is-"

"I know how it sounds," Drake interrupted, a hint of desperation creeping into his tone. "But I swear to you, it's real. These aren't just dreams or hallucinations. I can feel, touch, smell... everything is vivid and tangible in both worlds."

As he spoke, Drake could feel the weight of his words, the enormity of what he was revealing. Part of him wanted to stop, to laugh it off as a stress-induced delusion. But the larger part, the part that ached for understanding and resolution, pushed him forward.

13 - 14

Drake took a deep breath, his hands clenching the hospital sheets. "I mean that whatever happens to me in one world seems to affect me in the other," he explained, his voice barely above a whisper. "When I passed out from the headache and nosebleed in the blue world, I woke up here in the green world with the same symptoms."

He watched Dr. Harmon's face carefully, searching for any sign of disbelief or judgment. The doctor's expression remained impassive, but Drake noticed a slight furrow in his brow.

'He thinks I'm losing my mind,' Drake thought, panic rising in his chest. 'Maybe I am.'

Dr. Harmon leaned back in his chair, his fingers steepled beneath his chin. The silence stretched between them, punctuated only by the rhythmic beeping of the heart monitor.

Finally, the doctor spoke, his voice measured and calm. "That's certainly... unusual. But it's not unheard of for trauma to manifest in unexpected ways."

Drake's heart raced. Was this a dismissal or an opening? He decided to press on. "But Doctor, it's more than just manifestations. These worlds, they're real. I can smell the coffee in my kitchen, feel the texture of my son's soccer ball..." His voice trailed off, choked with emotion.

Dr. Harmon's eyes softened slightly. "Drake," he said gently, "I understand this feels real to you. And we'll work through this together. But for now, let's focus on your physical recovery. We can explore these experiences in depth during your therapy sessions."

Drake nodded, a mix of relief and frustration washing over him. At least the doctor wasn't calling for a psych evaluation on the spot. But he couldn't shake the feeling that there was more to his situation than simple trauma. As Dr. Harmon stood to leave, Drake's mind raced with unanswered questions and the growing certainty that he was on the edge of uncovering something far beyond his understanding.

15 - 16

Drake's fingers tightened on the crisp hospital sheets, his knuckles turning white. The sterile smell of disinfectant filled his nostrils, a stark reminder of his current reality. He took a deep breath, steadying himself.

"I know it sounds crazy," Drake said, his voice barely above a whisper, "but I can't shake the feeling that there's something more to it. Something I'm missing." He searched Dr. Harmon's face, looking for any sign of disbelief or judgment.

To his surprise, Dr. Harmon's expression remained neutral, his piercing gaze fixed on Drake. The older man leaned forward, his glasses catching the fluorescent light. "I'll do everything I can to help you figure it out, Drake," he said, his tone serious. "But it's going to take time. And patience."

Drake felt a glimmer of hope spark within him. Maybe, just maybe, he wasn't losing his mind after all. He wondered if Dr. Harmon had encountered anything like this before. The thought both terrified and excited him.

"Time," Drake repeated, letting out a mirthless chuckle. "That's the one thing I'm not sure I have, Doctor. Every moment I spend here feels like I'm losing time in the other world. My son..." His voice cracked, and he swallowed hard.

Dr. Harmon's eyebrows furrowed slightly, a flicker of concern crossing his features. "Tell me more about this other world, Drake. What makes it feel so real to you?"

17 - 18

Drake nodded, feeling a weight lift off his shoulders. The constant tension he'd been carrying since awakening in this fractured reality seemed to ease, if only slightly. His eyes met Dr. Harmon's, searching for any hint of doubt or dismissal, but found only steady compassion.

"Thank you, Doctor. I appreciate your support," Drake said, his voice heavy with emotion. He ran a hand through his disheveled hair, a habit born of stress and uncertainty. "It means more than you know to have someone believe me, or at least... not think I'm completely insane."

Dr. Harmon's stern features softened, the corners of his mouth turning up in a warm smile that reached his eyes. The doctor leaned back slightly in his chair, his posture relaxing as he regarded Drake with a mix of professional interest and genuine concern.

"Anytime, Drake. Anytime," Dr. Harmon replied, his tone reassuring. He adjusted his glasses, a thoughtful expression crossing his face. "The mind is a complex thing, and trauma can manifest in ways we don't always understand. But that doesn't make your experiences any less real or invalid."

Drake felt a surge of gratitude, tinged with a lingering fear of what lay ahead. He couldn't shake the feeling that he was standing on the edge of something vast and terrifying, a mystery that threatened to consume him. But for now, in this moment, he allowed himself to feel a glimmer of hope.

19 - 20

Drake's fingers traced the edge of his hospital blanket, the coarse fabric grounding him as his mind raced. The sterile scent of disinfectant mingled with the faint aroma of coffee from Dr. Harmon's mug, creating a surreal backdrop for the weight of his thoughts.

"There's more," Drake began, his voice barely above a whisper. He swallowed hard, his throat constricting around the words he needed to say. "I've been experiencing... memories. But they're not just memories. They're like glimpses into another life."

Dr. Harmon leaned forward, his brow furrowing with interest. Drake could almost see the gears turning in the doctor's mind, analyzing and cataloging every word.

"In this other life, this other world," Drake continued, his gaze fixed on a point beyond the hospital room walls, "I'm not a Detective. I'm a lawyer. And I'm investigating a mysterious accident with my partner, Richard Vega."

As he spoke, images flashed through Drake's mind: the sound of a gavel, the weight of a case files at his side, the smell of stale coffee in the firm. He could almost feel the rough texture of case files beneath his fingertips, hear the buzz of clients chattering in the background.

"It feels so real," Drake murmured, more to himself than to Dr. Harmon. "Like I'm living two lives simultaneously. And somehow, they're connected. I can feel it."

He turned back to Dr. Harmon, searching the doctor's face for any sign of disbelief or concern. Instead, he found only patient understanding, which both relieved and unnerved him.

"I know how this sounds," Drake added quickly, his words tumbling out in a rush. "But I can't shake the feeling that understanding this connection is crucial. That it might be the key to... to everything."

21 - 22

Dr. Harmon's brow furrowed in concern as he listened intently to Drake's words. "Tell me more about these memories, Drake. What do you remember?"

Drake's gaze drifted to the window, where raindrops chased each other down the pane. He took a deep breath, the sterile hospital air filling his lungs as he tried to grasp the elusive fragments swirling in his mind.

"It's... fragmented," he began, his voice low and hesitant. "Bits and pieces of conversations, glimpses of familiar places." Drake's fingers tightened on the bedsheet, knuckles whitening. "But there's something... ominous about it all. Like I'm on the verge of uncovering something dark and dangerous."

As he spoke, vivid flashes erupted behind his eyes: a dimly lit alley, the presence of something viral, hushed voices in a shadowy room. The acrid taste of fear coated his tongue, as real as if he were there in that moment.

"I remember... the accident," Drake continued, his brow furrowing. "The road was slippery The air was heavy with mist from the rain and... something else. Something worse." He shuddered involuntarily, causing Dr. Harmon to lean in closer, his eyes sharp with interest.

Drake's mind raced, trying to piece together the disjointed images. "There was this figure looking in through the broken windshield at me. He starred as the car sank; his face was disfigured."

He turned to face the doctor, noting the mixture of concern and fascination etched on his face. "I know it sounds crazy," Drake said, a hint of desperation creeping into his voice. "But these aren't just dreams or hallucinations. They're too vivid, too consistent. It's like I'm actually there, living another life."

23 - 24

Dr. Harmon nodded, his expression grave. The lines around his eyes deepened as he clasped his hands together, leaning forward in his chair. "It's possible that these memories are a manifestation of your subconscious mind, trying to make sense of the trauma you've experienced."

Drake felt a surge of frustration rise within him. He clenched his jaw, fighting the urge to lash out at the doctor's clinical assessment. Instead, he took a deep breath, tasting the sterile hospital air on his tongue.

"No," Drake said, shaking his head. A sense of urgency crept into his voice, causing it to tremble slightly. "It's more than that. There's a connection, a link between the two worlds." He locked eyes with Dr. Harmon, willing him to understand. "And I need to understand it, before it's too late."

As he spoke, Drake's mind raced with images from both realities – the grief-stricken faces of his family members, the mysterious warehouse, the cryptic symbols. They swirled together in a dizzying kaleidoscope, threatening to overwhelm him.

Dr. Harmon's piercing gaze seemed to cut through Drake's agitation. The doctor's calm demeanor stood in stark contrast to Drake's growing anxiety. Drake found himself wondering if Dr. Harmon truly believed him or if he was simply humoring a traumatized patient.

25 - 26

Dr. Harmon's eyes narrowed, his gaze penetrating as he studied Drake's face. The silence stretched between them, heavy with unspoken implications. Finally, the doctor spoke, his voice low and measured.

"I believe you, Drake," he said, each word carefully chosen. "And I'll do everything in my power to help you uncover the truth." He paused, his expression softening slightly. "But you must be careful. Sometimes, the truth can be more dangerous than we realize."

Drake felt a mix of relief and trepidation wash over him. He's taking me seriously, he thought, but there's something he's not saying. His hands clenched the bedsheets, knuckles white with tension.

"I know," Drake replied, his voice steady despite the turmoil within. A steely determination settled over him, pushing back against the fear that threatened to paralyze him. "But I can't let fear hold me back. Not when there's so much at stake."

As he spoke, images of his family flashed through his mind – his wife's smile, his son's laughter. In one world or another, he had lost them. The pain of that loss, even if only half-real, was unbearable.

Dr. Harmon leaned back in his chair, his brow furrowed in thought. "Your determination is admirable, Drake," he said softly. "But remember, you're not alone in this. We'll navigate these waters together."

Drake nodded, grateful for the doctor's support but acutely aware of the weight of his own responsibility. Whatever was happening, whatever force was tearing his reality apart, he knew he had to face it head-on.

27 - 28

Dr. Harmon reached for Drake's arm; his touch gentle but clinical. "We'll need to run some tests," he explained, his voice low and measured. "Starting with a blood sample."

Drake felt the cool antiseptic swab on his skin, followed by the sharp pinch of the needle. He winced, the sensation grounding him in the present moment. Despite the discomfort, his mind raced, grasping at fragments of memory and half-formed theories.

"Dr. Harmon," Drake began, his voice steady even as he felt the needle withdraw. "I need to ask you about someone." He paused, searching the doctor's face for any hint of recognition. "A janitor who used to work here, named Gabriel. Do you remember him?"

As he spoke, Drake's heart pounded, each beat echoing in his ears. Gabriel's face, blurred and indistinct, floated at the edges of his consciousness. Who was he? What role did he play in this twisted puzzle?

Dr. Harmon's eyebrows lifted slightly, a flicker of surprise crossing his features. "Gabriel?" he repeated, his tone careful and measured. "Now that's a name I haven't heard in quite some time."

Drake leaned forward, ignoring the dull ache in his arm where the needle had been. "So you do remember him," he pressed, his voice tinged with urgency. "What can you tell me about him?"

29 - 30

Dr. Harmon's brow furrowed; his eyes distant as he secured the vial of Drake's blood. The silence stretched, punctuated only by the soft beeping of nearby medical equipment.

"Gabriel..." Dr. Harmon finally spoke, his voice low and contemplative. "Yes, I remember him. A quiet, unassuming man. Kept to himself mostly." He paused, adjusting his glasses with a subtle frown. "But he always seemed... troubled, somehow."

Drake's pulse quickened, his mind racing with possibilities. Gabriel's enigmatic presence had haunted the edges of his fractured memories, and now, finally, a tangible connection. He leaned forward, wincing slightly as the movement pulled at his IV.

"Troubled?" Drake echoed, his voice barely above a whisper. "In what way?"

He studied Dr. Harmon's face intently, searching for any hint of hesitation or deception. The doctor's words about Gabriel felt like pieces of a puzzle, ones that might finally help him make sense of the bizarre duality he was experiencing.

As Dr. Harmon opened his mouth to respond, Drake's thoughts whirled. What secrets had Gabriel carried? And how did they connect to his own predicament, trapped between two realities?

31 - 32

Dr. Harmon sighed, his gaze drifting to the window, as if searching for answers in the gray Maine sky. "It's hard to explain," he said, his voice tinged with a mix of sympathy and frustration. "Gabriel had this... air of sadness about him. Like he was carrying a heavy burden, one that weighed him down every moment of every day."

Drake nodded slowly, absorbing the information. His mind raced, trying to connect this description of Gabriel to the fragmented memories and strange occurrences he'd been experiencing. The constant weight of grief he felt in both realities suddenly seemed to echo Gabriel's described demeanor.

"I know that feeling all too well," Drake thought, a wave of empathy washing over him for the mysterious janitor.

Leaning forward slightly, Drake lowered his voice, aware of the delicate nature of his next question. "Did he ever mention anything about a cult, or any strange beliefs?"

As the words left his mouth, Drake watched Dr. Harmon's reaction intently. He noted the slight widening of the doctor's eyes, the almost imperceptible tightening of his jaw. Drake's heart rate increased, his palms growing clammy with anticipation.

"Why would I ask about a cult?" Drake questioned internally, realizing the oddity of his inquiry. "But something tells me it's important, a key to understanding what's happening to me."

The silence stretched between them, charged with unspoken tension. Drake found himself holding his breath, waiting for Dr. Harmon's response, knowing that whatever came next could potentially reshape his understanding of his fractured reality.

33 - 34

Dr. Harmon's brow furrowed, casting deep shadows across his weathered face. He shook his head, his expression grave. "Not to me, but then again, Gabriel wasn't one to share much about his personal life. He was a mystery, even to those who worked alongside him."

Drake felt a chill run down his spine, the doctor's words confirming his suspicions about Gabriel's enigmatic nature. He watched as Dr. Harmon carefully withdrew the needle from his arm, pressing a cotton swab to the puncture site.

"A mystery," Drake mused internally, his mind racing. "Just like these parallel worlds I'm experiencing. Could there be a connection?"

As Dr. Harmon secured the vial of blood, Drake's gaze drifted to the crimson liquid. He couldn't shake the feeling that the answers he sought might be flowing through his very veins.

"Dr. Harmon," Drake started, his voice low and urgent, "have you ever encountered patients with... unusual experiences? Like living in two realities simultaneously?"

The doctor paused, his eyes meeting Drake's with a mix of concern and curiosity. "That's quite an unusual question, Drake. May I ask why you're interested in such phenomena?"

Drake hesitated, weighing the risks of revealing too much. "Just... professional curiosity," he replied, not entirely convinced by his own lie.

As Dr. Harmon finished with the blood sample, Drake couldn't shake the feeling that there was more to Gabriel than met the eye. The weight of unspoken secrets hung heavily in the air, mirroring the burden Gabriel reportedly carried.

"I need to find out everything I can about him," Drake thought, determination coursing through him. "Gabriel might be the key to understanding these strange occurrences in both worlds."

35 - 36

Drake took a deep breath, his tired eyes flickering with resolve. "Thank you, Dr. Harmon," he said, his voice tinged with determination. "I appreciate your help. I'll let you know if I find out anything else."

Dr. Harmon nodded; his brow furrowed with concern. "Drake, just... be careful. Sometimes the answers we seek can lead us down unexpected paths."

Drake's hand hesitated on the doorknob, his mind churning with the implications of Dr. Harmon's words. He turned back, offering a weak smile that didn't quite reach his eyes. "I will. But I have to know the truth, no matter where it leads."

As he stepped into the sterile hallway, the hospital's fluorescent lights cast harsh shadows across Drake's face, emphasizing the weariness etched into his features. His footsteps echoed in the quiet corridor, each one carrying him further from the safety of ignorance and closer to the dangerous unknown.

"Gabriel," Drake muttered under his breath, the name tasting like a riddle on his tongue. "Who are you really? And what do you have to do with all of this?"

His mind buzzed with possibilities, each thought more outlandish than the last. Could Gabriel be some sort of interdimensional traveler? A figment of his fractured psyche? Or something far more sinister?

Drake's pace quickened; driven by an urgency he couldn't fully explain. He had to find answers, had to piece together the puzzle of his shattered reality before it was too late. Gabriel was the key, the enigmatic figure who seemed to dance on the edges of both his worlds.

As he pushed through the hospital's main doors, the cool air hit his face, grounding him in the present moment. Drake's determination solidified into a steely resolve. Whatever secrets lay hidden beneath the surface, he would uncover them, no matter the cost.

Identity Uncovered

Green World – 2024

1 - 2

The dim light from Holly's desk lamp cast long shadows across the cluttered office, illuminating stacks of case files and scattered coffee cups. Drake's eyes darted from one photo to another pinned on the corkboard behind her desk, each image a frozen moment of violence and despair. The weight of what Holly had just revealed pressed down on him, making the air feel thick and oppressive.

Drake ran a hand through his unkempt hair, wincing as his fingers caught in a tangle. When was the last time I even looked in a mirror? he wondered, the thought flitting away as quickly as it came. There were more pressing matters at hand.

"So, this Gabriel guy... he's a janitor at Saint Montague Hospital?" Drake asked, his brow furrowing with concern. The words came out slowly, each syllable carefully considered as he tried to piece together the fragments of information they'd uncovered.

Holly nodded; her sharp features accentuated by the harsh lighting. "That's what our sources tell us," she replied, her voice tinged with a mixture of frustration and determination. "But there's something off about him, Drake. I can feel it in my gut."

Drake leaned forward, his elbows resting on his knees as he processed this new information. A janitor. It seemed so mundane, so ordinary. And yet, nothing about this case had been ordinary so far. The accident, the missing girl, the symbol... how did it all fit together?

"What makes you say that?" Drake probed, his eyes meeting Holly's intense gaze. He admired her intuition, the way she could sense the undercurrents of a situation that others might miss.

Holly's lips pressed into a thin line as she considered her response. "It's just... too convenient," she finally said, gesturing to the evidence spread out before them. "A janitor would have access to nearly every part of the hospital. Perfect cover for someone who doesn't want to be noticed."

Drake nodded, feeling a chill run down his spine. The implication was clear – if Gabriel was involved in something sinister, he was in the perfect position to carry out his plans undetected.

As the silence stretched between them, Drake's mind raced with possibilities. What if Gabriel was more than just a janitor? What if he was the key to unlocking this entire mystery? And more importantly, what dangers might they face if they started digging too deep?

3 - 4

Holly nodded, her fingers flying across the keyboard as she pulled up a series of files on her computer. The blue glow of the screen cast eerie shadows across her determined face. "That's right. We're still trying to track down more information on him, but so far, it's like he doesn't exist. No record of him anywhere."

Drake's brow furrowed deeper, his mind churning with the implications. A man with no past, working in a hospital where he could blend into the background. It was too perfect, too calculated. He leaned back in his chair, the old wood creaking under his weight, mirroring the tension in the room.

"How is that even possible in this day and age?" Drake mused, more to himself than to Holly. His fingers absently traced the stubble on his chin, a nervous habit he'd developed since the accident. "Everyone leaves a trace, a digital footprint. Unless..."

Unless someone had gone to great lengths to erase Gabriel's existence. The thought sent a chill down Drake's spine, making him acutely aware of the dangers they might be facing.

"And the taxi driver..." Drake's voice trailed off, his mind conjuring images he'd rather not see. "They found his body in the alleyway?"

The words hung heavy in the air, laden with the weight of a life lost and the growing realization that they were dealing with something far more sinister than they'd initially thought. Drake's eyes met Holly's, searching for confirmation, dreading what he might find there.

As he waited for Holly's response, Drake couldn't shake the feeling that they were standing on the edge of something vast and dangerous. Whatever was going on, it was clear that Gabriel – if that was even his real name – was at the center of it all. And finding him might be the key to unraveling this entire mystery, or it might be the thing that put them both in grave danger.

5 - 6

Holly's face tightened, her eyes reflecting a mix of determination and concern. "Yeah," she confirmed, her voice low and grave. "The CCTV footage is... disturbing, to say the least." She swiveled her computer screen towards Drake, revealing a grainy black-and-white video.

Drake leaned forward, his heart pounding as he watched a masked figure emerge from the shadows, brutally attacking the unsuspecting taxi driver. The violence was swift, efficient, and chillingly precise. As the attacker drove off in the cab, Drake felt his stomach churn.

"Jesus," he muttered, running a hand through his disheveled hair. "And you can't ID the suspect?"

Holly shook her head, frustration evident in her tense shoulders. "No luck so far. The perp knew exactly where the cameras were, kept their face hidden the whole time."

Drake's mind raced, connecting invisible dots. The symbol in the glove box suddenly felt like a burning presence in his thoughts. "And the symbol," he began, his voice tinged with urgency. "The one we found in the cab's glove box. What does it mean?"

As he awaited Holly's response, Drake couldn't shake the feeling that this symbol was the key to everything – his accident, the missing girl, and now this brutal murder. It all had to be connected, and the weight of that realization pressed down on him like a physical force.

7 - 8

Holly sighed deeply, running a hand through her short, dark hair. Her piercing eyes, usually sharp with determination, now reflected a mix of frustration and concern. "We're not sure yet," she admitted, her voice tinged with a hint of defeat. "But it's definitely connected to something bigger. The fact that it's tied to your accident, the missing girl, and now this murder... it can't be a coincidence."

Drake felt a chill run down his spine as Holly's words sank in. He leaned back in his chair, the leather creaking under his weight. His tired eyes scanned the cluttered office, taking in the stacks of files and the wall covered in crime scene photos. Each image seemed to pulse with hidden meaning, taunting him with secrets just out of reach.

"Christ," he muttered, his voice barely above a whisper. The weight of the revelation settled on his shoulders like a heavy blanket. His mind raced, piecing together fragments of information, searching for a pattern in the chaos.

After a moment of tense silence, Drake straightened up, his eyes locking onto Holly's. "We need to find out more about this Gabriel guy," he said, his tone laced with determination. "If he's involved in all of this, he might hold the key to unlocking the truth."

As he spoke, Drake couldn't shake the feeling that Gabriel was more than just a janitor at Saint Montague Hospital. The man's piercing eyes and cryptic manner haunted his thoughts, like a shadow lurking at the edge of his consciousness.

Holly nodded, her expression mirroring Drake's resolve. "Agreed. But where do we start? It's like he's a ghost – no records, no history, nothing."

Drake's brow furrowed as he considered their options. "We might need to go back to the hospital," he suggested, his voice low and contemplative. "Maybe there's something we missed, some clue about who Gabriel really is or where he came from."

As the words left his mouth, Drake felt a sudden surge of urgency. Time was slipping away, and with each passing moment, he sensed they were falling further behind whoever was orchestrating this intricate web of crime and deception.

9 - 10

Holly met his gaze, her expression hardening with determination. "Agreed. We'll keep digging. But we need to tread carefully, Drake. Whoever's behind all of this... they're playing for keeps."

The weight of her words settled over Drake like a shroud. He leaned back in his chair, the leather creaking beneath him, as his mind raced through the implications. The missing girl, his accident, the murdered taxi driver – all pieces of a puzzle he couldn't quite assemble.

"You're right," Drake murmured, his voice barely above a whisper. "We're dealing with something... bigger than we imagined." He ran a hand through his disheveled hair, feeling the weight of his dual realities pressing down on him. In one world, the absence of his wife's laughter echoed in empty rooms; in the other, his son's bedroom remained untouched, a shrine to what was lost.

Holly's eyes softened for a moment, catching a glimpse of the turmoil behind Drake's tired gaze. "We'll figure this out," she assured him, her tone carrying a mix of professional determination and personal empathy.

As they exchanged a meaningful glance, Drake felt a chill run down his spine. They were only scratching the surface of a conspiracy that ran deeper than either of them could have ever imagined. The stakes were higher than ever, and every instinct told him that danger lurked around every corner.

"Let's start with Gabriel," Drake said, leaning forward, his voice low and urgent. "We need to find out everything we can about him – his background, his connections, anything that might give us a lead."

Holly nodded, already turning to her computer. "I'll reach out to my contacts at Saint Montague, see if we can get access to their employee records."

As Holly began typing furiously, Drake closed his eyes, trying to center himself. He couldn't shake the feeling that every step forward was bringing them closer to an unseen threat, waiting patiently in the shadows. The road ahead was fraught with danger, but he knew they had no choice but to press on.

11 - 12

Drake's gaze drifted across Holly's cluttered office, taking in the organized chaos of case files, sticky notes, and half-empty coffee mugs. His eyes lingered on a framed photograph tucked behind a stack of papers – a younger Holly, beaming beside an older woman with the same piercing eyes. The image stirred something within him, a curiosity that had been building since they'd begun working together.

He watched Holly for a moment, her brow furrowed in concentration as she scanned through records on her computer. There was an intensity to her, a fire that seemed to burn just beneath the surface. Drake found himself wondering about the woman behind the detective, the experiences that had shaped her into this formidable force.

Clearing his throat softly, Drake broke the silence. "Holly," he began, his voice tentative, almost hesitant. "Can I ask you something personal?"

As soon as the words left his mouth, Drake felt a twinge of uncertainty. Was he overstepping? They were partners in this investigation, but did that give him the right to pry into her life? Still, he couldn't shake the feeling that understanding Holly better might be crucial to unraveling the mystery before them.

He held his breath, waiting for her response, acutely aware of the weight of his question hanging in the air between them.

13 - 14

Holly's eyes flicked up from her computer screen, a hint of surprise flickering across her features. The harsh glow of the monitor cast shadows on her face, accentuating the sharp angles of her cheekbones and the intensity in her gaze.

"Sure, Drake. What's on your mind?" Her voice was steady, but Drake detected a subtle shift in her posture, a slight tensing of her shoulders.

Drake hesitated, his fingers drumming an anxious rhythm on the armrest of his chair. The weight of his own past pressed down on him, reminding him of the delicate nature of personal inquiries. He took a deep breath, steeling himself.

"You mentioned earlier that you used to be in a relationship..." he began, his words coming out more cautiously than he'd intended. Drake's mind raced, questioning whether he should continue. But curiosity won out over caution. "What happened?"

As soon as the words left his mouth, Drake felt a pang of regret. Had he crossed a line? He watched Holly intently, trying to gauge her reaction. The air in the cramped office seemed to thicken with tension, and Drake found himself holding his breath, waiting for her response.

Internally, he chastised himself. 'Smooth move, Miller. Way to potentially alienate your partner in the middle of a crucial investigation.' But beneath his self-reproach, a part of him knew that understanding Holly – her past, her motivations – might be key to unraveling the complex web they found themselves entangled in.

15 - 16

Holly's expression softened, the hard lines of determination melting into something more vulnerable. She let out a weary sigh, her gaze drifting to a framed photo on her cluttered desk. Drake's eyes followed, catching a glimpse of a smiling couple - Holly, looking years younger, and a woman with kind eyes.

"It's a long story," Holly replied, her voice barely above a whisper. She traced the edge of the frame with her fingertip, lost in memory. "We were together for years, but... things just fell apart. We wanted different things, I guess."

Drake nodded, a familiar ache resonating in his chest. The weight of his own fractured family life pressed down on him, making Holly's pain all too relatable. He leaned forward, his voice gentle.

"I'm sorry to hear that," he offered, genuine sympathy coloring his words. "Must have been tough."

As he spoke, Drake's mind raced. He couldn't help but draw parallels to his own situation - the strain his career had put on his relationships, the guilt that gnawed at him daily. He wondered if Holly's dedication to her work had played a role in her relationship's demise, just as his own ambition had cost him so dearly.

17 - 18

Holly's eyes met Drake's, a faint smile playing at the corners of her mouth. Despite the sadness lingering in her gaze, there was a spark of resilience that caught Drake off guard.

"Yeah, it was," she admitted, her voice steady. "But hey, life goes on, right? You learn to pick up the pieces and move forward."

Drake felt a surge of admiration wash over him. Here was a woman who had faced heartbreak yet stood tall in its wake. He couldn't help but compare her strength to his own struggle, torn between two realities, constantly grappling with loss.

"You're a strong person, Holly," he said earnestly, his voice thick with respect. "I can tell."

As the words left his mouth, Drake found himself studying Holly more intently. The determined set of her jaw, the quiet fire in her eyes - they spoke volumes about her character. He noticed the slight tremor in her hand as she pushed a strand of hair behind her ear, a small sign of the vulnerability beneath her tough exterior.

She's like me, Drake thought, *carrying her pain close, but refusing to let it define her.*

The air between them seemed to shift, a newfound understanding blossoming in the cluttered confines of Holly's office. Drake felt a connection forming, born of shared struggle and mutual respect.

19 - 20

Holly's smile widened, a hint of genuine warmth breaking through her professional demeanor. "Thanks, Drake," she said softly, her eyes meeting his with a flicker of gratitude. "That means a lot."

Drake felt emboldened by this moment of connection. The walls of formality between them seemed to crumble just a bit, and he found himself leaning forward in his chair, curiosity piqued.

"What made you want to become a detective?" he asked, his voice tinged with genuine interest. "It's not exactly an easy job."

As the words left his mouth, Drake realized how much he wanted to understand Holly better. In the chaos of his fractured existence, she had become an anchor - someone who believed him, who was fighting alongside him to uncover the truth. He watched her intently, noticing the way her fingers absently traced the edge of a case file on her desk.

What drives her? Drake wondered. *What made her choose this path of relentless pursuit of justice?*

The air in the office seemed to thicken with anticipation as he waited for her response. Outside, the muffled sounds of Bridgewaters bustling streets filtered through the window, a stark contrast to the intensity of the moment unfolding between them.

21 - 22

Holly's expression turned thoughtful, her gaze drifting to a point beyond Drake as if peering into her past. The sharp lines of her face softened momentarily, revealing a vulnerability Drake hadn't seen before.

"Honestly?" she began, her voice taking on a reflective tone. "I've always had a knack for solving puzzles." A faint smile played at the corners of her mouth. "Growing up, I saw a lot of injustice in the world. It ate at me, you know?"

Drake nodded, his own memories of courtroom battles and moral compromises flashing through his mind. He leaned in, captivated by this glimpse into Holly's motivations.

"I wanted to be someone who could make a difference," Holly continued, her eyes refocusing on Drake with renewed intensity. "Someone who could help bring justice to those who needed it most."

As she spoke, Drake couldn't help but notice the passion igniting behind her words. It reminded him of his own drive, the one that had once pushed him to become a ruthless lawyer. But where his ambition had led him astray, Holly's seemed to have forged her into a beacon of integrity.

"Sounds like you found your calling," Drake responded, genuinely impressed. He felt a twinge of envy mixed with admiration. How different might his life have been if he'd channeled his own determination into such a noble pursuit?

23 - 24

Holly chuckled softly, a sound that seemed to brighten the cluttered office. "Yeah, I guess I did." Her eyes darted to a stack of case files on her desk, and Drake noticed her fingers tighten almost imperceptibly around her coffee mug. "It's not always easy, but... it's worth it. Knowing that I can make a difference, even in small ways."

Drake leaned back in his chair, studying Holly's face. The weight of unsolved cases, of lives hanging in the balance, was etched in the subtle lines around her eyes. He recognized that look – he'd seen it in the mirror countless times during his days as a lawyer.

"Small ways add up," he offered, his voice low and thoughtful. "One case at a time, one person at a time. It matters."

Holly's gaze met his, and for a moment, a current of understanding passed between them. Drake felt a swell of respect rising in his chest. This wasn't just another detective going through the motions. Holly was a force of nature, driven by an unwavering sense of justice.

As the silence stretched between them, Drake's mind raced. He thought about his own fractured existence, the two realities he was forced to navigate. How different would things have been if he'd had someone like Holly in his corner? Someone who refused to give up, who saw the humanity behind every case?

"You know," Drake started, breaking the quiet, "in my line of work – my old line of work – I saw a lot of darkness too. But I didn't always handle it the right way."

Holly tilted her head, curiosity evident in her expression. "How so?"

Drake sighed, the weight of his past decisions pressing down on him. "I focused on winning at all costs. Forgot about the people behind the cases." He paused, meeting Holly's gaze. "What you're doing here... it's important. Don't ever lose sight of that."

25 - 26

Holly's gaze drifted to the wall behind Drake, her eyes clouding over with memories. The fluorescent light flickered, casting shadows across her face as she spoke.

"I became a detective because... of a case," she began slowly, her voice a mixture of determination and sorrow. "It was a gruesome one, one that still haunts me to this day."

Drake leaned forward, his brow furrowing. He could sense the weight of her words, the pain lurking beneath the surface. His own experiences with trauma made him acutely aware of the toll such memories could take.

As Holly continued, the room seemed to darken, the air growing thick with unspoken horrors. "It was a serial killer," she said, her tone steady despite the visible tremor in her hands. "He preyed on young men and women, leaving behind nothing but death and devastation in his wake."

Drake's stomach clenched. He'd seen his fair share of darkness as a lawyer, but this... this was something else entirely. He watched Holly's face, noting the tightness around her eyes, the way her jaw clenched as she fought to maintain composure.

"Jesus," Drake breathed, his mind racing. "How did you get involved?"

Holly's fingers tapped nervously on the desk. "I was fresh out of the academy," she replied, her gaze distant. "Eager to prove myself. I thought I could make a difference; you know?"

Drake nodded, understanding all too well the drive to succeed, to stand out. He thought of his own relentless pursuit of victory in the courtroom, often at the expense of everything else.

"What happened?" he asked softly, dreading the answer but knowing Holly needed to share this burden.

27 - 28

Drake leaned forward; his brow furrowed with concern. "Go on," he urged softly, sensing the raw pain behind Holly's words. His own experiences with trauma made him acutely aware of the weight such memories could carry.

Holly's eyes, usually sharp and focused, now seemed to look through Drake, lost in the shadows of her past. She took a deep, shuddering breath, her fingers drumming an anxious rhythm on the desk.

"I was just a rookie back then," she began, her voice tinged with a bitterness that seemed out of place in someone so young. "Eager to prove myself, you know? I thought I could..." She paused, swallowing hard. "I thought I could make a real difference."

Drake nodded, understanding all too well the drive to succeed, to stand out. He thought of his own relentless pursuit of victory in the courtroom, often at the expense of everything else. "We all start out that way," he offered gently.

Holly's lips twisted in a humorless smile. "Yeah, well, nothing prepares you for the reality of it. The victims, the families... the sheer evil you're up against." She shook her head, as if trying to dislodge the memories. "I was so determined to bring justice, to be the one who cracked the case."

As Drake watched Holly struggle with her past, he couldn't help but wonder about the toll this job had taken on her. How many more dark secrets were hidden behind those piercing eyes?

29 - 30

"But..." Drake prompted gently, sensing there was more to the story. His brow furrowed, eyes fixed on Holly's face as he leaned forward slightly, unconsciously bracing himself for what was to come.

Holly's gaze dropped to her hands, which had balled into tight fists on the desk. "But I was wrong," she admitted, her voice barely above a whisper. The words seemed to physically pain her as they left her lips. "No matter how hard I tried, no matter how many hours I spent poring over evidence and chasing down leads, I couldn't catch him."

Drake felt a chill run down his spine. The raw anguish in Holly's voice was palpable, filling the cramped office with an almost tangible despair. He wanted to reach out, to offer some comfort, but held back, sensing she needed to get this out.

"He was always one step ahead of me," Holly continued, her voice gaining a hard edge. "Taunting me with his cruelty and his cunning." She looked up then, her eyes blazing with a mixture of fury and helplessness that made Drake's breath catch. "Do you know what it's like, Drake? To know there's a monster out there, to see the devastation he leaves behind, and be powerless to stop it?"

Drake's mind flashed to his own sense of powerlessness, the agony of living two lives, unable to save both his wife and son. "I... I think I might," he replied softly, more to himself than to Holly.

31 - 32

Drake reached out, his hand gently resting on Holly's trembling fist. The simple gesture seemed to bridge the chasm of pain between them. "It's not your fault," he assured her, his voice filled with a compassion that surprised even him. "You did everything you could."

Holly's eyes, glistening with unshed tears, met his. For a moment, Drake saw beyond the tough exterior of the determined detective to the vulnerable woman beneath. A single tear escaped, tracing a silvery path down her cheek.

"Maybe," she whispered hoarsely, her voice thick with emotion. "But... I couldn't save them." Her words hung heavy in the air, laden with years of guilt and regret. "And that's something I'll have to live with for the rest of my life."

Drake felt a sharp pang in his chest, recognizing the weight of her burden. It mirrored his own in so many ways. He wanted to tell her about his own struggles, the constant guilt of not being able to save both his wife and son. But he held back, knowing this moment was about Holly's pain, not his.

Instead, he squeezed her hand gently, offering silent support. "We can't save everyone," he said softly, "but that doesn't mean we stop trying."

Holly nodded almost imperceptibly; her eyes still fixed on some distant point. Drake wondered what horrors she was reliving, what faces haunted her sleepless nights. He knew all too well the power of such ghosts.

Unraveling DNA Secrets

Green World – 2024

1 - 2

Dr. Jesse Harmon's eyes widened as he stared at the computer screen, the ghostly blue glow illuminating his weathered features. Three distinct DNA profiles flickered before him, each as unique as a fingerprint. But it was the third profile that sent a chill down his spine—a faint, eerie luminescence pulsed from the data, defying everything he thought he knew about human biology.

"This can't be right," he muttered, adjusting his glasses and leaning closer to the monitor. His fingers flew across the keyboard, rechecking the analysis parameters. The results remained unchanged.

Harmon's mind raced, grappling with the implications. Drake Miller's blood sample held an impossible secret. Three DNA profiles in one person? And one exhibiting unexplained radioactivity? It challenged the very foundations of genetic science.

He pushed back from the desk, his chair squeaking in protest. "My God," he whispered, running a hand through his graying hair. "What are you, Drake?"

The weight of the discovery pressed down on him like a physical force. Harmon's thoughts turned to his patient—the troubled man with the haunted eyes who sat across from him just days ago, desperately seeking answers.

"I need to call him," Harmon decided, reaching for the phone. His hand trembled slightly as he dialed, the magnitude of what he was about to share settling over him like a shroud.

As the phone rang, Harmon's gaze drifted back to the screen. The faint glow from the third DNA profile seemed to pulse in time with his racing heartbeat. What dark secrets lay hidden within Drake Miller's genetic code? And more importantly, what danger might they pose?

3 - 4

Just as Harmon's fingers brushed the phone, a flicker of movement in his peripheral vision made him pause. The hairs on the back of his neck stood on end as an inexplicable chill permeated the air. He turned, his eyes widening in shock.

A shadowy figure loomed behind him, seeming to materialize from the darkness itself. The air around it pulsed with malevolent energy, and Harmon felt his breath catch in his throat.

"Who—" he began, but the word died on his lips as a searing pain exploded across his throat. Warm blood gushed forth, staining his pristine lab coat a horrifying crimson.

Harmon's mind reeled, unable to process the sudden turn of events. His hand flew to his neck, desperately trying to stem the flow of blood. "No," he gasped, the word barely audible as he staggered backward. "The results... Drake must know..."

His legs gave way, and he stumbled against the lab bench, knocking over vials and equipment. The crash echoed through the sterile room, a cacophony that seemed distant to Harmon's fading senses.

The figure remained motionless; its features obscured by the dim light of the lab. Harmon's vision began to blur, but he could still make out the ominous silhouette, a harbinger of death standing before him.

"Why?" Harmon choked out, his scientific mind still grasping for answers even as his life ebbed away. "What... what are you protecting?"

5 - 6

"Who are you?" Harmon managed to choke out, his voice barely a whisper as he struggled to comprehend the surreal scene unfolding before him. His analytical mind, even in these dire moments, sought to understand, to categorize the inexplicable horror before him.

The figure remained immobile, a silent specter in the sterile confines of the laboratory. Its silence was deafening, more oppressive than any verbal threat could have been. Harmon's eyes darted frantically, searching for any distinguishing features, any clue to the assailant's identity.

Is this retribution for my research? Harmon wondered, his thoughts growing hazy. *Or something more sinister tied to Drake's anomalous blood work?*

He opened his mouth to speak again, to demand answers, but only a gurgling sound escaped. The taste of copper flooded his mouth, and he felt his strength rapidly fading. His legs buckled beneath him, and he collapsed to the floor with a dull thud.

As his consciousness ebbed away, Harmon's last coherent thought was of his life's work. *All those years of study, of pushing the boundaries of human understanding... ending like this.*

With a final, agonized gasp, Harmon slumped completely, his lifeblood pooling around him in a macabre tableau of crimson. The pristine white tiles of the office floor transformed into a grotesque canvas, painted with the last vestiges of a brilliant mind snuffed out too soon.

7 - 7

The shadowy figure loomed over Harmon's prone form, its presence an oppressive weight in the now-silent laboratory. Harmon's vision swam, the world around him fading to a blurry haze. Yet, in this fleeting moment of clarity before the darkness consumed him, his mind raced with terrifying implications.

Drake's blood... three DNA profiles... the radioactivity... Harmon's thoughts whirled frantically. *What have I uncovered?*

The figure shifted slightly; its movement barely perceptible. Harmon's fading gaze locked onto it, a chill of recognition coursing through his dying body. Though he couldn't make out any distinct features, there was something hauntingly familiar about its stance, its presence.

The figure remained silent, but Harmon sensed a subtle change in its demeanor. Was it surprise? Anger? He couldn't tell.

As his consciousness slipped away, Harmon's analytical mind made one last desperate attempt to piece together the puzzle. *The fractures in Drake's reality... the impossible blood results... it's all connected. And it's far more dangerous than I ever imagined.*

With his final breath, Dr. Jesse Harmon knew that he had stumbled upon a truth so profound, so terrifying, that it had cost him his life. And Drake Miller, the man he had been trying to help, was at the center of it all.

Burden of Home

1 - 2

The door creaked open, a sound that echoed through Drake Miller's weary bones. He stepped inside, the weight of the day's revelations pressing down on his shoulders like an invisible burden. The familiar scent of home—a mixture of old books and Harrison's favorite cinnamon air freshener—enveloped him, offering a momentary respite from the maelstrom of questions swirling in his mind.

As Drake's eyes adjusted to the dim light of the living room, he caught sight of Harrison perched on the edge of the couch, his mop of curly hair silhouetted against the soft glow of a nearby lamp. The boy's posture was tense, his fingers fidgeting with the hem of his shirt—a habit he'd had since childhood.

"Dad?" Harrison's voice cut through the silence, a mix of concern and that unmistakable teenage cockiness. "You look like you've been through the wringer."

Drake forced a smile, the muscles in his face straining with the effort. He crossed the room, each step feeling like a monumental task. "Just a long day at the office, kiddo," he lied, the words tasting bitter on his tongue. How could he explain the truth to his son? How could he burden him with the knowledge of parallel worlds and fractured realities?

As he sank into the armchair across from Harrison, Drake's mind raced. Should I tell him? Can I protect him from this chaos? The weight of his dual existence pressed down on him, threatening to crush his resolve.

Harrison leaned forward, his bright eyes searching Drake's face. "Dad, what's really going on? You've been acting weird for weeks now."

Drake's heart clenched. He'd always prided himself on his ability to compartmentalize, to keep his work separate from his family life. But now, as he looked into his son's eyes—so full of trust and curiosity—he realized that the lines had blurred beyond recognition.

"Harrison, I—" Drake began, his voice catching in his throat. He paused, weighing each word carefully. "There's something I need to tell you. Something that might be hard to understand."

As the words hung in the air between them, Drake felt a shift in the atmosphere of the room. The once-comforting space now seemed charged with an electric tension, as if the very walls were holding their breath in anticipation of what was to come.

3 - 4

I should tell him everything, Drake thought, his mind racing. But how can I burden him with this madness? How can I explain that in another reality, he doesn't exist?

"Dad?" Harrison's voice cut through Drake's internal struggle. "You look like you're a million miles away. What's going on?"

Drake forced a weak smile, trying to mask the turmoil within. "Just a long day at work, that's all," he lied, hating himself for every word. "You know how it is."

But even as the words left his mouth, Drake knew he couldn't keep up this charade much longer. The weight of his secret was crushing him, threatening to tear apart the very fabric of his relationship with his son. And as he sat there, caught between two worlds, Drake realized that the time for truth was rapidly approaching, whether he was ready for it or not.

5 - 6

Drake chuckled softly, ruffling Harrison's hair affectionately. The familiar texture beneath his fingers grounded him, a reminder of the precious reality before him. Sinking down onto the couch beside Harrison. The worn leather creaked under his weight, a comforting sound in the quiet room. "I've got something for you."

Harrison's eyebrows shot up, curiosity sparking in his eyes. "Oh yeah? What is it? A new gaming console? Car keys?" He grinned, clearly enjoying the guessing game.

Drake's heart clenched. If only it were something so simple, so innocent. He reached into his pocket, his fingers brushing against the crisp edge of the envelope. With a tired sigh, he retrieved the letter he had found earlier that day.

"Not quite," Drake said, his voice barely above a whisper. He held the envelope in his hands, studying the hurried scrawl of Harrison's name across its front. The weight of its contents seemed to pull at him, threatening to drag him into an abyss of uncertainty.

7 - 8

Drake's hand trembled slightly as he extended the envelope towards Harrison. "I found this today," he explained, his voice low and tinged with apprehension. "I thought you might want to take a look."

Harrison's eyebrows knitted together; his usual cockiness replaced by a wary curiosity. He reached out, his fingers brushing against Drake's as he took the letter. The teenager turned it over in his hands, examining the hurried scrawl of his name.

"What is it?" Harrison asked, his tone uncharacteristically serious. "Is this about... mom?"

Drake's heart clenched at the mention of his wife, the duality of his realities threatening to overwhelm him. He shook his head, unable to find the words to explain the inexplicable.

With a shrug that seemed more like a nervous twitch, Harrison tore open the envelope. Drake watched intently; his breath caught in his throat as his son pulled out the contents.

Harrison's eyes widened, his mouth falling open in a silent gasp. Drake leaned in, his gaze fixed on the symbol that had haunted his thoughts since he first laid eyes on it – a vibrant green dragon, its sinuous body winding around a gnarled tree. The creature's wings spread wide, adorned with intricate symbols that seemed to shimmer and pulse with an otherworldly energy.

"Dad..." Harrison whispered, his voice trailing off as he traced the outline of the dragon with his finger. "What the hell is this?"

Drake's mind raced, searching for the right words to explain something he himself didn't fully understand. How could he tell his son that this symbol might be the key to unraveling the fractured reality they were living in?

9 - 10

Drake ran a hand through his disheveled hair, his tired eyes fixed on the pulsing symbol. "I don't know, Harrison," he admitted, his voice heavy with the weight of uncertainty. "But it's connected to everything that's been happening lately."

Harrison's brow furrowed, his usual cockiness replaced by a look of genuine concern. "What do you mean, 'everything'? Dad, what's going on?"

Drake hesitated, torn between his instinct to protect his son and the growing realization that Harrison deserved the truth. He could feel the walls of his dual realities pressing in, threatening to collapse.

"It's... complicated," Drake began, choosing his words carefully. "Remember those weird dreams I've been having? The ones where..." He paused, swallowing hard. "The ones where sometimes Mom is gone, and sometimes you are?"

Harrison nodded slowly, his eyes never leaving the mysterious symbol. "Yeah, you've been acting pretty strange lately. I thought it was just work stress or something."

Drake sighed, the sound filled with a mix of exhaustion and relief. "I wish it were that simple, kiddo. But this symbol, it's shown up in both... versions of my life. And now it's here, in our reality. I can't help but think it means something."

As he spoke, Drake couldn't shake the feeling that they were standing on the precipice of something monumental, something that would forever change the fabric of their existence.

11 - 12

The dim light of the living room cast long shadows across their faces, deepening the lines of worry etched on Drake's features. Harrison's fingers traced the contours of the green dragon, his touch hesitant as if the symbol might come to life at any moment.

"Dad," Harrison began, his voice uncharacteristically quiet, "you're scaring me a little. What aren't you telling me?"

Drake ran a hand through his disheveled hair, his exhaustion palpable. "There's someone... a man named Gabriel. He seems to be at the center of all this. And now, somehow, he's drawn you into it too."

Harrison's eyes widened, a spark of recognition flashing across his face. "Gabriel? The guy with the burned face and the limp?"

Drake's head snapped up, his heart racing. "You've met him? When? Where?"

"He... he came to school last week. Said he was a guest speaker for our mythology class. He talked about ancient symbols and their power. I thought it was just some weird coincidence, but now..."

Drake's mind reeled, pieces of the puzzle shifting into place. He leaned forward, fighting against the weight of exhaustion threatening to pull him under. "Harrison, listen to me. Whatever Gabriel told you, whatever he's planning, we need to be careful. I don't understand it all yet, but I know he's dangerous."

As the words left his mouth, Drake's eyelids grew heavy, the room blurring at the edges. He struggled to focus on Harrison's worried face, knowing he needed to stay awake, to explain more, to protect his son. But the pull of sleep was inexorable, dragging him down into the depths of unconsciousness.

His last coherent thought was a mixture of fear and determination. Tomorrow, he vowed silently. Tomorrow, he would tell Harrison everything, no matter the consequences. They would face this together, father and son against the enigmatic forces threatening to tear their world apart.

Conflict and Inner Turmoil

1 - 2

Drake's fingers dug into the frayed arms of the old chair; his knuckles white with tension. The living room, once a haven of family warmth, now felt suffocating. Shadows danced across the walls, cast by the flickering light of the old table lamp, mirroring the turmoil in Drake's mind.

Across from him, Harrison slouched on the couch, his lanky frame exuding a mix of teenage nonchalance and palpable concern. Drake's gaze flickered to his son's face, taking in the furrowed brow and the tight set of his jaw. The weight of what he was about to say pressed down on Drake's chest, making each breath a labored effort.

"Harrison," Drake began, his voice rough with exhaustion. He paused, searching for the right words. How do you tell your son that reality isn't what it seems? That the very fabric of their existence was fraying at the seams?

Harrison leaned forward, his curly hair falling into his eyes. "What's going on, Dad? You're kind of freaking me out here."

Drake ran a hand through his disheveled hair, buying time. The scent of stale coffee and sleepless nights clung to him like a second skin. "I need to tell you something," he finally managed, each word heavy with the burden of truth. "Something that might be hard to believe."

Harrison's eyes narrowed, a flicker of that beyond-his-years wisdom shining through. "Try me," he said, his voice a challenge tinged with worry.

Drake took a deep breath, steeling himself. The words hovered on the tip of his tongue, threatening to spill out in a torrent of impossibility. But how could he explain the inexplicable? How could he make Harrison understand when he barely understood it himself?

The silence stretched between them, thick with unspoken truths and mounting tension. Drake's mind raced, replaying the surreal events of the past few days like a fever dream. The dual lives, the impossible choices, the constant feeling of being torn in two – how could he possibly convey all of that to his son?

"Dad?" Harrison's voice cut through Drake's spiraling thoughts. "Whatever it is, we can handle it. Together."

Those words, so simple yet so powerful, broke something loose inside Drake. A sob caught in his throat, threatening to escape. He looked at his son – really looked at him – and saw not just the cocky teenager, but the brave, compassionate young man he was becoming.

"You're right," Drake said, his voice barely above a whisper. "We can handle it together. But Harrison, what I'm about to tell you... it's going to change everything."

3 - 4

Harrison leaned forward, his eyes locked on Drake's face, waiting for him to continue. The intensity of his gaze reminded Drake of his own courtroom days, when he'd scrutinize witnesses for any hint of deception. But there was no deception here, only an impossible truth.

Drake's throat constricted, his next words feeling like shards of glass. "I've been living two lives," he explained, his words slow and measured. "In one, your mother is alive, and in the other, you are."

The moment the words left his mouth, Drake felt a seismic shift in the room. Harrison's eyes widened, a mixture of disbelief and something else – fear, perhaps? – flashing across his features. Drake's heart raced, his palms growing clammy as he waited for his son's reaction.

'He thinks I've lost my mind,' Drake thought, fighting the urge to backpedal. 'But I have to make him understand. I have to try.'

"I know it sounds impossible," Drake continued, leaning forward to match Harrison's posture. "Trust me, I've been grappling with this reality for days. But somehow, I'm existing in two parallel worlds, and I can't... I can't reconcile them."

Drake's voice cracked on the last word, the weight of his dual existence pressing down on him like a physical force. He searched Harrison's face for any sign of comprehension, any flicker of belief amidst the shock.

5 - 6

Harrison's brow furrowed; his teenage cockiness momentarily replaced by genuine confusion. "What do you mean, Dad?" he asked, his voice tinged with uncertainty. His eyes darted around the room, as if searching for some hidden explanation. "Are you saying you're, like, time traveling or something?"

Drake's heart clenched at the bewilderment in his son's voice. He took a deep breath, steeling himself for Harrison's reaction. The worn leather of the armchair creaked as he shifted, trying to find the right words.

"I know it sounds crazy," he continued, running a hand through his disheveled hair. "But somehow, I'm able to move between these two worlds – one where I'm a detective working on a case, and the other where I'm just... me."

As the words left his mouth, Drake watched Harrison's face carefully. He could almost see the gears turning in his son's mind, trying to process this impossible information.

'God, what must he think of me?' Drake thought, his stomach churning. 'Have I just shattered his world?'

He leaned forward, elbows on his knees, desperate to make Harrison understand. "In one world, I'm investigating a series of bizarre murders. In the other, I'm... here, with your mother. But both feel equally real, equally important."

Drake's voice trailed off, the weight of his confession hanging in the air between them. He waited, breath held, for Harrison's response, praying that his son's natural curiosity would win out over disbelief.

7 - 8

Harrison's eyes widened in disbelief, his curly hair seeming to stand even more on end as he processed his father's words. Drake pressed on, determined to make him understand, even as doubt gnawed at his insides.

"It's like I'm living two separate lives, but they're both real," Drake explained, his words tinged with urgency. He leaned forward, hands gesticulating as if trying to grasp the intangible concept. "And everything that happens in one world affects the other."

Harrison's brow furrowed; his teenage cockiness momentarily replaced by genuine concern. "Dad, that's... that's impossible. Are you feeling, okay?"

Drake's heart sank, but he pushed through. "I know how it sounds, Harrison. But I need you to listen." He paused, collecting his thoughts. "When I close my eyes in one world, I open them in the other. Your mother is there, alive and well, but you..." His voice cracked. "You're not."

Harrison's face paled. "So, in this other world, I'm... dead?"

Drake nodded solemnly, the admission tearing at his soul. "And in that world, I'm trying to solve a case that might explain all of this. But I can't do it alone. I need you to believe me, son."

As he spoke, Drake's mind raced, wondering if he'd made a terrible mistake in sharing this burden with his son. But the weight of carrying this secret alone had become unbearable, and Harrison was the only person he could trust with the truth.

9 - 10

Harrison sat in stunned silence, his curly hair falling over his eyes as he stared at the worn carpet. The ticking of the old grandfather clock in the corner seemed deafening in the quiet room. Drake watched his son intently, noticing the subtle changes in his expression as he grappled with the impossible reality just presented to him.

"Dad," Harrison finally spoke, his voice barely above a whisper, "this is... insane." He looked up, his bright eyes now clouded with confusion and a hint of fear. "But the way you're talking, it's like..." He trailed off, unable to finish the thought.

Drake leaned forward; his tired eyes locked on his son's face. He could see the conflict playing out, the battle between disbelief and the trust Harrison had always placed in him. The weight of his dual lives pressed down on Drake's shoulders, threatening to crush him.

"I know it's a lot to take in," Drake said, reaching out to place a comforting hand on Harrison's shoulder. His touch was gentle, a stark contrast to the turmoil raging inside him. "But I need you to believe me. I need you to understand that I'm doing everything I can to make sense of this – for both of us."

As he spoke, Drake's mind raced with the implications of his confession. Would Harrison think he was losing his mind? Would this revelation drive a wedge between them? The fear of losing his son's trust gnawed at him, but he pushed it aside. He had to make Harrison understand, no matter the cost.

11 - 11

Harrison nodded slowly, his mop of curly hair bobbing with the movement. His eyes, usually sparkling with mischief, now held a depth of understanding beyond his years. He swallowed hard, his Adam's apple bobbing in his throat.

"Dad, I... I believe you," he said, his voice cracking slightly. "I mean, it's crazy, but you've never lied to me before. Why start now with something this bonkers?"

Drake felt a wave of relief wash over him, but it was quickly replaced by a renewed sense of urgency. Harrison continued, his words tumbling out faster now.

"So, what does this mean for us? Are we, like, dimension-hopping now? Do I have a doppelganger out there somewhere?" A hint of his usual enthusiasm crept into his voice, despite the gravity of the situation.

Drake shook his head, a small smile tugging at the corners of his mouth. Even in the face of the impossible, Harrison's imagination ran wild. "I don't know, son. But whatever comes next, we're in this together."

Harrison leaned back in his chair, running a hand through his unruly hair. His mind was racing, trying to process the implications of his father's revelation. He thought about his mother, alive in another world, and felt a pang of longing mixed with confusion.

"Dad," he said, his voice soft but determined, "whatever's going on, whatever we have to face... I'm with you. We're family, right? That's what matters."

Drake felt a lump form in his throat, overwhelmed by his son's unwavering support. In that moment, despite the uncertainty that lay ahead, he knew they would find a way through this labyrinth together.

Dragon's Embrace

1 - 2

Harrison's fingers traced the intricate lines of the green dragon symbol, its scales seeming to shimmer in the dim light of his desk lamp. The tree it encircled appeared to sway, branches reaching out like grasping fingers. He squinted, leaning closer to examine the cryptic symbols adorning the dragon's wings.

"What are you?" he muttered, cocking his head. "Some kind of ancient rune? Or just random squiggles?"

His mind raced with possibilities, each more outlandish than the last. Could it be an alchemical formula? A map to hidden treasure? The key to unlocking supernatural powers? The curly-haired teenager chuckled at his own wild imagination, but the laughter died in his throat as an eerie chill ran down his spine.

Harrison's bright eyes darted to the crumpled letter from his father, lying discarded at the edge of the desk. "Thanks for the nightmare fuel, Dad," he grumbled, running a hand through his unruly mop of hair. "Couldn't you have just sent a normal birthday card like other parents?"

As the hours ticked by, Harrison pored over the pages of his notebook, searching for any clue that might shed light on the symbol's meaning. His usual confidence waned with each fruitless attempt at decoding its secrets.

"Come on, Harrison," he chided himself, tapping his pen against the desk in frustration. "You're supposed to be the clever one. Figure it out already!"

But the more he stared at the symbol, the more unsettled he felt. What had initially seemed like an intriguing puzzle now loomed before him like a harbinger of something dark and unknowable. Harrison couldn't shake the feeling that he was being watched, as if the dragon's emerald eyes were following his every move.

"This is ridiculous," he muttered, pushing back from the desk. "It's just a drawing. Get a grip, Miller."

Yet even as he tried to reassure himself, Harrison's gaze was inexorably drawn back to the symbol. The shadows in his room seemed to deepen, swallowing the warm glow of his desk lamp. A cold sweat broke out on his forehead as he realized that the unease settling over him was more than simple frustration – it was fear.

3 - 4

Harrison's fingers trembled as they traced the intricate lines of the symbol, the cool paper a stark contrast to his feverish skin. His mind drifted, seeking solace in the familiar realms of his imagination.

"The Green Knight," he whispered, his voice barely audible in the hushed room. "Camelot's enigmatic challenger."

The world he had crafted for his creative writing class materialized around him – verdant forests, mist-shrouded castles, and the glint of armor in torchlight. For weeks, this story had been his refuge, more vibrant and alive than the mundane reality of his everyday life.

"It can't be," Harrison muttered, shaking his head in disbelief. "It's just a coincidence. It has to be."

But even as he spoke the words, a chill ran down his spine. The symbol before him was undeniably familiar – the very emblem he had designed for the Green Knight, his own creation brought to life on the page.

"How is this possible?" he asked the empty room, his voice cracking with a mixture of awe and fear. "I made you up. You're not real. You can't be real."

Harrison's heart raced as he struggled to reconcile the impossible. His mind reeled, grasping for a logical explanation. "Maybe I saw this somewhere before," he reasoned aloud, "and it just... stuck in my subconscious. That has to be it, right?"

But deep down, he knew. This was no coincidence, no trick of memory. The symbol was exactly as he had imagined it, down to the last intricate detail. Harrison's hands shook as he leafed through his notebook, searching for the original sketch.

"This can't be happening," he whispered, his voice trembling. "How can something from my imagination be here, in the real world?"

The silence that followed his question was deafening, broken only by the pounding of his heart and the rustle of pages as he frantically searched for answers that refused to reveal themselves.

5 - 6

Harrison's fingers trembled as he finally located the page he sought, his breath catching in his throat as he laid eyes on the sketch. "Oh God," he muttered, his voice barely above a whisper. "It's identical. Every. Single. Detail."

He traced the intricate patterns on the dragon's wings, his mind reeling with the implications. The symbols weren't just similar – they were exact replicas of what he had conjured in his imagination. A bead of cold sweat trickled down his temple as he compared the sketch to the mysterious letter.

"This can't be real," Harrison said, his voice shaking. "I'm losing my mind. That's the only explanation." But even as he spoke the words, he knew they rang hollow.

He stood abruptly, pacing the small confines of his room. "Think, Harrison, think!" he commanded himself. "There has to be a rational explanation for this."

But as he moved, he couldn't shake the feeling of being watched. The shadows in the corners of his room seemed to deepen, writhing with an unnatural life of their own. Harrison spun around, his eyes darting from corner to corner.

"Is someone there?" he called out, hating the tremor in his voice. Only silence answered him, but it was a silence pregnant with malevolent possibility.

Turning back to his desk, Harrison's gaze locked onto the symbol once more. "What are you?" he whispered, a mixture of fear and fascination coloring his words. "What does this mean?"

As if in response, a sudden gust of wind swept through the room, rustling the pages of his notebook. Harrison's heart leapt into his throat as he watched the pages flip on their own, finally settling on a sketch he didn't remember drawing – a dark, formless shape with glowing eyes that seemed to stare right through him.

7 - 8

Harrison stumbled backward, his breath catching in his throat. "This... this isn't possible," he muttered, his eyes wide with disbelief. The sketch seemed to pulse with an otherworldly energy, the eyes boring into his very soul.

"I never drew this," he whispered, his voice barely audible even in the oppressive silence of his room. "How could I have forgotten something like this?"

As if responding to his words, the shadows in the room seemed to deepen, creeping closer to where he stood. Harrison's heart raced, pounding so loudly he was sure it would burst from his chest.

"Who's there?" he called out, his voice cracking with fear. "Show yourself!"

Silence answered him, broken only by the sound of his ragged breathing. Harrison's eyes darted around the room, searching for any sign of movement, any hint of an intruder. But there was nothing – nothing except the ever-present feeling of being watched.

Swallowing hard, Harrison forced himself to turn back to his notebook. "Think rationally," he told himself, running a trembling hand through his hair. "There has to be an explanation for all of this."

But as he stared at the symbol and the terrifying sketch, rationality seemed to slip further and further away. "What if..." he began, his voice barely above a whisper, "what if I'm not imagining things? What if somehow, someway, my stories are becoming real?"

The very thought sent a chill down his spine, and Harrison found himself glancing over his shoulder, half-expecting to see the Green Knight or some other creation of his imagination lurking in the shadows.

"No," he said firmly, shaking his head. "That's impossible. It has to be."

Yet even as he spoke the words, doubt gnawed at him. If it was impossible, how could he explain the symbol? The sketch he didn't remember drawing? The oppressive feeling of being watched?

Harrison's gaze fell once more on his notebook, and a thought occurred to him – a thought so terrifying it made his blood run cold. "What other secrets," he whispered, his voice trembling, "what other horrors might be hiding in these pages?"

With shaking hands, he reached for the notebook, both dreading and needing to know what other impossible things might have sprung from his imagination into reality.

9 - 10

Harrison's trembling fingers traced the contours of the green dragon symbol, its scales seemingly rippling beneath his touch. "This isn't just a drawing anymore," he muttered, his voice quavering. "It's... alive somehow."

The dragon's emerald eyes seemed to follow him as he paced the room, its coiled form wrapped protectively around the tree at its center. Harrison paused, struck by a sudden realization. "Wait a second," he said, leaning in closer. "The tree... it's not just any tree. It's Yggdrasil, the World Tree from Norse mythology."

He ran a hand through his unruly curls, his mind racing. "But why would I combine that with the Green Knight? Unless..." His eyes widened. "Unless it's trying to tell me something."

Harrison spun back to his desk, rifling through his notes with newfound urgency. "The Green Knight in my story, he wasn't just a villain," he mused aloud. "He was a force of nature, a test for the heroes. And now..."

He trailed off, his gaze drawn back to the symbol. The dragon's wings, adorned with intricate patterns, seemed to pulse with an otherworldly energy. "Now it's a test for me," Harrison whispered, a mix of fear and excitement coursing through him.

Grabbing a fresh sheet of paper, he began to sketch furiously, his pen flying across the page. "If this symbol is more than just my imagination," he said, his voice gaining strength, "if it really is some kind of... I don't know, cosmic sign or something, then maybe I can use my stories to understand it."

As he drew, adding details to the dragon and the tree, Harrison felt a surge of creative energy unlike anything he'd experienced before. "It's like... like I'm tapping into something bigger than myself," he murmured, his eyes gleaming with intensity. "The dragon, it's not just power. It's the cycle of life itself. And the tree..."

He paused, staring at his creation with a mixture of awe and trepidation. "The tree connects everything. Past, present, future. Reality and imagination." Harrison swallowed hard, his voice dropping to a whisper. "What if... what if I'm not just writing stories? What if I'm shaping reality itself?"

The thought both thrilled and terrified him. Harrison looked around his room, suddenly seeing it with new eyes. "If that's true," he said, his voice filled with a combination of wonder and fear, "then everything I write, everything I imagine... it could all become real."

He turned back to his notebook, his hand hovering over the page. "The question is," Harrison said, his voice steady despite the tremor in his hand, "do I keep writing and risk unleashing who knows what into the world? Or do I stop, and potentially lose the chance to understand what's really going on?"

With a deep breath, Harrison made his decision. He put pen to paper and began to write, knowing that each word could potentially alter the very fabric of reality itself.

11 - 12

Harrison's pen danced across the page, his brow furrowed in concentration as he traced the intricate symbols adorning the dragon's wings. "These aren't just random doodles," he muttered, his voice thick with realization. "They're runes, ancient and powerful."

He leaned back, running a hand through his unruly curls. "But how did I know that? How am I suddenly understanding their meaning?"

As if in response, the symbols seemed to shimmer on the page, each one pulsing with an otherworldly energy. Harrison's eyes widened, his cocky demeanor momentarily shaken. "Fire, earth, air, water," he whispered, pointing to each symbol in turn. "And this one... knowledge. And here, enlightenment."

He stood abruptly, pacing the room as his mind raced. "It's like they're alive, like they're speaking to me. But that's impossible, right?" He laughed nervously, the sound echoing in the quiet room.

Turning back to his desk, Harrison's gaze was drawn inexorably to the central image of the dragon and tree. "It's more than just a cool design," he said, his voice filled with a mixture of excitement and trepidation. "It's a gateway, isn't it? To something... bigger."

As he spoke, the air in the room seemed to thicken, charged with an electric energy that made the hairs on the back of his neck stand up. Harrison swallowed hard, his earlier bravado replaced by a growing sense of awe.

"I always thought I was just making stuff up," he murmured, tracing the outline of the dragon with a trembling finger. "But what if... what if I've been tapping into something real all along? Something ancient and powerful?"

The symbols on the page seemed to pulse in response, as if confirming his suspicions. Harrison felt a surge of excitement mixed with fear. "This is way bigger than some creative writing assignment," he said, his voice filled with wonder. "I think I've stumbled onto something huge here. Something that could change... everything."

He paused, the weight of his realization settling over him. "The question is," Harrison said slowly, his eyes never leaving the mesmerizing symbol, "am I ready for what comes next?"

13 - 14

Harrison's heart pounded as he reached for his notebook, his fingers trembling slightly as they grazed the worn leather cover. "Okay, let's see what we've got here," he muttered, flipping through the pages with frantic energy.

Each turn of a page revealed another intricate sketch, another fragment of the world he'd created. The familiar drawings now seemed to pulse with an otherworldly energy, as if they were trying to leap off the page and into reality.

"This is insane," Harrison breathed, his eyes widening as he recognized elements from his story mirrored in the mysterious symbol before him. "It's all here. The dragon, the tree, even these weird runes on the wings. How is this possible?"

He ran a hand through his unruly curls, his mind racing. "I mean, I've always had a pretty wild imagination, but this... this is something else entirely." Harrison's gaze darted between his notebook and the symbol, searching for answers.

Harrison leaned back in his chair, his eyes never leaving the symbol. "But that's crazy, right?" he asked the empty room, his cocky teenager facade cracking under the weight of his confusion. "I'm just a kid with an overactive imagination. I can't actually be... what? Some kind of conduit for ancient magical forces?"

He let out a nervous laugh, but it did little to dispel the growing sense of unease that had settled over him. "Get it together, Harrison," he chided himself. "There's got to be a logical explanation for this. Maybe Dad's just messing with me. Yeah, that's got to be it."

But even as he spoke the words, Harrison knew they rang hollow. The connection between his creations and the symbol was too precise, too intricate to be a mere prank. Something much stranger was at play here, something that defied easy explanation.

With a determined set to his jaw, Harrison turned back to his notebook. "Alright, if this is real, then there's got to be more clues in here somewhere," he said, his voice regaining some of its usual confidence. "I created this world. If anyone can figure out what's going on, it's me."

As he dove back into his notes and sketches, Harrison couldn't shake the feeling that he was standing on the precipice of something monumental. Whatever mysteries lay hidden in the pages of his notebook, he was determined to uncover them, no matter where they might lead.

15 - 16

As Harrison's eyes darted across the pages, the familiar sketches and scribbles seemed to come alive, pulsing with an otherworldly energy he'd never noticed before. The Green Knight's armor gleamed with an eerie viridescence, while the dragon's scales rippled as if caught in an unseen breeze. He found himself muttering under his breath, "This can't be happening. It's just ink on paper, for God's sake."

But the more he stared, the more real it all became. The forest of Brocéliande, once just a figment of his imagination, now seemed to stretch out before him, its ancient trees whispering secrets long forgotten. He could almost smell the damp earth and hear the rustle of leaves in the wind.

"What if..." Harrison's voice trailed off, his mind reeling at the implications. "What if I'm not just writing a story? What if I'm somehow... channeling something real?"

The thought both thrilled and terrified him. He'd always dreamed of his stories coming to life, but not like this. Not in a way that blurred the lines between fiction and reality, that made him question his very sanity.

Just as he was about to delve deeper into a particularly intricate passage about the magical properties of the dragon's scales, a sound from outside his room made him freeze. Footsteps, slow and deliberate, echoing in the hallway beyond his door.

Harrison's heart leapt into his throat. "Hello?" he called out, his voice cracking slightly. "Dad, is that you?"

No response came, just the steady, rhythmic sound of approaching footsteps. Harrison's eyes darted to the clock on his desk – 2:37 AM. Who could be wandering the house at this hour?

"Okay, Harrison, get a grip," he whispered to himself, trying to steady his nerves. "It's probably just Dad checking on you. Or maybe the house is settling. Yeah, that's it. Old houses make weird noises all the time, right?"

But even as he tried to rationalize the sound, a chill ran down his spine. The footsteps had stopped, right outside his door. In the sudden silence, Harrison could hear his own heartbeat, pounding in his ears like a war drum.

"Who's there?" he called out again, hating how small and frightened his voice sounded. "Seriously, this isn't funny anymore."

The doorknob began to turn, slowly, agonizingly slowly. Harrison found himself holding his breath, his eyes fixed on the door, his mind racing with possibilities. Was it his father, coming to explain the mysterious symbol? Or was it something else entirely, something born from the pages of his notebook, crossing the threshold between imagination and reality?

As the door began to open, Harrison braced himself for whatever was about to be revealed, his hand instinctively clutching his notebook as if it were a talisman against the unknown.

17 - 18

Harrison's heart thundered in his chest as he lunged for the door, his hand grasping the cold metal of the handle. With a surge of adrenaline, he yanked it open, bracing himself for whatever nightmarish creature his imagination had conjured.

"Show yourself!" he shouted, his voice cracking with fear and determination.

But as the door swung wide, revealing the hallway beyond, Harrison's breath caught in his throat. There was... nothing. Just an empty corridor bathed in the ethereal glow of moonlight streaming through the window at the far end.

"What the hell?" he muttered, confusion replacing fear as he took a tentative step into the hallway. His eyes darted from shadow to shadow, searching for any sign of movement. "I could've sworn I heard..."

The floorboards creaked beneath his feet as he ventured further, the sound seeming to echo in the eerie silence. Harrison's mind raced, trying to reconcile what he'd heard with the emptiness before him.

"Maybe I'm losing it," he said to himself, running a hand through his curly hair. "All this stress, the symbol, the story... it's getting to me."

As he spoke, a cool breeze ghosted across his skin, causing goosebumps to rise on his arms. Harrison froze, his gaze snapping to the window at the end of the hall. It was closed.

"Where did that come from?" he whispered, his earlier bravado evaporating.

The moonlight seemed to flicker, as if something had passed in front of the window, casting a momentary shadow. Harrison's breath caught in his throat as he stared, wide-eyed, at the play of light and shadow.

"Is someone there?" he called out, hating how small and uncertain his voice sounded. "Dad? Is that you?"

Only silence answered him, broken only by the pounding of his own heart. Harrison took another step forward, drawn by a mix of fear and curiosity. As he moved, the floorboard beneath his foot gave a long, low groan, the sound seeming to reverberate through the entire house.

Harrison jumped, a small yelp escaping his lips. "Get it together," he chastised himself. "It's just an old house. There's nothing here. Nothing real, anyway."

But even as he tried to reassure himself, a nagging doubt gnawed at the back of his mind. If there was truly nothing there, why did he feel so watched? And why couldn't he shake the feeling that something was lurking just beyond his perception, waiting for the right moment to reveal itself?

19 - 20

Harrison's eyes darted frantically around the dimly lit hallway, his breath coming in short, sharp gasps. The shadows seemed to stretch and contort, taking on impossible shapes that danced at the edges of his vision. He blinked hard, trying to clear his head, but the unsettling sensation persisted.

"This isn't real," he muttered, clenching his fists at his sides. "It can't be real."

But even as the words left his lips, a chill ran down his spine. There, just beyond the reach of the moonlight, something moved. It was quick, almost too fast to register, but Harrison caught a glimpse of something dark and formless slithering across the wall.

"Who's there?" he called out, his voice cracking with fear. "Show yourself!"

Silence answered him, heavy and oppressive. Harrison took a hesitant step backward, his heart hammering against his ribs. His mind raced, trying to make sense of what he'd seen. Was it a trick of the light? A shadow cast by a passing car? Or was it something more sinister, something pulled straight from the pages of his story?

"This isn't happening," he whispered, his eyes wide and searching. "It's just my imagination. It has to be."

But even as he spoke, doubt gnawed at him. The symbol from his notebook, the inexplicable feeling of being watched – it all seemed too real, too tangible to be dismissed as mere fantasy. Harrison's gaze flicked nervously between the shadows, half-expecting to see the green dragon from his story materialize before his eyes.

"What if it's real?" he breathed, the question hanging in the air like a physical presence. "What if I've somehow brought it to life?"

The thought sent a fresh wave of terror coursing through him. If his creations could manifest in the real world, what other horrors might he have unknowingly unleashed?

Shadows of Intrigue

Green World – 2024

1 - 2

The darkness envelops me like a shroud as I crouch in the hallway, my back pressed against the cool wall outside Harrison's bedroom. Every nerve in my body is on high alert, my senses straining to detect the slightest disturbance in the oppressive silence of the Miller home. The steady thrum of my heartbeat echoes in my ears, a relentless reminder of the gravity of my intrusion.

"Focus, Gabriel," I whisper to myself, barely audible. "You're here for a reason."

My fingers brush against the rough texture of the carpet, grounding me in this moment of suspense. The darkness seems to pulse around me, alive with unspoken secrets and the weight of my conflicted conscience.

A sudden shuffling sound from behind Harrison's door sends a jolt of adrenaline through my system. I freeze, willing my body to meld with the shadows.

"Shit," I think, my mind racing. "Is he awake? Did he hear me?"

I hold my breath, counting the seconds as they tick by with agonizing slowness. The silence stretches on, broken only by the faint creaking of the house settling around me.

"Please, Harrison," I plead silently, "go back to sleep. Don't make this harder than it already is."

"I'm doing this for love," I reassure myself, though the words ring hollow even in my own mind. "To fix everything. To make it right."

The shuffling behind the door grows more pronounced, and I press myself further into the shadows, my heart pounding so loudly I fear it might give me away. I close my eyes, focusing on steadying my breath, on becoming one with the darkness that surrounds me.

"Dad?" Harrison's muffled voice carries through the door, laced with sleep and confusion. "Is that you?"

I bite my lip, torn between the instinct to respond and the desperate need to remain undetected. The silence stretches on, thick with tension and unspoken words.

"It's nothing, buddy," I whisper, my voice barely a breath. "Just go back to sleep."

3 - 4

The door creaks open, its hinges groaning in protest as Harrison's silhouette emerges into the dimly lit hallway. His curly hair is tousled from sleep, a stark contrast against the shadows that dance across his face. I hold my breath, pressing myself further into the darkness, willing my racing heart to slow its frantic rhythm.

Harrison's voice breaks the silence, tinged with uncertainty. "Is anyone there?" he calls out, his teenage bravado wavering slightly. "Dad?"

I remain motionless, watching as Harrison's eyes dart nervously from side to side, searching for any sign of movement. His hand trembles as he reaches for the light switch, and I silently pray he'll change his mind.

"Come on, Harrison," I think desperately. "It's just your imagination. Go back to bed."

"H-hello?" Harrison's voice cracks, betraying his fear. He takes a hesitant step forward, his bare feet padding softly against the wooden floor. "If this is some kind of joke, it's not funny."

I can see the internal struggle playing out on his face – the desire to appear brave warring with the instinct to retreat to the safety of his room. His hand hovers near the wall, ready to flip the switch that would flood the hallway with light and expose my presence.

"It's probably nothing," Harrison mutters to himself, his voice barely above a whisper. "Just the house settling or something. Yeah, that's it."

I hold my breath, willing him to turn back, to dismiss the noises that drew him from his room. The tension in the air is palpable, each second stretching into an eternity as I wait for Harrison's next move.

5 - 6

Finally, Harrison's shoulders slump, the fight draining out of him as he shakes his head. "Man, I'm losing it," he chuckles nervously, running a hand through his unruly curls. "Next thing you know; I'll be seeing ghosts in the mirror or something."

With a final, uncertain glance down the shadowy corridor, Harrison retreats into his room. The soft click of the door closing behind him is like thunder in the silence, and I feel my body uncoil, muscles I didn't even realize were tense finally relaxing.

"That was too close," I think, exhaling slowly as my heartbeat gradually returns to normal. The darkness of the hallway seems to press in around me, a reminder of how precarious my position is. "I can't afford any more slip-ups."

Gathering my wits, I begin to move, each step calculated and silent. The floorboards that had creaked under Harrison's weight remain mercifully quiet beneath my practiced tread. As I glide towards the staircase, I can't help but cast a final glance at Harrison's door.

"Sorry, kid," I murmur, barely audible even to my own ears. "But trust me, you're better off not knowing what goes bump in the night."

With the stealth of a shadow, I descend the stairs, my form melding with the darkness. The front door looms before me, both an obstacle and an escape. As I reach for the handle, a sudden thought strikes me.

"What if Harrison heard that?" The paranoia whispers in my mind. I pause, listening intently for any sign of movement from upstairs. The house remains silent, save for the gentle hum of the refrigerator in the kitchen.

Shaking off the moment of doubt, I twist the doorknob, wincing at the barely audible click. "Get it together," I chastise myself. "You're almost out. Don't blow it now."

With a final breath, I slip out into the night, the cool air a stark contrast to the stifling tension of the house. As I melt into the shadows of the suburban street, Harrison's words echo in my mind: "Next thing you know, I'll be seeing ghosts in the mirror."

"If only you knew, Harrison," I think grimly, disappearing into the darkness like the phantom I've become. "If only you knew."

7 - 8

The night air clings to me like a second skin as I move swiftly down the quiet suburban streets, my footsteps barely a whisper against the pavement. My mind races, grappling with the weight of my actions and the enigma of my purpose.

"Why am I doing this?" I mutter under my breath, the question hanging unanswered in the still night air. "What force compels me to invade the sanctity of the Miller home?"

As if in response, a memory of Drake Miller's face flashes before my eyes - his tired, conflicted gaze haunting me even now. I shake my head, trying to dispel the image.

"No," I growl, clenching my fists. "I can't afford to second-guess myself now. There are answers hidden within those walls, answers that Drake needs... even if he doesn't know it yet."

The streetlights cast long shadows as I make my way towards the looming silhouette of the hospital in the distance. With each step, my resolve strengthens, pushing aside the lingering doubts.

"Harrison," I whisper, the boy's name a prayer and a curse on my lips. "Linda. Drake. If you only knew the storm that's coming. Maybe then you'd understand why I had to do this."

As I approach the hospital grounds, a chill runs down my spine that has nothing to do with the night air. The task ahead looms large, fraught with danger and the potential for discovery.

"One step at a time," I remind myself, drawing a deep breath to steady my nerves. "Get in, get the blood sample, get out. Simple as that."

But even as I steeled myself for what lay ahead, a part of me knew that nothing about this night - or the secrets it held - would be simple at all.

9 - 10

The antiseptic smell of the hospital assaults my senses as I slip through the automatic doors, my footsteps echoing softly in the near-empty lobby. A lone nurse glances up from her station, her eyes sliding past me without recognition. I offer a curt nod, my heart thundering in my chest as I stride purposefully towards the elevator banks.

"Just another late-night visitor," I mutter under my breath, willing the universe to make it so. The elevator doors slide open with a soft ding, and I step inside, my fingers hovering over the panel of buttons. "Fourth floor," I remind myself, Dr. Harmon's office location etched into my memory from careful reconnaissance.

As the elevator ascends, I close my eyes, centering myself. "Focus," I whisper, clenching and unclenching my fists. "You're here for the blood. Nothing else matters."

The doors open, and I step out into a dimly lit corridor. The quiet hum of medical equipment fills the air, punctuated by the occasional distant sound of footsteps or hushed voices. I move swiftly, my eyes darting left and right, scanning for any signs of movement.

"Room 412," I breathe, spotting Dr. Harmon's nameplate on a door at the end of the hall. My pulse quickens as I approach, every nerve on high alert. Pressing my ear against the cool wood, I listen intently for any sound from within.

Silence.

With trembling fingers, I reach for the handle, my other hand instinctively patting the concealed blade at my hip. "Just in case," I reassure myself, though the weight of it feels more like a burden than comfort.

The door opens with a soft click, and I slip inside, my eyes adjusting to the darkness. The faint glow of a computer screen casts eerie shadows across the room. "Alright, Harmon," I murmur, scanning the office. "Where do you keep your secrets?"

As I move towards his desk, a sudden creak from the hallway freezes me in place. My breath catches in my throat as I strain to listen, every muscle taut with tension.

"Please," I plead silently to whatever higher power might be listening. "Not now. Not when I'm so close."

The moment stretches, an eternity compressed into seconds. Then, mercifully, the sound of retreating footsteps reaches my ears. I exhale slowly, my heart still racing.

"Focus," I command myself once more, turning back to the task at hand. "Find the blood sample. Find the truth. And pray to God that Dr. Harmon doesn't decide to work late tonight."

11 - 12

My eyes dart across the room, finally settling on a small refrigerator tucked in the corner. "Bingo," I whisper, a surge of adrenaline coursing through my veins. With swift, practiced movements, I cross the office and pull open the fridge door, wincing at the soft hum that seems to echo in the stillness.

Row upon row of neatly labeled vials greet me, their contents glinting in the dim light. My fingers dance across the labels, searching desperately. "Come on, Drake Miller, where are you?" I mutter, frustration mounting with each passing second.

Then, like a beacon in the darkness, I spot it. Drake Miller's name, stark black letters against white. A strangled laugh of relief escapes my lips as I carefully extract the vial, cradling it as if it were the most precious thing in the world.

"I've got you now," I whisper, staring at the crimson liquid within. "The key to unlocking your secrets, Drake. What makes you so special? Why are you trapped between two realities as well?"

As I turn to leave, a sudden noise from behind freezes me in place. The soft squeak of rubber soles on linoleum, barely audible but unmistakable in the silence. My heart leaps into my throat as I slowly pivot, my hand instinctively reaching for the concealed blade at my side.

13 - 14

The dim light of the office suddenly feels oppressive as I squint into the shadows, my fingers tightening around the hilt of my blade. A figure emerges from the darkness, and I feel my breath catch in my throat as I recognize Dr. Jesse Harmon, his silver hair gleaming faintly in the low light.

"Who...?" Dr. Harmon's voice is low and controlled, but I can hear the underlying tension. His eyes, magnified behind his glasses, dart from my face to the vial clutched in my hand.

Without hesitation, I lunge forward, the blade flashing as it slices through the air.

Dr. Harmon's eyes widen in horror as the blade finds its mark, a spray of crimson staining the sterile white walls. With a gurgling gasp, he collapses to the floor, his lifeblood pooling around him in a dark, viscous puddle.

"Why?" he chokes out, his stern features contorted in pain and disbelief.

I stand over him, my chest heaving, the weight of my actions crashing down upon me. "You wouldn't understand," I whisper, more to myself than to the dying man at my feet. "Drake Miller's blood... it's the key to everything. To realities we can't even begin to comprehend."

As Dr. Harmon's life ebbs away, I can't help but wonder: how many more lives will be sacrificed in my pursuit of the truth? And will I be able to live with the consequences when all is said and done?

15 - 16

A sense of grim satisfaction washes over me as I watch Dr. Harmon's eyes flutter closed, his labored breathing growing fainter with each passing second. The vial of Drake Miller's blood feels heavy in my hand, its contents gleaming dully in the dim light of the hospital room.

"It's done," I murmur, my voice barely audible over the steady hum of medical equipment. "The first step towards unraveling the mystery that binds us all."

I turn the vial over in my scarred hands, my disfigured face reflected in its surface. The burns that mar my features serve as a constant reminder of the price I've paid for knowledge, for justice. "Drake," I whisper, "you have no idea what lies dormant in your veins, do you?"

With practiced efficiency, I secure the vial in a protective case and tuck it into my coat pocket. As I move towards the door, I cast a final glance at Dr. Harmon's crumpled form. "Your sacrifice won't be in vain," I promise, my voice tinged with a mix of regret and determination. "The truth will come to light, no matter the cost."

The hallway outside is deserted, the late hour ensuring minimal staff presence. I slip through the corridors like a shadow, my footsteps silent on the polished floors. As I near the exit, a night nurse rounds the corner, her eyes widening as she takes in my appearance.

"Sir, are you alright?" she asks, concern evident in her voice. "You look-"

I cut her off with a raised hand and a disarming smile. "Just visiting a friend," I lie smoothly, my voice carrying a warmth that doesn't reach my eyes. "Late nights and worry can take their toll on anyone, wouldn't you agree?"

She nods hesitantly, and I brush past her before she can ask any more questions. The cool night air greets me as I step outside, carrying with it the promise of secrets yet to be uncovered. I disappear into the darkness, my resolve strengthened by the weight of the vial in my pocket and the knowledge that I, Gabriel Angel, am one step closer to unraveling the truth that binds Drake Miller's fate to my own.

17 - 18

As I navigate the labyrinthine corridors of the hospital, the fluorescent lights cast harsh shadows that seem to dance accusingly across the walls. My heart pounds in my chest, each beat a reminder of the life I've just extinguished. Dr. Harmon's startled expression flashes before my eyes, his final moments etched into my memory like a macabre photograph.

"Why did he have to be there?" I whisper to myself, my voice barely audible over the hum of the building's ventilation system. The weight of the blood vial in my pocket feels impossibly heavy, a physical manifestation of my guilt.

I pause at an intersection, leaning against the wall to catch my breath. A nearby mirror reflects my haggard appearance, and for a moment, I hardly recognize the man staring back at me.

"You did what was necessary," I mutter to my reflection, trying to convince myself. "For myself. For justice."

The words sound hollow, even to my own ears. I push off from the wall, continuing my journey through the maze-like halls. My mind races, grappling with the enormity of my actions.

"Why?" I question silently, my inner voice a cacophony of doubt and justification. "Why did it have to come to this?"

As I round another corner, I nearly collide with a young orderly pushing a cart of medical supplies. He looks up, startled, and I force a smile onto my face.

"Excuse me," I say, my voice steadier than I feel. "I seem to have lost my way. Could you point me towards the exit?"

The orderly nods, gesturing down the hall. "Take the next left, then follow the signs. You can't miss it."

"Thank you," I reply, my gratitude genuine despite the circumstances. As I move past him, a thought strikes me. "One more thing – did you happen to see Dr. Harmon tonight?"

The orderly shakes his head. "No, sir. Last I heard, he was working late in his office."

I nod, suppressing a shudder. "Of course. Thank you again."

As I follow the orderly's directions, my mind continues its relentless interrogation. What drove me to such extremes? Was there truly no other way? The answers remain elusive, hidden in the recesses of my fractured psyche.

"You're doing this for a reason," I remind myself, my voice barely a whisper. "Remember why you started. Remember Gabriel."

But even as I try to justify my actions, a part of me recoils at the memory of Dr. Harmon's life slipping away, of all the lives I've taken. The stark reality of what I've become weighs heavily upon me, a burden I fear I may never be able to shed.

19 - 20

The automatic doors slide open with a soft hiss, and a gust of cold night air hits me like a physical blow. I inhale sharply, the metallic scent of blood still clinging to my nostrils, mingling with the crisp scent of approaching rain. Bridgewater stretches out before me, a tapestry of streetlights and shadowed buildings, oblivious to the horror that just unfolded within the hospital walls.

"What have I done?" I mutter, my voice barely audible above the whisper of wind through the palm trees lining the parking lot.

A passing nurse glances at me curiously, and I force a smile, nodding in acknowledgment. As she disappears back into the hospital, I can't shake the feeling that her eyes linger on me a moment too long.

"Get it together," I hiss to myself, clenching my fists. "You can't fall apart now."

My fingers brush against the vial in my pocket, the weight of it both comforting and damning. I pull it out, studying the dark liquid within, my reflection distorted in the curved glass.

"This better be worth it," I murmur, addressing the vial as if it could answer. "Worth... everything."

A car alarm suddenly blares in the distance, making me jump. My paranoia kicks into overdrive, every shadow suddenly a potential threat.

"Time to go," I decide, slipping the vial back into my pocket and setting off at a brisk pace.

As I walk, the wind picks up, carrying with it the promise of impending storm and retribution. Each gust feels like an accusation, each rustle of leaves a whispered threat.

"They'll find out soon," I think, my steps quickening. "How long before they connect the dots? Before they come for me?"

I pause at a crosswalk, the 'Don't Walk' sign glowing an ominous red. A police cruiser rolls by, and I feel my heart rate spike.

"Easy," I breathe, willing myself to appear calm and collected. "You're just a guy out for a late-night walk. Nothing suspicious here."

The light changes, and I hurry across the street, my limp more pronounced as fatigue and stress take their toll. The shadows of Bridgewater's familiar streets now seem menacing, hiding potential dangers around every corner.

"Focus on the mission," I remind myself, ducking into an alley to catch my breath. "Lucian's waiting. He'll know what to do next."

As I lean against the cool brick wall, I can't help but wonder if I've crossed a line from which there's no return. The weight of my actions presses down on me, threatening to crush what's left of my sanity.

"One step at a time," I mutter, pushing off the wall and continuing my journey into the night. "Just keep moving forward."

21 - 22

As I emerge from the alley, the streetlights flicker ominously, casting long shadows that seem to reach for me with grasping fingers. I pull my collar up, trying to shield my face from any prying eyes.

"You're nothing but a ghost now, Gabriel," I whisper to myself, my voice barely audible above the distant hum of traffic. "A phantom slipping through the cracks of society."

A group of late-night revelers stumbles past, their laughter jarring in the otherwise quiet night. I press myself against a storefront, willing myself to become invisible.

"Hey, you alright there, mate?" one of them calls out, his words slurred.

I force a smile, waving them off. "Just waiting for a ride. Carry on."

As they move away, I let out a shaky breath. "Unseen and untouchable," I remind myself. "That's what you need to be."

But even as I try to convince myself of my ghostly nature, a nagging voice in the back of my mind whispers, "Even ghosts must face their demons eventually."

I pause at a corner, my eyes drawn to the silhouette of the hospital in the distance. The weight of the blood vial in my pocket feels heavier than ever.

"What have I become?" I mutter, running a hand through my disheveled hair. "How far am I willing to go for the truth?"

A car horn blares nearby, startling me out of my reverie. I realize I've been standing still for too long, exposed.

"Keep moving," I hiss, forcing my feet forward. "You can't afford to linger."

As I walk, my mind races with the implications of my actions. The image of Dr. Harmon's shocked face flashes before my eyes, and I stumble slightly.

"No turning back now," I say, gritting my teeth against the wave of guilt threatening to overwhelm me. "Justice must be served, no matter the cost."

With a final glance back at the hospital, I steel myself for what's to come. "Into the night," I whisper, my voice barely audible. "Let the darkness consume me."

And with that, I vanish into the shadows, leaving behind nothing but echoes of the man I once was and the uncertain future that awaits.

DNA Answers

Blue World – 2024

1 - 2

The harsh fluorescent lights stabbed at Drake's eyes as he slowly regained consciousness, the antiseptic smell of the hospital room assaulting his nostrils. His head throbbed, each pulse sending waves of nausea through his body. As his vision swam into focus, he saw Linda sitting beside his bed, her blonde hair falling in messy waves around her face. Her blue eyes, usually so vibrant, were clouded with worry, dark circles underneath betraying her exhaustion.

Drake's throat felt like sandpaper as he tried to speak, his voice coming out as a hoarse whisper. "Linda," he managed to croak out, wincing at the effort. "What... happened?"

Linda leaned forward, her hand instinctively reaching for his but stopping short, hovering uncertainly in the air between them. Drake's heart clenched at the hesitation, a painful reminder of the chasm that had grown between them since the accident.

"You collapsed at work," Linda said softly, her voice carrying that soothing tone she'd always used when Harrison was sick or scared. "They brought you here yesterday afternoon."

Yesterday afternoon? Drake's mind reeled, trying to piece together the fragments of his memory. The last thing he remembered was being in the firm, getting a pounding headache. Then... nothing.

"I don't... I can't remember," Drake mumbled, frustration coloring his words. He'd always prided himself on his sharp mind, his ability to recall every detail of a case. Now, he couldn't even remember how he'd ended up in this sterile hospital room.

Linda's expression softened, a ghost of a smile touching her lips. "It's okay, Drake. The doctors said some confusion is normal. You've been through a lot."

Drake closed his eyes, trying to shut out the harsh lights and the worried look on Linda's face. A lot. That was an understatement. He'd been through more than anyone could possibly understand, living two separate lives, grieving for a son in one world and a wife in another. The weight of it all threatened to crush him.

"I'm sorry," Drake whispered, the words feeling wholly inadequate. "I should have been more alert. If I hadn't been working so late those past nights..."

Linda's hand finally made contact with his, her touch warm and comforting despite the circumstances. "Don't," she said firmly. "We can't change the past, Drake. We can only move forward."

Drake squeezed her hand, drawing strength from her presence. Even after everything, Linda remained his anchor, keeping him tethered to reality when he felt like he might drift away entirely.

3 - 4

Linda's eyes softened as she reached out to grasp his hand, her touch warm and reassuring against his clammy skin. "You passed out, Drake," she said, her voice barely above a whisper. "Dr. Lee ran some tests and found something... unusual in your blood."

Drake's heart skipped a beat, his mind racing with possibilities. He frowned, trying to make sense of her words, the weight of uncertainty pressing down on him like a physical force. "Unusual? What do you mean?" he asked, his voice hoarse and tinged with apprehension.

Linda's gaze flickered away for a moment, as if she were struggling to find the right words. Drake could see the worry etched in the lines of her face, the way her brow furrowed slightly as she spoke. It was a look he had grown all too familiar with since the accident that had torn their family apart.

"I don't know exactly," Linda admitted, her grip on his hand tightening. "Dr. Lee said he's never seen anything like it before. He's running more tests to try and figure out what's going on."

Drake's mind whirled with possibilities, each more terrifying than the last. Was this somehow connected to his dual existence? To the other world where Linda was gone, and Harrison was still alive? The thought sent a shiver down his spine.

"I don't understand," Drake muttered, more to himself than to Linda. "How could there be something unusual in my blood? I feel fine... well, aside from passing out."

Linda's eyes met his, filled with a mixture of concern and determination. "We'll figure this out together, Drake. Whatever it is, we'll face it as a family. Just like we always have."

Her words, meant to comfort, only served to intensify the ache in Drake's chest. Family. The word held such different meanings in his fractured realities. In this world, their family was broken, missing the vital piece that was their son. In the other, it was Linda's absence that left a gaping hole in their lives.

As Drake opened his mouth to respond, a wave of dizziness washed over him, causing the room to spin. He closed his eyes, gripping Linda's hand tighter as he fought to regain his equilibrium. When he opened them again, for just a split second, he could have sworn he saw the other hospital room, the one where Harrison sat by his bedside instead of Linda.

The vision vanished as quickly as it had appeared, leaving Drake feeling disoriented and shaken. He knew he couldn't tell Linda about what he'd just experienced. How could he explain something he barely understood himself?

"Drake? Are you alright?" Linda's voice cut through his thoughts, laced with worry.

He forced a weak smile, trying to reassure her. "Yeah, just... a little dizzy. It's probably nothing."

But as he met Linda's concerned gaze, Drake couldn't shake the feeling that whatever was happening to him was far from nothing. It was something that threatened to unravel the very fabric of his existence, and he had no idea how to stop it.

5 - 6

As Drake struggled to regain his composure, the door swung open, revealing Dr. Lee's imposing figure. The physician's normally kind eyes were clouded with concern, his brow furrowed as he clutched a manila folder tightly to his chest. The air in the room seemed to thicken, charged with an unspoken tension that made Drake's skin prickle.

"Mr. Miller," Dr. Lee began, his voice low and measured, "I'm afraid I have some rather... unusual news." He paused, as if weighing his words carefully before continuing. "Your blood tests revealed something quite extraordinary. There are three separate DNA profiles present, one of which is highly radioactive."

Drake's mind reeled, his heart hammering against his ribcage as he tried to process the information. Three DNA profiles? Radioactive? The words echoed in his head; each repetition more surreal than the last. He glanced at Linda, whose face had drained of color, her grip on his hand tightening painfully.

"I... I don't understand," Drake stammered, his voice barely above a whisper. "How is that even possible?"

Dr. Lee's expression softened, a flicker of empathy crossing his features. "To be honest, Mr. Miller, I'm not entirely sure. In all my years of practice, I've never encountered anything like this."

Drake's thoughts raced, fragments of memories from both his realities colliding in a chaotic whirlwind. Could this be related to his dual existence? Was his body somehow manifesting the physical evidence of his fractured life?

"What does this mean for Drake?" Linda interjected, her voice trembling slightly. "Is he in danger?"

Dr. Lee hesitated, his fingers drumming lightly against the folder. "At this point, it's difficult to say. We'll need to run more tests to determine the full extent of the situation and its potential effects on Mr. Miller's health."

Drake closed his eyes, trying to steady his breathing. When he opened them again, he fixed Dr. Lee with a determined gaze. "Whatever it takes, Doctor. I need to know what's happening to me."

As the gravity of the situation settled over him, Drake couldn't help but wonder if this bizarre discovery might somehow be the key to unlocking the mystery of his dual existence – and perhaps, just perhaps, a way to reunite his fractured family once and for all.

7 - 8

Drake's mind reeled, his fingers digging into the starched hospital sheets as he struggled to process Dr. Lee's words. The sterile air of the room seemed to thicken, making it harder to breathe. He swallowed hard, his throat dry and constricted.

"What does this mean?" Drake asked, his voice barely above a whisper. The words hung in the air, heavy with the weight of their implications. His dark eyes, usually sharp and determined, now held a glimmer of fear as they searched Dr. Lee's face for answers.

Dr. Lee hesitated, his kind eyes clouding with concern. He adjusted his glasses, a nervous habit that betrayed his own unease. "It's difficult to say for certain," he began, choosing his words carefully. "But it appears as though you were exposed to a significant amount of radiation, as if you were near the epicenter of a nuclear explosion."

Drake's heart hammered against his ribcage, each beat echoing in his ears. Nuclear explosion? The absurdity of it all threatened to overwhelm him. He ran a hand through his disheveled black hair, trying to ground himself in the moment.

"That's... that's impossible," Drake muttered, more to himself than to Dr. Lee. "I would remember something like that, wouldn't I?" His mind raced, desperately trying to reconcile this information with his fractured memories.

Dr. Lee leaned forward; his voice soft but firm. "Mr. Miller, I understand this is a lot to take in. But I assure you, the test results are clear. Your body shows signs of extreme radiation exposure, unlike anything I've seen in my career."

Drake's gaze drifted to the window, watching as a gentle rain began to fall outside. Each droplet seemed to mirror the confusion and fear cascading through his mind. How could he have been exposed to such radiation without knowing? And what did it mean for his already complicated existence?

9 - 10

Drake's brown eyes, heavy with exhaustion and confusion, darted back to Dr. Lee. "I... I think I might know what happened," he said, his voice barely above a whisper. The weight of his dual existence pressed down on him, a secret he'd carried alone for so long. "There's something I haven't told you, something that might explain this."

Dr. Lee leaned in, his expression a mixture of concern and curiosity. "Go on, Mr. Miller. Anything you can tell us might help us understand your condition better."

Drake took a deep breath, his hands trembling slightly as he clasped them together. "This is going to sound crazy, but as you know I... I exist in two separate worlds. Two realities, running parallel to each other." He paused, searching Dr. Lee's face for any sign of disbelief or judgment. "In one world, I lost my wife. In the other, my son. And I... I think something happened to me in that other world. Something that caused this."

The room fell silent, save for the steady beep of the heart monitor. Drake's admission hung in the air, heavy and surreal. He could feel his heart racing, the truth of his fractured existence finally laid bare.

"I passed out because of it," Drake continued, his voice trembling with the weight of his confession. "One moment I was there, in that other world, and the next... I was here, collapsing on the floor of my office."

Dr. Lee's brow furrowed, his professional demeanor wavering for a moment as he processed Drake's words. "Mr. Miller, I... I'm not sure I understand. Two separate worlds? How is that possible?"

Drake let out a hollow laugh, the sound tinged with desperation. "I don't know, Doctor. I've been living this nightmare for months, and I still can't explain it. But I know it's real. As real as you and me sitting here right now."

11 - 12

Linda's grip tightened on Drake's hand, her slender fingers intertwining with his as her eyes searched his face, probing for any hint of deception. The warmth of her touch provided a stark contrast to the sterile chill of the hospital room. "Drake, I want to believe you," she said softly, her voice barely above a whisper. Her blue eyes, usually so full of light, now swam with a mixture of hope and trepidation. "If there's even a chance that Harrison is still alive..."

Drake's heart clenched at the mention of their son, a visceral pain that seemed to radiate through his entire being. The image of Harrison's mischievous grin and unruly curls flashed through his mind, as vivid and real as if the boy were standing right there in the room with them. The thought of Harrison still being out there, somewhere in that other reality, filled Drake with a desperate hope that threatened to overwhelm him.

"Linda," he began, his voice hoarse with emotion, "I know how this sounds. Hell, I can barely believe it myself." He paused, swallowing hard against the lump in his throat. "But I swear to you, on everything we've ever shared, that I'm telling you the truth. Our boy... he's alive. In that other world, he's alive and well, and I... I see him every day."

Linda's eyes widened, a glimmer of something – hope? fear? – flashing across her face. "You see him?" she breathed, her grip on Drake's hand tightening even further. "What's he like? Is he happy? Does he... does he ask about me?"

Drake closed his eyes, overwhelmed by the flood of memories and emotions. How could he possibly convey the reality of his experiences? The joy of hearing Harrison's laughter, mixed with the gut-wrenching knowledge that in this world, that laughter was silenced forever? He took a deep breath, steeling himself to meet Linda's gaze once more.

"He's beautiful, Linda," Drake said, his voice cracking. "So full of life and curiosity. He's grown into a remarkable young man, with your kindness and...and my stubbornness." A wry smile tugged at the corners of his mouth, despite the gravity of the situation. "And yes, he asks about you. All the time. He misses you terribly."

As the words left his mouth, Drake felt a surge of guilt. Was it cruel to give Linda this glimpse of a life she could never truly be part of? But as he looked into her eyes, he saw not anguish, but a fierce determination that took his breath away.

13 - 14

Drake leaned forward, his voice dropping to a low, urgent whisper. "We need to find out what's going on," he said, determination flashing in his eyes. The sterile hospital room seemed to fade away as he focused solely on Linda's face, searching for understanding. "We can't ignore this, Linda. Not when there's a chance that our son might still be alive."

His heart raced, the steady beep of the heart monitor echoing his rising excitement. The possibility of reuniting their fractured family, of bridging the gap between two realities, felt tantalizingly close. Drake's mind whirled with half-formed plans and desperate hopes, each thought tinged with the fear of disappointment.

Linda's expression shifted, her initial shock giving way to a steely resolve that Drake recognized all too well. It was the same look she'd worn when Harrison had been diagnosed with a rare illness as a toddler, the same unwavering determination that had seen them through countless sleepless nights and terrifying hospital visits.

"I'll do whatever it takes, Drake," she said, her voice strong despite the slight tremor in her hand as she squeezed his. "We'll get through this together."

Drake felt a lump form in his throat, overwhelmed by the depth of Linda's commitment. How many times had he taken her strength for granted in the past, prioritizing his career over their family? The guilt threatened to consume him, but he pushed it aside, focusing on the task at hand.

"It won't be easy," he warned, his voice rough with emotion. "We're dealing with something beyond our understanding. The radiation, the different realities... it's like something out of a science fiction novel."

Linda's lips quirked into a small, sad smile. "Our life hasn't exactly been normal for a while now, has it?" she said softly. "But if there's even the slightest chance of bringing Harrison back to us, I'm ready to face whatever comes our way."

Drake nodded, feeling a surge of love and gratitude for the remarkable woman beside him. "We'll need help," he mused, his mind already racing ahead. "Someone who can make sense of these test results, someone who might believe our story without thinking we're completely insane."

"What about Dr. Lee?" Linda suggested, her brow furrowed in thought. "He seemed... open to the possibility that something extraordinary was happening."

Drake considered this, weighing the risks and potential benefits. "It's a start," he agreed cautiously. "But we'll need to be careful. If word gets out about my condition, who knows what kind of attention it might attract."

As if on cue, a chill ran down Drake's spine, and he couldn't shake the feeling that they were being watched. He glanced towards the partially open door, half-expecting to see a shadowy figure lurking in the hallway. The paranoia that had become his constant companion in recent months surged to the forefront of his mind.

"Linda," he whispered, his grip on her hand tightening. "Promise me you'll be careful. If anything happens to me, if I... disappear, you need to keep searching. For Harrison. For the truth."

15 - 16

Dr. Lee cleared his throat, the sound cutting through the tense atmosphere like a scalpel. His kind eyes met Drake's; a flicker of concern evident beneath his professional demeanor. "I'll need to run some further tests to determine the extent of the radiation exposure and its potential effects on your health, Mr. Miller," he explained, his voice gentle yet tinged with urgency. "In the meantime, try to get some rest."

Drake nodded, his mind whirling with possibilities and fears. "How long will these tests take, Doctor?" he asked, unable to keep the tremor from his voice. The thought of waiting, of being trapped in this sterile room while answers eluded him, was almost unbearable.

Dr. Lee's expression softened. "I'll expedite the process as much as possible, Mr. Miller. But these are... unusual circumstances. We need to be thorough."

As the doctor turned to leave, Drake felt Linda's hand tighten around his own. He squeezed back, drawing strength from her unwavering presence. The door clicked shut, leaving them alone in the oppressive silence of the hospital room.

"Linda," Drake murmured, his voice barely above a whisper. "What if... what if this is the key to everything? To finding Harrison?" He couldn't bring himself to look at her, fear and hope warring within him.

Linda's free hand came to rest on his cheek, gently turning his face towards hers. "Then we'll face it together," she said, her eyes shining with determination. "Whatever comes next, Drake, I'm here. We'll find the truth."

Drake felt a surge of emotion, a complex mix of love, gratitude, and a desperate desire to protect her from the unknown dangers that lay ahead. Despite the uncertainty swirling around them, a tiny spark of hope ignited in his chest. Maybe, just maybe, they were on the brink of uncovering the truth behind his inexplicable condition.

"I don't know what I'd do without you," he admitted, his voice rough with emotion. "This whole situation... it's like something out of a nightmare. But having you here, it makes me believe we can actually get through this."

Linda smiled, a soft, sad expression that spoke volumes. "We've been through so much already, Drake. We'll face this too, one step at a time."

As they sat there, hand in hand, Drake couldn't shake the feeling that they were standing on the precipice of something monumental. The world as they knew it was about to change, and he could only hope they were ready for whatever lay ahead.

17 - 18

The sterile hospital room seemed to shrink around Drake as the hours crawled by, each tick of the clock on the wall a thunderous reminder of the uncertainty hanging over him. Linda's presence was a lifeline, her hand never leaving his as they waited in tense silence. Drake's mind raced, conjuring increasingly dire scenarios with each passing moment.

"What if they can't figure out what's wrong with me?" Drake murmured; his dark eyes fixed on the ceiling. "What if this... this radiation, or whatever it is, is changing me somehow?"

Linda's fingers tightened around his, her voice soft but steady. "We don't know anything yet, Drake. Let's not jump to conclusions. Dr. Lee is doing everything he can."

Drake turned to look at her, drinking in the sight of her gentle face, her blue eyes a calm sea in the storm of his thoughts. "How can you be so strong?" he asked, a hint of wonder in his voice.

She smiled, a small, sad quirk of her lips. "Because one of us has to be, and right now, it's my turn."

Just then, the door opened, and Dr. Lee stepped in, his face a mask of professional concern. Drake's heart leapt into his throat as he struggled to sit up, Linda's steadying hand on his shoulder.

"Mr. Miller, the results of the tests are... perplexing, to say the least," Dr. Lee began, his expression troubled. He paused, seemingly searching for the right words, and Drake felt the weight of dread settling in his stomach.

"Perplexing how?" Drake pressed, his voice hoarse with tension. "What did you find?"

Dr. Lee's brow furrowed as he continued, "The radiation levels in your blood are unlike anything I've ever seen before. It's as if..."

Drake leaned forward, his heart pounding so loudly he was sure the others could hear it. As Dr. Lee's words trailed off, a chill ran down Drake's spine. What could be so unprecedented that it left even a seasoned physician at a loss for words? The possibilities raced through his mind, each more terrifying than the last.

19 - 20

"As if what?" Drake pressed, his heart pounding in his chest. The sterile hospital room seemed to close in around him, the faint beeping of monitors a stark reminder of his precarious situation. He gripped the edge of the bed, knuckles turning white as he braced himself for Dr. Lee's response.

Dr. Lee hesitated, his kind eyes clouded with concern. He took a deep breath, as if steeling himself for the weight of his next words. "As if you were exposed to a highly concentrated source of radiation, far beyond anything that could occur naturally. It's... unprecedented."

The words hung in the air, heavy and ominous. Drake's mind reeled, struggling to process the implications. He glanced at Linda, her face a mirror of his own shock and confusion.

"How is that even possible?" Drake muttered, more to himself than anyone else. His thoughts raced back to his experiences in the other world, searching for any clue that might explain this bizarre revelation. "I don't understand. I haven't been near any nuclear facilities or... anything like that."

Dr. Lee's brow furrowed deeper; his professional demeanor tinged with a hint of frustration at the inexplicable nature of the situation. "That's what makes this so perplexing, Mr. Miller. The levels we're seeing... they're off the charts. It's as if you've been at ground zero of a nuclear explosion, yet you're sitting here, relatively unharmed."

Drake's gaze fell to his hands, half-expecting to see them glowing or somehow changed. They looked normal, belying the extraordinary situation unfolding around him. He couldn't shake the feeling that this was somehow connected to his dual existence, to the accident that had split his life in two.

"What does this mean for Drake?" Linda's voice cut through his thoughts, laced with fear and determination. "Is he in danger?"

As Dr. Lee began to respond, Drake found himself torn between the urge to confess everything about his fractured reality and the fear of being seen as completely insane. How could he explain something he barely understood himself? The weight of his secret pressed down on him, threatening to suffocate him with its implications.

21 - 22

Drake exchanged a worried glance with Linda, their eyes locking in a moment of shared trepidation. The gravity of the situation sank into his bones, chilling him to his core. Whatever had happened to him in the other world—that parallel existence he'd been living—had left an indelible mark on his body, one that defied all logical explanation.

"Linda," Drake whispered, his voice hoarse with emotion, "I... I think this is connected to what's been happening to me. The other world, the accidents, everything." He paused, swallowing hard against the lump in his throat.

Linda's fingers tightened around his, her blue eyes shimmering with unshed tears. "Drake, I want to believe that more than anything, but..." She trailed off, her gaze darting to Dr. Lee, who stood silently observing their exchange.

Drake's mind raced, memories of his time in the other world flashing through his consciousness. The bustling office of Bridgewater Police Department, the sense of purpose he'd found there—it all seemed so far removed from this sterile hospital room and the terrifying reality of his condition.

"What do we do now?" Linda asked, her voice tinged with fear. The question hung in the air, heavy with implications.

Drake closed his eyes, drawing a deep breath. When he opened them again, determination blazed in their depths. "We find answers," he said firmly. "We can't just sit here and wait for something to happen. If this radiation is connected to the other world, then that's where we need to start looking."

"Drake, you can't be serious," Linda protested, her brow furrowing with concern. "We don't even know if it's safe for you to—"

"I have to try," Drake interrupted, his voice softening as he met her gaze. "For Harrison. For us. I can't keep living this half-life, Linda. I need to know the truth, no matter how dangerous or impossible it might seem."

As the words left his mouth, Drake felt a strange sense of calm settle over him. For the first time since the accident that had torn his world apart, he felt a glimmer of hope—a chance to unravel the mystery that had consumed his existence and perhaps, just perhaps, find a way to bring his family back together.

23 - 24

Dr. Lee sighed heavily, running a hand through his salt-and-pepper hair, his kind eyes clouded with concern. "I'm afraid there's very little we can do at this point," he said, his voice soft but tinged with resignation. "We'll continue to monitor your condition closely and explore possible treatment options, but..." He paused, meeting Drake's gaze with unwavering honesty. "I won't sugarcoat it, Mr. Miller. This is uncharted territory."

Drake felt a knot form in his stomach, twisting and churning as the weight of Dr. Lee's words settled upon him. He swallowed hard, his throat suddenly dry. "Uncharted territory," he repeated, his voice barely above a whisper. "That's a polite way of saying you have no idea what's happening to me, isn't it?"

Dr. Lee nodded solemnly. "I've never seen anything like this before. The radiation levels in your blood, the multiple DNA profiles... it's beyond the scope of conventional medical science."

Linda's grip on Drake's hand tightened, her touch a lifeline in the storm of uncertainty. "But there must be something we can do," she insisted, her voice trembling with a mixture of fear and determination.

Drake closed his eyes, drawing a deep breath as he tried to center himself. When he opened them again, a fire of resolve burned in their depths. "We may not know what's happening," he said, his voice growing stronger with each word, "but I refuse to give up. For Harrison's sake, for Linda's sake... I'll find a way to unravel this mystery."

As he spoke, images flashed through Drake's mind: Harrison's soccer games, Linda's loving smile, the life they'd once shared. The road ahead would be fraught with uncertainty and danger, but he couldn't—wouldn't—let fear paralyze him.

"Dr. Lee," Drake said, sitting up straighter in the hospital bed, "I need to understand everything you've found. Every detail, no matter how small or seemingly insignificant. If we're going to navigate this uncharted territory, we need a map... even if we have to draw it ourselves."

Dr. Lee nodded, a hint of admiration flickering in his eyes. "Of course, Mr. Miller. I'll gather all the data we've collected and break it down for you. But I must caution you—the answers you seek may lead to even more questions."

"I'm prepared for that," Drake replied, his jaw set with determination. "Whatever it takes, I'll uncover the truth hidden within the shadows of my past. I owe it to my family... and to myself."

As the words left his mouth, Drake felt a strange sense of purpose wash over him. The fear and uncertainty were still there, coiled in his gut like a restless serpent, but alongside them burned a fierce determination. He would find a way to bridge the gap between his fractured realities, to bring his family back together, no matter the cost.

After the Diagnosis

Blue World – 2024

1 - 2

Drake Miller stumbled out of the hospital; his legs unsteady as he navigated the crowded sidewalk. Dr. Lee's words echoed in his mind, a cacophony of medical jargon and dire warnings that made his head spin. He caught a glimpse of Linda's retreating form, her shoulders hunched with worry and felt a pang of guilt twist in his gut.

"I have to fix this," he muttered, clenching his fists at his sides. "For Linda, for the kid... for myself."

The police station loomed before him, a stark concrete monolith that seemed to mock his desperation. Drake took a deep breath, steeling himself for what lay ahead. As he pushed through the heavy glass doors, the familiar scent of stale coffee and bureaucracy assaulted his nostrils.

Approaching the front desk, Drake cleared his throat. "Excuse me, I need to speak with Detective Keirstead. It's urgent."

The officer behind the desk, a paunchy man with thinning hair, frowned. "I'm sorry, sir, but there's no detective here by that name."

Drake's heart plummeted. "That's impossible. I just spoke with her the other day about..." He trailed off, realizing how insane he must sound.

"Are you sure?" he pressed, leaning forward. "Maybe she's new, or—"

"Sir, I've been at this desk for fifteen years," the officer said, his tone tinged with annoyance. "I know every detective in this precinct. There is no Keirstead."

Drake ran a hand through his disheveled hair, his mind racing. How could this be? Was he losing his grip on reality entirely? Before he could voice another question, a presence at his elbow made him turn.

A woman stood there; her piercing gaze locked onto his face. She exuded an aura of authority that made Drake straighten instinctively. Something about her seemed achingly familiar, yet he couldn't quite place it.

"Can I help you?" she asked, her voice crisp and professional.

Drake hesitated, suddenly unsure of himself. "I... I'm looking for information about a case. A hit and run, and... something more. I think they're connected."

The woman's eyebrow arched slightly. "And you are?"

"Drake Miller," he replied, extending his hand. "I'm a lawyer, but I'm here as a victim. And maybe... maybe something more."

As their hands met, Drake felt a jolt of recognition. This woman, whoever she was, held the key to unraveling the mystery that had consumed his life. He only hoped she would believe the impossible tale he had to tell.

3 - 4

The woman's firm handshake matched her commanding presence as she introduced herself, "I'm Detective Holly Sharp. You must be Mr. Miller. What can I do for you? I hope you've been recovering well since the accident."

Drake's eyes widened, a mixture of relief and confusion washing over him. He stammered, "Y-yes, thank you. I'm... I'm doing better." His gaze lingered on Detective Sharp's face, drinking in every detail. The resemblance was uncanny, and he found himself wondering if he had finally lost his grip on reality.

"Would you like to discuss this in my office?" Detective Sharp asked, her tone softening slightly as she noted Drake's evident distress.

Drake nodded, following her through the bustling precinct. His mind raced, trying to reconcile the familiar yet alien surroundings. As they entered her office, he couldn't help but marvel at how even the placement of her desk mirrored Keirstead's.

Once the door closed behind them, Drake took a deep breath. "Detective Sharp, I'm not sure where to begin. The accident... it's just the tip of the iceberg." He paused, running a hand through his disheveled hair. "There's a man, Gabriel. I believe he's connected not just to my accident, but to something much bigger, much darker."

Detective Sharp leaned forward, her piercing gaze fixed on Drake. "Start from the beginning, Mr. Miller. Tell me everything."

And so, Drake began his tale, his words tumbling out in a frantic cascade. He recounted the night of the accident, the mysterious figure on the road, the whispered words that still haunted his dreams. As he spoke, he watched Sharp's expression, searching for any sign of recognition or disbelief.

"I know it sounds insane," Drake admitted, his voice hoarse from the lengthy explanation. "But I swear to you, Detective, every word is true. Gabriel is out there, and I fear he won't stop until he's finished whatever he started that night."

5 - 6

Drake hesitated, his eyes scanning Detective Sharp's face, searching for any hint of familiarity beyond their brief encounter. The question burned on his tongue, and he couldn't resist asking, "Are you by chance formally known as Detective Keirstead?"

Sharp's eyebrows shot up, a flicker of surprise crossing her otherwise stoic features. She leaned back in her chair, the leather creaking softly as she folded her arms across her chest. "Keirstead?" she repeated, her voice tinged with curiosity. "Now that's a name I haven't heard in a while."

Drake's heart raced, hope surging through him. Could this be the connection he was looking for? He leaned forward, eager for her response.

Detective Sharp's piercing gaze softened slightly as she continued, "Wasn't a detective back when I went by my maiden name. I was just a rookie at the time." She paused, a ghost of a smile playing at the corners of her mouth. "But now I'm married to my spouse Rebekah Sharp. Been married six long years."

Drake's mind reeled with this information. The similarities were uncanny, yet the differences were equally striking. He found himself grappling with a strange mix of familiarity and disorientation.

"I see," Drake managed, trying to keep his voice steady. "It's just... you remind me of someone I used to know. The resemblance is remarkable."

Sharp nodded, her expression thoughtful. "Life has a way of taking unexpected turns, Mr. Miller. Sometimes we end up in places we never imagined." She leaned forward, her intense gaze locking with Drake's. "Now, about this Gabriel character you mentioned..."

7 - 8

Drake's mind raced, processing the implications of Detective Sharp's words. Some things were different in this world, yet others remained eerily similar. The fact that she was still a lesbian and with the same partner—albeit married in this reality—sent a chill down his spine. He cleared his throat, pushing aside his swirling thoughts to focus on the urgent matter at hand.

"Detective Sharp," he began, his voice low and urgent, "did you find out anything about the symbol found in the car or anything more about the Janitor Gabriel from Saint Montagues? Richard Vega was supposed to give you a call requesting further details. He may have forgotten after this past day."

Sharp's brow furrowed, her piercing gaze intensifying. "Symbol? Gabriel?" she repeated, her voice tinged with confusion and a hint of suspicion. "Mr. Miller, I'm afraid I don't have any information about a symbol, or a janitor named Gabriel. And I haven't received any calls from a Richard Vega."

Drake's heart sank, the weight of disappointment settling in his chest. He ran a hand through his hair, frustration mounting. "But surely there must be something," he pressed, leaning forward in his chair. "The accident, the strange occurrences—they're all connected, I'm sure of it."

Detective Sharp studied him for a long moment, her expression unreadable. "Mr. Miller," she said slowly, choosing her words carefully, "I understand you've been through a traumatic experience. But I need you to understand that we don't have any evidence linking your accident to a janitor or a mysterious symbol."

Drake's mind raced, desperately trying to find a way to make her understand. "But Gabriel," he insisted, his voice rising slightly, "he's out there, Detective. He's dangerous, and he's connected to all of this somehow. We need to find him before—"

"Before what, Mr. Miller?" Sharp interjected, her tone sharpening. "I'm sorry, but without concrete evidence or any leads to follow, there's not much we can do."

Drake slumped back in his chair, feeling defeated. How could he make her see the truth when he barely understood it himself? The image of Gabriel's disfigured face flashed in his mind, sending a shiver down his spine. He knew, with a certainty that defied explanation, that the man was out there, waiting, planning his next move.

"I know it sounds crazy," Drake said softly, meeting Sharp's gaze, "but I can't shake the feeling that something terrible is about to happen. And Gabriel is at the center of it all."

9 - 10

Detective Sharp's piercing gaze softened slightly as she observed Drake's distress. She leaned forward, her elbows resting on the desk, fingers steepled beneath her chin. "Listen, Mr. Miller," she began, her voice low and measured, "I can see this is weighing heavily on you. While I can't act on hunches alone, I'm not dismissing your concerns entirely."

Drake's heart quickened, a glimmer of hope breaking through his despair. He watched intently as Sharp's fingers danced across her laptop keyboard; her brow furrowed in concentration. The gentle hum of the computer filled the tense silence between them.

"Here, I want to show you something," Sharp announced, turning the laptop screen towards Drake. "Do you recognize this man?"

Drake leaned forward, his breath catching in his throat as he peered at the image on the screen. His mind raced, trying to reconcile the face before him with the fragmented memories swirling in his head. Was this the elusive Gabriel? Or another piece of the puzzle he couldn't quite place?

As he studied the image, Drake's inner turmoil intensified. Part of him longed to shout recognition, to finally have concrete evidence of Gabriel's existence. Yet another part hesitated, wary of jumping to conclusions in this world that seemed both familiar and alien.

"I..." Drake began, his voice trailing off as he struggled to form a coherent response. The weight of potential consequences pressed down on him, making each word feel like a monumental decision.

11 - 12

Drake's words caught in his throat as his eyes locked onto the figure in the CCTV footage. The man's face was a grotesque canvas of scars, twisted and mottled as if he'd been caught in an inferno. His gait was unmistakable - a pronounced limp that sent chills down Drake's spine. Recognition hit him like a freight train, memories of the accident surging back with vivid clarity.

"Oh God," Drake whispered, his voice barely audible as he gripped the edge of Sharp's desk. "That's him. That's Gabriel."

Sharp leaned in, her eyes darting between Drake and the screen. "You're certain?"

Drake nodded, his breath coming in short, sharp bursts. "I remember now. He... he came down over the embankment after the crash. I was trapped, disoriented, but I saw him clear as day."

As he spoke, the scene unfolded in his mind's eye - the crumpled metal, the acrid smell of smoke, and Gabriel's face looming in the shattered window.

"He was wearing this... this white robe. Like some kind of ceremonial garb," Drake continued, his voice gaining strength as the memories solidified. "And he said something. Something I couldn't understand at the time, but now..."

Drake trailed off, his brow furrowing as he struggled to recall the exact words. Sharp leaned closer, her pen poised over her notepad. "What did he say, Drake?"

"He whispered," Drake said, his eyes unfocused as he relived the moment. "'Remember my face, daddy.' That's what he said. 'Remember my face, daddy.'"

The words hung in the air between them, heavy with implication. Drake's mind raced, trying to make sense of it all. Why would Gabriel call him 'daddy'? What did it mean? The questions swirled in his head, threatening to overwhelm him.

"I don't understand," he murmured, more to himself than to Sharp. "None of this makes any sense."

13 - 14

Detective Sharp's eyes narrowed, her pen tapping rhythmically against her notepad. "Why would he call you daddy? You sure that's what he said?"

Drake ran a hand through his disheveled hair, his mind a tumultuous sea of confusion and half-formed theories. "Yes, I'm positive," he replied, his voice hoarse with the weight of certainty. "And no, I'm not sure why. It's... it's just another piece of this nightmarish puzzle."

He paused, weighing his next words carefully. The memory of another world, another life, pressed against the edges of his consciousness. Drake leaned forward, his elbows on his knees, and fixed Sharp with an intense gaze. "This is going to sound odd, but did you by chance find a dead taxicab driver in the city, say in an alleyway?"

The question hung in the air, pregnant with implications Drake couldn't fully articulate. He watched Sharp's face, searching for any flicker of recognition, any sign that the pieces might be falling into place. As he waited for her response, Drake's mind raced through the possibilities, each more unsettling than the last.

What if Gabriel was somehow connected to both worlds? What if the taxi driver's death was the key to unraveling this whole mystery? The questions piled up, threatening to suffocate him with their weight. Drake's hands clenched involuntarily; his knuckles white with tension. He needed answers, and he needed them now.

15 - 16

Detective Sharp's eyes narrowed, a flicker of surprise crossing her face before her professional mask slipped back into place. "There was a dead taxi driver found recently," she confirmed, her voice grim as she leaned back in her chair. "Behind a bowling alley downtown. But how do you know all this?"

The tension in the room thickened, pressing against Drake's chest like a physical weight. He could feel Sharp's piercing gaze boring into him, her suspicion palpable in the air between them. His mind raced, fragments of memories from both realities colliding in a chaotic dance. How could he possibly explain without sounding completely insane?

Drake hesitated, his fingers drumming an erratic rhythm on the arm of his chair. The truth hovered on the tip of his tongue, threatening to spill out in a torrent of impossible revelations. He drew in a deep breath, the musty scent of old case files and stale coffee filling his nostrils.

"I..." he began, then faltered. The words felt heavy, laden with consequences he couldn't fully fathom. Drake's gaze darted around the cluttered office, taking in the peeling paint on the walls, the overflowing inbox on Sharp's desk, anything to avoid meeting her scrutinizing stare.

Finally, he spoke, his voice steady despite the turmoil churning within him. "Detective Sharp, what I'm about to tell you is going to sound completely unbelievable. But I need you to hear me out." He leaned forward, his elbows on his knees, hands clasped tightly together. "I'm not just the man you think I am. There's more to this story – to my story – than either of us fully understands."

17 - 18

Drake's heart pounded in his chest as he continued, his voice barely above a whisper, "This is going to sound strange, but that car that caused my accident belonged to that dead cab driver. My son's killer – this Gabriel Angel person – and the cab driver's killer are one and the same."

Detective Sharp's eyebrows shot up, her piercing gaze intensifying as she processed his words. The office seemed to shrink around them, the tension palpable in the air. Drake could almost hear the gears turning in her mind, piecing together the fragments of information he'd just dropped in her lap.

After a moment that felt like an eternity, Sharp leaned back in her chair, the leather creaking under her weight. Her fingers drummed a staccato rhythm on the desk, betraying her agitation. "How do you know all this?" she demanded, her voice a mixture of confusion and irritation. The unspoken question hung between them: How had a lawyer somehow solved her case before her?

Drake's mind raced, searching for an explanation that wouldn't sound completely insane. He could feel Sharp's eyes boring into him, dissecting his every movement, every micro-expression. The weight of his knowledge – of the impossible truth – pressed down on him like a physical force.

"I..." he started, then faltered, his throat constricting. How could he possibly explain the inexplicable? The memory of Gabriel's scarred face flashed before his eyes, those haunting words echoing in his mind: "Remember my face, daddy." A chill ran down his spine as he realized the full implications of what he was about to reveal.

19 - 20

Drake took a deep breath, steeling himself for the revelation he was about to make. His eyes locked onto Sharp's, searching for any hint of the partner he knew in another life. "I know because... because I'm not just a lawyer," he began, his words hesitant yet resolute. The fluorescent lights buzzed overhead, casting harsh shadows across the cramped office. "I'm a detective. In another world. And you, Detective Sharp, are my partner."

The words hung in the air, heavy with implications. Sharp's eyes widened; disbelief etched across her features. For a moment, the only sound was the muffled noise of the precinct beyond the office door.

"You're what?" Sharp finally managed, her voice a mixture of incredulity and barely contained anger. "If this is some kind of joke, Miller, I swear-"

"It's not a joke," Drake interrupted, leaning forward in his chair. His heart pounded in his chest, but he pressed on. "I know it sounds impossible, but I can prove it to you." He paused, gathering his thoughts before continuing. "The case with the Bridgewater Strangler – you never told anyone how close you came to catching him that night by the docks. Or the time you confided in me about your father's struggle with alcoholism, and how it drove you to become a cop."

Sharp's face paled, her lips parting in shock. Drake could see the conflict in her eyes – the desire to dismiss his words warring with the undeniable truth of what he was saying.

"How could you possibly..." she whispered, her tough exterior cracking for just a moment.

Drake's mind raced, searching for more details that would convince her. "The scar on your left shoulder – you got it during a struggle with the Bridgewater strangler, not from a car accident like you told everyone else. And that night after we closed the Hartley case, you confessed how terrified you were of failing, of not living up to your own expectations."

Sharp's hand unconsciously moved to her shoulder, her fingers tracing the outline of the scar hidden beneath her blazer. Her eyes narrowed, a mix of suspicion and growing recognition flickering across her face.

"This is insane," she muttered, more to herself than to Drake. "Completely insane."

Drake leaned back, his voice softening. "I know how it sounds, believe me. I've been living this nightmare, trying to make sense of it all. But in that other world, we've been partners for months. We've faced down killers, corruption, our own demons – together."

Sharp's gaze locked onto his, searching for any sign of deception. "And in this... other world," she said slowly, the words sounding foreign on her tongue, "what happened to Gabriel?"

Drake's stomach clenched at the mention of Gabriel's name. "That's just it," he replied, frustration seeping into his voice. "He doesn't exist there. At least, not that we've ever encountered. But here, he's the key to everything – my accident, the cab driver, maybe even the reason I'm caught between these two realities."

Sharp exhaled heavily, running a hand through her short hair. "This is... a lot to process, Miller. Even if I believed you – and I'm not saying I do – what does it mean for our investigation?"

Drake leaned forward; his eyes intense. "It means we have an advantage. My knowledge from that world, combined with your skills here – we might be able to piece together what Gabriel's after and stop him before he strikes again."

As he spoke, Drake could see the wheels turning in Sharp's mind. Her skepticism was still evident, but there was something else there now – a spark of curiosity, maybe even hope.

"Alright," she said finally, her voice regaining some of its usual steel. "Let's say, for argument's sake, that I believe this crazy story. Where do we start?"

21 - 22

Sharp's eyes narrowed, a flicker of recognition crossing her face. "You know I almost had him. The one that got away. Shot him in the knee. But somehow, he just got away on me." She paused, her voice dropping to barely above a whisper. "I don't know how you know all this, but if what you're saying is true, then... then we need to find Gabriel before it's too late."

Drake's heart raced, a mixture of vindication and urgency coursing through him. "Tell me everything about that encounter," he pressed, leaning forward in his chair. "Every detail could be crucial."

Sharp's gaze grew distant, her fingers absently tracing the edge of her desk. "It was a cold night, about three years ago. We'd been tracking a series of ritualistic murders, and finally got a lead on the suspect." She swallowed hard, the memory clearly painful. "I cornered him in an alley. He was dressed all in white, like some kind of twisted angel. I ordered him to freeze, but he lunged at me. I fired, hit him square in the knee. But then..."

Drake finished her sentence, his voice hoarse. "He disappeared."

Sharp nodded, her eyes refocusing on Drake with newfound intensity. "How could you possibly know that?"

"Because in my world, you told me about this case. It's haunted you ever since," Drake explained, his mind racing. "Sharp, we need to go through every piece of evidence from that night. There might be something we missed, something that connects to what's happening now."

Without another word, Sharp stood and strode to a file cabinet, pulling out a thick folder. "Let's get to work then," she said, her professional demeanor returning despite the lingering disbelief in her eyes.

As they poured over case files and witness statements, Drake couldn't shake the feeling that they were running out of time. Each photograph, each report, seemed to taunt him with its inadequacy. His fingers trembled slightly as he flipped through pages, his exhaustion warring with the adrenaline coursing through his veins.

"What are we missing?" he muttered, more to himself than to Sharp. "There has to be a connection, something we're not seeing."

Sharp looked up from her stack of papers, her brow furrowed. "Miller, I've been meaning to ask. In this... other world of yours, are we... close?"

The question caught Drake off guard, pulling him momentarily from his frantic search. He met Sharp's gaze, seeing a vulnerability there he'd rarely witnessed in either version of his partner. "We're... complicated," he admitted. "Partners, friends. But always there for each other, no matter what."

A ghost of a smile played at Sharp's lips. "Sounds about right," she murmured, before turning back to the evidence with renewed determination.

As the hours ticked by, Drake felt the weight of their mission pressing down on him. Every dead end, every inconclusive lead, seemed to whisper of Gabriel's growing threat. Yet he pushed on, driven by the knowledge that somewhere in this maze of information lay the key to unraveling the mystery – and perhaps, to finding his way home.

23 - 24

Drake's eyes burned as he stared at the city map pinned to the wall, red strings crisscrossing between potential sightings of Gabriel. The pattern seemed random, chaotic, yet he couldn't shake the feeling that there was a method to the madness.

"He's playing with us," Drake growled, his frustration bubbling to the surface. "Every move calculated; every step planned. But why? What's his endgame?"

Sharp approached, coffee in hand. "Here," she offered, her voice tinged with concern. "You look like you need this more than I do."

Drake accepted the mug gratefully, the warmth seeping into his trembling hands. "Thanks," he murmured, taking a sip. "I just can't shake this feeling that we're missing something obvious."

As if on cue, Sharp's phone buzzed. Her face paled as she read the message. "Another sighting," she announced grimly. "Downtown, near the old theater district. Witness claims they saw a man matching Gabriel's description entering an abandoned building."

Drake's heart raced. "We need to go. Now."

As they rushed to the car, Drake's mind whirled with possibilities. Was this another of Gabriel's tricks, or had they finally caught a break? The streets blurred past as Sharp navigated through traffic, the city seeming to hold its breath in anticipation.

"What if it's a trap?" Drake voiced his concern, his hand instinctively reaching for a weapon that wasn't there in this reality.

Sharp's grip tightened on the steering wheel. "Then we spring it," she replied, her jaw set with determination. "It's time we turned the tables on this bastard."

As they neared their destination, Drake couldn't help but feel a sense of dread settling in his stomach. Gabriel's words echoed in his mind: "Remember my face, daddy." What did it mean? And how was it connected to the life he'd left behind?

The abandoned theater loomed before them, its once-grand facade now a crumbling reminder of faded glory. Drake and Sharp exchanged a look, years of partnership – across realities – conveying volumes without a word.

"Ready?" Sharp asked, her hand on the door handle.

Drake nodded, steeling himself for whatever lay ahead. "Let's end this," he said, his voice low and determined. As they stepped out into the night, Drake couldn't shake the feeling that whatever awaited them inside would change everything.

25 - 26

Drake's heart pounded in his chest as they entered the dilapidated theater, the musty air thick with decades of neglect. Shadows danced across peeling wallpaper, cast by the beam of Sharp's flashlight. Every creak of the floorboards sent a jolt through Drake's nerves, his mind racing with possibilities.

"I can't shake this feeling," Drake whispered, his voice barely audible. "It's like Gabriel's always watching, always one step ahead."

Sharp's eyes narrowed as she swept her light across the lobby. "Maybe that's exactly what he wants you to think, Miller. Don't let him get in your head."

But it was too late. As they moved deeper into the theater, Drake's thoughts spiraled. The image of Gabriel's scarred face, illuminated in the car's headlights that fateful night, flickered behind his eyelids with each blink. Those piercing eyes, filled with an unsettling mix of pain and purpose, seemed to follow him through the darkness.

"What if we're missing something obvious?" Drake mused, running a hand through his disheveled hair. "Gabriel's motives, they don't add up. Why me? Why my family?"

Sharp paused, turning to face him. "Look, Drake," she said, her tone softening slightly. "I may not understand all this parallel world stuff, but I know one thing. We're damn good detectives, in any reality. Trust your instincts."

Drake nodded, grateful for her steadying presence. As they approached the main auditorium, a flicker of movement caught his eye. He held up a hand, signaling Sharp to stop. The air grew heavy with anticipation as they both strained to listen.

"I know you're here," a familiar voice called out, sending chills down Drake's spine. Gabriel's words seemed to come from everywhere and nowhere at once. "Have you figured it out yet, Drake? Do you remember?"

Drake's mind raced, fragments of memories and clues swirling together. There was something there, just beyond his grasp. A connection he was missing. As he struggled to piece it together, doubt began to gnaw at the edges of his resolve. What if he was wrong? What if he couldn't save them?

"No," Drake muttered, clenching his fists. "I won't let you win, Gabriel. Whatever game you're playing, it ends now."

With a shared nod of determination, Drake and Sharp pushed open the auditorium doors, ready to face whatever lay beyond. The faint glimmer of hope in Drake's chest burned brighter, fueled by his refusal to give up. As they stepped into the unknown, he silently vowed to unravel the truth, no matter the cost.

Shadows of Uncertainty

Blue World – 2024

1 - 2

The shadows dance on the walls of my dimly lit apartment, casting eerie patterns that seem to mock my predicament. I slump in my threadbare armchair, the weight of Dr. Lee's words pressing down on me like an invisible force. My hands tremble as I replay his gentle, empathetic voice in my mind:

"I'm afraid the blood test results are... concerning. There are anomalies we can't explain."

I clench my fists, nails digging into my palms. "Damn it," I mutter, my voice barely above a whisper. "How could I have been so careless?"

The room feels suffocating, the air thick with tension and unspoken fears. I force myself to take deep breaths, trying to calm the racing thoughts that threaten to overwhelm me. But it's futile. The gravity of the situation crashes over me in waves, each realization more terrifying than the last.

Dr. Lee's kind eyes and soothing tone flash through my mind again. I can almost hear him saying, "Drake, remember, knowledge is power. We can work through this together." As I overheard standing outside the hospital room door.

But can they? The doubt gnaws at me, a relentless predator feasting on my vulnerabilities. I rise from the chair, pacing the small room like a caged animal. My footsteps echo in the silence, a rhythmic reminder of my isolation.

"I should have been more careful," I berate myself aloud, running a hand through my disheveled hair. "I should have known better than to let my guard down, even for a moment."

The gravity of my mistake threatens to crush me. I pause at the window, staring out at the city lights that seem so distant, so disconnected from the turmoil raging within me. My reflection in the glass looks haunted, a shadow of the man I once was.

"What now?" I whisper to my ghostly image. "How do I fix this?"

But the silence offers no answers, only the oppressive weight of uncertainty and fear. I turn away from the window, my gaze falling on the pile of medical documents scattered across my desk. Each page represents a piece of the puzzle, a fragment of the truth I've worked so hard to conceal.

I approach the desk slowly, my hand hovering over the papers. "I won't let this be the end," I vow, my voice gaining strength. "I've come too far, sacrificed too much."

With renewed determination, I begin to sift through the documents, searching for any clue, any piece of information that might help me regain control of the situation. As I work, Dr. Lee's words echo in my mind once more, a beacon of hope in the darkness:

"Remember, Drake, you're not alone in this. We'll find a way forward, together."

I cling to that promise, desperate for any shred of comfort in the storm that rages around me. But deep down, I know the truth: I am alone in this fight, and the battle has only just begun.

3 - 4

I pace the room, my thoughts swirling like a maelstrom. Drake's face flashes in my mind, his determined eyes boring into me. "Damn it," I mutter, running a hand through my hair. "How much does he really know?"

The question hangs in the air, unanswered and menacing. I turn to the window, watching my reflection in the darkened glass. "He knows about the blood," I say to my mirror image, "but does he understand what it means?"

My fingers trace the outline of my veins, feeling the power pulsing beneath my skin. The radioactive blood, my greatest strength and most dangerous secret. I close my eyes, remembering the moment I first discovered its potential.

"He can't possibly comprehend," I whisper, trying to convince myself. "The abilities it grants, the things I can do…"

But even as I speak the words, doubt gnaws at me. Drake Miller is no ordinary man. I've seen his resourcefulness, his relentless pursuit of the truth. He's like a bloodhound, never losing the scent once he's caught it.

I turn back to the room, my gaze falling on a framed photograph. It's Drake, from a newspaper clipping – the day he won a high-profile case. His eyes gleam with triumph, a hint of the ruthlessness that made him such a formidable lawyer.

"You're different now, aren't you?" I muse aloud, picking up the frame. "The accident changed you, but that drive… that's still there."

I set the photo down, a chill running through me. "And now you're coming for me."

The realization hits me like a physical blow. Drake isn't just a nuisance anymore; he's a genuine threat. With his knowledge of the blood, he could unravel everything I've worked for.

"I underestimated you once," I say, my voice barely above a whisper. "I won't make that mistake again."

As I stand there, surrounded by the shadows of my sanctuary, I feel the weight of my choices bearing down on me. The path ahead is treacherous, fraught with danger and uncertainty. But I've come too far to turn back now.

"So be it, Drake," I declare to the empty room. "If it's a battle of wits you want, then that's what you'll get. May the best man win."

5 - 6

A slow smile spreads across my face, the thrill of the challenge sending a surge of adrenaline through my veins. I pace the room, my mind racing with possibilities.

"You think you've got me cornered, don't you, Drake?" I mutter, running a hand through my hair. "But you have no idea what you're up against."

I stop at the window, peering out into the darkness. The city lights flicker in the distance, a stark reminder of the world beyond these walls – a world that Drake is desperately trying to protect.

"It's almost… exciting," I admit to myself, surprised by the rush of anticipation I feel. "A worthy opponent at last."

The phone on my desk buzzes, startling me from my reverie. I snatch it up, my heart racing as I see the caller ID.

"Lucian," I answer, my voice cool and controlled. "What news?"

"Gabriel," his voice crackles through the speaker, tense and urgent. "We've got a problem. Drake's been asking questions – dangerous questions."

I grip the phone tighter, my knuckles turning white. "What kind of questions?"

"About the blood, about its properties," he hesitates, then adds, "About you."

I close my eyes, taking a deep breath. "And what does he know?"

"Nothing concrete, but…" Lucian pauses, and I can almost see him wringing his hands. "He's persistent, Gabriel. And smart. He's piecing things together faster than we anticipated."

"I see," I reply, my mind already formulating plans and countermoves. "Thank you for the warning, master. I'll handle it from here."

As I end the call, I can't help but feel a mix of dread and exhilaration. Drake is proving to be even more resourceful than I'd imagined, pushing me to the limits of my cunning.

"Alright, Drake," I say to the empty room, a fierce determination settling over me. "You want to play? Let's play. But remember, in this game, there are no second chances."

I move to my desk, pulling out a locked drawer. Inside lies a small vial of glowing, radioactive blood – my trump card. As I hold it up to the light, I can't help but wonder: how far am I willing to go to keep my secrets? And more importantly, how far is Drake willing to go to uncover them?

7 - 8

I set the vial down, its eerie glow casting shadows across my face. My fingers trace the cool glass as I contemplate my next move. "Patience," I whisper to myself, "is the key to victory."

The silence of the room is broken by the soft ticking of a clock, each second a reminder of the precious time slipping away. I lean back in my chair, eyes fixed on the ceiling, mind racing with possibilities.

"Drake Miller," I muse aloud, my voice barely audible. "You think you've got me figured out, don't you? But you have no idea what you're truly up against."

I stand abruptly, pacing the room with measured steps. The floorboards creak beneath my feet, a rhythmic accompaniment to my turbulent thoughts.

"I can't rush this," I tell myself, running a hand through my hair. "One wrong move and it's all over. But I can't sit idle either."

I pause at the window, peering out into the night. The city lights flicker in the distance, a stark reminder of the world beyond these walls – a world that Drake threatens to upend with his relentless pursuit.

"What's your next move, Drake?" I ask the darkness. "What will you sacrifice to uncover the truth?"

The urgency of the situation weighs heavily on me, spurring me into action. I return to my desk, pulling out a notepad and pen. "Time to get to work," I mutter, jotting down ideas and strategies. "I won't let you catch me off guard again, Drake. This time, I'll be the one calling the shots."

As I write, a plan begins to take shape – a dangerous gambit that could either secure my victory or lead to my downfall. But in this high-stakes game we're playing, there's no room for half-measures.

"Ready or not, Drake," I say, a grim smile playing on my lips. "Here we come."

9 - 10

As I rise to my feet, a sudden wave of unease washes over me. The shadows in the room seem to deepen, closing in around me like hungry predators. I grip the edge of the desk, my knuckles turning white.

"What if I'm wrong about Drake?" I whisper to myself, my voice barely audible. "What if he's already ten steps ahead?"

The thought sends a chill down my spine, and I can't shake the image of Drake's tired, determined eyes. Those eyes that have seen two worlds, two realities. What secrets do they hold?

"No," I mutter, shaking my head vigorously. "I can't afford to second-guess myself now."

I pace the room, my footsteps echoing in the silence. "Focus, Gabriel," I command myself. "Drake is resourceful, but he's also vulnerable. Use that."

My mind races, formulating plans and discarding them just as quickly. I need something foolproof, something that will neutralize Drake without leaving any loose ends.

"If he knows about the blood," I reason aloud, "then he's already a threat. And threats need to be eliminated."

The word 'eliminated' hangs in the air, heavy with implications. I pause, considering the weight of what I'm contemplating. Drake Miller, once a ruthless lawyer, now a man torn between two realities. A man with a family he's desperate to save.

"It's him or me," I say, trying to convince myself. "And I've come too far to let him ruin everything now."

I turn to the window, staring out at the city lights. Somewhere out there, Drake is plotting his next move. But this time, I'll be ready. This time, I'll strike first.

"I'm sorry, Drake," I whisper to the night. "But in this game, there can only be one winner."

11 - 12

As I slip out into the night, the crisp autumn air of Bridgewater bites at my skin, carrying the faint scent of pumpkin spice from B&J Bistro. The weight of my decision presses down on me, each step feeling like I'm wading through molasses.

"It's necessary," I mutter to myself, my breath visible in the cold air. "For the greater good."

But even as I try to justify my actions, Linda's warm smile flashes through my mind, followed by Harrison's mischievous grin. Drake's family - the ones he's fighting so desperately to protect. My chest tightens.

I pause under a streetlight, its golden glow illuminating the mums in a nearby planter. "What am I becoming?" I whisper, running a hand through my hair.

A couple stumbles out of the Bulldog Bar and Grill, their laughter piercing the quiet night. I shrink back into the shadows, my heart racing.

"You're doing what needs to be done," I remind myself sternly. "Drake would do the same if he were in your shoes."

But would he? The Drake I've come to know, the one torn between two realities, seems a far cry from the ruthless lawyer he once was.

I continue walking, my footsteps echoing off the storefronts of Main Street. "It doesn't matter," I say aloud, my voice harsh in the stillness. "I've come too far to turn back now."

As I reach the edge of town, I turn back for one last look. The stained-glass windows of Bridgewater Baptist Church gleam softly in the moonlight, a silent witness to my internal struggle.

"I'm sorry," I whisper to the night, to Drake, to his family. "But this is the only way."

With a deep breath, I steel myself for what's to come. The game is far from over, and I intend to win - no matter the cost.

Green Dragon Symbol

Blue World – 2024

1 - 2

Linda Miller's heels clicked against the hardwood floor as she entered the foyer, her mind still swirling with the day's events at the hospital. The setting sun cast long shadows through the windows, painting the entrance in a warm, amber glow. As she shrugged off her coat, her gaze fell upon a small, cream-colored envelope resting on the hallway table.

"That's odd," she murmured, her brow furrowing as she approached the table. "I don't remember seeing this this morning."

Her fingers brushed against the smooth paper, tracing the elegant cursive of her name on the front. A familiar scent wafted up from the envelope – a hint of Harrison's favorite cologne. Her heart clenched at the memory of her son's infectious laughter echoing through these very halls.

Linda picked up the envelope, turning it over in her hands. The back was unmarked, sealed with a simple adhesive strip. No return address, no postmark. Just her name, written in an unfamiliar hand.

"Drake?" she called out, her voice wavering slightly. "Did you leave this for me?"

Silence answered her query, the house remaining still and empty. Of course, she thought, Drake wouldn't be home for hours yet. Linda's fingers itched to tear open the envelope, but a nagging doubt held her back.

"Get a grip, Linda," she chastised herself, running a hand through her wavy blonde hair. "It's just a letter. Nothing to be afraid of."

Yet as she stood there, envelope in hand, Linda couldn't shake the feeling that this innocuous piece of paper held something that would irrevocably change her life. The weight of recent events – Harrison's death, Drake's increasingly erratic behavior – pressed down on her shoulders like a physical force.

"Whatever it is," she whispered, her blue eyes fixed on her name written in that elegant script, "we'll face it together. As a family."

With a deep breath, Linda squared her shoulders and made her way towards the kitchen, the envelope clutched tightly in her hand. Whatever news it held, good or ill, she would meet it head-on. It was what she had always done, what she would always do – for Drake, for Harrison, for the family she loved more than life itself.

3 - 4

Linda's trembling fingers tore open the envelope, her heart pounding so loudly she could hear it in her ears. As she unfolded the letter, her eyes widened, breath catching in her throat.

"Oh my God," she whispered, her gaze fixed on the intricate drawing at the bottom of the page. "It can't be."

But there it was, unmistakable – a green dragon intertwined with a scarred tree. The symbol of the Green Knight, Sir Lancelot. Harrison's creation.

Linda's mind raced. "How is this possible? Who could have...?" Her words trailed off as she scanned the elegant script above the symbol, searching for answers.

Fear and confusion swirled within her as she clutched the letter tightly, her feet carrying her towards Harrison's room almost of their own accord. She paused at the door, her hand hovering over the knob.

"Harrison?" she called out, a flicker of hope igniting in her chest despite knowing the impossibility of a response.

Silence greeted her, as it had for months now. Linda pushed open the door, stepping into the room bathed in the soft, golden glow of evening light. The familiar space, unchanged since that fateful day, seemed to hold its breath.

"What does this mean?" Linda murmured, her eyes sweeping the room as if searching for clues. "Is this... is this a message from you, sweetheart?"

She sank onto the edge of Harrison's bed, the letter trembling in her hands. "Whatever this is, wherever you are, I promise we'll find you," Linda vowed, her voice thick with emotion. "We won't give up, Harrison. Not ever."

5 - 6

Linda's gaze drifted across the room, taking in the familiar tapestry of Harrison's imagination. Posters of mythical creatures and fantastical landscapes adorned the walls, interspersed with Harrison's own sketches – each one a window into the vibrant world he'd created. Her eyes settled on his desk, cluttered with notebooks and loose papers, the organized chaos of a mind constantly in motion.

"Oh, Harrison," Linda whispered, her voice catching as she rose and approached the desk. "Your stories, your drawings... they're everywhere, aren't they?"

Her fingers trailed over the notebooks, each one filled with Harrison's neat handwriting and intricate illustrations. She paused, her attention caught by a particular journal bound in deep green leather. With trembling hands, she picked it up, recognizing it as the one Harrison had been most secretive about in recent months.

"What were you working on, my love?" Linda murmured, opening the journal. Her breath caught as she beheld page after page of exquisitely detailed drawings – dragons with scales that seemed to shimmer on the paper, knights in gleaming armor, and landscapes that stretched beyond the confines of the page.

As she leafed through, tears welled in her eyes. "It's all here," she said softly, her voice filled with wonder and heartache. "Your whole world, Harrison. It's... it's beautiful."

Her fingers traced a particularly intricate drawing of a knight – the Green Knight, she realized – standing before a gnarled tree. The same symbol from the letter was etched into the tree's bark.

"What were you trying to tell us?" Linda asked, her words barely above a whisper. "What secrets did you discover?"

The weight of Harrison's absence pressed down on her, threatening to overwhelm. Linda clutched the journal to her chest, her tears falling freely now. "I miss you so much, sweetheart," she choked out. "Every day, every moment. Your imagination, your laughter, your... your everything."

She sank back onto the bed, still holding the journal close. "We'll figure this out, Harrison," Linda promised, her voice growing stronger despite her tears. "Whatever this means, whatever's happened... we'll bring you home. I swear it."

As the last light of day faded, Linda remained there, surrounded by the echoes of her son's creativity, clinging to the tangible pieces of him left behind – and to the hope that somewhere, somehow, Harrison was reaching out to them through the very world he'd created.

7 - 8

The front door creaked open, followed by the thud of Drake's briefcase hitting the floor. Linda's heart clenched, knowing the moment of revelation had arrived. She stood in the hallway, the letter clutched in her trembling hand, as Drake's footsteps drew nearer.

"Linda?" Drake called out; his voice tinged with concern. "Is everything alright?"

She stepped into view, her blue eyes meeting his tired brown ones. "Drake," Linda began, her voice barely above a whisper, "we need to talk."

Drake's brow furrowed, the lines of worry etching deeper into his face. "What's wrong?" he asked, closing the distance between them.

Linda held out the letter, her hand shaking. "This... this came today," she explained, her voice quavering. "It's about Harrison."

Drake's eyes widened, a mix of hope and fear flashing across his features. He reached for the letter, his fingers brushing against Linda's as he took it. "What does it say?" he asked, his voice hoarse with emotion.

Linda watched as Drake unfolded the paper, his eyes scanning the contents. She could see the moment realization hit him – his body tensed, his breath catching in his throat.

"The Green Dragon," Drake murmured, his voice filled with disbelief. "But how... how is this possible?"

Linda stepped closer, placing a comforting hand on Drake's arm. "I don't know," she admitted, her voice trembling. "But there's more. I found one of Harrison's journals today, and it's filled with drawings – drawings of knights and dragons, and that same symbol."

Drake looked up from the letter, his eyes meeting Linda's. She could see the turmoil swirling within them, a mirror of her own conflicted emotions. "What does this mean?" he asked, his voice barely above a whisper.

Linda took a deep breath, steeling herself. "I think... I think Harrison might be trying to reach us," she said, her voice gaining strength. "Through his stories, through this world he created. I don't understand how, but I feel it in my heart, Drake. Our son is out there, and he needs us."

Drake's hand found hers, squeezing it tightly. "We'll figure this out," he promised, his voice thick with determination. "Whatever it takes, we'll bring him home."

As they stood there, united in their resolve, Linda couldn't shake the feeling that they were standing on the precipice of something far greater and more terrifying than they could possibly imagine. But with Drake by her side, she found the courage to face whatever lay ahead – for Harrison, for their family, for the truth that awaited them in the pages of a fantasy world come to life.

9 - 10

Drake's brow furrowed as he traced the intricate lines of the green dragon symbol with his finger. "This... this changes everything, Linda," he said, his voice a mix of awe and trepidation. "The symbol, it's not just a figment of Harrison's imagination. It's a key, a bridge between our world and wherever he is now."

Linda's heart raced as she absorbed Drake's words. "But how is that possible?" she asked, her blue eyes widening with a mixture of hope and fear. "So you were telling the truth. You're saying our son is... in another realm?"

Drake ran a hand through his disheveled dark hair, his tired eyes betraying the weight of his internal struggle. "I don't know for certain, but these occurrences, they're too precise to be coincidental. The dreams, the symbols appearing in our reality – it's as if the boundaries between worlds are blurring."

As Linda listened, she felt a strange sense of clarity wash over her. Despite the fantastical nature of Drake's explanation, something deep within her resonated with the truth of his words. She reached out, grasping Drake's hand in hers. "I don't understand it all," she admitted, her voice soft but resolute, "but I know we're in this together. Whatever it takes to bring Harrison home, we'll face it side by side."

Drake squeezed her hand, a small smile breaking through his worried expression. "Together," he echoed, his voice gaining strength. "We'll unravel this mystery, Linda. For Harrison."

As the evening wore on, they pored over Harrison's journals, piecing together the fragments of his imaginary world that now seemed all too real. The weight of their mission was palpable, but so was the love that bound them.

Later, as they prepared for bed, Linda felt a lightness in her heart that had been absent for weeks. She turned to Drake, who was setting his alarm for the morning. "You know," she said, a hint of her old warmth creeping into her voice, "I never thought I'd say this, but I'm almost grateful for all those late nights you spent at the office."

Drake looked up; confusion etched on his face. "What do you mean?"

Linda smiled, moving closer to him. "Your determination, your ability to piece together complex cases – we need that now more than ever. You're no longer just fighting for clients, Drake. You're fighting for our family."

Touched by her words, Drake pulled her into an embrace. As Linda leaned in to kiss him goodnight, she felt a renewed sense of purpose. Their silent promise to Harrison hung in the air between them, a beacon of hope in the uncertainty that lay ahead.

11 - 12

Linda's lips brushed Drake's ear as she whispered, her voice trembling with quiet resolve, "Say hello to Harrison for me. Wherever he may be, let him know that we love him, and that we'll find a way to be together again." Her words hung in the air, a mixture of hope and heartache that seemed to permeate the very walls of their bedroom.

Drake pulled back slightly, his tired eyes meeting Linda's. "I will," he promised, his voice hoarse with emotion. "Every night, in both worlds, I'll make sure he knows." He paused, running a hand through his disheveled hair. "Do you think we can bring him back?"

Linda's brow furrowed as she considered the question. "I have to believe we can," she replied, her fingers absently tracing the pattern on their comforter. "It's what keeps me going."

As Drake settled into bed beside her, the mattress dipping under his weight, Linda couldn't shake the feeling of unease that lingered in the air like a heavy fog. She turned to face him, her blue eyes searching his face in the dim light. "Drake," she began hesitantly, "what aren't you telling me?"

Drake's expression tightened, a flicker of guilt passing over his features. "What do you mean?"

"I can't help but feel there's more to this than you're letting on," Linda pressed, her voice soft but insistent. "What other secrets are hiding beneath the surface? What other mysteries are we facing?"

Drake sighed heavily, the weight of their situation evident in the slump of his shoulders. "Linda, I..." he trailed off, seemingly at a loss for words. "There's so much I don't understand yet. So many pieces that don't fit together."

As they lay there in the darkness, the moonlight casting long shadows across their room, Linda's mind raced with possibilities. What other worlds might exist beyond their understanding? And how deep did this rabbit hole of parallel realities truly go?

13 - 14

Linda's eyes fluttered closed, her exhaustion finally overtaking her racing thoughts. As she drifted towards sleep, her mind swirled with a tempest of questions and fears. "Harrison," she murmured, her son's name a prayer on her lips. "Where are you, sweetheart?"

In the hazy realm between wakefulness and dreams, Linda's imagination conjured vivid images. Harrison, his curly hair wild and eyes sparkling with mischief, stood before her in a misty forest. "Mom," he called, his voice echoing strangely, "I'm on an adventure!"

"But where, Harrison?" Linda cried out, reaching for him. "How can I find you?"

The scene shifted, and suddenly Gabriel's scarred face loomed before her, his piercing eyes boring into her soul. "The answers lie within the symbol," he intoned cryptically, his voice smooth yet tinged with an otherworldly quality. "The green dragon and the scarred tree hold the key."

Linda tossed and turned, her fingers clutching at the sheets. "I don't understand," she whispered frantically. "What does it all mean?"

As the moon's silver glow filtered through the curtains, casting eerie shadows across the room, Linda's fitful sleep deepened. Her subconscious mind wove a tapestry of fantastical imagery – knights in shining armor battling fierce dragons, their scales glinting emerald in the sunlight. And there, at the center of it all, stood Harrison, wielding a sword etched with the mysterious symbol that haunted their waking hours.

"Mom! Dad!" Harrison's voice rang out, clear and strong. "I'm okay! I'm learning to be a hero!"

Linda's heart ached with a mixture of pride and fear. "Be careful, my brave boy," she murmured in her sleep, a single tear sliding down her cheek. "We'll find a way to bring you home."

15 - 15

As the kaleidoscope of dreams swirled around her, Linda felt a sudden warmth envelop her, like a gentle embrace from an unseen force. The chaotic images began to settle, coalescing into a serene landscape bathed in soft, golden light. At its center stood an ancient, gnarled tree, its bark etched with intricate patterns that seemed to pulse with life.

"Linda," a familiar voice called out, causing her heart to leap. She turned to see Harrison, his eyes twinkling with excitement and wisdom beyond his years. "Don't be afraid, Mom. This is all part of something bigger than we could have ever imagined."

Tears welled up in Linda's eyes as she reached out to touch her son's face. "Oh, Harrison," she breathed, her voice thick with emotion. "We miss you so much. Are you truly safe?"

Harrison smiled, a mixture of reassurance and adventure dancing in his expression. "I am, Mom. And I'm learning incredible things. But I need you and Dad to be strong. There's still so much to uncover."

Linda's brow furrowed, her maternal instincts warring with the surreal nature of their encounter. "But how can we help you? We don't understand any of this."

"Trust in the symbol, Mom," Harrison replied, his voice taking on an almost mystical quality. "The green dragon and the scarred tree – they're not just drawings. They're a map, a key to bringing us back together."

As the dream began to fade, Linda felt a surge of determination course through her. "We won't give up, Harrison," she promised, her voice steady and resolute. "No matter what it takes, we'll solve this puzzle and bring you home."

The last thing she saw before waking was Harrison's radiant smile, filled with love and hope. As Linda's eyes fluttered open, the weight of uncertainty still pressed upon her, but now it was tempered by a newfound sense of purpose. She turned to Drake, who was stirring beside her, and whispered, "Our journey's just beginning, love. And I have a feeling it's going to be more extraordinary than we could have ever imagined."

Shadows in the Dark

Green World – 2024

1 - 2

The flickering glow of the computer monitor cast eerie shadows across Drake Miller's face, his tired eyes scanning the grainy security footage with laser-like focus. Beside him, Detective Keirstead leaned forward, their shoulders nearly touching in the cramped confines of the dimly lit room. The air felt thick with tension, each passing frame ratcheting up the anticipation coiling in Drake's gut.

"Come on, you bastard," Drake muttered under his breath, his fingers tapping an impatient rhythm on the desk. "Show yourself."

As if in response to his silent plea, a flicker of movement caught his eye. Drake's hand shot out, finger jabbing at the screen. "Whoa. Right there."

Keirstead leaned in closer, his breath hot on Drake's neck. "What've you got, Miller?"

Drake's mind raced, analyzing every pixel of the frozen image before them. A shadowy figure lurked at the edge of the frame, barely visible in the low-resolution footage. But something about the stance, the predatory stillness, sent a chill down Drake's spine.

"I think this is our guy," Drake said, his voice low and intense. "Look at how he's positioned, like he's waiting for something... or someone."

As he spoke, Drake couldn't shake the nagging feeling that this case was about to consume him, just like so many others before. He thought of Linda and Harrison, of the promises he'd made to be more present, to put family first. But the pull of the mystery before him was undeniable, a siren song he couldn't resist.

"Let's see what happens next," Keirstead urged, reaching for the controls.

Drake nodded, bracing himself for whatever horrors the next few frames might reveal. As the footage began to play, he silently prayed that this time, just this once, he could solve the case without losing himself in the process.

3 - 4

The grainy footage sprang to life, its eerily silent narrative unfolding before their eyes. Drake's fingers tightened on the edge of the desk, his knuckles turning white as he watched the shadowy figure glide across the screen with predatory grace. Each movement seemed calculated, deliberate, sending a chill down his spine.

Beside him, Keirstead leaned forward, her dark eyes gleaming with an unsettling excitement. "Could hardly ask for a better angle," she said, her voice laced with a mixture of professional satisfaction and morbid fascination.

Drake shot her a sideways glance, momentarily taken aback by her enthusiasm. He couldn't help but wonder if her eagerness stemmed from a genuine desire for justice or something darker lurking beneath the surface.

"Better angle for what, exactly?" he muttered, more to himself than to his partner. "We're watching a man's final moments, Holly. This isn't a spectator sport."

Keirstead's lips twitched, her expression hardening slightly. "You know what I mean, Miller. The clearer the footage, the better our chances of identifying this bastard."

As they continued to watch, Drake's mind raced, cataloging every detail. The killer's fluid movements, the way they seemed to anticipate the victim's reactions – it all spoke of meticulous planning and experience. This wasn't some random act of violence; it was the work of a professional.

"Look at how he moves," Drake said, gesturing at the screen. "It's almost... choreographed. Like he's done this before."

Keirstead nodded, her earlier excitement tempered by the gravity of their observations. "You think we're dealing with a serial killer?"

Drake's response was cut short as the figure on screen made a sudden, chilling gesture...

5 - 6

The figure on screen emerged from the cab with an eerie grace, its movements fluid yet purposeful. Drake leaned forward, his breath catching in his throat as he watched the masked assailant close in on the unsuspecting driver.

"Jesus," Drake muttered, his fingers digging into the armrests of his chair. "This is..."

His words trailed off as the attacker struck, a lightning-fast punch to the driver's throat followed by a swift takedown. The brutality of the act was jarring, yet there was an undeniable precision to it that made Drake's skin crawl.

"It's almost like he's putting on a show," Keirstead observed, her voice barely above a whisper.

Drake nodded, his eyes never leaving the screen. "Yeah, and we're his unwitting audience."

As if on cue, the killer turned to face the camera directly. Even through the grainy footage, Drake could sense the murderer's eyes boring into him. The masked figure bowed with a flourish, as if basking in imaginary applause.

"What the hell?" Drake breathed, leaning even closer to the monitor. "Is he... is he bowing?"

Keirstead's reply was cut short as Drake held up a hand, his mind racing. "This isn't just a killer," he said, his voice tight with a mixture of dread and realization. "This is someone who wants to be seen, to be recognized. But for what?"

As the footage continued to play, Drake couldn't shake the feeling that they were dealing with something far more complex and sinister than they had initially thought. The theatrical nature of the kill, the deliberate acknowledgment of the camera – it all pointed to a killer with a message, a purpose beyond mere violence.

"We need to dig deeper," Drake said, finally tearing his eyes away from the screen to look at Keirstead. "This isn't random. There's a pattern here, a motive we're not seeing yet."

7 - 8

"Wow. Part murder, part performance piece," Keirstead continued, her voice a mixture of awe and disgust.

Drake's jaw clenched, his tired eyes narrowing as he absorbed the chilling spectacle before them. Without a word, he reached for the controls, rewinding the footage with a deliberate press of his finger. The masked figure moved backwards, rising from their bow, retreating from the camera's unblinking eye.

"Let's take another look," Drake muttered, his voice low and gravelly. He leaned in closer, the flickering light of the monitor casting harsh shadows across his scruffy features. "There's got to be something we're missing."

As the footage played again in slow motion, Drake scrutinized every detail of the killer's disguise. The mask, a featureless white oval, seemed to mock them with its blank expression. The killer's clothing was nondescript - dark, loose-fitting, carefully chosen to reveal nothing.

"What do you see, Miller?" Keirstead asked, her eyes flicking between the screen and her partner's intense expression.

Drake's mind raced, memories of his past cases intertwining with the present mystery. "The mask," he began, his voice thoughtful. "It's not just for concealment. It's a statement. This killer wants to be faceless, a blank canvas for us to project our fears onto."

He paused the footage, zooming in on the killer's gloved hands. "Look at the way they move," Drake continued, his finger tracing the air in front of the screen. "There's a... grace to it. Almost like they're dancing. This isn't just about killing. It's about the artistry of it."

The weight of his words hung heavy in the air, mingling with the low hum of the computer. Drake felt a familiar knot forming in his stomach, the same one he'd felt countless times before when faced with the darkest aspects of humanity. But now, it was tinged with something else - a nagging sense that this case would push him to confront not just the killer, but his own fractured reality.

"We're not just dealing with a murderer," Drake said, his voice barely above a whisper. "We're dealing with someone who sees death as their masterpiece."

9 - 10

Drake leaned back in his chair, his eyes never leaving the screen as he rubbed his stubbled chin. The killer's masked face seemed to taunt him, a blank canvas hiding untold horrors. He could feel Keirstead's eyes on him, waiting for his next move.

"Disguise doesn't give us a lot to go on," Drake finally said, his voice low and gravelly. "Let's pull a still and put it out to all the local-"

Before he could finish his thought, the door burst open, startling both detectives. An anxious young officer, his face flushed and breathing heavy, poked his head into the room. Drake's heart rate spiked, recognizing the look of urgency in the officer's eyes.

"What is it?" Drake demanded, rising from his chair. His mind raced with possibilities, each more grim than the last. Had there been another murder? Or worse, had the killer left them another cryptic message?

The officer opened his mouth to speak, but Drake held up a hand, suddenly overwhelmed by a vivid flash of memory - his son Harrison's laughter echoing through their home, a sound he feared he might never hear again in this reality. He closed his eyes, willing the bittersweet recollection away.

"Give me a moment," Drake said, his voice softer now. He turned to Keirstead, his expression a mixture of determination and vulnerability. "Whatever this is, we need to be prepared. This killer... he's not just taking lives. He's putting on a show, and we're his unwilling audience."

Keirstead nodded, her face mirroring his concern.

Drake took a deep breath, steeling himself for what was to come. He turned back to the officer, his jaw set. "Alright," he said, "let's hear it."

11 - 12

The young officer, Franklin Bird, swallowed hard, his Adam's apple bobbing nervously as he stammered out, "Detectives? We've got another one."

Drake's stomach lurched, a cold dread seeping into his bones. He exchanged a quick glance with Keirstead, noting the tightening of her jaw and the sharp intake of breath. The autumn wind outside seemed to howl in sympathy, rattling the windows of the small police station.

"Another what?" Drake asked, his voice low and gravelly, though he already knew the answer. He could taste the acrid tang of fear in the back of his throat, feel the weight of impending tragedy settling on his shoulders like a lead blanket.

Keirstead stepped forward, her piercing eyes locked on the young officer. "Spit it out, rookie," she commanded, her tone leaving no room for hesitation. "We need details, and we need them now."

Drake's mind raced, flashing through possibilities. Another victim? Another cryptic clue? Or worse, had the killer escalated, leaving a more gruesome scene for them to untangle? The silence stretched, thick and oppressive, as they waited for the officer's response.

13 - 14

The young officer's face paled as he uttered the words that sent a chill down Drake's spine: "Dead cabbie."

Drake's world seemed to tilt on its axis, the fluorescent lights of the station suddenly too harsh, too bright. He ran a hand through his disheveled hair, his fingers trembling slightly as the implications of this new development crashed over him like a tidal wave. His mind flashed to the security footage they'd just watched, the masked figure's theatrical bow burned into his retinas.

"Christ," Keirstead muttered under her breath, her usual composure cracking for a moment. She turned to Drake, her eyes wide with a mix of shock and grim determination. "Miller, you thinking what I'm thinking?"

Drake nodded slowly; his throat dry as sandpaper. "Yeah," he croaked, clearing his throat before continuing. "This is no coincidence. We're dealing with something far more sinister than we anticipated."

The weight of realization hung heavy in the air, an almost tangible presence in the cramped room. Drake's mind raced, piecing together the fragments of information they had. Two dead cabbies, a missing girl, a masked killer with a flair for the dramatic - it all pointed to a chilling conclusion.

"Serial killer," Drake whispered, the words barely audible but carrying the weight of a thunderclap. He locked eyes with Keirstead, seeing his own fear and determination mirrored in her gaze.

Keirstead nodded grimly, her lips pressed into a thin line. "We need to move fast," she said, already reaching for her coat. "Every second counts now."

As they prepared to head out, Drake couldn't shake the feeling that they were stepping into something much larger and more dangerous than they'd ever encountered before. The image of his son, Harrison, flashed in his mind, reminding him of what was at stake. He had to stop this killer, had to protect his family and his city. With renewed resolve, he squared his shoulders and followed Keirstead out into the night, ready to face whatever horrors awaited them.

15 - 16

The city pulsed with frenetic energy as Drake Miller and Detective Keirstead wound their way through the labyrinthine streets, their footsteps echoing off rain-slicked pavement. Neon signs flickered like dying fireflies, casting an eerie glow over their determined faces. Drake's heart hammered in his chest; each beat a reminder of the urgency that propelled them forward.

"Another dead cabbie," Drake muttered, his brow furrowed deeply as he glanced at Keirstead. "What are the odds?"

The question hung in the air, unanswered but laden with implications. Drake's mind raced, conjuring images of his son Harrison, safe at home, blissfully unaware of the darkness that stalked the city streets. He swallowed hard, pushing the thought away. Focus, he told himself. Lives depended on it.

"Two victims in one night," Keirstead responded, her voice tight with tension. "This killer's escalating, and fast."

Drake nodded grimly, his eyes scanning the faces of passersby, searching for... what? A glimpse of the masked figure from the security footage? He knew it was futile but couldn't help himself. Every shadow seemed to harbor potential danger.

"We need to establish a pattern," Drake said, thinking out loud. "Cab companies, routes, anything that links these victims together."

As they rounded a corner, the flashing lights of police cruisers came into view, illuminating the crime scene in stark bursts of red and blue. Drake felt a familiar tightness in his chest, the weight of responsibility settling over him like a shroud. He'd seen too many crime scenes in his life, but this... this felt different. Personal, somehow.

"Ready?" Keirstead asked, her hand hovering over her holstered weapon.

Drake took a deep breath, steeling himself for what lay ahead. "As I'll ever be," he replied, his voice a mixture of determination and dread. Together, they stepped into the chaos of the crime scene, ready to confront the darkness that threatened to engulf their city.

17 - 18

Drake's eyes swept over the grim tableau before him, his jaw clenching as he took in the abandoned taxi, its yellow paint a stark contrast to the somber mood enveloping the area. Police officers bustled about, their voices a low murmur against the backdrop of city noise. The acrid scent of fear and death hung heavy in the air, a familiar yet unwelcome companion.

"Christ," Drake muttered under his breath, his mind racing with possibilities. He couldn't shake the image of the masked killer from the security footage, bowing to the camera like some twisted performer. Was this another act in the same macabre play?

Keirstead's voice cut through his thoughts. "Too coincidental to ignore. We need to find out if there's any connection between the two incidents."

Drake nodded; his brow furrowed in concentration. "Agreed. Let's start with the basics - time of death, method, any witnesses."

As they approached the cordoned-off area, Drake felt a familiar hollowness in his chest. How many times had he prioritized scenes like this over his family? The guilt gnawed at him, a constant reminder of the life he'd lost - or rather, the two lives he was desperately trying to hold onto.

"What do we know so far?" he asked a nearby officer, forcing himself to focus on the present. The past - both versions of it - would have to wait.

The officer began rattling off preliminary details, but Drake found his attention drawn to a small pool of blood on the pavement. It glistened under the harsh streetlights, a stark reminder of the violence that had occurred here. He couldn't help but wonder - if he'd made different choices, would he be at home now, blissfully unaware of this darkness?

"Drake?" Keirstead's voice snapped him back to reality. "You with me?"

He nodded, pushing aside his internal struggle. "Yeah, sorry. Just... processing. Let's get to work. We've got a killer to catch."

19 - 20

Drake's eyes scanned the grim tableau before him, the shattered glass from the taxi's windows glittering like malevolent stars under the harsh streetlights. He turned to Keirstead, his voice low and gravelly with fatigue and determination.

"Let's see what we can find. Anything out of the ordinary could be a clue."

As they approached the abandoned taxi, evidence markers dotting the scene like macabre confetti, Drake couldn't shake the feeling that this case was going to drag him deeper into the abyss he'd been teetering on since the accident. He ran a hand through his disheveled hair, his mind racing with possibilities and regrets.

"What do you make of this, Keirstead?" Drake asked, gesturing towards the vehicle's mangled door. "Looks like our perp didn't waste time on subtlety."

Keirstead crouched down, examining the twisted metal. "Brute force, definitely. But there's something... deliberate about it. Almost like he wanted us to see his handiwork."

Drake nodded, a chill running down his spine. He couldn't help but think of Harrison, wondering if his son was safe in this reality while he investigated this horror. The weight of his dual existence pressed down on him, threatening to crush his resolve.

"We need to check for prints, DNA, anything that might give us a lead," Drake said, forcing himself to focus on the task at hand. "This psycho's got to slip up sometime."

As they circled the taxi, Drake's keen eyes caught something glinting beneath the driver's seat. He leaned in, careful not to disturb the scene, his heart pounding with a mixture of anticipation and dread.

"Keirstead," he called out, his voice tight. "I think I've got something here."

21 - 22

Drake's attention was suddenly drawn away from the glinting object as Keirstead's voice cut through the tense atmosphere.

"Miller," Keirstead called out, his tone urgent. "Look over there. Bloodstains on the pavement."

Drake straightened up, his tired eyes following Keirstead's outstretched arm. Sure enough, a dark, wet patch marred the cracked asphalt a few feet from the taxi. He approached cautiously, his mind racing with possibilities. The coppery scent hit him as he knelt, bringing back memories of countless crime scenes and the weight of lives lost.

"It's fresh," Drake observed, his voice low and gravelly. He reached out, hovering his hand just above the stain to feel its warmth. "The killer must have left in a hurry."

As he examined the blood, Drake's thoughts drifted to Linda. In one reality, she was waiting for him at home, her blue eyes filled with worry. In another, her absence left a gaping hole in his heart. The dichotomy threatened to overwhelm him, but he pushed it aside, focusing on the task at hand.

"What do you think, Keirstead?" Drake asked, looking up at his partner. "Victim's blood, or did our perp get sloppy?"

Keirstead crouched beside him, his brow furrowed in concentration. "Hard to say without lab results, but the pattern suggests arterial spray. Could be from the cabbie's throat if the killer used the same M.O. as before."

Drake nodded, a grim expression settling on his face. "We need to work fast. This bastard's escalating, and I'll be damned if we let another innocent die on our watch."

As he stood, Drake's hand unconsciously went to his pocket, fingers brushing against the photo of Harrison he always carried. The thought of his son's bright eyes and mischievous grin steeled his resolve. He had to solve this case, not just for the victims, but for the family he was fighting to protect across two realities.

"Let's get forensics down here ASAP," Drake said, his voice taking on a determined edge. "Every second counts, and I've got a feeling we're just scratching the surface of this nightmare."

23 - 24

Drake's mind raced as he scanned the crime scene, the image of the masked figure from the security footage burning in his thoughts. The theatrical bow, the deliberate movements - it all spoke of a killer who reveled in the spotlight, who saw murder as performance art. A chill ran down his spine as he considered the implications.

"What are you thinking, Miller?" Keirstead's voice cut through his reverie.

Drake ran a hand through his disheveled hair, his tired eyes narrowing. "I can't shake the feeling that this isn't just about killing cabbies. The mask, the bow to the camera - it's like he's putting on a show. But for who? And why?"

He paused, the weight of his dual realities pressing down on him. In one world, Linda would be waiting at home, her gentle presence a balm to his troubled soul. In the other, the empty space where she should be ached like a physical wound. Drake pushed the conflicting memories aside, forcing himself to focus.

"We need to dig deeper," he said, turning to Keirstead with renewed determination. "This killer, he's not just choosing victims at random. There's a pattern here, a message we're missing."

Keirstead nodded, his expression grim. "Agreed. But where do we start?"

Drake's gaze swept the area, taking in the curious onlookers gathering at the edges of the crime scene tape. "We start with the eyes and ears of the city," he said, gesturing towards the crowd. "Someone must have seen something, heard something. We need to track down every potential witness, leave no stone unturned."

As they approached the gathering of spectators, Drake couldn't help but think of Harrison. His son's uncanny ability to notice details others missed, to ask the questions that cut to the heart of matters - it was a gift Drake wished he had now. He made a mental note to call Harrison later, to hear his voice and draw strength from his unwavering spirit.

"Alright," Drake said, his voice taking on the authoritative tone that had served him well in his previous life as a lawyer. "Let's split up and start interviewing. Anyone who was in the area in the last few hours, anyone who might have seen our cabbie or his last fare. We're looking for anything out of the ordinary, no matter how small it might seem."

25 - 26

Keirstead nodded, her piercing eyes reflecting a mix of determination and curiosity. "Agreed. Let's split up and cover more ground," she said, her voice carrying the crisp efficiency that had become her trademark.

As they divided the tasks between them, Drake couldn't help but admire Keirstead's razor-sharp focus. She was already scanning the crowd, her analytical mind no doubt categorizing potential witnesses and formulating questions. "I'll take the east side of the street," Drake offered, "you handle the west. We'll reconvene in an hour to compare notes."

Keirstead gave a curt nod and strode off, her athletic build allowing her to weave through the crowd with ease. Drake watched her go, a sense of unease settling in his gut. There was something about this case that felt... off. As he approached his first witness, an elderly woman clutching her purse like a lifeline, he couldn't shake the feeling that they were only scratching the surface of something far more sinister.

"Ma'am," Drake began, flashing his badge, "I'm Detective Drake Miller. Did you happen to see anything unusual in the area tonight?"

The woman's eyes darted nervously. "I... I'm not sure. There was a man, earlier. He seemed... wrong, somehow."

Drake leaned in, his interest piqued. "Wrong how?"

"His eyes," she whispered, her voice trembling. "They were... empty. Like looking into a void."

As Drake jotted down notes, his mind raced. Empty eyes, a masked figure bowing to the camera... What kind of monster were they dealing with? He glanced across the street, catching sight of Keirstead interviewing a young couple. Her brow was furrowed, her posture tense. Whatever she was hearing, it wasn't good.

An hour later, as they reconvened, the weight of their findings hung heavy in the air. Keirstead's usually confident demeanor seemed shaken. "Drake," she said, her voice low, "I think we're dealing with something... something beyond our usual scope."

Drake nodded grimly. "I was afraid you'd say that. The witnesses on my side... their descriptions. It's like we're chasing a ghost."

As they compared notes, a chilling picture began to emerge. Multiple witnesses describing a figure that seemed to materialize out of thin air, eyes that held no humanity, a presence that left people feeling cold and afraid long after it had passed.

"This isn't just a serial killer," Keirstead murmured, her analytical mind struggling to make sense of the impossible. "It's something... else."

Drake felt a shiver run down his spine. In all his years on the force, he'd never encountered anything like this. As they stood there, surrounded by the bustle of the crime scene, he couldn't shake the feeling that they were staring into an abyss. And somewhere in the darkness, something was staring back.

Shadows of the Warehouse

1 - 2

Drake Miller's heart pounded in his chest as he stood shoulder to shoulder with Detective Keirstead, their eyes transfixed on the grotesque symbol etched into the wall before them. The dim light of the abandoned warehouse cast eerie shadows across the crude marking, its jagged lines reminiscent of a twisted, deformed face. Miller's breath caught in his throat as he took in the gruesome sight, his mind racing with memories of similar crime scenes he'd witnessed in both of his fractured realities.

Keirstead's voice cut through the suffocating silence, her words dripping with a mixture of disgust and determination. "This symbol... It's the same one we found at the other crime scenes."

Miller nodded grimly, his tired eyes never leaving the haunting image. He could feel the weight of his dual existence pressing down on him, the burden of knowledge from two parallel worlds threatening to overwhelm his senses. In one life, he was a seasoned detective working alongside Holly Kierstead; in another, he was an lawyer thrust into a world of murder and mayhem. The dichotomy was maddening.

"It's like looking into the eyes of evil itself," Miller murmured, his voice barely above a whisper. He ran a hand through his disheveled hair, the stubble on his chin rough against his palm. "What kind of monster are we dealing with here, Keirstead?"

The detective turned to face him, her expression a mask of professional detachment tinged with a hint of concern. "The worst kind, Miller. The kind that enjoys the game as much as the kill."

Miller's mind raced, piecing together fragments of information from both his realities. He wanted to tell Keirstead everything he knew about Gabriel, about the parallel worlds he was living in, but he held his tongue. How could he explain something he barely understood himself?

Instead, he stepped closer to the symbol, his eyes tracing every line and curve. "There has to be more to this than just a calling card," he mused aloud, his lawyer's mind searching for hidden meanings and clues. "What if it's not just a signature, but a message?"

Keirstead raised an eyebrow, her interest piqued. "What kind of message?"

Miller shook his head, frustration evident in the set of his shoulders. "I don't know yet, but I can't shake the feeling that we're missing something crucial." He turned back to his partner, determination blazing in his dark eyes. "We need to dig deeper, Keirstead. There's more to this case than meets the eye, and I intend to uncover every last secret."

As they stood there, surrounded by the oppressive atmosphere of the crime scene, Miller couldn't help but think of his family—of Linda and Harrison, existing in separate realities, both waiting for him to come home. The thought steeled his resolve. He would solve this case, he would catch Gabriel, and somehow, he would find a way to bridge the gap between his two worlds.

With a deep breath, Miller squared his shoulders and met Keirstead's gaze. "Let's get to work. We've got a killer to catch."

3 - 4

Miller's words hung in the air, heavy with implication. "Gabriel's calling card," he repeated, his voice low and gravelly. The scruffy-bearded detective ran a hand through his disheveled dark hair, his tired brown eyes never leaving the chilling symbol before them.

Keirstead turned to face Miller, her expression a complex mixture of curiosity and skepticism. Her piercing gaze bore into him, searching for answers. "How can you be so sure?" she asked, her tone carefully measured.

Miller's mind raced, weighing his words carefully. How could he explain his certainty without revealing the impossible truth of his dual existence? "I've... seen it before," he finally offered, his voice trailing off as he struggled to find the right balance between honesty and secrecy.

"Where else?" Keirstead pressed, her eyebrows knitting together in confusion.

Miller's heart pounded in his chest as he formulated his response. "It's complicated," he began, his words slow and deliberate. "But I've been piecing together information from various sources. This symbol, it's like a signature—unique to Gabriel."

As he spoke, Miller's thoughts drifted to the other reality, where Holly Sharp had shared crucial information about Gabriel. The weight of his knowledge from both worlds pressed down on him, a constant reminder of the bizarre situation he found himself in.

Keirstead's eyes narrowed, her skepticism evident. "And you didn't think to share this information earlier?"

Miller sighed, the guilt of his secrecy weighing heavily on him. "I wanted to be sure," he explained, his voice tinged with a mix of determination and vulnerability. "This case, it's unlike anything I've ever encountered. We can't afford to make assumptions."

As they stood there, surrounded by the grim reality of another crime scene, Miller couldn't shake the feeling that they were on the precipice of something monumental. The symbol before them wasn't just a calling card—it was a challenge, a taunt from a killer who believed himself untouchable.

"We need to dig deeper," Miller said, his resolve strengthening with each word. "Gabriel's leaving us breadcrumbs, and we need to follow them, no matter where they lead."

5 - 6

Keirstead's brow furrowed, her eyes searching Miller's face for any sign of deception or instability. "How do you know about Gabriel?" she pressed, her voice laced with incredulity. "And what does he have to do with your accident?"

The questions hung in the air, heavy and demanding. Miller felt the weight of them pressing down on his chest, constricting his breathing. He inhaled deeply, his tired eyes scanning the crime scene around them as he steeled himself for what was to come. The metallic scent of blood mingled with the acrid odor of fear, a potent reminder of the stakes at hand.

"I..." Miller began, his voice faltering. He cleared his throat and tried again, "It's not an easy explanation, Keirstead. You might not believe me."

Keirstead's skepticism deepened, etching lines into her forehead. "Try me," she challenged, crossing her arms over her chest.

Miller's mind raced, searching for the right words. How could he possibly explain the inexplicable? The parallel realities, the knowledge that seemed to bleed between them? He ran a hand through his disheveled hair, buying time as he formulated his response.

"Ever since the accident," he started, his voice low and gravelly, "things have been... different. I've been experiencing something I can't fully explain. It's as if I'm living two lives simultaneously, and in both of them, Gabriel is a threat we need to stop."

He paused, gauging Keirstead's reaction. Her expression remained guarded, but there was a glimmer of curiosity in her eyes that encouraged him to continue. Miller took another deep breath, bracing himself for what he was about to reveal.

7 - 8

Miller's gaze locked onto Keirstead's, his brown eyes intense with a mixture of desperation and conviction. "It's... complicated," he admitted, his voice barely above a whisper. "But I know Gabriel is the same person who killed the taxi driver and the family from the other night."

The words hung heavy in the air between them, laden with implications that seemed to stretch the boundaries of reality. Miller's heart raced, pounding against his ribcage as he awaited Keirstead's response. Would she believe him? Or would she dismiss his claims as the ravings of a man unhinged by trauma?

Keirstead's brow furrowed, her lips pursing into a thin line. The skepticism etched across her features deepened, but to Miller's surprise, she didn't immediately shut him down. Instead, she tilted her head slightly, a gesture that invited him to continue.

"Go on," she said, her voice carefully neutral. "I'm listening."

Miller felt a surge of relief, tempered by the weight of the task ahead. How could he possibly convey the bizarre nature of his experiences without sounding completely insane? He ran a hand through his scruffy beard, buying himself a moment to gather his thoughts.

"I know it sounds crazy," he began, his words tumbling out in a rush. "But ever since the accident, I've been experiencing... flashes. Memories, knowledge, details about cases I shouldn't know." He paused, swallowing hard. "Details about Gabriel."

As he spoke, Miller's mind raced, grappling with the duality of his existence. In thisreality, he was a seasoned detective, while in the other, he was a novice thrust into a world of crime and danger. The cognitive dissonance was maddening, yet he clung to the conviction that both realities held the key to stopping Gabriel.

Keirstead listened intently, her expression a mask of professional detachment. But Miller could see the wheels turning behind her eyes, weighing his words against the evidence they'd gathered. He pressed on, desperate to make her understand.

"I can't explain how I know, but I'm certain Gabriel is behind these killings. The symbol, the method, it all fits." Miller's voice grew more urgent. "We need to stop him before he strikes again."

9 - 10

Miller took a deep breath, steeling himself for what he was about to reveal. His tired eyes locked onto Keirstead's, searching for any sign of understanding or belief.

"You see, I've been dealing with something... unusual since my accident," he began, his voice gaining confidence as he spoke. "I've been living in two worlds, parallel realities, if you will." He paused, gauging Keirstead's reaction before continuing. "In one world, you're a seasoned detective named Holly Sharp. You and Rebekha got married. I'm a lawyer, just like I was before the accident. I was never a detective. This is all new to me."

Miller's words hung in the air between them, heavy with implications. He could see the skepticism etched on Keirstead's face, her sharp features tightening with each passing second. But he pressed on, his tone earnest and unwavering.

"You may think I'm crazy, and you have every right to think that," he admitted, running a hand through his disheveled dark hair. "But in the other reality, you revealed a secret to me. You told me about your first case, the reason why you became a detective. The killer that got away – you shot him in the knee."

As the words left his mouth, Miller watched Keirstead's eyes widen in disbelief. Her usual confident demeanor faltered, replaced by a mixture of shock and uncertainty. The young detective's short, dark hair seemed to bristle as she processed the information, her athletic frame tensing visibly.

"How could you possibly know that?" Keirstead whispered, her voice barely audible. The intensity in her piercing eyes betrayed a cocktail of emotions – surprise, fear, and a hint of curiosity.

Miller felt a glimmer of hope. He had struck a chord, revealing something that only Keirstead could have known. It was a small victory, but a crucial one in his quest to make her understand the gravity of their situation.

11 - 12

Miller leaned in, his voice dropping to a low, urgent whisper. "I know it sounds crazy, but it's true," he insisted, his tired eyes boring into Keirstead's with an intensity that made her shift uncomfortably. "And in both worlds, Gabriel is a dangerous killer who leaves behind that symbol as his signature."

The symbol - that chilling, intricate design etched in blood - flashed through Miller's mind, sending a shiver down his spine. He watched Keirstead closely, noting the subtle changes in her expression as she absorbed his words. Her brow furrowed, creating deep lines of concentration that seemed out of place on her youthful face.

Keirstead's gaze darted away, fixing on a point in the distance as she wrestled with the implications of Miller's revelation. The crisp autumn air swirled around them, carrying the faint scent of fallen leaves and wood smoke from a nearby chimney. It was a stark reminder of the peaceful town they were tasked to protect, now threatened by an unseen evil.

"This is... a lot to process," Keirstead finally murmured, her voice tinged with a mix of skepticism and growing unease. She turned back to Miller, her eyes searching his face for any sign of deception. "Parallel worlds? It's just... it's hard to believe."

Miller nodded, understanding her hesitation. "I know," he said softly, his heart heavy with the weight of his impossible story. "But think about it. How else could I know about your first case? About the shooter you wounded?"

As Keirstead fell silent, Miller could almost see the gears turning in her mind. Her analytical nature was at war with the impossible facts before her. Could there be some truth to his bizarre claims? The possibility, however remote, seemed to unsettle her deeply.

"If what you're saying is true," Keirstead began slowly, her words careful and measured, "then we're dealing with something far beyond our usual cases." She paused, her gaze drifting to the symbol they had uncovered earlier. "And this Gabriel... he's active in both of these... worlds?"

Miller nodded grimly, relief washing over him at this small concession. "Yes," he confirmed, his voice thick with emotion. "And in both realities, he's leaving a trail of bodies behind him. We have to stop him, Keirstead. Before anyone else dies."

13 - 14

Keirstead's brow furrowed, her eyes narrowing as she contemplated the gravity of their situation. The weight of Miller's revelation hung heavy in the air between them, a palpable tension that seemed to crackle with each passing second. Finally, she broke the silence, her voice low and guarded.

"So, what now?"

Miller's tired eyes sparked with renewed determination; his jaw set in a firm line as he met Keirstead's gaze. He could feel the familiar pull of both realities tugging at the edges of his consciousness, but he pushed it aside, focusing on the here and now.

"Now, we follow the evidence," he declared, his voice carrying a strength that belied his inner turmoil. "We track down Gabriel and bring him to justice, in both worlds."

As the words left his mouth, Miller's mind raced with the implications. How could they possibly navigate this impossible situation? He could see the doubt still lingering in Keirstead's eyes, but there was something else there too – a glimmer of curiosity, perhaps even belief.

"Look," Miller continued, running a hand through his disheveled hair, "I know it sounds insane. Hell, I'm living it, and I can barely believe it myself. But we can't ignore the facts. Gabriel is out there, and he's not going to stop unless we make him."

Keirstead nodded slowly, her analytical mind already working through the possibilities. "Alright, Miller. Let's say I believe you. How do we even begin to tackle something like this? We can't exactly put out an APB for a suspect in two different realities."

Miller couldn't help but let out a bitter chuckle at that. "Trust me, I've been grappling with that very question since this whole thing started. But we have to start somewhere. We need to pool our resources, compare notes from both... timelines, I guess you could call them."

As he spoke, Miller's hand unconsciously drifted to his pocket, fingering the worn edge of the photograph he always carried – a snapshot of happier times, before the accident that had shattered his world. Or worlds, as it were. The memory of his family, whole and intact in one reality, fractured in another, fueled his resolve.

"We need to look for patterns," he continued, his voice growing stronger with each word. "Similarities between the victims, locations, anything that might give us a clue to Gabriel's next move. And we need to do it fast. Every moment we waste is another opportunity for him to strike again."

15 - 16

Keirstead's eyes narrowed, a mix of skepticism and intrigue dancing across her features. She opened her mouth to respond, but before she could utter a word, the crackle of the police radio cut through the air like a knife.

"All units, we have a 187 at 1542 Oakwood Avenue. Possible connection to the ongoing Green Dragon case. Requesting immediate backup."

Miller's heart plummeted, his face draining of color. "No," he whispered, his voice barely audible. "Not again."

Keirstead was already moving, her hand instinctively reaching for her gun. "Let's go, Miller. We can continue this... unconventional brainstorming session on the way."

As they rushed towards the car, Miller's mind raced. He couldn't shake the feeling of déjà vu, the sickening certainty that he'd lived through this exact moment before, in another life, another world. The weight of his dual existence pressed down on him, threatening to crush him under its impossible burden.

"I just don't understand," he muttered, more to himself than to Keirstead as they peeled out of the parking lot, sirens wailing. "How can he be so far ahead of us in both realities? It's like he's playing some sick game, always one step ahead."

Keirstead's knuckles were white on the steering wheel, her jaw clenched tight. "Focus, Miller. We need to approach this logically. Tell me everything you know about Gabriel from both... timelines. Leave nothing out, no matter how insignificant it might seem."

As the city blurred past them, Miller closed his eyes, desperately trying to piece together the fragments of information scattered across two lives. "He's meticulous," he began, his voice low and intense. "Every crime scene is immaculate, save for that damned symbol. It's like he's taunting us, daring us to catch him."

17 - 18

The car screeched to a halt as they arrived at the grisly scene, the flashing lights of police vehicles casting an eerie blue and red glow across the darkened street. Miller's stomach churned as he stepped out, the acrid smell of blood hitting him like a physical force. He steeled himself, drawing on years of courtroom composure to maintain a professional facade.

"You ready for this?" Keirstead asked, her voice low and tense.

Miller nodded, swallowing hard. "As I'll ever be."

They approached the crime scene, ducking under the yellow tape. The victim lay sprawled in the center of the room, surrounded by a halo of crimson. Miller's breath caught in his throat as he took in the gruesome tableau.

"Jesus," he whispered, his eyes scanning the room, searching for any detail that might give them an edge. "It's just like the others."

Keirstead crouched beside the body, her face a mask of grim determination. "Same MO, same lack of evidence. It's like he's a ghost."

Miller's mind raced, trying to reconcile the scene before him with the memories of similar crimes from his other life. He couldn't shake the feeling that he was missing something crucial, some vital piece of information that existed just beyond his grasp.

Unable to contain his frustration any longer, Miller grimaced and muttered, "Another one... How many more will it take before we catch him?"

19 - 20

Keirstead's eyes flashed with steely resolve as she stood, her jaw set in determination. "We'll catch him, Miller. We have to." Her voice carried a weight of conviction that seemed to steady the room.

Miller nodded, drawing a deep breath to center himself. The coppery scent of blood hung thick in the air, a grim reminder of the stakes they faced. He watched as Keirstead pulled on a pair of latex gloves with practiced ease, her movements fluid and purposeful.

"Where do we start?" he asked, his eyes darting around the room, trying to take in every detail at once.

"We start with the basics," Keirstead replied, her voice low and focused. "Work our way out from the body. Look for anything out of place, anything that doesn't fit."

Together, they began to comb through the scene, their movements careful and methodical. Miller's heart raced as he knelt beside a discarded shoe, examining it closely. "Is this the victim's?" he asked, holding it up for Keirstead to see.

She shook her head, her brow furrowed in concentration. "No, it's too small. Could be a clue, or just unrelated debris. Bag it anyway."

As they worked, Miller couldn't help but marvel at Keirstead's efficiency. In this world, she was a seasoned detective, and it showed in every precise movement, every astute observation. He found himself relying on her expertise, grateful for her steady presence in the face of such horror.

"What about this?" Miller called out; his voice tight with tension as he pointed to a faint smudge on the wall. "It looks like... could it be part of the symbol?"

Keirstead hurried over, her eyes widening as she examined the mark. "Good catch, Miller. It's subtle, but definitely intentional. Let's get forensics on this ASAP."

As they continued their search, Miller's mind raced with possibilities. Every piece of evidence, no matter how small, could be the key to unraveling Gabriel's identity and bringing him to justice. The weight of responsibility pressed down on him, a constant reminder of the lives at stake.

"We're missing something," he muttered, more to himself than to Keirstead. "There has to be a pattern, a reason he's choosing these victims."

Keirstead paused, turning to face him with a thoughtful expression. "You might be onto something there. Let's review the victims' backgrounds again, see if we can find any connections we missed before."

As they worked tirelessly through the night, the determination in their eyes never wavered. They knew that somewhere in this gruesome puzzle lay the answers they sought, and they were resolved to find them, no matter the cost.

21 - 22

Miller nodded, his eyes scanning the room with an intensity that belied his exhaustion. The flickering crime scene lights cast eerie shadows across the walls, creating a disorienting kaleidoscope of shapes that seemed to dance and shift with each passing moment. As he meticulously examined every inch of the room, a nagging sense of familiarity crept over him, causing the hairs on the back of his neck to stand on end.

"Keirstead," he called out, his voice barely above a whisper, "does this feel... I don't know, familiar to you somehow?"

The detective turned; her sharp features etched with concentration. "What do you mean, Miller?"

He shook his head, trying to articulate the strange sensation. "It's like I've been here before, done this exact same thing. But not just here - everywhere we go, every clue we find. It's as if I'm reliving a memory I shouldn't have."

Keirstead's eyebrow arched skeptically, but her voice remained neutral. "Focus, Miller. We can't afford to get distracted by déjà vu right now."

Miller nodded, forcing himself to push aside the unsettling thoughts. He returned his attention to the grisly scene before them, his mind racing to connect the disparate pieces of evidence. As he crouched down to examine a blood spatter pattern, he couldn't shake the feeling that he was missing something crucial, something just beyond the reach of his conscious mind.

Suddenly, the silence was shattered by Keirstead's sharp intake of breath. Miller's head snapped up, his heart rate instantly accelerating as he locked eyes with his partner.

23 - 24

Keirstead's eyes were wide, her normally composed features contorted with a mix of shock and recognition. Her arm shot out, finger pointing towards the far wall of the dimly lit room.

"Look at this..." she breathed, her voice barely above a whisper.

Miller rose slowly, his tired muscles protesting as he straightened. He moved closer to where Keirstead stood, his eyes narrowing as they adjusted to the shadows. The coppery scent of blood hung heavy in the air, making his stomach churn as he approached. Then he saw it, and his breath caught in his throat.

There, etched into the wall with what could only be blood, was the symbol they'd been chasing – Gabriel's unmistakable calling card. The crude lines formed a twisted, inverted dragon, its edges dripping with macabre precision.

"Jesus," Miller muttered, his mind reeling. "It's exactly the same as the others."

Keirstead nodded grimly. "Down to the last detail. He's nothing if not consistent."

As Miller stared at the gruesome artwork, a wave of conflicting emotions washed over him. Part of him felt a grim satisfaction at finding concrete evidence, while another part recoiled at the horror of what it represented. His thoughts raced, trying to piece together the implications of this discovery.

"What do you think it means?" he asked, turning to Keirstead. "Is he trying to tell us something, or is this just his sick way of signing his work?"

Keirstead's brow furrowed in concentration. "I'm not sure, but whatever it is, we're dealing with someone who takes pride in his... craftsmanship. This isn't random, Miller. Every line, every drop of blood – it's all deliberate."

Miller nodded, a chill running down his spine as he contemplated the mind of a killer who could create such a horrific tableau with such meticulous care. He couldn't shake the feeling that they were being led down a very specific path, but to what end?

25 - 26

Miller's eyes traced the grotesque symbol once more, his jaw clenching as the reality of their situation sank in. The coppery scent of blood hung thick in the air; a constant reminder of the lives lost to Gabriel's twisted game.

"He's taunting us," Miller said quietly, his voice barely above a whisper. The words felt heavy on his tongue, laden with frustration and a growing sense of dread. In his mind, he could almost picture Gabriel's smug satisfaction as he left behind this grisly calling card.

Keirstead's lips pressed into a thin line, her eyes hardening as she surveyed the scene. "It's like he's always one step ahead," she replied, her tone grim and laced with a hint of anger. She ran a hand through her hair, a gesture Miller recognized as a sign of her mounting frustration.

Miller's thoughts drifted to Harrison, his son who existed only in one of his realities. The weight of protecting him, of stopping this killer before he could claim more victims, pressed down on Miller's shoulders like a physical burden. He clenched his fists, nails digging into his palms.

"We need to figure out his pattern," Miller said, turning to face Keirstead. "There has to be something we're missing, some connection between the victims or the locations. Gabriel can't be omniscient – he's human, and humans make mistakes."

Keirstead nodded, her expression softening slightly at Miller's determination. "You're right. We'll go over everything again, piece by piece if we have to. There's got to be a thread we can pull on to unravel this whole thing."

As they spoke, Miller couldn't shake the unsettling feeling that they were being watched, as if Gabriel's eyes were upon them even now. He glanced over his shoulder, half-expecting to see a shadowy figure lurking in the corners of the room. The emptiness that greeted him was almost more unnerving than if he had actually spotted someone.

27 - 28

Miller turned back to Keirstead; his brow furrowed in concentration. "We need to look at this from a different angle," he said, his voice low and intense. "Gabriel's not just killing randomly. There's a purpose to all of this, a message he's trying to send."

Keirstead leaned in, her eyes bright with renewed focus. "What are you thinking, Miller?"

He began to pace, his mind racing through the possibilities. "The symbol, the locations, the victims – they're all pieces of a larger puzzle. We've been looking at them individually, but what if we step back and see the bigger picture?"

As he spoke, Miller couldn't help but feel a strange sense of déjà vu, as if he'd had this conversation before in another life. He pushed the feeling aside, focusing on the task at hand.

"Let's map out all the crime scenes," Keirstead suggested, already moving towards the evidence board. "Maybe there's a geographical pattern we've missed."

Miller nodded, joining her at the board. As they worked, pinning locations and connecting them with red string, he couldn't shake the nagging feeling that Gabriel was always one step ahead. It was as if the killer knew their every move before they made it.

"What if," Miller began hesitantly, "what if Gabriel isn't working alone? What if he has eyes and ears everywhere?"

Keirstead paused, her hand hovering over the map. "You think there's a larger organization involved?"

Miller's mind flashed to the cult symbol, the eerie similarities between his two realities. "I think we might be dealing with something bigger than we ever imagined," he said quietly, a chill running down his spine.

As they continued to work, the pieces slowly began to fall into place. With each connection they made, Miller felt a growing sense of both dread and anticipation. They were getting closer to the truth, but at what cost?

Then the image appeared before, as they pinned each location to the map of one of Gabriel's murders a image formed. Staring back at them was a dragon, if the pins were green then you could say it was exactly like the symbol they've encountered across both timelines.

Chaos in the Crowd

Green World – 2024

1 - 2

The acrid smell of burnt rubber and gasoline assaulted Drake Miller's nostrils as he and Keirstead pushed their way through the frantic crowd. His eyes darted from face to face, searching for anything out of place amidst the chaos. The cacophony of sirens and panicked voices grated against his ears, threatening to overwhelm his senses.

"Over there," Keirstead shouted, pointing towards a yellow cab with its front end accordion-folded around a steel pole.

Miller's stomach clenched as he spotted the motionless figure slumped over the steering wheel. Is this how it ends? Another life snuffed out in an instant, leaving behind a shattered family? The memory of his own loss threatened to surface, but he forced it down, steeling himself for what lay ahead.

As they approached the wreckage, Miller's gaze locked onto the shattered windshield, a spiderweb of cracks obscuring the driver's face. He couldn't help but wonder if the man had a family waiting for him at home, unaware that their world was about to be turned upside down.

"What do we know?" Miller asked, his voice gruff with tension.

An officer stepped forward, his face grim. "Not much, Detective. It happened fast—"

"They always do," Miller interjected, his mind racing with possibilities. Was this a random act of violence or something more sinister? The weight of responsibility settled heavily on his shoulders as he realized that finding the truth now rested squarely on him and his partner.

The officer continued, gesturing towards the cab. "We've got multiple witnesses, but their stories are all over the place. It's a mess."

Miller nodded, his eyes never leaving the crumpled vehicle. "Any surveillance footage?"

"We're working on it," the officer replied. "Mall security is pulling the tapes now."

As Miller surveyed the scene, his thoughts drifted to Linda and Harrison. What would they think if they could see him now, thrust into the middle of this chaos? Would they be proud of his determination to uncover the truth, or would they resent the danger that seemed to follow him like a shadow?

"Miller," Keirstead's voice cut through his reverie. "We should start interviewing witnesses before their memories get too muddled."

He turned to his partner, grateful for her focus. "You're right. Let's split up, cover more ground."

As they prepared to dive into the sea of confused and frightened faces, Miller couldn't shake the feeling that this case would test him in ways he wasn't prepared for. But he had to press on—for the victim, for the truth, and for the family he was desperately trying to hold onto across two fractured realities.

3 - 4

The officer's voice cut through the chaos, his words painting a vivid picture of the violent scene that had unfolded mere moments ago. "Cab pulls up, door opens, three shots ring out. Driver tries to flee but ends up crashing into that pole over there."

Miller's eyes followed the officer's outstretched arm, his gaze settling on the mangled metal wrapped around the unforgiving concrete pillar. The sight sent a chill down his spine, reminding him of the fragility of life and the brutal efficiency of death.

"Jesus," Miller muttered under his breath, his mind racing with possibilities. He turned to Keirstead, noticing the tightness in her jaw as she absorbed the information. "Holly, what do you make of this?"

Keirstead's piercing eyes narrowed as she surveyed the scene, her voice low and determined. "Premeditated. The shooter knew exactly when and where to strike. This wasn't random."

Miller nodded, his thoughts aligning with his partner's assessment. "Agreed. But why here? Why now?" He ran a hand through his hair, frustration evident in his gesture. "We need to figure out who the victim was and if they had any connections that might explain this."

As they spoke, Gabriel Angel appeared at the edge of the crime scene, his presence sending a ripple of unease through Miller. The man's piercing gaze seemed to absorb every detail; his limp barely noticeable as he moved with eerie grace.

'There he is,' Drake thought to himself. Our suspect returned to the scene of the crime. "Mr. Angel," Miller called out, his voice tinged with suspicion. "We'd like to have a word with you."

Gabriel's lips curled into a enigmatic smile. "Merely a concerned citizen, Detective. One can't help but be drawn to such... unfortunate events."

Miller felt a knot forming in his stomach. Something about Gabriel's presence felt off, pinning Drake to the very spot he stood at. But before he could press further, Keirstead's hand on his arm pulled his attention back to the immediate task at hand.

"He was just there Kierstead. Did you see him?"

Kierstead looking in the direction Drake was looking, "See who? I don't see anything but an empty street over there."

Drake shrugged, he must have been seeing things. This case was starting to wear him down.

"We should start interviewing witnesses," she urged, her tone brooking no argument. "Every minute we wait, memories fade and details get lost."

Miller nodded, pushing thoughts of Gabriel to the back of his mind. "You're right. Let's get to work." As they moved to separate, he couldn't shake the feeling that this case was about to take them down a path far darker and more twisted than they could imagine.

5 - 6

The officer's words hung in the air, heavy with implication. "Witnesses describe a man with a limp, burned face and glasses, but he disappeared into the crowd before we could catch him."

Miller's mind raced; the description eerily reminiscent of Gabriel Angel. Could it be mere coincidence? He clenched his jaw, pushing the unsettling thought aside. "Any other distinguishing features?" he pressed, hoping for more concrete details.

Before the officer could respond, a new voice cut through the chaos. "No heroes today, just a hundred witnesses with a hundred stories."

Miller turned to see Rookie Officer Franklin Bird approaching, a wry smile playing on his lips. The young man's cavalier attitude grated on Miller's already frayed nerves.

"Care to elaborate on that, Bird?" Miller asked, his tone sharp.

Bird shrugged, seemingly unfazed by Miller's intensity. "Just saying, sir. Everyone's got their own version of events. One guy swears the shooter had a tattoo on his neck, another says he was wearing a red hat. It's a mess."

Miller fought the urge to snap at the rookie. Instead, he took a deep breath, his gaze sweeping across the chaotic scene. "That's why we're here, Bird. To sift through the mess and find the truth."

As he spoke, Miller couldn't shake the image of Gabriel Angel from his mind. The man's burned face, his subtle limp – it all fit too perfectly. But why would Gabriel insert himself into the investigation if he was the perpetrator? It didn't make sense.

"Keirstead," Miller called out to his partner. "Let's start with the most reliable-looking witnesses. We need to build a consistent picture of what happened here."

As they moved through the crowd, Miller's thoughts drifted to his wife, Linda. What would she make of all this? Would she understand the weight pressing down on him, the constant struggle to discern reality from delusion? He pushed the thoughts aside, focusing on the task at hand. There would be time for personal reflection later. Right now, a killer was on the loose, and it was his job to bring them to justice – no matter where the evidence might lead.

7 - 8

Miller's gaze flickered between Bird and the scene before him, a sense of unease settling over him like a heavy cloak. The rookie's cavalier attitude grated against his nerves, a stark contrast to the gravity of the situation. He clenched his jaw, fighting the urge to reprimand the young officer.

"Bird," Miller said, his voice low and measured, "I need you to take this seriously. Every detail matters, no matter how insignificant it might seem."

Bird's smile faltered, replaced by a look of chastened determination. "Yes, sir. I apologize."

Turning his attention back to the cab, Miller's mind raced with possibilities. The crumpled metal and shattered glass told a story of violence and desperation. He approached the vehicle cautiously, his eyes scanning every inch for potential evidence.

"What are you thinking, Drake?" Keirstead asked, her voice cutting through his concentration.

Miller ran a hand through his disheveled hair, the weight of his dual realities pressing down on him. "I'm thinking our shooter knew exactly what he was doing. This wasn't random. The precision, the escape... it's too clean."

As he spoke, an image of Harrison flashed through his mind – his son's mischievous grin, the sparkle in his eyes. The memory brought a sharp pang of grief, reminding Miller of all he had lost – and all he still stood to lose if he couldn't solve this case.

"We need to look beyond the obvious," Miller continued, his voice tinged with a mixture of determination and weariness. "The witnesses saw what the shooter wanted them to see. But what didn't they see? What are we missing?"

Keirstead nodded, her expression mirroring his intensity. "You think this might be connected to something bigger?"

Miller's gaze swept across the chaotic scene once more, taking in the frightened faces of the witnesses, the bustling activity of the first responders. "I don't know yet," he admitted. "But my gut tells me we're just scratching the surface of something much deeper."

9 - 10

Miller's eyes narrowed as he surveyed the bustling mall, his mind racing with possibilities. "Let's get the security footage," he said, his voice carrying a mix of urgency and determination. "We need to see if we can identify our shooter."

Keirstead nodded, her expression mirroring his intensity. "Good call. I'll get the mall security to pull it up for us."

As they made their way to the security office, Miller's thoughts drifted to Harrison. Would his son have been proud of him in this moment, or would he have seen right through his father's facade of control? The weight of his dual realities pressed down on him, threatening to overwhelm his focus.

Inside the cramped security office, Miller, Keirstead, and a portly mall security officer huddled around a bank of flickering monitors. The air was thick with tension as they watched the events unfold on the grainy screen before them.

"Can you zoom in on that area?" Miller asked, pointing to a section of the footage. His eyes never left the screen, searching for any detail that might crack the case wide open.

The security officer obliged, his fingers flying over the keyboard. "That's as clear as it gets, I'm afraid," he said apologetically.

Miller leaned in closer, his brow furrowed in concentration. "There's got to be something here," he muttered, more to himself than to the others. "Something we're not seeing."

As they watched the scene play out, Miller couldn't shake the feeling that they were missing a crucial piece of the puzzle. The shooter's movements, the timing of the attack – it all seemed too calculated, too precise to be random.

"Keirstead," he said, turning to his partner. "What do you make of this? Does anything stand out to you?"

She studied the footage intently, her eyes narrowed. "The way he moves... it's almost like he knows exactly where the cameras are. Like he's performed this routine before."

Miller nodded, a chill running down his spine. "My thoughts exactly. This isn't some amateur job. We're dealing with a professional here."

As they continued to analyze the footage, Miller's mind raced with possibilities. Who was this mysterious shooter? What was their motive? And most importantly, how were they going to catch them before they struck again?

The weight of responsibility settled heavily on Miller's shoulders, reminding him of all he had at stake. In one world, Linda waited for him, her love a beacon of hope in the darkness. In another, Harrison's memory drove him forward, pushing him to be the father he should have been.

As they turned back to the monitors, Miller couldn't shake the feeling that this case was about to change everything. For better or worse, he was on a collision course with a truth that threatened to shatter the fragile balance of his fractured existence.

11 - 12

The grainy security footage flickered to life, casting an eerie glow across Miller's face as he leaned in, his eyes sharp and focused. A yellow cab pulled into frame, its tires crunching over fallen leaves that had blown onto the mall parking lot. Miller's breath caught in his throat as the rear door swung open.

"Here we go," he muttered, more to himself than anyone else.

Three sharp cracks pierced the air, the muzzle flashes briefly illuminating the interior of the cab. Miller's jaw clenched, his mind racing back to another time, another tragedy. He pushed the memories aside, forcing himself to stay present.

The shooter emerged, a nondescript figure in a dark coat, face obscured by a beard and glasses. As if sensing the camera's gaze, the killer turned, staring directly into the lens for a heart-stopping moment before melting into the panicked crowd.

"Freeze it there!" Miller barked; his voice tight with frustration. The image stuttered to a halt, the shooter's hidden face taunting them from the screen.

Miller leaned back, running a hand through his disheveled hair. "Dammit," he growled, the weight of failure settling on his shoulders. "He knew exactly where the camera was. This wasn't some random act of violence."

His mind whirled with possibilities, each more unsettling than the last. Was this connected to one of his old cases? Or was it something far more personal, reaching across the divide between his fractured realities?

"What are you thinking, Miller?" Keirstead's voice cut through his spiraling thoughts.

He turned to her, seeing the same determination mirrored in her eyes. "I'm thinking we're dealing with someone who knows what they're doing. The disguise, the crowd... it's all too perfect."

Miller's gaze drifted back to the frozen image, a chill running down

13 - 14

Miller's gaze drifted back to the frozen image, a chill running down his spine as he studied the killer's obscured features. He leaned in closer, squinting at the screen, desperate for any detail that might crack the case wide open.

"We need to enhance this image, see if we can get a clearer picture of our suspect," Miller declared, his voice low and intense. He tapped the screen, indicating the shooter's face. "Focus on the eyes. Even with the glasses, there might be something we can use."

As he spoke, Miller's mind raced, recalling countless cases from his past. The meticulous planning, the calculated escape – it all pointed to a professional hit. But why here? Why now? The questions gnawed at him, echoing the constant battle between his two realities.

Keirstead nodded, her determination matching Miller's own. "I'm on it," she affirmed, already reaching for her phone to call in the tech team. "We'll run it through every facial recognition software we've got. If there's anything to find, we'll find it."

Miller watched her, grateful for her unwavering support. In both his worlds, Keirstead remained a constant, a partner he could rely on when everything else seemed to be falling apart. He allowed himself a brief moment of appreciation before refocusing on the task at hand.

"While we're waiting on that," Miller said, his eyes never leaving the screen, "let's go over the witness statements again. Someone must have seen something useful." He paused, a thought occurring to him. "And check for any similar MOs in recent cases. This level of precision... it feels familiar somehow."

"Focus, Drake," he muttered to himself, pushing aside the existential dread that threatened to overwhelm him. "One step at a time. Solve the case, save lives. That's what matters now."

With renewed determination, Miller turned back to the frozen image of the killer, ready to unravel the mystery that lay before him – no matter which reality it might lead him to.

15 - 16

Keirstead nodded, her eyes flashing with determination. "I'll start interviewing the witnesses, see if anyone caught a better glimpse of our guy," she said, already moving towards the crowd of shaken onlookers.

"What would you say, Linda?" he murmured, his voice barely audible above the chaotic din of the crime scene. "How do I explain that I'm living two lives, grieving you in one and our son in another?"

A nearby officer shot him a quizzical look, and Miller quickly straightened, pushing aside his personal concerns. He couldn't afford to let his guard down, not here, not now. The case demanded his full attention, and he owed it to the victims – both in this world and the other – to give it his all.

As he made his way back to the monitors, Miller's mind raced with possibilities. Could this killer be connected to his fractured reality? To the Green Dragon Killings? Or was it just another cruel twist of fate, designed to test his already strained sanity?

"One step at a time, Drake," he muttered, his eyes fixed on the frozen image of the suspect. "Solve the case, find the truth. Everything else can wait."

But even as he dove back into the investigation, a part of him longed for the comfort of Linda's embrace, for the simple joy of Harrison's laughter. Two worlds, two lives, and a mystery that seemed to span them both. Miller took a deep breath, steeling himself for whatever revelations lay ahead.

17 – 18

Blue World - 2024

The stark white walls of Dr. Lee's office seemed to pulse with an ethereal blue glow, a constant reminder of the surreal nature of this world. Drake Miller sat rigid in the plush armchair, his fingers digging into the soft leather as Dr. Lee leaned back, his piercing gaze never leaving Miller's face.

"So, 'Detective' Miller," Dr. Lee began, his voice a soothing balm in the tense atmosphere, "how have you been coping since our last session?"

Miller's jaw clenched, his dark eyes darting around the room as if searching for an escape. "I'm... managing," he finally replied, the words feeling hollow even as they left his lips.

Dr. Lee's eyebrow arched slightly, a subtle indication that he wasn't convinced. "Managing? That's quite a neutral term for someone in your unique situation."

A humorless chuckle escaped Miller's throat. "What would you prefer I say, Doc? That I'm thriving while living a double life? That I'm perfectly fine with the constant fear of losing my grip on reality?"

"I'd prefer you to be honest, Drake," Dr. Lee responded, his tone gentle but firm. "Both with me and with yourself."

Miller's gaze dropped to his hands, noticing for the first time how they trembled slightly. "Honest?" he murmured, more to himself than to Dr. Lee. "The truth is, I'm terrified. Every time I close my eyes, I don't know which world I'll wake up in. And Linda... God, Linda doesn't even know how to take any of this."

Dr. Lee leaned forward, his elbows resting on his knees as he regarded Miller with a mix of concern and curiosity. "And why did you tell her, Drake? Did you think she deserved to know what you're going through?"

The question hung in the air, heavy with implications. Miller's mind raced, images of Linda's tear-stained face flashing before his eyes. How could he burden her with this impossibility when she was already grappling with the loss of their son?

"I can't tell her about the case," Miller finally whispered, his voice thick with emotion. "She's been through so much already. How can I tell her that her husband is losing his mind, that he's living two lives, grieving you in one and our son in another? All the while being hunted by their son's murderer."

19 - 20

Dr. Lee's eyes softened with understanding, his voice carrying a gentle tone as he posed his next question. "What about your wife, Mr. Miller? How does she perceive your condition?"

The words hit Miller like a physical blow, causing him to shift uncomfortably in his seat. His brow furrowed with uncertainty, creating deep lines across his forehead as he struggled to formulate a response. The weight of unspoken truths pressed down on him, making the air in the room feel thick and oppressive.

"Linda, she..." Miller began, his voice trailing off as he searched for the right words. His hands clenched and unclenched in his lap, a physical manifestation of his internal turmoil. "She doesn't know," he finally admitted, the words barely above a whisper. "I haven't told her about... the killer."

Dr. Lee remained silent, his gaze steady and encouraging, inviting Miller to continue. The detective took a deep breath, his eyes darting around the room as if seeking an escape from the conversation.

"How can I?" Miller asked, his voice tinged with desperation. "After everything we've been through, after losing Harrison... I can't burden her with this too." He ran a hand through his disheveled hair, a gesture of frustration and helplessness. "She's already carrying so much pain. I see it in her eyes every day, that mix of sorrow and hope. How can I add to that?"

As he spoke, Miller's mind drifted to Linda's face, her blue eyes that once sparkled with joy now often clouded with grief. He could almost hear her soothing voice, always trying to comfort him even as she battled her own demons. The thought of her reaction to his fractured reality sent a shiver down his spine.

"I'm afraid," Miller confessed, his voice barely audible. "Afraid that if I tell her, it'll be the final straw. That she'll look at me and see a broken man, someone she can't rely on anymore. And I can't lose her too, Dr. Lee. I just can't."

21 - 22

Miller's words hung heavy in the air; the silence punctuated only by the soft ticking of a clock on Dr. Lee's desk. The detective's gaze fell to his hands, now clenched tightly in his lap, knuckles white with tension.

"We don't talk about it," Miller finally admitted, his voice a hoarse whisper. The words seemed to physically pain him as they left his lips, each syllable a reminder of the growing chasm between him and Linda. "It's easier to pretend everything's fine, to keep up the façade of normalcy. But every day, it feels like we're drifting further apart."

Dr. Lee raised an eyebrow, his keen eyes sensing the tension radiating from Miller's hunched form. The psychiatrist leaned forward slightly, his body language open and inviting, silently encouraging Miller to continue. The detective glanced up, meeting Dr. Lee's gaze, and found himself compelled to elaborate.

"I catch her looking at me sometimes," Miller continued, his voice thick with emotion. "There's concern in her eyes, maybe even fear. I think she knows something's wrong, but she doesn't push. And I... I don't have the courage to bring it up." He paused, swallowing hard against the lump forming in his throat. "How do you tell the person you love most in the world that you're losing your grip on reality?"

As he spoke, Miller's mind raced with images of Linda – her soft smile, the way she'd reach for his hand across the dinner table, the sound of her laughter that had become increasingly rare. The weight of his unspoken truths pressed down on him, threatening to suffocate him right there in Dr. Lee's office.

23 - 24

Dr. Lee's voice cut through Miller's swirling thoughts, gentle yet probing. "I see. And how does that make you feel?"

The question hung in the air, heavy with implications. Miller's hands clenched involuntarily, his knuckles whitening as he grappled with the maelstrom of emotions churning within him. The ticking of the clock on Dr. Lee's wall seemed to grow louder, each second stretching into an eternity as he searched for the right words.

Finally, Miller spoke, his voice barely above a whisper. "It's complicated. Linda has been through so much already..." He trailed off, his gaze drifting to the window, where the city sprawled out beneath them, oblivious to his inner turmoil. The detective's mind raced, recalling Linda's tear-stained face at Harrison's funeral, the nights he'd found her clutching their son's favorite stuffed animal, the forced smiles that never quite reached her eyes.

"I want to protect her," Miller continued, his words coming faster now, tumbling out like a confession. "But every time I look at her, I see the pain she's trying to hide. And I know that my... condition... it's just another burden she doesn't need." He ran a hand through his disheveled hair, frustration etched into every line of his face. "How can I add to her suffering when she's already lost so much?"

25 - 26

Dr. Lee leaned forward, his eyes radiating compassion as he studied Miller's hunched form. "Go on, Mr. Miller," he urged gently, his voice a soothing balm in the charged atmosphere of the office. "It's important to express your feelings, especially in times of distress."

Miller's gaze drifted back to the window, seeking solace in the sprawling cityscape below. The afternoon sun cast long shadows across the buildings, mirroring the dark thoughts that threatened to engulf him. He took a deep, shuddering breath, feeling the weight of his unspoken fears pressing down on his chest.

"I'm terrified," Miller admitted, his voice barely audible. "Terrified that if I tell Linda about these... episodes, about the other world I keep slipping into, she'll think I've lost my mind." He paused, swallowing hard against the lump in his throat. "Or worse, that she'll believe me and realize she's married to a man who's living two lives. How can I ask her to bear that burden?"

As he spoke, Miller's hands fidgeted restlessly, tracing invisible patterns on the armrest of his chair. His mind raced, conjuring images of Linda's face contorted with worry, disappointment, or worst of all, pity. The thought made his stomach churn.

"Sometimes," he continued, his voice gaining strength as the words poured out, "I wonder if it would be easier for her if I just... disappeared. If I stayed in that other world and let her move on with her life." The moment the words left his lips, Miller felt a pang of guilt. He knew he could never abandon Linda, not really, but the temptation to shield her from his fractured reality was overwhelming.

27 - 28

Miller's gaze drifted back to the window, his eyes tracing the outline of the city skyline as he wrestled with the weight of his confession. "Linda lost our son... Harrison," he said, his voice cracking on the name. "She's been trying to move on, but it's like there's a wall between us. I can't bear to burden her with my own struggles."

The words hung heavy in the air, each syllable a testament to the pain etched deep within Miller's heart. He could feel Dr. Lee's eyes on him, patient and understanding, but he couldn't bring himself to meet the doctor's gaze. Instead, he focused on the steady rhythm of his own breathing, willing himself to maintain composure.

"Every time I look at her," Miller continued, his voice barely above a whisper, "I see the ghost of our boy in her eyes. And I wonder... does she see the same in mine?" He paused, running a hand through his disheveled hair. "How can I tell her that sometimes, in that other world, Harrison is alive? That I get to hold him, to hear his laugh? It would break her all over again."

Dr. Lee nodded in understanding; his expression sympathetic. The doctor's silence spoke volumes, offering Miller the space to continue if he wished. And in that moment, Miller found himself caught between the overwhelming desire to unburden himself and the paralyzing fear of what that unburdening might cost him.

29 - 30

Dr. Lee leaned forward, his kind eyes meeting Miller's tired gaze. "It's natural to want to protect those we love, but keeping your feelings bottled up won't make them disappear. Communication is key to healing, Mr. Miller."

The words struck Miller like a physical blow, forcing him to confront the wall he'd built between himself and Linda. He could feel his heart racing, the familiar tightness in his chest a stark reminder of the burden he carried alone.

"But how?" Miller asked, his voice cracking with emotion. "How do I tell her about this... this other world? She'll think I've lost my mind."

Dr. Lee's expression softened, a gentle smile playing at the corners of his mouth. "Sometimes, Mr. Miller, the fear of sharing our truth is far worse than the reality of doing so. Your wife has shown incredible strength in the face of loss. Don't underestimate her capacity for understanding."

Miller nodded, the weight of Dr. Lee's words sinking in. His mind raced with possibilities, both terrifying and liberating. Perhaps it was time to open up to Linda, to share the burden of his reality with her. The thought sent a shiver down his spine, a mixture of anticipation and dread.

"You're right," Miller admitted, his voice barely above a whisper. "Linda deserves to know. We've always faced things together, even when it felt impossible. This shouldn't be any different."

As he spoke the words, Miller felt a glimmer of hope, fragile but persistent, taking root in his heart. The path ahead was uncertain, fraught with potential pitfalls, but the prospect of no longer carrying this weight alone filled him with a tentative sense of relief.

31 - 31

Miller's hand hovered over the doorknob of Dr. Lee's office, his fingers trembling slightly as he steeled himself for what lay ahead. The fluorescent lights in the hallway buzzed faintly, a discordant hum that matched the nervous energy coursing through his body. He took a deep breath, the scent of antiseptic and stale coffee filling his nostrils, reminding him of the stark reality he was about to face.

"I can do this," he muttered to himself, his voice barely audible. "For Linda. For us."

As he stepped into the corridor, his mind raced with potential scenarios, each more daunting than the last. How would Linda react? Would she believe him, or think he'd finally cracked under the weight of their shared grief?

"Hey, Drake," called out a passing nurse, her cheerful tone a stark contrast to his inner turmoil. "Heading home?"

Miller managed a weak smile, nodding in response. "Yeah, Sarah. Big night ahead."

He couldn't help but chuckle darkly at the understatement. 'Big night' didn't begin to cover the conversation he was about to have with his wife.

As he made his way to the elevator, Miller's thoughts drifted to Linda's face - those expressive blue eyes that had seen so much pain, yet still held so much love. He pictured her sitting at their kitchen table, waiting for him with a cup of coffee and a gentle smile. The image both comforted and terrified him.

"Linda," he practiced under his breath as the elevator descended, "there's something I need to tell you. About me, about... everything."

The words felt clumsy, inadequate. How could he possibly explain the inexplicable? But as the elevator doors opened and he stepped out into the lobby, Miller felt a surge of determination. This conversation had to happen, no matter how difficult. For their sake, and for his own.

Murder in the Office

1 - 2

The acrid smell of copper assaulted Drake Miller's nostrils as he stood beside the yellow police tape, his eyes fixed on the gruesome tableau before him. Dr. Jesse Harmon's body lay sprawled on the polished hardwood floor of his office, limbs akimbo, surrounded by an ever-expanding pool of crimson that seemed to mock the pristine white walls. The psychologist's sharp features, once animated with stern intensity, were now slack and lifeless, his eyes staring unseeing at the ceiling.

Detective Keirstead shifted beside Miller, her seasoned gaze sweeping methodically over the crime scene. With a heavy sigh that seemed to carry the weight of countless similar tragedies, she muttered, "What a mess."

Miller nodded grimly, his mind racing with the implications of Harmon's death. The doctor had been one of the few people who understood the bizarre duality of Miller's existence, straddling two parallel realities. Now, that lifeline of understanding had been viciously severed, leaving Miller feeling more alone than ever in his fractured world.

"He didn't deserve this," Miller said softly, his voice thick with emotion. "Whatever his methods, he was trying to help people. To understand."

Keirstead glanced at Miller, his expression softening slightly. "You knew him well?"

Miller ran a hand through his disheveled hair, the stubble on his chin catching against his palm. "Well enough to know he was onto something big. Something that might have explained..." He trailed off, unwilling to voice the impossible truth of his dual lives.

As they stood in somber silence, Miller couldn't shake the feeling that Harmon's death was somehow connected to his own strange predicament. The loss hit him doubly hard, resonating with the grief that constantly churned within him - for his wife in one reality, his son in another. He clenched his fists, determination rising through the fog of sorrow. Whoever had done this, whatever the reason, Miller vowed to uncover the truth - not just for Harmon, but for himself and the fractured existence he now endured.

3 - 4

Miller's eyes narrowed as he examined the scene more closely, his gaze sweeping over the gruesome tableau before him. The metallic scent of blood mingled with the sterile smell of the laboratory, creating a nauseating cocktail that made his stomach churn. His mind raced with questions, each one more unsettling than the last.

"Who could have done this? And why?" Miller asked, his voice low and gravelly. He ran a hand through his dark, disheveled hair, the weight of his dual existence pressing down on him more heavily than ever. In one reality, he could almost feel Linda's comforting presence beside him, while in the other, he ached for Harrison's youthful energy to dispel the gloom.

Keirstead stepped closer, her eyes scanning the room. "That's what we're here to find out, Miller. But I have to admit, this is no ordinary homicide."

Miller nodded grimly, his tired brown eyes reflecting the chaos within. "No, it's not. Harmon was onto something big, something that could've changed everything." He paused, weighing his next words carefully. "I can't help but think this is connected to... to my situation."

"Your situation?" Keirstead raised an eyebrow, curiosity piqued.

Miller sighed, the burden of his secret weighing heavily on him. "It's complicated, Detective. Let's just say Harmon was helping me understand some... unusual aspects of my life."

As they stood in contemplative silence, Miller's mind raced with possibilities. Could Gabriel, the elusive killer they'd been tracking, be behind this? And if so, what did it mean for Miller's fractured existence? The questions swirled in his mind, a maelstrom of uncertainty and fear.

"Whatever the reason," Miller said, his voice tinged with determination, "we need to find who did this. Harmon deserves justice, and I have a feeling that solving his murder might be the key to understanding a lot more."

5 - 6

Keirstead shook her head, her piercing gaze methodically scanning the blood-spattered room. The air hung heavy with the metallic scent of death, a grim reminder of the brutality they faced. She turned to Miller, her expression a mask of professional detachment tinged with a hint of frustration.

"We won't know anything concrete until we gather more evidence," Keirstead said, her voice low and measured. "This scene is a labyrinth of potential clues, Miller. We need to approach it systematically."

Miller nodded, his tired eyes darting from the lifeless body of Dr. Harmon to the chaotic disarray of the room. His mind, already burdened with the weight of his own fractured identity, now grappled with the implications of this gruesome murder. Could this be another piece of the puzzle that was his existence?

"You're right," Miller replied, his voice rough with fatigue and tension. "Where do you suggest we start?"

Keirstead's lips tightened into a thin line as she surveyed the crime scene once more. "First things first, we need to secure the area. Then we'll start interviewing anyone who might have seen or heard something suspicious."

As she spoke, Miller's thoughts drifted to Gabriel, the enigmatic figure who seemed to be pulling strings from the shadows. He couldn't shake the feeling that this murder was somehow connected to his own mysterious condition. The weight of uncertainty pressed down on him, threatening to overwhelm his already fragile psyche.

"I'll coordinate with the forensics team," Keirstead continued, pulling Miller from his introspection. "You start canvassing the building. Someone must have noticed something out of the ordinary."

Miller nodded, grateful for the direction. As he turned to leave, he cast one last glance at Harmon's body, a silent promise forming in his mind. "We'll find who did this, Doc," he whispered. "And maybe, just maybe, we'll uncover the truth about what's happening to me in the process."

7 - 8

As Miller began to move away from Dr. Harmon's lifeless form, a sudden glint caught his eye, stopping him in his tracks. He paused, his brow furrowing as he crouched down, his knees creaking in protest. There, nestled among the crimson pools staining the floor, lay a small, ornate card. Miller's heart raced as he reached out with a gloved hand, carefully plucking the object from its macabre resting place.

"What have you found?" Keirstead's voice floated over, tinged with curiosity and a hint of apprehension.

Miller didn't respond immediately, his eyes fixed on the card's surface. A chill ran down his spine as he took in the twisted, serpentine symbol etched into its face. The intricate design seemed to writhe before his eyes, as if alive and malevolent. He swallowed hard, his throat suddenly dry.

"Look at this," he said quietly, his voice barely above a whisper. As he held up the card, memories flooded his mind - fragmented images of similar symbols, whispered conversations, and a growing sense of dread.

Miller's thoughts raced, each possibility more terrifying than the last. He felt the weight of his complicated existence bearing down on him, threatening to crush him under its immense pressure. Yet, beneath the fear and uncertainty, a spark of determination ignited. This card, this symbol, might be the key to unlocking the mysteries that had plagued him for so long.

"What do you make of it?" he asked Keirstead, his eyes never leaving the sinister design. "We're always seeing this symbol, aren't we?"

9 - 10

Keirstead knelt beside Miller, her sharp features etched with concentration as she leaned in to examine the card. Her dark eyes narrowed, scanning every intricate detail of the serpentine symbol. Miller watched her closely, searching for any flicker of recognition in her expression.

"What is that?" Keirstead murmured, her voice low and tinged with a mix of fascination and unease. She reached out, her fingers hovering just above the card's surface as if afraid to touch it. "I've never seen anything quite like it before."

Miller's heart sank a little at her words. He'd hoped that perhaps Keirstead's keen detective instincts might have provided some immediate insight. Still, he couldn't shake the feeling that this symbol was significant, a piece of a larger puzzle he was desperately trying to solve.

"We've seen this before. The dead cabbies, the missing Johnson girl, my accident. It's all connected. Connected by a shared common element. This symbol." Miller replied, his voice rough with tension. He turned the card over in his hands, searching for any additional clues. "The way it's designed, it almost seems to move when you look at it. Like it's alive somehow."

Keirstead nodded, her brow furrowed in deep thought. "It definitely doesn't look like any gang symbol or calling card I've come across in my work. This feels... different. More ominous, somehow. Why is it, every time we find this symbol, that each design is more intricate then the last. Like he's adding details to the design each time."

As they studied the card together, Miller couldn't help but feel a growing sense of urgency. This symbol, whatever it represented, could be the key to understanding his fractured existence, to saving his family. He needed answers, and he needed them soon.

"We need to get this analyzed right away," Miller said, carefully placing the card into an evidence bag. "Maybe forensics can tell us something about its origin or composition."

11 - 12

Miller hesitated for a moment, his mind racing as he weighed the potential consequences of sharing his knowledge. The crisp autumn air carried the distant laughter from the Bulldog Bar and Grill, a stark contrast to the grim scene before them. Finally, he spoke, his voice low and tinged with a mix of trepidation and certainty.

" It's Gabriel's calling card."

The words hung heavy in the air between them, laden with implications. Miller watched Keirstead closely, noting the subtle shift in her expression as recognition dawned. Her eyes widened, the seriousness of the situation etching itself across her features.

"Gabriel?" Keirstead breathed, her voice barely above a whisper. "You mean..."

Miller nodded grimly, his heart pounding in his chest. He could almost hear the gears turning in Keirstead's mind, connecting the dots he'd been struggling with for so long. The weight of his dual existence pressed down on him, the memories of both realities vying for dominance in his thoughts.

"I know it sounds crazy," Miller continued, his voice rough with emotion, "but this symbol, it's tied to everything that's been happening. To me, to the murders, to the fractured reality I've been experiencing."

Keirstead's gaze darted between Miller and the card, her professional skepticism warring with the trust she'd built with her partner. "Drake, that's... that's a lot to process. Are you absolutely certain?"

Miller ran a hand through his disheveled hair, frustration and determination mingling in his voice. "As certain as I can be about anything these days. Linda, my family, they're caught up in this somehow. I need you to believe me, Kierstead. We need to follow this lead, wherever it takes us."

13 - 14

Keirstead's brow furrowed, her eyes narrowing as she processed the gravity of Miller's words. "Gabriel?" she repeated, her voice a mix of disbelief and growing concern. "The same Gabriel linked to the other murders?"

Miller nodded, his mind racing with possibilities. The weight of his fractured existence bore down on him as he considered the implications. Two lives, two realities, and at the center of it all, this enigmatic figure named Gabriel. He could feel the pieces of the puzzle shifting, rearranging themselves in his mind, but the full picture remained frustratingly out of reach.

"It has to be," Miller replied, his voice low and intense. "The symbol, the murders, the way he seems to appear and disappear at will - it all fits. But what I can't figure out is why. Why me? Why these victims?"

Keirstead's hand moved instinctively to her holster, her eyes scanning the crime scene with renewed vigilance. "If you're right about this, Drake, we're dealing with something far bigger than we initially thought. A serial killer with some sort of... what? Supernatural abilities?"

Miller's tired eyes met Keirstead's, a flicker of vulnerability passing across his face. "I know how it sounds, Holly. But after everything I've experienced, I'm starting to believe that anything's possible. We need to approach this with an open mind if we're going to have any chance of stopping him."

As he spoke, Miller's thoughts drifted to his family - to the wife he mourned in one reality and the son he'd lost in another. The pain of both losses intertwined, fueling his determination to unravel this mystery and find a way to make things right.

15 - 16

Miller's jaw clenched, his eyes narrowing as he surveyed the grim scene before him. The weight of Dr. Harmon's death pressed heavily on his conscience, a stark reminder of the dire stakes they faced. "It looks like our killer has struck again," he said, his voice rough with tension. "We need to find Gabriel before he claims another victim."

Holly's eyes widened; her sharp features etched with surprise as she processed Miller's revelation. "Gabriel?" she echoed, her mind racing with the implications of his words. "You mean we're dealing with the serial killer?"

Miller nodded grimly, running a hand through his disheveled hair. "Not just any killer, Holly. This one's different. Dangerous in ways we can't even begin to comprehend."

As he spoke, Miller's gaze drifted to the ornate card lying near Dr. Harmon's body, its twisted serpentine symbol seeming to mock him. He couldn't shake the feeling that Gabriel was always one step ahead, playing a game whose rules remained frustratingly opaque.

"What makes you so sure it's him?" Holly pressed, her analytical mind already working to connect the dots.

Miller sighed, feeling the weight of his fractured reality bearing down on him. "It's complicated," he admitted. "But trust me when I say that Gabriel is at the center of all this. And if we don't stop him soon, I fear the consequences will be catastrophic."

Holly's brow furrowed, her expression a mix of concern and determination. "Alright, Drake. I'm with you on this. But we're going to need more than just hunches to track this guy down. What's our next move?"

As Miller considered their options, he couldn't help but wonder how much he should reveal about his unique condition and the bizarre connection he shared with Gabriel. The fate of both his realities hung in the balance, and one wrong move could spell disaster for everyone he loved.

17 - 18

Holly's piercing gaze bore into Miller, her dark eyes narrowing as she processed the implications of what he'd just revealed. "Wait, you're saying your blood has three different DNA profiles?" she asked, her voice a mixture of disbelief and fascination.

Miller felt the weight of her stare, his shoulders tensing as he met her eyes. The fluorescent lights of the lab cast harsh shadows across his weathered face, accentuating the lines of worry etched deep into his skin. He nodded grimly, his expression serious as he held Holly's gaze.

"I know it sounds impossible," he said, his voice low and gravelly. The words seemed to catch in his throat, as if admitting this truth aloud made it all the more real. "But it's true. And it's connected to everything that's happening – to Gabriel, to these murders, to... to me."

As he spoke, Miller's mind raced, grappling with the implications of his condition. How could he possibly explain the fractured nature of his existence, the way his consciousness seemed to straddle multiple realities? The burden of this knowledge pressed down on him, threatening to crush him under its weight.

Holly leaned in closer, her brow furrowed in concentration. "How is that even possible, Drake? And what does it mean for our investigation?"

Miller ran a hand through his disheveled hair, buying himself a moment to gather his thoughts. "I wish I had all the answers, Holly. But what I do know is that understanding this – understanding me – is the key to stopping Gabriel and preventing more deaths."

The silence that followed was heavy with unspoken questions and the looming specter of a killer who seemed to defy the laws of nature itself.

19 - 20

Miller inhaled deeply, his tired eyes reflecting a mix of resignation and determination. " One of them is highly radioactive, as if I were exposed to nuclear radiation," he revealed, his voice barely above a whisper, as if speaking the words too loudly might trigger some catastrophic event.

The fluorescent lights of the lab seemed to flicker momentarily, casting eerie shadows across Miller's face. He clenched his fists, knuckles whitening, as he battled the urge to flee from this impossible truth. The weight of his fractured existence pressed down on him, threatening to suffocate him with each passing second.

Holly's sharp intake of breath cut through the silence. Her piercing eyes widened, a kaleidoscope of emotions flashing across her face - disbelief, concern, and a hint of fear. She leaned forward, her athletic frame tense as if ready to spring into action. "Radioactive?" she echoed, her voice a mix of incredulity and professional curiosity. "Drake, that's... How is that even possible?"

Miller watched as Holly's brow furrowed deeply, her analytical mind visibly working overtime to process this new information. He could almost see the gears turning behind her eyes, piecing together the implications of his condition with the broader scope of their investigation.

"I don't know, Holly," Miller admitted, his voice rough with frustration. "But I'm sure it's connected to everything - the murders, Gabriel, the gaps in my memory. It has to be." He paused, his gaze distant as he wrestled with the fragments of his shattered reality. "Whatever happened to me, whatever caused this... it's the key to understanding what we're up against."

21 - 22

Holly's sharp gaze locked onto Miller, her expression a mixture of awe and disbelief. "That's... unprecedented. I've never heard of anything like it," she breathed, her voice barely above a whisper. The gravity of the situation seemed to settle around them like a heavy fog, making the air thick with tension.

Miller nodded slowly, his tired eyes clouding with introspection. The weight of his condition pressed down on him, each heartbeat a reminder of the inexplicable anomaly coursing through his veins. He ran a hand through his disheveled hair, the gesture betraying a vulnerability rarely seen in the usually composed lawyer-turned-investigator.

"Neither have I," Miller admitted, his voice rough with fatigue and frustration. He leaned back against the wall, his gaze distant as he wrestled with the implications. "What does it mean, Holly? Am I... am I even human anymore?" The question hung in the air, laden with fear and uncertainty.

As he spoke, Miller's mind raced through a labyrinth of possibilities. Was this the reason for his fractured memories, the conflicting realities of his family? The thought of his wife and son - both alive and dead in his mind

- sent a fresh wave of anguish through him. He clenched his fists, the physical pain a welcome distraction from the emotional turmoil.

Holly stepped closer, her presence a steadying force in the chaos of Miller's thoughts. "Human or not, you're still you, Drake," she said firmly, her tone leaving no room for argument. "And we'll figure this out together. Whatever's happening, it's clear that Gabriel is at the center of it all."

Miller met her gaze, drawing strength from her unwavering determination. He nodded, feeling a renewed sense of purpose cutting through his despair. "You're right," he said, straightening up. "We need to focus on finding Gabriel. He's the key to unraveling all of this."

As they stood there, united in their resolve, Miller couldn't shake the feeling that they were standing on the precipice of something far larger and more terrifying than they could imagine. But with Holly by his side, he felt ready to face whatever horrors lay ahead.

23 - 24

Miller's brow furrowed; his eyes distant as he pieced together the horrifying puzzle. "Neither have I," he admitted, his voice low and gravelly. "But it explains why Gabriel targeted Dr. Harmon. He must have known about the blood sample and wanted to eliminate any evidence that could lead back to me."

As he spoke, Miller's hand unconsciously moved to his chest, feeling the phantom ache of a wound that didn't exist in this reality. The memory of Dr. Harmon's lifeless body flashed before his eyes, and he suppressed a shudder. What kind of monster was Gabriel, to go to such lengths? And what did it mean for Miller's own humanity?

Holly listened intently; her sharp features etched with concern. Her piercing eyes never left Miller's face, as if trying to read the secrets hidden beneath his scruffy exterior. She nodded slowly, her expression grave as she absorbed the weight of his words.

"It's a chilling thought," she murmured, her normally direct tone softened by the gravity of the situation. "To think that someone would go to such lengths... it speaks to a level of desperation and ruthlessness that's truly terrifying."

Miller watched as Holly's mind worked, her brow furrowing in that familiar way that told him she was connecting dots, formulating theories. He felt a surge of gratitude for her presence, her unwavering support in the face of this madness. Without her, he might have already lost himself to the chaos of his fractured existence.

"We're dealing with forces beyond our understanding," Miller said, his voice barely above a whisper. "Whatever Gabriel is, whatever I am... it's clear that the stakes are higher than we ever imagined."

25 - 26

Holly's dark eyes flashed with determination as she leaned forward, her voice low and urgent. "It's clear that Gabriel is determined to cover his tracks at any cost. We need to find him before he strikes again."

The gravity of her words hung in the air, heavy and oppressive. Miller felt his jaw tighten, the muscles in his face tensing as he nodded in grim agreement. His mind, already a tumultuous landscape of fractured memories and conflicting realities, began to race with potential strategies to track down the elusive killer.

"You're right," he muttered, running a hand through his disheveled hair. "But where do we even start? Gabriel's always been ten steps ahead of us."

As he spoke, Miller's eyes darted around the room, as if searching for answers in the shadows. His gaze lingered on the case board, covered in photos and notes that seemed to mock their efforts. The face of Gabriel Angel, heavily scarred and hauntingly familiar, stared back at him from multiple angles.

"We need to think like him," Holly suggested, her voice cutting through Miller's spiraling thoughts. "What's his next move? Who else might know about your... condition?"

Miller's mind reeled at the implications. Who else indeed? The list of potential targets sent a chill down his spine, each name carrying the weight of a possible death sentence. He couldn't shake the image of Dr. Harmon's lifeless body, wondering who might be next to pay the price for his fractured existence.

"We need to protect them," he said, his voice rough with emotion. "But we also need to use this. Gabriel's desperation might be our best chance to catch him off guard."

As the words left his mouth, Miller felt a familiar duality settling over him. Part of him, the dedicated detective, was already formulating plans and contingencies. But another part, the part that understood the otherworldly nature of their adversary, whispered warnings of caution.

Holly nodded, her eyes glinting with a mixture of concern and determination. "It's risky, but you're right. We can't just wait for him to strike again. We need to force his hand."

27 - 28

Miller ran a hand through his disheveled hair, his tired eyes reflecting the weight of their task. "Agreed. Let's get to work. We can't afford to waste any time."

The words hung in the air, charged with urgency. Holly's piercing gaze met Miller's, a silent understanding passing between them. She reached for her tablet, fingers flying across the screen as she pulled up a map of the city.

"We should start by mapping out potential targets," Holly suggested, her voice crisp and focused. "Anyone connected to your past, your condition, or the investigation."

Miller nodded, his mind racing. "Good idea. We'll need to set up surveillance, maybe even protective details." He paused, a flicker of vulnerability crossing his face. "My family... they need to be our top priority."

As they huddled over the tablet, Miller couldn't shake the image of Gabriel's disfigured face, those piercing eyes that seemed to hold untold secrets. The memory sent a shiver down his spine, a stark reminder of the danger they faced.

"What about your contacts in the department?" Holly asked, her brow furrowed in concentration. "Anyone who might have access to sensitive information about the case?"

Miller's jaw tightened, weighing the implications. "I'll make some calls, discreetly. We can't risk tipping off Gabriel if he has eyes inside."

As they worked, the gravity of their situation settled over them like a heavy cloak. Every name they added to their list was a potential victim, every location a possible crime scene. Miller felt the familiar pull of his dual nature – the detective driven to solve the case, and the man grappling with the otherworldly implications of his fractured existence.

"We're racing against time," Holly murmured, voicing the thought that hung unspoken between them.

Miller nodded grimly. "And Gabriel's always one step ahead. We need to change that."

With a shared sense of purpose, Miller and Holly dove deeper into their plans, knowing that their investigation could mean the difference between life and death for those caught in the killer's path. The clock ticked relentlessly, each second bringing them closer to Gabriel's next move – and their chance to finally bring him down.

Unspoken Tensions

Miller House – Blue World – 2024

1 - 2

The weight of unspoken words settled heavily on Drake Miller's shoulders as he lowered himself onto the worn leather couch beside Linda. The scent of her familiar lavender perfume mingled with the musty odor of old case files scattered across the coffee table, a poignant reminder of the life they once shared. Drake's fingers trembled slightly as he reached for Linda's hand, his calloused skin rough against her soft palm.

"Linda," he began, his voice barely above a whisper, "there's something I need to tell you."

Drake's heart raced, pounding so forcefully he was certain Linda could hear it. He struggled to maintain his composure, acutely aware that what he was about to say would shatter the fragile peace they'd managed to construct in the aftermath of their tragedy. The words he needed to speak felt like shards of glass in his throat, threatening to tear him apart from the inside out.

As he gazed into Linda's eyes, those same blue eyes that had captivated him years ago, Drake found himself transported back to happier times. Memories of family picnics, Harrison's laughter echoing through their backyard, and quiet evenings spent in each other's arms flooded his mind. The stark contrast between those joyful moments and the harsh reality of their current situation threatened to overwhelm him.

Drake took a deep breath, steeling himself for what was to come. He knew that once he spoke, there would be no going back. The truth would be out there, raw and painful, forever altering the delicate balance they'd struck between hope and despair. Yet, he also knew that he couldn't keep this secret any longer. The burden of knowledge weighed too heavily on his conscience, threatening to crush him beneath its weight.

With a gentle squeeze of Linda's hand, Drake prepared to unleash the words that would either bring them closer together or drive them irreparably apart. The air between them crackled with tension, thick with unspoken fears and desperate longing. In that moment, as he teetered on the precipice of revelation, Drake Miller felt more vulnerable than he ever had in his life, acutely aware that the next few minutes would determine the course of their future—both in this world and the other.

3 - 4

Linda's piercing blue eyes locked onto Drake's face, searching every crease and shadow for a clue to the weight behind his words. Her gaze, once a source of comfort, now felt like a spotlight, exposing every ounce of turmoil churning within him. Drake's throat tightened, his carefully prepared words suddenly evaporating under the intensity of her scrutiny.

"What is it, Drake?" Linda's voice trembled slightly, a mix of concern and trepidation coloring her tone. She leaned forward, her blonde hair cascading over her shoulders, creating a curtain between them and the rest of the world.

Drake's mind raced, grappling with the enormity of what he was about to reveal. How could he possibly explain the inexplicable? The parallel worlds, the duality of his existence, the son who was both lost and found? He opened his mouth, then closed it again, words failing him in this crucial moment.

Linda's brow furrowed, her concern deepening with each passing second of silence. "Drake, you're scaring me. Whatever it is, we can face it together. We always have."

Her words, meant to reassure, only intensified the ache in Drake's chest. He thought, 'If only it were that simple. If only we could truly face this together without tearing apart the fabric of our reality.' The weight of his dual lives pressed down on him, threatening to crush him under the strain of keeping both worlds intact.

Finally, Drake found his voice, rough with emotion. "Linda, I... I'm not sure how to explain this. It's going to sound impossible, maybe even cruel. But I need you to listen, to try and understand." He paused, gathering his courage. "It's about Harrison. There's something you need to know, something that changes everything."

5 - 6

Drake's hand moved almost of its own accord, reaching out to grasp Linda's. His grip was firm, reassuring, anchoring them both in this moment of impending revelation. He could feel the slight tremor in her fingers, the warmth of her skin against his palm, and it grounded him, giving him the strength to continue.

"It's about Harrison," he began, his voice low and steady despite the tempest of emotions raging within him. "In the other world, he's... he's doing well." Drake's eyes never left Linda's face, watching intently for her reaction as he continued, "He's taken up tennis, your favorite sport, and he even has a date for senior prom."

The words hung in the air between them, heavy with implications that Drake knew Linda couldn't yet fully comprehend. He held his breath, waiting for her response, his mind racing. 'How can I make her understand without shattering her completely? How do I explain that our son is both gone and thriving, existing in a reality just beyond our reach?'

Linda's expression shifted, a kaleidoscope of emotions playing across her features - confusion, hope, disbelief, and a flicker of something that looked dangerously like anger. Her grip on Drake's hand tightened, her knuckles turning white with the force of it.

"Drake," she whispered, her voice barely audible, "what are you saying? What... about Harrison? What's really going on?"

Drake swallowed hard, knowing that his next words would irrevocably change everything. He leaned in closer, his free hand coming up to cup Linda's cheek, his thumb brushing away a tear she hadn't even realized had fallen. "Linda, I know this sounds impossible, but I need you to listen. There's so much more I have to tell you..."

7 - 8

Linda's breath caught in her throat, her eyes widening as the full weight of Drake's words crashed over her. Tears welled up, spilling down her cheeks in silent streams as she struggled to process the impossible information. Her chest heaved with ragged breaths, each one a battle against the overwhelming tide of emotion threatening to drown her.

"Harrison... alive?" she choked out, her voice barely above a whisper. "But how... I don't understand... I thought this was a mere delusion of yours/ A way you found to help cope with his loss. Drake, I want to believe I really do, but how can I?"

Drake's heart clenched at the raw pain in her voice. He wanted nothing more than to pull her into his arms, to shield her from the cruel reality of their fractured existence. But he knew he had to give her time, to let her work through the shock.

"It's complicated, Linda," he began, his tone gentle. "I know it sounds insane, but—"

Before he could finish, Linda's expression shifted. The initial shock and grief morphed into something darker, more volatile. Her tears, once born of sorrow, now fueled by a rising anger that seemed to radiate from her very core.

"No," she hissed, jerking her hand away from Drake's grasp. "No, this isn't possible. This isn't fair!"

Drake recoiled slightly, taken aback by the sudden vehemence in her voice. "Linda, please, I know it's hard to believe, but—"

"Hard to believe?" Linda's voice rose, cracking with emotion. "It's impossible! How dare you sit here continuing to spew with these... these fantasies?" She stood abruptly, her whole body trembling. "Do you have any idea what you're doing to me?"

As Linda's anger boiled over, Drake found himself caught between the desire to comfort her and the need to make her understand. His mind raced, searching for the right words to bridge the chasm that seemed to be widening between them with each passing second.

9 - 10

Linda's eyes blazed with a fury Drake had never seen before, her voice rising to a crescendo as she unleashed her anguish. "How dare you?! How dare you come here and taunt me with fantasies of our son's life when I'm left here to grieve for him every single day?!"

The force of her words hit Drake like a physical blow, causing him to recoil involuntarily. His heart shattered anew at the sight of Linda's pain, raw and unfiltered. He longed to reach out, to pull her close and whisper reassurances, but the chasm between them seemed insurmountable.

"Linda, I—" Drake's voice cracked, thick with emotion. He swallowed hard, struggling to find the right words. "I never meant to cause you more pain. I thought... I thought knowing he was alive somewhere might bring you comfort."

Linda's fists clenched at her sides; her blonde hair wild around her tear-stained face. "Comfort? You think this brings me comfort?" She laughed bitterly, the sound devoid of any warmth. "It's torture, Drake. Pure torture."

Drake's mind raced, desperately trying to make her understand. "I know it seems impossible, but I swear to you, it's real. In that other world, Harrison is living the life we always dreamed for him. He's happy, Linda. He's thriving."

"Stop it!" Linda cried, pressing her hands to her ears. "I can't bear to hear this. Our son is gone, Drake. Gone! And no amount of fantastical stories will bring him back to me."

As he watched Linda crumble before him, Drake felt the weight of his dual existence more acutely than ever. How could he reconcile these two realities? How could he ease Linda's pain when he couldn't even fully comprehend the situation himself?

"I'm sorry," he whispered, his own tears falling freely now. "I'm so sorry, Linda. I never meant to hurt you like this."

11 - 12

"Linda, I..." Drake's voice cracked, his outstretched hand trembling in the space between them. The afternoon sun filtering through the stained-glass windows of their Bridgewater home cast a kaleidoscope of colors across Linda's grief-stricken face, accentuating the raw anguish etched into every line.

But before he could finish his thought, Linda pushed past him with unexpected force, her sobs echoing through the room like a haunting melody. The scent of her favorite lavender perfume lingered in the air, a cruel reminder of happier times. Drake watched helplessly as she retreated down the hallway, her footsteps heavy with the weight of her sorrow.

"Linda, please," he called after her, his voice barely above a whisper. He longed to chase after her, to gather her in his arms and somehow make this all right. But he knew, deep in his bones, that there was nothing he could say or do to ease this pain.

As Linda's cries faded into the depths of their home, Drake felt his own tears begin to fall. They mingled with the dust motes dancing in the autumn sunlight, each droplet a testament to the depth of their shared suffering. He sank onto the worn leather couch, the same one where they'd spent countless evenings cuddled with Harrison, watching movies and dreaming of the future.

"What have I done?" Drake thought, burying his face in his hands. The weight of his dual existence pressed down on him, threatening to crush him under its impossible burden. How could he bridge the gap between these two realities when he could barely make sense of them himself?

The clock on the mantel ticked relentlessly, each second a reminder of the life they'd lost and the fractured existence they now endured. Drake lifted his head, his gaze falling on a framed photo of Harrison, his son's infectious grin frozen in time. "I'm sorry, buddy," he whispered to the empty room. "I'm so sorry I couldn't protect you both."

13 - 14

Drake rose slowly, his body heavy with exhaustion and grief, and made his way to Linda's side. She sat curled on the window seat, her gaze fixed on the world outside, a world that seemed to mock their pain with its normalcy. He lowered himself beside her, close enough to offer comfort but not so close as to intrude on her space.

"Linda," he began, his voice rough with emotion, "I know there's nothing I can say to make this better. But please, don't shut me out. We need each other now more than ever."

She turned to him, her blue eyes red-rimmed and swimming with tears. "How can you even be here, Drake? How can you sit there and talk about Harrison as if... as if he's still alive somewhere?"

Drake's heart clenched at the raw anguish in her voice. He longed to tell her everything, to explain the impossible duality of his existence, but he knew she wasn't ready to hear it. Instead, he reached out tentatively, his hand hovering over hers.

"Because I have to believe there's still hope," he said softly. "I have to believe that our love for Harrison, for each other, means something. That it can somehow bridge this... this chasm between us."

Linda's fingers twitched, almost imperceptibly, towards his. "I want to believe that too, Drake. But it hurts so much. Every time I close my eyes, I see his face. I hear his laugh. And then I wake up, and he's gone all over again."

Drake swallowed hard, fighting back a fresh wave of tears. "I know, sweetheart. I feel it too. Every second of every day." He paused, searching for the right words. "Maybe... maybe we can find a way to honor his memory together. To keep him alive in our hearts, even if we can't have him here with us."

15 - 16

Miller's words hung in the air, heavy with the weight of their shared grief. He watched Linda's face intently, noting the subtle shifts in her expression as she processed his suggestion. Her eyes, still glistening with unshed tears, seemed to soften ever so slightly.

"Linda, I understand your pain. I feel it too, every moment of every day," Drake said, his voice barely above a whisper. He fought to keep his tone steady; to be the anchor she needed in this storm of emotions. But inside, he was drowning in the duality of his existence, torn between the world where Harrison lived and this one where they mourned him.

Linda turned to him, her eyes red-rimmed and raw with emotion. The sight of her anguish made Drake's heart constrict painfully in his chest. He longed to pull her into his arms, to shield her from the cruel reality that had shattered their lives. But he held back, uncertain if his touch would bring comfort or provoke more pain.

"How?" Linda's voice cracked on the single syllable. "How can you understand when I can barely breathe some days? When every little thing reminds me of him?"

Drake closed his eyes briefly, wrestling with the urge to reveal the truth about his split reality. Instead, he reached for her hand, relieved when she didn't pull away. "Because he's a part of me, just as he's a part of you. And that connection... it's both beautiful and excruciating."

17 - 18

Linda's fingers tightened around Drake's; her grip almost painful as she searched his face. Her blue eyes, once so full of warmth and laughter, now held an ocean of grief that threatened to drown them both.

"Do you? Do you really understand, Drake?" Linda's voice trembled, raw with emotion. "Because it feels like you're living in a different world, a world where our son is still alive, while I'm left here drowning in grief."

The words hit Drake like a physical blow, knocking the air from his lungs. He swallowed hard, fighting against the tide of guilt that threatened to overwhelm him. How could he explain the impossible truth without shattering what little stability they had left?

"Linda, I..." Drake began, his voice hoarse. He ran his free hand through his disheveled dark hair, a nervous habit he'd developed since the accident. "I wish I could make you understand. The pain, it's... it's with me every moment, just in a different way."

As he spoke, Drake's mind raced with images of Harrison in that other reality – laughing, growing, living. The joy of those moments collided violently with the stark emptiness of this world, where Harrison's absence was a constant, aching void.

Miller's heart broke at her words, knowing that no matter how much he longed to bridge the gap between them, he could never truly understand the depth of her sorrow. The weight of his dual existence pressed down on him, a secret burden he couldn't share.

"I know it seems impossible," Drake continued, his brown eyes searching Linda's face, desperate to connect. "But please believe me when I say that I'm right here with you in this pain. Every. Single. Day."

19 - 20

Drake leaned forward, his tired eyes brimming with a desperate intensity. "I know it's hard to believe, Linda, but in the other world... it's not just a fantasy. It's real." His voice cracked, raw with emotion. "And I promise you, I would give anything to bring him back to us if I could."

The words hung in the air between them, heavy with the weight of impossible truths and shared grief. Drake's hand trembled slightly as he reached out, longing to bridge the chasm that had opened between them. He watched Linda's face, searching for any sign that his words had reached her.

Linda's blue eyes, usually so warm and understanding, had been clouded with pain and anger moments before. But as she processed Drake's words, something shifted in her expression. The hard lines of anguish softened, ever so slightly, as she looked at him.

Drake held his breath, his heart pounding. He could see the conflict playing out across Linda's features – the desire to believe warring with the crushing reality of their loss. Her long blonde hair fell across her face, and he resisted the urge to brush it back, to offer some small comfort.

"Linda," he whispered, his voice barely audible. "I know how crazy it sounds. But please, try to understand. I'm living this nightmare right alongside you, just... differently."

Linda's gaze met his, and for a moment, Drake saw a glimmer of the connection they'd once shared. Her expression softened, not with forgiveness or acceptance, but with a hint of the empathy that had always been at her core.

21 - 22

Linda's voice quivered as she spoke, her words cutting through the heavy silence. "I know you would, Drake. And I'm sorry for lashing out at you. It's just... sometimes it's easier to be angry than to face the pain head-on."

The rawness in her voice tore at Drake's heart. He could see the toll their fractured reality had taken on her – the dark circles under her eyes, the slight tremor in her hands. Linda had always been his rock, but now she seemed as fragile as spun glass.

Without hesitation, Drake reached out, his calloused hand finding hers. He marveled at how small and delicate her fingers felt in his grasp, a stark contrast to the strength he knew she possessed. As he held her hand, he felt the familiar warmth of her skin, a sensation that anchored him in this moment, in this version of reality.

"I understand," Drake murmured, his thumb tracing gentle circles on the back of her hand. "Anger is... easier. Simpler. But Linda, we can't let it consume us. Harrison wouldn't want that."

He watched as Linda's eyes welled with fresh tears at the mention of their son's name. Drake's mind raced, torn between the grief of this world and the bittersweet knowledge of Harrison's existence in another. He longed to share more, to paint a vivid picture of their son's life, but he knew it would only deepen Linda's pain.

Instead, he simply held her hand tighter, offering what little comfort he could in the face of their shared loss. The silence between them was thick with unspoken words and impossible longings.

23 - 24

Drake took a deep breath, his voice low and steady as he spoke, "You don't have to face it alone, Linda. We'll get through this together, one day at a time."

As the words left his lips, he felt a subtle shift in the air, a lightening of the oppressive weight that had been bearing down on them both. Linda's fingers tightened around his, a silent acknowledgment of his promise.

Drake's mind wandered to the courtrooms of his past, where he had once wielded words like weapons, caring little for the collateral damage. Now, each syllable felt heavy with responsibility, laden with the power to heal or harm. He chose them carefully, like a man diffusing a bomb.

"I know I wasn't always there before," he confessed, his voice barely above a whisper. "Work consumed me, and I... I lost sight of what truly mattered. But I'm here now, Linda. For you. For us."

Linda's blue eyes met his, a storm of emotions swirling within them. "Drake," she began, her voice catching. "I want to believe that. I do. But how can we move forward when half of our heart is missing?"

The question hung between them, heavy and unanswerable. Drake felt the familiar pull of his other reality, where Harrison was alive and well, playing tennis and going to prom. The contrast was a cruel joke of the universe.

"We honor him," Drake finally replied, surprised by the strength in his own voice. "We live for him, Linda. We carry his memory with us, in everything we do."

As they sat together in the quiet of the room, the fading sunlight casting long shadows across the floor, Drake felt a glimmer of hope amidst the darkness. It was fragile, barely perceptible, but it was there. He knew that no matter how difficult the journey might be, they would always have each other to lean on. In this world, and perhaps, somehow, in others too.

Night Shift Secrets

Blue World – 2024

1 - 2

Drake Miller's eyes stung as he stared at the glowing computer screen, the harsh fluorescent light of his cramped office casting long shadows across stacks of case files and discarded coffee cups. His fingers flew across the keyboard, each click echoing in the stillness of the night as he delved deeper into the gruesome details of the recent murders plaguing the city.

"Damn it," he muttered, running a hand through his disheveled dark hair. "There has to be something here, some connection I'm missing."

The faces of the victims flashed before him - young, old, men, women - seemingly random targets of a depraved killer. But as Drake's tired eyes scanned row after row of data, a faint pattern began to emerge from the chaos.

He leaned in closer, brow furrowed in concentration. "Wait a second..."

Forensic reports blurred together as he scrolled frantically, heart pounding. There - a shared chemical compound found at multiple crime scenes. And here - trace DNA evidence that didn't match the victims but appeared across several cases.

"It can't be a coincidence," Drake murmured, mind racing. "These murders, they're connected somehow."

He pushed back from the desk, pacing the small office as pieces started falling into place. The killer wasn't choosing victims at random - there was a method to the madness, a sinister design hidden beneath the surface.

"What am I missing?" he growled in frustration, raking his fingers through his hair again. "What's the link?"

Drake's gaze fell on a framed photo of Linda and Harrison, their smiling faces a stark contrast to the grim reality surrounding him. A pang of guilt twisted in his gut as he realized how long it had been since he'd seen them.

"I'm sorry," he whispered to the photograph. "I have to do this. I have to stop whoever's behind these killings before anyone else gets hurt."

With renewed determination, he returned to the computer, diving back into the data. The thread connecting the cases grew stronger with each new revelation, weaving an intricate web of secrets and lies that threatened to ensnare the entire city.

As dawn broke outside his window, Drake knew he was on the verge of uncovering something big - something that could change everything. The truth was out there, hidden in the shadows, and he would stop at nothing to bring it into the light.

3 - 4

Drake Miller slumped back in his chair, his tired eyes burning as he rubbed them roughly. The harsh glow of the computer screen illuminated his haggard face, casting deep shadows that accentuated the lines of exhaustion etched into his features. His gaze fixed on the data before him, disbelief warring with a growing sense of excitement.

"It can't be," he murmured, leaning forward to scrutinize the results once more. "A shared genetic trait among all the victims? How is that even possible?"

His mind raced, recalling the faces of those who had fallen victim to the killer's brutal spree. They had seemed so different, so disconnected. Yet here, hidden in their very DNA, was an undeniable link.

Drake's heart began to pound, a mix of anticipation and trepidation coursing through his veins. He pushed back from the desk, pacing the cluttered office as the implications of his discovery began to sink in.

"This could be it," he said aloud, his voice rough with emotion. "The key to unlocking this whole damn case."

He paused, his eyes falling on the framed photo of Linda and Harrison. Their smiling faces seemed to mock him, a reminder of the life he'd left behind in his relentless pursuit of justice. Drake picked up the frame, his fingers tracing the outline of his son's face.

"I'm doing this for you," he whispered. "For both of you. To make the world safer."

Setting the photo down, Drake turned back to his computer, his mind already racing with possibilities. "If we can identify others with this genetic marker," he mused, "we might be able to predict the killer's next move. Maybe even catch the bastard before they strike again."

The weight of his discovery pressed down on him, a mixture of hope and fear twisting in his gut. This breakthrough could change everything, but it also opened up a Pandora's box of new questions and challenges.

"One step at a time, Miller," he reminded himself, sinking back into his chair. "First, we need to confirm these findings. Then we can start piecing together the bigger picture."

As he began compiling his notes, Drake couldn't shake the feeling that he was standing on the precipice of something monumental. The truth was within reach, and he was determined to grasp it, no matter the cost.

5 - 6

Drake Miller's heart pounded in his chest as he strode through the precinct's bustling corridors, his footsteps echoing off the polished linoleum floors. The manila folder clutched tightly in his hands felt like it contained dynamite, ready to explode and reshape the entire investigation. He navigated past chattering officers and ringing phones, his mind racing with the implications of his discovery.

Reaching Detective Holly Sharp's office, Drake paused, taking a deep breath to steady himself. He rapped his knuckles against the door frame, the sound sharp and urgent.

"Come in," Holly's crisp voice called from within.

Drake stepped inside, immediately noting the organized chaos of Holly's workspace. Case files were stacked in neat piles, post-it notes adorned her computer monitor, and a half-empty cup of coffee sat precariously close to the edge of her desk.

Holly glanced up, her piercing eyes locking onto Drake's disheveled appearance. "Drake, what brings you here?" she asked, her tone direct and to the point.

Drake's fingers tightened around the folder as he approached her desk. "Holly, I've found something that could blow this case wide open," he said, his voice low and intense. "It's big, possibly game-changing."

He couldn't help but notice the slight raise of Holly's eyebrow, a telltale sign of her interest piqued. As he prepared to lay out his findings, Drake's mind raced. 'This is it,' he thought. 'The moment that could change everything. But am I ready for what comes next?'

7 - 8

Drake laid the files on Holly's desk with a decisive thump, his heart pounding with a mixture of excitement and trepidation. "I think I've found something," he said, his voice tinged with urgency. "A genetic trait shared by all the victims."

Holly's sharp eyes narrowed as she reached for the files, her efficient movements betraying her keen interest. Drake watched intently as she flipped through the reports, her brow furrowing in concentration. The silence in the room was thick with anticipation, broken only by the soft rustle of papers and the distant hum of the precinct beyond the office door.

"This is... incredible," Holly murmured, her eyes scanning the data with lightning speed. Drake could almost see the gears turning in her mind, piecing together the implications of his discovery. "If what you're saying is true, it could be a major breakthrough in the case."

Drake leaned forward, resting his palms on the edge of her desk. "I've been poring over these files for weeks," he said, his voice low and intense. "At first, I thought I was seeing patterns where there weren't any. But the more I dug, the clearer it became. This genetic marker... it's like a signature, Holly. It's there in every victim."

As Holly continued to study the reports, Drake's mind raced with possibilities. 'Could this be the key we've been searching for?' he wondered. 'Or am I grasping at straws, desperate for any lead in this seemingly unsolvable case?'

He watched Holly's face carefully, searching for any sign of doubt or dismissal. But her expression remained focused, her eyes darting back and forth across the pages with fierce concentration. The tension in the room was palpable, charged with the potential of this new discovery.

9 - 10

Drake's pulse quickened with anticipation as he watched Holly absorb the information. The weight of his discovery hung heavy in the air, mingling with the scent of stale coffee and the faint whir of the office's aging air conditioner.

"We need to confirm this link," Drake said, his voice tight with urgency. "Inform the lab to run further tests. And we need to track down anyone else who shares this trait. It could be our best lead yet."

Holly looked up from the files, her eyes meeting Drake's with a mix of excitement and trepidation. "Agreed," she said, her tone matching the seriousness of the situation. "I'll assemble a team to follow up on your findings immediately."

As Holly reached for her phone, Drake's mind raced with the implications of their next steps. 'This could be it,' he thought, a flicker of hope igniting in his chest. 'The break we've been waiting for. But what if it leads us down another dead end?'

The memory of his family flashed through his mind - Linda's warm smile, Harrison's mischievous grin. For a moment, the weight of his dual existence pressed down on him, threatening to overwhelm his focus. Drake shook his head slightly, forcing himself back to the present.

"What's our next move?" he asked Holly, his voice slightly hoarse with emotion. "We need to be careful how we proceed. If the killer catches wind of what we've found..."

11 - 12

Drake's voice trailed off as the implications hung heavy in the air. Holly leaned forward, her brow furrowed in concentration.

"We'll need to keep this under wraps," she said, her fingers drumming a nervous rhythm on the desk. "Limit the information to a select few. Maybe start with a discreet search of medical records?"

Drake nodded, his mind already racing ahead. "Good idea. We could cross-reference with our database of known offenders, see if any red flags pop up."

As they delved deeper into their brainstorming session, the office seemed to fade away, leaving only the electric current of their shared focus. Drake found himself pacing, his restless energy a stark contrast to Holly's steady presence at her desk.

"What if," Drake mused, running a hand through his disheveled hair, "what if this trait isn't just a coincidence? What if the killer is specifically targeting individuals with this genetic marker?"

Holly's eyes widened at the implication. "That would mean our perpetrator has access to genetic information. Medical records, DNA databases..."

"Exactly," Drake said, his voice tight with a mix of excitement and dread. "We could be looking at someone with insider knowledge. A doctor, a lab technician, maybe even someone in law enforcement."

The weight of this possibility settled over them like a heavy blanket. Drake's mind flashed to his son Harrison, his curious nature and inquisitive eyes. What if he carried this genetic trait? The thought sent a chill down Drake's spine.

"We need to cast a wide net," Holly said, breaking into Drake's spiraling thoughts. "But carefully. If we're right about this, we can't risk tipping off our suspect."

Drake nodded, forcing himself to focus. "Agreed. Let's start by..."

Hours melted away as they pored over the evidence, their voices rising and falling in a steady rhythm of theories and counterarguments. The weight of their discovery hung in the air, mingling with the tension and excitement that crackled between them.

As the night wore on, Drake found his thoughts drifting to Linda, wondering which version of her he'd see when he finally made it home. The duality of his existence pressed upon him, a constant reminder of the fragility of his reality.

"Drake?" Holly's voice cut through his reverie. "You still with me?"

He blinked, refocusing on the task at hand. "Yeah, sorry. Just... thinking about the implications of all this."

Holly's expression softened with understanding. "It's a lot to process. But we're on to something here, I can feel it."

Drake nodded, a small smile tugging at his lips despite the gravity of the situation. "You're right. Let's keep going. We're close to cracking this, I know it."

With renewed determination, they dove back into their work, the night stretching endlessly before them, full of possibilities and hidden dangers.

13 - 14

The fluorescent lights flickered, casting long shadows across the nearly deserted precinct as Drake Miller gathered his belongings, his mind a whirlwind of theories and half-formed connections. He paused, running a hand through his disheveled hair, the weight of the case pressing down on his shoulders like a physical burden.

"You heading out?" Holly Sharp's voice cut through the silence, her tone laced with a mixture of exhaustion and lingering excitement.

Drake nodded, his tired eyes meeting hers. "Yeah, I think we've done all we can for tonight. But this genetic link... it's big, Holly. Really big."

She leaned against her desk, arms crossed. "I know. It's like we've stumbled onto the edge of something massive. But Drake, be careful. We don't know how deep this rabbit hole goes."

A wry smile tugged at the corner of his mouth. "Careful? When have you known me to be careful?"

Holly's laugh was tinged with concern. "That's exactly what worries me. Just... watch your back, okay?"

Drake nodded, his mind already racing ahead to the next steps. As he made his way through the quiet corridors, he couldn't help but wonder which version of his life he'd be stepping into tonight. Would it be the world where Linda waited for him, her presence a balm to his troubled soul? Or the one where Harrison's laughter echoed through an empty house, a bittersweet reminder of what he'd lost?

The cool night air hit him as he stepped outside, bringing with it a moment of clarity. He stood there, letting the breeze wash over him, his thoughts a tumultuous sea of possibilities.

"We're close," he muttered to himself, stuffing his hands into his pockets. "So damn close to cracking this thing wide open."

As he walked to his car, the city's nighttime bustle faded into the background. Every shadow seemed to hold a secret, every passerby a potential lead. The genetic revelation they'd uncovered was just the tip of the iceberg, he was sure of it.

Drake paused, his hand on the car door, as a familiar figure caught his eye across the street. For a moment, he could have sworn he saw Holly Keirstead, her long black hair unmistakable even in the dim streetlight. But when he blinked, she was gone, leaving him to wonder if his exhausted mind was playing tricks on him.

"Get it together, Miller," he chastised himself, sliding into the driver's seat. "You're seeing ghosts now?"

As he started the engine, Drake couldn't shake the feeling that they were standing on the precipice of something monumental. The genetic link, the shared traits among the victims – it all pointed to a conspiracy far larger and more insidious than they'd initially suspected.

"What are we missing?" he mused aloud, his fingers drumming an erratic rhythm on the steering wheel. "What's the piece we can't see yet?"

With a deep breath, Drake pulled away from the curb, the city's nightlife blurring past his windows. Tomorrow would bring new challenges, new leads to chase. But for now, he allowed himself a moment of hope. They were close – closer than they'd ever been before. And no matter which version of his fractured reality he returned to tonight, Drake knew one thing for certain: he wouldn't rest until he uncovered the truth lurking in the shadows, no matter the cost.

15 - 15

Drake's car wound through the labyrinthine streets of the city, streetlights casting intermittent shadows across his furrowed brow. The genetic revelation gnawed at him, each passing moment birthing new theories and questions that demanded answers.

"It can't be coincidence," he muttered, his knuckles white on the steering wheel. "But what's the connection?"

As he approached a red light, Drake's gaze fell on a bustling 24-hour diner. The neon sign flickered, casting an eerie glow that seemed to beckon him. Without fully realizing his decision, he found himself pulling into the parking lot.

The bell chimed as he entered, the aroma of coffee and grease enveloping him. Drake slid into a booth, his mind racing as he absently ordered a black coffee from a tired-looking waitress.

"What would Harrison make of all this?" he wondered, a pang of longing striking his heart. In one reality, his son's insightful observations might have provided a fresh perspective. In the other, Linda's unwavering support would have been a balm to his troubled soul.

The waitress returned, setting down a steaming mug. "Anything else, hon?"

Drake looked up, his exhausted eyes meeting hers. "No, thanks. Actually, wait—" He paused, an idea forming. "You see a lot of people come through here, right?"

She shrugged, "Sure do. All sorts."

"Ever notice any... similarities? People who look related, maybe?"

The waitress's brow furrowed. "Can't say I have. Why? You looking for someone?"

Drake sighed, running a hand through his disheveled hair. "I'm not sure yet. But I think I'm onto something big."

As she walked away, Drake pulled out his phone, fingers flying over the keys as he typed out a message to Detective Sharp:

"Need to expand search parameters. Look for family connections, distant relatives. The genetic link might go deeper than we thought."

He hit send, then leaned back, taking a long sip of coffee. The diner's quiet hum faded into the background as his mind raced, connecting invisible threads between victims and suspects.

"I'm coming for you," Drake whispered to the unseen killer. "And when I find you, I'll make sure you pay for every life you've destroyed."

With renewed determination, he stood, leaving a generous tip before striding back into the night. The truth was out there, hidden in the darkness, and Drake Miller was ready to chase it down, no matter where it led.

Tension in the Interrogation Room

Blue World - 2024

1 - 2

Drake Miller's chest tightened as he stared at the forensic report, the dimly lit interrogation room doing nothing to quell the churning in his stomach. He swallowed hard, his eyes darting over the cold, clinical text, desperate for any shred of answers to the enigma that had consumed his life. The tragic car accident that had ripped his reality in two, leaving him straddling two divergent worlds, plagued him relentlessly. Each day was a constant battle to reconcile the two lives he led, both equally vivid, both equally devastating.

Detective Holly Sharp studied him with a clinical gaze, her sharp features softening ever so slightly as she noticed the anguish etched into his weary face. She knew all too well the burden of secrets, of being ostracized for daring to speak the unspeakable. As a woman in a predominantly male profession, she'd encountered her fair share of skepticism and disdain. But she'd persevered, her determination fueling her success. And now, sitting across from this desperate man, she found herself unable to turn away from the depth of his despair.

Miller's voice, when it finally emerged, was barely a whisper, yet it resonated through the room like a gunshot. 'So, what's the verdict?' He held his breath, as if the very air had been siphoned from the room, his entire existence hanging on her reply.

Sharp hesitated, her fingers drumming against the report. 'The results... they're...' she trailed off, hunting for the right words. How could she possibly explain the inexplicable? The evidence before them defied all logic and reason. But the unmistakable truth stared her in the face, as clear as day: the samples they'd collected from Miller were a perfect match to those at the crime scene.

Drake Miller's world began to crumble around him. The harsh reality of the situation, the gravity of the implications, crashed down on him like a ton of bricks. 'I... I can't have...' he stuttered, the words catching in his throat. 'I didn't...'

His face, already pale, blanched to an ashen hue, and Sharp felt a pang of empathy for the man before her. She'd seen criminal masterminds, hardened by years of callousness and deceit, confess without an ounce of remorse. But never had she seen such genuine disbelief, such a complete and utter lack of comprehension as she did now.

'I...' he began, the words catching in his throat. 'I...'

As the weight of the revelation crushed him, Drake Miller's legs gave out, and he collapsed to the floor in a heap, trembling uncontrollably. Sharp watched, frozen in place, her heart aching for the man before her. This couldn't be the same monster she'd been chasing, could it? The man in front of her seemed nothing more than a broken shell of the cold-blooded killer she'd envisioned.

Slowly, Holly Sharp knelt down and placed a hand on his shaking shoulder, her eyes haunted by the horror reflected in his. "Drake... I... I...," she stuttered, at a loss for words. "I don't know what to say. I don't... I don't understand this either."

The room fell silent, save for the erratic breathing of the two lost souls caught in the eye of a twisted storm. Outside, the storm raged on, a fitting metaphor for the maelstrom that had

3 - 4

Detective Sharp's piercing eyes narrowed as she traced her finger along the report, her lips pursed in concentration. The fluorescent lights buzzed overhead, casting harsh shadows across her stern features. Drake Miller leaned forward, his heart racing, as Sharp finally broke the tense silence.

"The DNA analysis confirms it," she said, her voice low and deliberate. "The genetic trait we discovered in the victims is present in the sample from the robe as well."

Miller's breath caught in his throat, a mixture of exhilaration and dread coursing through his veins. This was the breakthrough they'd been hoping for, the missing piece that could finally crack the case wide open. But as he studied Sharp's grave expression, a chill crept down his spine, settling like ice in the pit of his stomach.

"My God," he whispered, his voice barely audible. "So it's true. The killer really does share this unique genetic marker." His mind raced, piecing together the implications. Could this trait be the key to understanding the murderer's motives? Or was it merely a coincidence, a cruel twist of fate that linked these victims together?

Sharp nodded grimly, her eyes never leaving the report. "It appears so, Miller. But there's more to it than that. This isn't just a simple genetic quirk we're dealing with."

Miller's heart pounded so loudly he was sure Sharp could hear it. He gripped the edge of the table, his knuckles turning white. "What do you mean?" he asked, dreading the answer but knowing he had to hear it.

As Sharp opened her mouth to respond, Miller's thoughts whirled chaotically. What other secrets did this DNA analysis hold? And how deep did this genetic connection truly go? The weight of the unknown pressed down on him, threatening to suffocate him with its dark possibilities.

5 - 6

Sharp's piercing gaze met Miller's, her eyes reflecting a mix of concern and professional detachment. "However," she continued, her tone somber, "there's something else. We found three distinct DNA profiles on the robe, all of which share the same genetic trait."

Miller's brow furrowed in confusion, his mind struggling to process this new information. The fluorescent lights hummed overhead, casting harsh shadows across Sharp's face as she waited for his response. He could feel sweat beading on his forehead, his heart pounding against his ribcage like a trapped animal.

"Three profiles? But that's..." Miller trailed off, the implications sinking in like lead weights in his gut. His fingers unconsciously traced the edge of the report, as if seeking some tangible connection to the truth hidden within its pages. "How is that even possible?" he murmured, more to himself than to Sharp.

The detective leaned forward, her voice dropping to a near whisper. "I don't know, Miller. But whatever we're dealing with here, it's far more complex than we initially thought."

Miller's mind raced, piecing together fragments of information like a deranged jigsaw puzzle. Three DNA profiles, all sharing the same rare genetic trait. The possibilities were staggering, each more terrifying than the last. Could they be dealing with multiple killers? Or was there something even more sinister at play?

"We need to consider every angle," Miller said, his voice hoarse with tension. "Could this be some kind of genetic manipulation? Or are we looking at a family connection?"

Sharp's eyes narrowed, her analytical mind clearly working overtime. "Those are all possibilities we need to explore. But Miller, you need to prepare yourself. This case... it might hit closer to home than any of us expected."

A cold dread settled in Miller's chest, threatening to suffocate him. He knew Sharp was right, but he couldn't shake the feeling that they were standing on the precipice of something far darker and more personal than he could have ever imagined.

7 - 8

Sharp's piercing gaze locked onto Miller's, her expression a mixture of professional detachment and barely concealed concern. "Exactly. One of those profiles is a perfect match to your son, Harrison."

The words hung in the air, heavy and oppressive, as Miller's world tilted on its axis. His heart hammered against his ribcage; each beat a thunderous echo in the suddenly stifling interrogation room. "Harrison?" he choked out, his voice barely above a whisper. "That's... that's impossible. He's just a kid, for God's sake! He's dead!"

Sharp leaned back in her chair, her posture rigid with tension. "I'm sorry, Drake. I know this is difficult to process, but the evidence doesn't lie. Your son's DNA was found on that robe, along with the other two profiles."

A maelstrom of emotions surged through Miller – disbelief, fear, and a sickening sense of betrayal. His hands clenched into fists, knuckles turning white as he struggled to maintain his composure. "There has to be some mistake," he insisted, his words tinged with desperation. "Harrison couldn't be involved in this. He's not capable of... of..."

"Of murder?" Sharp finished softly, her tone devoid of judgment.

Miller's mind reeled, fragments of memories flashing before his eyes – Harrison's laughter, his inquisitive nature, the way his eyes lit up when he talked about his latest scientific discovery. How could that same boy be connected to such horrific crimes?

"I had known there was a connection between the murders and my accident," Miller murmured, more to himself than to Sharp. "But this... this is like a bolt of lightning. It changes everything."

Sharp nodded grimly, her eyes never leaving Miller's face. "You need to bring Harrison in for questioning, Drake. You understand that, don't you? In your other reality, that's what you need to do."

The very thought sent a chill down Miller's spine. He could feel the weight of his dual existence pressing down on him, the fractured realities of his life colliding in this singular, devastating moment. "I need to talk to him first," he said, his voice thick with emotion. "I need to understand... to hear it from him."

As the implications of the revelation sank in, Miller felt a fierce, primal protectiveness surge through him. Despite the evidence, despite the horrors they were investigating, Harrison was still his son. And he would move heaven and earth to protect him, no matter the cost.

9 - 10

Miller leaned forward, his hands gripping the edge of the table so tightly his knuckles turned white. The fluorescent light buzzed overhead, casting harsh shadows across his face as he struggled to process the information. His voice, barely above a whisper, trembled with a mixture of fear and desperation as he asked, "And the other two profiles?"

Detective Sharp's piercing gaze met his, her eyes a storm of sympathy and concern. She hesitated, her usual direct manner faltering for a moment. The silence stretched between them, thick and oppressive, before she finally spoke. "They're identical to yours," she said quietly, her words hanging heavy in the air. Then, with a slight catch in her voice, she added, "But one of them... it's highly radioactive."

Miller's breath caught in his throat, his mind racing to make sense of this new information. "Radioactive?" he repeated, his voice hoarse. "Like mine. How is that even possible?"

Sharp shook her head, her brow furrowing. "We're not sure yet. Our lab techs are baffled. It's like nothing they've ever seen before."

As the implications of Sharp's words sank in, Miller felt a cold dread seeping into his bones. He closed his eyes, trying to steady his breathing. "This can't be happening," he thought, his inner voice a tumult of confusion and fear. "How can there be two profiles identical to mine? And radioactive? What does this mean for Harrison?"

Opening his eyes, Miller met Sharp's gaze once more. "Holly," he said, using her first name in a rare moment of vulnerability, "what does this mean? For me, for Harrison... for the case?"

Sharp leaned back in her chair, her fingers drumming a restless rhythm on the table. "I wish I had answers for you, Drake," she replied, her tone softening slightly. "But right now, we have more questions than answers. You need to bring Harrison in, run more tests, and figure out what's connecting all of this."

Miller nodded slowly, his mind still reeling from the revelations. As he sat there, under the harsh glare of the interrogation room lights, he couldn't shake the feeling that his world was about to change irrevocably. Whatever lay ahead, he knew one thing for certain: he would do whatever it took to protect his son, no matter where this twisted path might lead.

11 - 12

Miller's fingers tightened around the edge of the table, his knuckles turning white as he processed the implications. The weight of Sharp's words settled over him like a suffocating blanket, threatening to crush the air from his lungs. He forced himself to take a deep breath, his mind racing with possibilities, each more terrifying than the last.

"Harrison," he murmured, his voice barely audible even in the stillness of the interrogation room. "My God, Holly, what if he's involved in this somehow?"

Sharp leaned forward, her eyes filled with a mixture of concern and determination. "Drake, we can't jump to conclusions. We need to approach this methodically, gather more information."

Miller shook his head, a bitter laugh escaping his lips. "Methodically? My son could be in danger, and you want me to be methodical?" He ran a hand through his disheveled hair, his internal struggle evident in every movement.

"I know it's difficult," Sharp replied, her tone softening, "but we need to keep a clear head. Tell me about Harrison. Has he been acting differently lately? Anything out of the ordinary?"

Miller's mind whirled, images of his son flashing before his eyes. Harrison's mischievous grin, his boundless energy, his insatiable curiosity. "He's always been an explorer," Miller said, his voice thick with emotion. "Always pushing boundaries, seeking out the next adventure. But lately..."

He trailed off, his brow furrowing as he recalled recent interactions with his son. "He's been more secretive, spending more time alone in his room. I thought it was just typical teenage behavior, but now..." The words hung in the air, heavy with unspoken fears.

Sharp nodded, jotting down notes. "Again you'll need to bring him in for questioning, run some tests. It's crucial we understand the extent of his involvement, if any."

Miller's head snapped up, his eyes blazing with a fierce protectiveness. "I'm not treating my son like a suspect, Holly. He's a victim in this, same as me. For frig sakes he's dead in this world. You suggest he can time jump as well?"

"Drake," Sharp said, her voice firm but compassionate, "we don't know what we're dealing with here. The radioactive DNA, the murders... we need to consider all possibilities."

As the weight of the situation settled over him, Miller felt his resolve harden. He leaned forward, his voice low and intense. "I'll bring Harrison in myself. But I'm not letting him out of my sight, not for a second. Whatever's going on here, whatever danger he might be in, I'm going to protect him. No matter what it takes."

13 - 14

"We need to find him, I need to get home to my son," Drake Miller said, his voice firm with determination, the words resonating through the now-empty interrogation room. Detective Sharp nodded grimly, gathering the scattered papers from the table.

Miller's mind raced, images of Harrison flashing before his eyes – his son's mischievous grin, his boundless energy, the sparkle of curiosity that always danced in his eyes. The thought of that light being snuffed out by some unknown threat sent a shudder through Miller's body.

"I'll drive you," Sharp offered, her tone softer than usual. "We can strategize on the way."

Miller shook his head, running a hand through his disheveled hair. "No, I need to do this alone. Harrison... he's always been sensitive to tension. If he sees us both, if he sees the other you, he'll know something's wrong."

Sharp hesitated, then nodded. "Alright, but I want updates. Every hour, Drake. And if anything seems off—"

"I'll call for backup immediately," Miller finished, already moving towards the door. The weight of the day's revelations pressed down on him, but the urgency of finding Harrison propelled him forward.

Hours later, the relentless tick of the clock echoed through the empty halls of the police station as Drake Miller paced restlessly. Night had fallen, but sleep eluded him like a shadowy phantom, taunting him with its elusive embrace. He had been haunted by the revelations of the day, the weight of the genetic trait discovery pressing down on him like a leaden shroud.

"Dammit, Harrison, what did you do?" he muttered, his voice barely above a whisper. The house had been empty when he'd arrived, no sign of his son. Linda was away visiting her sister, unreachable. Miller's calls in the other world to Harrison's friends had yielded nothing but confusion and concern.

He paused by the window, staring out at the darkness that seemed to press against the glass. His reflection stared back at him – a man haunted, eyes sunken with worry, the scruffy beard a testament to days of neglect.

"I should have seen it," he berated himself, memories of recent weeks flooding back. "The late nights, the secretive behavior. God, I was so caught up in work, in my own guilt... I missed the signs."

The silence of the station seemed to mock him, amplifying every creak and groan of the old building. Miller resumed his pacing, his mind racing through possibilities, each more terrifying than the last.

"Harrison," he whispered, as if his son might somehow hear him across the vast unknown. "Whatever you're mixed up in, whatever's happening... I'm coming for you. I won't let you face this alone. Not this time."

15 - 16

Miller's gaze drifted to the evidence closet, its metal door gleaming dully in the dim light. He approached it slowly, his footsteps echoing in the empty corridor. Standing before it, he could almost hear the siren song of relief emanating from within.

"Just a few hours of sleep," he murmured, his hand hovering over the door handle. "That's all I need to clear my head, to figure this out."

The weight of his badge seemed to grow heavier with each passing moment. Miller's fingers trembled as he grasped the handle, the cool metal a stark contrast to his feverish skin.

"What would Linda say?" he whispered, his voice cracking. "Or Harrison? God, I'm supposed to be setting an example."

He leaned his forehead against the door, closing his eyes. The image of Harrison's face flashed in his mind - not the cocky teenager of recent months, but the wide-eyed boy who used to look at him with such admiration.

"I can't," Miller said, his voice firmer now. "I won't. There has to be another way."

He stepped back from the door, his heart pounding. The temptation still clawed at him, but he clenched his fists, fighting against it.

"Think, Drake," he muttered, pacing again. "What would Harrison do if he was in trouble? Where would he go?"

17 - 18

Drake Miller slipped into the evidence closet, his heart hammering against his ribs like a caged animal desperate for escape. The metallic click of the door echoing in the small space seemed to mock his moment of weakness. Rows of neatly labeled evidence bags stretched before him, a veritable pharmacy of illicit substances and confiscated medications.

"What am I doing?" he muttered, his voice barely above a whisper. His gaze swept over the shelves, each label a silent accusation until his eyes locked onto a familiar bottle. The sedative, potent enough to knock out the most stubborn insomniac, seemed to call out to him.

Miller's hand trembled as he reached for the bottle, his fingers closing around its cool surface. "This isn't me," he said, even as he uncorked it and poured a generous dose. The bitter scent filled the air, promising sweet oblivion.

As he lifted the glass to his lips, Linda's voice echoed in his mind. "Drake, you're stronger than this. Remember who you are."

He hesitated, the liquid inches from his mouth. "But I'm so tired, Linda. So damn tired of fighting."

Harrison's cocky grin flashed before his eyes. "Come on, Dad. You always told me to face my problems head-on. Is this what you meant?"

Miller's hand shook violently, spilling drops of the sedative onto his shirt. With a strangled cry, he slammed the glass down on the shelf, liquid sloshing over the rim.

"No," he growled, gripping the edge of the shelf until his knuckles turned white. "I won't do this. I can't." He looked at the spilled sedative, its promise of relief now nothing more than a puddle of shame. "I have to be better. For Harrison. For Linda. For the man I want to be."

19 - 20

The silence of the evidence closet pressed in on Miller, suffocating as the weight of his decision. For a long moment, he stood motionless, his breath coming in ragged gasps. The sedative's scent still hung in the air, tempting him with its siren call of oblivion.

"I thought it would be instant," Miller whispered, his voice hoarse. "But nothing's changed. The world's still crushing me, Linda. The darkness... it's everywhere."

He closed his eyes, willing the drug to take effect, to numb the pain that had become his constant companion. Slowly, almost imperceptibly at first, the edges of his consciousness began to blur. The sharp contours of his thoughts, once razor-edged with worry and fear, softened into a hazy fog.

"It's... happening," he murmured, his words slurring slightly. "I can feel it, Harrison. The weight... it's lifting."

Miller stumbled, catching himself against the shelf. Evidence bags rattled, their contents a grim reminder of the line he'd just crossed. But as the sedative took hold, even that guilt began to fade, replaced by a wave of blessed relief.

"Is this what peace feels like?" he wondered aloud, a sad smile tugging at his lips. "I'd almost forgotten."

The worries that had plagued him for so long – the fractured realities, the missing pieces of his life – began to recede. In their place, a soothing calm settled over him, as comforting as Linda's embrace.

"I'm sorry," Miller whispered to the empty room, to the ghosts of his family that haunted his every waking moment. "I just needed... a moment. Just one moment without the pain."

As he sank to the floor, his back against the cold metal shelves, Miller felt a temporary respite from the turmoil of his waking hours. In this chemically induced twilight, he found a fragile solace, knowing it couldn't last but clinging to it nonetheless.

"I'll be stronger tomorrow," he promised, his words barely audible as consciousness slipped away. "I'll find you, Harrison. I'll make things right, Linda. I swear..."

21 - 21

Drake Miller's eyelids fluttered, heavy as lead, as he slumped further down onto the cold, hard floor of the evidence closet. The harsh fluorescent light above him blurred into a soft, hazy glow, casting long shadows across the cramped space.

"Harrison," he mumbled, his voice thick with the encroaching sedative, "I can see you, son. You're... you're smiling."

In the fading edges of consciousness, Miller's mind conjured an image of his boy – not as the sullen teenager he'd last seen, but as the bright-eyed child who once looked at him with unabashed adoration.

"Dad!" Dream-Harrison's voice echoed, filled with a warmth that made Miller's heart ache. "You made it! I knew you would."

Miller's hand reached out, trembling, grasping at empty air. "I'm here, buddy. I'm... I'm trying to be here."

The world tilted and swayed around him, reality blending seamlessly with the realm of dreams. He could almost feel the softness of Harrison's curls beneath his fingers, smell the familiar scent of his son's shampoo.

"You always work so hard, Drake," Linda's soothing voice drifted through his mind. "It's okay to rest sometimes. We'll be here when you wake up."

A single tear slipped down Miller's cheek as he surrendered to the pull of unconsciousness. "I miss you both... so much," he whispered, his words barely audible. "Please... don't leave me again."

As the sedative finally claimed him completely, Drake Miller sank into a world where the fractured pieces of his life knitted back together. For now, at least, there was no mystery to solve, no parallel realities to navigate. In the realm of dreams, there was only the warmth of his family's love, a balm to his wounded soul.

His last coherent thought before succumbing entirely was a mix of relief and regret: "Just for tonight... let me pretend it's all okay."

Awakening in Confusion

Green World – 2024

1 - 2

Drake Miller's eyes fluttered open, the world around him a swirling kaleidoscope of muted colors and indistinct shapes. His head throbbed with a dull, persistent ache as he struggled to push himself upright, his limbs heavy and uncooperative. "What... what happened?" he mumbled, his voice thick and slurred.

The bedroom slowly came into focus, familiar yet strangely alien in the dim light of dawn filtering through the curtains. Drake blinked hard, trying to clear the fog from his mind. Every movement felt like wading through quicksand, his thoughts scattered and elusive.

"Linda?" he called out, his wife's name barely more than a whisper. No response came, the silence of the house pressing in around him. Drake's heart began to race, a cold tendril of fear worming its way into his gut. Something was wrong, terribly wrong.

He swung his legs over the side of the bed, the room tilting alarmingly as he fought to stand. "Get it together, Miller," he growled to himself, gripping the bedpost for support. "You've got to find Harrison."

The thought of his son cut through the haze like a knife, bringing a sudden clarity to Drake's muddled mind. Harrison. Where was Harrison? The last thing he remembered was...

"The sedative," Drake muttered, pieces of memory slowly falling into place. "I took a damn sedative to sleep."

With unsteady steps, he made his way to the bedroom door, each movement a monumental effort. The hallway beyond seemed to stretch and warp before his eyes, the familiar family photos on the walls taking on a sinister quality in the half-light.

"Harrison?" Drake called out, his voice stronger now, tinged with desperation. "Harrison? Where are you?"

Silence was his only answer, broken only by the pounding of his own heart. Drake leaned against the wall, closing his eyes as a wave of dizziness washed over him. "Think, damn it," he hissed through clenched teeth. "What happened last night?"

But the memories remained frustratingly out of reach, like wisps of smoke slipping through his fingers. All he knew with certainty was that his son was in danger, and he had to find him before it was too late.

With a deep breath, Drake pushed himself away from the wall, determination overriding the lingering effects of the sedative. "I'm coming, Harrison," he whispered, his voice thick with emotion. "Whatever's happened, whatever I have to do, I'll find you. I promise."

And with that vow echoing in his mind, Detective Drake Miller stumbled forward into the uncertain dawn, driven by a father's love and the desperate need to unravel the mystery that had shattered his world.

3 - 4

Drake's heart lurched as he reached Harrison's room, the door standing ajar like an ominous invitation. He pushed it open with trembling fingers, his breath catching in his throat as he took in the scene before him.

"No," he whispered, his voice barely audible. "Harrison?"

The room lay in disarray, a stark contrast to the usual meticulousness of his son's space. Drake's eyes darted frantically from the rumpled bed to the scattered belongings, each detail painting a picture of hasty departure.

"This can't be happening," Drake muttered, running a hand through his disheveled hair. "Not again. Not my boy."

He stumbled towards the bed, his legs still unsteady. The twisted sheets seemed to mock him, a tangle of fabric that held no answers. Drake's mind raced, memories of his fractured reality blurring with the present moment.

"Was it real?" he wondered aloud, his voice cracking. "Did I dream it all? Or is this the nightmare?"

His gaze fell upon Harrison's desk, where a notebook lay open, its pages covered in cryptic symbols. Drake's brow furrowed as he struggled to make sense of the scrawling's.

"What were you working on, son?" he murmured, tracing a finger over the ink. "What secrets were you trying to uncover?"

A chill ran down Drake's spine as he realized the gravity of the situation. His son, always curious, always pushing boundaries, might have stumbled upon something far more dangerous than he could have imagined.

"I should have been there for you," Drake choked out, guilt washing over him in waves. "I should have protected you. I'm so sorry, Harrison."

He sank onto the edge of the bed, his head in his hands, the weight of his failures threatening to crush him. But beneath the despair, a spark of determination flickered to life.

"No," Drake growled, his hands clenching into fists. "I won't lose you. Not to this world, not to any other."

He stood, swaying slightly but steadier now, resolve burning in his tired eyes. "I'll find you, Harrison. Whatever it takes, wherever you are, I'll bring you home."

5 - 6

Drake stumbled out of Harrison's room, his mind a whirlwind of terrifying possibilities. The hallway seemed to stretch endlessly before him, each step a monumental effort as he fought against the lingering effects of the sedative.

"Harrison!" he called out, his voice echoing through the empty house. "Son, where are you?"

Only silence answered him, amplifying the dread that coiled in his gut. Drake's hand trembled as he reached for his phone, fumbling with the screen as he dialed Harrison's number.

"Please, pick up," he muttered, pressing the device to his ear. "Come on, Harrison."

The call went straight to voicemail, Harrison's cheerful greeting a stark contrast to the fear gripping Drake's heart.

"Dammit!" he cursed, slamming his fist against the wall. The pain brought a moment of clarity, and Drake took a deep breath, trying to center himself.

"Think, Drake," he urged himself. "Where would he go? What was he looking for?"

His mind raced back to the symbols in Harrison's notebook, the cryptic drawings that had seemed so innocuous just moments ago. Now, they took on a sinister significance.

"Could he have figured it out?" Drake wondered aloud, his voice barely above a whisper. "Did he find a way to cross over?"

The thought sent a chill down his spine. If Harrison had indeed found a way to navigate between the fractured realities, he could be in grave danger.

"I can't lose him," Drake said, his voice thick with emotion. "Not to this. Not to the nightmares that haunt me."

He made his way downstairs, each step more determined than the last. As he reached for his car keys, a new resolve settled over him.

"I'll find you, son," he promised to the empty house. "Whatever it takes, whatever world you're in, I'll bring you home."

Drake paused landing, his hand on the bannister. "And this time," he added, his voice low and fierce, "I won't let you down. I'll be the father you deserve, Harrison. Just... just be safe until I get there."

With that, he stepped out into the cool morning air, ready to face whatever horrors awaited him in his search for his son.

7 - 8

Drake's hand trembled as he reached for the banister, his mind a whirlpool of anxiety and determination. Each creaking step down the stairs echoed his racing heartbeat, a grim reminder of the urgency that propelled him forward. As he descended, his gaze drifted towards the closed bedroom door where Linda would have slept, blissfully unaware of the chaos unfolding.

"Linda," he whispered, his voice barely audible. "How can I explain this to you?"

He paused, his hand resting on the cool wood of their bedroom door. The weight of his dilemma pressed down on him, threatening to crush his resolve. Would she understand? Or would she look at him with that mix of concern and disbelief he'd grown all too familiar with?

"I can't go back and wake her," Drake muttered, running a hand through his disheveled hair. "She'd think I've finally lost it completely."

He turned away, his shoulders slumping under the burden of his secret. The living room loomed before him, bathed in the eerie pre-dawn light that filtered through the curtains. Drake's eyes darted around, searching for any clue, any hint of where Harrison might have gone.

"I should have seen this coming," he berated himself, pacing the room. "I should have known he'd try to unravel the mystery himself. God, Harrison, why couldn't you just talk to me?"

The irony of his words wasn't lost on Drake. How many times had he pushed his son away, too consumed by his own fractured reality to truly listen?

As he reached for the front door, a sudden wave of dizziness washed over him. The lingering effects of the sedative clouded his judgment, making him question his own actions.

"Am I doing the right thing?" he asked the empty room. "Or am I chasing shadows across realities that don't exist?"

Drake shook his head, trying to clear the fog. "No, I have to believe. For Harrison's sake, I have to trust what I know is real."

He stepped out into the cool morning air, the first rays of sunlight painting the sky in hues of pink and gold. The beauty of the dawn stood in stark contrast to the turmoil in Drake's heart.

"I'm coming, son," he whispered, his voice carrying a mix of determination and fear. "Whatever it takes, whatever world you're in, I'll find you. And this time, I won't let you down."

As Drake moved towards his car, each step felt like a choice between two worlds – the safe, familiar reality he was leaving behind, and the uncertain, potentially dangerous path he was about to embark on. The weight of responsibility pressed down on him, a constant reminder of what was at stake.

"We're on the edge of something big, Harrison," he murmured, fumbling with his car keys. "I just hope we both make it through to the other side."

9 - 10

Harrison Miller's footsteps echoed off the quiet suburban sidewalks as he strode purposefully away from his house, his mind racing with unanswered questions. The crisp morning air nipped at his cheeks, but he barely noticed, too consumed by the burning curiosity that had driven him from his bed at this early hour.

"What do they mean?" he muttered to himself, his fingers tracing the outline of the notebook in his pocket. "Why can't I shake the feeling that these symbols are important?"

As he rounded a familiar corner, Harrison's gaze swept across the neighborhood he'd known all his life. The manicured lawns and picket fences seemed oddly alien now, as if he were seeing them through a new lens.

"It's like everything's changed overnight," he mused aloud, his voice tinged with a mixture of excitement and apprehension. "Or maybe I'm the one who's changed."

A jogger passed by, offering a friendly wave. Harrison returned it half-heartedly, his thoughts elsewhere. He pulled out the notebook, flipping through its pages with trembling fingers.

"Dad would probably tell me I'm overthinking this," he said, a hint of his typical teenage cockiness creeping into his voice. "But he doesn't understand. These symbols... they're calling to me. Like they're trying to tell me something important."

Harrison paused at a crosswalk; his eyes fixed on a particularly intricate symbol. "What are you trying to say?" he whispered, tracing its curves with his fingertip. "And why me? Why now?"

As the light changed, Harrison stepped off the curb, his mind awash with possibilities. "Maybe it's connected to Dad's accident," he speculated, his imagination running wild. "Or maybe it's something bigger. Something that could change everything."

The weight of uncertainty bore down on him like a heavy cloak, but Harrison pressed on, determined to unravel the mystery that had captured his thoughts. With each step, he felt as if he were moving closer to some grand revelation, teetering on the edge of a discovery that could reshape his understanding of the world.

"Whatever it is," he declared to the empty street, his voice filled with determination, "I'm going to figure it out. No matter what it takes."

11 - 12

Harrison's footsteps echoed against the quiet streets of Bridgewater, the familiar storefronts and autumn-adorned planters blurring into a kaleidoscope of muted colors as he lost himself in thought. The scent of pumpkin spice wafting from B&J Bistro barely registered in his consciousness, his mind consumed by the enigmatic symbols that seemed to dance before his eyes.

"It's like they're alive," he muttered, his brow furrowed in concentration. "Like they're trying to tell me something, if I could just crack the code."

His reverie was shattered by a sudden movement in his peripheral vision. Harrison's head snapped up, his eyes widening as they locked onto a figure lurking in the shadows between two buildings. The man was tall and gaunt, his face a map of scars and twisted flesh. But it was the pronounced limp in his gait that sent a chill down Harrison's spine.

"Hey, are you okay?" Harrison called out, his voice cracking slightly. "Do you need help or something?"

The man didn't respond, instead taking a halting step forward. Despite his obvious physical impairment, there was an unsettling grace to his movements, like a predator stalking its prey. Harrison's heart leaped into his throat as he stumbled to a halt, his palms growing clammy with sudden fear.

"I should probably get going," Harrison said, trying to inject some of his usual cockiness into his tone. "My dad's a detective, you know. He'll be wondering where I am."

The man's eyes, dark and intense, remained fixed on Harrison as he took another step forward. Harrison's mind raced, his thoughts a jumbled mess of fear and confusion.

"This can't be happening," he thought, his chest tightening. "This is Bridgewater, for crying out loud. Nothing bad ever happens here."

Yet as the disfigured man drew closer, Harrison couldn't shake the feeling that he had stumbled into something far beyond his understanding. The symbols in his notebook seemed to burn in his pocket, a tangible reminder of the mysteries that had led him to this moment.

"Look, I don't want any trouble," Harrison said, his voice trembling despite his best efforts. "Just tell me what you want, okay?"

The man's lips curved into what might have been a smile, but on his scarred face, it looked more like a grimace. Harrison's heart pounded in his chest; each beat a thunderous reminder of the danger he now faced.

13 - 14

Harrison swallowed hard; his throat dry as sandpaper. His mind raced, searching for a way out of this nightmarish situation. With a burst of teenage bravado, he squared his shoulders and locked eyes with the disfigured stranger.

"Who are you?" Harrison demanded, his voice quivering with a mixture of fear and defiance. He silently cursed the tremor in his words, wishing he could summon the unwavering confidence he usually wore like armor.

The man's lips curved into a twisted smile, revealing a row of jagged teeth that seemed more suited to a shark than a human. "I am Gabriel," he replied, his voice a low, rasping whisper that sent shivers down Harrison's spine. "And you, young Harrison, are coming with me."

Harrison's eyes widened, his heart hammering against his ribcage. How did this man know his name? The realization hit him like a punch to the gut – this was no random encounter.

"Like hell I am," Harrison retorted, attempting to inject some of his typical cockiness into his voice. "I don't know who you are or what you want, but I'm not going anywhere with you."

Gabriel's piercing gaze seemed to bore into Harrison's soul, making him feel exposed and vulnerable. "Oh, but you will," Gabriel said, his tone eerily calm. "You see, Harrison, you're part of something much bigger than yourself. Those symbols you've been obsessing over. They're just the beginning."

Harrison's hand instinctively moved to his pocket, where his notebook rested. His mind reeled with questions. How did Gabriel know about the symbols? What did they mean? And most importantly, how was he going to get out of this?

"Look, man," Harrison said, desperately trying to keep his voice steady, "I don't know what you're talking about. I'm just a kid, okay? Whatever this is, I'm not part of it."

Gabriel's laugh was a harsh, grating sound that set Harrison's teeth on edge. "Oh, but you are," he rasped. "Whether you know it or not, you're at the center of it all. And it's time for you to embrace your destiny."

As Gabriel took another step forward, Harrison's fight-or-flight instinct kicked into overdrive. His eyes darted around, searching for an escape route, his muscles tensing in preparation to run.

15 - 16

Harrison's heart thundered in his chest as Gabriel closed the distance between them, the man's disfigured face twisted into a predatory grin. "Stay back!" Harrison shouted, his voice cracking with fear as he stumbled backward. But before he could turn to run, Gabriel's strong hands shot out with surprising speed, seizing Harrison's arms in an iron grip.

"Let go of me!" Harrison yelled, thrashing against Gabriel's hold. His mind raced, desperately trying to recall the self-defense moves his dad had taught him. But panic clouded his thoughts, making it impossible to focus.

Gabriel's raspy chuckle sent chills down Harrison's spine. "Such spirit," he mused, effortlessly dragging the struggling teenager into the shadows of a nearby alley. "Your father would be proud."

"My dad?" Harrison gasped, momentarily ceasing his struggles. "What do you know about my dad?"

"More than you could possibly imagine," Gabriel replied cryptically, his grip never loosening. "But all will be revealed in due time."

As they moved deeper into the alley, away from the street and any potential witnesses, Harrison's mind whirled with a mix of fear and curiosity. How did this stranger know about his father? What did it have to do with the symbols in his notebook?

"Look," Harrison said, trying to sound braver than he felt, "if this is about my dad's work or something, just tell me. You don't have to do... whatever this is."

Gabriel's laugh echoed off the brick walls surrounding them. "Oh, Harrison," he said, his voice dripping with amusement, "this is so much bigger than your father's work. You're about to enter a world beyond your wildest imagination."

As the shadows engulfed them, Harrison realized with growing dread that he was completely at the mercy of this enigmatic and terrifying man. His attempts to break free proved futile against Gabriel's superhuman strength.

"Where are you taking me?" Harrison demanded, his voice trembling despite his efforts to sound defiant.

Gabriel's response sent a chill through Harrison's very core: "To meet your destiny, young Harrison. And to unlock the secrets that have been waiting for you all along."

17 - 18

Harrison's heart raced as they descended deeper into the labyrinth of narrow alleys and forgotten streets, the familiar cityscape fading into an otherworldly realm of shadows and whispers. Gabriel's grip remained unyielding, his disfigured face a mask of eerie calm as he guided his captive through the urban maze.

"You can't just kidnap me," Harrison protested, his cocky teenage bravado warring with the fear that threatened to overwhelm him. "People will notice I'm gone. My dad—"

"Your father," Gabriel interrupted, his voice a low rasp, "is precisely why you're here, Harrison. The symbols in your notebook? They're just the beginning."

Harrison's eyes widened, his curiosity momentarily eclipsing his terror. "How do you know about that? Have you been watching me?"

A twisted smile played across Gabriel's scarred lips. "I've been watching you both for longer than you can imagine. Your father's journey and yours are inexorably linked."

As they rounded another corner, Harrison caught sight of a strange, glowing symbol etched into the brickwork—eerily like the ones he'd been obsessively sketching. His mind reeled, grasping for some logical explanation.

"What is all this?" he demanded, gesturing with his free hand toward the ethereal marking. "Why me? Why now?"

Gabriel paused, his piercing gaze locking onto Harrison's. "Because, my boy, you're the key to unlocking a power beyond mortal comprehension. And it's time for you to fulfill your destiny."

With each step deeper into this hidden world, Harrison felt the boundaries of reality blur. His desperate desire for escape warred with an insatiable need to uncover the truth behind Gabriel's cryptic words and his own inexplicable connection to this shadowy realm.

19 - 20

The shrill ring of Drake Miller's phone pierced the oppressive silence of his darkened bedroom, jolting him from his restless contemplation. His heart thundered in his chest as he fumbled for the device, fingers trembling with a mixture of anticipation and dread. The cool glass of the screen felt almost alien against his clammy palm as he swiped to answer, bringing the phone to his ear with agonizing slowness.

"Hello?" Drake breathed; his voice barely audible even to his own ears. The word hung in the air, pregnant with fear and desperate hope.

As he waited for a response, Drake's mind raced, replaying the events of the past few hours in vivid detail. Harrison's empty room, the twisted sheets, the scattered belongings – each image flashed before his eyes like frames from a nightmarish film.

'Please, let it be him,' Drake thought, his free hand clenching into a tight fist. 'Let him be safe. Let this all be some terrible misunderstanding.'

The silence on the other end of the line stretched on, each second feeling like an eternity. Drake's breath caught in his throat, the weight of uncertainty pressing down on him like a physical force. He could hear his own ragged breathing, amplified in the stillness of the room.

"Harrison?" he ventured, unable to bear the silence any longer. "Son, is that you?"

Drake's eyes darted around the shadowy bedroom, as if searching for some sign, some clue that might shed light on his son's whereabouts. The familiar contours of the room seemed alien and threatening in the gloom, twisted by his fear and guilt.

'I should have been there for him,' Drake berated himself silently. 'I should have seen this coming. What kind of father am I?'

As the silence on the phone continued, Drake's mind spiraled further into a maelstrom of worst-case scenarios. Each passing moment without a response only served to heighten his anxiety, pushing him closer to the brink of panic.

"Please," he whispered, his voice cracking with emotion. "If someone's there, if you have my son... just tell me what you want. I'll do anything. Just let me know he's okay."

21 - 22

The response came not from Harrison, but from a voice that sent chills racing down Drake's spine. Deep and gravelly, it resonated with a menacing undertone that made his blood run cold.

"Mr. Miller," the voice rasped, each syllable dripping with malevolent intent. "I have something that belongs to you."

Drake's grip on the phone tightened, his knuckles turning white as he processed the stranger's words. His mind raced, a torrent of emotions threatening to overwhelm him. Fear, anger, and desperation warred within him, each vying for dominance.

"Who are you?" Drake demanded, his voice trembling despite his efforts to remain calm. "Where's my son? What have you done with Harrison?"

He paced the room, unable to stay still, his free hand running through his disheveled hair. The weight of his past negligence bore down on him, fueling his determination to make things right.

'I won't fail Harrison again,' Drake thought fiercely. 'Whatever it takes, I'll bring him home.'

The voice on the other end chuckled, a sound devoid of any warmth or humanity. "All in good time, Mr. Miller. Your boy is... safe, for now. But his continued well-being depends entirely on you."

Drake's mind whirled, trying to piece together the puzzle before him. "What do you want from me?" he asked, his tone a mixture of defiance and desperation. "Money? Information? Whatever it is, we can work something out. Just don't hurt my son."

As he awaited the response, Drake's gaze fell on a family photo on the nightstand. Harrison's smiling face stared back at him, a stark reminder of what was at stake. The guilt of his past negligence threatened to consume him, but he pushed it aside, focusing on the present crisis.

'I won't let you down this time, Harrison,' he vowed silently. 'I'll find you, no matter what it takes.'

23 - 24

Gabriel's raspy voice sliced through Drake's thoughts like a cold blade. "Unfinished business, Mr. Miller. That's what we have between us." The words dripped with malice; each syllable carefully enunciated to maximize their impact.

Drake's blood ran cold as the realization hit him. This wasn't a random kidnapping; this was personal. His mind raced, desperately trying to connect the dots. "Who are you?" he demanded, his voice thick with desperation. "What do you want with my son?"

A sardonic chuckle echoed through the phone, sending shivers down Drake's spine. "Oh, come now, Detective. Surely you haven't forgotten me so easily. After all, you're the one who made me what I am today."

Drake's grip on the phone tightened, his knuckles turning white. He paced the room, his free hand running through his disheveled hair as he tried to place the voice. "I don't understand," he muttered, more to himself than to Gabriel. "What are you talking about?"

"Think back, Miller," Gabriel taunted, his tone dripping with barely contained rage. "Think back to another life. Long ago and long forgotten."

Drake's mind reeled, memories of an old case flooding back. The weight of his past decisions crashed down upon him, amplifying the urgency of the present situation. 'How could I have been so blind?' he thought, self-recrimination gnawing at his insides. 'Harrison's paying for my mistakes.'

Swallowing hard, Drake forced his voice to remain steady. "Listen, whatever happened in the past, we can work this out. Just tell me where Harrison is. Please."

Gabriel's laughter, cold and mirthless, filled the line. "Oh, Detective. You still don't get it, do you? This isn't about negotiation. This is about justice. My justice."

25 - 26

Drake's fingers tightened around the phone, his knuckles turning white as he fought to control the tremor in his voice. The weight of his past decisions pressed down on him like a physical force, threatening to crush him beneath their burden. His mind raced through a labyrinth of possibilities, each more terrifying than the last, as he struggled to piece together the fragments of this nightmarish puzzle.

"Your justice?" Drake echoed, his voice barely above a whisper. He closed his eyes, drawing in a deep breath to steady himself. "Gabriel, I... I know I've made mistakes. But Harrison is innocent in all of this. He's just a boy."

There was a moment of heavy silence on the line, broken only by the sound of Drake's ragged breathing. When Gabriel spoke again, his voice was eerily calm, almost contemplative. "Innocence is a luxury, Detective Miller. One that was stolen from me long ago. By you."

Drake's free hand clenched into a fist, nails digging into his palm. The pain grounded him, helping him focus through the haze of fear and guilt. "What do you want?" he asked, forcing his voice to remain steady despite the terror gnawing at his insides. "Whatever it is, I'll do it. Just... just don't hurt my son."

As he waited for Gabriel's response, Drake's mind whirled with a maelstrom of thoughts and emotions. 'I should have seen this coming,' he berated himself silently. 'All those years of putting work first, of thinking I was untouchable... and now Harrison's paying the price.' The irony of it all wasn't lost on him – the very cases that had made his career were now threatening to destroy everything he held dear.

"What I want," Gabriel replied, his words dripping with malice, "is for you to experience the same pain, the same loss that I did. To watch everything, you love crumble before your eyes, knowing that you're powerless to stop it."

Drake's breath caught in his throat, a chill running down his spine at the raw hatred in Gabriel's voice. "Please," he found himself saying, pride abandoned in the face of his son's peril. "I'll do anything. Just tell me what you want me to do."

27 - 28

Gabriel's laughter echoed through the phone, chilling Miller to the bone. The sound was like nails scraping across a chalkboard, sending shivers down Drake's spine. "You'll find out soon enough," Gabriel taunted, his voice dripping with malicious glee. "But for now, let's just say I have a proposition for you."

Drake's grip tightened on the phone, his knuckles turning white as he fought to keep his composure. "What kind of proposition?" he asked, his words measured and deliberate, each syllable a struggle against the panic threatening to overwhelm him.

"Oh, Detective Miller," Gabriel purred, drawing out each word with sadistic pleasure. "Where would be the fun in revealing all my cards at once? Let's just say it involves a little... scavenger hunt. One where the prize is your son's life."

Drake's free hand clenched into a fist, his nails digging into his palm as he battled to keep his voice steady. "If you hurt him, I swear to God-"

"Tsk, tsk," Gabriel interrupted, his tone mocking. "Threats will get you nowhere, Detective. Remember, I hold all the cards here. Your son's fate rests entirely in my hands... and yours, if you choose to play along."

As Gabriel's words sank in, Drake's heart plummeted, the full weight of the situation crashing down upon him. His son – his precious Harrison – was now a pawn in some twisted game orchestrated by this madman. Every fiber of his being screamed to lash out, to threaten, to do something, anything to save his child. But the cold, logical part of his mind – the detective that had solved countless cases – knew he had to tread carefully.

"What do you want me to do?" Drake asked, his voice barely above a whisper, the words tasting like ash in his mouth.

"That's more like it," Gabriel replied, satisfaction evident in his tone. "I'll be in touch with your first task soon. And remember, Detective Miller – time is of the essence. The clock is ticking, and with each passing moment, your son's chances grow slimmer."

As the line went dead, Drake stood frozen, the phone still pressed to his ear. His mind raced, analyzing every word, every inflection of Gabriel's voice, searching for any clue that might lead him to Harrison. With a steely resolve, he forced himself to take a deep breath, knowing that panic would only cloud his judgment.

"I'm coming for you, Harrison," he murmured, his voice thick with determination. "Whatever it takes, I'll find you. I promise."

Lingering Absence

Blue World – 2024

1 - 2

Linda's trembling fingers traced the edges of Harrison's leather-bound notebook, its pages worn and dog-eared from constant use. The familiar scent of her son's cologne lingered in the air, a bittersweet reminder of his absence. She perched on the edge of his unmade bed, surrounded by the chaos of a teenager's room—discarded clothes, scattered video game cases, and half-finished sketches pinned haphazardly to the walls.

"Oh, Harrison," she whispered, her voice catching. "Are you really out there, sweetheart?"

Her eyes scanned the intricate drawings that filled the pages, a kaleidoscope of fantastical creatures and abstract shapes that seemed to dance across the paper. Harrison had always possessed a vivid imagination, but these—these were different. Darker. More urgent.

Linda's heart raced as she flipped through the notebook, her maternal instincts screaming that something was terribly wrong. "This isn't like you," she murmured, tracing a particularly disturbing image with her fingertip. "What were you trying to tell us?"

As she turned another page, a chill ran down her spine. There, in the bottom corner, was a symbol that made her blood run cold. The same intricate design that had arrived in that cursed letter weeks ago, the one that had sent her husband spiraling into obsession.

"No," Linda gasped, her hand flying to her mouth. "No, it can't be."

She stared at the symbol; its lines seeming to writhe and twist before her eyes. How could Harrison have known about this? What did it mean? The questions swirled in her mind, a dizzying whirlpool of fear and confusion.

"I should have seen it," she whispered, hot tears spilling down her cheeks. "I should have known something was wrong. Oh God, Harrison, what have they done to you?"

Linda clutched the notebook to her chest, rocking back and forth as waves of guilt and terror washed over her. She had to find him. She had to make this right. But as she sat there, surrounded by the remnants of her son's life, she couldn't shake the feeling that she was already too late.

3 - 4

Linda's heart pounded as she forced herself to her feet, the notebook clutched tightly against her chest. "There has to be more," she muttered, her eyes darting frantically around Harrison's room. "Something, anything to tell me where you are, sweetheart."

She yanked open his dresser drawers, tossing clothes aside with trembling hands. "Come on, Harrison," she pleaded, her voice cracking. "You always left clues for your treasure hunts. Please, baby, give me something to find you."

As she rifled through the contents, Linda's mind raced. "Why would you draw that symbol? What does it mean to you?" She paused, holding up one of Harrison's favorite t-shirts. "Were you trying to warn us? Or... or were you already under some sort of influence?"

The thought made her stomach churn. Linda moved to the closet, flinging open the door with such force it slammed against the wall. "I should have been paying closer attention," she berated herself, pushing aside hangers and shoeboxes. "I was so caught up in my own grief, I didn't see what was happening right in front of me."

Her fingers brushed against something taped to the back of the closet. "What's this?" Linda murmured, carefully peeling away a folded piece of paper. As she opened it, her breath caught in her throat. It was a crude map, with the same haunting symbol marking a location.

"Oh, Harrison," she whispered, studying the map with growing dread. "What have you gotten yourself into?"

5 - 6

Linda's heart pounded in her chest as she stared at the drawing, her fingers tracing the ominous symbol that had become the focal point of her nightmares. With a shaky exhale, she reached for her phone on the bedside table, her mind made up.

"I have to do this," she whispered to herself, her voice barely audible in the oppressive silence of Harrison's room. "For Harrison. For all of us."

Her thumb hovered over Vega's contact, a war raging within her. Every instinct screamed at her to run, to hide, to protect herself from the man who had brought so much pain into their lives. But the fierce love of a mother overpowered her fear.

As she pressed the call button, Linda's free hand clutched Harrison's t-shirt to her chest, drawing strength from the familiar scent of her son. The phone rang once, twice, three times, each second stretching into an eternity.

Suddenly, a chill ran down her spine as a voice whispered directly into her ear, "Hello, Linda. I've been expecting your call."

Linda whirled around, her blue eyes wide with terror, but the room was empty. She realized with growing horror that Gabriel's voice was coming through the phone..

"H-how did you..." she stammered, her voice trembling.

Gabriel's laugh was cold and mirthless. "Oh, Linda. You should know by now that I'm always one step ahead. Your predictability is... disappointing."

Linda's fear quickly gave way to anger, her maternal instincts flaring. "Where is my son, you monster?" she demanded, her voice stronger now. "What have you done with Harrison?"

"Tsk, tsk," Gabriel chided, his tone dripping with condescension. "Always so quick to accuse. Perhaps you should be asking what Harrison has done for us."

Linda's breath caught in her throat. "What do you mean?"

"Your boy is special, Linda. He has a gift, a purpose. One that you, in your ignorance, have been stifling all these years."

"No," Linda shook her head vehemently, even though Gabriel couldn't see her. "You're lying. Harrison would never willingly join your... your cult!"

Gabriel's laugh sent shivers down her spine. "Are you so sure? Children often seek what their parents deny them. And Harrison... well, let's just say he's found a family that truly appreciates his talents."

Linda's mind reeled, memories of Harrison's recent withdrawn behavior flooding back. Had she truly been so blind? "I want to see him," she said, her voice barely above a whisper.

"All in due time, my dear," Gabriel purred. "But know this – your journey is far from over. The path ahead is treacherous, and the price of failure... well, I think you can imagine."

As the line went dead, Linda sank to her knees, the weight of Gabriel's words crushing her. She clutched Harrison's shirt tighter, tears streaming down her face. "I'll find you, baby," she vowed, her voice thick with determination. "No matter what it takes, I'll bring you home."

Bound and Confused

Green World – 2024

1 - 2

Harrison's heart thundered in his chest as he thrashed against the ropes biting into his wrists, his breath coming in ragged gasps. The empty room before him seemed to mock his confusion, the space where Gabriel had stood just moments ago now hauntingly vacant.

"Gabriel?" Harrison called out, his voice cracking with a mixture of fear and desperation. "Where the hell did you go?"

Silence answered him, broken only by the frantic pounding of his own pulse in his ears. Harrison's mind raced, trying to piece together the fragments of what he'd just witnessed. Gabriel had been there, talking on the phone, his scarred face contorted with an urgency that sent chills down Harrison's spine.

"Dad?" Gabriel had said, his usually smooth voice tight with tension. "It's happening sooner than we thought. We need to move now."

Harrison strained his memory, fighting against the fog of panic clouding his thoughts. What had Gabriel meant? What was happening? And why did it involve his father?

"Hey!" Harrison shouted again, his teenage bravado wavering. "This isn't funny, man. You can't just disappear like that!"

But even as the words left his mouth, Harrison knew this was no trick. The air in the room felt different, charged with an energy he couldn't explain. It was as if the very fabric of reality had shifted, leaving him alone and bound in this featureless space.

"Think, Harrison, think," he muttered to himself, closing his eyes and taking a deep breath. "There's got to be an explanation for this. People don't just vanish into thin air."

But the image of Gabriel's intense gaze, those eyes that seemed to hold secrets beyond Harrison's comprehension, flashed in his mind. Maybe, he thought with a shudder, there were things in this world he didn't understand. Things that defied explanation.

"Dad," Harrison whispered, a tremor in his voice. "What have you gotten us into?"

3 - 4

Harrison's heart thundered in his chest; each beat a desperate reminder of his predicament. He twisted his wrists against the coarse ropes, wincing as they bit into his skin. The empty room seemed to mock him with its silence, the absence of Gabriel more terrifying than any visible threat.

"This is insane," Harrison muttered, his eyes darting around the barren space. "People don't just disappear. It's not possible." But even as he said it, doubt crept into his voice. He'd always prided himself on his vivid imagination, but this... this was beyond anything he could have conjured up.

Sweat beaded on his forehead as he struggled, his mind racing. "Okay, Harrison, think. What would the hero in one of your stories do?" He let out a bitter laugh. "Probably not get kidnapped by a guy with freaky burn scars in the first place."

The memory of Gabriel's disfigured face flashed in his mind, and Harrison shuddered. There had been something in those eyes, something ancient and knowing that had made him feel like a child again. "What did you want with me?" he called out, his voice echoing in the empty room. "Why drag me into whatever crazy stuff you and Dad are mixed up in?"

As the silence stretched on, panic clawed at Harrison's throat. "Where are you?" he screamed, his cocky facade crumbling. "What's happening? Someone answer me!"

But there was no response, just the sound of his own ragged breathing. Harrison slumped in the chair, exhaustion warring with fear. "Dad," he whispered, his voice cracking. "I don't know what's going on, but... I need you. Please."

Call of Desire

Blue World – 2024

1 - 2

Linda's trembling fingers hovered over Drake's contact, her heart hammering against her ribs as she finally pressed 'call'. The phone's harsh ring pierced the suffocating silence of the bedroom, each unanswered tone driving a spike of dread deeper into her chest. She paced frantically, her blonde hair disheveled from running her hands through it repeatedly.

"Please, Drake, pick up," she whispered, her voice cracking. "I need you now more than ever."

As the rings continued, Linda's mind raced. She knew Drake was likely lost in slumber in that other world, oblivious to the terror unfolding here. The thought of him peacefully dreaming while their son was missing tore at her heart.

"Drake, it's me," she began as the voicemail beeped. "Something terrible has happened. Harrison is—" Her voice broke, and she took a shuddering breath. "Please, call me back as soon as you get this. I don't know what to do."

She ended the call, her blue eyes brimming with unshed tears. The phone slipped from her grasp, clattering to the floor as panic threatened to overwhelm her. Linda sank onto the edge of the bed, her shoulders shaking with silent sobs.

"I can't do this alone," she murmured, wrapping her arms around herself. "Drake, where are you when I need you most?"

The silence of the room pressed in on her, a stark reminder of her isolation in this moment of crisis. Linda's gaze fell on a family photo on the nightstand—happier times, before the accident that had fractured their lives. She reached out, tracing Drake's face with a trembling finger.

"You promised you'd always be there for us," she whispered, a hint of bitterness creeping into her voice. "But you're trapped in another world, and our son is gone."

Linda closed her eyes, trying to summon the strength that had carried her through so many hardships. But the weight of this new tragedy threatened to crush her resolve. She needed Drake's steady presence, his unwavering determination. Without him, she felt adrift in a sea of fear and uncertainty.

"I have to be strong," she told herself, her voice barely audible. "For Harrison. For our family."

But as the minutes ticked by with no response from Drake, Linda felt her hope slipping away like sand through her fingers. She was alone in this nightmare, and the realization chilled her to her core.

3 - 4

Suddenly, a thought pierced through Linda's fog of despair. Richard Vega. Drake's partner and trusted colleague might have some insight into Drake's whereabouts, or at the very least, offer a lifeline in this moment of crisis.

With renewed purpose, Linda lunged for her phone, her fingers trembling as she scrolled through her contacts. Finding Vega's other number, she pressed call, her heart pounding in sync with each ring.

"Please, please answer," she whispered, pacing the room with frenetic energy.

The line clicked. "Vega here," came the gruff, sleep-laden voice.

Linda's words spilled out in a frantic torrent. "Richard, it's Linda Miller. I'm sorry to wake you, but it's an emergency. Harrison's alive and has been taken, and I can't reach Drake. I don't know what to do—"

She paused, choking back a sob. "I think... I think it has something to do with that symbol Drake's been investigating. The one that's been haunting him across both worlds."

Linda's free hand clutched at her throat, her voice dropping to a hoarse whisper. "Richard, I'm scared. What if this is connected to Drake's... condition? What if whoever took Harrison knows about the two realities?"

She closed her eyes, trying to steady her breathing. "I need your help, Richard. You're the only one who understands what Drake's going through, the only one who might be able to make sense of this nightmare."

5 - 6

Linda's voice quivered as she forced herself to continue, her words barely above a whisper. "Vega, please it's Linda," she said, struggling to keep her voice steady despite the fear gripping her like an icy vise. "I... I don't know where Drake is. Please, you have to help me find them."

The silence on the other end of the line stretched for what felt like an eternity, each second amplifying Linda's dread. Her mind raced, conjuring terrifying scenarios of what might have befallen her husband and son. She pressed the phone closer to her ear, straining to hear any sign of life on the other end.

Finally, Vega's voice crackled through, grave with concern. "Linda, stay calm," he said, his tone a mixture of reassurance and urgency. "I'll do everything I can to help. Tell me everything you know, and we'll figure this out together."

Linda's knees weakened with relief, and she sank onto the edge of the bed, her free hand gripping the comforter. "Oh, thank God," she breathed, closing her eyes momentarily. The weight of Vega's support, his unwavering loyalty to Drake, washed over her like a comforting wave.

"Richard, I'm sorry to drag you into this," Linda began, her words tumbling out in a rush. "But Harrison's gone, and Drake... Drake's unreachable. I think he might be trapped in the other world, and I don't know how to reach him there."

She paused, taking a shaky breath, her mind reeling with the absurdity of their situation. How had their lives become so entangled in this impossible reality? Linda's gaze fell on a family photo on the nightstand, Drake's tired eyes and forced smile a stark reminder of the toll his dual existence had taken on them all.

"There's more," she continued, her voice barely above a whisper. "The man who took Harrison... he knew things, Richard. Things about Drake, about the two worlds. I'm afraid this is bigger than we ever imagined."

7 - 8

Linda's fingers traced the outline of the symbol etched into Harrison's notebook, which lay open on her lap. The intricate design seemed to pulse with an otherworldly energy, sending a chill down her spine. "And there's this symbol," she said, her voice trembling. "Harrison drew it, but I've seen it before. In Drake's notes, in his nightmares. It's everywhere, and I can't shake the feeling that it's the key to all of this."

As she spoke, her mind raced with possibilities, each more terrifying than the last. "What if Gabriel isn't working alone? What if there's a whole group out there, watching us, waiting for the right moment to strike?"

Linda's breath caught in her throat as a new thought occurred to her. "Oh God, Richard. What if they've known about Drake all along? What if they've been manipulating us from the shadows, pulling strings we couldn't even see?"

She stood abruptly, pacing the room as her anxiety mounted. "And Harrison... why him? Is it because he's Drake's son? Does he have some connection to the other world that we don't understand?"

Linda's voice dropped to a whisper, fear evident in every syllable. "Richard, what if we can't get them back? What if this symbol, this... whatever it is, has the power to keep them trapped forever?"

9 - 10

Vega listened intently, his brow furrowed with concern as Linda's words poured out in a torrent of fear and confusion. The weight of the situation seemed to press down on him, his shoulders hunching slightly as he absorbed the gravity of her revelations.

"Linda," he said softly, his voice a steady anchor in the storm of her emotions, "I need you to take a deep breath. We're going to figure this out, I promise."

She paused in her pacing, her blue eyes wide and glistening with unshed tears. "But how? Drake's gone, Harrison's gone, and we're left with nothing but this... this symbol and a man who seems to have appeared out of thin air."

Vega leaned forward, his gaze intense. "Not nothing, Linda. We have each other, and we have Drake's research. His condition, living between two worlds, it's always made him vulnerable, but it's also given him insights that no one else has. We need to use that."

Linda sank back onto the couch, her hands trembling as she clutched the notebook. "You're right," she whispered, "but I'm so scared. Gabriel, he... there was something about him, Richard. Something that felt... wrong."

"I understand," Vega said, his voice steady despite the urgency thrumming beneath his words. "Linda, I'll start looking into Gabriel's background right away. We need to find out everything we can about him—his motives, his connections. And we'll do whatever it takes to bring Harrison back safely."

Linda nodded, a spark of determination igniting in her eyes. "What can I do? I can't just sit here and wait."

"Drake's notes," Vega replied, gesturing to the notebook. "Go through them, see if there's anything we've missed. Any connection to Gabriel, or to that symbol. And Linda," he added, his voice softening, "take care of yourself. We need you strong for when we find them."

As Linda ended the call, she felt a complex mix of emotions swirling within her. Fear still gnawed at her insides, but Vega's words had kindled a flame of hope. She looked down at the notebook, her fingers tracing the outline of the symbol. "I'm going to find you," she whispered, her voice barely audible. "Both of you. No matter what it takes."

11 - 12

Linda's blue eyes narrowed as she stared at the symbol in Harrison's notebook, her blonde hair falling in a curtain around her face. "What are you hiding?" she murmured, her fingertips tracing the intricate lines. The crisp autumn air drifted through the open window, carrying with it the faint scent of pumpkin spice from B&J Bistro down the street.

She set the phone down on the kitchen table, her mind racing. "Richard," she said aloud, as if he were still on the line, "I don't know if I can do this alone." The words hung in the air, a testament to her vulnerability.

Linda closed her eyes, taking a deep breath. When she opened them, a steely resolve had settled in her gaze. "No," she said firmly, "I have to be strong. For Harrison. For Drake."

She flipped through the notebook, scanning each page with renewed intensity. As she did, a memory surfaced – Harrison, hunched over this very table, his young face screwed up in concentration as he drew. "Mom," he had said, looking up at her with those innocent eyes, "do you think Dad will like my drawing?"

The recollection sent a pang through her heart. "Oh, Harrison," she whispered, her voice thick with emotion, "where are you, sweetheart?"

Linda set the phone down, her gaze drawn back to the symbol. In the soft glow of the kitchen light, it seemed to pulse with an otherworldly energy. A chill ran down her spine as she realized that this simple drawing might be the key to unraveling a mystery far more complex and dangerous than she could have ever imagined.

"Drake," she whispered, her voice barely audible, "what have you gotten us into?" The question lingered in the air, unanswered, as Linda steeled herself for the challenges that lay ahead, knowing that her life – and the lives of those she loved – would never be the same.

Shadows of the Past

Green World – 2024

1 - 2

Detective Holly Keirstead's fingers trembled as she flipped through the worn case files spread across her desk, the familiar ache of frustration settling in her chest. The harsh fluorescent lights of her office cast eerie shadows over the gruesome crime scene photos, a grim reminder of her past failures.

"Damn it," she muttered, running a hand through her long dark hair. "How did I miss this before?"

Her piercing eyes scanned the images, searching for the elusive thread that had eluded her for years. As she examined each photo, a chill ran down her spine. There, hidden in plain sight, was a recurring motif—a serpentine figure drawn in blood at every crime scene.

Holly leaned back in her chair, her mind racing. "It can't be a coincidence," she whispered to herself, her voice barely audible over the hum of the air conditioning. "But what does it mean?"

She stood abruptly, pacing the small confines of her office as she wrestled with the implications. The weight of unsolved cases pressed down on her shoulders, threatening to crush her resolve. But Holly Keirstead was nothing if not determined.

"I won't let you win this time," she declared to the empty room, her voice gaining strength. "Whatever game you're playing, I'll figure it out."

As she spoke, Holly's gaze fell on a photo of Gabriel Angel, the enigmatic figure who had haunted her investigations for years. His piercing eyes seemed to mock her from the glossy surface, challenging her to unravel the mystery.

"What are you hiding, Gabriel?" she murmured, tracing the outline of his face with her finger. "How are you connected to all of this?"

The questions swirled in her mind, each one leading to another in a dizzying spiral. Holly closed her eyes, taking a deep breath to center herself. When she opened them again, her expression was one of steely resolve.

"I'll find you," she promised, her voice barely above a whisper. "And this time, I'll make sure you pay for what you've done."

With renewed purpose, Holly turned back to her desk, determined to uncover the truth that had eluded her for so long. As she dove back into the files, a small voice in the back of her mind whispered a warning—be careful what you wish for, Detective Keirstead. Some truths are better left buried.

3 - 4

Detective Holly Keirstead's fingers trembled slightly as she dialed the forensics lab, her voice steady despite the storm of emotions raging within her.

"This is Detective Keirstead. I need a full genetic analysis on all blood samples from the unsolved cases, including our latest victim. Look for any unique markers or patterns. And I want it expedited."

As she hung up, Holly's mind raced with possibilities. Could this finally be the key to unlocking Gabriel Angel's sinister secrets?

"You've evaded me for too long, Gabriel," she muttered, her eyes fixed on his disfigured face in the case file photo. "What kind of monster are you?"

The wait for results felt interminable. Holly paced her office, each step echoing her mounting tension. She paused at the window, her reflection a ghostly overlay on the city beyond.

"What if I'm wrong?" she whispered to herself, doubt creeping in. "What if this leads nowhere, just like before?"

Shaking off the negative thoughts, Holly squared her shoulders. "No, I can't think like that. This time is different. This time, I'll find the truth."

As she turned back to her desk, a chill ran down her spine. The memory of Gabriel's piercing gaze, even through a photograph, made her shudder. Those eyes seemed to hold untold horrors, secrets that both repelled and drew her in.

"What will I find when I look into your past, Gabriel?" Holly mused aloud, her voice a mix of determination and trepidation. "And am I prepared for what I might uncover?"

The weight of unsolved cases pressed down on her, a constant reminder of past failures. But now, with this new lead, hope flickered like a fragile flame. Holly clung to it, knowing that it might be her last chance to bring justice to the victims and their families.

"Whatever demons I have to face," she vowed, her jaw set with determination, "I'll face them. For the victims. For the truth."

As the hours ticked by, Holly immersed herself in the case files once more, searching for any detail she might have missed. All the while, the specter of Gabriel Angel loomed in her mind, a shadowy figure whose secrets threatened to unravel everything she thought she knew about these crimes.

5 - 6

Holly's eyes burned as she pored over the case files, the harsh fluorescent light of her office a stark contrast to the deepening twilight outside. She rubbed her temples, willing away the exhaustion that threatened to overtake her.

"There has to be something here," she muttered, spreading out crime scene photos across her desk. "Some connection I've missed."

Her gaze fell on a photo of Drake Miller, his tired eyes staring back at her. She couldn't shake the feeling that he was somehow central to this mystery, despite his apparent innocence.

"What's your role in all this, Drake?" Holly wondered aloud. "Are you a victim, or something more?"

A soft knock at her door startled her from her thoughts. Rookie Franklin Bird, her colleague, leaned against the doorframe, concern etched on his face.

"Holly, it's past midnight. You should get some rest," he said gently.

She shook her head, gesturing to the files spread before her. "I can't, Franklin. Not when we're so close. I can feel it."

Bird sighed, stepping into the office. "I know that look. What's got you so worked up?"

Holly hesitated, then pointed to Gabriel's photo. "Him. There's something about him that doesn't add up. The burns, the limp... it's like he's a ghost from the past."

"You think he's connected to the old cases?"

"I don't know," Holly admitted, frustration coloring her voice. "But I can't shake the feeling that he's the key to everything. His presence at the crime scenes, the way he speaks in riddles... it's like he's taunting us."

Franklin nodded, his expression thoughtful. "What about Drake? You've been fixating on him too."

Holly leaned back in her chair, her mind racing. "Drake's story is bizarre, Bird. Living in two worlds? It sounds crazy, but what if there's some truth to it? What if it's connected to Gabriel somehow?"

"That's a big leap, Holly," Bird cautioned.

"I know, I know," she said, standing up to stretch her stiff muscles. "But my gut tells me there's more to this than meets the eye. I just need to find the missing piece."

As she gazed out the window at the city skyline, bathed in the soft glow of twilight, Holly felt a renewed sense of purpose wash over her. She turned back to the rookie, her eyes blazing with determination.

"I made a vow, Franklin. No matter what it costs me, I won't rest until I uncover the truth and bring justice to the victims. Even if it means confronting my own demons along the way."

Bird nodded, understanding the weight of her words. "Just don't lose yourself in the process, Holly. We're here to help, remember that."

As he left, Holly returned to her desk, diving back into the evidence with renewed vigor. The city slept, but for her, the night was young, and the hunt for answers had only just begun.

7 - 8

The shrill ring of her desk phone shattered the tense silence of Holly Keirstead's office. Her heart leapt into her throat as she snatched up the receiver, her knuckles white with anticipation.

"Keirstead," she barked, her voice tight with barely contained excitement.

"Detective, it's Dr. Ramirez from the lab. We've finished processing those samples you sent over."

Holly's breath caught. "And?" she pressed, leaning forward in her chair.

"It's... well, you'd better come down and see for yourself. The results are... unusual."

Fifteen minutes later, Holly burst through the lab doors, her dark hair disheveled from her harried drive across town. Dr. Ramirez stood waiting, a thick folder clutched in her trembling hands.

"What have you got for me, Doc?" Holly demanded, her piercing eyes fixed on the folder.

Dr. Ramirez hesitated, then spread the papers across the gleaming steel table. "It's unprecedented, Detective. The DNA from all the crime scenes? It's an exact match to your latest victim."

Holly's brow furrowed. "That's impossible. Are you saying our killer is—"

"No, no," Ramirez interrupted. "It's not just similar. It's identical. Down to the last marker. It's as if the same person was both the killer and the victim at every single crime scene."

Holly's mind reeled as she stared at the damning evidence before her. "How is that even possible?" she whispered, more to herself than to the doctor.

As she pored over the data, a chill ran down her spine. The implications were staggering, defying everything she thought she knew about the case. And somewhere in the back of her mind, unbidden, the image of Gabriel's piercing eyes and enigmatic smile rose to the surface.

"What the hell are we dealing with here?" Holly muttered, her fingers tracing the perplexing results laid out before her.

9 - 10

Holly's piercing gaze darted between the lab results and Dr. Ramirez's concerned face, her mind racing to connect the impossible dots. "This can't be right," she muttered, running a hand through her dark hair. "It's like we're chasing a ghost."

Dr. Ramirez cleared her throat. "Detective Keirstead, I've triple-checked the results. There's no mistake."

Holly's eyes narrowed as she leaned in, her voice dropping to a whisper. "What if it's not a mistake, but something we've never seen before? Something... beyond our understanding?"

The scientist shifted uncomfortably. "I'm not sure I follow."

"Neither do I," Holly admitted, her tone a mixture of frustration and curiosity. She straightened up, her athletic frame taut with tension. "But whatever this is, it's connected. All of it. And we need to figure out why."

As she spoke, images flashed through her mind: crime scenes drenched in blood, the mysterious figure always lurking just out of sight, and now this impossible DNA evidence. What kind of monster were they dealing with?

"I need copies of everything," Holly demanded, her voice sharp with urgency. "And I mean everything, Dr. Ramirez. Every test, every analysis, every wild theory you've got."

The doctor nodded, hurrying to comply as Holly turned to stare out the lab's window, her reflection ghostly in the glass. Her thoughts drifted to Drake Miller, the man at the center of this maelstrom. What was his connection to all of this? And more importantly, where was he now?

"Time's running out," she murmured to herself, her fists clenching at her sides. "I can feel it. We need to move fast before—"

The shrill ring of her phone cut through the tense silence, making both women jump. Holly snatched it up, her heart pounding. "Keirstead," she barked into the receiver.

As she listened, her eyes widened, and a mix of emotions played across her face: shock, fear, and beneath it all, a spark of fierce determination. "I'm on my way," she said tersely, ending the call.

She turned to Dr. Ramirez, her voice tight with barely contained energy. "Get me those copies. I've got a lead to chase down, and I can't waste another second."

With that, Holly strode out of the lab, her mind already racing ahead to the next step in this twisted investigation. Whatever dark forces were at play, she was determined to bring them into the light, no matter the cost.

11 - 12

Holly's mind whirled as she sped through the autumn-kissed streets of Bridgewater, the crisp air rushing through her open window doing little to cool her feverish thoughts. The genetic marker in the report – immunity to radiation – pulsed like a neon sign in her mind's eye, connecting invisible dots.

"Serpentine," she muttered, her knuckles white on the steering wheel. "How could I have missed it?" The blood drawings from her old case flickered in her memory, suddenly taking on a new, sinister shape.

She pulled over abruptly, tires screeching on fallen leaves as her phone rang. From an unknown caller.

"Gabriel," she breathed when the line connected. "It's you, isn't it? The man I shot all those years ago."

A pause, then that smooth, deliberate voice that sent chills down her spine. "Detective Keirstead. I wondered when you'd put it together."

"How?" she demanded, her free hand clenching into a fist. "How did you survive? And what's your connection to Drake and Harrison?"

Gabriel's chuckle was low, almost fond. "So many questions, Holly. But time is short, and answers are... complicated."

Holly's mind raced. "Drake's story about living in two worlds – it's not just an insanity plea, is it? There's more to this than I thought."

"Perhaps," Gabriel replied enigmatically. "But consider this – if Drake is your killer, how could he orchestrate his family's accident? And if not him, then who?"

Holly's breath caught. "Harrison? But he was just a child during the first—"

"Was he?" Gabriel interrupted softly. "Time is a fickle thing, Detective. As for me... well, let's just say I have a vested interest in how this plays out."

"Are you working with Drake?" Holly pressed, frustration mounting. "Or is someone framing him?"

"Find Drake," Gabriel said, his voice suddenly urgent. "Find him before it's too late. The answers you seek – and the danger – are closer than you realize."

The line went dead, leaving Holly with more questions than answers. She slammed her palm against the steering wheel, her mind a maelstrom of possibilities.

"Damn it!" she hissed, starting the car again. "I need to find Drake. Now."

As she pulled back onto the road, the autumn sun dipped low, casting long shadows across Bridgewater's quaint streets. Holly couldn't shake the feeling that time was running out – for her, for Drake, and for the truth she'd spent years chasing.

Descent into Darkness

Green World – 2024

1 - 2

Drake's hands trembled as he stuffed his gun into his waistband and grabbed his jacket, his mind a whirlwind of fear and determination. "Hold on, Harrison," he muttered, his voice barely above a whisper. "Daddy's coming."

As he sped through the darkened streets toward the abandoned Bridgewater Amusement Park, memories assaulted him like a barrage of bullets. Harrison's fifth birthday party at the park, his son's laughter echoing as they rode the merry-go-round together. The day he'd promised to take Harrison back, only to cancel at the last minute for an important case. The guilt gnawed at him, threatening to consume him whole.

"I won't fail you again," Drake vowed, his knuckles white as he gripped the steering wheel.

The rusted gates of the amusement park loomed before him, a twisted mockery of their once-welcoming presence. Drake's breath caught in his throat as he stepped out of the car, his eyes drawn to the dilapidated funhouse that stood like a sentinel in the moonlight. Faded knights and a snarling green dragon adorned its facade, their paint peeling and chipped.

"Jesus," Drake whispered, a shiver running down his spine. "What have you done, Gabriel?"

He approached the entrance, each step heavy with the weight of apprehension and nostalgia. The cheerful music that once filled the air had long since faded, replaced by an eerie silence broken only by the creak of rusted metal in the breeze.

"Harrison!" Drake called out, his voice echoing through the empty park. "Harrison, can you hear me?"

No response came, save for the mocking whisper of the wind through decaying rides. Drake's heart pounded in his chest, a frantic rhythm that matched the urgency of his thoughts. What if he was too late? What if Gabriel had already...

No. He couldn't afford to think like that. He had to stay focused, had to keep moving forward. For Harrison. For redemption.

As Drake approached the funhouse, a flicker of movement caught his eye. A shadow, darting between the weathered columns of the entrance. His hand instinctively moved to his gun, muscles tensing in anticipation.

"Gabriel?" he called out, trying to keep his voice steady. "I know you're here. Let's talk about this."

A low chuckle emanated from the darkness, sending chills down Drake's spine. "Oh, Drake," Gabriel's smooth voice replied, dripping with condescension. "Always the negotiator, aren't you? Even now, when your son's life hangs in the balance."

Drake's jaw clenched, anger surging through him. "Where is he, Gabriel? What have you done with my son?"

"Your son?" Gabriel's voice grew harder, his words laced with venom. "You lost the right to call him that long ago, Drake. When you chose your precious career over your family."

The words hit Drake like a physical blow, dredging up memories of missed birthdays, broken promises, and tearful goodbyes. But he pushed them aside, focusing on the present, on the urgency of the moment.

"I've made mistakes," Drake admitted, his voice raw with emotion. "But I'm here now. I'm not leaving without Harrison."

Gabriel stepped into view; his scarred face illuminated by the pale moonlight. His piercing eyes locked onto Drake's, a smirk playing at the corners of his mouth. "Then by all means," he said, gesturing toward the funhouse entrance. "Come and find him."

As Drake took a step forward, his heart racing with a mixture of fear and determination, he couldn't shake the feeling that he was walking into a trap. But for Harrison, he would face any danger, confront any demon – even the ones that lurked within himself.

3 - 4

Drake stepped into the funhouse, his footsteps echoing ominously in the cavernous space. The air was thick with dust and decay, the faint scent of rust mingling with the musty odor of abandonment. His senses were on high alert as he scanned his surroundings, every instinct screaming danger.

"Harrison?" he called out, his voice wavering slightly. "Can you hear me, son?"

Only silence answered him, broken by the creaking of aged wood beneath his feet. Drake's hand instinctively reached for the small of his back, where he'd tucked away his service pistol. The cold metal against his palm provided little comfort as he ventured deeper into the funhouse.

Distorted mirrors lined the walls, reflecting grotesque versions of himself. Drake caught a glimpse of his own reflection – disheveled, tired eyes haunted by guilt and fear. He barely recognized the man staring back at him.

"You know, Drake," Gabriel's voice echoed from somewhere in the shadows, "I always admired your determination. Even when it meant neglecting those closest to you."

Drake's jaw clenched. "I'm not here to discuss the past, Gabriel. Where's Harrison?"

A chuckle resonated through the funhouse. "Oh, but the past is precisely why we're here. Or should I say the future. Your choices, your priorities – they've led us to this moment."

As Drake rounded a corner, his mind raced with thoughts of Harrison. The image of his son's bright eyes and mischievous grin flashed before him, a stark contrast to the darkness surrounding him now. He couldn't afford to let fear paralyze him, couldn't allow himself to be consumed by doubt.

"I've made mistakes," Drake admitted, his voice thick with emotion. "But I'm here now, and I'm not leaving without my son."

"Your son?" Gabriel's voice grew harder. "Tell me, Drake, do you even know his favorite color? His dreams? His fears?"

The words cut deep, but Drake pushed forward. "I may not know everything about him, but I know I love him. And I know he needs me now more than ever."

With each step, Drake drew closer to the truth, closer to the confrontation that would determine Harrison's fate. The funhouse seemed to stretch endlessly before him, a maze of mirrors and shadows, each turn potentially hiding danger – or salvation.

"Love," Gabriel scoffed. "Is that what you call it? Abandoning him for case files and courtrooms?"

Drake's fists clenched at his sides. "I'm not the same man I was, Gabriel. The accident... it changed everything. Opened my eyes to what truly matters."

As he spoke, Drake realized the truth in his words. The parallel lives he'd been living, the grief and guilt he'd carried – they had transformed him. He was no longer the cutthroat lawyer who'd put career before family. Now, he was a father willing to face any danger to save his son.

"Well then, Drake," Gabriel's voice seemed closer now, "let's see just how much you've changed. How far you're willing to go to prove your love."

Drake's heart pounded in his chest as he stepped into a circular room, mirrors surrounding him on all sides. In the center stood Gabriel, a menacing smile on his scarred face. And there, behind him, bound and gagged, was Harrison – his eyes wide with fear and desperation.

"Dad!" Harrison's muffled cry pierced through Drake's soul.

In that moment, as father and son locked eyes across the room, Drake knew with absolute certainty that he would stop at nothing to save Harrison. The past, with all its regrets and mistakes, fell away. All that mattered now was the present – and the fight that lay ahead.

5 - 6

Drake's eyes darted between Gabriel's disfigured face and Harrison's terrified expression, his mind racing to formulate a plan. The funhouse mirrors distorted their reflections, creating a disorienting maze of images that seemed to mock his desperation.

"Let him go, Gabriel," Drake growled, his voice low and dangerous. "This is between you and me."

Gabriel's laugh echoed off the mirrored walls, a chilling sound that sent shivers down Drake's spine. "Oh, but Drake, it's so much more than that. Your son is the key to everything."

Drake took a cautious step forward, his hands clenched into fists at his sides. "What do you mean? What could you possibly want with Harrison?"

As he inched closer, Drake's mind whirled with possibilities. Was this about revenge? Or was there something more sinister at play? The weight of his past decisions pressed down on him, threatening to crush his resolve.

Gabriel's piercing gaze locked onto Drake. "You know about the blood, don't you? The genetic anomaly that makes us... special."

Drake's breath caught in his throat. How could Gabriel know about that? He'd kept it hidden for so long, buried beneath layers of denial and fear.

"I don't know what you're talking about," Drake lied, buying time as he edged closer to Harrison.

Gabriel's eyes narrowed. "Don't play dumb with me, Drake. Your son carries the same gift – or curse, depending on how you look at it. And I need him to unlock its full potential."

Drake's heart raced as the pieces began to fall into place. The murders, the symbol, the blood – it all led back to this genetic quirk that had plagued him his entire life. And now, it threatened to destroy everything he held dear.

"Dad, please," Harrison whimpered through his gag, tears streaming down his face.

Drake's resolve hardened. He squared his shoulders, facing Gabriel head-on. "I won't let you use him for your twisted experiments. Whatever you're planning, it ends here."

Gabriel's smile widened, revealing teeth that gleamed in the dim light. "Oh, Drake. It's only just beginning."

7 - 8

Drake's jaw clenched as he stared down Gabriel, the weight of their confrontation settling heavily in the musty air of the dilapidated funhouse. His eyes darted briefly to Harrison, bound and gagged, before snapping back to the disfigured face of his adversary. The burn scars that marred Gabriel's features seemed to writhe in the flickering shadows, lending an otherworldly quality to his already menacing presence.

"Let him go," Drake growled, his voice low and dangerous. "This is between you and me, Gabriel. Harrison has nothing to do with it."

Gabriel's lips curled into a sardonic smile, his piercing gaze never wavering. "On the contrary, Drake. Your son has everything to do with it. He's the key to unlocking our true potential."

Drake took a cautious step forward, his muscles coiled and ready to spring. "I won't let you use him as a lab rat for your twisted experiments."

"Still clinging to your moral high ground, I see," Gabriel sneered, his words dripping with disdain. "Tell me, how does it feel to be so... righteous? Does it help you sleep at night, knowing you've abandoned one life to save another?"

The taunt hit Drake like a physical blow, stirring up the guilt and anguish he'd been desperately trying to suppress. Images of his wife in the other reality flashed through his mind, her face twisted in grief and betrayal. He shook his head, forcing himself to focus on the present danger.

"You don't know anything about me," Drake spat, his fists clenching at his sides.

Gabriel's laugh echoed off the warped mirrors surrounding them, a chilling sound that sent shivers down Drake's spine. "Oh, but I do, Drake. I know everything about you. Your fears, your failures, your deepest, darkest secrets. I know the weight you carry, trying to balance two impossible realities."

Drake's mind raced, searching for a way to turn the tables on Gabriel, to find some weakness he could exploit. But as he stared into those cold, calculating eyes, he realized with growing dread that he was facing an opponent who had planned for every contingency.

"What do you want?" Drake asked, his voice barely above a whisper.

Gabriel's smile widened, a predatory gleam in his eyes. "I want you to embrace your true nature, Drake. To stop fighting against the gift we've been given and use it to reshape the world in our image."

As Gabriel spoke, Drake inched closer to Harrison, his heart pounding in his chest. He knew he had only one chance to save his son and put an end to Gabriel's madness. With a silent prayer, he prepared himself for the fight of his life, knowing that the fate of both his realities hung in the balance.

9 - 10

Gabriel's piercing gaze locked onto Drake, his disfigured face twisting into a cruel smile. "You know about the blood," he said, his voice cutting through the silence like a knife, cold and calculated. "You know about the genetic anomaly that binds us together."

Drake's breath caught in his throat, his mind reeling from the implications of Gabriel's words. He struggled to maintain his composure, but the trembling in his hands betrayed his inner turmoil. "What are you talking about?" he managed to choke out, desperately clinging to the hope that Gabriel was bluffing.

Gabriel's laugh echoed through the funhouse, a hollow, mirthless sound that sent chills down Drake's spine. "Oh, come now, Drake. Don't play coy with me. I know you've felt it – the pull between realities, the constant struggle to keep your worlds from colliding. It's in our blood, you see. A genetic quirk that allows us to exist in multiple dimensions simultaneously."

Drake's heart clenched, a surge of adrenaline coursing through his veins. He had suspected as much, had felt the inexplicable connection between his two lives, but hearing it confirmed sent a jolt of fear through him. How could Gabriel know about his condition, about the secrets he had kept hidden for so long?

"How?" Drake whispered; his voice barely audible over the pounding of his own heart. "How could you possibly know about this?"

Gabriel's eyes glinted with malicious glee. "I've been watching you, Drake. Studying you. You're not as alone in this as you think. There are others like us, scattered throughout the world, each struggling with their own fractured existences. But you... you're special. You're the key to unlocking our true potential."

Drake's mind raced, trying to process the flood of information. He thought of his wife, his son, the two lives he'd been desperately trying to balance. "What do you want from me?" he asked, his voice hoarse with emotion.

Gabriel took a step closer, his limp barely noticeable as he moved with predatory grace. "I want us to work together, Drake. To harness the power of our unique condition and reshape reality itself. Imagine it – a world where we're no longer torn between lives, where we can exist fully in every dimension simultaneously."

Drake shook his head, revulsion rising in his throat. "You're insane," he spat. "I won't help you destroy the fabric of reality. I won't risk losing my family – either of them."

Gabriel's expression hardened, the burns on his face contorting into a mask of fury. "You don't have a choice, Drake. You're part of this whether you like it or not. And if you won't join me willingly... well, I have ways of persuading you."

As Gabriel's words hung in the air, Drake's resolve hardened. He knew he had to find a way to stop this madman, to protect his loved ones and the very nature of reality itself. With determination burning in his eyes, he prepared himself for whatever came next, knowing that the fate of everything he held dear hung in the balance.

11 - 12

Gabriel's piercing eyes bore into Drake, a cruel smile playing at the corners of his scarred mouth. "There's a mole in your midst, Drake," he said, his voice low and menacing, each word dripping with malice. "Someone close to you who betrayed your trust, who shared your secrets with me."

Drake's heart pounded against his ribcage, his mind reeling from the implications. He struggled to keep his voice steady as he replied, "You're lying. No one would—"

"Oh, but they did," Gabriel interrupted, his tone laced with mock sympathy. "Your condition, your struggles, your fears... I know it all, Drake. Every little detail."

The funhouse mirrors surrounding them distorted Drake's reflection, fracturing his image into a thousand broken pieces – a fitting metaphor for the shattered trust he now felt. He clenched his fists, fighting to maintain his composure. "Who?" he demanded, his voice barely above a whisper.

Gabriel merely chuckled, the sound echoing ominously through the abandoned amusement park. "Now, where's the fun in revealing all my cards at once? Let's just say it's someone you'd never suspect."

Drake's mind raced, cycling through faces of friends, colleagues, even family members. Who could have betrayed him so completely? The thought sent a wave of nausea crashing over him, mingling with the fear and uncertainty that already gripped his heart.

"You're trying to manipulate me," Drake said, more to convince himself than Gabriel. "This is just another one of your mind games."

Gabriel's eyes flashed dangerously. "Is it, Drake? Or are you simply afraid to face the truth? The truth that someone you trust implicitly has been feeding me information all along?"

Drake's resolve wavered, doubt creeping into his thoughts like poison. He tried to push it away, to focus on the immediate threat before him, but the seed of suspicion had been planted. As he stood there, facing his nemesis in the twisted ruins of a once-joyful place, Drake felt more alone and vulnerable than ever before.

13 - 14

Drake's thoughts whirled, a maelstrom of confusion and betrayal threatening to overwhelm him. But as he stared into Gabriel's piercing eyes, he forced himself to focus on the present danger. There was no time for dwelling on the past, no time for regret or recrimination. He needed answers, and he needed them now.

"Enough games, Gabriel," Drake growled, his voice rough with emotion. "What do you want?"

Gabriel's lips curled into a cold smile, his scarred face twisting grotesquely in the dim light. "What I've always wanted, Drake. A future where we're not held back by the small-minded masses."

Drake felt a chill run down his spine, but before he could respond, Gabriel continued, his voice devoid of emotion, his gaze unwavering. "I killed those people, Drake. I killed them because they posed a threat to our future. Because someday, somewhere, they would have stood in my way."

The words hit Drake like a physical blow, stealing the air from his lungs. He stumbled back a step, his mind reeling. "You... what?" he gasped, struggling to comprehend the enormity of Gabriel's confession.

"You heard me," Gabriel replied, his tone matter of fact, as if discussing the weather rather than multiple murders. "Every single one of them - obstacles removed. Efficiently. Permanently."

Drake's stomach churned, bile rising in his throat. He thought of the victims, their faces flashing before his eyes - lives snuffed out by the man standing before him. "How could you?" he whispered, horror and revulsion warring within him.

Gabriel tilted his head, regarding Drake with something akin to pity. "How could I not? They were holding us back, Drake. Holding you back. Don't you see? I did this for us."

"Us?" Drake spat, anger flaring hot and bright within him. "There is no 'us,' Gabriel. You're a monster."

A flicker of something - pain? regret? - passed across Gabriel's face, so quickly Drake thought he might have imagined it. Then the mask of cold indifference slipped back into place. "A monster?" Gabriel mused. "Perhaps. But a necessary one. Someone has to make the hard choices, Drake. Someone has to pave the way for our kind."

Drake shook his head, trying to clear it of the poisonous words. He couldn't let Gabriel's twisted logic infect him. "You're wrong," he said firmly. "There's always another way. Always."

Gabriel's laugh was brittle, like breaking glass. "Such naivety. I expected better from you, Drake. After everything you've seen, everything you've experienced... how can you still cling to such childish ideals?"

As Gabriel spoke, Drake's hand inched towards the concealed weapon at his hip. He knew he might only get one chance. One shot to end this madness once and for all.

15 - 16

Drake's fingers curled around the cold metal of his concealed weapon, his heart pounding so loudly he was certain Gabriel must hear it. The abandoned funhouse seemed to close in around them, shadows dancing on the peeling walls like macabre spectators to their confrontation.

"You don't have to do this, Gabriel," Drake said, his voice hoarse with tension. "We can find another way. There's still time to—"

"Time?" Gabriel interrupted, his scarred face twisting into a sardonic smile. "Time is a luxury we no longer have, Drake. Our genetic anomaly ensures that. Every moment we waste in pointless debate is a moment closer to our extinction."

Drake's mind reeled, struggling to process the implications of Gabriel's words. The weight of their shared condition, the blood that tied them together in ways he was only beginning to understand, pressed down on him like a physical force.

"So that's your justification?" Drake asked, fighting to keep his voice steady. "Murder? Genocide? All to protect a genetic quirk?"

Gabriel's eyes flashed dangerously. "A quirk? Is that what you think this is?" He took a step forward, his limp barely noticeable as he moved with predatory grace. "This is evolution, Drake. We are the next step. And I will do whatever it takes to ensure our survival."

As Gabriel advanced, Drake's fingers tightened on his weapon. He knew he should act, should end this threat before it was too late. But something held him back—a mixture of fear, doubt, and a lingering hope that there might be another way.

"And what about Harrison?" Drake asked, desperation creeping into his voice. "Where does he fit into your grand plan?"

A flicker of emotion passed across Gabriel's face, gone so quickly Drake couldn't be sure he'd seen it. "Your son is safe, for now. His fate, like ours, hangs in the balance of the choices we make here today."

Drake's blood ran cold at the implication. "If you've hurt him, I swear I'll—"

"You'll what?" Gabriel cut him off, his voice dripping with contempt. "Kill me? Go ahead, Drake. Pull that trigger you've been fingering. See if it makes you feel better. See if it brings back all those lives I've taken. See if it makes you any different from me."

The words hit Drake like a physical blow, forcing him to confront the darkness that lurked within his own heart. He had always known Gabriel was dangerous, but hearing the cold calculation in his voice, seeing the utter lack of remorse in those piercing eyes, sent a shiver down his spine that seemed to reach into his very soul.

As Gabriel spoke, Drake's mind raced with the realization of the true extent of his enemy's ruthlessness. He knew now, with a certainty that chilled him to his core, that Gabriel would stop at nothing to achieve his goals. That he would use any means necessary to eliminate anyone who stood in his path—be it friend, foe, or even family.

"You're wrong, Gabriel," Drake said, his voice barely above a whisper. "There's always a choice. Always another way."

Gabriel's laugh echoed through the decrepit funhouse, a sound devoid of joy or warmth. "Then choose, Drake. Here and now. Your son's life, or the lives of countless strangers. Your ideals, or your family. What's it going to be?"

As the weight of Gabriel's ultimatum settled over him, Drake felt the world narrow to a single, terrible moment of decision. His hand trembled on his weapon as he stared into the abyss of Gabriel's eyes, knowing that whatever choice he made would forever alter the course of both their lives.

17 - 18

Drake's jaw clenched, his eyes never leaving Gabriel's disfigured face as he fought against the wave of despair threatening to engulf him. The dilapidated funhouse seemed to close in around them, the faded images of knights and dragons on the walls a mocking reminder of simpler times.

"You don't get to dictate the terms, Gabriel," Drake growled, his voice low and steady despite the turmoil within. "I won't choose between my son and my humanity. That's not a choice at all."

Gabriel's scarred lips twisted into a sneer. "Always the righteous lawyer, aren't you, Drake? Even now, you can't see the bigger picture."

Drake took a step forward, his resolve hardening with each passing moment. "The bigger picture? You mean your twisted vision of the future? I see it clearly, Gabriel. I see the darkness you're trying to unleash."

As he spoke, Drake's mind raced, memories of his past life as a ruthless attorney mingling with the desperation of a father fighting for his son. He couldn't go back to being that man, the one who sacrificed everything for success. But he also couldn't lose Harrison.

"You think you know darkness, Drake?" Gabriel's voice dripped with contempt. "You haven't even scratched the surface."

Drake's eyes blazed with determination. "Maybe not. But I know light, Gabriel. I know what it means to love, to protect. And that's something you'll never understand."

With each word, Drake felt his resolve strengthen, the fear and doubt that had clouded his judgment burning away in the face of his unwavering love for his son. He knew, with a clarity that surprised even him, that he couldn't let Gabriel's darkness consume them both.

"This ends now," Drake declared, his voice echoing through the abandoned funhouse. "One way or another, we finish this. For Harrison. For all the lives you've destroyed."

Gabriel's eyes narrowed, a flicker of something—surprise? respect?—passing across his scarred features. "So be it, Drake. Let's see if your light can withstand the coming storm."

As they faced each other in the dim light, the air crackled with tension. Drake knew that this confrontation would determine not just Harrison's fate, but the very essence of who he was as a man, a father, and a protector. The battle for their souls had begun, and Drake was ready to fight with everything he had.

19 - 20

Drake lunged forward, his muscles coiled with tension, every fiber of his being focused on ending this nightmare. But as he charged, Gabriel's hand moved with lightning speed, a metallic glint catching Drake's eye.

"Did you really think it would be that easy?" Gabriel's voice was eerily calm as he leveled the sleek handgun at Drake's chest.

Time seemed to slow as Drake registered the weapon, his mind racing. "Gabriel, don't—"

The deafening crack of the gunshot tore through the air, drowning out Drake's words. A searing, white-hot pain exploded in his hip, the force of the impact sending him crashing to the ground.

"You see, Drake," Gabriel mused, his disfigured face twisting into a grotesque smile, "your light, your love—they make you predictable. Weak."

Drake gasped, his vision blurring as he clutched his wound. The taste of copper filled his mouth as he struggled to form words. "You're... wrong," he managed, each syllable a herculean effort.

Gabriel loomed over him, his piercing eyes reflecting a mix of triumph and curiosity. "Am I? Look at you now, Drake. Where's your strength? Where's your resolve?"

Through the haze of pain, Drake's thoughts turned to Harrison. He couldn't fail, not now. Not when his son needed him most. "My strength," he rasped, fixing Gabriel with a defiant glare, "comes from something you'll never understand."

The world tilted and spun around Drake as he fought to stay conscious, the agony in his hip threatening to pull him into darkness. But he clung to his purpose, to the love that had driven him this far. He wouldn't let Gabriel win. He couldn't.

21 - 22

Drake's vision swam, the dilapidated funhouse walls melting into a kaleidoscope of faded colors and twisted shapes. He gritted his teeth, fighting against the waves of pain that threatened to drag him under. "Harrison," he whispered, his son's name a talisman against the encroaching darkness.

Gabriel's laugh echoed through the chamber; a chilling sound devoid of warmth. "Still clinging to hope, Drake? How very... predictable of you."

With a herculean effort, Drake pushed himself up onto his elbows, his breath coming in ragged gasps. "You don't... understand," he panted, fixing Gabriel with a steely gaze. "This isn't about winning or losing. It's about... family."

"Family?" Gabriel spat, his face contorting with disgust. "That's your great motivation? How pathetically sentimental."

As Gabriel's words washed over him, Drake's mind raced. He thought of the man he used to be—the ruthless lawyer who'd sacrifice anything for victory. How different he was now, lying broken on the floor of an abandoned funhouse, fighting for his son's life.

"You're right," Drake conceded, his voice barely above a whisper. "I am sentimental. But that's not weakness, Gabriel. It's strength."

Gabriel's eyebrows shot up, a flicker of uncertainty crossing his face. "Strength? Look at you, Drake. You're bleeding out on the floor. How is that strength?"

Drake's lips curled into a pained smile. "Because I'll never stop fighting. For Harrison. For my family. Can you say the same?"

As the words left his mouth, Drake felt a surge of resolve course through him. But even as he clung to this newfound determination, he could feel his strength ebbing away, the harsh reality of his situation crashing over him like a tidal wave.

23 - 23

The world around Drake began to blur, the dim lights of the funhouse smearing into a hazy, kaleidoscopic nightmare. Gabriel's figure loomed above him, a dark silhouette against the fading backdrop of reality. Drake's ears rang with the lingering echoes of the gunshot, each reverberation seeming to pull him further into the abyss.

"Oh, Drake," Gabriel's voice cut through the fog, dripping with mock pity. "Your sentimentality has always been your downfall. Family, love, loyalty—they're all weaknesses to be exploited."

Drake tried to respond, to rally against Gabriel's cruel words, but his tongue felt leaden in his mouth. His thoughts, once razor-sharp, now drifted like smoke, impossible to grasp.

"You... don't... understand," Drake managed to rasp, his words slurring together. "Love... makes us... stronger."

Gabriel's laughter, cold and mirthless, pierced through Drake's fading consciousness. "Strong enough to bleed out on a dirty floor? I think not."

As darkness encroached on the edges of his vision, Drake's mind conjured an image of Harrison—his son's smile, bright and hopeful. He clung to that image, a lifeline in the encroaching void.

"Harrison," Drake whispered, his voice barely audible. "I'm... sorry."

The last thing Drake heard before consciousness slipped away entirely was Gabriel's voice, low and triumphant: "Sleep now, Drake. When you wake—if you wake—your world will be forever changed."

Then, mercifully, there was only silence and darkness.

Adrenaline and Agony

Green World – 2024

1 - 2

Drake's body hit the ground with a sickening thud, his limbs twitching as pain coursed through him. I couldn't help but admire the way his scruffy beard twitched with each labored breath; his tired eyes squeezed shut against the agony. A rush of adrenaline flooded my system as I gazed down at my handiwork.

"You never could stay down, could you, Drake?" I mused aloud, my voice eerily calm in the stillness of the night. "Always getting back up, no matter how hard life knocks you down."

His eyes fluttered open, those brown orbs filled with a mix of pain and determination. "Why... why are you doing this?" he rasped, each word a struggle.

I chuckled, taking a step back to survey the scene. My heart pounded in my chest, the thrill of victory mingling with something darker, more primal. The dilapidated funhouse loomed around us, a grotesque monument to forgotten joy. Outside rusted Ferris wheel cars creaked in the gentle breeze, casting elongated shadows across the building.

"You know why, Drake," I replied, my gaze drawn to the twisted metal of a nearby mirror. "This is where it all began, isn't it? Where your perfect little world came crashing down around you."

Drake's fingers clawed at the dirt as he tried to push himself up. "My family... they have nothing to do with this," he growled, his normally contemplative tone edged with desperation.

I crouched down beside him, close enough to see the flecks of gray in his disheveled black hair. "Oh, but they have everything to do with this," I whispered. "Your wife, your son – they're the reason you're here, fighting so hard to stay alive."

A look of anguish crossed Drake's face; his internal struggle evident in the set of his jaw. "You don't understand," he muttered, more to himself than to me. "I have to make it right... I have to save them both."

Standing once more, I cast my gaze over the eerie landscape of the funhouse. The full moon hung low in the sky, bathing everything in an otherworldly glow. It was a fitting backdrop for our confrontation – a place where reality seemed to bend and warp, much like Drake's fractured existence.

"Two worlds, Drake," I said, my voice barely above a whisper. "Two lives. How long did you think you could keep juggling them before everything came crashing down?"

Drake's eyes met mine, a spark of his old determination shining through the pain. "As long as it takes," he growled. "I won't give up on either of them."

I couldn't help but admire his resilience, even as I reveled in his defeat. Drake Miller, once the ruthless lawyer who would do anything to win, now brought low by the very thing he had once neglected – his family.

3 - 4

A wave of conflicting emotions washed over me as I gazed down at Drake's crumpled form. His disheveled appearance, the dark circles under his eyes, the stubble on his chin – it all spoke to the toll this dual existence had taken on him. Yet even now, beaten and broken, there was a fire in those tired eyes that I couldn't extinguish.

"You know, Drake," I said, my voice laced with a mixture of admiration and contempt, "in another life, we might have been on the same side. But you represent everything I've come to hate – the man who puts ambition above all else, who thinks he can have it all without consequence."

Drake's lips curled into a bitter smile. "And what about you?" he rasped, each word clearly causing him pain. "You think you're any different? You're just as consumed by this... this madness as I am."

I paused, considering his words. The nagging sense of unease that had been gnawing at me grew stronger. "Maybe you're right," I admitted, more to myself than to him. "Maybe we're both just pawns in a game we don't understand."

As I turned to leave, the floorboards creaked ominously under me, as if agreeing with my assessment. The taste of copper filled my mouth, a reminder of the violence that had just transpired.

"This isn't over," Drake called out, his voice growing stronger with each word. "I'll find the truth, no matter what it takes. For my wife, for my son... for both of them."

I looked back one last time, meeting his determined gaze. "I know you will, Drake. That's what I'm counting on."

5 - 5

As I melted into the shadows of the dilapidated amusement park, Drake's labored breathing faded behind me. The moonlight cast eerie silhouettes of broken rides and abandoned booths, a twisted funhouse mirror reflecting the fractured realities we both inhabited.

"You don't understand," I whispered to the night, knowing Drake couldn't hear me. "The truth... it's a labyrinth of mirrors, each reflection more distorted than the last."

My mind raced, contemplating the intricate web of deception I'd woven. Drake's determination was admirable, but it was also his greatest weakness. He couldn't see that his relentless pursuit was leading him further from the truth he so desperately sought.

"Why can't you just let it go?" I muttered, pushing through a tangle of overgrown vines. "Your obsession... it's tearing apart both versions of your life."

I paused, leaning against the rusted frame of a carnival game booth. The irony wasn't lost on me – here I was, equally obsessed, equally entangled in this mess. But unlike Drake, I knew the full scope of our shared predicament.

"He thinks he's fighting for his family," I mused aloud, "but he doesn't realize he's fighting against himself."

As I resumed my retreat, a chilling thought struck me. What if Drake's dual existence wasn't just a result of the accident? What if it was a symptom of something far more sinister, something that threatened the very fabric of reality itself?

I shook my head, trying to dispel the unsettling notion. "Focus," I chided myself. "One step at a time. Drake will come for you, and when he does, you need to be ready."

The distant wail of sirens pierced the night, reminding me that time was running short. As I quickened my pace, dragging Harrison along with me, I couldn't shake the feeling that our next encounter would be pivotal – not just for Drake and me, but for the countless unseen players in this cosmic game of chess.

"Until next time, Drake Miller," I whispered to the wind. "May your demons grant you the strength you'll need for what's to come."

Crimson Confession

1 - 2

Holly's heart pounded in her chest as she dropped to her knees beside Drake's prone form, her eyes fixating on the dark crimson stain blooming across his shirt. The metallic scent of blood filled her nostrils as she gently peeled back the fabric, revealing an angry wound just below his ribcage. Her trained eyes quickly assessed the injury, noting the jagged edges and steady flow of blood with mounting concern.

"Drake, what happened?" Holly's voice came out steadier than she felt, her hands moving swiftly to apply pressure to the wound. "Who did this to you?"

Drake's face contorted in pain; his usually thoughtful brown eyes now clouded with agony. He drew in a ragged breath before speaking, each word seeming to cost him dearly. "He shot me, Holly. In the other world... Gabriel shot me."

Holly's brow furrowed deeply, her mind reeling at his words. Another world? Gabriel? The surreal nature of the situation threatened to overwhelm her, but she forced herself to focus on the immediate danger. "Drake, you're not making sense. We need to get you help."

"You don't understand," Drake insisted, his voice growing more urgent despite the strain. "It's all connected. The realities... they're bleeding into each other." He gripped Holly's arm with surprising strength, his eyes boring into hers with an intensity that sent a shiver down her spine.

As Holly maintained pressure on the wound, her mind raced through possibilities. Was this some kind of delusion brought on by blood loss? Or was there truth to Drake's ramblings about other worlds? The detective in her couldn't help but search for connections, even as she prioritized his immediate medical needs.

"Drake, I need you to stay with me," Holly urged, her voice taking on a gentle yet authoritative tone. "We'll figure this out together, but right now, you need to conserve your strength."

Drake's grip on her arm loosened slightly, his eyes growing unfocused. "Holly, you have to believe me. Gabriel... he's the key to all of this. He knows about the split realities."

As Drake's words trailed off, Holly felt a chill run through her body. The name Gabriel echoed in her mind, conjuring an image of piercing eyes and a heavily scarred face. She had encountered him briefly during her investigation, and something about the man had set her on edge. Now, hearing Drake connect him to this bizarre situation only amplified her unease.

"I hear you, Drake," Holly assured him, her free hand moving to check his pulse. "But right now, we need to focus on getting you stable. Can you tell me anything else about what happened?"

Drake's eyes fluttered, his breathing becoming more labored. "The accident... it wasn't an accident. Gabriel... he's been manipulating both worlds. We have to stop him before—" His words cut off abruptly as a spasm of pain wracked his body.

Holly leaned in closer, her heart racing as she tried to make sense of Drake's fragmented revelations. "Before what, Drake? What is Gabriel trying to do?"

But Drake's eyes had rolled back, his body going limp beneath her hands. Panic surged through Holly as she quickly checked his vitals, relief washing over her as she confirmed he was still breathing, albeit shallowly.

As she reached for her phone to call for help, Holly's mind whirled with the implications of Drake's words. Two worlds, a manipulative Gabriel, and a wounded Drake caught in the middle. Whatever was going on, Holly knew one thing for certain – she was now entangled in a mystery far more complex and dangerous than she could have ever imagined.

3 - 4

"We'll talk about that later," Holly said, her voice steady despite the chaos swirling around them. She squeezed Drake's hand reassuringly, her piercing eyes meeting his pain-filled gaze. "Right now, we need to get you to the hospital."

Drake nodded weakly, his disheveled appearance a stark contrast to Holly's composed demeanor. "Holly, I—" he began, but she cut him off gently.

"Save your strength," she insisted, already reaching for her phone. "I'm calling an ambulance now."

As Holly dialed, her fingers moving with practiced efficiency, she couldn't help but notice the way Drake's eyes darted around the room, as if searching for unseen threats. His earlier words about Gabriel and another world echoed in her mind, sending a chill down her spine.

"This is Detective Holly Kierstead," she spoke into the phone, her voice clear and authoritative. "I need an ambulance at the Bridgewater Police Department. Male, mid-fourties, gunshot wound to the abdomen. Victim is conscious but losing blood rapidly."

As she relayed the details, Holly's free hand instinctively moved to apply pressure to Drake's wound. She could feel the warm, sticky blood seeping through her fingers, a grim reminder of the urgency of the situation.

"They're on their way," Holly informed Drake as she ended the call. "Just hang in there, okay?"

Drake's eyes locked onto hers, a mix of gratitude and fear evident in his gaze. "Holly, if I don't make it—"

"Don't you dare," she interrupted, her tone fierce. "You're going to be fine. We have too many questions that need answering for you to check out now."

As they waited for the ambulance, Holly's mind raced with possibilities. If Drake's wounds from another reality had manifested here, what did that mean for the nature of their world? And who was this Gabriel that seemed to pose such a threat?

"Drake," Holly ventured, her curiosity getting the better of her, "what did you mean about Gabriel shooting you in another world?"

Drake's response was cut short by the distant wail of sirens. Holly felt a wave of relief wash over her, knowing help was near. Yet, as she looked down at Drake's pale face, she couldn't shake the chilling thought that had taken root in her mind: If she hadn't found him when she did, Drake might have bled out alone on this floor, a victim of a crime committed in a world she couldn't even comprehend.

5 - 6

The ambulance screeched to a halt outside, its flashing lights painting the room in an eerie red glow. Paramedics burst through the door, their faces a mask of professional urgency.

"Over here!" Holly called, her voice steady despite the turmoil in her chest.

As the paramedics swarmed around Drake, Holly's athletic build came in handy. She helped lift his limp form onto the stretcher, her movements quick and precise.

"I'm coming with him," she stated, her tone brooking no argument.

The ride to the hospital was a blur of sirens and tense silence. Holly's mind whirled with unanswered questions, chief among them the fate of Linda. She pulled out her phone, dialing the number again.

"Come on, Linda," she muttered, her free hand clasping Drake's. "Pick up, damn it."

No answer. Holly's stomach twisted with worry.

"Holly," Drake's voice was barely a whisper. "Gabriel... he's dangerous. More than you know."

She leaned in close, her piercing eyes locked on his. "We'll deal with him, Drake. But right now, you need to focus on staying with me, okay?"

As they arrived at the emergency room, the reality of the situation hit Holly like a physical blow. Gabriel was out there, a shadowy threat looming over them all. Her analytical mind raced, trying to piece together the fragments of information she had.

"Ma'am, we need to take him now," a nurse said, gently but firmly pushing Holly aside.

She watched as they wheeled Drake away, her heart pounding. "I'll be right here, Drake," she called after him. "You're not alone in this."

Left standing in the bustling ER, Holly took a deep breath, steeling herself. She might not understand everything that was happening, but one thing was clear: Drake needed her, and she wouldn't let him down. Whatever dangers lay ahead, whatever mysteries needed solving, Holly was determined to face them head-on.

7 - 8

The fluorescent lights of the waiting room buzzed incessantly, their harsh glare amplifying Holly's growing sense of unease. She paced the worn linoleum floor, her footsteps echoing in the near-empty space. The clock on the wall seemed to mock her, its hands moving with agonizing slowness.

"This can't be happening," Holly muttered, running her fingers through her short, dark hair. Her mind raced, replaying the night's events in vivid detail. Drake's words about Gabriel and another world haunted her, each repetition in her thoughts sending a chill down her spine.

A nurse approached, clipboard in hand. "Mrs. Sharp? Any update on contacting Mr. Miller's next of kin?"

Holly's jaw clenched. "Still working on it," she replied, her voice tight with frustration. "His partner isn't answering her phone."

As the nurse nodded sympathetically and walked away, Holly slumped into an uncomfortable plastic chair. She leaned forward, elbows on her knees, and closed her eyes.

"Come on, Drake," she whispered fiercely. "You're tougher than this. You have to be."

The minutes stretched into hours, each one feeling like an eternity. Holly's analytical mind wouldn't shut off, cycling through scenarios and possibilities, each one more dire than the last. She tried to focus on the facts, on what she knew for certain, but the unknown variables kept intruding.

"I should have seen this coming," she berated herself. "I should have protected him better."

Just as Holly was about to make another attempt at reaching Linda, movement caught her eye. A doctor, his face etched with exhaustion, was approaching. Holly's heart leapt into her throat as she stood, her legs trembling slightly.

"Detective Sharp?" the doctor asked, his voice low and grave.

Holly nodded, unable to form words. She searched the doctor's face for any hint of good news, but his somber expression offered no comfort.

"How is he?" she finally managed to ask, her voice barely above a whisper.

The doctor took a deep breath, and Holly braced herself for whatever was coming next.

9 - 10

The doctor's weary eyes met Holly's as he began, "Drake Miller is stable for now." His measured tone sent a chill through Holly's body. "But he's lost a significant amount of blood, and the gunshot wound was severe. He's in critical condition."

Holly's breath caught in her throat, her mind reeling with the gravity of the situation. She clenched her fists, willing herself to stay composed. "What are his chances?" she asked, her voice tight with suppressed emotion.

The doctor hesitated before responding, "It's touch and go at this point. The next 24 hours will be crucial."

Holly nodded, her piercing eyes never leaving the doctor's face. "Can you tell me more about his injuries? Where exactly was he shot?"

As the doctor explained the extent of Drake's wounds, Holly's analytical mind kicked into overdrive, processing the information while simultaneously grappling with the emotional toll. She knew Drake was tough—she'd seen his determination firsthand—but the thought of him fighting for his life sent a shiver down her spine.

"Thank you, doctor," Holly said, her voice steadier than she felt. "I appreciate your honesty."

As the doctor turned to leave, Holly called out, "Wait! Is there anything I can do? Anything he needs?"

The doctor's expression softened slightly. "Just be here for him. Your presence might make a difference."

Left alone once more, Holly sank back into her chair, her mind a whirlwind of conflicting thoughts and emotions. "Dammit, Drake," she muttered under her breath, "you can't give up now. We've got too much left to figure out."

11 - 12

Holly took a deep breath, steeling herself before asking, "Can I see him?" Her voice, barely above a whisper, trembled with a mixture of fear and anticipation.

The doctor nodded, his expression softening. "Of course. Follow me."

As they navigated the labyrinth of sterile corridors, Holly's mind raced. What would she find? How bad was it really? The antiseptic smell burned her nostrils, a stark reminder of the dire situation.

"He's still unconscious," the doctor explained as they walked. "Try not to be alarmed by the equipment. It's all there to help him."

Holly nodded; her throat too tight to speak. She thought of Drake—the man who existed in two realities, torn between grief and hope. How cruel that he should suffer in both worlds now.

They reached a door, and the doctor paused. "Are you ready?"

"As I'll ever be," Holly managed, her heart pounding.

The door swung open, and Holly's breath caught in her throat. There lied Drake, pale and still, a far cry from the determined, conflicted man she knew. Machines beeped rhythmically, their cold efficiency a counterpoint to the fragility of human life.

"Oh, Drake," she whispered, her heart breaking at the sight. She stepped closer, her eyes taking in every detail—the tubes, the monitors, the bandages. This was Drake Miller, the man who fought to save his family across realities, now fighting for his own life.

"I'll give you some time," the doctor said softly, retreating from the room.

Holly approached the bed, her mind reeling. "What happened to you in that other world, Drake?" she murmured. "And how are we going to get you out of this one?"

13 - 14

Holly approached Drake's bedside cautiously, her footsteps echoing in the sterile room. The rhythmic beeping of the heart monitor seemed to underscore the fragility of the moment. She reached out, her hand trembling slightly as she took Drake's in hers. His skin felt cool and clammy, a stark contrast to the warmth she remembered from their previous encounters.

"Oh, Drake," she whispered, her voice catching as she studied his face. The scruffy beard she'd grown accustomed to seemed more unkempt now, his features etched with lines of pain even in unconsciousness. His chest rose and fell in shallow, labored breaths, each one a reminder of how close he'd come to slipping away entirely.

Holly felt a lump form in her throat, her analytical mind struggling to find the right words in this emotional minefield. She was used to interrogating suspects, piecing together clues, but this—comforting a man who lived between two realities—this was uncharted territory.

"I'm here, Drake," she finally managed, her voice thick with emotion. She squeezed his hand gently, hoping that somehow, he could feel her presence. "You're going to make it through this. I won't let anything happen to you."

As the words left her lips, Holly was struck by their weight. She'd sworn to protect and serve, but this felt different—more personal, more vital. Drake's revelation about Gabriel and the other world swirled in her mind, a puzzle she was determined to solve.

"We've got so much to figure out," she continued, her thumb tracing small circles on the back of his hand. "But first, you need to fight. Fight like you've been fighting for your family, Drake. They need you—both versions of them."

Holly's eyes darted to the monitors, willing them to show some sign of improvement. "And I... I need you too," she admitted softly, surprising herself with the depth of feeling behind those words.

15 - 15

Holly's gaze lingered on Drake's pale face, her brow furrowing as doubt crept into her mind like a sinister fog. She leaned closer, her voice barely above a whisper, "But Gabriel's still out there, isn't he? Waiting in the shadows, plotting his next move."

The steady beep of the heart monitor seemed to grow louder, matching the increasing tempo of Holly's own pulse. She stood abruptly, pacing the small hospital room, her detective's instincts kicking into high gear.

"How did he do it, Drake?" she muttered, more to herself than her unconscious partner. "How did he hurt you in one world and have it affected you here?"

Holly paused at the window, her reflection ghostly in the darkness beyond. Her eyes narrowed as she recalled Gabriel's piercing gaze, his cryptic words, the burn scars that marred his face. "What game is he playing?"

She turned back to Drake, her voice tight with determination. "I won't let him win, Drake. Whatever he's planning, whatever this... this other world is, we'll figure it out together."

But even as the words left her lips, Holly felt the weight of uncertainty pressing down on her. She sank into the chair beside Drake's bed, her hand finding his once more. "I just hope..." she began, her voice catching, "I hope I'm strong enough to protect you. To protect us all."

The night stretched on, filled with the hum of machines and the whisper of Holly's racing thoughts. As she kept her vigil, she couldn't shake the feeling that this was just the beginning of a much darker, more dangerous journey.

Mole Revealed

1 - 2

Linda's heart raced as Richard Vega's iron grip tightened around her arm, dragging her through the dimly lit alleyway. The cool night air whipped her blonde hair across her face, stinging her eyes as they moved swiftly between towering brick buildings.

"Richard, please," Linda pleaded, her voice barely above a whisper. "Why are you doing this? I thought we were friends."

Vega's face remained an impassive mask, his jaw clenched tightly as he pulled her along. The silence that followed her question was deafening, broken only by the sound of their hurried footsteps echoing off the walls around them.

Linda's mind reeled, struggling to comprehend how someone she had trusted, someone who had been a source of support during her darkest days, could betray her so completely. The weight of his betrayal crushed against her chest, threatening to overwhelm her. But as she stumbled over an uneven patch of pavement, nearly losing her footing, a spark of determination ignited within her.

"I won't let you do this," she hissed, attempting to wrench her arm free. "Whatever you're planning, whatever you think you're going to accomplish, it won't work."

Vega's grip only tightened in response, his fingers digging painfully into her flesh. "Save your breath," he muttered, his voice low and cold. "You don't understand what's at stake here."

With each step they took, Linda's heart pounded harder, the rhythm seeming to sync with their hurried pace. The sound filled her ears, drowning out the ambient noise of the city around them. She stole a glance at Vega's face, illuminated briefly by a passing streetlight, and felt a chill run down her spine at the cold determination etched into his features.

"Richard," she tried again, her tone softer this time, appealing to the man she thought she knew. "Whatever trouble you're in, whatever's forcing you to do this, I can help. We can figure this out together."

For a moment, she thought she saw a flicker of something—regret, perhaps—in Vega's eyes. But it vanished as quickly as it had appeared, replaced by a steely resolve that made Linda's blood run cold.

"There's no going back now," Vega replied, his voice barely audible. "For either of us."

As they rounded another corner, Linda's mind raced, searching for a way out of this nightmare. She knew she couldn't afford to underestimate Vega or whatever forces were at play here. Her survival instinct kicked in, pushing aside the hurt and betrayal, forcing her to focus on the immediate danger.

"You don't have to do this," Linda said, her voice steady despite the fear coursing through her veins. "Whatever they have on you, whatever they're threatening, we can fight it. I won't give up on you, Richard."

Vega's pace faltered for a split second, and Linda felt a glimmer of hope. But then his grip tightened once more, and he pulled her forward with renewed determination.

"It's too late for that," he growled, his words laced with a mixture of anger and resignation. "Just... just stop talking and keep moving."

As they pressed on through the labyrinth of city streets, Linda's mind whirled with possible escape plans, each one seeming more impossible than the last. But she refused to give up hope, drawing on the inner strength that had carried her through so much heartache in the past.

I will survive this, she thought to herself, her resolve hardening with each step. I have to. For Drake, for my family. I won't let them down.

3 - 4

The acrid stench of decay assaulted Linda's senses as they rounded the final corner, her stomach lurching in protest. There, bathed in the sickly glow of a flickering streetlight, stood Gabriel. His disfigured face twisted into a grotesque imitation of a smile, sending chills down Linda's spine. The man responsible for so much pain and suffering cast a long, menacing shadow across the cracked pavement.

"Ah, Mrs. Miller," Gabriel's smooth voice belied his monstrous appearance. "So good of you to join us."

Linda's heart thundered in her chest as Vega roughly shoved her forward. She stumbled, her blonde hair falling across her face as she struggled to regain her footing. When she looked up, she found herself mere inches from Gabriel's piercing gaze.

"What do you want from me?" Linda demanded, her voice wavering despite her best efforts to remain strong. She could feel the weight of Gabriel's cold, calculating stare boring into her.

Gabriel's lips curled into a cruel smirk. "Oh, my dear, it's not about what I want from you. It's about what you represent in the grand scheme of things."

A shiver ran down Linda's spine, her mind racing to decipher his cryptic words. She thought of Drake, of her family, and the crushing realization that she was powerless to protect them crashed over her like a tidal wave.

"I don't understand," she whispered, her blue eyes searching Gabriel's face for any hint of humanity.

Gabriel leaned in close, his breath hot against her ear. "Understanding is not required, Linda. Only obedience."

In that moment, as Gabriel's words hung in the air between them, Linda felt a sense of helplessness unlike anything she had ever known before. Her nurturing instincts, her strength, her very identity – all seemed to crumble in the face of this enigmatic monster.

5 - 6

Linda's heart pounded in her chest as she struggled to process Gabriel's chilling words. She clenched her fists, summoning every ounce of courage she possessed.

"Why are you doing this?" Linda demanded, her voice trembling with a mixture of anger and fear. Her blue eyes flashed defiantly, even as her body shook. "What could you possibly gain from terrorizing innocent people?"

Gabriel's scarred face remained impassive, his piercing gaze never wavering from Linda's. He tilted his head slightly, as if considering her question. "Innocence," he mused, his voice smooth yet laced with malice, "is such a subjective concept, don't you think?"

Before Linda could formulate a response, Gabriel raised a hand, silencing her. With a slight nod to Vega, he spoke again, his tone eerily calm. "I'm afraid our little chat must come to an end, my dear. There's much work to be done."

Linda felt Vega's iron grip on her arm tighten as Gabriel motioned for them to leave. As they began to move, Linda's mind raced frantically. 'This can't be happening,' she thought, her maternal instincts kicking into overdrive. 'Drake, my family... they're all in danger because of me.'

"You won't get away with this!" Linda shouted, her voice echoing in the darkness as Vega dragged her away. "Whatever you're planning, it won't work!"

Gabriel's cold laughter followed them, sending chills down Linda's spine. As they disappeared into the shadows, Linda's heart sank with the realization that she was facing a danger unlike any she had ever known—one that threatened not only her own life but the lives of everyone she loved.

7 - 8

Richard Vega's grip on Linda's arm loosened slightly as they moved through the dimly lit corridor, his facade of stern professionalism cracking under the weight of his inner turmoil. Linda sensed the change, her eyes darting to his face, searching for any sign of compassion or weakness she could exploit.

"You don't have to do this, Richard," she whispered urgently, her voice barely audible above the sound of their footsteps echoing off the cold concrete walls. "Whatever Gabriel has on you, we can figure it out together. There's always another way."

Vega's jaw clenched, his dark eyes flickering with a mix of emotions - fear, regret, and something else Linda couldn't quite place. He opened his mouth to speak, then closed it again, as if wrestling with his own inner demons.

Linda pressed on, desperation coloring her words. "Think about your family, Richard. Would they want you to be part of this? To be responsible for harming innocent people?"

For a moment, Vega's steps faltered, and Linda felt a glimmer of hope. But then his expression hardened once more, his grip tightening as he propelled her forward. "You don't understand," he muttered, his voice low and strained. "None of us have a choice anymore."

As they rounded a corner, Linda's mind raced, frantically searching for a way out. She thought of Drake, of their children, of the life they had built together. 'I can't let it end like this,' she thought, her heart pounding in her chest. 'I have to find a way to warn them, to stop whatever Gabriel is planning.'

Suddenly, a distant sound caught her attention - the faint wail of sirens in the distance. Vega tensed beside her, his eyes widening with a mixture of fear and... was that relief? Linda's pulse quickened as she realized this might be her only chance.

"It's not too late," she said, her voice stronger now, filled with a determination she didn't know she possessed. "We can still make this right, Richard. Help me stop him, and I promise I'll do everything I can to protect you and your family."

9 - 10

Richard Vega's jaw clenched, his eyes darting nervously between Linda and the shadowy path ahead. The distant sirens faded, leaving only the sound of their footsteps echoing off the damp pavement. He drew in a sharp breath, his voice barely above a whisper. "You don't know what you're asking, Linda. Gabriel... he's not just dangerous. He's something else entirely."

As they turned down a narrow alley, the flickering streetlights cast long, menacing shadows. Linda suppressed a shudder, her mind racing with terrifying possibilities. "What do you mean, 'something else'? What aren't you telling me, Richard?"

Vega's pace slowed, his grip on her arm loosening slightly. His eyes, when they met hers, were filled with a haunted look that sent chills down her spine. "The deal I made... it wasn't just about protection. Gabriel, he... he knows things. Things that shouldn't be possible."

Linda's heart pounded in her chest as she pressed further. "What kinds of things? Richard, please, I need to understand."

He hesitated, glancing over his shoulder as if expecting Gabriel's disfigured face to materialize from the darkness. "He showed me... visions. Of my family, of terrible things that would happen if I didn't cooperate. And then, they started coming true."

Linda's breath caught in her throat. "That's impossible. He must have set it up, manipulated events somehow."

Vega shook his head, his voice trembling. "You don't understand. The things I saw... no one could have orchestrated them. It's like he can see the future, or... or shape it somehow. And now, I'm trapped. We all are."

As they approached the meeting point, Linda felt a wave of dread wash over her. She knew that whatever awaited them in the shadows ahead would change everything. Her voice was barely audible as she whispered, "There has to be a way out, Richard. For all of us."

11 - 12

The air grew thick with tension as they rounded the final corner, the crunch of autumn leaves beneath their feet echoing ominously in the deserted street. Linda's heart hammered against her ribs as she caught sight of a figure emerging from the inky darkness ahead, his presence commanding an instinctive fear that made her blood run cold.

Gabriel Angel stepped into the dim light cast by a flickering streetlamp; his heavily scarred face twisted into what might have been a smile. "Ah, Richard," he purred, his voice smooth as silk yet laced with venom. "I see you've brought our guest. How... thoughtful of you."

Vega's grip on Linda's arm tightened reflexively, his own face a mask of barely concealed terror. "I've done what you asked, Gabriel. Now please, just... just let this be over."

Linda's eyes darted between the two men, her mind racing. "What is this? Richard, you can't seriously be handing me over to him!"

Gabriel's piercing gaze locked onto Linda, sending a shiver down her spine. "My dear Linda," he said, taking a step closer. "You have no idea how long I've waited for this moment. The pieces are finally falling into place."

Vega's voice trembled as he spoke. "I'm sorry, Linda. I never wanted it to come to this, but I... I had no choice."

With a gentle yet firm motion, Vega pushed Linda towards Gabriel. As their hands made contact, Linda felt a jolt of something cold and alien course through her body. Gabriel's grip was like iron, his scarred fingers digging into her flesh.

"You've done well, Richard," Gabriel said, his eyes never leaving Linda's face. "Your family will be safe... for now."

Linda struggled against Gabriel's hold, her voice rising in panic. "Richard, please! Don't do this! Whatever he's promised you, it's not worth it!"

But as she looked into Vega's eyes, she saw only resignation and guilt. He took a step back, his shoulders slumping in defeat. "I'm sorry," he whispered again, the words barely audible.

Gabriel's lips curled into a cruel smile. "Now, Linda," he said, his voice sending chills down her spine, "we have so much to discuss. The future awaits us, and you have a vital role to play."

As Gabriel began to lead her away, Linda's mind raced with fear and confusion. What did he mean by 'the future'? What role was she meant to play in his twisted plans? And how could she possibly escape the grasp of a man who seemed to know far more than any human should?

13 - 13

Vega's footsteps echoed hollowly on the damp pavement as he retreated from the scene, his heart pounding a frantic rhythm against his ribcage. The weight of his actions pressed down on him like a physical force, threatening to crush him beneath its immensity.

"What have I done?" he muttered, his voice barely above a whisper as he ran a trembling hand through his hair. "God, what have I done?"

The darkness seemed to close in around him, the shadows taking on a menacing quality as if they were alive and reaching for him with grasping tendrils. Vega quickened his pace, his breath coming in short, sharp gasps.

"I had no choice," he argued with himself, his inner voice rising in pitch as panic set in. "It was them or my family. I had to protect my own."

But even as he tried to justify his actions, the image of Linda's terrified face as he handed her over to Gabriel burned in his mind. The cold, calculating look in Gabriel's eyes as he took possession of her haunted Vega, sending shivers down his spine.

"This isn't over," Vega murmured, his hands clenching into fists at his sides. "There has to be a way to make this right."

As he turned a corner, the streetlights flickered ominously, casting eerie shadows that danced and twisted around him. Vega couldn't shake the feeling that he was being watched that Gabriel's influence stretched far beyond what he could see or understand.

"Have I made a deal with the devil himself?" The question hung in the air, unanswered and terrifying in its implications. Vega knew, deep in his bones, that the consequences of his choices would ripple outward, affecting not just Linda and his family, but potentially countless others.

With each step he took, the weight of his guilt seemed to grow heavier, threatening to drag him down into the depths of despair. Yet he pressed on, driven by a desperate hope that somehow, someway, he might find a path to redemption.

In The Doctor's Chair

Blue World – 2024

1 - 2

The sterile white walls of Dr. Lee's office seemed to close in on Drake as he sank deeper into the leather armchair, his fingers absently tracing the worn armrests. The scent of antiseptic hung in the air, a constant reminder of the clinical nature of this space that had become all too familiar over the past month. Drake's weary eyes darted around the room, taking in the framed diplomas on the wall and the neatly arranged bookshelf, anything to avoid meeting Dr. Lee's penetrating gaze.

"How are you feeling today, Drake?" Dr. Lee's gentle voice broke through the oppressive silence, his tone carrying a mix of professional concern and genuine empathy.

Drake's shoulders tensed as he shifted in his seat, the leather creaking beneath him. He ran a hand through his unkempt hair, wincing as his fingers caught on tangled knots. "I'm... I'm here," he managed, his voice rough from disuse. The words felt hollow, inadequate to express the storm of emotions raging within him.

Dr. Lee leaned forward slightly, his kind eyes never leaving Drake's face. "And how are you really feeling?" he probed, his voice soft but insistent.

Drake's mind raced, images of that fateful night flashing before his eyes - the blinding headlights, the sickening crunch of metal, Linda's terrified scream cut short. He swallowed hard, his throat constricting. "I can't... I can't stop seeing it," he whispered, his voice barely audible. "Every time I close my eyes, it's like I'm right back there, and Linda..." His voice cracked, unable to finish the sentence.

Dr. Lee nodded slowly, his expression a mask of understanding. "It's natural to experience flashbacks after such a traumatic event," he said, his words measured and calm. "Have you been practicing the grounding techniques we discussed?"

Drake's fingers curled into fists, his nails digging into his palms. "I've tried," he admitted, frustration seeping into his tone. "But it's like... it's like I'm trapped in this endless loop, and no matter what I do, I can't break free." He looked up at Dr. Lee, his eyes pleading for understanding, for some magic words that could make everything right again.

As Dr. Lee opened his mouth to respond, Drake's gaze drifted to the window behind him, where the world outside continued on, oblivious to the turmoil within these four walls. How many times had he sat in this very spot, pouring out his fears and frustrations? And yet, Linda was still missing, the truth still maddeningly out of reach. The weight of uncertainty pressed down on him, threatening to crush what little hope remained.

3 - 4

Drake sighed heavily, his thoughts drifting back to the void left by Linda's absence. "Physically, I'm recovering," he began, his voice tinged with weariness. His fingers traced the fading scar on his hip, a tangible reminder of that fateful night. "But emotionally... I don't know how to describe it. It's like a part of me is missing, like I'm trapped in a nightmare that I can't wake up from."

He paused, his gaze flickering to the framed photograph on Dr. Lee's desk - a serene landscape that seemed to mock the chaos of his inner world. "Every morning, I wake up hoping it was all just a bad dream," Drake continued, his voice barely above a whisper. "But then I reach for Linda, and she's not there. It's like losing her all over again, every single day."

Dr. Lee leaned forward, his kind eyes reflecting the compassion that had made him such a trusted confidant. "It's natural to feel that way after everything you've been through," he offered reassuringly, his voice a soothing balm to Drake's raw emotions. "But it's important to remember that healing takes time, both physically and emotionally."

Drake nodded, though the words felt hollow in the face of his overwhelming grief. "I know that, logically," he admitted, running a hand through his disheveled hair. "But how do I keep going when half of me is missing? How do I face a world where Linda might be..." He couldn't bring himself to finish the thought, the possibility too painful to voice aloud.

5 - 6

Drake's fingers trembled as they raked through his unkempt hair, frustration etching deep lines across his weary face. The sterile office seemed to close in around him, amplifying the suffocating sense of helplessness that had become his constant companion.

"I just can't shake this feeling of powerlessness," he admitted, his voice cracking with raw desperation. "Every lead turns cold, every hope snuffed out. I want to find Linda, to bring her back home where she belongs, but I don't even know where to begin." His eyes, once bright with determination, now held a haunted look as they met Dr. Lee's steady gaze. "What if I never see her again? What if I've failed her?"

Dr. Lee leaned forward, his calm demeanor a stark contrast to Drake's agitation. The soft rustle of his crisp white coat seemed to punctuate the gravity of the moment. "We'll find her, Drake," he said firmly, his words carrying a weight of conviction that Drake desperately wanted to believe. "But it's crucial not to lose sight of yourself in this process. You've endured a profound trauma, and it's perfectly natural to feel overwhelmed."

As Dr. Lee spoke, Drake's mind raced, replaying the countless sleepless nights, the fruitless searches, the gnawing fear that tightened around his heart with each passing day. He clenched his fists, nails digging into his palms, as if the physical pain could anchor him to reality.

"But how?" Drake whispered; his voice barely audible. "How can I focus on myself when Linda's out there, possibly hurt or..." He couldn't finish the thought, the possibilities too horrific to voice.

Dr. Lee's expression softened, a glimmer of understanding in his eyes. "You're stronger than you realize, Drake," he said, his tone gentle yet resolute. "I believe that together, we can navigate through this darkness. Your determination, your love for Linda – these are powerful forces. But to harness them effectively, you must also care for yourself."

7 - 8

Drake nodded, a flicker of determination igniting within him. He leaned forward, his gaze locking with Dr. Lee's. "Thank you, Dr. Lee," he said, gratitude coloring his words. The weight of his scruffy beard seemed to mirror the heaviness in his heart, but there was a new spark in his tired eyes. "I'll do whatever it takes to find Linda and bring her back home."

As he spoke, Drake felt a surge of energy coursing through his veins, a renewed sense of purpose pushing back against the suffocating darkness that had consumed him for so long. His fingers drummed against the arm of the chair, a physical manifestation of his restless resolve.

"I know it won't be easy," Drake continued, his voice growing stronger with each word. "But Linda... she's my anchor, my compass. Without her, I'm adrift in a storm I can't navigate." He paused, swallowing hard against the lump in his throat. "I need to find her, not just for her sake, but for mine. For us."

Dr. Lee nodded, a gentle smile tugging at the corners of his mouth. "That's the spirit, Drake. Your love for Linda is a powerful motivator, but remember, it's also okay to lean on others for support. You don't have to face this alone."

Drake's mind raced with possibilities, plans beginning to form even as he sat there. "I'll start by retracing our steps from that night," he mused aloud, his brow furrowing in concentration. "There has to be something we missed, some clue that can point us in the right direction."

As he spoke, Drake felt a glimmer of hope blooming in his chest, a tiny flame pushing back against the oppressive darkness. With Dr. Lee's guidance by his side, he knew that he would stop at nothing to uncover the truth and reunite with his beloved wife, no matter the obstacles that lay ahead.

9 - 10

Drake shifted uncomfortably in his seat, the leather creaking beneath him as he struggled to find the words. The sterile white walls of Dr. Lee's office seemed to close in, amplifying the weight of his uncertainty. He ran a hand through his disheveled dark hair, his tired brown eyes fixed on a point somewhere beyond the present.

"And then there's the other world," Drake added, his voice barely above a whisper, tinged with a frustration that bordered on despair. "I haven't been able to go back since waking up from the coma. For all I know, in that world, I'm... I'm dead."

The words hung heavy in the air, each syllable a testament to the bizarre duality of his existence. Drake's mind reeled, caught between two realities, neither of which felt wholly real or wholly false. He clenched his fists, knuckles whitening as he fought against the overwhelming sense of helplessness threatening to engulf him.

Dr. Lee leaned forward, his kind eyes radiating empathy behind his glasses. "It's understandable that you would feel disconnected from that world," he acknowledged, his tone gentle yet firm. "But it's important to remember that the events there are beyond your control. Right now, your focus needs to be on your recovery here in the present."

Drake nodded, though the furrow in his brow deepened. "I know you're right, Dr. Lee," he conceded, his voice thick with emotion. "But how can I just... let go? That world it's as real to me as this one. My son..." He trailed off, unable to complete the thought.

Dr. Lee's expression softened further. "Your feelings are valid, Drake. The connection you feel to both realities is profound. But healing requires us to focus on what we can influence, in the here and now."

As the doctor spoke, Drake's mind wandered to the life he'd left behind in that other world – the cases he'd been working on, the promises he'd made. The guilt of his potential absence there gnawed at him, a constant reminder of the complex web of responsibilities he'd become entangled in.

11 - 12

Drake's fingers drummed restlessly on the arm of his chair; his gaze fixed on the autumn leaves swirling past the office window. The vibrant oranges and reds seemed to mock the turmoil churning within him. He turned back to Dr. Lee, his eyes pleading. "But what if Harrison is still out there, waiting for me to find him?" he mused aloud, his voice laced with uncertainty. "What if I'm the only one who can bring him back?"

The weight of those words hung heavy in the air, filling the room with an almost palpable tension. Drake could feel his heart racing, the possibility of reuniting with his son both thrilling and terrifying. What if he failed? What if he was already too late?

Dr. Lee leaned forward, his calm demeanor a stark contrast to Drake's agitation. He placed a comforting hand on Drake's shoulder, offering silent support. "We'll find a way to uncover the truth, Drake," he reassured him, his voice steady and grounding. "But it's going to take time and patience. Right now, the most important thing is to focus on your recovery and trust that everything will fall into place in due time."

Drake wanted to believe him, desperately so. But the gnawing doubt persisted, whispering insidiously in the back of his mind. How could he sit idly by when his son might be out there, lost and alone? The conflict tore at him, leaving him feeling raw and exposed.

"I hear you, Dr. Lee," Drake finally managed, his voice barely above a whisper. "But every moment I spend here, focusing on myself... it feels like I'm abandoning him all over again."

13 - 14

Drake's eyes flickered to the window, watching as raindrops began to streak down the glass, mirroring the turmoil within him. He could feel Dr. Lee's gaze, patient and understanding, but it did little to quell the storm of emotions raging inside.

"I know you're right," Drake admitted, his voice rough with resignation. "I need to heal, to be strong enough to face whatever lies ahead. But..." He trailed off, struggling to articulate the weight pressing down on his chest.

Dr. Lee leaned back in his chair; his expression thoughtful. "But the guilt is eating at you," he finished softly, prompting Drake to nod.

A heavy sigh escaped Drake's lips as he ran a hand through his disheveled hair. "It's not just guilt," he confessed, his brown eyes dark with turmoil. "It's this constant ache, this... this emptiness where Harrison should be. And now, with Linda gone too..." His voice cracked, the pain of his losses threatening to overwhelm him.

Silence stretched between them for a moment, broken only by the gentle patter of rain against the window. Drake's mind raced, memories of his family flickering like a bittersweet slideshow behind his eyes.

Finally, he leaned forward, his gaze intense as he locked eyes with Dr. Lee. "There's something else," Drake began, his voice low and tinged with disbelief. "Something that doesn't make sense about my recovery."

Dr. Lee's eyebrows raised slightly, encouraging Drake to continue.

"The bullet," Drake explained, gesturing vaguely towards his hip. "They never found it. It's like... like it just vanished into thin air."

15 - 16

Dr. Lee's eyes widened, his calm demeanor giving way to genuine astonishment. He leaned forward, his elbows resting on the polished surface of his desk. "That's remarkable," he murmured, his voice barely above a whisper. Drake could almost see the gears turning in the doctor's mind, possibilities unfolding like a complex equation.

"It suggests that there's some kind of... connection between the two realities," Dr. Lee continued, his tone gaining momentum as he spoke. "A bridge, if you will, that allows events in one world to influence the other."

Drake felt a shiver run down his spine, the implications of Dr. Lee's words sinking in. He glanced down at his hands, noticing for the first time how they trembled slightly. The room suddenly felt too small, too confining for the enormity of what they were discussing.

"But how is that possible?" Drake wondered aloud, his brow furrowing deeply. He looked up at Dr. Lee, searching the doctor's face for answers. "And what does it mean for me... for all of us?"

The question hung in the air between them, heavy with potential and fear. Drake's mind raced, memories of his two lives colliding and intertwining. He thought of Linda's smile, of Harrison's laugh, of the pain and joy that existed in both worlds. The weight of it all threatened to crush him.

"I don't know," Dr. Lee admitted softly, his usual confidence tempered by the mystery before them. "But Drake, this could be the key to understanding your unique situation. To finding a way forward."

Drake nodded slowly; his throat tight with emotion. "A way to bring my family back together," he whispered, hope and dread warring within him. The possibility was both exhilarating and terrifying, a lifeline thrown into a stormy sea of uncertainty.

17 - 18

Dr. Lee's expression grew thoughtful, his kind eyes narrowing as he leaned forward in his chair. The soft leather creaked beneath him, a sound that seemed to echo in the suddenly charged atmosphere of the office. "It's possible that your blood holds the key," he mused, his voice tinged with excitement that he was clearly trying to temper. "Perhaps there's something unique about its composition that allows it to transcend the boundaries between realities."

Drake felt his heart rate accelerate, a rush of adrenaline coursing through his veins at Dr. Lee's words. His fingers gripped the armrests of his chair tightly, knuckles whitening as he processed the implications. The idea was simultaneously thrilling and terrifying, a potential lifeline in the sea of confusion he'd been drowning in since waking from his coma.

"So, you're saying that my blood could be the key to unlocking this... this connection?" Drake asked, his voice tinged with a mix of anticipation and disbelief. He leaned forward, mirroring Dr. Lee's posture, as if physical proximity might bring him closer to understanding. "But how? I mean, I'm just... me. How could my blood be special?"

As he spoke, Drake's mind raced with possibilities. Images flashed through his consciousness: Linda's smile, Harrison's laugh, the life he'd lost and the one he was desperately trying to hold onto. Could his blood really be the bridge between these two realities? The thought was dizzying, almost too much to comprehend. Dr. Lee's words echoed Gabriels revelation.

Dr. Lee's calm voice cut through Drake's whirlwind of thoughts. "It's just a theory at this point, Drake," he cautioned, his tone gentle but firm. "But given what we know about your unique situation, it's a possibility we can't ignore. Your experiences, the physical manifestations like the missing bullet... they all point to something extraordinary happening on a cellular level."

Drake nodded slowly, trying to ground himself in the present moment even as his mind threatened to spiral into a labyrinth of 'what ifs'. He took a deep breath, feeling the air fill his lungs, reminding himself that regardless of the mysteries surrounding him, he was still here, still alive, still fighting.

"What's our next step then?" Drake asked, determination creeping into his voice. The spark of hope that had ignited within him was growing, fueled by the possibility of answers, of reuniting his fractured family. "How do we... how do we test this theory?"

19 - 20

Dr. Lee leaned forward, his eyes alight with a mix of professional curiosity and genuine compassion. "We'll need to start with a comprehensive analysis of your blood," he explained, his voice taking on a thoughtful cadence. "We'll look for any anomalies, any unique markers that might explain your ability to traverse between realities."

Drake's fingers drummed nervously on the armrest of his chair, his mind racing ahead. "And if we find something?" he pressed, barely able to contain the urgency in his voice. "What then?"

"Then," Dr. Lee continued, his tone measured but tinged with excitement, "we explore ways to harness that unique property. It could involve developing a targeted treatment, or perhaps even finding a way to... amplify the effect."

Drake's heart pounded in his chest, hope and fear intertwining in a dizzying dance. He closed his eyes for a moment, trying to steady himself. When he opened them again, his gaze was resolute. "I'm willing to do whatever it takes," he declared, his voice low and intense. "If there's even a chance of bringing my family back together, of understanding what's happening to me... I have to try."

Dr. Lee nodded, a small smile playing at the corners of his mouth. "Your determination is admirable, Drake," he said softly. "But remember, this is uncharted territory. We must proceed with caution."

Drake's mind whirled with possibilities, memories of his past life colliding with the harsh reality of his present. The ruthless lawyer he once was seemed like a distant shadow, replaced by a man driven by love and an insatiable need for answers. "I understand the risks," he said, his voice barely above a whisper. "But I can't just sit back and do nothing. Not when there's a chance to make things right."

As the words left his mouth, Drake felt a surge of excitement course through him, electric and alive. For the first time since waking from his coma, the fog of despair that had clouded his vision began to lift. He leaned forward, meeting Dr. Lee's gaze with newfound intensity. "When can we start?"

Dying in the Funhouse

Green World – 2024

1 - 2

Detective Holly Kierstead's heart pounded in her chest as she rounded the corner of the funhouse, her flashlight beam cutting through the oppressive darkness. The acrid smell of rust and decay assaulted her nostrils as she stepped into what once must have been a hall of mirrors, now reduced to shattered glass and twisted metal frames. Her light caught a glimpse of something on the ground ahead, and as she moved closer, her breath caught in her throat.

"Oh God, Drake," she whispered, her voice barely audible over the creaking of the old structure around her.

There he lay, sprawled on the grimy floor, his usually meticulously pressed suit now rumpled and stained dark with what she feared was blood. Holly rushed forward, her training kicking in even as her mind reeled with questions and fears.

"Drake! Can you hear me?" she called out, dropping to her knees beside him. Her hands, usually steady in even the most intense situations, trembled as she pressed her fingers to his neck, searching desperately for a pulse. "Come on, come on," she muttered, leaning in close to listen for breath.

A faint, thready pulse met her fingertips, and she let out a shaky sigh of relief. "Thank God," she breathed, before turning her attention to assessing his injuries. Her eyes scanned his body, taking in the pallor of his skin, the dark circles under his eyes that seemed more pronounced than ever.

"Drake, it's Holly. Can you open your eyes for me?" she urged, gently tapping his cheek. Her mind raced, torn between the urgent need to get help and the fear of leaving him alone in this godforsaken place. "What happened to you? Who did this?"

As she spoke, her gaze darted around the room, searching for any clue, any sign of what might have transpired. The funhouse's warped mirrors reflected fractured images of herself and Drake, creating a disorienting kaleidoscope that seemed to mock her efforts to make sense of the situation.

"I swear, Drake," she murmured, her voice taking on a determined edge, "I'm going to figure this out. I'm going to find whoever did this to you." She squeezed his hand, hoping that somehow, he could hear her, that he knew he wasn't alone. "Just hang on, okay? Don't you dare give up on me now."

3 - 4

With trembling hands, Holly reached for her phone, her fingers flying across the screen as she dialed 911. The eerie silence of the abandoned funhouse was broken only by the sound of her rapid breathing and the faint beeps of the keypad.

"This is Detective Holly Kierstead," she spoke into the phone, her voice steady despite the fear gripping her heart. "I need an ambulance at the old Bridgewater Amusement Park, in the funhouse. I have an officer down, male, mid-forties, unconscious with unknown injuries. Possible blood loss." Her words echoed in the empty space, a stark reminder of their isolation.

As she waited for the dispatcher's response, Holly's eyes never left Drake's pale face. "Yes, that's correct. Please hurry," she urged, her free hand instinctively reaching out to check his pulse again.

After ending the call, Holly leaned closer to Drake, her voice barely above a whisper. "Helps on the way, Drake. Just hold on." She brushed a strand of his dark hair from his forehead, noting how cold and clammy his skin felt beneath her touch.

Her mind raced with questions, each more unsettling than the last. "What were you doing here, Drake?" she muttered, more to herself than to him. "This isn't like you to go off alone without backup."

Holly's gaze darted around the room, taking in the distorted mirrors and faded carnival props. The once-cheerful decorations now seemed sinister in the dim light, hiding potential dangers in every shadow. "Who did this to you? And why here, of all places?"

She shook her head, trying to focus. "I should have known something was wrong when you missed our check-in. I should have come sooner." Guilt gnawed at her, mixing with the fear and uncertainty that threatened to overwhelm her.

As the minutes ticked by, each feeling like an eternity, Holly couldn't shake the growing dread that time was running out. "Come on, Drake," she pleaded, her voice cracking slightly. "You've got to pull through this. Your family needs you. We need you."

5 - 6

Holly's jaw clenched, her determination hardening into an unbreakable resolve. "I won't let you down, Drake," she whispered fiercely, her hand gripping his limp one. "Whatever it takes, I'll get you through this."

The eerie silence of the abandoned funhouse pressed in around her, broken only by Drake's shallow breathing. Holly's keen eyes scanned the area, searching for any clues that might shed light on the situation. A glint of something metallic caught her attention near one of the distorted mirrors.

"What's this?" she murmured, carefully making her way over without letting go of Drake's hand. As she bent down to examine it, her heart raced. "A cufflink? But it's not yours, is it, Drake?"

Her mind whirled with possibilities. "This wasn't just a random attack. Someone lured you here, didn't they?" She turned back to her unconscious partner, her voice low and intense. "What were you onto, Drake? What did you discover that was worth silencing you for?"

A creaking sound from somewhere in the funhouse made Holly's head snap up, her free hand instinctively moving to her holstered weapon. "We're not alone," she breathed, eyes darting to every shadow. "I need to get you out of here, now."

As she contemplated how to move Drake safely, a chilling realization dawned on her. "Your accident... the split realities you've been experiencing... it's all connected, isn't it?" Her voice trembled slightly as the pieces began to fall into place. "Gabriel's been manipulating you, Drake. Playing with your mind, your very reality. But why?"

The distant wail of sirens pierced the air, bringing both relief and a new sense of urgency. Holly leaned in close to Drake, her voice barely above a whisper. "I promise you; I'll uncover the truth. I'll find out who did this to you, and I'll make them pay. Just stay with me, partner. Stay with me."

7 - 8

Holly's heart raced as she scanned the dimly lit funhouse, her senses on high alert. The warped mirrors and faded carnival props cast eerie shadows; their once-cheerful facades now sinister in the gloom. She leaned in close to Drake, her voice a tense whisper.

"I don't like this, Drake. We're exposed here." Her eyes darted to a nearby alcove. "I need to move you somewhere more defensible."

With a grunt of effort, Holly began to drag Drake's unconscious form towards the alcove. Her muscles strained as she pulled him across the dusty floor, her mind racing.

"Who would go to such lengths to get to you?" she muttered, more to herself than her unresponsive partner. "And why an abandoned amusement park? It's like something out of a nightmare."

As she settled Drake into the relative safety of the alcove, a glint of metal caught her eye. Holly reached down, plucking a small object from the floor near where Drake had fallen.

"Another cufflink?" she mused, turning the ornate piece over in her hand. "Definitely not standard issue for a lawyer turned reluctant detective."

The wail of approaching sirens grew louder, but Holly's relief was tempered by a growing sense of dread. She crouched beside Drake, her voice low and urgent.

"I don't think this is over, Drake. Whoever did this to you... they're playing a bigger game. And I'm starting to think your accident, your split realities – it's all connected somehow." She squeezed his hand. "I promise you; I'll figure this out. I'll find the truth, no matter where it leads."

A sudden creak from deeper within the funhouse made Holly freeze. Her hand instinctively moved to her weapon as she positioned herself protectively in front of Drake.

"Come on," she whispered fiercely to the approaching sirens. "We need to get out of here. Fast."

9 - 9

The ambulance screeched to a halt outside the dilapidated funhouse, its flashing lights casting eerie red and blue shadows across the crumbling facade. Holly Kierstead stood rooted to the spot, her eyes never leaving Drake's unconscious form as paramedics burst through the door, equipment in hand.

"Over here!" she called, her voice cracking with a mixture of relief and lingering fear. "He's unresponsive, possible head trauma."

The paramedics swarmed around Drake, their movements swift and practiced. Holly found herself pushed back, watching helplessly as they worked to stabilize her partner. Her mind raced, trying to piece together the fragments of this bizarre puzzle.

"Detective," one of the paramedics addressed her, "do you know what happened?"

Holly shook her head, her eyes still fixed on Drake. "I found him like this. No visible assailant, no weapon that I could see." She paused, swallowing hard. "Will he be, okay?"

The paramedic's face remained neutral. "We're doing everything we can. We need to get him to the hospital immediately."

As they lifted Drake onto the stretcher, Holly's hand instinctively reached out, brushing his arm. She leaned in close, her voice barely above a whisper. "Hang in there, Drake. I'm not giving up on you."

The stretcher wheeled past her, and Holly felt a surge of determination rising within her. She turned to the remaining paramedic, her voice steely. "Which hospital are you taking him to?"

"Saint Montagues," he replied. "It's the closest trauma center."

Holly nodded, already formulating her next moves. As she watched the ambulance pull away, sirens blaring, she made a silent vow. Her voice was low, intense, meant for her ears alone. "I swear, Drake, I will uncover the truth. Whatever's going on here, whatever twisted game is being played – I'll figure it out. And I'll make damn sure you make it through this to see the end of it."

With one last glance at the ominous funhouse, Holly strode towards her car, her posture rigid with resolve. The hunt for answers had only just begun, and she was determined to see it through, no matter the cost.

I Am Gabriel

1 - 2

I lean in close, my breath hot on Linda's ear as she strains against the ropes binding her to the chair. Her blonde hair, usually so meticulously styled, hangs in damp tangles around her face. Those expressive blue eyes, once warm and comforting, now dart wildly about the dimly lit room.

"Where's Harrison? What have you done with my son?" Linda's voice trembles, a far cry from her usual soothing tones.

I straighten, allowing a cruel smile to play across my lips. "Your concern is touching, Linda. But I'm afraid Harrison is... indisposed at the moment."

Her struggles intensify, the chair creaking beneath her. "Please," she begs, "he's just a boy. He doesn't deserve this."

I circle her slowly, savoring her distress. Linda Miller, the pillar of strength, reduced to this quivering mess. It's almost poetic. "Oh, but he does," I murmur. "More than you could possibly imagine."

Linda's eyes lock onto mine, a flicker of defiance breaking through her fear. "Whatever you want, take it from me. Leave Harrison out of this."

I chuckle, the sound echoing in the oppressive silence. "Always the protective mother, aren't you? But you see, Linda, you're not the one I need. You're merely... collateral."

With a wave of my hand, the air before us shimmers and parts, revealing a window into another world. And there, bound just as securely as his mother, is Harrison.

The boy's curly hair is matted with sweat, his usually bright eyes wide with terror as he sees me approach.

"Mom!" Harrison cries out, his voice cracking. "Mom, I'm scared!"

Linda lurches forward in her chair, nearly toppling it. "Harrison! Baby, it's okay. Mommy's here. Everything's going to be alright."

I watch the interplay between mother and son, marveling at the strength of their bond even across the divide between worlds. Such a pity it will soon be severed forever.

"You won't get away with this," Harrison spits, mustering all the bravado a terrified teenager can manage. "My dad will find us. He'll stop you."

I turned back to Linda, raising an eyebrow. "Such faith in his father. Tell me, Linda, have you ever wondered why Drake was so... special?"

Linda's brow furrows, confusion momentarily overriding her fear. "What are you talking about?"

I lean in close once more, my voice barely above a whisper. "Your husband, your son... they're far more than they appear. And soon, very soon, Harrison will fulfill the destiny that's been waiting for him since before he was born."

As I straighten, I catch sight of my reflection in the shimmering portal. My eyes gleam with anticipation, for I know that the culmination of all my plans is finally at hand.

3 - 4

I turn back to Harrison, his defiant glare a mirror of his mother's. In my hand, I hold the vial of blood, its crimson contents seeming to pulse with an otherworldly energy. The boy's eyes widen as I approach, his bravado faltering.

"What... what is that?" Harrison stammers, his cocky facade crumbling.

I hold the vial up to the light, admiring its viscous contents. "This, my dear boy, is the key to unlocking your true potential. The essence that will bridge worlds."

With practiced precision, I uncap the vial and ready the syringe. Harrison thrashes against his bonds, but they hold firm.

"No! Don't touch me!" he shouts, his voice cracking with fear.

I place a hand on his shoulder, steadying him. "Shh... This won't hurt. Much."

In one swift motion, I plunged the needle into Harrison's neck. He gasps, more from shock than pain, as I depress the plunger. The crimson fluid flows into his veins, disappearing beneath his skin.

"What did you do to me?" Harrison whispers, his eyes wide with a mixture of fear and... something else. Curiosity? Anticipation?

I step back, watching as the blood begins its work. "I've given you a gift, Harrison. The power to transcend the boundaries that separate realities."

Harrison's breathing quickens, his pupils dilating as the blood courses through his system. I can almost see the changes beginning, subtle but profound.

"It's time to reunite with your father," I declare, my voice resonating with chilling certainty. "Time to embrace your destiny."

Harrison's eyes lock onto mine, confusion warring with a dawning realization. "My... my father? But he's..."

"Not lost," I interrupt. "Merely... displaced. And you, my boy, are the key to bringing him back."

As the full weight of my words sinks in, I see a flicker of something new in Harrison's eyes. Fear, yes, but also a spark of excitement. The allure of the unknown, the promise of power – it calls to him, just as I knew it would.

"Who are you?" Harrison asks, his voice barely above a whisper. "What are you?"

I smile, a predator's grin. "I am the architect of your destiny, Harrison. And together, we're going to reshape the very fabric of reality itself."

5 - 6

Harrison's body tenses, his muscles rippling beneath his skin as the blood I've injected begins to take hold. His eyes, once filled with confusion, now shimmer with an otherworldly gleam. I watch, transfixed, as the subtle shift in his demeanor unfolds before me.

"I... I can feel something," Harrison gasps, his voice trembling with a mix of awe and trepidation. "It's like... like I'm connected to everything."

I nod, satisfaction curling my lips. "That's just the beginning, Harrison. Soon, you'll be able to see beyond the veil that separates our world from others."

As Harrison grapples with his newfound sensations, I turn my attention to Linda. She strains against her restraints, her blue eyes blazing with a mother's fury and fear.

"Let him go!" Linda screams, her blonde hair whipping around her face as she struggles. "Whatever you're doing to my son, stop it now!"

I approached her, my voice low and menacing. "Oh, Linda. If only you could understand the gift I'm giving your boy. He's about to become something... extraordinary."

Linda's defiance falters for a moment, uncertainty creeping into her expression. "What do you mean? What are you turning him into?"

I laugh, the sound echoing ominously in the room. "A bridge, Linda. A conduit between worlds. And the key to my grand design."

Turning back to Harrison, I see his eyes dart between his mother and me, conflict etched across his features. The cockiness of his teenage years seems to have evaporated, replaced by a dawning comprehension of the magnitude of his situation.

"Mom," Harrison calls out, his voice cracking. "I... I think I can see Dad. He's... he's calling to me."

Linda's face contorts with a mix of hope and horror. "Drake? Harrison, what do you mean you can see him?"

I stand between them, reveling in the palpable tension. With Linda bound and helpless, and Harrison poised on the brink of transformation, I feel the thrill of impending victory course through my veins.

"This is just the beginning," I declare, my voice resonating with dark promise. "Soon, the barriers between worlds will crumble, and reality itself will bow to my will."

As Harrison's transformation continues and Linda's anguished cries fill the air, I allow myself a moment of triumphant reflection. The pieces are falling into place, and the universe trembles on the precipice of change. My grand design, born of blood and ambition, is about to reshape existence itself.

7 - 8

The air grows thick with tension as Linda's muffled cries echo through the shadowy chamber. I turn to face her, drinking in the sight of her bound form, her blonde hair disheveled and blue eyes wild with a mixture of fear and... something else.

"You can't win," Linda spits out, her words barely audible through her gag. "Whatever you're planning, it won't work."

I stride towards her, my footsteps echoing ominously. "Oh, Linda," I crooned, reaching out to brush a strand of hair from her face. She flinches away, but I catch the defiant glint in her eyes. "Your strength is admirable, truly. But it's misplaced."

Linda's gaze flicks past me, seeking Harrison. I turn, following her line of sight to where Harrison writhes in the adjacent portal.

"What have you done to him?" Linda demands, her maternal instincts overriding her fear.

I smile, savoring the moment. "I've given him a gift, Linda. A destiny."

In the other room, Harrison's body contorts violently. His curly hair is plastered to his forehead with sweat, his eyes rolling back as spasms wrack his frame. The injection of my blood courses through his veins, awakening potentials long dormant.

"Stop it!" Linda screams, her voice raw with anguish. "You're killing him!"

I shake my head, tsking softly. "No, Linda. I'm birthing him anew. Your son will be the key to unlocking the boundaries between worlds."

Harrison's back arches off the table, a guttural cry tearing from his throat. "Mom!" he calls out, his voice thick with pain and confusion. "Something's... happening to me!"

"Yes," I whisper, more to myself than anyone else. "Embrace it, Harrison. Embrace your destiny."

Linda struggles against her bonds, her nurturing nature driving her to reach her son. "Harrison, baby, hold on! I'm here, I'm right here!"

I turn back to Linda, my eyes gleaming with dark triumph. "Your love for him is touching, truly. But it can't save him from what he's meant to become."

As Harrison's cries of agony mix with Linda's desperate pleas, I feel a surge of exhilaration. The pieces of my grand design are falling into place, and soon, reality itself will bend to my will.

9 - 10

As Harrison's convulsions begin to subside, I sense a palpable shift in the air. The room crackles with an unseen energy, emanating from the boy's trembling form. His eyes snap open, revealing pupils dilated to pinpricks, surrounded by irises that now swirl with an otherworldly iridescence.

"What... what's happening to me?" Harrison gasps, his voice carrying an ethereal echo that wasn't there before. His gaze darts around wildly, as if seeing beyond the confines of the room.

I lean in closer, my voice barely above a whisper. "You're becoming something extraordinary, Harrison. Can you feel it? The power coursing through your veins?"

Linda's voice cuts through the air, sharp with maternal concern. "Harrison! Baby, look at me. Are you okay?"

Harrison's head snaps towards his mother's voice, but his eyes seem to look through her rather than at her. "Mom? I... I can see... everything. It's like the world is made of light and shadow, and I can touch it all."

I can see Harrison's convulsions begin to subside; I sense a palpable shift in the air. The room thrums with an otherworldly energy, emanating from the boy's prone form. His eyes snap open, no longer the innocent grey of a carefree teenager, but swirling with an iridescent power that seems to pierce through the very fabric of reality.

"What... what's happening to me?" Harrison gasps, his voice trembling with a mixture of fear and exhilaration. He raises his hands, staring at them in wonder as tendrils of energy dance between his fingertips.

I lean in closer, my voice barely above a whisper. "You're becoming something more, Harrison. Something... transcendent."

Linda's voice cuts through the air, thick with desperation. "Harrison! Baby, look at me! Don't listen to him!"

But Harrison's gaze is fixed on his own hands, his expression a mix of awe and confusion. "I can feel... everything. It's like I'm connected to... to..."

"To the very essence of existence itself," I finish for him, unable to keep the pride from my voice. "You're tapping into powers beyond mortal comprehension, Harrison. You're becoming a conduit between worlds."

As I step back, watching Harrison's transformation near its completion, I can't help but marvel at the raw potential now coursing through his veins. Soon, he will be able to traverse the boundaries of reality with ease, opening doorways I've only dreamed of.

"Mom," Harrison calls out, his voice stronger now, laced with an otherworldly resonance. "I can see... I can see so much. It's beautiful and terrifying all at once."

Linda's sobs echo through the room, a counterpoint to the hum of energy surrounding her son. "Please," she begs, her eyes locked on mine. "Don't do this to him. He's just a boy!"

I turn to her, my expression softening for just a moment. "He was a boy, Linda. Now, he's becoming something far greater. A bridge between worlds, a key to unlocking the very foundations of reality."

As Harrison rises from the table, his body seemingly weightless, I feel a surge of anticipation. The culmination of years of planning and sacrifice stands before me, raw power incarnate.

"What happens now?" Harrison asks, his voice resonating with newfound strength and uncertainty.

I smiled, extending my hand towards him. "Now, Harrison, we reshape the universe itself."

11 - 12

I take a step towards Harrison, my hand still outstretched and feel the crackle of energy in the air around us. The room seems to pulse with an otherworldly glow, emanating from Harrison's transformed form.

"Can you feel it, Harrison?" I ask, my voice barely above a whisper. "The threads of reality, weaving through your very being?"

Harrison's eyes, now shimmering with an ethereal light, dart around the room. "I... I can see them," he stammers, his cocky teenage bravado replaced by awe. "It's like a tapestry, but alive and constantly shifting."

Linda writhes against her restraints, her maternal instincts screaming against the unnatural scene before her. "Harrison, baby, please! Fight it!"

I turn to her, my patience wearing thin. "Enough, Linda. Your son is fulfilling a destiny beyond your comprehension."

Returning my attention to Harrison, I continued, "Focus on those threads, Harrison. Feel how they bend to your will."

As Harrison raises his hand, the air around it seems to ripple and distort. A small tear in reality opens, revealing glimpses of another world beyond.

"I did it," Harrison breathes, his voice a mix of excitement and fear. "I actually did it."

I nod, satisfaction coursing through me. "Yes, you did. And this is just the beginning."

Linda's sobs have quieted, replaced by a steely determination in her eyes. "You won't get away with this," she declares, her voice steady despite her tears. "Someone will stop you."

I can't help but laugh, the sound echoing ominously in the charged atmosphere. "Oh, Linda. You still don't understand. With Harrison's power and my knowledge, we're unstoppable."

As I speak, I feel a tremor of doubt. Is it truly that simple? Are there forces out there, beyond even my reckoning, that might seek to intervene?

I push the thought aside, focusing on the task at hand. "Harrison, it's time to take the next step. Are you ready to see what lies beyond?"

Harrison hesitates, glancing at his mother. For a moment, I see the conflict in his eyes, the pull of familial bonds warring with the intoxicating lure of his newfound abilities.

"I..." he begins, uncertainty clear in his voice.

I step closer, my voice low and persuasive. "Think of the worlds waiting to be explored, Harrison. The mysteries to be unraveled. You hold the key to it all."

As Harrison's resolve strengthens, I can't shake the nagging feeling that our journey is far from over. What challenges await us beyond the veil of reality? What forces might stand in our way?

But as I watch Harrison tentatively reach out to widen the portal, I know one thing for certain: whatever comes, I'm prepared to face it head-on.

13 - 13

I stand before the widening portal, my disfigured face illuminated by its otherworldly glow. The air crackles with potential, and I can feel the fabric of reality bending to my will. My piercing eyes sweep over Linda and Harrison, both instruments in my grand design.

"Behold," I declare, my voice smooth yet commanding, "the dawn of a new era."

Harrison's eyes widen in a mixture of awe and terror. "What... what is this?" he stammers, his body still trembling from the aftermath of the injection.

I smile, a gesture that doesn't quite reach my eyes. "This, my boy, is the culmination of years of planning. The merging of worlds, the rewriting of destiny itself."

Linda struggles against her bonds, her voice muffled but desperate. "Gabriel, please! You don't have to do this!"

I turn to her, my gaze intense. "Oh, but I do, Linda. You see, I am more than just a man. I am the architect of destinies, the master of realms."

As I speak, I can't help but reflect on the path that led me here. The burns that mar my face, the limp in my left leg - badges of honor from my journey across realities. Each scar is a testament to my unwavering resolve.

"You don't understand the power you're dealing with," Harrison interjects, a spark of defiance in his eyes.

I laugh, the sound echoing ominously in the charged atmosphere. "Oh, but I do. With your power and my knowledge, we're unstoppable."

As the portal pulses with energy, I feel a surge of triumph. Yet, beneath it all, a flicker of doubt. What forces might yet stand in my way? What unforeseen challenges await beyond the veil of reality?

I push the thoughts aside, focusing on the moment at hand. "It's time," I announce, my voice resonating with finality. "Time to reshape existence itself." Then I step into the portal, closing the portal between Harrison and Linda.

Still Bound

Green World – 2024 – moments later

1 - 2

Harrison's wrists burned as he thrashed against the unyielding restraints, each desperate movement only causing the bindings to bite deeper into his flesh. His heart pounded in his chest, a frantic rhythm that echoed the panic surging through his veins. But there was something else too—an unfamiliar power coursing through him, hot and electric, making every nerve ending tingle with an alien energy.

"What have you done to me?" he gasped, his voice cracking with fear and confusion as he glared at Gabriel's disfigured face.

Gabriel's piercing eyes locked onto Harrison's; his gaze unnervingly calm in contrast to the chaos of emotions swirling within the young man. "I've given you a gift, Harrison," he replied, his voice smooth and deliberate. "Your fathers blood now flows through your veins, opening doors you never knew existed."

Harrison's mind reeled, trying to process Gabriel's words while fighting against the overwhelming sensations assaulting his body. "What are you talking about? What doors?"

A hint of a smile played at the corners of Gabriel's scarred lips as he leaned in closer, his voice dropping to a near whisper. "Imagine, Harrison, a tapestry of infinite possibilities—countless timelines branching out from every decision ever made. Your blood, infused with your fathers, has become a key to unlock these alternate realities."

The implications of Gabriel's words hit Harrison like a physical blow, leaving him breathless and dizzy. His thoughts raced, trying to grasp the enormity of what he was hearing. Other timelines? Alternate realities? It was too much, too vast, too terrifying to comprehend.

"You're insane," Harrison spat, his teenage bravado warring with the growing dread in the pit of his stomach. "This isn't possible. It can't be."

Gabriel's eyes flashed with something akin to amusement. "Oh, but it is, my young friend. And you're about to discover just how possible it truly is."

As Gabriel's words sank in, Harrison felt a wave of nausea wash over him. The room seemed to spin, and he squeezed his eyes shut, desperately wishing he could wake up from this nightmare. But when he opened them again, Gabriel was still there, watching him with that unsettling intensity.

"Why me?" Harrison choked out, his voice barely above a whisper. "Why did you choose me for this... this madness?"

Gabriel tilted his head, regarding Harrison with a mixture of curiosity and something that might have been pity. "Because, Harrison, you possess a unique quality—an openness to possibility that most adults have long since lost. Your imagination, your curiosity... they make you the perfect vessel for this power."

Harrison shook his head violently, curls bouncing wildly as he tried to deny the reality of his situation. "No, no, no. This isn't happening. It can't be real."

But even as the words left his mouth, Harrison could feel the truth of it thrumming through his veins. Something had changed within him, something fundamental and irreversible. And as that realization settled over him like a suffocating blanket, Harrison felt the last vestiges of his childhood innocence slipping away, replaced by a terrifying new awareness of the vastness and complexity of the universe.

3 - 4

As the weight of his new reality crashed down upon him, Harrison felt a spark ignite deep within his core—a fierce, primal determination that refused to be extinguished. His jaw clenched, teeth grinding together as he fixed Gabriel with a defiant glare.

"I won't be your puppet," Harrison spat, his voice low and trembling with rage. "Whatever sick game you're playing, I refuse to be a part of it."

Gabriel's scarred face twisted into a mirthless smile, his piercing eyes never leaving Harrison's. "Oh, my dear boy," he purred, his voice a silky caress that sent shivers down Harrison's spine, "you're already a part of it. The moment blood entered your veins, your fate was sealed."

Harrison's nostrils flared as he drew in a sharp breath, his heart thundering in his chest. "No," he growled, muscles straining against the unyielding restraints. "I don't accept that. I won't!"

With a sudden burst of energy, Harrison thrashed violently against his bonds, the chair creaking ominously beneath him. Adrenaline surged through his system, lending him a strength he didn't know he possessed. Each movement sent shockwaves of pain through his battered body, but he welcomed it, used it to fuel his desperate struggle for freedom.

"Your determination is admirable," Gabriel observed, his tone maddeningly calm as he watched Harrison's futile efforts. "But you fail to understand the true nature of your predicament. The power within you now—it's not something you can simply reject or ignore."

Harrison's mind raced, grasping for any shred of hope or possibility. "There has to be a way," he panted, sweat beading on his forehead as he continued to fight against his restraints. "I won't let you use me for whatever twisted purpose you have in mind."

Gabriel's lips curled into a sneer, his disfigured features casting eerie shadows in the dim light. "Use you? Oh, Harrison, you still don't see. I'm not using you—I'm liberating you. The knowledge, the power, the infinite possibilities... they're all yours now. Whether you choose to embrace them or not, that's up to you."

As Gabriel's words sank in, Harrison felt a curious sensation spreading through his body—a tingling warmth that seemed to pulse in time with his racing heartbeat. For a moment, he faltered, wondering if this strange new energy could indeed be the key to his escape.

"That's it," Gabriel murmured, leaning in closer, his eyes glittering with an almost feverish intensity. "Can you feel it? The power coursing through your veins? Don't fight it, Harrison. Let it in. Let it show you the truth of your potential."

Harrison squeezed his eyes shut, torn between the temptation to give in and his desperate need to resist. "No," he whispered, more to himself than to Gabriel. "I won't let you win. I won't let you break me."

5 - 5

Harrison's eyes snapped open, blazing with defiance. "You're wrong," he spat, his voice trembling with a mixture of fear and determination. "This isn't liberation. It's manipulation, and I won't be your pawn."

He twisted his wrists against the bindings, feeling the rough material bite into his skin. The pain was grounding, a reminder of his humanity in the face of Gabriel's otherworldly influence. "There's always a way out," Harrison muttered, more to himself than his captor. "Always."

Gabriel's laughter echoed through the room, a chilling sound that sent shivers down Harrison's spine. "Such spirit! But tell me, boy, how do you plan to escape when you don't even understand the nature of your cage?"

As Harrison's mind raced, searching for an answer, he felt that strange warmth pulsing through him again. It whispered of possibilities, of realities beyond his comprehension. For a fleeting moment, he wondered if he could harness this new power, use it against Gabriel somehow.

"I don't need to understand it," Harrison retorted, his teenage bravado shining through despite the dire circumstances. "I just need to beat it. And I will. You don't know me, Gabriel. You don't know what I'm capable of."

Even as the words left his mouth, Harrison felt a surge of... something. Not quite hope, but a fierce, unyielding resolve. He might be trapped, he might be scared out of his mind, but he refused to give up. There had to be a way out of this nightmare, and he would find it.

"Oh, but I do know you, Harrison," Gabriel purred, his disfigured face twisting into a grotesque smile. "Better than you know yourself. And soon, you'll see the truth of it all."

Harrison closed his eyes again, blocking out Gabriel's unsettling visage. In the darkness behind his eyelids, he pictured his family, his friends, the life he'd left behind. "They're waiting for me," he thought fiercely. "I have to get back to them. I have to find a way."

When he opened his eyes again, they gleamed with renewed determination. "You're wrong about me, Gabriel," Harrison declared, his voice steady despite his racing heart. "And I'm going to prove it. Whatever it takes, however long it takes, I will find a way out of here. Count on it."

Momma Bound

Blue World – 2024

1 - 2

As the dim light of the room cast long shadows across the walls, Linda's heart pounded in her chest, each beat a thunderous reminder of her dire situation. She sat bound to the chair, her wrists chafing against the rough rope that held her fast, feeling the fibers dig into her soft skin with every subtle movement. Her blue eyes darted around the room, searching for any sign of hope or escape, but finding only darkness and despair. Vega's troubled expression was a stark contrast to his usual composed demeanor as he paced back and forth before her, his footsteps echoing in the tense silence like a metronome counting down to some unknown fate.

Linda's mind raced, trying to piece together how she had ended up in this nightmarish scenario. She thought of Drake, her son, and a wave of maternal worry washed over her. Would she ever see him again? The thought threatened to overwhelm her, but she pushed it aside, forcing herself to focus on the present moment.

Vega's voice cut through the silence, tinged with a desperation that Linda had never heard from him before. "Linda, please," he implored, his eyes meeting hers with an intensity that made her breath catch in her throat. "You don't understand. Gabriel, he'll—"

As Vega's words trailed off, Linda felt a chill run down her spine. Gabriel's name hung in the air like a dark cloud, promising storm and destruction. She remembered the man's piercing gaze, his face heavily disfigured with burns, and the way he seemed to look right through her, as if reading her very soul. What hold did this enigmatic figure have over Vega?

"What, Vega?" Linda pressed, her voice steadier than she felt. "What will Gabriel do?" She watched as Vega's face contorted with internal conflict, his steps faltering as he turned to face her fully.

"He'll..." Vega began, then shook his head, running a hand through his hair in frustration. "You can't imagine what he's capable of, Linda. The things I've seen him do..."

Linda leaned forward as much as her bonds would allow, her blonde hair falling around her face. "Then tell me, Vega. Help me understand." She infused her words with all the warmth and compassion she could muster, drawing on the strength that had seen her through so much loss and heartache.

3 - 4

Linda's blue eyes locked onto Vega's troubled gaze, her voice steady despite the rapid pounding of her heart. "Gabriel isn't here, Vega," she interjected, her words cutting through the tension like a knife. "It's just you and me. You have a choice, Vega. You can let me go. You can do the right thing."

The room fell silent, save for the soft creaking of floorboards as Vega paused mid-stride. His brow furrowed deeply, the weight of Linda's words seeming to press down on his shoulders. She watched intently as his eyes flickered with uncertainty, a storm of conflicting emotions playing across his face.

"I... I can't just..." Vega stammered, his voice barely above a whisper. "Gabriel, he's everywhere, Linda. Even when he's not here, it's like he knows..."

Linda leaned forward, ignoring the bite of the ropes against her wrists. "But he's not here now, Vega. This is your chance to break free from his control. To be the person I know you can be."

For a moment, hope blossomed in Linda's chest as she saw a glimmer of resolve in Vega's eyes. Could her words have finally reached him? Could he find the courage to defy Gabriel's hold?

"You don't understand the depths of his influence," Vega murmured, his gaze distant. "The things he's capable of... the secrets he knows..."

Linda's mind raced, searching for the right words to break through Vega's hesitation. She thought of her own struggles, the strength she'd found in the face of overwhelming grief. "We all have choices, Vega," she said softly. "Even in the darkest moments. What kind of person do you want to be when this is all over?"

5 - 6

But then, with a resigned sigh, Vega shook his head, his expression falling into a mask of defeat. "I can't, Linda. You don't understand what he's capable of. I can't risk—"

Linda's blue eyes flashed with a mix of frustration and determination. She tugged at her bonds, her blonde hair falling across her face as she leaned forward. "Risk what, Vega?" Her voice rose, edged with frustration that belied her usual calm demeanor. "Risk doing the right thing? Risk standing up to a man who's using you as a pawn in his twisted game?"

Vega flinched at her words, his hands clenching and unclenching at his sides. He turned away, unable to meet Linda's piercing gaze. "It's not that simple," he muttered, his voice barely audible.

Linda's mind raced, searching for a way to reach him. She thought of her own struggles, the strength she'd found in the face of overwhelming loss. "Nothing worth doing ever is, Vega," she said, her tone softening. "But that doesn't mean we shouldn't try."

She watched as Vega's shoulders tensed; his internal conflict palpable in the air between them. Linda's heart pounded; each beat a reminder of the precious seconds ticking away. She had to make him understand, had to find a way to break through the fear that held him captive as surely as the ropes that bound her.

"Look at me, Vega," Linda urged, her voice steady despite the tremor of adrenaline coursing through her. "Really look at me. Do you see a victim? Or do you see someone who's faced unimaginable pain and come out stronger?"

7 - 8

Vega turned slowly, his gaze reluctantly meeting Linda's. She saw the conflict in his eyes, the guilt that shadowed his features like a heavy shroud. His voice was barely above a whisper, cracking with emotion. "I didn't sign up for this, Linda. I never wanted—"

"None of us did," Linda interrupted, her voice softening with empathy. She felt a sudden surge of compassion for this man, caught in Gabriel's web just as surely as she was. Her blue eyes, usually so warm, now blazed with intensity as she leaned forward in her chair. "But here we are. And now you have a choice. You can continue to serve Gabriel blindly, or you can choose to do what's right. The choice is yours, Vega."

Linda's words hung in the air between them, charged with the weight of their shared predicament. She watched Vega closely, noting the subtle shift in his posture, the flicker of uncertainty that crossed his face. Her own heart raced, hope and fear warring within her chest. She thought of her family, of Drake, wondering if she'd ever see them again. The memory steeled her resolve.

"I know you're scared," Linda continued, her voice low and urgent. "I am too. But fear doesn't have to define us, Vega. We can choose to be more than our fears."

9 - 10

The silence stretched on, thick and oppressive, broken only by Vega's ragged breathing. Linda's eyes never left his face, searching for any sign of the internal struggle she knew he must be experiencing. Her wrists ached from the rope binding them, but she pushed the discomfort aside, focusing all her energy on the man before her.

"What would happen if you let me go?" Linda whispered; her voice barely audible. "What's the worst Gabriel could do?"

Vega's head snapped up; his eyes wide with terror. "You don't understand, Linda. He'd—" He cut himself off, swallowing hard.

Linda leaned forward as much as her bonds would allow. "Tell me, Vega. Help me understand."

For a moment, it seemed as though Vega might speak, might finally unburden himself of the weight he'd been carrying. But then, as if some unseen strings had been cut, his shoulders slumped. With a defeated sigh that seemed to come from the depths of his soul, Vega sank to his knees before her.

Linda's heart clenched at the sight. This broken man kneeling before her was a far cry from the confident captor who had first brought her here. She longed to reach out, to offer some comfort, but her bindings held her fast.

"Oh, Vega," she murmured, her voice thick with emotion. "It doesn't have to be this way. We can find another path, together."

But even as the words left her lips, Linda knew that time was slipping away. She could almost feel Gabriel's presence looming over them, an unseen specter waiting to strike. Her mind raced, searching for a way out of this nightmare, even as Vega remained motionless before her, a portrait of resignation.

11 - 12

"I'm sorry, Linda," Vega murmured, his voice barely above a whisper, the words hanging heavy in the air between them. "I wish things could be different. But I can't—"

Linda's heart raced as she watched Vega, his eyes downcast and shoulders slumped. In that moment of his vulnerability, she saw her chance. With a swift, practiced motion honed by years of determination, she twisted her wrists, feeling the rough fibers of the rope give way.

As the bindings fell away, Linda's mind flooded with memories of her life back in Bridgewater – the crisp autumn air, the warmth of B&J Bistro, the comforting rhythm of small-town life. These thoughts fueled her resolve, reminding her of all she had to fight for.

"Vega," she said softly, her blue eyes fixed on him as she slowly rose to her feet, "you don't have to finish that sentence. You don't have to be trapped in this life anymore."

Adrenaline coursed through her veins as she stood, her legs trembling slightly from disuse. She took a cautious step forward, her motherly instincts urging her to comfort the broken man before her, even as her survival instincts screamed at her to run.

"We can both walk away from this," Linda continued, her voice gentle yet firm. "It's not too late to make things right."

As she spoke, Linda's mind raced, calculating her next move. The door was only a few feet away, but could she make it before Vega realized what was happening? And even if she escaped this room, how would she navigate the unfamiliar terrain beyond?

"Linda, please," Vega pleaded, finally looking up at her. "You don't know what you're saying. Gabriel will—"

"Gabriel isn't here," Linda interrupted, taking another careful step. "It's just us, Vega. We can make our own choices."

With each passing second, Linda felt her chance at freedom slipping away. She knew she had to act, but a part of her ached at the thought of leaving Vega behind, trapped in the web of Gabriel's influence.

"I'm sorry," she whispered, more to herself than to Vega, as she made her decision. In one fluid motion, she turned and bolted for the door, her heart pounding in her chest as she reached for the handle, praying it wasn't locked.

13 - 14

Linda's fingers closed around the cold metal of the door handle, her heart thundering in her chest as she yanked it open. The sudden rush of cool air from the hallway beyond hit her face, carrying with it the promise of freedom. She didn't hesitate, her body propelling forward on pure instinct and adrenaline.

"No!" Vega's startled cry echoed behind her, followed by the sound of his scrambling footsteps.

Linda's mind raced as she sprinted down the dimly lit corridor, her blonde hair whipping behind her. "I have to keep moving," she thought, her breaths coming in short gasps. "I can't let him catch me. I can't go back to that room."

She could hear Vega's frantic pursuit, his footfalls growing louder with each passing second. The hallway seemed to stretch endlessly before her, a maze of shadows and uncertainty.

"Linda, wait!" Vega's voice rang out, desperation clear in his tone. "Please, don't—"

She didn't slow down, didn't look back. Her blue eyes darted from side to side, searching for an escape route, a hiding place, anything that could give her an advantage. The motherly instinct that had made her want to comfort Vega earlier now fueled her determination to survive, to return to those who needed her.

"I'm sorry, Vega," Linda thought, her heart aching despite the urgency of her situation. "But I have to get back to my family. I have to keep fighting."

As she rounded a corner, Linda's mind raced with possibilities. Would she find an exit? Or would she merely be trading one prison for another? The unknown loomed before her, both terrifying and full of potential. But one thing was certain – she wouldn't go down without a fight.

15 - 16

Linda's lungs burned as she pushed herself harder, her legs trembling with exertion but propelled by sheer will. The corridor ahead split into two paths, and without hesitation, she veered left, praying it would lead her to freedom.

"You can't escape, Linda!" Vega's voice echoed behind her, tinged with a mix of frustration and concern. "Gabriel will find you – he always does!"

The mention of Gabriel sent a chill down her spine, but Linda refused to let fear paralyze her. "I won't let him control me," she muttered through gritted teeth, her blonde hair plastered to her forehead with sweat. "I won't become another pawn in his twisted game."

As she rounded another corner, Linda's heart leapt at the sight of a stairwell. Hope surged through her veins, giving her a second wind. She grabbed the railing, taking the steps two at a time, her footsteps echoing in the narrow space.

"Think, Linda, think," she urged herself, her mind racing. "There has to be a way out of this nightmare."

Reaching the landing, Linda paused for a split second, her blue eyes scanning her surroundings. The air felt different here – fresher, somehow. Could it mean...?

"Linda!" Vega's voice was closer now, snapping her back to reality.

With renewed determination, she pushed through a heavy door, emerging into a dimly lit parking garage. The sight of cars and the faint glow of exit signs ignited a spark of hope in her chest. For the first time since her captivity began, Linda allowed herself to believe that escape might truly be possible.

17 - 17

Linda's eyes darted from vehicle to vehicle, her mind racing as she weighed her options. "I need to find a way out, fast," she whispered to herself, her voice barely audible over the pounding of her heart. The cool air of the garage kissed her skin, a stark contrast to the stifling atmosphere of her captivity.

As she crouched behind a parked SUV, Linda's thoughts turned to Drake, and her son. "I have to make it back to him," she murmured, her voice thick with emotion. "He needs me now more than ever."

The sound of a door slamming echoed through the garage, followed by Vega's frantic footsteps. "Linda! Please, you don't understand the danger you're in!" His voice reverberated off the concrete walls, laced with desperation.

Linda's jaw clenched, her resolve hardening. She wouldn't let Vega's pleas sway her, not when freedom was so tantalizingly close. With careful movements, she began to edge her way towards a distant exit sign, its soft red glow a beacon of hope in the shadowy expanse.

"I understand more than you think, Vega," she called out, her voice steady despite her racing pulse. "I understand that I have a choice – and I choose to fight."

As she moved, Linda's eyes fell upon a discarded tire iron lying near one of the vehicles. Without hesitation, she scooped it up, the cold metal a comforting weight in her hand. "I won't go back," she thought fiercely. "Whatever lies ahead, I'll face it head-on."

The sound of Vega's approach grew louder, and Linda knew she had to act fast. With a deep breath, she stood up, brandishing the tire iron like a weapon. "Stay back, Vega," she warned, her blue eyes flashing with determination. "I don't want to hurt you, but I will if I have to."

The Return

1 - 2

Drake's heart thundered in his chest as the familiar creak of the front door shattered the oppressive silence. He froze, hardly daring to breathe, his senses heightened to a razor's edge. Could it be? After all this time? A trembling whisper floated through the air, his name on her lips, and suddenly he was moving, his feet carrying him towards the sound before his mind could catch up.

"Linda!" The name tore from his throat, raw with emotion, as he caught sight of her silhouette in the dimly lit hallway. Without hesitation, he closed the distance between them, his arms enveloping her in a desperate embrace. She felt so fragile in his arms, yet so wonderfully real, and he clung to her as if she might vanish at any moment.

"You're here," he murmured into her hair, his voice thick with disbelief. "You're really here." His mind raced, a torrent of questions threatening to spill forth, but he held them back, focusing instead on the solid warmth of her presence.

Linda's arms tightened around him, her fingers digging into the fabric of his shirt. "Drake," she breathed, her voice muffled against his chest. "I... I didn't know if I'd make it back."

Drake pulled back slightly, his hands moving to cradle her face. In the dim light, he could see the exhaustion etched into her features, the shadows under her eyes speaking volumes of the ordeal she must have endured. His heart clenched painfully at the sight, guilt and anger warring within him. How could he have let this happen? He should have protected her, should have seen the danger coming.

"I'm so sorry," he whispered, his thumbs gently stroking her cheeks. "I should have—"

"No," Linda cut him off, her blue eyes fierce despite her weariness. "This isn't your fault, Drake. You couldn't have known."

He wanted to argue, to shoulder the blame that felt so rightfully his, but the determined set of her jaw silenced him. Instead, he pressed his forehead to hers, drinking in her presence. "I thought I'd lost you," he admitted, the words barely audible. "I thought..."

"I'm here now," Linda reassured him, her hands coming up to cover his. "We're together. That's what matters."

Drake nodded, trying to let her words sink in, to push away the fear and guilt that still gnawed at him. He took a deep breath, steadying himself. "Are you hurt? Do you need anything?"

Linda shook her head slightly. "Just... just hold me for a moment. Please."

Without a word, Drake pulled her close again, enveloping her in his arms. As he held her, feeling her heartbeat against his chest, he made a silent vow. He would never let her go again. Whatever dangers lay ahead, whatever threats still lurked in the shadows, they would face them together. And this time, he would be ready.

3 - 4

Drake's heart thundered in his chest as he cradled Linda in his arms, the warmth of her body a stark contrast to the cold dread that had gripped him for days. His fingers tangled in her wavy hair, still soft despite whatever ordeal she had endured. He pulled back just enough to search her face, his dark eyes roaming over every detail as if to reassure himself she was truly there.

"Linda, where have you been?" he asked, his voice ragged with concern. "Are you alright?" The words tumbled out, urgent and pleading.

Linda's blue eyes, usually so warm and calm, now shimmered with unshed tears. Her fingers curled into the fabric of his shirt, gripping tightly as if he might vanish at any moment. "I don't know," she whispered, her voice trembling. "It's all a blur, Drake. I—" She swallowed hard, her gaze darting around the dim hallway as if expecting shadows to come alive.

Drake's protective instincts flared. He cupped her face gently, trying to ground her. "It's okay, you're safe now. Take your time."

Linda drew a shaky breath, her words coming out in a rush. "Vega... he betrayed you, Drake. He... he held me hostage for Gabriel."

The name hit Drake like a physical blow. Gabriel. The man with the burned face and cryptic words, always hovering at the edges of this nightmare. Drake's mind raced, piecing together fragments of memories and clues. "Gabriel?" he repeated, his voice low and dangerous. "What does he want with you?"

But Linda only shook her head, burying her face in his chest. "I don't know," she murmured. "There was so much I didn't understand. But Drake, I'm scared. I think... I think this is bigger than we realized."

Drake tightened his embrace, his jaw clenching as he stared into the shadows beyond. Whatever game Gabriel was playing, whatever twisted plot he had set in motion, Drake knew one thing with absolute certainty: he would do whatever it took to keep Linda safe and unravel this mystery, no matter the cost.

5 - 6

Drake's blood ran cold, a surge of anger and fear coursing through his veins like ice water. He held Linda tighter, his arms forming a protective barrier against the encroaching darkness that seemed to seep into every corner of their once-safe haven. "I should've known," he murmured, his voice heavy with regret, each word weighed with the burden of his perceived failure. "I should've seen it coming."

Linda's fingers curled into the fabric of Drake's shirt; her grip desperate yet reassuring. She pulled back just enough to meet his gaze, her blue eyes shimmering with a fierce determination that pierced through the haze of his self-doubt. "It's not your fault, Drake," she insisted, her voice low but unwavering. "We'll find a way to stop Gabriel, together."

Drake's mind whirled, a tempest of emotions and fragmented thoughts. How could he have been so blind? The signs were there, subtle but present, like a malevolent undercurrent beneath the surface of their lives. He closed his eyes, inhaling deeply, trying to center himself. "But I should have protected you, Linda. I promised—"

"No," Linda cut him off, her tone brooking no argument. "You can't shoulder this alone. We're in this together, remember?" Her hand found his cheek, her touch grounding him in the present. "We've faced worse, Drake. We'll face this too."

Drake leaned into her touch, drawing strength from her unwavering resolve. "You're right," he conceded, his voice growing steadier. "But Gabriel... he's unlike anyone we've dealt with before. The way he manipulates, the reach he seems to have—it's terrifying."

Linda nodded, a shadow passing over her features. "I know. But that's why we need each other now more than ever. We're stronger together, Drake. Always have been."

As Drake gazed into Linda's eyes, he felt a spark of hope ignite within him. Despite the darkness closing in, despite the betrayals and the lurking danger, they still had each other. And maybe, just maybe, that would be enough to see them through this nightmare.

7 - 8

Drake nodded, his jaw clenching with resolve. "We will," he vowed, his eyes flashing with determination. "But first, we need to get you somewhere safe." His gaze darted around the room, assessing potential threats lurking in the shadows.

"Drake, I—" Linda began, her voice wavering, but he was already in motion, his protective instincts kicking into overdrive.

"Come on," he urged, gently guiding her towards the living room. "We need to regroup, gather our thoughts." His hand trembled slightly as he flicked on the lights, illuminating the familiar space that now felt alien and hostile.

Linda sank onto the couch, her exhaustion evident in the slump of her shoulders. Drake's heart constricted at the sight. He grabbed a soft blanket from the nearby armchair, draping it carefully around her. "Here," he murmured, his voice thick with emotion. "Try to relax, if you can."

"How can I relax when our world is falling apart?" Linda whispered, her blue eyes glistening with unshed tears.

Drake knelt before her, taking her hands in his. "We'll figure this out, I promise. But you need to regain your strength." He squeezed her hands gently before rising. "I'll get you some water and painkillers. You look like you could use them."

As he moved towards the kitchen, Drake's mind raced. How had everything gone so wrong? The weight of his past choices pressed down on him, threatening to crush his resolve. He fumbled with the glass, nearly dropping it as his hands shook with a mixture of adrenaline and fear.

"Steady," he muttered to himself, gripping the counter's edge. "Linda needs you to be strong now." Taking a deep breath, he filled the glass and grabbed the bottle of painkillers from the cupboard.

Returning to Linda, Drake couldn't help but notice how small and vulnerable she looked, huddled beneath the blanket. It was a stark contrast to the fierce, determined woman he knew her to be. "Here," he said softly, offering her the water and pills. "This should help take the edge off."

As Linda accepted them gratefully, Drake settled beside her on the couch, his arm instinctively wrapped around her shoulders. "We're going to get through this," he assured her, even as doubt gnawed at the edges of his consciousness. "Together."

9 - 10

As Linda sipped the water, Drake found himself unable to sit still. He rose abruptly, his legs carrying him back and forth across the living room in long, purposeful strides. His mind whirred with possibilities, each more desperate than the last.

"We can't stay here," he muttered, more to himself than to Linda. "Gabriel's reach... it's too far. He got to you right under our noses." Drake's voice cracked with emotion, his dark eyes flashing with a mixture of fear and determination. "We need to end this. Put a stop to his reign of terror once and for all."

Linda's soft voice cut through his frenzied thoughts. "Drake, love, slow down. You're making me dizzy."

He paused mid-stride, turning to face her. The sight of her, pale and exhausted, struck him like a physical blow. Her usual warmth and strength seemed diminished, replaced by a fragility that tore into his heart.

"I'm sorry," Drake said, running a hand through his disheveled hair. "I just... I can't bear the thought of losing you again. Of Gabriel getting his hands on you or Harrison."

Linda reached out, her slender fingers intertwining with his. "I know, Drake. I'm scared too. But we can't rush into this blindly. Gabriel's too smart, too prepared for that."

Drake sank down beside her, his shoulders sagging under the weight of their predicament. "You're right," he admitted, his voice barely above a whisper. "We need a plan. A real strategy to outmaneuver him and his cronies."

"Together," Linda reminded him, her blue eyes holding his gaze steadily. "We'll figure this out together."

Drake nodded, feeling a small spark of hope ignite in his chest. "Together," he agreed, squeezing her hand. "Now, let's start from the beginning. Tell me everything you remember about your time with Vega. Every detail could be crucial."

As Linda began to speak, Drake listened intently, his mind already working to piece together the puzzle that had become their lives. They had a long night ahead of them, but with Linda by his side, he felt ready to face whatever challenges lay ahead.

11 - 12

Drake's calloused hand enveloped Linda's, his grip firm yet gentle, anchoring them both in the tumultuous sea of uncertainty that threatened to engulf them. The warm glow of the living room lamp cast long shadows across their faces, accentuating the lines of worry etched into their features. "We'll get through this, Linda," Drake promised, his voice steady despite the maelstrom of emotions churning within him. His dark eyes, typically sharp and analytical, now brimmed with a mix of determination and vulnerability.

Linda's fingers tightened around his, drawing strength from his touch. "I hope you're right, Drake," she whispered, her voice trembling like a autumn leaf in the wind. "Because what I'm about to tell you... it's worse than we imagined."

Drake leaned in; his brow furrowed with concern. "Tell me everything, Linda. Don't hold back."

She took a shaky breath, her blue eyes clouding with the memory of her ordeal. "It started with a letter," Linda began, her words halting and uncertain. "A simple envelope, but when I opened it... God, Drake, that symbol. The green dragon. It was there, staring back at me, and I felt this... this cold dread wash over me."

As Linda spoke, Drake felt a chill crawl up his spine, his lawyer's instincts screaming that this was more than just a random act of intimidation. "What was in the letter?" he pressed gently, fighting to keep his voice calm.

"Threats," Linda replied, her free hand clenching into a fist. "Vague at first, but then... they mentioned Harrison, Drake. They knew things about our son that no one should know."

Drake's breath caught in his throat, a surge of protective fury rising within him. "How?" he demanded more to himself than to Linda. "How could they possibly...?" He trailed off, his mind racing through possibilities, each more terrifying than the last.

"I don't know," Linda admitted, her voice barely above a whisper. "But that symbol, Drake... why does it feel so familiar? Like I've seen it before, long ago?"

Drake shook his head, frustration etched into every line of his face. "I wish I knew, Linda. But I promise you, we'll figure this out. We'll find Harrison, and we'll put an end to Gabriel's sick games once and for all."

As he spoke the words, Drake felt a renewed sense of purpose flood through him. The tired, guilt-ridden lawyer was pushed aside, replaced by the determined father and husband who would stop at nothing to protect his family. Whatever challenges lay ahead, whatever dark secrets the green dragon symbol held, Drake knew that with Linda by his side, they stood a fighting chance.

13 - 14

Linda's eyes suddenly widened, a spark of recognition flashing across her face. "The symbol... I know it from somewhere," she murmured, her brow furrowed in concentration. Drake leaned forward, his heart rate quickening as he watched his wife's mind work furiously to piece together the puzzle.

"What is it, Linda?" Drake pressed, his voice low and urgent. "Where have you seen it before?"

She shook her head, frustration evident in the set of her jaw. "I can't quite... Wait here, Drake. I need to show you something."

With a burst of energy that belied her earlier exhaustion, Linda rose from the couch, determination etched on her face. Drake watched as she strode purposefully towards Harrison's room, her movements carrying a mix of urgency and trepidation.

As the sound of Linda's footsteps faded, Drake found himself alone with his tumultuous thoughts. His mind raced, conjuring up a myriad of possibilities, each more unsettling than the last. What connection could Gabriel possibly have to Harrison? The very idea sent a chill down his spine.

"Come on, Drake," he muttered to himself, running a hand through his disheveled hair. "Think. What are you missing?"

He paced the living room, his steps matching the frantic rhythm of his heart. The green dragon symbol danced mockingly behind his eyelids every time he blinked. It seemed to hold the key to everything – Gabriel's motivations, Harrison's disappearance, the fractured reality he found himself trapped in.

"What did you draw, buddy?" Drake whispered; his voice thick with emotion as he thought of his son. "What did you see?"

The wait for Linda's return felt interminable, each second stretching into an eternity. Drake's mind conjured images of Harrison's room – the colorful drawings pinned to the walls, the scattered toys, the empty bed that hadn't been slept in for far too long. What clue had been hiding there all this time, right under their noses?

As he turned to make another circuit of the room, Drake caught sight of his reflection in the window. The man staring back at him looked haggard, eyes sunken with worry and lack of sleep. But beneath the exhaustion, there was a fire burning – a determination that would not be extinguished until he had answers, until his family was whole again.

"Whatever it takes," Drake vowed to his reflection, his voice barely above a whisper. "Whatever it takes to bring you home, Harrison. To end this nightmare."

The sound of Linda's returning footsteps jolted Drake from his reverie. He spun towards the hallway, every muscle in his body tense with anticipation. Whatever Linda had found, he knew it would change everything. For better or worse, they were about to take another step deeper into the labyrinth of secrets that surrounded them.

15 - 16

Linda appeared in the doorway, her face a mask of conflicting emotions – hope warring with fear, determination tinged with uncertainty. In her hands, she clutched a worn notebook, its edges frayed, and its cover adorned with Harrison's name in childish scrawl. Drake's heart lurched at the sight, a bittersweet reminder of their son's vibrant presence.

"I found it," Linda said, her voice barely above a whisper as she approached Drake. Her fingers trembled slightly as she flipped through the pages, each one filled with colorful sketches and doodles that spoke of Harrison's boundless imagination.

Drake watched, his breath caught in his throat, as Linda's fingers danced over the pages. He could almost hear Harrison's laughter, see the mischievous glint in his son's eyes as he proudly showed off his latest creation. The memory was so vivid, so painfully real, that for a moment, Drake forgot the horror of their current situation.

Finally, Linda stopped on a page, her sharp intake of breath drawing Drake's attention. "Here," she said, her voice quavering as she held the notebook out to him. "This is what was in the letter. It's... it's something Harrison drew."

Drake's eyes locked onto the page, and he felt the world tilt beneath his feet. There, rendered in vibrant green crayon, was the dragon symbol that had been haunting their nightmares. The same symbol that had adorned the letter that had lured Linda into danger.

"How..." Drake began, his voice trailing off as he struggled to process what he was seeing. "Linda, how is this possible? How could Harrison have known about this symbol?"

17 - 18

Drake's mind reeled as he stared at the crude green dragon, its childish lines a stark contrast to the sinister implications it held. His fingers traced the outline, half-expecting the drawing to come to life and snap at him. "This can't be a coincidence," he murmured, his voice thick with disbelief.

Linda leaned in closer, her warmth a stark contrast to the chill that had settled over Drake. "What do you think it means?" she asked, her voice barely above a whisper.

Drake shook his head, his brow furrowed in concentration. "I don't know, but it can't be good. Gabriel, Harrison, this symbol... it's all connected somehow." He paused, his eyes meeting Linda's. "Did Harrison ever mention anything about this drawing? Anything at all?"

Linda's eyes clouded with frustration. "No, nothing. It was just another doodle to me at the time. God, Drake, how could we have missed this?"

Drake's hand found Linda's, squeezing it reassuringly. "We couldn't have known. But now..." He trailed off, his gaze drifting back to the notebook. The green dragon seemed to mock him, a taunting reminder of how little they truly understood.

"What if Gabriel's been watching Harrison all along?" Drake voiced the terrifying thought that had been forming in his mind. "What if our son is somehow part of his twisted game?"

Linda's sharp intake of breath was the only sound in the room for a long moment. When she spoke, her voice was steel. "Then we put an end to this game, Drake. We find our son and we bring him home."

Drake nodded, feeling a surge of determination course through him. He stood, pulling Linda to her feet. "We need to find him, Linda," he said, his voice urgent as he met her gaze. "We need to find Harrison before it's too late."

As the words left his mouth, Drake felt a shift in the air, as if the very universe was aligning to set their quest in motion. Whatever Gabriel's plan was, whatever role Harrison played in it, Drake knew one thing with absolute certainty: he would move heaven and earth to bring his son back safely.

Mole Extinguished

Blue World – 2024

1 - 2

The room seemed to constrict around them, shadows dancing on the walls like spectral observers to the brewing confrontation. Gabriel's scarred face twisted into a mask of barely contained fury as he fixed his piercing gaze on Richard Vega, the man who had shattered months of meticulous planning with a single act of incompetence. The air crackled with tension, heavy and suffocating in the cramped space.

Gabriel's fingers twitched at his sides as he advanced, each step measured and purposeful. His mind raced, calculating the ramifications of Linda's escape, the delicate web of his carefully laid plans now in tatters. The burns that marred his features seemed to pulse with his anger, a physical manifestation of the rage that threatened to consume him.

"Richard Raymond Vega," Gabriel's voice was low, a dangerous whisper that sliced through the silence. "I trusted you with one simple task. One. Task." His words dripped with venom, each syllable a dagger aimed at Vega's heart.

Vega's eyes darted frantically, seeking an escape that didn't exist. Gabriel allowed himself a moment of cruel satisfaction at the fear he saw reflected in those desperate orbs. Good. Let him tremble. Let him taste the consequences of his failure.

"You've made a grave mistake, Vega," Gabriel growled, his voice low and menacing as he closed the distance between them. "You were supposed to keep her captive, to ensure she didn't escape. And yet here we are, with her out there, free to tell anyone who will listen about our little arrangement."

The weight of Linda's potential revelations pressed down on Gabriel, threatening to crush the empire of secrets he had so painstakingly built. He could almost see her now – blonde hair catching the light, those expressive blue eyes filled with determination as she sought help. The very thought made his blood boil.

"Gabriel, please," Vega whimpered, his earlier bravado evaporating like mist in the morning sun. "I can fix this. I can find her again. Just give me another chance!"

Gabriel's lip curled in disgust. Pathetic. He had no use for groveling cowards. "Another chance?" he hissed, leaning in close enough that Vega could surely feel the heat of his breath. "You squandered the only chance you'll ever get."

His mind raced, considering options, weighing consequences. Linda was out there, a ticking time bomb of information. How much did she truly know? How much damage could she do? Gabriel's fingers clenched involuntarily; his limp more pronounced as he circled Vega like a predator toying with its prey.

"Tell me, Raymond," Gabriel's voice was eerily calm now, a stark contrast to the storm raging within. "Did you ever stop to consider the ripple effects of your incompetence? The lives you've put at risk? The secrets you've endangered?"

He didn't wait for an answer. In truth, he didn't care for Vega's excuses or pleas. The die was cast. Now, there was only damage control and retribution.

3 - 4

Gabriel's scarred face contorted into a grimace, the burn marks stretching grotesquely as he towered over Vega. The dim light cast long shadows across the room, turning Gabriel's disfigured features into a nightmarish mask.

Vega recoiled, his back pressed against the wall, eyes darting frantically for an escape that didn't exist. "I-I'm sorry, Gabriel," he stammered, his voice a pathetic whimper. "I didn't mean for her to get away. It was a mistake, I swear."

A humorless chuckle escaped Gabriel's lips, the sound chilling in its emptiness. He leaned in, his piercing gaze boring into Vega's soul. "A mistake?" he repeated, his voice dripping with disdain. "Your entire existence is a mistake, Vega."

Gabriel's mind raced, calculating the ramifications of Linda's escape. How much did she know? Who might she contact? Every second she remained free was a threat to everything he'd built.

"You know," Gabriel continued, his tone deceptively conversational, "I've always prided myself on my ability to read people. To see the truth beneath their lies." He paused, letting the silence stretch uncomfortably. "But you, Vega... you've surprised me. I never thought you'd be foolish enough to betray me."

Vega's eyes widened, a flicker of hope igniting. "No, Gabriel! I'd never betray you! I-"

"Silence," Gabriel commanded, his voice cutting through Vega's protests like a knife. "Your words are as worthless as your loyalty."

Gabriel's expression remained cold and unforgiving; his features cast in shadow as he loomed over Vega like a specter of death. "Sorry won't cut it, Vega," he spat, his voice laced with venomous disdain. "You've outlived your usefulness to me. And now..."

He let the threat hang in the air, savoring the fear that radiated from Vega in palpable waves. In that moment, Gabriel knew that no matter what happened next, Richard Vega would never again know a moment's peace.

5 - 6

Without warning, Gabriel lunged forward, his scarred hand closing around Vega's throat with a vice-like grip. Vega's eyes widened in terror, bulging as he struggled against Gabriel's iron grasp, his legs kicking uselessly at the air.

"Did you think I'd let this slide, Raymond?" Gabriel hissed, his face inches from Vega's, close enough for the man to see the intricate network of burn scars etched across his features. "Did you believe your incompetence would go unpunished?"

Vega clawed desperately at Gabriel's fingers, his mouth opening and closing like a fish out of water. The room seemed to shrink around them, the shadows deepening as if to bear witness to this brutal act.

Gabriel's mind raced, a mix of cold calculation and burning rage. He had trusted Vega, had believed him capable of this one simple task. Now, with Linda free, everything hung in the balance. Years of meticulous planning, all jeopardized by one man's failure.

"I was going to kill you anyway," Gabriel whispered, his voice a sinister caress in Vega's ear. "But now... now I'm going to enjoy it even more." He tightened his grip, feeling Vega's pulse flutter frantically beneath his fingers. "Your death will serve as a reminder to others of the price of betrayal."

Vega's struggles grew weaker, his face turning an alarming shade of purple. Gabriel watched dispassionately, his piercing eyes never leaving Vega's face. He wanted to see the moment life left those panicked eyes, to witness firsthand the consequences of crossing Gabriel Angel.

7 - 7

As Vega's struggles grew weaker, his vision fading to black, Gabriel leaned in closer, his scarred face contorting into a twisted smile. "Do you see now, Raymond?" he hissed, his voice a low, menacing growl. "This is the price of failure."

Vega's eyes, wide with terror, locked onto Gabriel's piercing gaze. In those final moments, he saw not just the face of his killer, but a glimpse of the depths of Gabriel's obsession - the cult, the symbol, the grand design that had consumed him.

"I... I didn't..." Vega choked out, his words barely audible as life drained from him.

Gabriel's grip tightened further, his disfigured face a mask of cold fury. "You didn't what, Raymond? Understand the stakes? Grasp the importance of your role?" He leaned in, his lips almost brushing Vega's ear. "Well, now you do. And your failure will serve as a lesson to others."

As consciousness slipped away from Vega, Gabriel's mind raced with the implications of this setback. Linda's escape threatened everything he had worked for, every carefully laid plan. But he would adapt, as he always had. This was merely a temporary setback in a game that spanned decades.

"Goodbye, Raymond," Gabriel whispered, watching the last flicker of life fade from Vega's eyes. "Your death brings us one step closer to our ultimate goal."

Awakening in the Unknown

1 - 2

Drake's eyes snapped open, his vision blurring as the harsh fluorescent lights assaulted his retinas. The sterile scent of antiseptic burned his nostrils, a stark contrast to the musty air of the abandoned funhouse where he'd last been conscious. His head throbbed; thoughts scattered like puzzle pieces as he struggled to make sense of his surroundings.

"Linda?" he croaked, his voice barely above a whisper. Where was she? They'd been huddled together, whispering furtively about their plans to escape Gabriel's iron grip. Now, he found himself alone in a stark hospital room, the steady beep of monitors his only companion.

Drake's heart raced, pounding against his ribcage as if trying to escape. He attempted to sit up, but a wave of dizziness sent him crashing back against the pillows. What had happened? How had he ended up here? The last thing he remembered was Linda's warm hand in his, her eyes wide with determination as they plotted their next move.

"Drake? Oh, thank God you're awake!" Holly's voice cut through the fog of his confusion; relief evident in her trembling tone. She appeared at his bedside, her face a mixture of worry and exhaustion. Her usually neatly styled hair was disheveled, as if she'd been running her fingers through it repeatedly.

"Holly, what's going on?" Drake asked, his words slurring slightly. He reached out a hand towards her, needing to feel the reassurance of her touch. "How did we get here? What happened?"

Holly's fingers intertwined with his, squeezing gently. "Shh, try to stay calm," she soothed, though the slight quiver in her voice betrayed her own unease. "You've been through a lot. We both have."

Drake's mind raced, trying to piece together the fragments of his memory. The funhouse, the hushed conversations, the constant fear of discovery – it all seemed like a distant nightmare now. Yet the reality of his current situation felt no less surreal.

"But Gabriel..." Drake started, his voice trailing off as a fresh wave of panic washed over him. Had their nemesis found them? Was this all part of some elaborate trap?

Holly leaned in closer, her warm breath tickling his ear as she whispered, "We're safe for now. But we need to be careful. There's so much I need to tell you, but not here. Not now."

Drake nodded, swallowing hard against the lump forming in his throat. The weight of their shared secrets pressed down on him, threatening to suffocate him in this sterile room. He clung to Holly's hand like a lifeline, anchoring himself in the storm of confusion and fear that raged within him.

As he lay there, surrounded by the rhythmic beeping of machines and the faint bustle of hospital activity beyond the door, Drake couldn't shake the feeling that this was merely the eye of the hurricane. Whatever force had landed him in this bed was still out there, waiting to strike again. And he knew, with a certainty that chilled him to his core, that he and everyone he loved were far from safe.

3 - 4

Drake's throat constricted, his parched lips struggling to form words as he gazed up at the stark white ceiling. The fluorescent lights above him seemed to pulse in sync with the throbbing pain in his head, intensifying his disorientation.

"What... what happened?" he finally managed to croak, his voice barely above a whisper. Drake attempted to push himself up, desperate for answers, but a sudden wave of dizziness sent him crashing back against the pillows.

The room spun violently, and he squeezed his eyes shut, fighting against the nausea that threatened to overwhelm him.

Holly Kierstead's sharp intake of breath cut through the haze of his confusion. Her hand, cool and steady, pressed gently against his shoulder, anchoring him to the present. When Drake opened his eyes again, he found himself staring into her intense gaze, noting the worry etched across her features.

"You were shot, Drake," she explained, her usually confident voice now trembling with a mixture of concern and something else—fear, perhaps? "I found you in an abandoned amusement park of all places. You know that green dragon symbol, eerily familiar to that statue at the funhouse."

Drake's mind reeled, struggling to process this information. Shot? Amusement park? The pieces refused to fit together, like a jigsaw puzzle with half its parts missing. He opened his mouth to ask more questions, but Holly continued, her words coming faster now, as if she couldn't hold them back.

"It was like something out of a nightmare, Drake. The park was deserted, rides frozen in time, and there you were, sprawled out in the hall of mirrors. I thought... I thought I'd lost you."

As Holly spoke, fragmented images flashed through Drake's mind—the glint of moonlight on rusted metal, the acrid smell of gunpowder, a looming shadow with emerald eyes. But try as he might, he couldn't string these fragments into a coherent memory.

"I don't... I can't remember," Drake admitted, frustration coloring his tone. He clenched his fists, the IV in his arm pulling uncomfortably at the motion. "Why can't I remember, Holly?"

Kierstead's expression softened, her hand moving from his shoulder to gently grasp his. "It's okay, Drake. You've been through a traumatic experience. The doctors say some memory loss is normal. What matters is that you're alive, and we're going to figure this out together."

As Drake looked into Holly's determined eyes, he felt a glimmer of hope amidst the chaos of his thoughts. Whatever had happened in that abandoned amusement park, whatever force was at play here, he knew he wasn't facing it alone. But as the pain medication began to pull him back towards unconsciousness, one thought persisted: what other secrets lay buried in the recesses of his fractured memory?

5 - 6

Drake's eyes fluttered, struggling to focus on Holly's face as the room seemed to tilt and sway around him. The conversation with Linda, their desperate plans to outwit Gabriel, it all felt like wisps of smoke, dissipating the harder he tried to grasp them. "Linda," he murmured, his voice barely above a whisper, "We were... we were planning something. Something important."

Holly Kierstead leaned in, her piercing gaze fixed on Drake's face. "Drake, we need to talk," she said, her voice low and urgent. "There's something you need to know about what happened to you... about what's really going on."

The gravity in her tone sent a chill down Drake's spine, cutting through the fog of his disorientation. "What do you mean?" he asked, his words slurring slightly as he fought against the pull of the painkillers. "Holly, what's happening?"

She glanced over her shoulder, as if checking for eavesdroppers, before turning back to him. "The shooting wasn't random, Drake. We have reason to believe it's connected to the case you've been working on. The green dragon symbol, the abandoned amusement park... it's all part of something bigger."

Drake's mind raced, trying to connect the dots that seemed just out of reach. "Gabriel," he muttered, the name tasting bitter on his tongue. "He's behind this, isn't he?"

Holly's eyes widened slightly, a mix of surprise and concern flashing across her face. "How much do you remember, Drake? This goes deeper than just Gabriel. We think there's a whole network involved, and you might have stumbled onto something big."

As she spoke, Drake's heart monitor began to beep more rapidly, mirroring the growing sense of dread in his chest. What had he uncovered? And more importantly, what dangers still lurked in the shadows of his fractured memory?

Flickering Truths

Green World – 2024

1 - 2

The fluorescent light above Holly's desk flickered intermittently, casting an eerie glow across the towering stacks of case files that threatened to topple at any moment. She squinted at the grainy photographs spread before her, each one a haunting reminder of Meghan Johnson's disappearance. The young girl's smiling face stared back at her, a stark contrast to the fear that had gripped the community in the weeks since she vanished.

Holly rubbed her temples, trying to ward off the headache that had been building for hours. "There has to be something I'm missing," she muttered, her voice barely audible above the hum of the ancient air conditioning unit. Her eyes darted from one piece of evidence to another, searching for the elusive thread that would unravel this mystery.

As she reached for her lukewarm coffee, a commotion in the hallway caught her attention. Footsteps pounded against the linoleum floor, growing louder with each passing second. Holly's hand instinctively moved to her holster, her body tensing in anticipation.

The door burst open, revealing a young officer whose chest heaved with exertion. His face was ashen, eyes wide with a mix of fear and excitement. "Detective Keirstead," he gasped, gripping the doorframe for support. "We found her."

Holly's heart raced, her mind struggling to process the officer's words. Could it be true? After weeks of dead ends and false leads, had they finally made a breakthrough? She leaned forward, her voice steady despite the adrenaline coursing through her veins. "Slow down, Officer. Take a deep breath and tell me exactly what's going on."

The officer nodded, gulping in air before continuing. "It's Meghan Johnson, Detective. She's alive. We got a call from a gas station attendant on the outskirts of town. Said a girl matching Meghan's description stumbled in, asking for help."

Holly's thoughts whirled as she processed this information. Relief warred with suspicion – she'd learned the hard way that hope could be a dangerous thing in their line of work. "Has her identity been confirmed?" she asked, already reaching for her jacket. "And what's her condition?"

"They're bringing her in now," the officer replied, his words tumbling out in a rush. "Paramedics are with her, but from what I heard, she's pretty shaken up. Keeps talking about some man and... and blood, I think?"

A chill ran down Holly's spine at the mention of blood. What horrors had Meghan endured during her captivity? And more importantly, was her captor still out there? Holly stood, her chair scraping against the floor as she moved with purpose. "I want a full briefing in five minutes," she ordered, her tone brooking no argument. "And get me everything we have on known offenders in the area. If this girl escaped, we need to move fast before the bastard responsible goes to ground."

As she strode towards the door, Holly's mind raced with possibilities. This could be the break they'd been waiting for, the key to unraveling not just Meghan's disappearance, but potentially other unsolved cases as well. But first, she needed answers – and she was determined to get them, no matter what it took.

3 - 4

Holly's heart hammered against her ribcage as she strode purposefully down the dimly lit corridor, her footsteps echoing off the cold, sterile walls. The fluorescent lights flickered overhead, casting eerie shadows that seemed to dance and twist with each passing second. She could feel the weight of responsibility pressing down on her shoulders, urging her forward with an almost palpable force.

"How long ago did she escape?" Holly demanded, her voice tight with a mixture of anticipation and dread. She glanced sideways at the officer struggling to keep pace beside her.

"About an hour ago," he panted, his face still ashen. "A couple found her wandering along the highway, barely coherent. They called it in immediately."

Holly's mind raced, calculating possibilities. "And the scene? Has it been secured?"

The officer nodded frantically. "Yes, ma'am. Units are already there, combing the area."

As they approached the interrogation room, Holly's steps faltered for a moment. She took a deep breath, steeling herself for what lay ahead. "Remember," she said, her voice low and intense, "this girl has been through hell. We need to tread carefully."

With a sharp nod to the guard, Holly pushed open the heavy door, her eyes immediately drawn to the small, huddled figure in the corner. The sight of Meghan Johnson, her clothes torn and caked with dirt, her eyes wide with terror, hit Holly like a physical blow. For a split second, she was transported back to her own childhood, to the fear and helplessness she'd once felt. She pushed the memory aside, forcing herself to focus on the present.

"Meghan?" Holly said softly, crouching down to the girl's level. "I'm Detective Kierstead. You're safe now. Can you tell me what happened?"

Meghan's eyes darted wildly around the room, her breath coming in short, panicked gasps. "He... he said I was special," she whispered, her voice barely audible. "That I could help him... open the door."

Holly's brow furrowed, a chill creeping down her spine. "What door, Meghan? What did he mean?"

But Meghan just shook her head, tears streaming down her dirt-streaked face. "The blood," she whimpered. "So much blood..."

As Holly watched the traumatized girl, her heart ached with a mixture of compassion and determination. Whatever nightmare Meghan had endured, Holly vowed silently to bring her captor to justice, no matter the cost. The pieces of this twisted puzzle were finally starting to fall into place, and she wouldn't rest until she'd uncovered the truth lurking in the shadows.

5 - 6

Meghan's voice trembled as she continued, her words spilling out in a frantic torrent. "There was another boy... in the room with me. The man, he... he did something terrible to him."

Holly leaned in; her voice gentle but urgent. "What did he do to the boy, Meghan?"

"He injected him with... with blood," Meghan choked out, her eyes wide with renewed terror. "Said it was a portal to other timelines. The boy screamed and screamed, then... then he just disappeared."

Holly's blood ran cold, her mind reeling at the implications. She struggled to keep her voice steady, fighting back the wave of nausea that threatened to overwhelm her. "Did the man say anything else about the blood, Meghan?"

The girl nodded; her gaze unfocused as if lost in the horrific memory. "He said it was special. That it could... could unlock doors between worlds."

As Holly listened, a chill crept down her spine, her thoughts racing. Could it be possible? The rational part of her mind rebelled against the idea, but years on the force had taught her that reality often defied logic. She found herself wondering, could this blood truly hold the key to unlocking the mysteries that had plagued them for so long?

"Meghan," Holly said softly, pushing aside her own tumultuous thoughts, "you've been incredibly brave. We're going to do everything we can to find this man and the other boy. You're safe now."

As she spoke the reassuring words, Holly couldn't shake the feeling that they were on the precipice of something far larger and more terrifying than she could have ever imagined. The weight of responsibility settled heavily on her shoulders, a grim determination taking root in her heart.

7 - 7

Holly's jaw clenched as she rose from her chair, her eyes blazing with a fierce determination that belied the turmoil churning within. "I swear to you, Meghan, we'll find this man," she vowed, her voice low and intense. "This Gabriel won't get away with what he's done."

As she strode out of the interrogation room, Holly's mind raced, piecing together the fragments of information they'd gathered. The enigmatic Gabriel, with his scarred face and cryptic words, seemed to be at the center of it all. She could almost see his piercing gaze, as if he were watching her even now.

"Kier!" Officer Bird called out, jogging to catch up. "What's our next move?"

Holly's steps didn't falter as she replied, "We need to cross-reference every detail Meghan gave us with our existing cases. There has to be a pattern, a connection we're missing."

Her fingers twitched, itching to dive into the mountain of files awaiting her. "And Bird," she added, her tone brooking no argument, "I want everything we have on blood rituals, portals, alternate timelines - no matter how far-fetched it seems."

As they reached her office, Holly paused, her hand on the doorknob. "What if it's true?" she murmured, almost to herself. "What if this blood really is a key to other worlds?"

Franklin Bird shifted uncomfortably. "Detective, you can't seriously believe-"

"I don't know what to believe anymore," Holly cut him off, her voice sharp. "But I do know that we're dealing with something far beyond our usual cases. And I'll be damned if I let Gabriel slip through our fingers because we were too close-minded to consider every possibility."

She pushed open the door, the familiar scent of coffee and old paper enveloping her. As she sank into her chair, Holly's resolve hardened. "No matter the cost," she whispered, her eyes falling on the photo of Meghan pinned to her board, "I'll uncover the truth behind Gabriel's sick game. And when I do, he'll wish he'd never set foot in this town."

Tension in the Hospital Room

Green World – 2024

1 - 2

The fluorescent lights flickered overhead, casting harsh shadows across Detective Holly Kierstead's face as she leaned across the cold metal table, her eyes locked on Drake Miller. The air in the cramped hospital room felt thick with tension, almost suffocating in its intensity. Holly's fingers drummed a nervous rhythm on the tabletop, betraying the gravity of the situation despite her outward composure.

"Drake, we need to talk," Holly began, her voice low and urgent, each word carefully measured. She paused, searching for the right way to convey the earth-shattering information she possessed.

Drake's weary eyes met hers, a flicker of apprehension crossing his scruffy features. He shifted in his bed, the metal frame scraping against the floor. His mind raced, trying to piece together what could have prompted this impromptu meeting. Was it about the case? Or something more personal?

"What is it, Holly? What's happened?" Drake asked, his tone tinged with a mixture of curiosity and dread. He leaned forward, narrowing his eyes as if he could discern the truth from Holly's expression alone.

As Holly opened her mouth to respond, Drake found himself studying the lines of fatigue etched into her face, the slight tremble in her usually steady hands. Whatever this was, it was big - and it was clear that it had shaken Holly to her core. A knot of anxiety formed in Drake's stomach, his thoughts spiraling through worst-case scenarios. What new twist in this already convoluted case could have rattled the unflappable Detective Kierstead?

3 - 4

Holly drew in a deep breath, her fingers interlacing tightly on the table before her. "It's about the blood," she replied, her words heavy with significance. The fluorescent light above cast harsh shadows across her face, emphasizing the gravity of her expression. "The blood we found on the robe, it's identical to yours. But that's not all. It also matches Gabriel's blood profile."

Drake felt as if the air had been sucked from his lungs. His mind reeled, struggling to process the implications of Holly's words. The room seemed to tilt on its axis, and he gripped the edge of the table to steady himself. "What?" he breathed, his voice barely above a whisper.

As the initial shock began to subside, Drake's brow furrowed in confusion. He ran a hand through his disheveled hair, his thoughts racing. "We've already gone over this. You, me, maybe the other you, I can't recall," he murmured, more to himself than to Holly. The weight of multiple realities pressed down on him, memories blurring and overlapping in his mind.

Drake's gaze snapped back to Holly, his eyes wide with a mix of disbelief and growing concern. "But how is that possible?" he asked, his voice hoarse with emotion. The impossibility of it all threatened to overwhelm him, but a nagging thought pushed its way to the forefront of his mind. "And what does it have to do with Harrison?"

As he spoke his son's name, Drake felt a surge of protective instinct. His hands clenched into fists on the table, knuckles white with tension. The thought of Harrison being involved in this twisted mystery filled him with a potent mixture of fear and determination. Whatever was happening, whatever impossible truths were unraveling before them, Drake knew one thing for certain: he would do whatever it took to keep his son safe.

5 - 6

Holly's expression darkened, her eyes filled with a mixture of concern and urgency. She leaned forward, her voice dropping to a near-whisper as she delivered the chilling news. "I don't know, Drake. But there's something else you need to know," she said, her words carrying the weight of a terrible secret. "Gabriel injected Harrison with blood, claiming it was a portal to other timelines."

The world seemed to tilt on its axis as Drake processed her words. His heart thundered in his chest; each beat a painful reminder of the danger his son might be in. "Harrison," he whispered, his voice barely audible, thick with fear and disbelief. The name hung in the air between them, charged with all the love and worry of a father facing an incomprehensible threat.

Drake's mind raced, images of his son's mischievous grin and curious eyes flashing before him. He could almost hear Harrison's excited voice, always ready for the next adventure. But this... this was beyond anything they could have imagined. "What does this mean for him?" Drake asked, his words tumbling out in a rush. "Is he in danger?"

As he spoke, Drake's hand unconsciously moved to his own arm, rubbing the spot where he imagined Gabriel might have injected Harrison. The thought of that enigmatic figure with his piercing eyes and cryptic words anywhere near his son sent a chill down Drake's spine. He looked at Holly, desperate for answers, his eyes silently pleading for some reassurance that his worst fears weren't coming true.

"God, Holly," Drake breathed, his voice cracking with emotion. "What kind of twisted game is Gabriel playing? And why involve Harrison?" The questions hung in the air, unanswered, as Drake grappled with the implications of this revelation. His son, unwittingly drawn into a web of alternate timelines and impossible blood matches. The weight of it all threatened to crush him, but beneath the fear, a spark of determination began to grow.

7 - 7

Holly's eyes softened with sympathy as she reached across the table, her hand resting gently on Drake's arm. "I don't know, Drake," she admitted, her voice soft with compassion. "We're in uncharted territory here."

Drake felt the warmth of Holly's touch, a stark contrast to the cold dread seeping through his veins. He closed his eyes, struggling to process the whirlwind of emotions threatening to overwhelm him. When he opened them again, his gaze was steely, determined.

"We need to find Harrison," Drake declared, his voice low and urgent. "Now."

Holly nodded, her expression mirroring Drake's resolve. "I've already put out an APB," she said, her detective instincts kicking in. "But Drake, we need to be careful. If what Gabriel said is true..."

"If it's true," Drake interrupted, his words laced with a mixture of fear and disbelief, "then my son could be anywhere. Or any when." He ran a hand through his disheveled hair, his mind reeling with the implications. "Christ, Holly, how do we even begin to search for him?"

As he spoke, Drake's thoughts raced back to the moment he'd last seen Harrison – his son's laughter echoing through their home, blissfully unaware of the danger lurking on the horizon. The memory cut like a knife, reminding Drake of all he stood to lose.

"We start with what we know," Holly replied, her voice steady and reassuring. "The blood, Gabriel, the timelines. There has to be a connection we're missing."

Drake nodded, clinging to Holly's words like a lifeline. "You're right," he said, his voice growing stronger with each word. "We'll find him. We have to."

The Black World

1 - 2

Harrison's eyes snapped open, his vision blurred by swirling dust particles that danced in the eerie, muted light. He blinked rapidly, confusion etching deep lines across his youthful face as he tried to make sense of the alien landscape before him. Gone were the familiar posters of his favorite bands and the comforting clutter of his bedroom; in their place stretched an endless expanse of desolation, a barren wasteland that seemed to mock his very existence.

"What the hell?" he muttered, his voice cracking with disbelief as he pushed himself up on trembling arms. The movement sent a cascade of grit tumbling from his curly hair, and he coughed, the acrid taste of dust coating his tongue. "This can't be real. I must be dreaming."

But as Harrison's gaze swept across the horizon, taking in the low, brooding sky and the oppressive silence that hung in the air like a shroud, a creeping sense of dread began to seep into his bones. This was no dream – the harsh reality of his surroundings was far too vivid, too visceral to be a product of his imagination.

Struggling to his feet, Harrison stumbled forward, his eyes widening in horror as he recognized the twisted remnants of what had once been his bustling hometown. Where once stood proud buildings and tree-lined streets, now lay only rubble and ruin, a grotesque parody of the place he had called home.

"No, no, no," he whispered, his voice rising in pitch as panic threatened to overwhelm him. "This can't be happening. Mom? Dad? Anyone?"

His desperate cries echoed across the desolate landscape, mocking him with their hollow return. The air, heavy with the stench of decay, seemed to press in on him from all sides, threatening to suffocate him with its oppressive weight.

As he stumbled through the debris-strewn streets, Harrison's mind raced, trying to piece together the fragments of his last memories. "I was in the room," he muttered to himself, kicking aside a chunk of concrete. "I was talking the girl in the next room over, and then... and then..."

His voice trailed off as a distant sound caught his attention – a low, ominous rumble that seemed to emanate from the very earth itself. Harrison froze, his heart pounding in his chest as he strained to identify the source of the noise.

"Hello?" he called out, his voice wavering with a mixture of hope and fear. "Is anyone there?"

The only response was the echo of his own words, bouncing back at him from the broken shells of buildings that loomed overhead like silent sentinels. Harrison shuddered, wrapping his arms around himself as a chill wind whipped through the desolate streets, carrying with it the faint whisper of forgotten memories and shattered dreams.

3 - 4

Harrison's eyes darted frantically from one crumbling structure to another, his teenage bravado crumbling like the ruins surrounding him. "This can't be real," he muttered, his voice cracking with disbelief. "It's got to be some kind of nightmare, right?"

But the acrid taste of ash on his tongue and the sting of dust in his eyes told a different story. This was no dream – this was a waking nightmare, a twisted version of reality that defied all logic and reason.

"Okay, Harrison, think," he said aloud, running a hand through his unruly curls. "What would Dad say? 'When in doubt, gather information.'" He forced a weak chuckle, the sound hollow in the oppressive silence.

Taking a deep breath, Harrison began to pick his way through the rubble, his eyes scanning for anything familiar, anything that might give him a clue as to where – or when – he was. As he rounded a corner, he came face to face with a half-collapsed billboard, its faded image barely visible beneath layers of grime and decay.

"No way," he breathed, his eyes widening in shock. "That's... that's impossible."

The billboard, weathered and torn, displayed a date – a date that was decades in the past. Harrison stumbled backward, his mind reeling with the implications. "Time travel? But how? Why?" His questions echoed unanswered in the empty streets, leaving him more lost and confused than ever.

Fear gripped his heart like an icy fist as the full weight of his situation crashed down upon him. "I'm alone," he whispered, his voice trembling. "I'm alone in a world that doesn't exist yet. How am I supposed to get back home?"

5 - 6

Harrison's legs trembled beneath him, but he forced himself to stand tall, his fists clenching at his sides. "No," he muttered, shaking his head vigorously. "I can't lose it now. I've got to keep it together."

He took a deep breath, the acrid air burning his lungs. "Okay, what do I know?" he asked himself, his voice steadying as he fell into the familiar pattern of problem-solving. "Gabriel's blood somehow brought me here. But why? And how?"

As he picked his way through the desolate landscape, Harrison's mind raced with possibilities. "Maybe it's some kind of genetic key?" he mused aloud, his sneakers crunching on broken glass. "Or a chemical reaction that triggered a temporal shift?"

A gust of wind howled through the empty streets, carrying with it the faint echo of a distant sound. Harrison froze, his ears straining. "Hello?" he called out, hope and fear mingling in his voice. "Is anyone there?"

The only response was the whistling of the wind through the skeletal remains of buildings. Harrison's shoulders slumped, but he pressed on, his determination growing with each step.

"I've got to find a way back," he said, his voice growing stronger. "Mom, Dad, my friends... they must be worried sick. And what about Gabriel? Is he behind all this?"

As he rounded a corner, Harrison stumbled upon the remains of what once might have been a library. Books lay scattered across the ground, their pages yellowed and brittle. He knelt down, carefully picking up a tattered volume.

"Maybe there are answers here," he murmured, flipping through the fragile pages. "Something about time travel, or parallel universes, or... anything that could explain this mess."

His fingers trembled as he turned each page, hope and desperation warring within him. "Come on," he whispered urgently. "Give me something, anything. I can't stay here. I don't belong in this world."

As the sun began to set, casting long shadows across the ruined cityscape, Harrison looked up, his eyes filled with a mix of fear and determination. "I'll find a way back," he promised himself, his voice echoing in the emptiness. "Whatever it takes, I'll figure this out. I have to."

7 - 7

Harrison clutched the book to his chest, his eyes scanning the desolate horizon. The fading light cast eerie shadows across the rubble-strewn landscape, sending a shiver down his spine.

"Okay, think Harrison," he muttered to himself, running a hand through his unruly curls. "What would the hero in one of your stories do?"

He squinted at a distant structure, its jagged silhouette piercing the sky. "Shelter," he decided, his voice tinged with both fear and determination. "That's step one. Can't solve interdimensional mysteries if I freeze to death."

As he picked his way through the debris, Harrison's mind raced. "This is just like that time I got lost in the woods during summer camp," he said, forcing a chuckle. "Except, you know, with more apocalyptic vibes and fewer mosquitoes."

The wind picked up, carrying with it the acrid scent of decay. Harrison pulled his shirt over his nose, his eyes watering. "God, what happened here?" he wondered aloud, his voice muffled. "It's like the whole world just... ended."

Reaching the building, he hesitated at the entrance, its gaping maw dark and forbidding. "Come on, Harrison," he urged himself. "Where's that adventurous spirit now?" Taking a deep breath, he stepped inside, the darkness swallowing him whole.

"Hello?" he called out, his voice echoing in the emptiness. "Any friendly post-apocalyptic survivors around? I come in peace, and I make a mean s'more."

Bullet Time

1 - 2

The searing pain in Drake Miller's hip pulsed in sync with the harsh fluorescent lights flickering overhead, each throb a stark reminder of the bullet lodged inside him. He sucked in a shallow breath, wincing as agony lanced through his body. "Linda... Harrison..." he whispered through gritted teeth, their faces flashing in his mind—one lost, one still within reach, both driving him forward.

A flurry of white coats swirled around him, the medical team's hushed voices carrying an undercurrent of urgency that set Drake's nerves on edge. He caught snippets of their hurried conversation:

"BP's dropping..."

"We need to get him into surgery, stat."

"Prep OR 3..."

Drake's eyes darted from face to face, searching for a hint of reassurance, but finding only tightly controlled professional masks. A young nurse approached, her smile not quite reaching her eyes as she adjusted his IV.

"How are you feeling, Mr. Miller?" she asked, her tone forcefully cheerful.

Drake managed a wry chuckle that quickly turned into a grimace. "Like I've been shot," he replied, his voice rough with pain and dark humor. "But I've had worse... in another life."

The nurse's brow furrowed in confusion, but Drake was already lost in thought. He'd faced death before—or had he? The memories of his dual realities swirled in his mind, leaving him dizzy and disoriented. Which world was real? Which family could he save?

"Stay with us, Mr. Miller," the nurse urged, her voice cutting through the haze. "The doctor will be here soon to explain the procedure."

Drake nodded, forcing himself to focus on the present. He had to survive this—for Linda, for Harrison, for the chance to become the man they deserved. The man he should have been before the accident tore his world apart.

"I'm here," he rasped, locking eyes with the nurse. "I'm not going anywhere. I can't... not when there's still so much left unsaid, so much to make right."

The nurse patted his arm gently, a flicker of genuine sympathy crossing her face. "That's the spirit, Mr. Miller. Hold onto that. It'll help you through what's coming."

As she turned away, Drake closed his eyes, trying to steady his racing thoughts. The chaos of the hospital room faded into the background as he clung to the images of his family—whole, happy, united. He would find a way to bridge the gap between his fractured realities, to heal the wounds of the past.

"I'm coming home," he whispered to the ghosts of his memory. "To both of you. Somehow."

3 - 4

The lead physician approached Drake's bedside, her footsteps echoing ominously in the stark hospital room. Drake's heart rate spiked, the quickening beep of the monitor betraying his rising anxiety. He swallowed hard, his throat dry and constricted.

"Mr. Miller," the doctor began, her voice steady but grave, "I'm Dr. Sanchez. We've assessed your condition, and I'm afraid we're facing a critical situation."

Drake's mind raced, flashing through a myriad of worst-case scenarios. He forced himself to meet the doctor's gaze, steeling himself for what was to come. "How bad is it, doc?" he managed to croak out, his voice barely above a whisper.

Dr. Sanchez's expression softened slightly, but her eyes remained serious. "We need to operate," she said, her words slicing through the fog of pain that had settled over Drake. "The bullet has caused extensive damage, and if we don't act quickly, there's a risk of internal bleeding."

Drake's breath caught in his throat. Surgery. The word hung in the air between them, heavy with implications. "What are my chances?" he asked, hating how vulnerable he sounded.

The doctor hesitated for a moment before responding. "Every surgery carries risks, Mr. Miller. But without it, your chances of survival are... slim."

Drake closed his eyes, allowing himself a brief moment of fear before pushing it aside. He thought of Linda and Harrison, their faces blurring together in his mind's eye. Which reality would he wake up to if he survived this? Which loved one would he be forced to mourn?

"I understand," Drake finally said, opening his eyes and fixing Dr. Sanchez with a determined stare. "Do what you have to do. I have too much to live for to give up now."

Dr. Sanchez nodded, a flicker of respect crossing her face. "We'll prepare you for surgery immediately. Is there anyone you'd like us to contact?"

Drake's heart clenched. In this fractured existence, who could he call? Who even knew he was here? "No," he said softly. "There's no one. Not here, anyway."

As the medical team began to bustle around him, preparing for the impending surgery, Drake steeled himself for the battle ahead. He would fight, not just for his life, but for the chance to unravel the mystery of his dual realities and find a way back to his family – in whichever world that might be.

5 - 6

Drake's fingers curled into the crisp hospital sheets, his knuckles turning white as he steeled himself against the wave of pain and uncertainty. "I'm ready," he said, his voice low and gravelly, masking the fear that threatened to overwhelm him.

Dr. Sanchez nodded, her eyes reflecting a mix of professional detachment and genuine concern. "We'll take good care of you, Mr. Miller. The anesthesiologist will be here shortly to begin the procedure."

As the medical team bustled around him, Drake's mind drifted to Linda and Harrison. The image of Linda's gentle smile, her blonde hair catching the sunlight, flickered in his mind's eye. It was quickly replaced by Harrison's mischievous grin, his curly hair a wild halo around his face.

"Doc," Drake called out, his voice cracking slightly. "If... if something goes wrong, is there any way to get a message to my family?"

Dr. Sanchez paused, her brow furrowing. "I thought you said there was no one to contact."

Drake swallowed hard, the conflicting realities warring in his mind. "It's complicated. They might not even know I'm here. But if I don't make it..."

"You're going to make it, Mr. Miller," Dr. Sanchez interrupted firmly. "But if it gives you peace of mind, write down their information. I'll make sure they're notified if necessary."

As a nurse handed him a pen and paper, Drake's hand trembled. Which address should he write? Which phone number? The weight of his fractured existence pressed down on him, making it hard to breathe.

"I can't lose them," he whispered, more to himself than anyone else. "Not again. Not like this."

The nurse placed a comforting hand on his shoulder. "Focus on getting through this, Mr. Miller. Your family needs you to fight."

Drake nodded, clinging to the image of Harrison's smile, Linda's warm embrace. They were his anchor, his reason to survive this ordeal. As the anesthesiologist approached with the mask, Drake closed his eyes, silently vowing to find his way back to them – in whatever reality awaited him on the other side of this surgery.

7 - 8

The anesthesia mask descended, and Drake's world began to blur at the edges. As consciousness slipped away, he clung to the image of Harrison's smile like a lifeline. "I'm coming back to you," he murmured, his words slurring. "Both of you... I promise."

Darkness enveloped him, and for a moment, Drake felt suspended between his two realities. In that liminal space, he let go of his fears, surrendering to the void.

When awareness returned, it came in fragments. The steady beep of a heart monitor pierced the fog. Harsh fluorescent light seeped through his eyelids. Drake's throat felt raw, his body leaden.

"Mr. Miller?" A voice called from far away. "Can you hear me?"

Drake struggled to open his eyes, blinking against the brightness. The world swam into focus, revealing a nurse leaning over him.

"Wha...?" he croaked, his mouth dry as sandpaper.

"You're in recovery, Mr. Miller. The surgery's over. How are you feeling?"

Drake's mind raced, trying to piece together his fractured memories. "Harrison?" he mumbled. "Linda?"

The nurse's brow furrowed. "I'm sorry, there's no one here by those names. Do you want us to call someone for you?"

Panic clawed at Drake's chest. Which reality was he in? Had the surgery somehow erased one of his lives? He tried to sit up, but pain lanced through his hip.

"Easy," the nurse cautioned, gently restraining him. "You need to stay still. The doctor will be here soon to explain everything."

Drake sank back, his heart pounding. "I need to know," he insisted, his voice hoarse. "My family... are they...?"

The nurse's expression softened. "I'm sorry, Mr. Miller. I don't have any information about your family. But let's focus on you right now. How's your pain level?"

Drake closed his eyes, fighting back tears of frustration and fear. "It doesn't matter," he whispered. "Nothing matters if I've lost them again."

9 - 10

As Drake wrestled with his tumultuous thoughts, the door opened, and the lead physician entered, her footsteps echoing in the sterile room. She approached his bedside, her expression a careful blend of professional detachment and cautious optimism.

"Mr. Miller," she began, her voice cutting through the haze of his anxiety, "I'm Dr. Reeves. I performed your surgery."

Drake's eyes snapped open, searching her face for any clue about his predicament. "My family," he rasped, his voice barely above a whisper. "Do you know...?"

Dr. Reeves held up a hand, her expression softening. "Let's focus on you for a moment, Mr. Miller. The surgery was a success," she said, her voice tinged with relief. "We were able to remove the bullet and repair the damage to your hip. You're going to be okay."

A wave of gratitude washed over Drake as he processed her words, momentarily overshadowing his fear about his dual realities. Despite the lingering pain and discomfort, he felt a profound sense of gratitude for the second chance he had been given.

"Thank you," he managed, his voice thick with emotion. "I... I don't know how to express..."

Dr. Reeves nodded, a small smile playing at the corners of her mouth. "You don't need to thank us, Mr. Miller. It's our job. Now, about your family—"

Drake's heart leapt into his throat. "Yes?" he asked, leaning forward despite the pain it caused.

"We couldn't reach anyone at the numbers you provided pre-surgery," Dr. Reeves explained gently. "Is there someone else we should contact?"

Drake's mind raced. Which reality was he in? Where was Harrison? Where was Linda? He closed his eyes, concentrating hard, and suddenly, like a bolt of lightning, clarity struck. He knew where to find Harrison, in both realities.

"I know where they are," he said, his voice growing stronger with each word. "I can find them. I just need to get out of here."

Dr. Reeves frowned, concern etching lines in her forehead. "Mr. Miller, you've just undergone major surgery. You need time to recover before—"

"You don't understand," Drake interrupted, his eyes blazing with a newfound determination. "My son... my wife... they're out there, and they need me. I can't waste another moment."

Echoes of a Forgotten Home

Apocalypse World – 20 A.C

1 - 2

Harrison's footsteps echoed through the empty shell of his childhood home, each creak of the floorboards sending a shiver down his spine. He stood frozen in the entryway, his eyes roving over peeling wallpaper and crumbling plaster, struggling to reconcile the desolation before him with the warm memories etched in his mind.

"This can't be real," he muttered, running a hand through his unruly curls. "It's like walking through a nightmare."

As he ventured deeper into the house, fragments of his past life seemed to flicker at the edges of his vision - phantom echoes of laughter, the ghost of his mother's perfume. Harrison paused in what had once been the living room, his gaze drawn to a faded rectangle on the wall where a family portrait had hung.

"We were so happy here," he whispered, his voice cracking. "What the hell happened?"

Unbidden, a memory surfaced - sprawling on the floor with his parents, engaged in an epic battle of Monopoly. His father's booming laugh, his mother's playful accusations of cheating. The weight of loss pressed down on Harrison's chest, threatening to suffocate him.

He stumbled into the kitchen, kicking aside debris as he went. "This is where Mom taught me to make pancakes," he said aloud, desperate to fill the oppressive silence. "I nearly burned the house down that first time."

A wry chuckle escaped him, quickly morphing into a choked sob. Harrison braced himself against the countertop, his knuckles white as he gripped the edge.

"Get it together, Miller," he growled, scrubbing at his eyes. "You can't fall apart now."

But as he gazed out the grimy kitchen window at the overgrown backyard beyond, another wave of memories crashed over him. Endless summer days spent chasing fireflies, building elaborate forts, letting his imagination run wild. The ache of nostalgia was almost physical, a hollow pain in the pit of his stomach.

"I'd give anything to go back," Harrison murmured, pressing his forehead against the cool glass. "Just for a moment."

He closed his eyes, willing himself to wake up from this surreal nightmare. But when he opened them again, nothing had changed. The devastation remained, a stark reminder of all he had lost.

With a heavy sigh, Harrison pushed away from the window. "Time to face reality, kid," he told himself, squaring his shoulders. "No use living in the past."

Yet even as he spoke the words, Harrison couldn't shake the feeling that something wasn't right. This house, this place - it held secrets he had yet to uncover. And deep down, a small voice whispered that perhaps the past wasn't as far behind him as he thought.

3 - 4

Harrison's footsteps echoed through the silent corridors, each step a thunderous intrusion in the eerie stillness. The sound reverberated off the crumbling walls like a haunting refrain, sending shivers down his spine. As he approached his old bedroom, a mixture of anticipation and dread churned in his gut.

"Come on, Harrison," he muttered to himself, his voice unnaturally loud in the oppressive silence. "It's just a room. Your room."

With a trembling hand, he pushed open the door, wincing at the ominous creak of rusty hinges. The sight that greeted him was like a snapshot frozen in time, preserved in dust and decay.

"Holy shit," Harrison breathed, his eyes wide as he took in the scene before him.

The furniture lay in disarray, a thick layer of dust coating every surface. Posters hung askew on the walls, faded remnants of his teenage obsessions. But amidst the chaos, one object caught his eye – his old notebook, its pages yellowed with age but still intact.

Harrison's heart raced as he approached the desk where the notebook lay. "I can't believe it's still here," he whispered, reaching out with trembling hands to pick it up.

As he flipped through the worn pages, a flood of memories washed over him. Sketches of fantastical creatures, scribbled notes about his dreams, and then... there it was. The intricate dragon symbol that had haunted his dreams for as long as he could remember.

"What the hell?" Harrison muttered, tracing the symbol with his finger. "Why does this feel so... familiar?"

A chill ran down his spine as he stared at the dragon, its serpentine form seeming to writhe on the page. It was as if a piece of a long-forgotten puzzle had suddenly fallen into place, connecting him to a past he had buried deep within his subconscious.

"This can't be a coincidence," he said, his voice barely above a whisper. "But what does it mean?"

As Harrison continued to study the symbol, a sense of unease settled over him. The room suddenly felt oppressive, the air thick with unseen presences. He glanced around nervously, half-expecting to see shadowy figures lurking in the corners.

"Get a grip, Miller," he chastised himself, shaking his head. "It's just an old drawing. Nothing to freak out about."

But even as he tried to reassure himself, Harrison couldn't shake the feeling that he had stumbled upon something significant. Something that might just hold the key to unraveling the mystery of his past – and perhaps, his future.

With a deep breath, he closed the notebook and tucked it under his arm. "Looks like I've got some research to do," he murmured, casting one last glance around the room before stepping back into the hallway, the weight of his discovery heavy on his shoulders.

5 - 6

Harrison's feet moved of their own accord, carrying him down the dim hallway towards the bathroom. The flickering light bulb cast eerie shadows that danced across the cracked tiles, making the hairs on the back of his neck stand on end.

"This is ridiculous," he muttered to himself, his cocky teenage bravado wavering. "It's just an old bathroom. Nothing to be afraid of."

But as he stepped inside, the oppressive atmosphere seemed to close in around him. Harrison found himself standing before the dusty mirror, his reflection staring back at him with hollow eyes that seemed to belong to someone else entirely.

"What the hell?" he breathed, leaning closer to examine his face.

The longer he stared, the more unsettling his reflection became. It was as if he was looking at a stranger wearing his skin - a stranger with piercing eyes that held a haunted wisdom far beyond his sixteen years.

"This can't be real," Harrison said, his voice trembling. "I look just like... but that's impossible."

As he studied his reflection, a chill ran down his spine. The face staring back at him bore an uncanny resemblance to the one that had haunted his nightmares ever since his abduction - the same intense gaze, the same rugged features, but unmarred by time or hardship.

"How is this possible?" he whispered, touching his cheek in disbelief. "I look like him, but... older? Unchanged?"

Harrison's mind raced, trying to make sense of what he was seeing. Was this some kind of trick? A hallucination brought on by stress and fear? Or was it something far more sinister - a glimpse into a reality he could scarcely comprehend?

"Get it together, Harrison," he said firmly, attempting to shake off the growing sense of dread. "There has to be a logical explanation for this. Maybe it's just the light, or... or..."

But even as he tried to rationalize what he was seeing, Harrison couldn't shake the feeling that he had stumbled upon something beyond his understanding. Something that tied directly into the mysteries surrounding his abduction and the strange symbol in his notebook.

"Whatever's going on," he said, his jaw set with determination, "I'm going to figure it out. No matter what it takes."

7 - 8

Harrison's heart pounded in his chest as he stared at the reflection, his teenage bravado crumbling in the face of this inexplicable phenomenon. "This can't be real," he muttered, running a trembling hand through his unruly curls. "It's like I've aged a decade in the blink of an eye."

The weight of the situation crashed down upon him, and Harrison felt his knees buckle. He gripped the edge of the cracked sink, his knuckles turning white. "Think, Harrison, think," he urged himself, his voice echoing in the desolate bathroom. "What would Dad say if he were here?"

As if in response to his thoughts, a memory of his father's words floated to the surface: "Sometimes, son, the world doesn't make sense. That's when you need to trust your instincts."

"My instincts?" Harrison scoffed, his eyes never leaving the mirror. "My instincts are telling me to run screaming into the night."

But even as the words left his mouth, Harrison felt a shift within himself. The initial shock was giving way to a familiar sense of curiosity - the same burning desire to understand that had always driven him.

"Okay, let's approach this logically," he said, straightening up. "I'm in a house that looks like mine but isn't. I look older but don't feel it. And there's that symbol..."

Suddenly, the air in the bathroom felt thick and oppressive. Harrison's breath came in short gasps as a wave of claustrophobia washed over him. "I can't... I can't stay here," he choked out, stumbling backwards.

With one last glance at the mirror, Harrison turned and bolted from the bathroom, his heart hammering against his ribs. The world around him seemed to blur and shift, reality bending in ways that defied explanation.

As he stumbled into the hallway, Harrison's mind raced with possibilities, each more outlandish than the last. "Time travel? Parallel universes? Or am I just losing my mind?" he wondered aloud, his voice tinged with hysteria.

One thing, however, was crystal clear - the familiar world he knew was gone, replaced by this twisted reflection of reality. "I'm definitely not in Kansas anymore," Harrison muttered, channeling his inner Dorothy as he tried to make sense of his surroundings.

9 - 10

Harrison's feet carried him swiftly through the decaying remnants of his once-familiar home, his mind reeling as he struggled to process the surreal landscape. The urgency of his situation crashed over him like a tidal wave, drowning out the myriad questions swirling in his head.

"Focus, Harrison," he muttered to himself, his voice cracking with a mixture of fear and determination. "You can figure this out later. Right now, you need to survive."

With a deep breath, he pushed open the front door, wincing as it creaked ominously on rusted hinges. The scene that greeted him stole the air from his lungs. Where once stood a vibrant neighborhood bustling with life, now lay a desolate wasteland stretching as far as the eye could see.

"Holy shit," Harrison breathed, his eyes wide with disbelief. "What the hell happened here?"

The acrid stench of decay assaulted his nostrils, causing him to gag reflexively. Covering his nose with the sleeve of his shirt, Harrison took a tentative step onto what used to be his front lawn, now nothing more than cracked earth and withered weeds.

"Okay, think," he said aloud, his voice trembling slightly. "You're in some kind of... apocalyptic version of your hometown. Priority one: find water, food, and shelter."

As he spoke, Harrison's gaze darted nervously from one crumbling structure to another, his senses on high alert for any sign of movement or danger. The eerie silence that blanketed the landscape only heightened his anxiety.

"This is insane," he muttered, running a hand through his unruly curls. "I'm sixteen, for crying out loud. I should be worrying about homework and girls, not... whatever the hell this is."

Despite the fear gnawing at his insides, a small part of Harrison couldn't help but feel a twinge of excitement. This was the kind of adventure he'd always dreamed about, the stuff of his wildest imaginings. But as he surveyed the lifeless streets before him, reality came crashing down.

"This isn't a game," he reminded himself sternly. "This is real, and if I don't get my act together, I might not make it out alive."

With renewed determination, Harrison set off down the desolate street, his eyes scanning the horizon for any sign of life or resources. As he walked, he couldn't shake the feeling that he was being watched, unseen eyes following his every move through the wasteland that had once been his home.

11 - 12

Harrison's footsteps echoed hollowly against the cracked pavement, the sound seeming to reverberate through the empty streets like a ghostly reminder of the life that once thrived here. He paused at an intersection, squinting against the harsh sunlight as he tried to get his bearings.

"Okay, think," he muttered to himself, his voice unnaturally loud in the stillness. "If this is really Bridgewater, then the old water tower should be... that way." He pointed towards what used to be the town center, now a jumble of twisted metal and shattered concrete.

As he made his way towards the tower, Harrison's mind raced with questions. "How did this happen? And why can't I remember anything?" He kicked at a piece of debris, sending it skittering across the road. "It's like I've been dropped into some messed-up video game, except there's no reset button."

The familiar landmarks of his hometown, now warped and decaying, only served to heighten his sense of disorientation. Where the Bulldog Bar and Grill once stood, there was now only a gaping hole, its edges jagged and menacing. The stained glass windows of Bridgewater Baptist Church lay shattered on the ground, their once-vibrant colors dulled by a thick layer of dust.

"This can't be real," Harrison whispered, his voice catching in his throat. "It just can't be."

But as the hours stretched on and the sun began to dip lower in the sky, the harsh reality of his situation became impossible to ignore. Harrison found himself talking out loud, if only to break the oppressive silence.

"Okay, Harrison, let's recap," he said, his tone dripping with false bravado. "You've woken up in some post-apocalyptic wasteland, with no memory of how you got here, and no idea what happened to everyone else. Just another Tuesday, right?"

He laughed bitterly, the sound echoing off the empty buildings around him. "God, what I wouldn't give for a cheeseburger from B&J Bistro right now. Or to hear Mom's voice, telling me everything's going to be okay."

As the reality of his isolation sank in, Harrison felt a lump forming in his throat. He swallowed hard, determined not to let his emotions get the better of him. "No time for a pity party, Miller," he chided himself. "You've got to figure this out. There has to be an explanation, and you're going to find it."

With renewed determination, he pressed on through the desolate streets, his eyes constantly scanning for any sign of life or clues to unravel the mystery of his surroundings. But as the day wore on and exhaustion began to set in, a nagging doubt crept into his mind.

"What if I'm the only one left?" he whispered, voicing his deepest fear. "What if this is all that's left of the world?"

13 - 14

The sun dipped below the horizon, casting long shadows across the barren landscape. Harrison's legs trembled, his muscles screaming in protest with each step. He stumbled, catching himself against a rusted lamppost.

"Shit," he muttered, his cocky facade crumbling. "I can't... I can't keep going like this."

His eyes, once bright with curiosity, now dulled by fatigue, scanned the desolate cityscape. A dilapidated structure loomed ahead, its windows dark and gaping like empty eye sockets.

"Well, it's not exactly the Ritz," Harrison quipped to himself, his voice hoarse. "But beggars can't be choosers, right?"

With a heavy sigh, he dragged himself towards the building, each step a monumental effort. As he approached, he couldn't shake the feeling of being watched. The hairs on the back of his neck stood on end.

"Hello?" he called out, his voice echoing in the eerie silence. "Anyone there? I come in peace, I swear. Just looking for a place to crash."

No response came, save for the whisper of wind through the abandoned streets. Harrison chuckled nervously, running a hand through his unruly curls.

"Great, now I'm talking to myself. Mom always said I had an overactive imagination."

He pushed open the creaking door, wincing at the sound. The interior was a mess of debris and shadows. Harrison's heart pounded as he made his way through the darkness, his fingers trailing along the wall for guidance.

"This is fine," he muttered. "Totally fine. Just like that time Dad and I went camping, right? Except, you know, with more apocalyptic vibes."

He settled into a corner, huddling against the cold concrete. As exhaustion washed over him, Harrison couldn't shake the unsettling feeling that eyes were upon him, watching from the shadows.

"If there's anyone out there," he whispered into the darkness, his voice trembling slightly, "I could really use a friend right now."

15 - 16

Harrison's eyes fluttered open, his body jerking awake at the slightest sound. The darkness pressed in around him, thick and oppressive. He rubbed his eyes, trying to shake off the lingering tendrils of fitful dreams.

"Well, that was about as restful as a rollercoaster ride," he muttered, his voice hoarse.

Memories of his past life flashed through his mind - birthday parties, family dinners, lazy summer afternoons. But they felt distant, like faded photographs. Harrison pressed his palms against his temples, trying to make sense of it all.

"Who am I now?" he wondered aloud, his words echoing in the empty room. "Am I still that kid from the suburbs? Or... something else?"

He stood up, stretching his aching muscles. "One thing's for sure, I'm definitely not cut out for this whole 'lone survivor' gig."

As dawn broke, Harrison ventured outside. The desolate landscape stretched before him, a stark reminder of his isolation. But then, something caught his eye - a figure in the distance, barely visible through the morning haze.

Harrison's heart raced. "No way," he breathed, squinting to get a better look. "It can't be..."

He took a tentative step forward, then another. The figure became clearer - a man, weathered by time and hardship, but with an unmistakable air of strength.

"Dad?" Harrison whispered, his voice a mix of hope and disbelief.

As he drew closer, a whirlwind of emotions surged through him. Relief, joy, confusion - all battling for dominance.

"If that's really you," Harrison called out, his voice cracking, "please tell me you brought a cheeseburger. I'm starving, and I've got about a million questions."

17 - 18

Harrison's voice carried across the barren wasteland, a fragile thread of hope in the desolate silence. "Father?" he called out again, louder this time, his heart pounding in his chest.

Drake Miller's head snapped up at the sound, his eyes widening in disbelief as they locked onto Harrison. For a moment, time seemed to stand still, the weight of their shared history hanging heavy between them.

"Harrison?" Drake's voice was barely above a whisper, rough with emotion. He took a halting step forward, his hands trembling at his sides. "Is that really you, son?"

Harrison swallowed hard, fighting back the lump in his throat. "Yeah, Dad. It's me. Though I gotta say, this whole post-apocalyptic reunion thing? Not exactly how I pictured our next father-son bonding experience."

Drake's weathered face cracked into a smile, a glimpse of the man Harrison remembered peeking through. "Always with the jokes, even now. Some things never change, do they?"

"Well, someone's gotta keep things light in the face of, you know, the end of the world and all," Harrison quipped, gesturing at the desolation around them. But his cocky grin faltered as he took in his father's appearance - the deep lines etched into his face, the haunted look in his eyes. "Dad, what happened to you? To... everything?"

Drake's expression grew somber, his gaze distant. "It's a long story, son. One I'm not sure I fully understand myself." He paused, studying Harrison intently. "But what about you? How did you end up here, in this... place?"

Harrison ran a hand through his unruly curls, a nervous habit from childhood. "Honestly? I have no idea. One minute I'm in this warehouse, the next I'm waking up in some twisted version of our old city. It's like I'm trapped in one of those parallel universe sci-fi flicks we used to watch."

As father and son stood facing each other, the air between them crackled with unspoken questions and long-buried emotions. Harrison felt a surge of conflicting feelings - relief at finding his father, confusion about their surroundings, and a gnawing fear of what might come next.

"Dad," he began hesitantly, "I know things weren't always great between us before, but... I'm really glad you're here." The words felt inadequate, but they were all he had.

Drake's eyes softened, a flicker of the loving father Harrison remembered shining through. "Me too, son. Me too." He reached out, clasping Harrison's shoulder firmly. "Whatever's happening, whatever brought us here - we'll figure it out together. I promise."

As they stood there, reunited against the backdrop of a shattered world, Harrison couldn't shake the feeling that this was just the beginning of something much bigger than either of them could imagine.

19 - 20

Drake's hand trembled slightly as it rested on Harrison's shoulder, his weathered face a canvas of conflicting emotions. "Harrison," he finally managed to say, his voice thick with a mixture of disbelief and hope, "Is it really you?"

The words hung in the air between them, heavy with the weight of lost time and unspoken regrets. Harrison felt a lump form in his throat, his own eyes brimming with unshed tears as he gazed at the man he'd once idolized, now looking so vulnerable and uncertain.

"Yes, Father. It's me," Harrison replied, his voice cracking slightly. He swallowed hard, fighting to maintain his composure. "I know I look different, older maybe, but it's still me."

Drake's eyes roamed over his son's face, drinking in every detail as if afraid Harrison might vanish at any moment. "You've grown so much," he murmured, his hand moving to cup Harrison's cheek. "How long has it been? How did you-"

"I don't know," Harrison interrupted, shaking his head. "Time feels... weird here. Fluid. One minute I'm sixteen, the next I'm waking up in some nightmare version of our old house." He paused, a flicker of his old cockiness returning. "Gotta say, Dad, your taste in alternate realities leaves a lot to be desired."

A ghost of a smile tugged at Drake's lips, but his eyes remained troubled. "Harrison, there's so much I need to tell you, so much you need to understand about what's happening."

Harrison nodded, his expression growing serious. "I know, Dad. I can feel it. Something big is going on, isn't it? Something to do with why we're both here, in this... place?"

21 - 22

Drake's eyes widened with a mixture of pride and concern as he took in his son's perceptiveness. "You always were too smart for your own good," he muttered, his hand falling away from Harrison's face. The weight of their shared predicament seemed to press down on him, aging him visibly in the span of a heartbeat.

Without warning, Drake surged forward, enveloping Harrison in a fierce embrace. His arms trembled as they wrapped around his son, clinging to him as if he were a lifeline in a storm-tossed sea. Harrison reciprocated instantly, burying his face in his father's shoulder, inhaling the familiar scent that brought a flood of memories cascading through his mind.

"I thought I'd lost you," Drake whispered, his voice raw with emotion. "When Gabriel took you, I... I didn't know if I'd ever see you again."

Harrison tightened his grip, fighting back the sob that threatened to escape. "I'm here, Dad," he choked out. "I'm here, and I'm not going anywhere."

They stood like that for what felt like an eternity, two figures locked in an embrace amidst the desolate landscape that surrounded them. The wind howled mournfully, whipping up eddies of dust that swirled around their feet, but neither man seemed to notice.

As they clung to each other, Harrison's mind raced. "Dad," he murmured, not lifting his head from Drake's shoulder, "what's happening to us? How are we here? And who's Gabriel?"

Drake's body tensed at the questions, but he didn't release his hold. "It's complicated, son," he replied, his voice muffled against Harrison's hair. "More complicated than I ever imagined possible. But I promise you, we'll figure this out together."

23 - 24

Harrison pulled back slightly, his eyes searching his father's weathered face. The desolate landscape around them seemed to fade into the background as he focused on Drake's tired eyes, noticing the new lines etched around them, testaments to the worry and strain of their separation.

"Dad," Harrison began, his voice cracking with a mix of fear and curiosity, "how did you end up here? What happened to Mom? And..." he paused, swallowing hard, "what's become of our home?"

Drake's shoulders sagged under the weight of his son's questions, his hand running through his disheveled hair - a nervous habit Harrison recognized from countless courtroom preparations. The older man opened his mouth to speak, but hesitated, his eyes darting across the barren wasteland surrounding them.

"Harrison," Drake finally said, his voice heavy with a regret that seemed to age him even further, "there's something you need to know. Something I should have told you long ago."

The teenager's heart raced, a chill running down his spine despite the arid heat. "What is it, Dad?" he pressed, his cocky teenage bravado faltering in the face of his father's grave demeanor.

Drake took a deep breath, his hand gripping Harrison's shoulder tightly. "Our family... our lives... they're not what we thought they were. The accident that tore us apart, it didn't just change our lives, it... it split reality itself."

Harrison's brow furrowed, his mind reeling. "Split reality? Dad, what are you talking about? That's impossible, it's-"

"I know how it sounds," Drake interrupted, his voice taking on the firm tone Harrison associated with his detective persona. "But I swear to you, it's the truth. And understanding it is the key to getting us home... if home even exists anymore."

As Drake's words hung in the air, Harrison felt the ground beneath his feet shift, as if reality itself was responding to this revelation. He looked at his father, seeing not just the tired detective he'd known, but a man carrying the weight of impossible truths.

"Tell me everything," Harrison demanded, his voice steadier than he felt. "No more secrets, Dad. Whatever's happening, whatever this is," he gestured at the wasteland around them, "I need to know. We're in this together now."

Drake nodded solemnly, a flicker of pride passing through his eyes at his son's determination. "You're right," he agreed, his hand squeezing Harrison's shoulder. "It's time you knew the whole story. But Harrison," he paused, his voice dropping to a near whisper, "once I tell you this, there's no going back. Are you sure you're ready?"

Harrison met his father's gaze, his jaw set with resolve. "I'm ready, Dad. Whatever it is, we'll face it together."

As Drake began to speak, the wind picked up around them, carrying whispers of a truth that would forever change their understanding of reality itself.

25 - 26

Drake's voice trembled as he began, his words carried on the desolate wind. "Richard Vega, the man I thought was my friend, my partner... he betrayed us all, Harrison. He's been working with Gabriel this whole time."

Harrison's stomach churned, his mind reeling at the implications Gabriel? The disfigured man who—"

"Yes," Drake cut in, his eyes haunted. "The very same. He's a madman with delusions of godhood, playing with forces beyond our comprehension."

As Drake spoke, the barren landscape seemed to pulse with an otherworldly energy, mirroring the growing dread in Harrison's heart. He listened, transfixed, as his father recounted the horrifying details of Linda's abduction.

"They took your mother, Harrison," Drake choked out, his composure cracking. "Gabriel's men snatched her right from our home. And I... I couldn't stop them."

Harrison's fists clenched involuntarily, rage and fear battling within him. "But why? What does Gabriel want with Mom?"

Drake's eyes met Harrison's, filled with a mixture of sorrow and determination. "It's all part of his grand plan. He believes he can manipulate reality itself, create portals between worlds. And somehow, our family is at the center of it all."

As the weight of their predicament settled over them, Harrison felt a chill run down his spine. The desolate wasteland around them suddenly seemed more sinister, as if it were a manifestation of Gabriel's twisted ambitions.

"Dad," Harrison whispered, his voice barely audible over the howling wind, "what are we going to do?"

Drake placed both hands on his son's shoulders, his grip firm and reassuring. "We're going to fight, Harrison. We're going to find your mother, stop Gabriel, and put an end to this madness. It won't be easy, and the odds are stacked against us, but we have something Gabriel doesn't."

Harrison looked up at his father, a glimmer of hope piercing through the darkness. "What's that?"

"Each other," Drake replied, a fierce determination in his eyes. "We're not alone in this, son. Together, we stand a chance of overcoming whatever Gabriel throws at us."

As father and son stood there, united in their resolve, the barren landscape seemed to shift around them. For a moment, Harrison could almost see a flicker of their old world superimposed over the wasteland a reminder of what they were fighting for, and the home they hoped to return to.

27 - 28

Harrison's brow furrowed as he processed his father's words, his mind reeling with the implications. The wind whipped around them, carrying dust and debris from the desolate landscape, a stark reminder of the strange reality they now inhabited.

"Blood? Portals between realities?" Harrison echoed, his voice a mix of disbelief and fascination. "Dad, this sounds like something out of one of my sci-fi novels."

Drake's eyes, tired but resolute, locked onto his son's. "I know it sounds incredible, Harrison, but it's the truth. Gabriel's blood... it has properties we can scarcely comprehend."

Harrison ran a hand through his unruly curls, his thoughts racing. "But how? I mean, what makes his blood so special?"

"It's not just his blood," Drake explained, his voice low and urgent. "It's ours too. We're connected to this somehow, in ways I'm only beginning to understand."

As his father spoke, Harrison felt a tingling sensation in his veins, as if his very blood was responding to the revelation. He glanced down at his hands, half expecting to see them glowing or changed in some way.

"So you're saying that Gabriel injected me with his blood, and that's what's allowing me to traverse between different timelines?" Harrison asked, struggling to wrap his mind around the concept. The words felt strange on his tongue, like speaking a foreign language.

Drake nodded, his expression grave. "Yes, that's exactly it. Gabriel's blood acts as a key, unlocking doors between realities that should remain closed."

Harrison's mind raced with questions, each more fantastical than the last. "But why me? Why us? And how did Gabriel figure all this out?"

As he awaited his father's response, Harrison couldn't help but feel a mix of terror and exhilaration. The world as he knew it had been turned upside down, yet a part of him – the part that had always dreamed of adventure and the extraordinary – couldn't help but feel a thrill at the possibilities that lay before them.

29 - 30

Drake's weathered face tightened, his dark eyes reflecting a mixture of determination and regret. "Yes, that's exactly it," he confirmed, his voice low and gravelly. "But we can't dwell on that now. We need to focus on finding a way out of here, back to our own reality."

The urgency in his father's tone sent a shiver down Harrison's spine. He ran a hand through his unruly curls, feeling the weight of their predicament settling on his shoulders. The desolate landscape around them seemed to blur at the edges, as if it might dissolve at any moment.

"Right," Harrison nodded, trying to muster the cocky confidence that usually came so easily to him. "Back to our reality. No biggie. Just hop between dimensions like we're catching the school bus." He let out a nervous laugh, his mind racing with the possibilities and dangers that lay ahead.

Swallowing hard, Harrison voiced the question that had been gnawing at him since his father's revelation. "But how do we do that? How do we even know if we're in the same reality as the one we came from?" The words tumbled out, laced with a mixture of curiosity and fear.

As he waited for his father's response, Harrison couldn't help but marvel at the absurdity of their situation. Here he was, standing in a world that felt like a post-apocalyptic movie set, discussing interdimensional travel with his dad as if it were the most normal thing in the world. A part of him wanted to laugh at the sheer impossibility of it all, while another part wanted to curl up and pretend this was all just a bizarre dream.

Drake's eyes narrowed as he considered Harrison's questions, his hand absentmindedly stroking his scruffy beard. The gesture reminded Harrison of countless evenings spent watching his father pore over case files, that same look of intense concentration etched on his face. It was oddly comforting, a slice of normalcy in their decidedly abnormal circumstances.

31 - 32

Drake's expression grew somber, the lines on his face deepening as he weighed his words carefully. "We don't know for sure," he admitted, his voice low and tinged with a mixture of frustration and determination. "But we have to try. We have to concentrate all our efforts on getting back to 2024, back to Linda and safety."

Harrison nodded, his teenage bravado faltering slightly as the gravity of their situation sank in. "And if we can't?" he asked, hating how small his voice sounded.

Drake's eyes softened, and he reached out to squeeze Harrison's shoulder. "We will," he said firmly. "We have to. Your mother... she's waiting for us, son."

As they spoke, an eerie change began to ripple through their surroundings. The desolate landscape that had seemed so solid just moments ago began to blur and shift, as if viewed through a heat haze. Harrison blinked rapidly, wondering if his eyes were playing tricks on him.

"Dad," he whispered, his voice tight with apprehension. "Are you seeing this?"

Drake nodded, his grip on Harrison's shoulder tightening. "I am. Stay close to me."

The air around them crackled with an otherworldly energy, raising the hair on Harrison's arms. He felt a strange sensation wash over him, as if reality itself were warping and twisting in response to their conversation. It was exhilarating and terrifying all at once, like being on the world's most intense roller coaster.

"What's happening?" Harrison asked, fighting to keep the tremor out of his voice. He wanted to appear brave, to be the son his father needed him to be, but the reality-bending scenario unfolding around them was testing the limits of his courage.

Drake's eyes darted around, taking in the shifting landscape with a mixture of awe and trepidation. "I think," he said slowly, "we might be onto something. This... this could be our way home."

33 - 34

Drake's eyes locked onto Harrison's, his gaze intense and unwavering. "We need to focus," he urged, his voice tinged with urgency. "Concentrate on where you want to go, on the life you want to return to. We can't let Gabriel's machinations hold us captive any longer."

Harrison swallowed hard, his heart pounding in his chest. "But how, Dad? How do we even begin to control... this?" He gestured at the swirling, shifting reality around them.

Drake's expression softened, a flicker of the father he used to be shining through the hardened exterior. "Trust me, son. Close your eyes. Picture home. Picture Linda. Picture everything we're fighting to get back to."

With a shared determination, father and son closed their eyes, their hands clasped tightly together. Harrison's mind raced, trying to conjure up images of the life they'd left behind. He thought of his mother's warm smile, the comforting scent of her perfume. He imagined the familiar creaks of their old house, the way sunlight filtered through the kitchen windows on lazy Sunday mornings.

"That's it," Drake murmured encouragingly. "Keep going. Remember the sound of Linda's laughter, the way she'd hum while cooking dinner. Remember the feeling of safety, of belonging."

As they focused, Harrison felt a strange sensation building within him, like a current of electricity coursing through his veins. He squeezed his father's hand tighter, clinging to the connection as the world around them seemed to dissolve.

"Dad," Harrison whispered, his voice trembling. "I can see it. I can almost feel it. It's like we're there, but not quite."

Drake's voice was strained with concentration. "Hold onto it, Harrison. Don't let go. This is our chance. We have to break free from Gabriel's influence, from this twisted reality he's trapped us in."

The air crackled with intensity, and Harrison felt as if he were being pulled in a thousand directions at once. His mind flooded with memories – birthdays, holidays, quiet evenings at home – each one a lifeline to the world they were desperately trying to reach.

"I love you, Dad," Harrison choked out, tears streaming down his face. "Whatever happens, I want you to know that."

Drake's grip tightened, his voice thick with emotion. "I love you too, son. More than you could ever know. Now, let's go home."

35 - 36

A kaleidoscope of swirling colors engulfed them, reality bending and twisting like a funhouse mirror. Harrison's stomach lurched as he felt himself hurtling through a void, his father's hand still clasped tightly in his own.

"Dad!" he cried out, his voice lost in the maelstrom. "What's happening?"

Drake's response came as if from a great distance. "Hold on, Harrison! Don't let go!"

The sensation intensified, a dizzying rush of vertigo threatening to tear them apart. Harrison's mind raced, clinging desperately to thoughts of home, of safety, of normalcy. Just when he thought he couldn't endure another moment, everything stopped.

Harrison's eyes snapped open, his heart pounding. He found himself lying in his own bed, sunlight streaming through the familiar curtains of his room. "What the..." he muttered, sitting up abruptly and running his hands over his face. "Was it all a dream?"

He glanced around, taking in the posters on his walls, the clutter on his desk. Everything was exactly as he remembered it, yet something felt... off. Harrison swung his legs over the side of the bed, his bare feet touching the cool hardwood floor.

"Dad?" he called out, his voice wavering. "Mom? Is anyone home?"

Silence answered him. Harrison stood, his legs shaky, and made his way to the bedroom door. As he reached for the handle, a chill ran down his spine. How had he gotten here? The last thing he remembered was being in Gabriel's clutches, and then...

"Focus, Harrison," he told himself, taking a deep breath. "One step at a time. Figure out what's going on."

He opened the door, peering out into the hallway. The house seemed eerily quiet, devoid of the usual morning bustle. "Hello?" he called again, his voice echoing through the empty corridors.

As Harrison made his way downstairs, a nagging doubt gnawed at him. Was this really his home? Or was it another of Gabriel's twisted illusions? He paused at the bottom of the stairs, his eyes darting around the living room.

"Think, Harrison," he muttered to himself. "What would Dad do in this situation?"

The thought of his father sent a pang through his chest. Where was Drake now? Had he made it back too? Harrison's mind raced with possibilities, each more unsettling than the last.

He moved to the front window, peering out at the familiar neighborhood. Everything looked normal, peaceful even. But appearances could be deceiving, he reminded himself. After everything they'd been through, Harrison knew better than to trust his eyes alone.

As he stood there, wrestling with his doubts, a sudden realization hit him. "The notebook," he whispered, his eyes widening. "If this is really our world, it should still be where I left it."

With renewed purpose, Harrison bounded back up the stairs, his heart pounding in his chest. He burst into his room, making a beeline for his desk. There, buried beneath a stack of comic books, lay the worn leather notebook.

His hands trembling, Harrison opened it to the page with the intricate dragon symbol. "It's here," he breathed, relief washing over him. "It's really here."

But as he stared at the familiar drawing, a new wave of uncertainty crashed over him. If he was truly home, safe from Gabriel's machinations, why did he feel so... alone?

37 - 37

Harrison traced the dragon symbol with his finger, a chill running down his spine as he remembered Gabriel's piercing gaze and cryptic words. He closed the notebook with a sharp snap, his mind racing.

"I need to call Dad," he muttered, fumbling for his phone. As he dialed, Harrison paced the room, his free hand running through his hair. The line rang once, twice, three times before a familiar voice answered.

"Harrison?" Drake's voice was thick with emotion. "Are you alright? Where are you?"

Relief flooded through Harrison. "Dad! I'm home, I'm safe. Are you still at the hospital?"

"Yes, I'm here. But Harrison, listen to me carefully," Drake's tone turned urgent. "We can't be sure we're out of danger yet. Gabriel—"

"I know," Harrison interrupted, his voice dropping to a whisper as if the very walls might be listening. "He's still out there. Dad, what do we do now?"

There was a pause on the other end of the line, and Harrison could almost see his father's furrowed brow as he considered their next move. Finally, Drake spoke, his words measured and deliberate.

"We need to meet. Not here, not at home. Somewhere public, but quiet. The old bookstore on Maple Street, do you remember it?"

Harrison nodded, then realized his father couldn't see him. "Yeah, I remember. When?"

"One hour. And Harrison," Drake's voice softened, "be careful. We don't know what Gabriel's capable of."

As Harrison ended the call, he couldn't shake the feeling of being watched. He moved to the window, scanning the street below. Everything looked normal, but the hairs on the back of his neck stood on end.

"Get it together," he muttered to himself, taking a deep breath. "You've made it this far. You can do this."

With trembling hands, Harrison gathered the notebook and a few other essentials. As he headed for the door, he caught a glimpse of himself in the hallway mirror. For a split second, he could have sworn he saw Gabriel's scarred face staring back at him, those piercing eyes boring into his soul.

Harrison blinked, and the illusion vanished. But the unease remained, a constant companion as he stepped out into the world, uncertain of what lay ahead but determined to face it head-on.

Haunted Confessions

1 - 2

Drake's eyes bore into Detective Kierstead's, his haunted gaze silently pleading for her to believe the impossible tale he was about to unfold. The harsh fluorescent lights of the hospital room cast deep shadows across his face, accentuating the lines of exhaustion etched into his features.

"It was like stepping into a nightmare," Drake began, his voice barely above a whisper. "The sky was a sickly yellow, choked with ash and smoke. Buildings lay in ruins, their skeletal frames reaching toward the poisoned heavens like the fingers of the damned."

He paused, swallowing hard as the vivid memories assaulted his senses. The acrid taste of sulfur on his tongue, the crunch of pulverized concrete beneath his feet, the eerie silence broken only by the howling wind—it all came rushing back with brutal clarity.

Detective Kierstead leaned forward, her brow furrowed in concentration as she struggled to process Drake's words. Her analytical mind rebelled against the fantastical nature of his account, yet she couldn't deny the raw emotion in his voice.

"Harrison and I wandered for what felt like an eternity," Drake continued, his hands clenching into fists at his sides. "We saw... things. Terrible things. Shadows that moved of their own accord, whispers in the darkness that spoke of unspeakable horrors."

He fell silent, lost in the grip of the memories. Kierstead's voice cut through the heavy silence, tinged with a mix of skepticism and curiosity. "So, you're saying that you and Harrison were able to focus your energy and will yourselves back to this timeline?"

Drake met her gaze, his eyes blazing with an intensity that made Kierstead's breath catch in her throat. "I know how it sounds," he said, his voice low and urgent. "But I swear to you, it's the truth. We stood there, in that godforsaken wasteland, and we concentrated every fiber of our being on coming home."

As he spoke, Drake's mind raced with the implications of what they had experienced. Had they truly traversed the boundaries between realities? Or had it all been some kind of shared delusion, born of fear and desperation? The weight of uncertainty pressed down on him, threatening to crush his fragile grip on sanity.

3 - 4

Drake nodded, his expression serious, the lines on his face deepening as he relived the harrowing experience. "Yes, that's exactly it. It was like we were in some kind of shared dream, and together, we were able to visualize our way back to our own reality." His voice wavered slightly, betraying the emotional toll of their ordeal. "We focused on memories of this world, of our home, of the people we love. It was as if we were weaving a tapestry of our lives with our minds, creating a bridge back to where we belonged."

Detective Kierstead leaned forward, her piercing eyes fixed on Drake's face, searching for any sign of deception or confusion. She found none. Instead, she saw only raw sincerity and a haunted look that spoke volumes about the trauma he'd endured. Her analytical mind grappled with the fantastical nature of his story, trying to reconcile it with her understanding of the world.

"I know it sounds impossible," Drake continued, running a hand through his disheveled hair. "Hell, if someone had told me this story a year ago, I'd have thought they were insane. But after everything I've seen, everything I've experienced..." He trailed off, lost in thought for a moment before meeting Kierstead's gaze again. "The boundaries between realities are more porous than we ever imagined, Kier. It's terrifying and awe-inspiring all at once."

Kierstead pondered Drake's words, her mind racing with questions and possibilities. The idea of traversing between different timelines seemed almost too fantastical to believe, yet Drake's earnest demeanor left little room for doubt. She found herself torn between her instincts as a detective, which demanded hard evidence, and her growing trust in Drake's integrity.

"I want to believe you, Drake," she said finally, her voice soft but firm. "It's just... it goes against everything we know about the nature of reality. How can we be sure that what you experienced wasn't some kind of shared hallucination?"

Drake's eyes flashed with a mixture of frustration and understanding. "I've asked myself the same question a thousand times," he admitted. "But the things we saw, the physical toll it took on us... it was real, Kier. As real as you and me sitting here right now."

5 - 6

Kierstead leaned forward, her brow furrowed in concentration, her voice dropping to a near whisper as she pressed, "And you're certain that it was Harrison you saw in that alternate reality?"

Drake's eyes flickered with a storm of emotions - pain, love, and an unwavering certainty that seemed to radiate from his very core. He nodded, his jaw clenching as he fought to keep his voice steady. "Yes, I'm certain. It was him, without a doubt," he said, his words heavy with the weight of his experience. "He looked older, worn down by the harshness of that world, but it was unmistakably my son."

As he spoke, Drake's mind raced back to that moment, the image of Harrison's gaunt face and haunted eyes seared into his memory. He could still feel the ache in his chest, the overwhelming desire to protect his child from the cruel reality he'd found himself in. "God, Kier, you should have seen him," Drake continued, his voice thick with emotion. "He was a man, not the boy I remember. His eyes... they'd seen things no person should ever have to witness."

Kierstead watched Drake intently, noting the way his hands trembled slightly as he recounted the encounter. "How can you be so sure it wasn't some kind of trick?" she asked, her detective's instincts warring with her growing belief in Drake's story.

Drake's gaze snapped to meet hers, a fire burning in his eyes. "Because I know my son," he said fiercely. "I may have failed him in the past, prioritized my work over our relationship, but I'd recognize Harrison anywhere, in any reality. It was him, Kier. And seeing him there, in that hellish place... it's lit a fire in me. I have to find him, to make things right. I can't fail him again."

As he spoke, Drake's resolve solidified, his earlier exhaustion giving way to a steely determination. He leaned forward, his voice low and intense. "I don't care if I have to tear apart the fabric of reality itself. I'm going to bring my son home."

7 - 8

Kierstead absorbed this revelation in silence, her sharp eyes studying Drake's face intently. The weight of his words hung heavy in the air, filling the room with an almost palpable tension. She leaned back in her chair, her brow furrowed in deep concentration as she processed the implications of Drake's extraordinary tale.

"If what you're saying is true," Kierstead began, her voice barely above a whisper, "then everything we thought we knew about the nature of reality... it's all up for grabs." She shook her head, a mix of awe and disbelief etched across her features. "Multiple timelines, alternate realities... it's like something out of a science fiction novel."

Drake nodded grimly, his eyes distant as he relived the surreal experience. "I know how it sounds, Kier. If I hadn't lived it myself, I wouldn't believe it either. But it's real. And it's terrifying."

Kierstead's analytical mind raced, trying to piece together the puzzle before her. She leaned forward, her voice quiet yet insistent as she asked, "And Gabriel? Did you encounter him in this alternate reality?"

The mention of Gabriel's name sent a visible shudder through Drake's body. He clenched his fists, knuckles turning white as he fought to maintain his composure. "Gabriel," he spat the name out like a curse, "No, he wasn't there. At least, not physically. But his presence... it was like a shadow looming over everything. I could feel him, Kier. Even in that other world, his influence was everywhere."

Kierstead's eyes narrowed, her detective instincts kicking into high gear. "What do you mean, his influence? How could you tell?"

Drake ran a hand through his disheveled hair, struggling to find the words to describe the indescribable. "It's hard to explain. But there were symbols, markings... they were similar to the ones we've seen here, associated with his cult. And the way people spoke about him... it was like he was some kind of dark messiah, bridging the gap between realities."

As Drake spoke, Kierstead's mind whirled with possibilities, each more unsettling than the last. If Gabriel truly had the power to influence multiple realities, the scope of their investigation had just expanded exponentially. She suppressed a shudder, forcing herself to focus on the task at hand.

"We need to dig deeper into Gabriel's past," she said, her voice taking on a determined edge. "If he's able to manipulate reality itself, we need to understand how and why. It might be the key to finding Harrison and putting an end to all of this."

Drake nodded, a flicker of hope igniting in his eyes. "Whatever it takes, Kier. I'm ready to face whatever comes next. For Harrison's sake, and for all of us."

As they sat there, united in their resolve, neither of them could shake the feeling that they were standing on the precipice of something far greater and more terrifying than they had ever imagined. The boundaries between realities were blurring, and in the shadows between worlds, a malevolent force was waiting, ready to plunge them all into darkness.

9 - 10

Drake's expression darkened at the mention of Gabriel's name, his jaw clenching with barely restrained anger. The lines etched deep into his face seemed to deepen, shadows dancing across his features in the dim light of the hospital room. He took a deep breath, his eyes flickering with a mix of rage and fear.

"No, it wasn't him," Drake said, his voice low and gravelly. "It was... an illusion, a trick of the mind." He paused, running a hand through his disheveled hair. "But it doesn't matter. What matters is that we're back here now, and we need to focus on finding Harrison and putting an end to this madness once and for all."

Detective Kierstead leaned forward, her piercing gaze locked onto Drake's face. She could feel the weight of his words, the desperation in his voice. Her mind raced, trying to piece together the fragments of this bizarre puzzle.

"You're right," she said, nodding slowly. "We can't let ourselves get distracted by what-ifs and maybes. Harrison is our priority." She hesitated for a moment, then added, "But Drake, we can't ignore the implications of what you've experienced. If Gabriel has the power to manipulate reality itself..."

Drake cut her off, his voice sharp. "I know, Kier. Believe me, I know. But right now, all I can think about is my son. Everything else... it's just noise."

Kierstead watched as Drake's hands clenched and unclenched, a physical manifestation of the turmoil within him. She felt a surge of admiration for his unwavering focus, even in the face of such overwhelming circumstances.

"Agreed," she said, her resolve hardening. "We'll do whatever it takes to bring Harrison home and stop Gabriel from hurting anyone else." She leaned back in her chair, her mind already formulating a plan. "I'll put out an APB on Gabriel, see if we can track down any leads on his whereabouts. And we should look into any properties he might own or have connections to."

Drake nodded, a glimmer of hope breaking through the storm of emotions on his face. "Thank you, Kier. I don't know what I'd do without you on this case."

As they sat there, united in their determination, Kierstead couldn't help but wonder what other impossible truths they might uncover in their search for Harrison. The boundaries of reality had been shattered, and she knew that nothing would ever be the same again.

11 - 12

The autumn sun filtered through the hospital room window, casting long shadows across Drake's haggard face. His dark eyes, usually sharp and calculating, now held a haunted look that spoke volumes about the ordeal he'd endured. Detective Kierstead leaned forward in her chair, her posture taut with anticipation.

"We're in uncharted territory here, Drake," Kierstead said, her voice low and intense. "But if anyone can navigate this, it's us."

Drake ran a hand through his disheveled hair, exhaling slowly. "You're right, Kier. We've come too far to back down now. Harrison's counting on us."

As he spoke, a palpable energy seemed to crackle between them, a shared resolve that transcended words. Drake's mind raced with possibilities, each more outlandish than the last. He found himself yearning for the simplicity of his old life, when the biggest challenge was winning a difficult case in court.

"What if—" Drake began, but was abruptly cut off by the shrill ring of Kierstead's cell phone.

The detective's hand flew to her pocket, retrieving the device with practiced ease. As she glanced at the caller ID, her eyes widened, and her breath caught in her throat. She looked up at Drake, an expression of disbelief etched across her features.

"Drake," she whispered, her voice trembling slightly, "I think you need to hear this."

With shaking hands, Kierstead answered the call, her gaze never leaving Drake's face. The tension in the room was palpable, thick enough to cut with a knife. Drake leaned forward, every muscle in his body coiled tight, ready to spring into action at a moment's notice.

As Kierstead listened to the voice on the other end of the line, her expression morphed from disbelief to shock, then to a cautious hope. Drake watched, his heart pounding so hard he could feel it in his temples, as relief flooded Kierstead's face.

She glanced at Drake, her eyes wide with a mix of emotions he couldn't quite decipher. The world seemed to slow down, each second stretching into an eternity as Drake waited for her to speak, to share whatever earth-shattering news had just come through that phone call.

13 - 14

Detective Kierstead's voice cut through the tension, her words barely above a whisper but carrying the weight of the world. "Hello? Harrison, is that you?" she asked, her voice tinged with urgency.

Drake's world tilted on its axis. His son's name, spoken aloud, sent a jolt of electricity through his body. He leaned forward, straining to hear any response from the other end of the line. His mind raced, a whirlwind of emotions threatening to overwhelm him. Could it really be Harrison? After everything they'd been through, all the impossible journeys across realities, was it possible his son had found his way back?

Drake's eyes widened in shock as he watched Kierstead's reaction, his heart pounding in his chest. The detective's face was a canvas of emotions – relief, disbelief, and a cautious hope that mirrored his own feelings. She nodded slightly, her brow furrowed in concentration as she listened intently to the voice on the other end.

"Is it really him?" Drake whispered, his voice hoarse with emotion. He ran a hand through his disheveled hair, a nervous habit he'd developed during this ordeal. "Kier, please, tell me what's happening."

Kierstead held up a finger, silencing him as she continued to listen. Drake's fingers dug into the arms of his chair, his knuckles turning white with the effort of restraining himself from snatching the phone away. Could it be true? Was his son really back at the house? The possibility seemed too good to be true, yet hope bloomed in his chest, threatening to burst forth at any moment.

"I can't believe it," Drake muttered to himself, his mind racing through the implications. "After everything we've been through, all the impossible things we've seen... Harrison, please be okay. Please be real."

15 - 16

Kierstead's expression softened, her eyes glistening with relief as she spoke into the phone, her voice trembling slightly, "Thank goodness you're okay, Harrison. Where are you exactly? We'll come to get you right away." She paused, listening intently, her free hand clenching and unclenching at her side.

Drake leaned forward, his breath caught in his throat. Every fiber of his being strained to hear his son's voice, to confirm that this wasn't some cruel trick of fate. His mind raced with possibilities, memories of their harrowing journey through the alternate reality flashing before his eyes.

"Is he hurt?" Drake mouthed urgently, his dark eyes searching Kierstead's face for any sign of concern. The detective shook her head slightly, offering a reassuring smile that did little to quell the storm of emotions raging within him.

After what felt like an eternity, Kierstead lowered the phone, her expression mirroring Drake's own disbelief. She turned to him, her voice barely above a whisper, "Drake, your son, he's back at the house. Says he just woke up there."

The words hit Drake like a physical force, knocking the air from his lungs. He staggered to his feet, his mind reeling. "How is that possible?" he breathed, running a hand over his scruffy beard. "We were just there, Kier. He wasn't... I mean, we would have seen him, right?"

Kierstead shook her head, her brow furrowed in confusion. "I don't know, Drake. But it's him. It's really him."

Drake's heart thundered in his chest, a mix of elation and fear coursing through his veins. "We need to go," he said, his voice thick with emotion. "Now. I need to see him, to make sure he's real, that he's okay. Give me the phone. I need to speak with him."

17 - 18

Drake's heart leaped with unbridled joy, a surge of adrenaline coursing through his veins like liquid fire. His tired eyes, once dulled by the weight of his dual existence, now blazed with renewed purpose. Without a moment's hesitation, he sprang to his feet, nearly toppling the nearby chair in his haste.

"Harrison," he whispered, his voice cracking with emotion. The name hung in the air, a talisman against the darkness that had threatened to consume him. Drake's mind raced, a kaleidoscope of memories flashing before him—Harrison's first steps, his kindergarten graduation, the fateful day of the accident that had torn their world asunder.

Turning to Kierstead, Drake's face was a canvas of conflicting emotions—hope warring with disbelief, joy grappling with fear. "We need to go. Now," he said, his voice trembling like a leaf in a storm. His hands shook as he fumbled for his jacket, fingers clumsy with urgency.

"Drake, wait," Kierstead cautioned, her tone gentle but firm. "We need to approach this carefully. What if—"

"What if it's not real?" Drake finished, his dark eyes meeting hers. "What if it's another trick, another fracture in reality?" He paused, drawing a shaky breath. "I can't... I won't let fear hold me back, Kier. Not now. Not when he's so close."

As they moved towards the door, Drake's mind whirled with possibilities. Was this the universe's way of mending the rift? Or was it merely setting the stage for a crueler twist of fate? Whatever awaited them, Drake knew one thing with certainty—he would face it head-on, for Harrison, for the chance to be the father he should have been all along.

19 - 20

Kierstead nodded, her sharp features softening with understanding. "Alright, let's go," she said, her voice steady as she matched Drake's urgent pace.

They burst through the hospital doors, the crisp evening air hitting Drake's face like a shock of cold water. He inhaled deeply, the scent of autumn leaves and distant rain filling his lungs. As they raced towards Kierstead's waiting car, Drake's thoughts tumbled over one another, a maelstrom of hope and fear.

"What if he doesn't remember?" Drake blurted out, his hand gripping the car door handle. "What if he's not the same Harrison?"

Kierstead paused, her piercing gaze meeting Drake's. "Then we'll face it together," she assured him, her tone firm yet compassionate. "Whatever version of Harrison we find, he's still your son."

As they sped through the darkening streets, Drake's heart hammered against his ribcage. The familiar landmarks of his neighborhood blurred past, each one bringing him closer to a reunion he'd dreamed of but never truly believed possible.

"I've missed so much," Drake murmured, more to himself than to Kierstead. "All those years I spent chasing success, thinking I was securing our future... and now..."

"Now you have a second chance," Kierstead interjected, her eyes flicking between the road and Drake's anguished expression. "Don't waste it on regrets, Drake. Focus on what's ahead."

Drake nodded, swallowing hard against the lump in his throat. As they turned onto his street, a wave of nostalgia washed over him. The old oak tree where Harrison had built his first treehouse, the driveway where they'd spent countless hours shooting hoops—each memory hit him with the force of a physical blow.

"We're here," Kierstead announced, bringing the car to a stop outside Drake's home. For a moment, Drake sat frozen, his hand on the door handle, overwhelmed by the enormity of what awaited him inside.

"Whatever happens," he said, his voice barely above a whisper, "thank you, Kier. For everything."

With a deep breath, Drake stepped out of the car, his eyes fixed on the front door of his home. Each step towards it felt like a journey across worlds, bringing him closer to the son he'd thought lost forever.

21 - 22

Drake's trembling hand grasped the cold doorknob, his heart thundering in his chest as he pushed the door open. The familiar creak of hinges echoed through the entryway, and his eyes darted frantically around the room, searching for any sign of Harrison. Suddenly, there he was—standing in the doorway of the living room, a lanky silhouette backlit by the warm glow of the table lamp.

"Dad?" Harrison's voice cracked, a mixture of relief and disbelief.

Drake felt his breath catch in his throat, overwhelmed by the sight of his son. Harrison looked older, more weathered than the boy in his memories, but unmistakably alive. The mop of curly hair was longer, wilder, framing a face that had lost some of its boyish roundness. But those eyes—those bright, curious eyes—were exactly as Drake remembered.

"Harrison," Drake breathed, his voice barely above a whisper. "Is it really you?"

For a moment, time seemed to stand still. Father and son locked eyes, a flood of unspoken emotions passing between them. Drake's mind raced, grappling with the surreal nature of their reunion. How could he explain the inexplicable journey that had brought them back together?

Without warning, Harrison closed the distance between them in three long strides, throwing himself into his father's arms. Drake staggered back, nearly knocked off balance by the force of the embrace and the torrent of emotions it unleashed.

"I thought I'd never see you again," Harrison choked out, his face buried in Drake's shoulder. "Everything was so messed up, Dad. I was lost, and scared, and—"

"Shh, it's okay," Drake soothed, his own tears flowing freely now. He held Harrison tightly, one hand cradling the back of his son's head as if he were still a small child. "I'm here now. We're together."

As they clung to each other, Drake's mind whirled with a thousand questions, a thousand apologies, a thousand promises. But for now, all that mattered was this moment—the solid warmth of his son in his arms, the miracle of their reunion.

"How did you find your way back?" Drake asked softly, pulling back just enough to look into Harrison's eyes.

Harrison shook his head, his brow furrowing in confusion. "I... I don't know. One minute I was somewhere else, somewhere dark and cold, and then... I just woke up here. Like coming out of a nightmare."

Drake nodded, understanding all too well the disorienting nature of shifting between realities. "We have so much to talk about, son. So much to figure out. But right now, I just want you to know how sorry I am for everything that's happened. For not being there when you needed me most."

Harrison's lips quirked into a small, sad smile. "You're here now, Dad. That's what matters."

As they stood there, locked in their embrace, Drake made a silent vow. No more chasing success at the expense of his family. No more divided loyalties or parallel lives. From this moment on, he would dedicate himself to being the father Harrison deserved—in this reality and any other.

23 - 23

Drake's heart swelled with a mixture of joy and fierce protectiveness as he held Harrison close, his fingers gripping the fabric of his son's shirt as if afraid he might vanish again at any moment. The familiar scent of Harrison's shampoo, the sound of his breathing—every sensation was a precious reminder that this was real, that they were truly reunited.

"I thought I'd lost you," Drake murmured, his voice thick with emotion. "God, Harrison, I've been searching for you across realities. I've seen things you wouldn't believe."

Harrison pulled back slightly, his eyes wide with curiosity and concern. "Across realities? Dad, what else has happened?"

"It's a long story," Drake said finally, running a hand through his disheveled hair. "One I'm not sure I fully understand myself. But I promise, I'll tell you everything."

Detective Kierstead cleared her throat softly, reminding them of her presence. Drake turned, keeping one arm around Harrison's shoulders, unwilling to break contact completely.

"I hate to interrupt," Kierstead said, her usually stern expression softened by the emotion of the moment, "but we need to make sure Harrison is okay. And... we need to talk about Gabriel."

At the mention of Gabriel's name, Drake felt Harrison stiffen beside him. A cold dread settled in his stomach as he realized that their ordeal might not be over yet. But as he looked at his son, saw the determination in his eyes, Drake knew that whatever came next, they would face it together.

"You're right," Drake nodded to Kierstead, then turned back to Harrison. "Son, I know you've been through hell, but we need to know what happened. Are you up for talking about it?"

Harrison took a deep breath, squaring his shoulders. "Yeah, Dad. I think I am. But first... can we just sit down for a minute? I feel like I haven't rested in years."

As they moved towards the living room couch, Drake's mind raced with questions and theories. What had Harrison experienced? How had he found his way back? And most importantly, what did Gabriel have to do with all of this? But for now, he pushed those thoughts aside, focusing on the warmth of his son beside him, the miracle of their reunion. Whatever challenges lay ahead, they would face them as a family—whole and united at last.

The Burden of your Choices

Green World – 2024

1 - 2

The weight of Harrison's limp body pressed against my shoulder, each step a painful reminder of the choices that had led us to this moment. The night air clung to my skin, thick with an oppressive silence that seemed to mock my inner turmoil. As I trudged along the deserted street, the distant glow of the Miller house flickered like a beacon of hope and damnation intertwined.

"Almost there, kid," I muttered, more to myself than to Harrison's unconscious form. My voice sounded hollow, swallowed by the darkness that surrounded us. I could feel the rapid beating of my heart, a stark contrast to the eerie stillness of the night.

Harrison's curly hair brushed against my cheek, and I was struck by how young he looked, how vulnerable. His face, usually alive with mischief and curiosity, was now pale and expressionless. The sight sent a pang of guilt through my chest, threatening to overwhelm me.

"You should be waking up very soon," I said softly, my words falling flat in the oppressive silence. I adjusted my grip on Harrison, his dead weight a constant reminder of my actions. "I'm sorry it had to come to this, but you left me no choice. You understand that don't you?"

The question hung in the air, unanswered. Of course, he couldn't respond, and part of me was grateful for that. What would I say if he were awake? How could I explain the tangled web of lies and half-truths that had led us here?

As I walked, my mind raced with possibilities, each more dire than the last. What if Harrison didn't wake up? What if Linda found out what I'd done? The thought of her face, filled with disappointment and horror, filled me with excitement.

"We're going to fix this," I promised, my voice barely above a whisper. "I'm going to make everything right, Harrison. I swear it."

But even as the words left my mouth, I couldn't shake the feeling that I was lying – to Harrison, to myself, to the very night that bore witness to our silent procession. The weight of my actions hung heavy on my shoulders, far heavier than Harrison's unconscious form.

As we neared the Miller house, I could feel my resolve wavering. The façade of control I had carefully constructed was beginning to crumble, revealing the scared and desperate man beneath. I took a deep breath, steeling myself for what was to come.

"Almost there," I repeated, the words a mantra against the encroaching darkness. "Just hold on, Harrison. Everything's going to be different very soon."

But as I gazed at his peaceful face, twisted in a slumber that belied the turmoil raging within him, I couldn't help but wonder if anything would ever be okay again.

3 - 4

The Miller house loomed before us, its familiar silhouette now ominous and foreboding. Shadows danced across the lawn, their elongated forms seeming to reach for us with grasping fingers. I swallowed hard, my throat dry as sandpaper.

"Home sweet home," I muttered, the words tasting like ash in my mouth. Harrison's weight shifted on my shoulder, and I stumbled slightly, my exhaustion threatening to overtake me.

As we approached the front door, I couldn't shake the feeling of being watched. My eyes darted from shadow to shadow, half-expecting to see Linda's accusing gaze or Detective Miller's stern face materializing from the darkness.

As I crossed the threshold, the house seemed to close in around us. The air felt thick, oppressive, laden with secrets and unspoken fears. I glanced down at Harrison's pale face, a wave of guilt washing over me.

The darkness of the house pressed in, a stark reminder of the twisted path I'd chosen. This house held a father's love, perverted into something unrecognizable. I'd told myself it was all for Harrison, for Linda, for my future family. But standing here, in the suffocating quiet of our home, I couldn't help but wonder if I'd lost sight of what truly mattered along the way.

5 - 6

With a heavy sigh, I gently lowered Harrison's limp form onto his bed, his curly hair splaying out against the cold mattress. The sight of him, so vulnerable and innocent, sent a sharp pang through my chest. I knelt beside him, my hand hovering uncertainly over his cheek.

"What have I done to you, kid?" I whispered, my voice thick with emotion. "How did we end up here?"

Harrison's chest rose and fell steadily, his face peaceful in unconsciousness. But I knew the moment he woke, that peace would shatter. The questions, the accusations, the fear – it would all come flooding back.

A wave of exhaustion crashed over me, threatening to pull me under. I stumbled to my feet, bracing myself against the wall. The room spun, memories and regrets swirling together in a dizzying haze.

"Can't rest yet," I muttered, shaking my head to clear it. "Too much left to do. Too many loose ends."

I glanced at the clock – 7:27 PM. Time was running out. Soon, Harrison would wake, and with him, the reckoning I'd been avoiding for so long.

"I know you won't understand, son," I said, my voice barely above a whisper. "Hell, I barely understand it myself anymore. But I promise you, everything I've done... it was all for us. For the betterment of the human race."

The lie tasted bitter on my tongue, but I clung to it like a lifeline. It was all I had left.

7 - 8

With a heavy sigh, I turned away from Harrison's prone form, my footsteps echoing in the oppressive silence of the Miller house. The weight of my decisions bore down on me, each step a Herculean effort as I made my way to the laundry room. The darkness seemed to pulse around me, a living entity threatening to swallow me whole.

"Get it together," I hissed to myself, clenching my fists until my nails bit into my palms. "You've come too far to fall apart now."

I positioned myself in the shadows of the dimly lit laundry room, my heart pounding a staccato rhythm against my ribs as I waited. Minutes stretched into eternities; the air thick with anticipation.

Finally, a soft groan broke the silence. Harrison stirred, his eyelids fluttering open, confusion etched across his youthful features. He reached up with a trembling hand, fingers gingerly probing the bruise forming on his temple.

"What... where am I?" he mumbled, his voice hoarse and uncertain.

I held my breath, watching as he struggled to make sense of his surroundings. The cockiness that usually colored his speech was gone, replaced by a vulnerability that made my chest ache.

"Mom?" Harrison called out, a tremor in his voice. "Dad? Is anyone there?"

The urge to rush to his side, to comfort him, was almost overwhelming. But I remained rooted in place, knowing that revealing myself now would unravel everything.

As Harrison's confusion gave way to frustration, I couldn't help but marvel at his resilience. Even in the face of the unknown, that spark of defiance – so much like his mother's – refused to be extinguished.

I watched him struggle to his feet, my heart breaking for the innocence I was about to shatter. The night was far from over, and the darkness that surrounded us threatened to consume everything in its path.

9 - 10

Harrison's eyes darted around the dimly lit laundry room, his gaze lingering on the shadowy corners as if expecting someone to leap out at any moment. I could see the gears turning in his mind, that quick intelligence I'd always admired now working against me as he pieced together the situation.

I pressed myself further into the shadows, my heart thundering so loudly I was sure he'd hear it. Every fiber of my being screamed to reveal myself, to explain, to comfort him. But I remained still, a silent observer to my son's mounting distress.

Harrison ran a hand through his unruly curls, wincing as his fingers brushed against the bruise on his head. "Okay, Harrison, think," he said to himself, his tone carrying a forced bravado. "You've read enough mystery novels. What would the hero do in this situation?"

Despite the gravity of the moment, I felt a flicker of pride at his attempt to stay calm and logical. It was so quintessentially Harrison – facing the unknown with a mix of imagination and determination.

As I watched him piece together the fragments of his ordeal, my mind raced with the implications of our encounter. How much did he remember? How much could I reveal without destroying everything?

Harrison's next words sent a chill down my spine. "Dad," he whispered, his voice barely audible. "Dad was there. But that doesn't make sense. Unless..."

I held my breath, waiting for the accusation, the horror, the realization of betrayal. But it didn't come. Instead, Harrison shook his head, as if dismissing the thought.

"No," he said firmly. "Dad wouldn't. He couldn't. There has to be another explanation."

The unwavering faith in his voice was like a knife to my heart. I remained frozen in the shadows, a silent witness to my son's struggle, knowing that soon, that faith would be shattered forever.

11 - 12

Harrison's trembling fingers fumbled with his phone, the device slipping in his sweaty grasp as he punched in a number. The tension in the air was so thick I could barely breathe, my heart pounding in sync with each ring that echoed through the silent room.

"Come on, come on," Harrison muttered, his voice a mix of frustration and fear. "Pick up, Detective Keirstead. Please."

I watched, torn between the urge to reveal myself and the paralyzing fear of what that revelation would mean. My son's face, illuminated by the harsh glow of his phone screen, was a canvas of emotions – fear, determination, and a flicker of hope that tore at my soul.

"Detective Keirstead?" Harrison's voice cracked with relief. "It's Harrison Miller. I... I think I've been kidnapped. I'm in my house, my bedroom exactly."

As Harrison conversed with the detective and then his father, the conversation went on for what felt like hours. After Harrison hung up he began to pack his things to leave. Moments went by and Harrison still stood rooted in place. Then a sound of footsteps approaching awakened him from his daydreams.

"Someone's coming," he whispered urgently into the air.

Harrison ran and burst the front door open, flooding the dim room with light. Detective Keirstead strode in, her face a mask of concern, with another figure close behind her – Drake, or rather, the other version of Drake that existed in this fractured reality.

"Harrison!" Drake exclaimed, rushing to our son's side. "Thank God you're alright."

I watched from the shadows as Harrison's face cycled through a whirlwind of emotions – relief, confusion, and then a dawning suspicion that made my blood run cold.

"Dad?" he said, his voice laced with uncertainty. "But how... I thought..."

Detective Keirstead's sharp gaze swept the room, her hand hovering near her holster. "Harrison, are you hurt? Can you tell us what happened?"

As Harrison began to recount his fragmented memories, I remained hidden, a silent observer to the unfolding drama. The weight of my actions pressed down on me, threatening to crush me under the weight of guilt and regret.

"I remember... darkness," Harrison said, his brow furrowed in concentration. "And... Dad? But that doesn't make sense. You were... different somehow."

The Drake of this reality – placed a comforting hand on Harrison's shoulder. "It's okay, son. You're safe now. We'll figure this out together."

The urge to step out of the shadows, to reveal myself and the truth of our fractured existence, was almost overwhelming.

But as Detective Keirstead's keen eyes scanned the room once more, I knew that my moment had not yet come. The truth would have to wait, buried beneath layers of lies and half-truths, until the time was right to shatter the fragile peace of this reality.

13 - 14

Drake's limp was pronounced as he moved closer to Harrison, his gait uneven and strained. I could see the pain etched in the lines of his face, a mirror of my own anguish. As he settled beside his son, his eyes flickered towards my hiding spot, a fleeting moment of recognition passing between us. The weight of our shared secret hung heavy in the air, unspoken but palpable.

Detective Keirstead's voice cut through the tension, sharp and authoritative. "Harrison, I need you to focus. Where were you before you woke up here?"

Harrison ran a hand through his unruly curls, his teenage bravado faltering. "I... I'm not sure. Everything's fuzzy. I remember leaving the house, and then... nothing."

"Nothing at all?" Keirstead pressed, her eyes narrowing. "No faces, no locations?"

"Leave him be," Drake interjected, his voice a low rumble. "He's been through enough."

I watched from the shadows, my heart racing. How much did Harrison remember? How much had I inadvertently revealed in my misguided attempt to renew him?

"With all due respect, Mr. Miller," Keirstead retorted, "your son's disappearance is part of an ongoing investigation. We need answers."

Harrison's eyes darted between the detective and his father, confusion and fear warring on his face. "I want to help, I really do. But it's like... like there's a wall in my mind. I can't get past it."

As I observed the scene unfolding before me, a whirlwind of thoughts crashed through my mind. Had I done the right thing? Or had I only succeeded in fracturing this family further, deepening the chasm between realities?

Drake's voice, tinged with a mixture of concern and frustration, broke through my reverie. "Detective, maybe we could continue this tomorrow. Harrison needs rest."

"Dad, I'm fine," Harrison protested, a flash of his usual cockiness breaking through. "I can handle this. I'm not a kid anymore."

The irony of his words struck me like a physical blow. In this reality, in this moment, he was still just a boy – a boy a father failed to protect, a boy I had inadvertently thrust into the heart of a mystery he couldn't begin to comprehend.

15 - 16

The walls of the dimly lit room seemed to pulse and contract, the air growing thick and oppressive as the interrogation dragged on. I pressed myself further into the shadows, my heart hammering against my ribcage as Detective Keirstead's piercing gaze swept the room, coming dangerously close to my hiding spot.

"Harrison," Drake interjected, his voice strained with a mixture of concern and barely concealed desperation, "you don't have to do this now. We can—"

"No, Dad," Harrison cut him off, a hint of defiance creeping into his tone. "I want to remember. I need to."

I felt a surge of pride mingled with gut-wrenching fear. Harrison, so brave, so determined – and so utterly unaware of the danger he was in. The weight of my actions pressed down on me, threatening to crush me beneath a mountain of guilt and regret.

"Take us through what you do remember," Keirstead prodded, her voice softening slightly. "Every detail counts."

Harrison furrowed his brow, concentrating. "I remember... a voice. Familiar, but... different. And then darkness."

My breath caught in my throat. How much had he retained? How close was he to unraveling the twisted web I'd woven?

"A voice?" Drake leaned forward, his eyes flickering with a mix of hope and trepidation. "Can you describe it?"

Harrison shook his head, frustration evident in the set of his jaw. "It's like... it's there, but just out of reach. Like trying to grab smoke."

As I watched the scene unfold, my resolve wavered. The urge to step forward, to confess everything, clawed at my insides.

"I won't push you further tonight," Keirstead conceded, her tone laced with reluctance. "But we'll need to continue this conversation soon."

Drake nodded, relief washing over his features. "Thank you, Detective. We appreciate your understanding."

As they began to wrap up, I steeled myself. The path ahead was fraught with danger, every step a potential misstep that could bring my carefully constructed world crashing down. But I had come too far to turn back now. For Linda, for Harrison, for the family I Loved in the future and would lose– I would see this through to the bitter end.

17 - 17

The air in the room grew thick with tension as Detective Keirstead and Drake exchanged knowing glances. I pressed myself further into the shadows, my heart pounding so loudly I feared it might give me away. Harrison's eyes darted around the room, searching for something – or someone – just beyond his grasp.

"There's something else," Harrison murmured, his brow furrowing. "A... a symbol, I think. It keeps flashing in my mind, but I can't quite..."

Drake's head snapped up; his gaze intense. "A symbol? Can you describe it?"

As Harrison struggled to articulate what he'd seen, I felt a chill run down my spine. The cult's mark – how much did he remember? My fingers instinctively traced the outline of the scar hidden beneath my shirt, a constant reminder of the choices that had led me here.

"It's... circular, I think," Harrison said hesitantly. "With lines, like... like a web, maybe?"

I watched as Drake's face paled, his eyes widening with recognition. He glanced at Detective Keirstead, who nodded almost imperceptibly.

"Harrison," Drake said, his voice low and urgent. "I need you to focus. This symbol – it's important. Can you remember anything else about it? Anything at all?"

As Harrison closed his eyes, concentrating, I felt the walls of my carefully constructed reality begin to crumble. The final pieces were falling into place, and I knew that soon, there would be nowhere left to hide.

"I... I think I saw it somewhere," Harrison whispered, his voice barely audible. "Not just in my mind, but... here. In this house."

The room fell silent, the weight of Harrison's words hanging heavy in the air. I held my breath, every muscle in my body tense as I waited for the inevitable fallout.

"Drake," Detective Keirstead said, her tone sharp. "We need to search the premises. Now."

As they moved to leave the room, I knew my time was running out. The truth was closing in, threatening to consume everything I had fought so hard to protect. But even as fear gripped my heart, a part of me felt an odd sense of relief. The end was near, and with it, perhaps, a chance for redemption.

Embrace of Change

Green World – 2024

1 - 2

Drake's arms tightened around Harrison, his son's lanky teenage frame trembling slightly in his embrace. The familiar scent of Harrison's shampoo—a blend of mint and something fruity—filled Drake's nostrils as he buried his face in his son's curly mop of hair, fighting back the sting of tears.

"Dad, I swear, I just made it up," Harrison's muffled voice vibrated against Drake's chest. "The dragon, I mean. I didn't think—I didn't know it would become... this."

Drake pulled back slightly, his hands gripping Harrison's shoulders as he searched his son's face. Those bright eyes, usually dancing with mischief, now shimmered with a mix of fear and defiance. A lump formed in Drake's throat as he struggled to reconcile the gravity of their situation with the innocence of his boy's explanation.

"I believe you, Harrison," Drake managed, his voice rough with emotion. "But why didn't you tell me sooner? Do you have any idea how worried I've been?"

Harrison's gaze dropped, his shoulders hunching beneath Drake's hands. "I thought... I thought you'd be mad. Or worse, disappointed. You're always so serious about your work, and I just wanted to create something cool, you know?"

Drake's heart clenched at his son's words, a tidal wave of regret threatening to overwhelm him. Had he really become so disconnected, so focused on his career that his own son felt he couldn't share his creativity?

"Harrison, look at me," Drake said softly, waiting until those familiar brown eyes—so like his own—met his gaze. "I could never be disappointed in you for using your imagination. I'm sorry if I ever made you feel that way. I love you, and I'm proud of you, always."

A ghost of Harrison's usual grin flickered across his face. "Even when I accidentally start a city-wide manhunt with my doodles?"

Drake couldn't help but chuckle, the sound feeling foreign in the tense atmosphere. "Well, let's call that a learning experience, shall we?"

The moment of levity was shattered as suddenly as a gunshot. A scraping noise emanated from the shadows beyond the dim circle of light surrounding them, followed by a soft thud. Drake's body tensed instinctively, every nerve in his body screaming danger.

"Drake? Harrison?" Detective Keirstead's voice cut through the silence, sharp and authoritative. The metallic click of a gun being cocked punctuated her words. "Don't move."

Drake's mind raced, his lawyer's instincts warring with his parental ones. Should he argue, try to explain? Or focus solely on protecting Harrison? His son's rapid breathing beside him made the decision for him.

"It's okay," Drake murmured, giving Harrison's shoulder a reassuring squeeze. "Just stay calm and let me handle this."

As he turned to face the direction of Keirstead's voice, Drake's thoughts whirled. How had she found them? What did she know? And most importantly, how could he shield his son from whatever was coming next?

3 - 4

Detective Keirstead's voice rang out again, steely and commanding, "Come out with your hands up."

Drake's heart hammered against his ribs as he instinctively shifted, placing himself between Harrison and the unseen threat. His muscles coiled, ready to spring into action at a moment's notice. The room seemed to close in around them, shadows dancing ominously at the edges of his vision.

"Detective," Drake called out, fighting to keep his voice steady, "there's been a misunderstanding. My son and I—"

"Save it, Miller," Keirstead cut him off. "I said hands up. Both of you. Now."

Drake felt Harrison's trembling fingers grip the back of his shirt. He wanted nothing more than to turn and comfort his boy, to shield him from this nightmare. Instead, he slowly raised his hands, palms out.

"Harrison," Drake said softly, not daring to look back, "do as she says, okay? Everything's going to be alright."

"Dad?" Harrison's voice cracked, thick with fear and confusion. "What's happening?"

Drake's mind raced, searching for a way out, a loophole, anything to protect his son. It was like preparing for a high-stakes court case, but with infinitely more on the line. He took a deep breath, channeling the determination that had once made him a formidable attorney.

"Detective Keirstead," he tried again, injecting a note of calm authority into his voice, "I understand how this looks, but I assure you, we can explain everything. The dragon symbol—it's not what you think. My son—"

"I don't want to hear it, Drake," Keirstead interrupted, her footsteps growing closer. "You're both coming with me. We'll sort this out at the station."

Drake's jaw clenched. He could feel Harrison's fear radiating behind him, could practically hear the rapid thoughts whirling through his son's mind. In that moment, Drake made a silent vow: no matter what happened next, he would protect Harrison. He'd failed his family once before; he wouldn't do it again.

"Alright," Drake conceded, his mind already formulating strategies, "we'll come quietly. But I want it on record that my son is innocent in all of this. Whatever you think I've done, Harrison has no part in it."

As Keirstead's shadowy figure emerged from the darkness, Drake steeled himself for what was to come. The familiar weight of guilt and regret pressed down on him, but alongside it burned a fierce determination. He'd navigate this labyrinth of parallel realities, of suspicion and danger, and he'd do it with Harrison by his side. No matter the cost.

5 - 6

Harrison's eyes darted frantically around the room, his gaze bouncing from shadow to shadow like a pinball in a machine. The teenager's breath came in short, sharp gasps, his chest heaving beneath his wrinkled T-shirt. "Dad," he whispered, his voice cracking with fear, "what's happening?"

Drake's mind raced, a thousand possibilities colliding like atoms in a particle accelerator. Friend or foe? Ally or enemy? The questions pounded against his skull, each one carrying the weight of their very survival. He reached back, gripping Harrison's trembling hand in his own.

"It's okay, son," Drake murmured, his eyes never leaving the shadows where Detective Keirstead had disappeared. "We're going to be fine. Just stay behind me."

The silence stretched between them, thick and oppressive, broken only by the sound of their ragged breathing. Drake's thoughts whirled, analyzing every angle, every potential outcome. Could it be another officer? A criminal who'd followed them? Or something far more sinister, tied to the fractured reality he'd been navigating?

"You said... you said the dragon was your creation," Drake said softly, his words barely audible. "Tell me more about that, Harrison. When did you start drawing it?"

Harrison swallowed hard, his voice quavering as he replied, "I... I don't know, Dad. It just came to me one day. I thought it looked cool, so I kept drawing it. I didn't think—"

A sudden creak from the floorboards to their left cut him off. Drake tensed, positioning himself more firmly in front of his son. "Whoever you are," he called out, infusing his voice with a strength he didn't entirely feel, "we're not a threat. Let's talk this through."

The shadows seemed to shift, and Drake's heart raced as he strained to make out any discernible shape or movement. Harrison's grip on his hand tightened, the boy's fear palpable in the air between them.

"Dad," Harrison whispered, his voice barely audible, "what if it's—"

Drake cut him off gently, "Shh, it's alright. We'll face this together." He kept his voice low, steady, hoping to project a calm he didn't feel. His mind raced through possibilities, each more alarming than the last. Could it be connected to the accident that split his reality? A threat from one of his past cases as a lawyer?

The silence stretched on, punctuated only by the sound of their shallow breathing. Drake's eyes darted around the room, searching for anything they could use as a weapon or shield. "Harrison," he murmured, "I need you to listen carefully. If I tell you to run, you go. No questions, no hesitation. Understand?"

Harrison's reply came as a choked whisper, "But Dad, I can't leave you—"

"Promise me, son," Drake insisted, his tone brooking no argument.

A tense moment passed before Harrison reluctantly agreed, "Okay, I promise."

As they stood there, trapped in this moment of uncertainty, Drake couldn't help but reflect on how far he'd come from the man he once was—the lawyer who'd sacrifice anything for a win, even his family. Now, here he stood, ready to lay down everything for his son. The irony wasn't lost on him.

"Whatever happens," Drake said softly, his eyes still scanning the shadows, "I want you to know I love you, Harrison. More than anything in this world or any other."

7 - 7

Drake's words hung in the air, heavy with emotion, as the tension in the room continued to build. His muscles coiled, ready to spring into action at a moment's notice. The shadows seemed to pulse with malevolent energy, threatening to engulf them at any second.

"Dad," Harrison whispered, his voice trembling, "I'm scared."

Drake swallowed hard, fighting back his own fear. "I know, son. But we're going to get through this. Together."

As if in response to his words, a floorboard creaked in the darkness. Drake's heart leapt into his throat. "Who's there?" he called out, his voice steadier than he felt. "Show yourself!"

Silence answered him, but Drake's instincts screamed that they weren't alone. He could almost feel the presence watching them, calculating, waiting for the right moment to strike.

"Listen to me, Harrison," Drake said, his voice low and urgent. "Whatever happens next, remember what I taught you about staying calm under pressure. It's just like preparing for a big case. Focus on the facts, not the fear."

Harrison nodded; his eyes wide but determined. "Like you always say, 'Emotion clouds judgment.'"

A ghost of a smile touched Drake's lips. "That's right. You remember."

As they stood there, father and son united against an unseen threat, Drake couldn't help but marvel at the turn his life had taken. Once, he would have given anything to win a case. Now, he'd give everything to protect his son.

Moonlite Confrontation

The cold barrel of Detective Kierstead's gun glinted in the moonlight as she leveled it at the shadows. "Come out with your hands up!" she shouted, her voice sharp and unwavering. Even in the darkness, I could see the determination etched on her face, those piercing eyes scanning for any sign of movement.

My heart pounded in my chest as I considered my options. This was it - the moment everything had been building towards. No more running, no more hiding. With a deep breath, I stepped out of the inky blackness, hands raised high above my head.

"Hello detectives," I called out, trying to keep my voice steady. "I hear you've been looking for me."

Detective Kierstead's eyes widened slightly, but her aim never faltered. "That's far enough," she barked. "On your knees, now!"

As I slowly lowered myself to the ground, I couldn't help but admire her poise. Even faced with a suspect she'd been hunting for months; she maintained perfect control. No hint of the small-town girl she'd once been - only the sharp, ambitious detective she'd become.

"You've led us on quite a chase," Kierstead said, her tone clipped and professional as she approached, gun still trained on me. "I have to admit, I'm almost impressed."

"High praise coming from you, Detective," I replied, forcing a grim smile. "I've heard about your reputation. The rising star of the department, isn't that, right?"

Her eyes narrowed slightly. "Flattery won't get you anywhere. You're under arrest for-"

"I know my rights," I interrupted, my mind racing. How much did they really know? How much evidence had they gathered? "And I know you don't have enough to make any charges stick. Not yet anyway."

Kierstead's jaw tightened, but she didn't rise to the bait. Smart. Collected. Everything I'd come to expect from studying her these past weeks. "We'll see about that," she said coolly. "For now, you're coming with us. And believe me, we'll get to the bottom of this."

As she reached for her handcuffs, I couldn't shake the feeling that this was only the beginning. The real challenge was yet to come.

Caught in the Act

Green World – 2024

1 - 2

The shadows seemed to coalesce, taking form as Gabriel emerged from the inky darkness. His scarred visage caught the dim light, casting eerie shadows across his disfigured features. Detective Holly Kierstead felt her breath catch in her throat as his piercing gaze locked onto her, radiating an intensity that made the air feel thick and oppressive. With deliberate slowness, Gabriel's hand descended, one long finger extending to point accusingly at his knee.

"Remember me, Detective?" The words slithered from his lips, low and menacing, each syllable dripping with barely contained rage. "How long ago was it that you gave me this to remember you by?"

Holly's mind raced, memories flooding back of that fateful night years ago. The warehouse raid gone wrong, the desperate chase through rain-slicked alleys, the moment of truth when instinct overrode protocol. Her fingers twitched, muscle memory recalling the weight of her service weapon as it discharged.

"The Bridgewater Strangler," she managed, fighting to keep her voice steady. "I... I didn't expect to see you here." The words felt hollow, inadequate in the face of his seething anger.

His lips curled into a mirthless smile, the scar tissue pulling taught across his cheek. "No, I don't imagine you did. Tell me, do you often forget the lives you've ruined, or am I special?"

Holly's jaw clenched, a familiar cocktail of guilt and defiance warring within her. "That night... things happened fast. I made a call—"

"A call?" Gabriel's voice rose, sharp as a knife's edge. "Is that what you call shooting an unarmed man? A 'call'?"

The detective squared her shoulders, meeting his gaze unflinchingly. "You were fleeing a crime scene, refusing to comply with—"

"I was scared!" The words exploded from Gabriel, echoing in the confined space. "I was young, and stupid, and scared. And you..." His voice dropped to a whisper, somehow more terrifying than his shout. "You took everything from me that night."

Holly felt the weight of her badge, suddenly heavy against her chest. She'd replayed that night a thousand times, questioned every decision. But faced with the living embodiment of her worst mistake, words failed her. The silence stretched between them, charged with years of pain and regret.

3 - 4

Holly's mind raced, searching for the right words, but found only a void where her usual confidence should be. She swallowed hard, her throat dry as sandpaper. "Gabriel, I—"

"Save it," he snarled, cutting her off with a sharp wave of his hand. The movement made Holly flinch, her right hand instinctively twitching towards her holster. Gabriel noticed, his eyes narrowing dangerously. "Still so quick to reach for that gun, aren't you, Detective?"

Holly forced her hand to relax, cursing herself for the involuntary reaction. She took a deep breath, trying to center herself. "I'm not here to fight you, Gabriel. I'm here to solve a case."

A bitter laugh escaped his lips. "Oh, the irony. The great Detective Kierstead, here to dispense justice once again. Tell me, do you sleep well at night knowing what your brand of justice did to me?"

The words hit Holly like a physical blow. She'd spent years building walls around that night, compartmentalizing it as a necessary evil in the line of duty. But now, faced with the living, breathing consequence of her actions, those walls came crumbling down.

"No," she admitted, her voice barely above a whisper. "I don't sleep well at all."

For a moment, a flicker of something—surprise? satisfaction? —crossed Gabriel's face. But it was gone in an instant, replaced by the same cold fury. "Good," he said, his voice low and dangerous. "Neither do I."

5 - 6

Holly swallowed hard; her throat suddenly dry. "It's been a long time," she admitted, her voice tinged with regret. "But I haven't forgotten." Her eyes traced the scars on Gabriel's face, each one a stark reminder of that fateful night. "Not a single day goes by that I don't think about what happened."

Gabriel's piercing gaze bore into her, his lips curling into a sneer. "How touching," he spat, venom dripping from every syllable. "Your guilt must be such a burden. Tell me, Detective, does it weigh as heavily as the metal buttle you shot through my knee?"

Holly flinched, the memory of bone crunching beneath her baton flashing unbidden through her mind. She fought to keep her voice steady. "I was doing my job, Gabriel. You left me no choice."

"No choice?" Gabriel's laugh was a harsh, grating sound that sent chills down Holly's spine. "There's always a choice, Detective. You chose to cripple me. You chose to destroy my life."

The tension in the room was palpable, a silent battlefield where old wounds and past sins collided with the present. Holly's fingers twitched, longing for the reassuring weight of her weapon, but she resisted the urge. She couldn't afford to make the same mistake twice.

"I'm not sorry," she whispered, the words feeling woefully inadequate. "If I could go back-"

"But you can't," Gabriel interrupted, his voice deathly quiet. He took a step closer, and Holly had to fight every instinct not to back away. "We're here now, Detective. And I intend to make sure you never forget the consequences of your actions."

As Gabriel's presence loomed over her, Holly's mind raced. How could she defuse this situation? How could she make amends for a past that seemed beyond redemption? The weight of their shared history hung heavy in the air, a reminder of their lives forever altered by their fateful encounter.

7 - 8

Drake watched the tense exchange unfold, his heart pounding in his chest. The air felt thick, oppressive, as if the very room was closing in around them. He swallowed hard, his mouth suddenly dry as sandpaper.

"This can't be happening," he muttered under his breath, his eyes darting between Gabriel and Detective Kierstead. The weight of their shared history hung heavy in the air, casting a long shadow over their uncertain future.

Gabriel's piercing gaze shifted, locking onto Drake with an intensity that made his blood run cold. In that moment, recognition dawned on him like a bolt of lightning, sending a shiver down his spine.

"You," Drake breathed, his voice barely audible. "I know you."

Gabriel's lips curled into a sardonic smile. "Ah, the esteemed lawyer finally remembers. How... touching."

Drake's mind reeled, memories flooding back with brutal clarity. "You shot me in the Funhouse. You kidnapped Harrison and Linda. You-"

"The one you so callously threw under the bus to win?" Gabriel finished, his voice dripping with venom. "How perceptive of you, Mr. Miller."

Drake's hands trembled, his lawyer's instinct to argue warring with the crushing weight of guilt. "if I've done something to you, I don't remember," he said weakly, even as the words rang hollow in his ears.

Gabriel's laugh was a harsh, mirthless sound. "Don't remember? Is that what you tell yourself to sleep at night? Tell me, does it help ease the guilt of destroying innocent lives for your precious career?"

Drake's throat constricted, his next words catching painfully. "I... I didn't know."

"Maybe not yet you don't," Gabriel snarled, taking a menacing step forward. "But you will. Eventually you'll make the mistake, and it'll set us done this road. You'll be too focused on your win record to see the truth."

As Gabriel's scarred face loomed closer, Drake found himself paralyzed, trapped between the man he once was and the man he was desperately trying to become. The face he had tried so hard to forget now stood before him, a living testament to his past sins.

"I'm sorry," Drake whispered, the words feeling woefully inadequate. "If I could go back-"

"But you can't," Gabriel interrupted, echoing his earlier words to Kierstead. "We're all here now, Mr. Miller. And I intend to make sure you never forget the consequences of your actions."

As the weight of Gabriel's words settled over him, Drake realized with chilling clarity that his past and present had collided in the most devastating way possible. There would be no escaping the reckoning that was to come.

9 - 10

Harrison's whisper cut through the tension like a knife, his voice trembling with a mixture of fear and recognition. "It's him," he breathed, his eyes wide and fixed on Gabriel's imposing figure. The words hung in the air, barely audible yet deafening in their implications.

Drake's arm instinctively tightened around his son's shoulders, pulling Harrison closer as if he could shield him from the danger that now stood before them. His heart raced, pounding a frantic rhythm against his ribs as he stared at the face he'd hoped never to see again. Every scar, every line etched into Gabriel's visage was a stark reminder of the pain he'd caused, the lives he'd altered with his careless pursuit of success.

"Harrison," Drake murmured, his voice low and urgent, "I need you to stay calm. Can you do that for me?" He felt his son nod against his side, the boy's frame tense with apprehension.

Swallowing hard, Drake forced himself to meet Gabriel's cold gaze. "I remember you," he admitted, the words tasting bitter on his tongue. "God help me, I remember everything."

Gabriel's lips curled into a sneer. "How touching. The great Drake Miller, finally facing the consequences of his actions. Tell me, does your son know what kind of man his father really is?"

Drake flinched, his grip on Harrison tightening reflexively. "Leave him out of this," he growled, a protective fire igniting in his chest. "This is between you and me."

"Dad?" Harrison's voice quavered; his earlier cockiness replaced by genuine fear. "What's going on? Who is this guy?"

The question hung heavy in the air, forcing Drake to confront the ugly truth he'd been running from for so long. How could he explain to his son the depths of his past mistakes, the lives he'd ruined in his relentless pursuit of success?

"He's..." Drake began, his voice faltering. "He's obviously someone I wronged, Harrison. Someone I hurt badly because I was too focused on winning to see the truth."

Gabriel's harsh laugh cut through the room. "Hurt? Is that what you call destroying a man's life, Mr. Miller? Tearing apart families for the sake of your precious sanctuary?"

Drake's mind raced, desperately searching for a way out of this nightmare. But as he looked into Gabriel's eyes, he saw only cold, implacable vengeance staring back at him. The reckoning he'd feared for so long had finally arrived, and he knew with sickening certainty that there would be no easy escape from the sins of his past.

11 - 12

Gabriel's piercing gaze shifted from Drake to Harrison, his scarred features twisting into a cruel smirk. The intensity of his stare bore into the boy's soul, a predatory gleam dancing in his eyes that sent shivers down Drake's spine. Harrison instinctively shrank back against his father, his earlier bravado crumbling under the weight of Gabriel's malevolent scrutiny.

"Such a brave little soldier," Gabriel purred, his voice dripping with venomous sarcasm. "Tell me, boy, do you know what kind of man your father really is?"

Drake's jaw clenched, his protective instincts flaring. "That's enough, Gabriel," he snarled, positioning himself more firmly between his son and the threat before them. "This is between us. Leave Harrison out of it."

But even as the words left his mouth, a sinking feeling settled in Drake's gut. He knew, with a certainty that chilled him to his core, that Gabriel had no intention of sparing anyone. The man's presence here, in this sleepy Indiana town so far from their shared past, was proof enough of his determination.

"It can't be," Drake muttered, more to himself than anyone else. His mind reeled, grasping for some rational explanation, some way to deny the horrifying reality standing before him. "How did you find us?"

Gabriel's laugh was a harsh, grating sound that seemed to suck the warmth from the room. "Oh, Drake," he said, shaking his head with mock pity. "Did you really think you could hide from me forever? That your sins wouldn't eventually catch up to you?"

As Gabriel spoke, memories flooded Drake's mind – late nights at the office, missed birthdays and soccer games, the gradual erosion of his marriage. All in pursuit of that next big case, the next rung on the corporate ladder. And at what cost? The weight of his choices pressed down on him, threatening to crush him under their enormity.

"Dad?" Harrison's voice quivered, confusion and fear evident in every syllable. "What's he talking about? What did you do?"

Drake swallowed hard, the lump in his throat making it difficult to breathe. How could he possibly explain the darkness of his past to his son? The compromises he'd made, the lives he'd ruined in his blind ambition? He opened his mouth, struggling to find the words, but Gabriel beat him to it.

"Yes, Drake," Gabriel taunted, his eyes glittering with malice. "Why don't you tell your boy all about the skeletons in your closet? I'm sure he'd love to hear how his father destroyed lives for a paycheck. You see Harrison it's not what your father did in the past, it's what he will do in the future that I'm here about."

13 - 14

Detective Kierstead's hand inched closer to her weapon, her fingers brushing against the cold metal as she locked eyes with Gabriel. The familiar face before her sent a jolt of recognition through her body, memories flooding her mind like a torrent of icy water. Each recollection was a dagger to her conscience, reminding her of the choices that had led them to this moment.

"You haven't changed a bit, Gabriel," she said, her voice steady despite the tremor in her heart. "Still holding onto old grudges, I see."

Gabriel's lips curled into a mirthless smile, his scarred face a mask of eerie calm. "Grudges?" he replied, his voice smooth as silk yet laced with venom. "I prefer to think of it as... unfinished business, Detective."

As he spoke, Kierstead's mind raced, recalling the fateful night that had altered both their lives forever. The rain-slicked streets, the chase, the gunshot that still echoed in her nightmares. She forced herself to maintain her composure, even as guilt gnawed at her insides.

"We all have regrets, Gabriel," she said, her eyes never leaving his. "But this isn't the way to make things right."

Gabriel's laugh was a harsh, grating sound that sent shivers down her spine. "Make things right?" he sneered. "Oh, my dear detective, I'm not here to make things right. I'm here to settle the score."

The tension in the room was palpable, a living thing that seemed to pulse with each passing second. Drake stood frozen, his arm still protectively around Harrison, watching the exchange with growing dread. He could feel his son trembling beside him, and a wave of guilt washed over him. How had he dragged his family into this nightmare?

"Holly," Drake said, his voice barely above a whisper. "What's going on? How do you know him?"

Kierstead's jaw tightened, her gaze still fixed on Gabriel. "It's a long story, Drake. One I'm not proud of."

Gabriel's eyes glittered dangerously in the dim light. "Oh, but it's such a riveting tale," he purred. "Shall I tell it, Detective? Or would you like to confess your sins to your friends here?"

Kierstead's hand tightened on her weapon, her heart pounding in her chest. She knew she should draw it, should end this threat before it escalated further. But something held her back – was it guilt? Fear? Or the nagging feeling that maybe, just maybe, she deserved whatever retribution Gabriel had in mind?

"That's enough, Gabriel," she said, fighting to keep her voice steady. "Whatever happened in the past, it's between you and me. Leave them out of it."

Gabriel's smile widened, revealing teeth that seemed unnaturally sharp in the shadowy room. "Oh, but Detective," he said, his voice dripping with false sweetness, "they're already a part of this. More than you know."

15 - 15

The air in the room grew thick, suffocating, as if the very walls were closing in around them. Drake's mind raced, desperately trying to piece together the fragments of this twisted puzzle. He glanced at Harrison, whose wide eyes reflected the terror that gripped them all.

"What does he mean, Dad?" Harrison whispered, his voice trembling.

Drake swallowed hard; his mouth dry. "I don't know, son," he murmured, pulling Harrison closer. "But we'll figure it out together."

Gabriel's piercing gaze shifted to Drake, his scarred face twisting into a grotesque smile. "Ah, the protective father," he mused, his voice a hypnotic drawl. "How touching. But tell me, Drake, have you shared with your boy the truth about your own past? About the choices that led you here?"

Drake felt a chill run down his spine. "I don't know what you're talking about," he said, struggling to keep his voice steady.

Gabriel chuckled, a low, menacing sound that seemed to reverberate through the room. "Of course you don't. That's the beauty of denial, isn't it? It's so... comforting."

Kierstead took a step forward, her eyes blazing. "That's enough, Gabriel. Whatever game you're playing, it ends now."

"Oh, but the game has only just begun, Detective," Gabriel replied, his tone eerily calm. "And I assure you, the stakes are higher than you could possibly imagine."

As Gabriel spoke, Drake's mind whirled with fragmented memories – flashes of a symbol, whispered conversations, and a nagging sense that he was missing something crucial. He glanced at Kierstead, noticing the tightness in her jaw, the barely contained fury in her eyes. What was the connection between her and Gabriel? And how did it all tie back to him?

"Listen," Drake said, his voice hoarse, "I don't know what happened between you two, between us, but surely we can talk this out. There must be a way to resolve this without–"

Gabriel's laughter cut him off, a harsh, bitter sound that sent shivers down Drake's spine. "Resolve? Oh, Drake, your naivety is almost endearing. Some wounds don't heal. Some betrayals can never be forgiven."

The room fell silent, the weight of Gabriel's words hanging heavy in the air. Drake felt as if he were standing on the edge of a precipice, one wrong move away from plunging into an abyss of secrets and lies. The truth was there, dancing just out of reach, but he knew that grasping it might shatter everything he thought he knew about himself and the world around him.

Facing the Millers

Green World – 2024

1 - 2

I stand before the Millers, my heart pounding in my chest as the gravity of this moment threatens to crush me. The dim light of the room casts long shadows across their faces, emphasizing the lines of worry and confusion etched into their features. I can feel the weight of their stares, a mixture of curiosity and suspicion that makes my skin crawl.

"I never thought it would come to this," I begin, my voice barely above a whisper. The words taste bitter on my tongue, a confession long overdue. "But I owe you the truth. All of you."

Drake's eyes narrow, his jaw clenching as he takes a step forward. "The truth? After everything you've done, you think we'll believe anything you say?"

I flinch at the venom in his words, a stark reminder of the pain I've caused. My gaze drifts to Harrison, who stands silently beside his father, his young face a mask of confusion and fear. The sight of him sends a pang of regret through my chest, knowing that my actions have irrevocably altered the course of his life.

"I know I've hurt you," I say, forcing myself to meet Drake's gaze. "I've manipulated and deceived you for far too long. But please, just hear me out. What I'm about to tell you will change everything you thought you knew about yourselves and the world around you."

I can see the conflict in Drake's eyes, the battle between his anger and his innate curiosity. It's Detective Kierstead who breaks the tense silence, her sharp voice cutting through the air like a knife.

"Then start talking, Gabriel," she says, her piercing eyes fixed on me. "And make it good, because right now, you're looking at a long time behind bars."

I take a deep breath, steeling myself for what's to come. The truth is a double-edged sword, and I know that once I start speaking, there's no going back. The world as they know it will crumble, and I'll be the one holding the sledgehammer.

"It all began with a group called the Temporal Guardians," I start, watching as confusion flickers across their faces. "An organization that you, Detective Miller, will form in the future. An organization dedicated to protecting the fabric of time itself."

The words hang in the air, heavy with implications. I can see the disbelief in their eyes, the struggle to comprehend the magnitude of what I'm saying. But I press on, knowing that every second counts, that the fate of countless timelines hangs in the balance.

As I continue to speak, I can feel the weight on my shoulders shifting. It's both a burden and a relief to finally reveal the truth, to lay bare the intricate web of lies and half-truths I've spun over the years. With each word, I'm dismantling the carefully constructed facade I've hidden behind for so long, exposing the raw, vulnerable core of who I really am and why I've done the things I've done.

The room seems to shrink around us as I delve deeper into my explanation, the air growing thick with tension and unspoken questions. I can see the gears turning in Detective Kierstead's mind, her analytical nature already working to piece together the fragments of this impossible puzzle. And through it all, I can't shake the feeling that this revelation is just the beginning of something much larger, much more dangerous than any of us could have imagined.

3 - 4

I watch as Detective Kierstead's piercing eyes narrow, her jaw clenching as she processes my words. The silence in the room is oppressive, broken only by the faint ticking of a clock that seems to echo the passage of time itself.

"Temporal Guardians?" Holly finally speaks, her voice laced with a mix of skepticism and barely contained frustration. "You expect us to believe this science fiction nonsense, Gabriel?"

I feel a rueful smile tugging at the corners of my mouth, the irony of her disbelief not lost on me. "I understand your skepticism, Detective," I say, my voice low and measured. "But the truth is often stranger than fiction."

As I speak, I can't help but notice the way Holly's hand instinctively moves towards the trigger, her body language screaming distrust. It's a stark reminder of the chasm that exists between us, the damage I've done in my misguided attempts to protect the future.

"You've manipulated us, lied to us, and now you're spinning tales about time travel?" Holly's words cut through the air like a knife. "Why should we believe anything you say?"

I take a deep breath, feeling the weight of their collective gazes upon me. "Because," I say, my voice barely above a whisper, "the fate of not just our world, but countless others, hangs in the balance. And whether you believe me or not, the truth remains unchanged."

As I speak, I can't help but reflect on the irony of my situation. I, who had dedicated my life to preserving the integrity of time, now find myself unraveling the very fabric I swore to protect. The burden of knowledge weighs heavily on my shoulders, and I wonder, not for the first time, if I've made the right choice in revealing these secrets.

5 - 6

I turn to Harrison, his youthful face a mix of confusion and intrigue. His curly hair seems to vibrate with the energy of his churning thoughts. "Harrison," I begin, my voice softening, "your genetic makeup is unique. It holds the key to unlocking portals between different timelines."

Harrison's eyes widen, a flicker of excitement dancing across his features. "What do you mean, 'unique'?" he asks, his voice cracking slightly with the cockiness of adolescence.

I press on, driven by the need to make them understand. "The Temporal Guardians have been monitoring you for years, waiting for the moment when your abilities would manifest."

Drake steps forward, his scruffy beard bristling with tension. "You expect us to believe that my son is some kind of... time traveler?" His voice is thick with skepticism, but I can see the wheels turning behind his tired eyes.

"Not just Harrison," I explain, my gaze sweeping across the room. "You too, Detective Miller. You see, the Temporal Guardians – or Guardians of the Roundtable, as denoted by the green dragon symbol – was an organization formed by you."

Linda gasps, her blonde hair falling across her face as she turns to look at her husband. Drake's expression is a storm of disbelief and dawning comprehension.

"You brought together a series of individuals who all shared the same genetic makeup," I continued, my words tumbling out faster now. "An aversion to high levels of radiation. When exposed to these levels, the genetic markup duplicates and multiplies, allowing the individual to transcend to other worlds and timelines."

As I speak, I can't help but marvel at the cruel irony of it all. Here I am, revealing the very secrets I've fought so hard to protect, to the very people I've hurt in my misguided attempts to change the future.

7 - 8

I pause, letting the weight of my words settle over the room. The silence is thick, palpable, broken only by the soft ticking of a clock on the wall. Detective Keirstead's sharp eyes bore into me, her analytical mind no doubt piecing together the implications of what I've just revealed.

After a moment, I draw a deep breath, steeling myself for what comes next. "I was working with the organization," I begin, my voice low and tinged with a mixture of regret and fear. "We were trying to stop a deadly explosive from going off when I was caught in the blast radius."

Drake's fists clench at his sides, his knuckles turning white. "What are you saying, Gabriel?" he demands, his voice a hoarse whisper.

I meet his gaze, unflinching. "That's why I'm so scared," I confess, the words tasting bitter on my tongue. "The explosion destroyed most of my timeline and sent me back years. I waited to be rescued, tried to go back to that moment and stop the crisis. But I failed, and no one came looking for me."

Linda reaches out, gripping Drake's arm as if to steady herself. Harrison, young and confused, looks between his parents and me, his brow furrowed in concentration.

"You see," I continue, my voice gaining strength as I delve deeper into the explanation, "if you harness your energy hard enough, you can just teleport between timelines. You don't need a body in one to go hopping to."

As I speak, I can't help but remember the moment of the explosion - the searing heat, the deafening roar, the feeling of being torn apart and reassembled across the fabric of time itself. The memory sends a shudder through me, one that I hope goes unnoticed by the others.

9 - 10

I take a deep breath, steeling myself for what comes next. "Since I was betrayed, I knew the only way to stop my timeline from being destroyed was by stopping the Temporal Guardians from ever forming." The words tumble out, heavy with the weight of my actions. "So, I set out on my mission to kill every single one of them."

Detective Kierstead's eyes narrow, her hand instinctively moving towards her holster. I raise my hands in a placating gesture, noting the tension in her shoulders.

"That was until a few years ago when Detective Keirstead here—or Sharp, whichever you go by—shot me," I continue, my gaze locked on her steely eyes. "I knew I was getting close to being discovered. I had to lay low."

Drake's face contorts, a mixture of disbelief and dawning comprehension. "The janitor at Saint Montague's," he murmurs, his voice barely audible.

I nod, a humorless smile tugging at my lips. "For years, I bid my time, working odd jobs until I landed that role. I knew the history—soon you would be brought in there after an accident, and the events leading to the Temporal Guardians would unfold."

My words hang in the air, heavy with implication. Drake's eyes widen, realization dawning on his face. I can almost see the pieces clicking into place in his mind, the lawyer in him connecting the dots of this bizarre puzzle.

"Here's the tricky part about messing with time," I say, my voice dropping to a near-whisper. "I didn't know it was to be me that caused the accident. I should have—I knew the history—but still, I didn't expect this to happen."

Suddenly, Drake speaks up, his voice tight with barely contained emotion. "You're saying..."

11 - 12

Drake's eyes narrow, his legal mind dissecting every word I've uttered. "If you wanted to stop the Temporal Guardians," he begins, his voice steady but tinged with a hint of disbelief, "then why not do so by killing me, letting me die in the crash? Without me, there would be no organization, right?"

The question hits me like a punch to the gut, forcing the air from my lungs. I blink rapidly, my mind racing to formulate a response. The autumn breeze wafting through the open window carries the faint scent of pumpkin spice from B&J Bistro down the street, a jarring contrast to the weight of our conversation.

"I..." I start, then pause, realizing I'm at a loss for words. My gaze darts between Drake and Detective Kierstead, whose piercing eyes seem to bore into my very soul. The silence stretches, punctuated only by the distant laughter drifting from the Bulldog Bar and Grill.

I swallow hard, my throat suddenly dry. "I hadn't... I didn't think that part through fully," I admit, the words tasting bitter on my tongue. My hands clench involuntarily at my sides, a physical manifestation of my internal struggle.

Detective Kierstead - or Sharp, I remind myself - leans forward, her sharp features accentuated by the golden sunlight filtering through the nearby window. "You mean to tell us," She says, her voice low and dangerous, "that in all your grand plans of time manipulation and murder, you overlooked the most obvious solution?"

I feel my face flushed with shame and frustration. How could I have been so shortsighted? The weight of my actions, the lives I've taken, suddenly feels impossibly heavy. "I was... I was focused on dismantling the organization," I stammer, knowing how weak the excuse sounds even as I utter it. "I thought by eliminating key members, I could prevent its formation without..."

My voice trails off as I realize the magnitude of my error. The room seems to close in around me, the warm, small-town charm of Minden, Indiana now feeling suffocating rather than comforting.

13 - 14

I take a deep breath, steeling myself for what I'm about to reveal. "I wanted to let you suffer," I confess, my voice barely above a whisper. Drake's eyes widen, a mix of shock and anger flashing across his tired features. "You were supposed to be in custody," I continue, the words tumbling out faster now. "The blood I left behind was supposed to indicate you in the murders. I wanted to ruin your life across time."

The confession hangs heavy in the air, the weight of my cruelty palpable. Drake's jaw clenches, his hand unconsciously moving to the small scar on his forehead - a remnant of the accident that had fractured his reality. For a moment, I see the shadow of the ruthless lawyer he once was, the man who would do anything to win a case.

Then, something shifts in his expression. The anger doesn't fade entirely, but it's tempered by a dawning realization. Drake leans forward, his voice low and intense. "And why does our blood match anyway?" he asks, his brown eyes boring into mine. "Why is it part mine and part Harrison's?"

I can see the gears turning in his mind, the lawyer in him piecing together the puzzle. His fingers drum against the table, a nervous habit I've noticed before. The silence stretches between us, charged with unspoken questions and barely contained emotions.

"You're right to ask that," I finally responded, my voice hoarse. "It's... complicated. More complicated than I think any of us realized." I pause, searching for the right words to explain the intricate web of time, genetics, and fate that binds us all together.

15 - 16

I take a deep breath, steeling myself for the revelation I'm about to unleash. "You see, while you were at the hospital, I injected you with a part of my blood," I confess, watching Drake's eyes widen in shock. "Your blood then awakened and took on the genetic marker."

Drake's hand flies to his arm, as if he can feel the foreign blood coursing through his veins. His face pales, and I can almost see the memories flooding back. "Don't you remember the doctor telling you that both your family was dead?" I press on, my voice barely above a whisper. "That's the timeline you come from. The more you visit, the more your blood multiplies."

The room falls into a stunned silence, the gravity of my words sinking in. I can see the gears turning in Detective Kierstead's mind, her sharp eyes narrowing as she processes this new information. Her hand instinctively moves to the holster at her hip, a reflex born from years of training and a deep-seated need to protect.

"You explain that like it makes sense as to why your blood matches Harrison's and Drake's," she interjects, her voice cutting through the tension like a knife. "It doesn't."

I turn to face her, recognizing the fierce determination in her gaze. Holly Kierstead, the young detective who had clawed her way up the ranks, was now standing at the precipice of a truth that could shatter her understanding of reality. Her short, dark hair frames her face, which is set in a mask of skepticism and barely contained frustration.

"Detective Kierstead," I begin, my tone measured, "I understand your confusion. The concept of blood altering timelines and genetic markers is... well, it's beyond what most people can comprehend." I pause, searching for a way to make her understand. "Think of it like this: the blood I injected into Drake was a key, unlocking a door to possibilities that were always there, just dormant."

Holly's eyes narrow further, her analytical mind working overtime to process this information. I can see the conflict in her expression - the part of her that wants to dismiss this as nonsense warring with the detective in her that senses there's more to uncover.

17 - 18

I take a deep breath, feeling the weight of every word as I continue, "When you inject someone with this blood, you take on a part of their genetic makeup. Since you created the Guardians, Drake, you made it your mission to awaken as many people as possible. Your blood is now their blood, your blood is the giver of life. So, in a sense, we are all the same."

Drake's eyes widen, a mixture of disbelief and dawning comprehension washing over his face. His hand trembles slightly as he reaches up to run it through his disheveled dark hair, a gesture I've come to recognize as a sign of his internal struggle. I can almost see the gears turning in his mind, trying to reconcile this new information with the fractured reality he's been living.

"But that's—" Drake begins, his voice hoarse with emotion. He takes a step forward, his tired eyes suddenly alight with a desperate need to understand.

I raise my hand, cutting him off before he can continue. The words I've spoken hang heavy in the air, and I know Drake needs time to process this revelation. His mouth closes, but I can see the questions burning behind his eyes, threatening to spill out at any moment.

In the tense silence that follows, I watch as Drake's gaze flicks between me and Detective Kierstead, as if searching for some sign that this is all an elaborate hoax. The weight of his dual existence—grieving a wife in one world, a son in another—seems to press down on him even more heavily now.

"I know this is a lot to take in," I say softly, my voice barely above a whisper. "But understanding this is crucial to comprehending the larger picture, Drake. Your blood, your very essence, is at the heart of everything that's happened."

Drake's shoulders slump slightly, the burden of this knowledge visibly settling upon him. I can see the conflict in his eyes—the lawyer in him wanting to argue, to find some flaw in my explanation, while the part of him that has experienced the impossible knows that there's truth in my words.

As I watch him grapple with this revelation, I can't help but feel a twinge of guilt. I've shattered his world once again, adding another layer of complexity to his already fractured existence. But there's no turning back now. The truth, as painful as it may be, is our only path forward.

19 - 19

I lock my eyes with Detective Kierstead, her penetrating gaze a mixture of skepticism and dawning realization. With a deep breath, I square my shoulders and declare, "The time has come for this to end. Take me away, officer, and I'll explain the remainder of my plan."

The words hang heavy in the air, charged with the weight of all that's been revealed. Drake's eyes widen, a flicker of fear crossing his face as he processes the implications of my statement. I can almost see the gears turning in his mind, trying to piece together how this connects to the loss of his family across different timelines.

Detective Kierstead takes a step forward, her hand instinctively moving towards her holster. "You're saying there's more?" she asks, her voice a mixture of professional detachment and barely concealed urgency.

I nod slowly, feeling the scarred tissue on the left side of my face pull taut with the movement. "Much more," I reply, my tone grave. "But it's not safe to discuss it here. There are ears everywhere, Detective. Ears that span across time and space."

As I speak, I can't help but let my gaze drift to Drake. The anguish etched on his face is palpable, a stark reminder of the pain I've caused. A part of me wants to reach out, to offer some form of comfort, but I know it would be hollow coming from me.

"Why should we trust you?" Drake suddenly interjects, his voice hoarse with emotion. "After everything you've done, all the lies and manipulation, why should we believe anything you say?"

I feel a sad smile tug at the corners of my mouth. "Because, Drake," I say softly, "despite everything, I'm your only chance at understanding the truth. At potentially saving your family."

The mention of his family sends a visible shudder through Drake's body. I can see the internal struggle playing out on his face—the desire to dismiss me warring with the desperate hope that I might hold the key to reuniting him with his loved ones.

Detective Kierstead clears her throat, breaking the tension. "Alright, Gabriel," she says, her voice firm but not unkind. "We'll do this your way. But I warn you, any tricks and you'll wish you'd never messed with time in the first place."

As she moves to handcuff me, I can't help but think about the irony of her words. If only she knew half of it. The real trick, I muse silently, is yet to come. And as we prepare to leave, I steel myself for what lies ahead, knowing that the fate of not just this timeline, but countless others, hangs in the balance

Viral Confession

Green World – 2024

1 - 2

I lean forward, my scarred hands clasped on the cold metal table, as Miller enters the interrogation room. His face is a mask of confusion and anger, but I can see the fear lurking beneath. I take a deep breath, steeling myself for the revelation to come.

"You may want to take a seat," I say, my voice low and steady. "Then after this, maybe a nap. You should go visit your wife while there's still time left."

Miller's brow furrows. "What are you talking about?"

I lock eyes with him, unflinching. "Remember how I said my world was ravaged by a bomb? I fought so hard to change that throughout my career. However, in the end, I failed, and you betrayed me. So I thought the best way to save my world was to destroy yours first. Take out all the temporal guardians at once, let there be no survivors."

Kierstead speaks up, her voice sharp with alarm. "What did you do?"

A humorless smile tugs at my lips. "I planted a biohazardous bomb in both timelines. Think of it as a token from the future. Let's break down what this virus does."

I pause, letting the weight of my words sink in. The room feels charged with tension, thick enough to cut with a knife. Miller's face has drained of color, while Kierstead's eyes burn with a mix of horror and determination.

"The virus belongs to a new strain of genetically engineered pathogens," I explain, my tone clinical and detached. "It's designed to be highly adaptable and resilient. The complex protein coat allows it to evade the body's immune system and replicate rapidly within host cells."

Miller slams his fist on the table, his voice hoarse with rage. "You're lying. This can't be real."

I shake my head slowly. "I wish I were, Miller. But this is very real. And it gets worse. The virus is primarily transmitted through respiratory droplets, making it highly contagious. It can also survive on surfaces for extended periods, increasing the risk of indirect transmission through contact with contaminated objects."

As I speak, I can see the horror dawning on their faces. Part of me wants to stop, to take it all back, but I know it's too late. The wheels are already in motion.

Kierstead leans forward, her voice barely above a whisper. "How long do we have?"

I meet her gaze, seeing the fierce determination burning behind her eyes. "Not long enough," I reply softly. "Time is of the essence."

3 - 4

I take a deep breath, steeling myself for the next wave of devastating information I must deliver. "The virus has a relatively short incubation period," I explain, my voice steady despite the gravity of the situation. "Typically ranging from one to fourteen days after exposure."

Miller's face contorts with a mix of anger and despair. "So, we could already be infected and not even know it?" he demands, his voice cracking.

I nod solemnly. "That's correct. During this time, infected individuals may show no symptoms, allowing the virus to spread silently. It's one of the most insidious aspects of this pathogen."

Kierstead's eyes narrow as she processes this information. "So, we're looking at a potential silent epidemic," she says, her tone clipped and professional despite the fear I can see lurking in her gaze.

"Precisely," I confirm. "And when the symptoms do manifest, they're severe and wide-ranging."

Miller slumps back in his chair, running a hand through his hair. "What kind of symptoms are we talking about?" he asks, his voice barely above a whisper.

I lean forward, my chains clinking against the table. "Upon infection, the virus targets various systems in the body," I explain. "High fever, cough, shortness of breath, severe fatigue. Muscle and joint pain that makes every movement agony. Splitting headaches that feel like your skull is being crushed. And that's not even mentioning the gastrointestinal issues – nausea, vomiting, diarrhea."

As I speak, I can see the color draining from their faces. The reality of what they're facing is sinking in, and I feel a pang of regret for the pain I'm causing. But it's too late to turn back now.

"This is why I said to say goodbye to your family, Miller," I add softly. "Time truly is of the essence."

5 - 6

Miller's face contorts with a mixture of rage and despair. "You bastard," he hisses, lunging forward only to be restrained by Kierstead. "How could you do this?"

I met his gaze unflinchingly, my voice calm despite the turmoil in my chest. "It's not just about the initial symptoms, Drake. The respiratory complications are where things get truly dire."

Kierstead's grip on Miller loosens as she turns to me, her professional facade cracking. "What do you mean?"

I take a deep breath, feeling the weight of my words. "The virus has a particular affinity for lung tissue. It leads to severe respiratory complications – pneumonia, acute respiratory distress syndrome. The kind of conditions that result in profound hypoxia."

Miller's face pales further. "Low oxygen levels," he whispers.

I nod grimly. "Exactly. It often progresses to respiratory failure, necessitating mechanical ventilation. But even that might not be enough."

"Why?" Kierstead demands, her voice tight with barely contained emotion.

"Because of the immune response," I explain, my eyes never leaving Miller's. "The virus triggers what we call a cytokine storm – a massive, uncontrolled release of inflammatory proteins. It's the body's attempt to fight off the infection, but it backfires spectacularly."

Miller slumps in his chair, his voice barely audible. "What does that mean for the infected?"

I lean forward, my chains rattling. "It means widespread tissue damage, Drake. Organ failure. The lungs, heart, kidneys – they're all vulnerable. It's like the body wages war on itself, and everyone loses."

The room falls silent, the weight of my words hanging heavy in the air. I can see the realization dawning on their faces – the true scale of the catastrophe I've unleashed.

"Why?" Miller finally asks, his voice breaking. "Why would you do this?"

I meet his gaze, my own eyes filled with a mixture of regret and determination. "Because sometimes, Drake, to save a world, you have to be willing to destroy one."

7 - 8

Gabriel leaned back in his chair, his disfigured face twisting into a grimace. "But that's not even the worst of it," he continued, his voice low and ominous. "The virus doesn't just stop at ravaging the body's organs. It goes for the brain too."

Detective Keirstead's eyes widened, her professional composure cracking. "What do you mean, Gabriel?" she demanded, her voice tight with barely contained fury.

I turned to face her, my chains clinking softly. "Neurological effects, Detective. The virus can invade the central nervous system, leading to a host of complications. Encephalitis, seizures, confusion... even coma in some cases."

Miller, who had been silent, suddenly slammed his fist on the table. "Damn it, Gabriel! Do you realize what you've done? You're talking about destroying entire populations!"

I nodded solemnly, feeling the weight of my actions. "I do, Drake. And it gets worse. As the infection progresses, it doesn't discriminate. It attacks everything."

Keirstead leaned forward, her voice barely above a whisper. "Multi-organ failure?"

"Precisely," I confirmed, my gaze sweeping between them. "The widespread tissue damage and inflammation lead to systemic complications. Liver, kidneys, heart - all of them start shutting down, one by one."

Miller stood up abruptly, pacing the small room. "This is insanity, Gabriel. You've potentially doomed both timelines. How could you possibly justify this?"

I closed my eyes, memories of my ravaged world flashing before me. "Because, Drake, in my timeline, the suffering was unimaginable. I thought... I thought by acting first, I could prevent that future from ever happening."

Keirstead's voice cut through the tension. "And now? Do you still believe that?"

I opened my eyes, meeting her intense gaze. "Now, Detective, I realize I may have become the very thing I sought to prevent. But the clock is ticking. If you want to save your world - both worlds - you need to act fast."

9 - 10

Drake's face contorted with a mix of anger and desperation as he turned to face me, his fists clenched at his sides. "Act fast? How the hell are we supposed to act fast against a virus that's already out there, Gabriel? You've unleashed a biological nightmare!"

I leaned forward, my handcuffs clinking against the metal table. "Listen, Drake. The mortality rate is astronomical, especially for vulnerable populations. The elderly, the immunocompromised, those with underlying conditions - they'll be hit the hardest. But make no mistake, this virus doesn't discriminate. Even the healthiest individuals are at risk."

Keirstead interjected, her voice tight with controlled fury. "What about treatment? There has to be something we can do."

I shook my head slowly, feeling the weight of my actions pressing down on me. "That's the crux of it, Detective. There's no specific antiviral treatment available. Management is purely supportive - alleviating symptoms, preventing complications. It's a losing battle against time."

Drake slammed his palm on the table, making me flinch. "Damn it, Gabriel! You're talking about millions of lives! There has to be something!"

I met his gaze, seeing the desperation in his eyes. "Prevention is our only real weapon now. Strict infection control measures are crucial. Vaccination, if we can develop one fast enough. Hand hygiene, masks, social distancing - it's all we've got."

Keirstead leaned in, her voice low and intense. "And how long do we have before this spirals out of control?"

I closed my eyes, calculations running through my mind. "Days, maybe a week at most. The virus spreads rapidly, and with no natural immunity..."

Drake's voice was barely a whisper, filled with horror. "We're looking at a potential extinction event."

I nodded solemnly, the full weight of my actions crashing down upon me. "Yes, Drake. Unless we can find a way to stop it, that's exactly what we're facing."

11 - 12

Drake stood motionless, his face a mask of shock and disbelief. The weight of my words seemed to physically crush him, his broad shoulders slumping as the full implications sank in. His eyes, usually so sharp and determined, now held a haunted look that spoke volumes about the turmoil raging within.

"A deadly virus..." he murmured, his voice barely audible. "One that could wipe out all timelines if not stopped." His gaze snapped back to me, a fierce intensity burning through the shock. "How could you do this, Gabriel? How could you condemn countless innocent lives?"

I opened my mouth to respond, but was cut off by a new voice. A man in a crisp suit stepped into the room, his presence commanding attention. He fixed Drake with a stern look, his tone brooking no argument.

"Time is of the essence, Miller," he stated flatly. "I suggest you say goodbye to your wife and son."

Drake's face paled further, if that was even possible. His mind seemed to race, thoughts of Linda and Harrison flashing across his features. I could almost see him reliving moments with them - Linda's warm smile, Harrison's infectious laughter. The weight of potential loss hung heavy in the air.

"No," Drake growled, his fists clenching at his sides. "I won't just say goodbye. There has to be a way to stop this, to save them and everyone else."

His eyes met mine, a mixture of desperation and determination blazing within them. "Gabriel, you created this virus. There must be something - anything - we can do to counteract it. Please, I'm begging you. Help me save my family, save all the families across every timeline."

I felt the crushing weight of guilt press down upon me, knowing that my actions had brought us to this point. But as I looked into Drake's pleading eyes, I felt a spark of something I hadn't felt in a long time - hope. Maybe, just maybe, there was still a chance to make things right.

Under the Subway Station

Green World – 2024

1 - 2

The fluorescent lights flickered overhead, casting harsh shadows across Gabriel's disfigured face as Detective Miller entered the sterile interrogation room. Gabriel's piercing eyes locked onto Miller, a hint of urgency breaking through his otherwise inscrutable expression. Without waiting for pleasantries, Gabriel leaned forward, his scarred hands clasped tightly on the metal table.

"Detective," Gabriel began, his voice low and smooth despite the tension evident in his rigid posture. "I have information you need to hear immediately."

Miller's brow furrowed, taken aback by Gabriel's directness. He opened his mouth to respond, but Gabriel cut him off with a raised hand.

"The bomb," Gabriel said tersely, his words carefully measured. "It's in the abandoned subway station under Fifth Avenue. East entrance, near the maintenance tunnel."

Gabriel's eyes never left Miller's face, watching intently for any reaction. The detective's mind raced, processing the implications of this unexpected revelation. Could he trust the words of this enigmatic man? The same man who had apparently kidnapped his son?

"How do you-" Miller started to ask, but Gabriel interjected again.

"There's no time for questions, Detective," Gabriel insisted, his voice taking on an edge of urgency. "Every second we waste here puts more lives at risk. You need to act now."

Miller's hand instinctively moved towards his radio, torn between his duty as a detective and his suspicion of Gabriel's motives. The weight of responsibility pressed down on him as he considered the potential consequences of both action and inaction.

Gabriel leaned back slightly; his piercing gaze still fixed on Miller. "I understand your hesitation, Detective," he said, his tone softening almost imperceptibly. "But ask yourself this - can you afford to ignore this information, knowing what's at stake?"

3 - 4

Miller's eyes narrowed, the lines around them deepening as suspicion mingled with a growing sense of urgency. He knew Gabriel wasn't one to offer information without a catch, and the man's disfigured face seemed to twist into an inscrutable mask as he awaited Miller's response.

"And why should I believe you?" Miller demanded; his tone clipped. He leaned forward, resting his palms on the cold metal table, his dark eyes boring into Gabriel's. The fluorescent lights overhead cast harsh shadows across the interrogation room, amplifying the tension crackling between them.

Gabriel's piercing gaze never wavered, his voice low and measured as he replied, "Because, Detective, time is a luxury we don't have. You know as well as I do that this isn't a game."

Miller's jaw clenched, his mind racing through possibilities. Could this be another of Gabriel's manipulations? Or was the threat real? The weight of potential lives at stake pressed down on him, making his next decision feel monumental.

"You've given me no reason to trust you, Gabriel," Miller growled, his fingers drumming an agitated rhythm on the table. "For all I know, this could be another one of your sick traps."

Gabriel leaned forward, his scarred face inches from Miller's. "Think, Drake," he urged, using the detective's first name with unsettling familiarity. "What do I have to gain by lying about this? If you ignore me and that bomb goes off, the blood will be on your hands, not mine."

Miller pulled back, running a hand through his disheveled hair. The exhaustion of the past weeks showed in the dark circles under his eyes, a stark contrast to Gabriel's unnervingly calm demeanor. He knew he had to make a decision, and fast.

5 - 6

Gabriel's lips curled into a sardonic smile, his scarred features twisting into an unsettling mask. "Because I have nothing left to lose," he replied cryptically, his voice a low rasp that sent chills down Miller's spine. "But you do. And if you want to prevent a catastrophe, you'll find that bomb before it's too late."

The words hung in the air, heavy with implication. Miller's mind raced, parsing through Gabriel's statement for hidden meanings or traps. He'd been burned by this man before, but the urgency in Gabriel's tone was impossible to ignore.

"What game are you playing at, Gabriel?" Miller demanded, leaning forward, his fists clenched on the table. "Why tell me this now? What's your angle?"

Gabriel's piercing gaze met Miller's, unflinching. "No game, Detective. Just the cold, hard truth. Time is ticking away, and with every second you waste questioning me, that bomb edges closer to detonation."

With that, Gabriel leaned back in his chair, his demeanor suddenly inscrutable. The shift was jarring, as if a switch had been flipped. Miller found himself studying the man's face, searching for any crack in the facade, any tell that might reveal his true intentions.

Seconds stretched into an eternity as Miller weighed his options. The rational part of his mind screamed caution, reminding him of Gabriel's history of deception. But deep in his gut, an instinct he couldn't ignore told him this threat was real.

"If you're lying..." Miller began, his voice trailing off as the implications of inaction crashed over him.

Gabriel's eyes glinted, a mixture of triumph and something else - was it fear? - flashing across his face. "Then you'll have plenty of time to punish me later," he finished. "But if I'm telling the truth, Detective, you don't have a moment to spare."

7 - 8

Without another word, Miller spun on his heel and strode out of the interrogation room, his mind racing as he formulated a plan. The weight of responsibility pressed down on him, each heartbeat a reminder of the lives hanging in the balance.

"Johnson! Martinez!" he barked, his voice echoing through the precinct. "Get a bomb squad to the abandoned subway station under Fifth Avenue, east entrance near the maintenance tunnel. Now!"

As he hurried through the bustling corridors, Miller's thoughts whirled. Was he making the right call? Gabriel's words haunted him: "Because I have nothing left to lose." What did that mean? And why now?

"Sir," Officer Chen intercepted him, her brow furrowed with concern. "What's going on?"

Miller barely broke stride as he replied, "Possible bomb threat. I need every available unit mobilized and ready to assist with evacuation if necessary."

He paused, running a hand through his disheveled hair. The image of his family flashed through his mind – their smiling faces a stark contrast to the chaos unfolding around him. He pushed the thought away, steeling himself for what lay ahead.

"Listen up, everyone!" Miller's voice boomed across the precinct, commanding instant attention. "We have a credible bomb threat at the abandoned subway station under Fifth Avenue. I need all hands-on deck for this one."

As his colleagues sprang into action, Miller felt the familiar surge of adrenaline coursing through his veins. He turned to his partner, Detective Kierstead, who had appeared at his side.

"You think Gabriel's intel is solid?" Kierstead asked, skepticism evident in her tone.

Miller hesitated, then nodded grimly. "We can't afford to take the chance that it's not. The stakes are too high."

As they rushed towards the exit, Miller's mind raced with possible scenarios, each more dire than the last. The weight of countless lives pressed down on him, a burden he'd carried for years but never quite this heavy.

"Let's move!" he shouted, leading the charge out of the precinct. With every passing second, the tension mounted, each moment bringing them closer to either averting disaster or facing unimaginable consequences.

9 - 10

The dank, musty air of the abandoned subway station assaulted Miller's nostrils as he led his team down the crumbling steps. His heart hammered against his ribs; each beat a stark reminder of the urgency that propelled them forward. The beam of his flashlight cut through the oppressive darkness, casting eerie shadows that seemed to dance and twist with malevolent intent.

"Stay alert," Miller barked, his voice echoing off the graffiti-covered walls. "We don't know what we're walking into here."

As they ventured deeper into the labyrinthine tunnels, Miller's mind raced. Images of Linda and Harrison flashed before his eyes, their faces a poignant reminder of what was at stake. He swallowed hard, pushing the thoughts aside. "Focus, Drake," he muttered to himself. "They're counting on you."

Detective Kierstead's voice cut through the tense silence. "Miller, you sure about this? What if it's a wild goose chase?"

Miller turned, his eyes locking with his partner's. "It's not. I can feel it in my gut. We're close."

The group pressed on, their footsteps echoing ominously through the abandoned corridors. With each passing moment, the air grew thicker with anticipation, the weight of their mission pressing down on them like a physical force.

Suddenly, Miller's flashlight beam caught something – a glint of metal amidst the rubble. "There!" he shouted, his voice tight with a mixture of relief and dread. "Everyone, hold position!"

As they approached the spot Gabriel had described, Miller's breath caught in his throat. There, nestled among the debris and decay, sat a small device, its blinking lights pulsing with sinister intent.

"Dear God," Kierstead whispered, her face pale in the dim light. "It's real."

Miller nodded grimly; his eyes fixed on the bomb. "Yeah, it is. And now we've got to figure out how to stop it before it's too late."

11 - 12

Miller knelt beside the device, his heart racing as he studied its intricate components. "Bomb squad's in route, but we can't wait," he said, his voice low and tense. "We've got to start now."

Holly Kierstead hesitated, her eyes wide with fear. "Drake, are you sure? We're not trained for this."

"We don't have a choice," Miller replied, his hands already moving towards the bomb. As his fingers brushed the cool metal, he couldn't help but think of Harrison, imagining his son's mischievous grin. "I can't let this thing take more lives," he muttered, more to himself than anyone else.

Time seemed to slow to a crawl as Miller and his team worked, their movements precise and methodical. Sweat beaded on his forehead, and he could hear his own heartbeat thundering in his ears. "Wire cutters," he demanded, his voice barely above a whisper.

As he carefully navigated the maze of wires, Miller's mind drifted to Linda. Her strength, her unwavering support – he drew on it now, channeling her resilience into his steady hands. "Come on, Drake," he urged himself. "You've got this."

Minutes stretched into what felt like hours, each second bringing them closer to potential catastrophe. The tension in the air was palpable, thick enough to choke on. Miller's team watched in silent anticipation; their breath held collectively.

Finally, after what seemed an eternity, Miller's fingers closed around the last wire. He hesitated for a split second, doubt creeping in. "If I'm wrong," he thought, "I'll never see them again." But the image of his family steeled his resolve.

With a deep breath, he made the cut.

For a heart-stopping moment, nothing happened. Then, with a soft click, the bomb's lights flickered and died. The oppressive silence that followed was deafening.

"Is it...?" Kierstead began, her voice trembling.

Miller nodded, a wave of relief washing over him. "It's done. We did it."

As the reality of their success sank in, Miller surveyed the scene, a complex mix of emotions swirling within him. Pride, relief, and lingering anxiety battled for dominance. He couldn't help but wonder about Gabriel's role in all this, the enigmatic figure whose warning had set this all in motion.

"Nice work, everyone," Miller said, his voice rough with emotion. "Let's get this secured and head back. We've got a lot of questions that need answering."

13 - 13

Drake Miller trudged up the grimy subway stairs, his footsteps echoing in the cavernous space as he emerged into the harsh glare of flashing police lights. He squinted, his tired eyes adjusting to the chaos above ground. As the cool night air hit his face, his thoughts inevitably drifted to Gabriel Angel, the man whose cryptic warning had set this night's events in motion.

"Sir," a young officer approached, clipboard in hand. "We need your statement for the—"

Miller held up a hand, cutting him off. "In a minute," he growled, his voice gravelly with exhaustion. He turned to his partner, Kierstead, who was busy coordinating with the bomb disposal unit. "I need to make a call."

As he pulled out his phone, Miller's mind raced. Gabriel's disfigured face flashed before him, those piercing eyes that seemed to bore into his soul. He dialed a familiar number, his fingers trembling slightly.

"This is Miller," he said as soon as the line connected. "I need everything we have on Gabriel Angel. And I mean everything."

There was a pause on the other end. "Sir, that's classified information. I'd need clearance from—"

"Damn it, Johnson!" Miller snapped, his frustration boiling over. "That man just helped us prevent a catastrophe. I need to know why."

As he hung up, Miller's gaze swept over the scene. Emergency vehicles, flashing lights, curious onlookers held back by yellow tape. It all felt surreal. He couldn't shake the feeling that this was just the beginning of something much bigger.

"What's your angle, Gabriel?" he muttered to himself, running a hand through his disheveled hair. "Why help us? What's your endgame?"

Kierstead approached, her face etched with concern. "Drake, you, okay? You look like you've seen a ghost."

Miller let out a humorless chuckle. "Maybe I have, Holly. Maybe I have." He turned to face her fully. "What do you make of all this? Gabriel's warning, the bomb... it doesn't add up."

Holly shrugged, her eyes darting around nervously. "I don't know, but I've got a bad feeling about this. Something tells me we're just scratching the surface."

Miller nodded; his expression grim. "I couldn't agree more. And I've got a feeling Gabriel Angel is at the center of it all."

As they stood there, the weight of the night's events pressing down on them, Miller couldn't help but feel a grudging sense of gratitude towards Gabriel. Despite his suspicions, the man had saved countless lives tonight. But at what cost? And to what end?

The questions swirled in Miller's mind, a relentless torrent of uncertainty. One thing was clear: this was far from over. And Drake Miller was determined to uncover the truth, no matter where it led.

Night Terrors Awakening

Blue World – 2024

1 - 2

Drake's eyes snapped open, his heart hammering against his ribs like a frantic prisoner. The dim glow of the bedside clock cast eerie shadows across the room, its red digits a stark reminder of the urgency that had jolted him from his fitful slumber. Beside him, Linda stirred, her blonde hair splayed across the pillow as she blinked groggily in the half-light.

"Linda, wake up," Drake urged, his voice hoarse with sleep and tinged with desperation. He reached out, gently shaking her shoulder as the weight of their impending mission pressed down on him. "We don't have much time."

Linda's blue eyes fluttered open, confusion giving way to concern as she registered the intensity in Drake's gaze. He could see the questions forming on her lips, but there was no time for explanations. Every second that ticked by was another moment lost; another step closer to catastrophe.

As Linda pushed herself up, Drake's mind raced, recalling the fragments of information that had led them to this moment. The parallel timelines, Gabriel's sinister plot, the ticking bomb that threatened to tear their world apart – it all swirled in his thoughts like a maelstrom of fear and determination.

"Drake, what's happening?" Linda's voice, still thick with sleep, cut through his spiraling thoughts. Her hand found his in the darkness, a lifeline amidst the chaos.

He turned to her, his brown eyes meeting her blue ones, trying to convey the gravity of their situation without words. "I'm sorry," he whispered, the weight of his past mistakes pressing down on him. "I should have been more vigilant, should have seen this coming."

Linda squeezed his hand, her touch a balm to his frayed nerves. "We're in this together," she said, her voice steady despite the fear he could see flickering in her eyes. "Whatever it is, we'll face it as a family."

Drake nodded, drawing strength from her unwavering support. He took a deep breath, steeling himself for what lay ahead. "We need to move fast," he said, already pushing back the covers and swinging his legs over the side of the bed. "Every moment counts now."

As they hurried to dress, Drake's mind raced with possibilities and strategies. The lawyer in him wanted to approach this methodically, to weigh every option and consider every angle. But the desperate father, the man who had already lost so much, knew that time was a luxury they couldn't afford.

"I never wanted to drag you into this," Drake murmured as he pulled on his shoes, guilt gnawing at him. "I thought I could protect you, protect our family, by keeping you in the dark."

Linda paused in the act of pulling her hair back, her eyes softening as she looked at him. "Drake, we're stronger together. You don't have to carry this burden alone anymore."

Her words washed over him, a soothing balm to his troubled soul. For a moment, he allowed himself to bask in the warmth of her love, to draw strength from her unwavering faith in him. Then, with a determined nod, he stood, ready to face whatever challenges lay ahead.

"Let's go," he said, his voice low but resolute. "We have a world to save."

3 - 4

Linda's eyes widened in alarm as she sat up, her gaze locking onto Drake's face. The soft light from the bedside lamp cast shadows across her features, accentuating the worry lines that had formed around her eyes. "What's wrong?" she asked, her voice laced with concern, a tremor barely concealed beneath her usual soothing tone.

Drake took a deep breath, his mind racing as he tried to find the right words. The weight of the information he carried pressed down on him, threatening to crush him under its enormity. He ran a hand through his disheveled hair, buying himself a few precious seconds to organize his thoughts. "There's a bomb," he explained quickly, the words tumbling out in a rush. "In this timeline. Gabriel planted it, and it's set to go off soon."

As he spoke, Drake's eyes darted around the room, as if expecting to see the device materialize in the shadows. His heart pounded in his chest; each beat a reminder of the urgency of their situation. He couldn't help but think of Gabriel's disfigured face, those piercing eyes that seemed to hold untold secrets. What game was he playing? What was his endgame?

"Gabriel?" Linda echoed, her brow furrowing as she processed the information. "The man with the burns? Drake, how do you know this?"

Drake's hands clenched into fists, his knuckles turning white with the pressure. "I can't explain it all right now," he said, his voice strained. "But I swear to you, Linda, this is real. We're in danger, and we need to act fast."

He could see the questions swimming in Linda's eyes, could almost hear the doubts forming in her mind. But beneath it all, he saw trust - unwavering, unshakeable trust in him. It both comforted and terrified him. What if he was wrong? What if he was leading them into even greater danger?

"Okay," Linda said softly, reaching out to place a reassuring hand on his arm. "I believe you. What do we need to do?"

Drake felt a surge of love and gratitude wash over him. Even in the face of this unbelievable threat, Linda remained his rock, his anchor in the storm. "We need to move fast," he said, already pushing back the covers and swinging his legs over the side of the bed. "Every moment counts now."

5 - 6

Linda's breath caught in her throat, her blue eyes widening in shock as the gravity of Drake's words sank in. "A bomb? Here?" she repeated, her voice barely above a whisper, trembling with the weight of disbelief and terror.

Drake nodded gravely, his dark eyes meeting hers with an intensity that spoke volumes. The lines on his face deepened, etched with the burden of knowledge and responsibility. "Yes," he confirmed, his voice low and urgent. "We need to warn Detective Sharp. She's the only one who can help us stop it."

His mind raced, calculating the risks, the precious minutes ticking away. How much time did they have? Where exactly was the bomb? Questions swirled in his head like a maelstrom, threatening to overwhelm him.

Linda's hand found his in the dim light of their bedroom, her touch anchoring him to the present. "Drake," she whispered, her voice steadier now, "how can, you be sure? This is... it's unthinkable."

He squeezed her hand, drawing strength from her unwavering presence. "I know it sounds crazy," Drake admitted, running his free hand through his disheveled black hair. "But after everything we've been through, after all the impossible things we've seen... Linda, I need you to trust me on this."

His wife's eyes searched his face, and he could see the moment when determination replaced fear. "I do trust you," she said firmly. "Always. What do we need to do?"

Drake felt a surge of love and gratitude, tempered by the urgency of their situation. "We need to contact Sharp immediately," he explained, already reaching for his phone. "She has the resources, the authority to mobilize quickly. If anyone can prevent this disaster, it's her."

As his fingers hovered over the keypad, a chilling thought struck him. What if they were too late? What if their warning came moments before devastation? The weight of countless lives pressed down on his shoulders, threatening to crush him under its immensity.

7 - 8

Drake's fingers trembled as he punched in Detective Sharp's number, each digit feeling like a lifeline cast into the darkness. The phone's shrill ring pierced the tense silence of the bedroom, each unanswered tone driving a spike of anxiety deeper into his chest.

"Come on, Sharp," he muttered, his free hand clenching and unclenching rhythmically. "Pick up, damn it."

As the seconds stretched into an eternity, Drake's mind raced with memories of his past life – the ruthless lawyer who'd sacrifice anything for a win. How different he was now, desperately trying to save lives instead of careers. The irony wasn't lost on him, a bitter taste in his mouth as he silently pleaded with a universe that seemed determined to fracture his existence.

Finally, blessedly, the line clicked. "Sharp," came the curt response, and Drake nearly sagged with relief.

"Detective," he blurted, words tumbling out in a frantic rush. "It's Drake Miller. There's a bomb – Gabriel planted it in this timeline. We don't have much time."

He could almost hear Sharp's posture stiffen through the phone. "Miller? Slow down. What exactly are you saying?"

Drake took a deep breath, forcing himself to speak clearly despite the panic clawing at his throat. "I know how this sounds, but please, you have to listen. There's an explosive device somewhere in the city. If we don't find it soon, people will die. Innocent people, Sharp. I can't... I can't let that happen. Not again."

His voice cracked on the last words, the weight of his dual realities pressing down on him. In one world, he'd lost his wife: in another, his son. The thought of more loss, more families torn apart, was unbearable.

"Drake," Sharp's voice cut through his spiraling thoughts, sharp and focused. "I need details. Everything you know, now."

9 - 10

Detective Sharp listened intently, her voice steady as she reassured Drake, "Thank you for letting me know. I'll mobilize my team right away." The calm professionalism in her tone was a stark contrast to Drake's frantic energy, but it carried an undercurrent of urgency that told him she understood the gravity of the situation.

"You believe me?" Drake asked, unable to keep the surprise from his voice. He'd half-expected to be dismissed, to have to fight to be taken seriously.

"Miller, in this line of work, I've learned to trust my gut," Sharp replied, a hint of wry humor in her words. "And right now, my gut's telling me you're not the type to cry wolf. Now, any idea where this bomb might be?"

Drake closed his eyes, trying to recall every detail from his fractured memories. "I... I'm not sure. But I think it might be near the city center. Gabriel always had a flair for the dramatic."

"Alright, I'm on it. We'll start there and fan out. I'll keep you updated," Sharp said, her voice becoming distant as she barked orders to someone on her end of the line.

As the call ended, relief flooded through Drake, a weight lifting from his shoulders. He turned to Linda, meeting her eyes with a determined expression. The fear in her blue gaze mirrored his own, but there was strength there too, a resilience that never failed to amaze him.

"She believed us," Drake said, his voice hoarse. "Sharp's mobilizing her team. We've taken the first step, Linda. We might actually be able to stop this."

Linda reached out, taking his hand in hers. "You did it, Drake. You got through to her."

Drake squeezed her hand, drawing strength from her touch. "We did it. I couldn't have done this without you, you know that, right?" He paused, a lump forming in his throat. "God, Linda, I'm so sorry. For everything. For not being there, for putting work first for so long..."

"Shh," Linda soothed, her free hand coming up to cup his cheek. "That's in the past. What matters is now, and right now, you're here. We're together, and we're fighting. That's what counts."

Drake leaned into her touch, closing his eyes briefly. When he opened them again, determination had replaced the guilt in his gaze. "You're right. We can't change the past, but we can shape the future. And I swear, Linda, I'm going to do everything in my power to make sure it's a future where we're all safe. Where our family is whole again."

11 - 12

Drake's eyes locked with Linda's, his voice steady despite the tremor in his hands. "We need to get to safety," he said, the weight of their situation hanging heavy in the air. "But first, we wait for Detective Sharp's next move. Together, we'll stop this bomb and make sure no one else gets hurt."

Linda nodded, her blonde hair catching the dim light as she moved. "What do you think Sharp will do?" she asked, her blue eyes searching Drake's face for reassurance.

Drake ran a hand through his dark hair, his mind racing. "Knowing Sharp, she'll act fast. She's not one to waste time," he replied, recalling the detective's no-nonsense attitude. "But we can't just sit here waiting. We need to be ready to move."

As he spoke, Drake's gaze darted around their bedroom, assessing what they might need. His lawyer's mind, once focused on winning cases at any cost, now channeled that same intensity into protecting his family. "Linda, can you grab a bag? Pack some essentials, just in case we need to leave quickly."

Linda nodded, her movements swift and purposeful as she retrieved a duffel bag from their closet. Drake watched her for a moment, marveling at her strength. Even in the face of unimaginable danger, she remained composed, her actions methodical and focused.

"I can't believe we're in this situation," Drake muttered, more to himself than to Linda. "A bomb, parallel timelines... it's like something out of a nightmare."

Linda paused in her packing, turning to face him. "Drake," she said softly, her voice a balm to his frayed nerves, "we've been through so much already. We've faced loss, grief, the impossible. If anyone can handle this, it's us."

Drake felt a surge of emotion at her words, remembering the accident that had torn their lives apart, splitting his reality in two. In one world, he had lost Linda; in another, their son. The pain of those memories threatened to overwhelm him, but he pushed it aside, focusing on the present.

"You're right," he said, moving to help her pack. "We're stronger together. And this time, I swear I won't let anything come between us. Not work, not danger, nothing."

As they finished packing, Drake's phone buzzed with a text from Detective Sharp. His heart raced as he read the message aloud: "Team mobilized. Stay put. Will contact soon with instructions."

Drake and Linda exchanged a look, a mix of relief and apprehension passing between them. "This is it," Drake said, his voice barely above a whisper. "Whatever happens next, we face it together."

Linda reached out, intertwining her fingers with his. "Together," she echoed, her grip firm and reassuring.

With that, Drake and Linda set their plan into motion, their minds focused on the task ahead as they prepared to face whatever challenges lay in their path. And as they braced themselves for the journey ahead, they knew that they would do whatever it took to protect the world they loved and the people they held dear.

City Under Threat

Blue World – 2024

1 - 2

Detective Sharp's pulse pounded in her ears as Miller's words echoed in her mind: "There's a bomb in the city." Her sharp eyes darted across the bustling precinct, assessing her team with laser focus.

"Listen up!" she barked, her commanding voice cutting through the din. "We have a critical situation. There's an explosive device somewhere in the city, and we need to find it before it's too late."

The room fell silent, all eyes fixed on Sharp as she continued, her words clipped and urgent. "I want every available officer on this. Check security footage, canvas neighborhoods, follow up on any suspicious activity reports. Leave no stone unturned."

As her team sprang into action, Sharp felt a familiar surge of adrenaline course through her veins. This was what she lived for—the thrill of the chase, the race against time to save innocent lives. But beneath her steely exterior, a flicker of doubt gnawed at her. What if they couldn't find it in time?

She pushed the thought aside, focusing on the task at hand. "Bird," she called out, her piercing gaze locking onto his weary face. "You're with me. We need to retrace Vega's steps, see if we can find any clues he might have left behind."

As they hurried out of the precinct, Sharp's mind raced, piecing together fragments of information. "Talk to me, Miller," she urged, her voice tight with tension. "What else can you tell me about Vega's movements before he died?"

Miller's response was thoughtful, measured. "He was... erratic in the days leading up to his death. Paranoid. Like he knew something was coming."

Sharp's brow furrowed as she processed this information. "And you're sure he didn't give you any indication of where the bomb might be?"

"No," Miller replied, his voice heavy with regret. "I wish he had. God, I wish he had."

Hours blurred together as Sharp, and her team combed through every lead, every possibility. The city became a labyrinth of potential hiding spots, each dead end more frustrating than the last. Sharp's determination never wavered, but as the clock ticked relentlessly forward, a creeping sense of dread began to take hold.

"Nothing at the docks," came a crackled report over her radio. "Warehouse district's clear too."

Sharp's jaw clenched as she surveyed the city map spread out before her, red pins marking each cleared location. "Where are you?" she muttered, her eyes scanning the vast expanse of urban sprawl. "Where would you hide a bomb in plain sight?"

She turned to Miller, noting the lines of exhaustion etched on his face. "We're missing something," she said, her voice a mix of frustration and determination. "What aren't we seeing?"

Miller shook his head, his eyes distant. "I don't know. But we can't give up. There are too many lives at stake."

Sharp nodded, her resolve hardening. "You're right. We keep looking until we find it or..." She left the alternative unspoken, the weight of it hanging heavy in the air between them.

As night fell over the city, Sharp stood at the precinct window, her reflection ghostly in the glass. The city lights twinkled below, oblivious to the danger lurking in their midst. She pressed her forehead against the cool pane, closing her eyes for a brief moment.

"Where are you?" she whispered, her words a desperate plea to the universe. "Where are you hiding?"

3 - 4

Sharp's eyes snapped open, her reflection staring back at her with a mixture of determination and despair. The city's twinkling lights seemed to mock her now, each one a potential hiding place for the bomb that threatened to tear everything apart. She turned away from the window, her heart heavy with the weight of her promise to Miller.

"Detective," Officer Chen called, his voice tight with urgency. "We've exhausted every lead. What's our next move?"

Sharp's gaze swept across the room, taking in the weary faces of her team. She squared her shoulders, pushing down the creeping sense of failure. "We go back to the beginning," she announced, her voice carrying a strength she didn't entirely feel. "Sometimes, the answer is right where we started."

As they drove through the darkening streets, Sharp's mind raced, replaying every detail of the case. The car screeched to a halt at the scene where Vega's body had been discovered, and she stepped out, the cool night air doing little to calm her nerves.

"Why here?" Miller asked, following close behind as they approached the taped-off area.

Sharp's eyes scanned the scene, her voice low and intense. "Because this is where it all began. If we're missing something, it might be here."

The sight of Vega's outline on the ground, now just a faded chalk mark, sent a chill down Sharp's spine. She crouched down, her fingers hovering just above the rough asphalt. "What were you trying to tell us, Vega?" she murmured, her brow furrowed in concentration.

Miller paced nearby, his anxiety palpable. "Sharp, we're running out of time. If we don't find that bomb soon..."

She stood abruptly, cutting him off. "I know, Miller. Believe me, I know." Her eyes locked with his, fierce determination blazing in their depths. "But we will find it. We have to."

As they combed through the scene once more, Sharp couldn't shake the feeling that they were on the precipice of something crucial. Each passing second felt like a hammer blow against her resolve, but she pushed on, driven by the knowledge that failure wasn't an option. The city's fate hung in the balance, and she was the thin blue line standing between order and chaos.

5 - 6

Sharp's eyes darted across the crime scene, her keen gaze searching for anything they might have missed. The flashing lights of nearby police vehicles cast an eerie glow, transforming familiar shadows into potential threats. Suddenly, a glint caught her attention, a tiny reflection amidst the chaos.

"Wait," she breathed, her heart rate quickening. "There's something here."

She moved closer, her steps measured and deliberate. As she approached, the object came into focus, and a sinking feeling settled in her stomach. There, discarded on the ground as if it were nothing more than trash, lay Vega's badge.

"Oh, God," Sharp whispered, her voice barely audible. She crouched down, her fingers trembling as she reached for the badge. The metal was cool against her skin, a stark contrast to the heat of her rising dread.

Miller's voice cut through her thoughts. "What is it, Sharp? What did you find?"

She stood slowly, turning to face him with the badge held out. "It's Vega's law badge. Just... tossed aside like it meant nothing."

Miller's face paled. "Jesus. What kind of monster are we dealing with here?"

Sharp's jaw clenched, her fingers tightening around the badge. "The kind that doesn't value life, Miller. The kind that sees people as disposable."

As she stared at the badge, a wave of despair washed over her. The weight of the situation pressed down on her shoulders, threatening to crush her resolve. In her mind's eye, she saw the faces of countless innocent civilians, unaware of the danger looming over their city.

"We're missing something," she muttered, more to herself than to Miller. "This badge, it's not just evidence. It's a message."

Miller stepped closer, his brow furrowed. "A message? What do you mean?"

Sharp's eyes narrowed as she turned the badge over in her hands. "Think about it. Vega was one of you. This badge represents everything you stand for – protection, justice, order. By discarding it like this, our bomber is telling us exactly what he thinks of those ideals."

7 - 8

Detective Sharp's fingers trembled as she pulled out her phone, the cool metal a stark contrast to her clammy skin. The weight of impending disaster bore down on her as she dialed Miller's number, each ring echoing the frantic beating of her heart. She paced the dimly lit crime scene, her eyes darting between Vega's discarded badge and the shadows that seemed to close in around her.

"Come on, Miller," she muttered, her free hand clenching and unclenching at her side. "Pick up, damn it."

The call connected, and Miller's gruff voice came through. "Sharp? What's the situation?"

She took a deep breath, steeling herself. "Miller," she began, her voice steady despite the maelstrom of emotions swirling within her. "I need you to listen carefully. I believe the bomb is in the law firm."

There was a sharp intake of breath on the other end of the line. Sharp could almost see Miller's tired eyes widening, his scruffy beard twitching as he processed her words.

"The law firm?" Miller repeated, his tone a mix of disbelief and dawning realization. "What makes you think that?"

Sharp's gaze fell once more on Vega's badge, glinting accusingly in the dim light. "It's the message, Miller. The disregard for authority, for justice. Where else would our bomber want to make his statement?"

She could hear Miller's heavy breathing; knew he was probably running his hand through his disheveled hair as he often did when deep in thought. "You're right," he finally said, his voice tight with urgency. "It fits the profile. But Sharp, if you're right, we don't have much time."

"I know," she replied, already moving towards her car. "Meet me there. And Miller? Be careful. This bastard's already taken one of our own."

As she ended the call, Sharp couldn't shake the feeling that they were racing against an invisible clock, each tick bringing them closer to catastrophe. The city's skyline loomed before her, a silent witness to the deadly game unfolding in its streets.

9 - 10

Miller's voice crackled through the phone, heavy with the weight of their dire situation. "I'm on my way. God, I hope we're not too late."

Sharp gripped the steering wheel tighter, her knuckles turning white as she weaved through late-night traffic. The city lights blurred past, a kaleidoscope of neon and shadow. Her mind raced, replaying every detail of the case, searching for any clue they might have missed.

"Miller," she said, her voice barely above a whisper, "what if we're wrong? What if—"

"We can't think like that," he cut in, his tone firm but tinged with an undercurrent of fear. "We have to trust our instincts. It's all we've got right now."

Sharp nodded, even though Miller couldn't see her. She could almost picture him, his dark eyes intense with determination, his normally disheveled appearance even more unkempt in the face of this crisis.

"I keep thinking about Harrison," Miller continued, his voice softening. "If anything happened to him... I can't lose him again, Sharp. I can't."

The raw emotion in his voice struck a chord within Sharp. She knew the depths of Miller's love for his son, how it drove him even in the face of his fractured reality.

"We won't let that happen," she assured him, her own resolve strengthening. "We're going to find this bomb, Miller. We're going to stop it."

As they neared the law firm, the gravity of what lay ahead settled over them like a heavy shroud. The fate of countless lives hung in the balance, and time was slipping away with each passing second.

11 - 12

Detective Sharp's grip tightened on her phone, her knuckles whitening as she nodded grimly, even though Miller couldn't see her. "Yes," she affirmed, her voice low and taut with tension. "It's the only lead we have left. We need to act fast." The words hung in the air, heavy with the weight of their implications. Sharp's mind raced, imagining the ticking clock, the lives at stake, the catastrophic consequences if they failed.

There was a beat of silence on the other end of the line, and Sharp could almost see Miller's face, his brow furrowed in concentration, his tired eyes blazing with renewed determination. When he spoke again, his voice carried a sense of urgency that matched her own. "I'm on my way," he said, the words clipped and decisive. "We'll find the bomb together."

Sharp felt a surge of relief mingled with apprehension. "Good," she replied, already moving towards her car. "Meet me at the south entrance. We'll need to coordinate with the bomb squad and—"

"No time," Miller interrupted, his voice rough with emotion. "Every second counts. We go in first, assess the situation. If we wait for backup, it might be too late."

Sharp hesitated, torn between protocol and the desperate need for immediate action. Her free hand clenched into a fist as she made her decision. "Agreed," she said, sliding into the driver's seat. "But Miller, we need to be smart about this. One wrong move and—"

"I know," he cut in, his tone softening slightly. "We've got this, Sharp. We have to."

As she started the engine, Sharp couldn't shake the image of Vega's discarded badge, a grim reminder of what was at stake. "See you in five," she said, ending the call and peeling out of the parking lot, her heart pounding in rhythm with the wailing sirens that cut through the night.

Detective on Edge

Blue World – 2024

1 - 2

The incessant buzzing of Detective Holly Sharp's phone cut through the tense silence like a knife, each vibration sending a jolt of adrenaline through her body. Her piercing eyes darted to the screen, recognizing Miller's name instantly. With a sharp intake of breath, she swiped to answer, her heart pounding in her ears.

"Miller, any luck on your end?" she asked, her voice tight with urgency. She paced the room, her free hand clenched at her side, knuckles white with tension.

"We're still searching, Sharp," Miller's gravelly voice crackled through the speaker. "This place is a maze. How about you?"

Holly's mind raced, analyzing every possible scenario. "Nothing concrete yet," she replied, frustration evident in her clipped tone. "But we can't afford to miss anything. The stakes are too high."

As she spoke, Holly's eyes scanned the room, taking in every detail with laser focus. The weight of responsibility pressed down on her shoulders, threatening to crush her resolve. But she pushed it aside, channeling her fear into determination.

"Listen, Miller," she said, her voice low and intense. "We need to think outside the box. Gabriel's clever, but he's also predictable in his unpredictability. What are we overlooking?"

There was a pause on the other end of the line, filled only by the sound of Miller's heavy breathing. Holly could almost see him, brow furrowed in concentration, his tired eyes reflecting the same desperate urgency she felt.

"I don't know, Sharp," he finally admitted, the weariness in his voice palpable. "But we can't give up. Too many lives are at stake."

Holly nodded, even though Miller couldn't see her. Her free hand unconsciously moved to her holster, feeling the reassuring weight of her weapon. "You're right," she agreed, her voice steely with resolve. "We keep looking. We keep pushing. We don't stop until we find that bomb."

As she ended the call, Holly took a deep breath, steadying herself for the challenge ahead. The clock was ticking, and failure wasn't an option. With renewed determination, she strode towards the door, ready to face whatever came next in this high-stakes game of cat and mouse.

3 - 4

Holly's mind raced as she paced the room, her footsteps echoing in the tense silence. The weight of countless lives pressed down on her, each passing second a reminder of their dwindling time. She ran her fingers through her hair, a nervous habit she'd never quite shaken, as she mentally catalogued every shred of information they had on Gabriel Angel.

"Think, Holly," she muttered to herself, her piercing eyes darting around the room as if the answer might materialize on the walls. "Where would a man with burns and a vendetta hide a bomb?"

She paused, her gaze falling on a photo of Gabriel, his disfigured face staring back at her with those unsettling eyes. A chill ran down her spine as she recalled their last encounter, his smooth voice laced with hidden meanings and cryptic clues.

"What are you trying to tell us, you bastard?" she growled, her fists clenching at her sides.

Just then, her phone buzzed again. It was Miller.

"Sharp," he said, his voice tight with tension, "I've been thinking. What if we're looking at this all wrong? What if it's not about where Gabriel would hide the bomb, but where he'd want it to be found?"

Holly's breath caught in her throat. "You might be onto something, Drake," she replied, her mind already spinning with possibilities. "Gabriel's not just after destruction. He wants to send a message."

"Exactly," Miller agreed, a hint of hope creeping into his tired voice. "So where would make the biggest statement?"

As Holly opened her mouth to respond, a sudden realization hit her like a thunderbolt. Her heart raced as the pieces began to fall into place, Gabriel's enigmatic words from their last encounter suddenly taking on a chilling new meaning.

"Miller," she said, her voice barely above a whisper, "I think I know where it is."

5 - 6

"Wait, I have an idea," she said suddenly, a glimmer of hope igniting within her. Detective Sharp's fingers trembled as she gripped her phone tighter, her mind racing with the implications of her revelation.

Miller's voice crackled through the speaker, urgent and desperate. "What is it?" he asked, his tone eager. The weariness that had been weighing him down seemed to evaporate, replaced by a renewed sense of purpose.

Sharp inhaled sharply, her eyes darting around the room as if searching for invisible threads connecting the clues. "Gabriel's always been about symbolism, hasn't he?" she began, her words tumbling out in a rush. "He's not just planting a bomb; he's making a statement."

"Go on," Miller urged, his breath audible through the phone.

Detective Sharp's eyes widened as a sudden realization struck her, the pieces of the puzzle finally falling into place. "The hospital," she breathed, her voice barely above a whisper. The words hung in the air, heavy with significance. "Gabriel has a history there, and it's a high-profile target."

Her mind raced, memories of Gabriel's past flashing before her eyes. The countless hours she'd spent poring over his case file, the intricate web of his life unraveling before her. She could almost see him now, his piercing eyes filled with that eerie calm as he plotted his next move.

"Sharp? You still there?" Miller's voice crackled through the phone, snapping her back to reality.

"Yes," she replied, her voice steadier now. "Think about it, Miller. The hospital where Gabriel was working, where you were taken after the accident. It's the perfect symbolic target for him."

She could hear Miller's sharp intake of breath, could almost see him running a hand through his disheveled hair as he processed the information. "Christ, you're right," he muttered, the weariness in his voice giving way to a renewed sense of urgency.

"It fits his pattern," Sharp continued, pacing the room as she spoke. "High impact, maximum casualties, and deeply personal. It's everything he stands for."

There was a moment of tense silence before Miller's voice crackled through again, determination evident in every word. "Let's move," he said, the urgency in his tone mirroring the adrenaline now coursing through Sharp's veins. "I'll meet you there in ten."

As Sharp grabbed her coat and badge, her mind was already racing ahead, formulating a plan. She knew they were walking into a potential disaster, but for the first time since this nightmare began, she felt a glimmer of hope. They had a lead, a target, and most importantly, they had each other. Whatever Gabriel had planned, they would face it together.

7 - 8

The world outside blurred into a chaotic tapestry of lights and shadows as Detective Sharp's car tore through the city streets, her knuckles white against the steering wheel. Every nerve in her body thrummed with tension, her mind laser-focused on the ticking clock they raced against.

"Come on, come on," she muttered under her breath, swerving around a slow-moving sedan. Her eyes darted to the rearview mirror, catching sight of Miller's car close behind. The familiar sight of his determined face gave her a momentary sense of calm amidst the storm.

As they rounded a corner, the hospital loomed into view, a behemoth of concrete and glass against the night sky. Sharp's heart hammered in her chest as she took in the scene unfolding before them.

"Jesus," she breathed, pulling up to the curb with a screech of tires.

The hospital entrance was a maelstrom of activity. Ambulances wailed, their lights painting the night in eerie flashes of red and blue. Panicked civilians streamed out of the building, their faces etched with fear and confusion. Hospital staff in scrubs rushed back and forth, trying to maintain order in the face of mounting chaos.

Miller's car pulled up beside her, and he was out in an instant, his eyes wide as he took in the scene. "Sharp," he called out, his voice taut with tension, "what's our play here?"

She turned to face him, her jaw set with determination. "We split up," she said, her voice steady despite the adrenaline coursing through her veins. "You take the east wing, I'll take the west. We need to find that bomb, and fast."

As they moved towards the hospital entrance, Sharp couldn't help but think of the last time she'd been here - a lifetime ago, it seemed, when the world made sense and Gabriel was just another name on a case file. Now, as they stood on the precipice of potential disaster, she felt the weight of every decision, every misstep that had led them to this moment.

"Miller," she said, grabbing his arm before they parted ways. "Whatever happens in there... we're in this together, alright?"

He nodded, his eyes meeting hers with a mix of fear and resolve. "Together," he echoed, squeezing her hand briefly before disappearing into the chaos of the hospital lobby.

Taking a deep breath, Sharp steeled herself and plunged into the fray, her mind racing with possibilities and prayers. The bomb was here, somewhere in this labyrinth of corridors and rooms. And they had to find it before it was too late.

9 - 10

Detective Sharp pushed through the crowded hallways, her eyes darting from face to face, searching for any sign of suspicion or fear that might betray the bomber's presence. The cacophony of panicked voices and hurried footsteps echoed off the sterile walls, amplifying the urgency of their mission.

"Excuse me," she barked, flashing her badge at a startled nurse. "I need access to the restricted areas. Now."

The nurse hesitated; her eyes wide. "I... I don't have clearance for that."

Sharp's patience wore thin. "Lives are at stake. Either you open those doors, or I'll break them down myself."

As they moved deeper into the hospital's maze-like corridors, Sharp's mind raced. "Think, Holly," she muttered to herself. "Where would Gabriel hide it?"

They encountered a locked door, and Sharp didn't hesitate. With a powerful kick, she forced it open, ignoring the twinge of pain in her leg.

"Miller," she called into her radio. "Anything on your end?"

His voice crackled back, strained and breathless. "Nothing yet. This place is a labyrinth."

Sharp's heart pounded as they descended into the basement, the air growing thick and oppressive. "It has to be here," she thought, her eyes scanning the dimly lit corridor. "Gabriel always did have a flair for the dramatic."

As they rounded a corner, Sharp froze. There, tucked away in a forgotten storage room, sat the bomb. Its digital display glowed an angry red, the numbers ticking down with merciless precision.

"Miller," she breathed into her radio. "I've found it. Basement, east wing, storage room B."

Her partner's voice came back, tight with tension. "On my way. What's our play here?"

11- 11

Sharp's eyes locked onto the bomb, her breath catching in her throat as she approached it with cautious steps. The red digits on the timer seemed to pulse with malevolent intent, each second bringing them closer to catastrophe.

"We don't have time to wait for the bomb squad," she said, her voice low and tense as Miller burst into the room. "We have to do this ourselves."

Miller's face paled, but he nodded grimly. "I've had some training, but this... this is way beyond anything I've dealt with before."

Sharp's mind raced, recalling every scrap of information she'd ever learned about explosives. "We need to identify the type of detonator," she muttered, more to herself than to Miller. "Look for anything unusual, any wires that don't seem to fit."

As they carefully examined the device, Sharp's thoughts drifted to Gabriel Angel. His cryptic words echoed in her mind, taunting her. "What game are you playing, Gabriel?" she wondered silently.

Miller's voice cut through her thoughts. "I think I've found the main power source," he said, pointing to a cluster of wires. "If we cut that, it should disable the whole thing."

Sharp nodded, her hand steady as she reached for the wire cutters. "Here goes nothing," she whispered, positioning the tool. With a deep breath, she made the cut.

The timer froze, its angry red glow fading to black. Sharp and Miller exhaled in unison, the tension draining from their bodies.

"We did it," Miller breathed, a hint of disbelief in his voice.

Sharp allowed herself a small smile, but her relief was short-lived. "This isn't over," she said, her eyes scanning the room. "Gabriel's still out there, and I have a feeling this was just the beginning."

As they secured the area, waiting for the bomb squad to arrive and properly dispose of the device, Sharp couldn't shake the feeling that they were being watched. Somewhere in the shadows, she sensed Gabriel's presence, his piercing gaze boring into her.

"What's your endgame, Angel?" she murmured, her voice barely audible. "What twisted path are you leading us down?"

Race Against Time

1 - 2

The deafening wail of the hospital's emergency sirens pierced the air as Detective Holly Sharp sprinted down the stark white corridor, her heart thundering in her chest. The floor beneath her feet trembled, a bone-chilling reminder of the reactivated bomb pulsing with deadly intent somewhere in the building's depths.

"Drake, we need to move faster!" she shouted over her shoulder, her piercing eyes scanning the chaos unfolding around them. Patients in wheelchairs and gurneys clogged the hallways, their faces etched with fear and confusion as staff members frantically tried to guide them to safety.

Drake Miller, his disheveled appearance a stark contrast to Sharp's crisp suit, stumbled behind her, his tired eyes wide with urgency. "I'm right behind you, Holly," he called back, his voice strained as he helped an elderly woman navigate her IV stand through the throng of panicked people.

Sharp's mind raced, calculating their odds of evacuating everyone in time. We can't let these people die. Not on our watch. She gritted her teeth, pushing aside the gnawing doubt threatening to consume her.

"This way!" Sharp bellowed, gesturing towards the emergency exit at the end of the corridor. "Everyone, move quickly but calmly. We're almost there!"

The detective's commanding presence seemed to cut through the pandemonium, bringing a semblance of order to the evacuation. As they neared the exit, Sharp could feel the weight of responsibility pressing down on her shoulders, threatening to crush her resolve.

Drake caught up to her, his breathing labored. "Holly, do you think we—"

His words were cut short as they burst through the emergency doors into the crisp night air. Sharp's momentary relief was shattered as she turned to see Drake's face, illuminated by the sickly green glow of the bomb's digital display he'd been carrying.

"Oh God," Drake whispered, his voice barely audible over the cacophony of sirens and panicked voices. "It's... it's still counting down. We failed."

Sharp's blood ran cold as she watched the numbers on the timer flicker and continue their relentless march towards zero. Time seemed to slow to an agonizing crawl as the full weight of their failure crashed over her.

"No," she breathed, her usually steely composure cracking. "There has to be something we can do. We can't just—"

But even as the words left her lips, Sharp knew the bitter truth. They were out of options, out of time. The bomb was going to detonate, and there was nothing they could do to stop it.

3 - 4

Drake's tired eyes flickered with a sudden, fierce determination as he locked gazes with Sharp. In that moment, a lifetime of choices, regrets, and unfulfilled promises seemed to crystallize into a single, irrevocable decision.

"Holly," he said, his voice steady despite the chaos swirling around them. "Get everyone as far away as possible. I've got an idea."

Sharp's brow furrowed, her piercing eyes searching Drake's face. "What are you talking about, Miller? We need to move, now!"

Drake shook his head, a sad smile playing at the corners of his mouth. "No, you need to move. I'm staying."

"That's insane!" Sharp protested, her usual brusque tone tinged with genuine concern. "You can't possibly—"

"I'll buy you some time," Drake interrupted, his voice calm but determined. He placed a hand on Sharp's shoulder, giving it a gentle squeeze. "It's the only way, Holly. You know that as well as I do."

Sharp's mind raced, desperately searching for an alternative. "Drake, think about Linda, about your family. You can't just—"

"Linda would understand," Drake said softly, his eyes distant for a moment. "She always did. And maybe... maybe this is how I make things right. For both of them."

As he spoke, Sharp could see the weight of Drake's dual existence—the grief for his lost wife in one life, the sorrow for his missing son in another—etched in the lines of his face. She opened her mouth to argue further, but the words died on her lips as she recognized the unwavering resolve in his expression.

"You're a good cop, Holly," Drake said, his voice barely above a whisper. "And a good friend. Take care of them for me, will you?"

Before Sharp could respond, Drake turned and strode back towards the hospital entrance, his shoulders set with grim determination. She watched him go, her heart heavy with the knowledge that she might never see her partner again.

"Damn it, Miller," she muttered, blinking back the sting of tears. Then, steeling herself, she turned to the panicked crowd and began shouting orders, her voice carrying the authority that had made her both feared and respected throughout her career.

As she worked to move people to safety, Sharp couldn't shake the image of Drake walking away, carrying the weight of two worlds on his shoulders. She silently vowed that whatever happened next, she would honor his sacrifice and uncover the truth behind the fractured reality that had brought them to this moment.

5 - 6

Drake's footsteps echoed through the emptying corridors as he raced back towards the bomb, his heart thundering in his chest. The fluorescent lights flickered ominously overhead, casting eerie shadows that seemed to reach for him with spectral fingers. With each step, he could feel the weight of his decision pressing down on him, a burden heavier than any he'd carried before.

"I'm sorry, Linda," he whispered, thinking of his wife in one reality. "I'm sorry, Harrison," he added, his missing son's face flashing before his eyes from the other. The duality of his existence had never felt more painfully real than in this moment.

As he rounded the corner to the room housing the bomb, Drake's breath caught in his throat. The device sat there, innocuous yet deadly, its digital display ticking away the seconds left until detonation. He approached it cautiously, his police training warring with the primal fear coursing through his veins.

"Well, you bastard," he muttered to the bomb, "looks like it's just you and me now."

Drake's hands hovered over the device, his mind racing through every bomb disposal technique he'd ever learned. But as the seconds ticked by, he realized the futility of his efforts. There wasn't enough time.

He closed his eyes, drawing a deep breath. "Holly," he thought, picturing his partner's face, "I hope you understand why I had to do this."

With a final, resolute exhale, Drake opened his eyes and threw himself over the bomb. As he lay there, shielding the device with his body, a strange calm washed over him. In that moment, suspended between two realities, Drake Miller found a peculiar sense of peace.

"At least in this moment," he whispered to himself, "I know exactly who I am and what I'm meant to do."

7 - 8

A blinding white light erupted, searing through Holly Sharp's eyelids as she instinctively threw her arms up to shield herself. The deafening explosion that followed rocked the very foundations of the hospital, the force of it slamming into her chest like a freight train. For a heart-stopping moment, the world around her dissolved into pure chaos, a maelstrom of flying debris and shattered glass.

"Miller!" Holly screamed, her voice lost in the cacophony of destruction. She stumbled forward, disoriented, her ears ringing as the shockwave rippled through her body. "Drake, where are you?"

The air thick with dust and smoke, Holly's sharp eyes darted frantically around the devastated corridor. Sparks rained down from exposed wiring, and the acrid smell of burnt plastic filled her nostrils. She coughed violently, her lungs burning as she pushed herself to keep moving.

"This can't be happening," she thought, her mind reeling. "He can't be gone. Not like this."

As suddenly as it had begun, the chaos subsided, leaving in its wake an eerie, deafening silence. Holly's ragged breathing seemed obscenely loud in the stillness. She emerged from behind a partially collapsed wall, her normally immaculate suit torn and covered in grime.

"Drake?" she called out again, her voice hoarse and trembling. "Answer me, damn it!"

The silence that greeted her was more devastating than any explosion could have been. Holly's legs gave way beneath her, and she sank to her knees amidst the rubble. For a moment, her tough exterior cracked, revealing the raw anguish beneath.

"You stupid, brave idiot," she whispered, her words choked with emotion. "Why did you have to play the hero?"

9 - 10

Holly's piercing gaze fell upon the smoldering crater where Drake had stood moments ago. The sight hit her like a physical blow, forcing the air from her lungs. Tears welled in her eyes, blurring her vision as she stared at the stark reminder of his ultimate sacrifice.

"No," she murmured, her voice barely audible. "This isn't how it was supposed to end."

She dragged herself to the edge of the crater, her hands trembling as they grasped at the scorched debris. The acrid smell of burnt flesh assaulted her nostrils, making her gag.

"Drake," Holly choked out, her usual composure shattered. "You stubborn bastard. Why couldn't you just let me help you?"

As the reality of the situation sank in, Holly's mind raced with memories of their partnership. Drake's disheveled appearance, his sardonic humor, the unwavering determination in his tired eyes – all gone in an instant of selfless heroism.

"You saved them all," she whispered, her words heavy with a mixture of pride and sorrow. "But at what cost?"

Holly's fingers curled into fists, her nails digging into her palms as she fought to regain control of her emotions. She took a deep, shuddering breath, forcing herself to look beyond her personal grief.

"Your sacrifice won't be in vain, Drake," she said, her voice growing stronger. "I'll make sure of it. Your courage, your selflessness – it won't be forgotten."

As she spoke, Holly's gaze swept across the devastated hospital corridor. Despite the destruction, she could hear distant voices – survivors, people Drake had given his life to protect.

"You hear that, Miller?" she said, a bittersweet smile tugging at her lips. "That's the sound of lives you saved. Your legacy, right there."

Holly pushed herself to her feet, wincing at the pain that shot through her battered body. She stood tall, her resolve hardening as she faced the daunting task ahead.

"Rest easy, partner," she murmured, casting one last glance at the crater. "I'll take it from here. Your memory will be a beacon for us all – a reminder of what true courage looks like in the face of adversity."

11 - 11

Holly took a deep breath, her piercing eyes scanning the wreckage around her. The acrid smell of smoke and destruction filled her nostrils, a grim reminder of the chaos that had unfolded mere moments ago. She clenched her jaw, pushing down the waves of grief threatening to overwhelm her.

"I won't let you down, Drake," she whispered, her voice barely audible above the distant sirens and cries for help. "Your fight becomes my fight now."

She turned, her movements deliberate and purposeful, as she began to navigate through the debris-strewn corridor. Each step felt heavier than the last, but she pressed on, driven by a newfound determination.

"Detective Sharp!" a voice called out, causing her to pause. It was one of the junior officers, his face streaked with soot and concern. "Are you alright? We need to get you checked out by the paramedics."

Holly shook her head, her eyes never leaving the path ahead. "I'm fine," she said, her tone brooking no argument. "There are others who need help more than I do. What's the situation outside?"

As the officer began to brief her, Holly's mind raced, already formulating plans and strategies. She could almost hear Drake's voice in her head, offering insights and observations as he always had.

"We'll find who's behind this," she muttered under her breath, her words a solemn vow. "For you, Drake. For everyone they've hurt. This ends now."

With renewed purpose, Holly strode towards the hospital exit, her steps growing more confident with each passing moment. The weight of her responsibility was immense, but she embraced it, drawing strength from the memory of her fallen partner.

"You always said I was too stubborn for my own good," she said softly, a ghost of a smile playing on her lips. "Well, partner, you're about to see just how stubborn I can be. Evil doesn't stand a chance."

Echoes of Absence

1 - 2

Harrison's eyes snapped open, his gaze immediately drawn to the empty space on the couch where his father had been sleeping just moments ago. The indent in the cushions was still warm, a ghostly reminder of Drake's presence. Harrison blinked rapidly, his heart pounding as he struggled to process what he was seeing—or rather, what he wasn't seeing.

"Dad?" Harrison called out, his voice cracking. "Dad, where are you?"

Silence answered him, heavy and oppressive. Harrison's mind raced, trying to conjure up a logical explanation. Maybe his father had just gotten up to use the bathroom or grab a midnight snack. But deep down, Harrison knew something was terribly wrong.

He leapt to his feet, nearly tripping over the coffee table in his haste. "This isn't funny, Dad!" he shouted, a hint of his usual teenage bravado creeping into his voice. "If this is some kind of weird test or lesson, I'm not impressed!"

Harrison's eyes darted around the room, taking in the familiar surroundings that now seemed alien and threatening. The family photos on the mantle stared back at him, his father's tired eyes and scruffy beard frozen in time. The old grandfather clock in the corner ticked away, each second feeling like an eternity.

"Think, Harrison, think," he muttered to himself, running his hands through his unruly curls. "There's got to be some explanation for this."

He began to search the room methodically, his movements growing more frantic with each passing moment. He checked behind the curtains, under the furniture, even in the potted plants. But there was no sign of his father, no clue to explain his sudden vanishing act.

"This can't be happening," Harrison whispered, his earlier cockiness replaced by raw fear. "People don't just disappear into thin air. It's not possible."

But as he stood in the middle of the living room, surrounded by the mundane trappings of their everyday life, Harrison was forced to confront the impossible truth. His father was gone, vanished without a trace, leaving behind nothing but questions and a growing sense of dread.

"Dad," he called out one last time, his voice barely audible. "Please come back. I need you."

The silence that followed was deafening, and Harrison felt a chill run down his spine as he realized he was truly alone.

3 - 4

Harrison's trembling fingers fumbled with his phone, nearly dropping it as he pulled it from his pocket. He punched in his father's number, each digit feeling like a lifeline to cling to in this surreal nightmare.

"Come on, Dad. Pick up, pick up," he muttered, his voice cracking with desperation.

The phone rang once, twice, and then... "Hey, this is Drake. Leave a message, and I'll get back to you."

"No!" Harrison shouted, his free hand clenching into a fist. "Dad, where are you? Please, call me back immediately. It's an emergency!"

He ended the call and immediately redialed, his heart pounding so hard he could feel it in his throat. Again, voicemail. And again. And again.

"This can't be happening," he groaned, running a hand through his unruly curls. "How can he just vanish and his phone goes straight to voicemail? It doesn't make any sense!"

Harrison's legs gave out beneath him, and he collapsed onto the couch, his lanky frame sinking into the cushions. The phone slipped from his grasp, clattering to the floor.

"Where did you go, Dad?" he whispered, his bright eyes now brimming with tears. "Are you okay? Did someone take you? Or did you... did you leave me?"

The silence of the room pressed in on him, suffocating in its intensity. Harrison's mind raced, conjuring up increasingly terrifying scenarios. Was his father hurt? Kidnapped? Or had he simply decided he'd had enough of dealing with a smart-mouthed teenager?

"No," Harrison said firmly, shaking his head. "Dad wouldn't do that. He wouldn't just abandon me. Something must have happened to him."

He leaned forward, elbows on his knees, head in his hands. "But how? How could someone just disappear without a trace? It's like something out of one of those crazy sci-fi movies we used to watch together."

The memory of those movie nights, curled up on this very couch with his dad, hit Harrison like a physical blow. A sob escaped his lips, quickly followed by another.

"I can't lose you, Dad," he choked out. "I can't do this alone. Please, wherever you are, be okay. Just be okay, and come back to me."

5 - 6

Harrison's gaze drifted to the crook of his elbow, where a small bandage still covered the spot where Gabriel had drawn his blood just days ago. The memory of that encounter sent a chill down his spine.

"What did you mean, Gabriel?" he muttered, his voice barely above a whisper. "What's so special about my blood?"

He closed his eyes, recalling Gabriel's piercing stare and cryptic words. "Your blood holds secrets, Harrison. Secrets that could change everything."

Opening his eyes, Harrison's gaze fell on a framed photo of him and his father, taken just last summer. "Dad, what aren't you telling me? What does all of this mean?"

He stood abruptly, pacing the room with nervous energy. "This can't be a coincidence. Gabriel, the blood test, and now Dad vanishing... it's all connected somehow."

Harrison paused, his hand hovering over the photo. "I can't just sit here and wait. I have to do something."

Determination surged through him, pushing back the tide of fear and confusion. "Okay, Harrison, think. Where would Dad go if he was in trouble? Who would he trust?"

Then is dawned on Harrison. "He trusts Detective Kierstead."

Threads of Fate

1 - 2

The fluorescent lights flickered overhead, casting eerie shadows across Gabriel's scarred face as Detective Keirstead leaned in, her voice low and insistent. "You know more than you're letting on, Gabriel. What's your connection to the cult?"

Gabriel's piercing eyes met hers, unflinching. "Detective, the threads of fate are woven in intricate patterns. My role, like yours, is but a single strand in a tapestry beyond your comprehension." His voice carried a hint of amusement, as if privy to some cosmic joke.

Keirstead's frustration was palpable. "Cut the cryptic bull—"

A deafening explosion rocked the building, cutting her off mid-sentence. The walls trembled, plaster raining down from the ceiling. In that instant of chaos, Gabriel's demeanor shifted, a predatory gleam replacing his enigmatic calm.

As the officers stumbled, disoriented by the blast, Gabriel surged forward with unexpected agility, his movements fluid despite his pronounced limp. "Fate, it seems, has other plans for me tonight," he mused, effortlessly breaking free from his restraints.

The detective lunged for him, but Gabriel was already in motion. "Your persistence is admirable, Detective," he called over his shoulder, dark hair whipping across his face as he darted towards the exit. "But some mysteries are not meant to be unraveled by mortal hands."

Gabriel's mind raced as he navigated the chaos. The explosion's timing was impeccable – too perfect to be coincidence. As alarms blared and officers shouted in confusion, a smile played at the corners of his lips. The pieces were falling into place, just as the prophecy had foretold.

3 - 4

Detective Keirstead's voice cut through the cacophony of alarms and panicked shouts, her words sharp and commanding. "Gabriel Angel, stop right there!" She leveled her weapon, its muzzle trained on Gabriel's retreating form. "All units, we have a fugitive on the loose. Secure all exits!"

Gabriel's footsteps echoed in the corridor, his limp barely noticeable as adrenaline coursed through his veins. He glanced back, his piercing eyes locking with Keirstead's for a moment. "Ah, Detective," he called out, his voice eerily calm amidst the chaos, "your determination is admirable, but futility often masquerades as bravery."

As he rounded a corner, Gabriel's mind raced, calculating his next move. The labyrinthine hallways of the station stretched before him, a maze of potential escape routes and dead ends. "The path of least resistance is not always the wisest choice," he muttered to himself, deliberately choosing a route that seemed counterintuitive.

Keirstead's pursuit was relentless, her voice growing closer. "We've got the building surrounded, Gabriel. There's nowhere to run!"

A wry smile played on Gabriel's scarred lips as he ducked into a narrow passage. "Oh, Detective," he thought, "if only you understood the true nature of confinement. These walls are but an illusion compared to the prison of ignorance."

The sound of multiple footsteps echoed from different directions, the police force mobilizing to corner their elusive prey. Gabriel's heart pounded, not from fear, but from a surge of exhilaration. He knew that every step, every decision in this moment was part of a greater design, a cosmic dance choreographed long before this night.

As he navigated the corridors, Gabriel's voice carried back to his pursuers, a tantalizing mix of warning and invitation. "The symbol you seek, Detective, is but a key to a door you may not wish to open. Some truths are better left in the shadows."

5 - 6

With a final burst of speed, Gabriel slammed his shoulder against the emergency exit, the metal bar giving way with a resounding clang. The cool night air rushed to greet him, a stark contrast to the stifling tension of the station. Sirens wailed in the distance, their piercing cries a symphony of approaching danger.

"Freedom," Gabriel whispered, his piercing eyes scanning the urban landscape before him. "But at what cost?"

Without hesitation, he melted into the shadows of a nearby alley, his movements fluid and purposeful despite the limp in his left leg. The disfigured contours of his face, usually a source of unwanted attention, now served as a perfect camouflage in the dim streetlights.

As he navigated the labyrinthine streets, Gabriel's mind raced. "They underestimate the power of the unseen," he mused, his voice barely audible. "The cult's influence runs deeper than they could ever imagine."

A police cruiser roared past, its lights painting the wet pavement in flashes of red and blue. Gabriel pressed himself against a brick wall, becoming one with the darkness. He could hear the frantic radio chatter of the officers inside.

"This chase," Gabriel thought, his eyes gleaming with an otherworldly intensity, "it's but a small piece in a grand cosmic puzzle. They hunt me, unaware that they too are being hunted by forces beyond their comprehension."

As he slipped from shadow to shadow, Gabriel's voice carried on the night breeze, a final taunt to his pursuers. "Chase me all you want, Detective Keirstead. But remember, the closer you get to me, the closer you get to truths that will shatter your world."

With that, he disappeared into the urban maze, leaving behind only questions and the lingering scent of mystery.

7 - 8

Gabriel's piercing eyes scanned the darkened alley, his mind churning with possibilities. "The symbol," he whispered to himself, his voice a low, melodic rumble. "It's the key to everything."

He pressed his hand against the rough brick wall, feeling the texture beneath his scarred fingers. The burns that marred his face seemed to throb with an otherworldly energy, a constant reminder of the power he wielded and the price he'd paid.

"They think they've cornered me," Gabriel mused, a wry smile playing on his lips. "But they don't realize I'm always three steps ahead."

As he moved deeper into the shadows, his thoughts drifted to the Temporal Guardians, to the intricate web of connections that had led him to this moment. The sirens in the distance faded, replaced by the ambient sounds of the sleeping city.

"I wonder," he pondered aloud, his voice carrying a hint of irony, "if Detective Keirstead has any inkling of how close she came to unraveling the truth tonight. So close, yet eternally far."

Gabriel's hand instinctively went to his pocket, feeling the outline of a small object hidden there. "The next phase begins now," he declared to the empty alley. "And this time, there will be no escape for any of them."

With renewed purpose, he limped forward, each step a testament to his unwavering resolve. The night enveloped him, a willing accomplice in his grand design.

9 – 10 – moments earlier

The interrogation room felt like a pressure cooker, its walls closing in as Detective Holly Keirstead's piercing gaze bore into me. I sat motionless, my exterior calm belying the storm brewing within. Every fiber of my being screamed for action, but I forced myself to remain still, knowing my moment would come.

"Gabriel," Holly's voice cut through the tension, "I'll ask you one more time. Where were you on the night of—"

Her words were swallowed by a deafening explosion that rocked the entire building. The fluorescent lights flickered, plunging us into momentary darkness. In that split second of chaos, I saw my chance.

"What the hell?" Holly exclaimed, her composure briefly shattered.

I lunged forward, my restraints snapping like brittle twigs. The surge of adrenaline coursing through my veins dulled the pain of my wrists tearing against the metal. Holly's eyes widened in shock as I sprang to my feet.

"Gabriel, don't—" she started, reaching for her weapon.

But I was already moving, my body acting on pure instinct. "Sorry, Detective," I growled, "but I can't afford to stick around for the finale."

I barreled past her, shouldering the door open with a force that surprised even me. The corridor beyond was a scene of pandemonium. Alarms blared, their shrill cry mixing with the panicked shouts of officers and civilians alike.

As I sprinted down the hallway, weaving through the chaos, my mind raced. What caused that explosion? Was it connected to the fractured reality I'd been experiencing? The questions swirled in my head, competing with the urgent need to escape.

"Stop! Miller!" Holly's voice echoed behind me, but it only spurred me to run faster.

I dodged a stumbling officer, narrowly avoiding a collision. "Out of my way!" I shouted, more to myself than anyone else. The exit sign glowed like a beacon of hope at the end of the corridor.

My heart pounded in my chest, each beat a reminder of what was at stake. My sanity, the truth – it all hinged on my escape. As I ran, faces flashed before my eyes: my wife's smile, my daughter's laugh. I had to make it out, had to find a way to save them both.

The sirens grew louder, their wail a constant reminder of the danger at my heels. But I couldn't afford to look back. Every second counted, every step bringing me closer to freedom and the answers I desperately sought.

11 - 12

As I neared the emergency exit, the weight of my situation bore down on me like a physical force. My lungs burned, muscles screaming with each stride, but I refused to let fear take hold. "This is what you're made for," I whispered to myself, teeth gritted. "Chaos, uncertainty - this is where you thrive."

The door loomed ahead, its glowing EXIT sign a lifeline in the madness. I slammed into the push bar with my shoulder, bursting out into the night. The cool air hit me like a slap, sharp and invigorating.

"Gabriel! Don't do this!" Holly's voice rang out behind me, closer than I'd expected. I could hear the conflict in her tone - duty warring with something else. Understanding? Concern?

I didn't pause to analyze it. "I have to, Holly!" I shouted back, feet pounding the pavement as I sprinted across the parking lot. "You don't understand what's at stake!"

The night embraced me, shadows offering cover as I weaved between parked cars. Shouts echoed off the buildings, a cacophony of pursuit growing more distant with each step. But I was already several moves ahead, my mind racing through escape routes and safe houses.

"I was born for this," I thought, a grim smile tugging at my lips. "Let them chase. They have no idea what they're dealing with."

13 - 14

Suddenly, the world around me exploded into blinding white light. It was as if the very fabric of reality had been torn asunder, bathing everything in an otherworldly glow. I skidded to a halt, momentarily disoriented by the sudden shift.

"What the hell?" I gasped, my heart pounding even harder than before. The light seemed to emanate from within me, pulsing in rhythm with my racing pulse.

As quickly as it had appeared, the disorientation vanished, replaced by an incredible surge of energy. It coursed through my veins like liquid fire, every nerve ending singing with power. I flexed my fingers, marveling at the sensation. Then I was gone, in a shroud of white light I disappeared away from the approaching officers and further into the city.

Drake Miller is Dead

Blue and Green World – 2024

1 - 2

Linda sat in the dimly lit living room, shadows dancing across the walls as the flickering light from the old table lamp cast an eerie glow. Her fingers traced the worn fabric of the armchair, a tangible connection to a world that suddenly felt alien and hostile. Detective Sharp's voice pierced the silence, each word a brutal assault on Linda's senses.

"I'm sorry, Mrs. Miller," Detective Sharp said, her usually stern voice tinged with a rare note of compassion. "We've done everything we could, but..."

Linda's breath caught in her throat, her heart pounding so loudly she could barely hear the detective's next words. She leaned forward, gripping the arm of the chair as if it were the only thing anchoring her to reality.

"Please," Linda whispered, her voice barely audible. "Just tell me."

Detective Sharp's voice was soft, a flicker of empathy crossing her face before her professional mask slipped back into place. "Miller is dead."

The words hung in the air, heavy and suffocating. Linda's mind reeled, desperately trying to reject the information, to find some loophole, some way this couldn't be true. She opened her mouth to speak, but no sound came out.

"Mrs. Miller," Detective Sharp continued, her tone softening slightly, "I know this is difficult to process. Is there someone I can call for you?"

Linda shook her head, her gaze unfocused as she stared at a point just beyond the detective's shoulder. How could this be happening? Drake had promised he'd come home. He'd promised Harrison he'd be there for his birthday next week. The lies we tell ourselves, Linda thought bitterly, to keep the darkness at bay.

"How?" Linda finally managed to choke out, her voice sounding foreign to her own ears.

Detective Sharp shifted in her seat, her posture rigid with tension. "The details are still unclear. There was an explosion at the hospital. We're doing everything we can to piece together what happened."

Linda's mind flashed to Drake's determined face as he'd left that morning, his promise to uncover the truth echoing in her ears. Had he known? Had he suspected the danger he was walking into?

"I need to see him," Linda said suddenly, her voice stronger now, fueled by a desperate need to deny the reality crashing down around her.

Detective Sharp's expression tightened, a flicker of something—pity? regret?—crossing her face. "I'm afraid that's not possible, Mrs. Miller. The explosion... there's nothing left to..."

The detective's words faded into the background as Linda's world imploded, the carefully constructed facade of normalcy shattering into a million jagged pieces. Drake was gone. Harrison had lost his father. And Linda... Linda was alone in a world that no longer made sense.

3 - 4

Linda's grip on the phone tightened, her knuckles turning white as she struggled to process the devastating news. The world around her blurred, shadows creeping in at the edges of her vision as Detective Sharp's voice continued, a distant echo in the storm of her grief.

"Mrs. Miller? Linda? Are you still there?" The detective's tone softened, laced with concern.

"I'm... here," Linda managed, her voice barely above a whisper. She swallowed hard, tasting the salt of her tears. "I just... I can't believe..."

"I know this is incredibly difficult," Detective Sharp said, her words measured and careful. "We have grief counselors available if you need—"

"No," Linda interrupted, a sudden flash of anger cutting through her despair. "What I need is answers. What happened to my husband?"

There was a pause on the other end of the line, heavy with unspoken tension. When Detective Sharp spoke again, her voice was tinged with a mix of professional detachment and genuine sympathy. "We're still investigating, Mrs. Miller. But I promise you, we will find out what happened. Drake was... he was one of our own."

Linda closed her eyes, memories of Drake's determined face flooding her mind. His passion for justice, his unwavering belief in doing what was right. It had drawn her to him, defined their life together. And now...

"He wouldn't have... it couldn't have been an accident," Linda said, her voice trembling with the weight of her conviction. "Drake was too careful, too..."

"We're exploring all possibilities," Detective Sharp assured her, but Linda could hear the hesitation in her voice.

As the detective continued to speak, offering platitudes and promises of further information, Linda found herself drifting, her mind reeling with the enormity of her loss. How could she face a world without Drake? How could she tell Harrison that his father would never come home again?

5 - 6

Linda's grip on the phone loosened, her arm dropping to her side as the device clattered to the floor. She barely registered Detective Sharp's voice, now tinny and distant, still emanating from the fallen handset. The floodgates of emotion burst open, and a guttural sob tore from her throat.

"Harrison," she choked out, her son's name a prayer and a lament. "Oh God, Harrison."

Her legs gave way, and she crumpled to the floor, her body wracked with violent tremors. Tears flowed freely, soaking into the plush carpet beneath her. Linda's mind reeled, assaulted by a barrage of memories—Harrison's first steps, his gap-toothed grin on his first day of school, the way his eyes lit up when Drake walked through the door after a long day at work.

"Why?" she screamed, her fists pounding against the floor. "Why them? Why my boys?"

The room seemed to tilt and spin around her, the familiar contours of her living room suddenly alien and oppressive. Her gaze fell on the mantelpiece, where a row of framed photographs stood like sentinels of happier times. Drake's proud smile as he held a newborn Harrison. The three of them at the beach, squinting into the sun. Harrison's sixteenth birthday, just months ago, Drake's arm draped around his son's shoulders.

Linda struggled to her feet, stumbling towards the photos. Her trembling fingers traced the outline of Drake's face, his kind eyes staring back at her from behind the glass.

"You promised," she whispered, her voice raw with anguish. "You promised you'd always be there for us. How could you leave us like this?"

She clutched the frame to her chest, sinking back to the floor. The weight of her grief threatened to crush her, each breath a monumental effort. In that moment, Linda felt as though she was drowning, pulled under by currents of sorrow too strong to resist.

"I can't do this alone," she sobbed, rocking back and forth. "Drake, please. I need you. Harrison needs you. How are we supposed to go on without you?"

The silence of the room seemed to mock her pleas, offering no comfort, no answers. Only the crushing weight of an unfathomable loss remained, settling over Linda like a shroud as she wept for the family that had been torn apart in an instant.

7 - 8

Linda's eyes fell upon Harrison's backpack, still slung over the armchair where he'd tossed it after school just months ago. The sight of it, so ordinary and yet now painfully poignant, sparked a sudden shift in her grief-stricken mind.

"No," she whispered, her voice gaining strength. "I can't give up. They wouldn't want that."

With trembling hands, Linda pushed herself up from the floor, her legs unsteady beneath her. She made her way to the backpack, unzipping it with care. Inside, she found Harrison's worn copy of "To Kill a Mockingbird," his favorite book. A yellow sticky note peeked out from between the pages, covered in his messy scrawl: "Mom, thanks for always believing in me. Love you."

Her breath caught in her throat as she read the words. "Oh, Harrison," she murmured, tears welling up once more. "I'll always believe in you, sweetheart. Always."

Linda's gaze drifted to a framed photo of Drake on the mantle, his eyes twinkling with that mischievous glint she'd fallen in love with years ago. She could almost hear his voice, gentle yet firm: "You're stronger than you know, Lin. You've got this."

She pressed her palm to her chest, feeling her heart thundering beneath. "I don't know if I can do this without you both," she admitted to the empty room. "But I have to try. For Harrison's dreams. For your legacy, Drake. For the love we shared."

With shaky steps, Linda made her way to the window, drawing back the curtains. The world outside seemed unchanged, oblivious to the devastation within these walls. Yet as the warm sunlight touched her tear-stained face, she felt a tiny spark of something she thought she'd lost forever – hope.

"One day at a time," she whispered to herself, clutching Harrison's book to her heart. "That's how we'll get through this. Together, even if you're not here. I promise."

9 - 10

The silence of the room was shattered by the shrill ring of Linda's phone, startling her from her reverie. She fumbled for it, her heart racing as she saw the caller ID: Detective Sharp.

"Hello?" Linda's voice wavered, bracing herself for more devastating news.

"Mrs. Miller," Detective Sharp's voice crackled through the speaker, terse and professional. "I'm at the scene. I... I think you should come down here."

Linda's breath hitched. "Is it... have you found something?"

There was a heavy pause before Sharp replied, "It's best if you see for yourself. I'll send a car for you."

As the call ended, Linda's mind raced with possibilities. Hope and dread warred within her as she grabbed her coat, hands trembling.

Across town, Detective Holly Sharp stood amidst the chaos, her piercing eyes scanning the devastation wrought by the explosion. The once-bustling hospital was now reduced to a heap of rubble and debris, with thick plumes of smoke billowing into the sky.

"Officer Chen!" Sharp barked, her voice cutting through the cacophony of sirens and shouting. "Secure that perimeter! I don't want a single unauthorized person within 100 yards of this site!"

As Chen scrambled to comply, Holly's gaze swept over the scene once more. Her jaw clenched, mind racing. Something about this didn't add up. The blast pattern, the timing... it was too perfect, too calculated.

"What the hell were you mixed up in, Drake?" she muttered under her breath, recalling her last conversation with her colleague and friend. He'd been onto something big, but now...

A junior officer approached, looking pale. "Detective Sharp, we've found something in the east wing. You... you need to see this."

Holly's eyes narrowed. "Lead the way," she commanded, steeling herself for whatever grim discovery awaited. As she picked her way through the debris, she couldn't shake the feeling that this was only the beginning of something much larger and far more sinister than anyone realized.

11 - 12

Holly followed the junior officer through the maze of twisted metal and crumbling concrete, her heart heavy with a mixture of dread and determination. As they approached the east wing, the acrid smell of smoke intensified, burning her nostrils and making her eyes water.

"This is where we last had contact with Detective Miller," the young officer explained, his voice wavering slightly. "But there's no sign of... well, anything."

Holly's brow furrowed as she surveyed the scene, her trained eye taking in every detail. The destruction was absolute, yet something felt off. Where there should have been evidence of human remains, there was nothing but ash and debris.

"It doesn't make sense," she muttered, more to herself than her companion. "Drake was right here, and now he's just... gone?"

Kneeling down, Holly began to sift through the wreckage with her gloved hands, ignoring the heat that still radiated from some of the debris. Her movements were methodical, almost desperate, as she searched for any trace of her friend and colleague.

"Detective Sharp," the junior officer began hesitantly, "do you think there's a chance he might have..."

"Survived?" Holly finished, her voice tight with emotion. "I don't know. But I do know Drake Miller. He's not the type to just disappear without a trace."

As she continued her search, Holly's mind raced with possibilities. Drake had been investigating something big, something that had him on edge in the days leading up to the explosion. What if this wasn't an accident at all?

"This doesn't add up," she said aloud, frustration seeping into her voice. "An explosion this size should leave more evidence behind. It's like he just vanished into thin air."

The junior officer shifted uncomfortably. "Maybe we should call in the forensics team, see if they can find anything we've missed?"

Holly nodded absently, her focus still on the debris in front of her. "Good idea. Get them here ASAP. And I want a full report on everyone who entered or left this hospital in the last 24 hours."

As the officer hurried away to make the necessary calls, Holly sat back on her heels, a heavy sigh escaping her lips. "Where are you, Drake?" she whispered, her eyes scanning the devastation once more. "And what the hell have you gotten yourself into?"

13 - 14

Holly Sharp pushed herself to her feet, her knees creaking in protest after hours of combing through the wreckage. She brushed the dust from her tailored suit, a futile gesture given the chaos surrounding her. The acrid smell of smoke and chemicals hung heavy in the air, a constant reminder of the devastation that had occurred.

"Detective Sharp," a young officer called out, jogging towards her with a tablet in hand. "We've got the security footage from the hospital's main entrance. Do you want to take a look?"

Holly's piercing eyes locked onto the officer. "Pull it up," she commanded, her voice tight with barely contained frustration. As the video began to play, she leaned in, scrutinizing every frame. "Stop. Rewind that last bit."

The officer complied, and Holly's breath caught in her throat. There, on the screen, was Drake Miller, entering the hospital just minutes before the explosion. But something was off about his demeanor, a tension in his shoulders that Holly recognized all too well.

"He knew," she muttered, more to herself than the officer beside her. "He knew something was going to happen."

"Ma'am?" the officer questioned, confusion evident in his voice.

Holly straightened, her mind racing. "Drake wasn't just in the wrong place at the wrong time. He came here for a reason. And now he's gone without a trace." She turned to face the younger man, her expression hardening. "I want every piece of evidence cataloged and analyzed. Leave no stone unturned. If there's even a hint of Drake's presence here, I want to know about it."

As the officer hurried off to relay her orders, Holly found herself alone once more, surrounded by the remnants of what was once a bustling hospital. The weight of unanswered questions pressed down on her, threatening to overwhelm her usually stoic demeanor.

"Dammit, Drake," she whispered, her fists clenching at her sides. "What were you into? And how the hell am I supposed to find you now?"

15 - 16

"Come on, come on," Harrison muttered, his voice cracking with desperation. He closed his eyes, visualizing his father's face, the warmth of his embrace. "Dad, where are you?"

The air around him seemed to crackle with an unseen energy, responding to his intense concentration. Harrison's hands trembled, and he clenched them into fists, willing himself to maintain his focus.

"I can do this," he said, his cocky teenage bravado masking the fear that threatened to overwhelm him. "I've jumped between realities before. This is just... a bigger leap."

As he spoke, memories flooded his mind – his mother's smile, his father's hearty laugh, the three of them together, a family whole and unbroken. The vivid images fueled his determination.

"Dad always said I had an overactive imagination," Harrison mused, a wry smile tugging at his lips. "Bet he never thought it'd come in handy like this."

He took a deep breath, centering himself. The world around him began to blur, colors bleeding into one another like a watercolor painting left in the rain. Harrison's heart leapt – it was working!

"Hold on, Dad," he whispered, his voice barely audible above the rushing in his ears. "I'm coming for you. Whatever it takes, I'll bring you back."

As the familiar surroundings of his home began to take shape around him, Harrison's resolve hardened. He was here, in this other reality, and nothing would stop him from finding his father and making their family whole again.

17 - 18

Harrison blinked rapidly, his vision clearing as the new reality solidified around him. The living room materialized, achingly familiar yet subtly different. A framed photo on the mantle caught his eye – his mother and father, smiling, with no trace of the grief that had haunted them in his world.

"Harrison? Is that you?" His mother's voice drifted from the kitchen, warm and alive, sending a jolt through his system.

He swallowed hard, his throat suddenly dry. "Yeah, Mom. It's me," he called back, his voice cracking slightly.

But as he turned to finally greet the mother he thought he lost all those months ago, a white light suddenly enveloped around Harrison and with that he was gone. Harrison Miller, just like his father, had vanished into thin air.

Another World

The flickering glow of computer monitors cast an eerie pallor across Dr. Rachel Summers' gaunt features as she hunched over her cluttered desk, surrounded by towering stacks of ancient tomes and dog-eared scientific journals. The setting sun painted long shadows across the university campus outside, but Dr. Summers barely registered the fading light, her eyes darting feverishly between screens displaying complex equations and arcane symbols.

"It has to be here somewhere," she muttered, fingers flying across the keyboard as she cross-referenced obscure theories and anomalous data points. The soft hum of laboratory equipment provided a soothing counterpoint to the frantic pounding of her heart.

For weeks, she had barely left this dimly lit sanctuary, driven by an insatiable thirst for knowledge that bordered on obsession. Sleep was a luxury she could ill afford, not when she stood on the precipice of a discovery that could reshape humanity's understanding of the universe itself.

Dr. Summers leaned back in her chair, rubbing her bleary eyes as she pondered the implications of her findings. An anomaly in the fabric of space-time, hinting at the existence of alternate timelines... it was almost too fantastical to believe, and yet the data didn't lie.

"What am I missing?" she wondered aloud, her voice barely above a whisper. "There has to be a connection I'm not seeing."

As if in answer to her plea, a gentle knock echoed through the lab. Dr. Summers startled, nearly knocking over a precarious stack of papers as she turned to face the door.

"Come in," she called, hastily attempting to smooth her disheveled hair and straighten her rumpled lab coat.

The door swung open to reveal Dr. Charles Lee, his kind eyes crinkling with concern as he took in her haggard appearance. "Rachel," he said softly, his voice warm and soothing, "I thought I might find you here. Have you been working all night again?"

Dr. Summers felt a pang of guilt at the gentle admonishment in his tone. "I'm close to a breakthrough, Charles," she explained, gesturing excitedly at the screens surrounding her. "I can feel it. Just a little more time, and I'll have concrete proof of—"

"Of alternate timelines, yes," Dr. Lee finished for her, a hint of skepticism creeping into his voice. "Rachel, I worry that you're pushing yourself too hard. Perhaps it's time to step back, take a breath, and approach this with fresh eyes."

She shook her head vehemently, her exhaustion momentarily forgotten in a surge of passionate conviction. "You don't understand," she insisted, her voice rising. "This isn't just some wild theory. The data supports it. If I'm right, it could change everything we thought we knew about the nature of reality itself!"

Dr. Lee held up his hands in a placating gesture, his expression softening. "I hear you, Rachel. Your dedication is admirable, truly. But remember, even the most groundbreaking discoveries require a clear mind and a healthy body. When was the last time you had a proper meal? Or a full night's sleep?"

Dr. Summers opened her mouth to argue, but the words died on her lips as she realized she couldn't remember the answer to either question. She slumped back in her chair, suddenly aware of the bone-deep weariness that had settled into her very being.

"You're right," she admitted reluctantly, her shoulders sagging. "I've been so focused on unraveling this mystery that I've neglected everything else. But Charles, if you could see what I've uncovered... it's extraordinary."

Dr. Lee's eyes sparkled with a mixture of curiosity and concern. "Then show me," he said gently, pulling up a chair beside her. "Walk me through your findings, and perhaps a fresh perspective will help you see something you've missed."

As Dr. Summers began to explain her research, her initial reluctance gave way to renewed enthusiasm. With each revelation, each carefully constructed theory, she felt her passion reigniting, fueled by the attentive presence of her colleague.

And as the night deepened around them, the two scientists delved deeper into the mysteries of the universe, unaware that their pursuit of knowledge was about to lead them down a path that would challenge the very foundations of reality itself.

3 - 4

Dr. Summers' fingers trembled as she caressed the brittle pages of the ancient tome, its leather binding cracked and worn with age. The parchment crackled ominously beneath her touch, as if warning her of the forbidden knowledge contained within.

"Look at this, Charles," she breathed, her voice barely above a whisper. "These symbols... they're unlike anything I've ever seen before. But there's a pattern, a rhythm to them that speaks of something beyond our understanding."

Dr. Lee leaned in, his brow furrowed in concentration. "Fascinating," he murmured. "What do you think it means?"

Rachel's eyes gleamed with a feverish intensity. "Parallel worlds, Charles. Alternate timelines existing alongside our own, separated by the thinnest of veils."

She traced her finger along a series of intricate glyphs, her excitement palpable. "Each of these represents a different reality, a different path that history could have taken. And here, at the center..." She tapped a complex symbol that seemed to pulse with an otherworldly energy. "This is the key to it all."

Dr. Lee's expression wavered between curiosity and concern. "Rachel, this is... extraordinary. But are you certain? The implications of such a discovery..."

"I know," she interrupted, her voice tight with a mixture of exhilaration and fear. "It's overwhelming. That's why I need help, Charles. I can't do this alone."

She turned to face him, her eyes pleading. "I need minds like yours, brilliant thinkers who aren't afraid to challenge the impossible. Together, we could unlock the secrets of the multiverse itself."

Dr. Lee sat back, his kind eyes searching Rachel's face. "You're treading dangerous ground, Rachel. The human mind isn't meant to comprehend such vastness. Are you prepared for what you might find?"

Rachel's jaw set with determination. "I have to be, Charles. This knowledge... it could change everything. Rewrite history, reshape the future. We can't turn our backs on it now."

As she spoke, a chill ran down her spine, a primal instinct warning her of the perilous path ahead. But the allure of discovery, the tantalizing promise of unlocking the universe's greatest mysteries, was too powerful to resist.

"Will you help me?" she asked, her voice barely above a whisper.

Dr. Lee hesitated, the weight of the decision heavy in the air between them. Finally, he nodded slowly. "I'll help you, Rachel. But we must proceed with caution. Some doors, once opened, can never be closed again."

Rachel felt a surge of relief and gratitude, even as a tendril of fear coiled in her gut. She knew, with a certainty that defied explanation, that they were about to embark on a journey that would challenge everything they thought they knew about reality itself.

5 - 6

Rachel's heart raced as she paced the dimly lit conference room, her footsteps echoing off the stark white walls. She paused, running her fingers through her disheveled hair, and turned to face the assembled group of scientists. "Thank you all for coming," she began, her voice tight with anticipation. "What we're about to embark on will change the course of human history."

Dr. Marcus Chen leaned forward, his keen eyes fixed on Rachel. "You've been rather cryptic about this project, Dr. Summers. Care to enlighten us?"

Rachel took a deep breath, steeling herself. "We're forming a clandestine research group - the Temporal Research Initiative. Our goal is to explore and potentially manipulate alternate timelines."

A hushed murmur rippled through the room. Dr. Harmon's stern voice cut through the whispers. "And how do you propose we do that, Dr. Summers? It sounds like science fiction."

"It's not fiction, Jesse," Rachel countered, her voice gaining strength. "I've uncovered evidence - ancient texts, anomalous data - that suggests the existence of parallel worlds. With your expertise in theoretical physics, Dr. Chen, and the combined brilliance in this room, we can push beyond the boundaries of known science."

Dr. Chen's eyes lit up with excitement. "You're talking about quantum entanglement on a macro scale. The implications are... staggering."

Rachel nodded, a spark of relief igniting in her chest. At least someone understood. "Exactly. But we'll be operating outside traditional institutions. The potential for misuse is too great to risk government oversight."

Dr. Lee's gentle voice interjected, "Rachel, have you considered the ethical ramifications? Altering timelines could have unforeseen consequences."

She met his concerned gaze, her own eyes blazing with determination. "That's why I need all of you. Your brilliance, your caution, your diverse perspectives. Together, we can navigate this uncharted territory responsibly."

As Rachel looked around the room, she saw a mix of excitement, skepticism, and fear on the faces before her. She swallowed hard, realizing the weight of what she was asking. "I know it's a lot to take in," she said softly. "But imagine the possibilities. We could prevent disasters, cure diseases before they happen, reshape the very fabric of reality."

Dr. Chen stood up, his voice filled with resolve. "I'm in. This is the kind of challenge I've been waiting for my entire career."

One by one, the other scientists nodded their agreement, until only Dr. Harmon remained silent. Rachel held her breath, knowing his expertise would be crucial to their success.

Finally, he spoke, his voice gruff but not unkind. "It's madness, Summers. But it's the kind of madness that changes the world. Count me in."

As the gravity of the moment settled over them, Rachel felt a mixture of exhilaration and terror coursing through her veins. They were about to embark on a journey that would challenge the very foundations of reality itself, and there was no turning back.

7 - 8

Dr. Maya Patel leaned forward, her dark eyes gleaming with intellectual fervor. "I've been working on a revolutionary gene-editing technique that could potentially stabilize our molecular structure during temporal shifts," she said, her voice brimming with excitement. "It's theoretical, of course, but combined with Dr. Chen's work on quantum entanglement, we might just crack this thing wide open."

Rachel felt a surge of hope as she watched Dr. Patel's enthusiasm spread through the room like wildfire. "That's brilliant, Maya," she breathed, her mind already racing with possibilities. "How soon can you start running simulations?"

"I can have preliminary results by tomorrow morning," Dr. Patel replied, her fingers flying across her tablet. "But we'll need to build a custom quantum computer to handle the complex calculations required for full-scale testing."

Dr. Chen chimed in, his normally reserved demeanor giving way to unbridled enthusiasm. "I know just the person who can help us with that. An old colleague from MIT—brilliant with hardware design."

As the scientists around her began to brainstorm, their voices overlapping in a cacophony of ideas and theories, Rachel felt a tremor of both excitement and trepidation run through her. We're really doing this, she thought, her heart pounding. We're about to rewrite the laws of physics as we know them.

"Hold on," Dr. Harmon's stern voice cut through the chatter. "Before we get carried away, we need to establish clear ethical guidelines. The implications of this research are staggering—we can't afford to be reckless."

Rachel nodded, grateful for his cautionary tone. "You're absolutely right, Jesse. We'll need to proceed with the utmost care and consideration. Dr. Lee, would you be willing to head up an ethics committee to oversee our work?"

Dr. Lee smiled warmly, his gentle demeanor a stark contrast to the intensity of the conversation. "Of course, Rachel. We'll need to tread carefully, balancing our pursuit of knowledge with the potential consequences of our actions."

As the meeting continued late into the night, Rachel found herself both exhilarated and terrified by the enormity of what they were undertaking. The mysteries of the multiverse beckoned, promising untold discoveries and unimaginable dangers. With this brilliant team by her side, she felt ready to face whatever lay ahead in the vast, uncharted territories of alternate timelines.

9 - 10

Rachel's eyes darted between her colleagues, their faces illuminated by the harsh glow of computer screens. The lab hummed with tension as Dr. Chen's voice cut through the silence.

"We've got a problem," he said, his normally calm demeanor tinged with urgency. "Someone's been probing our security protocols. I think we've been compromised."

Rachel's stomach clenched. "How bad is it, Marcus?" she asked, leaning forward.

Dr. Chen's fingers flew across his keyboard. "Bad enough. They haven't breached our core systems yet, but they're getting close. And I'm detecting similar attempts from multiple sources."

Dr. Patel interjected, her voice tight with concern. "Could it be rival research groups? Or worse, government agencies?"

"Both, potentially," Rachel murmured, her mind racing. She turned to Dr. Harmon, who stood silently observing. "Jesse, what's your take on this?"

Dr. Harmon's stern features hardened. "We're treading dangerous waters here, Rachel. The ethical implications alone are staggering. If our research falls into the wrong hands..."

"I know," Rachel nodded, feeling the weight of responsibility settle on her shoulders. "But we can't stop now. We're too close to a breakthrough."

Dr. Lee, ever the voice of reason, spoke up. "Perhaps we should consider bringing in outside help? A neutral party to oversee our work and ensure its integrity?"

Rachel pondered this, her thoughts a whirlwind of possibilities and potential consequences. The power to reshape history, to rewrite the future – it was intoxicating, but terrifying in equal measure.

"No," she decided finally, her voice firm. "We keep this in-house. Tighten security, implement new protocols. We press on, but with extreme caution."

As her team nodded in agreement, Rachel felt a surge of determination. They were walking a razor's edge between scientific triumph and potential catastrophe, but the promise of unlocking the secrets of alternate timelines was too tantalizing to abandon.

"Let's get back to work," she said, her eyes gleaming with resolve. "The multiverse is waiting for us."

11 - 11

Rachel turned back to the holographic display, her fingers dancing across the interface as she manipulated complex equations and multidimensional models. The air in the lab crackled with tension and anticipation.

"Dr. Summers," Dr. Chen's voice cut through the silence, his tone laced with a mix of awe and trepidation. "I think you should see this."

Rachel hurried over to his workstation, her heart pounding. "What is it, Marcus?"

Dr. Chen's eyes were wide behind his glasses. "I've been running simulations based on our latest data, and... well, look."

The screen before them flickered to life, displaying a dizzying array of intersecting timelines and quantum probabilities. Rachel leaned in, her breath catching in her throat as she absorbed the implications.

"My God," she whispered. "Are you saying that..."

"Yes," Dr. Chen nodded gravely. "Our attempts to manipulate alternate timelines aren't just affecting parallel worlds. They're causing ripples across the entire multiverse."

Dr. Patel joined them, her brow furrowed with concern. "But that's impossible. The energy required to influence multiple realities simultaneously would be..."

"Incalculable," Rachel finished, her mind reeling. "Unless..."

She trailed off, a chilling realization dawning on her. The room seemed to spin as she grappled with the enormity of what they'd stumbled upon.

"Unless what, Rachel?" Dr. Patel pressed, her voice tinged with urgency.

Rachel swallowed hard, her throat suddenly dry. "Unless we've tapped into something far more powerful and fundamental than we ever imagined. Something that underpins the very fabric of existence itself."

The silence that followed was deafening. Rachel could feel the weight of her team's gazes upon her, a mixture of fear and excitement palpable in the air.

"What do we do now?" Dr. Chen asked, his voice barely above a whisper.

Rachel straightened, her jaw set with determination. "We proceed with extreme caution. This changes everything we thought we knew about the nature of reality. The potential for both discovery and disaster is... unimaginable."

As she spoke, a nagging doubt gnawed at the edges of her consciousness. Had they gone too far? Were they meddling with forces beyond their comprehension?

"Team," she addressed the room, her voice steady despite her inner turmoil. "We're standing on the precipice of something monumental. But we must remember that with great power comes great responsibility. From this moment on, we move forward with the utmost care and consideration for the consequences of our actions."

Little did Rachel know that her words would prove prophetic in ways she could never have anticipated. For in their relentless pursuit of knowledge, they had set in motion events that would challenge not just their understanding of the universe, but the very foundations of reality itself.

Tendrils of Pain

Blue World – 2024

1 - 2

Linda's eyes fluttered open as an unsettling warmth radiated from the wound on her hand, spreading through her body like tendrils of electricity. She flexed her fingers, wincing at the lingering ache. "It's nothing," she whispered to herself, her soothing voice a stark contrast to the unease churning in her stomach. "Just stress. It has to be."

As she settled back against the cool pillows, Linda's thoughts drifted to Drake, worry etching lines across her forehead. "I hope he's sleeping peacefully," she murmured, her maternal instincts kicking in even as exhaustion tugged at her consciousness. The events of the past few days played through her mind like a fractured film reel, disjointed and haunting.

Sleep finally claimed her, but instead of respite, Linda found herself plunged into a dreamscape of swirling shadows and half-formed memories. She stumbled through a vast, undulating darkness, her bare feet sinking into ground that felt both solid and ephemeral.

"Hello?" Linda called out, her normally calm voice tinged with fear. "Is anyone there?"

Whispers surrounded her, a cacophony of indistinct voices that seemed to emanate from the very air itself. Linda spun around, her long blonde hair whipping about her face as she tried to locate the source. "Please," she pleaded, "I don't understand. What's happening?"

From the corner of her eye, Linda caught glimpses of shadowy figures darting just beyond her field of vision. Her heart raced, pounding a frantic rhythm against her ribs. "Drake?" she called out, hoping against hope to see her son's familiar face. "Harrison?"

But the figures remained elusive, their forms shifting and melting back into the darkness before she could focus on them. Linda's empathetic nature, usually a source of strength, now left her overwhelmed by the raw emotions permeating this strange dreamworld.

"I have to wake up," Linda told herself, squeezing her eyes shut and willing herself back to reality. "This isn't real. It can't be real." But when she opened her eyes, the surreal landscape remained, stretching endlessly in all directions.

A memory flashed before her – Drake's laughter echoing through their home, a sound she hadn't heard in what felt like an eternity. "My sweet boy," Linda whispered, tears welling in her eyes. "What's happened to us?"

As she continued to wander, more fragmented images assaulted her senses: Harrison's kind smile, now tinged with an otherworldly sadness; the amusement park where her family had shared so many joyful moments, now twisted and decaying in her mind's eye.

"This has to mean something," Linda muttered, her analytical mind struggling to make sense of the dreamscape even as fear threatened to overwhelm her. "But what? What are you trying to tell me?"

The whispers grew louder, more insistent, but still maddeningly incomprehensible. Linda clasped her hands over her ears, her fingers brushing against the wound that had started this strange journey. "Please," she begged, her voice cracking with emotion, "I just want to understand. I want to help my family. Tell me how to fix this!"

But the dream offered no answers, only more questions as Linda continued to wander through the vast, shadowy landscape, searching for a truth that remained frustratingly out of reach.

3 - 4

Linda stumbled forward, her feet sinking into the soft, ashen ground as she approached the ruins of the once-vibrant amusement park. The Ferris wheel, now a skeletal silhouette against the inky sky, creaked ominously in a non-existent wind. Twisted metal and shattered remnants of carnival games littered the desolate landscape, casting long, grotesque shadows that seemed to reach for her with gnarled fingers.

"Drake?" Linda called out, her voice trembling. "Harrison? Are you here?"

As she ventured deeper into the decaying park, memories flooded her mind – Drake's booming laughter as he won a stuffed animal for Harrison, the boy's eyes sparkling with delight as he bit into a cloud of cotton candy. Now, those happy scenes felt like relics from another lifetime, tainted by the oppressive darkness surrounding her.

"This can't be real," Linda whispered to herself, her heart racing. "It's just a dream. It has to be."

But even as she tried to reassure herself, a flicker of otherworldly light caught her attention. There, in the center of the ruined park, stood a familiar figure bathed in an ethereal glow. Linda's breath caught in her throat as she recognized Drake, but not as she remembered him.

"Drake?" she called out, her voice barely above a whisper.

As she drew closer, Linda could see that Drake's eyes blazed with an unearthly light, his gaze fixed on something beyond her comprehension. When he spoke, his voice echoed strangely, as if coming from everywhere and nowhere at once.

"Linda," Drake said, his tone filled with a mixture of sorrow and urgency. "I've been trying to reach you."

Linda reached out to touch him, but her hand passed through his form like smoke. "What's happening, Drake? Where's Harrison? Why are we here?"

Drake's expression twisted with pain. "I don't have much time. The accident... it changed everything. We're trapped, Linda. All of us. And I don't know how to fix it."

As Linda struggled to process his words, the ground beneath them began to tremble, and the ruins of the amusement park seemed to shift and warp around them. "Drake, please," she pleaded, tears streaming down her face. "I don't understand. How can I help you? How can I save our family?"

5 - 6

"Linda," he said, his voice echoing through the darkness. "You shouldn't be here." Drake's words hung in the air, heavy with an otherworldly resonance that sent chills down Linda's spine. His ethereal form seemed to flicker and waver, as if struggling to maintain its presence in this surreal dreamscape.

Linda's heart raced, her maternal instincts kicking into overdrive despite the bizarre circumstances. She opened her mouth to speak, to cry out, to demand answers about Harrison's whereabouts and what was happening to their family. But as she tried to form the words, her voice caught in her throat, strangled by an unseen force.

Panic rising in her chest, Linda attempted to move towards Drake, to embrace her husband and never let go. But her body refused to cooperate. It felt as if she were wading through thick, viscous molasses, her limbs heavy and unresponsive. The harder she fought against this invisible restraint, the more exhausted she became.

'What's happening to me?' Linda thought, her mind reeling as she struggled to make sense of the situation. 'Why can't I speak? Why can't I move?' The frustration and fear threatened to overwhelm her, but she clung to her deep-rooted strength, the same resilience that had carried her through countless hardships.

Drake's glowing eyes softened with a mixture of concern and resignation as he watched his mother's struggle. "Linda," he said, his voice softer now but still carrying that eerie echo. "I know you want to help, but you can't stay. It's not safe."

Linda's thoughts raced, desperately trying to convey her love, her worry, her determination to save her family. 'Drake, please,' she pleaded silently. 'Don't push me away. Let me help you. Let me understand.'

As if hearing her unspoken words, Drake's form shimmered and began to fade. "I'm sorry, Lin," he whispered, his voice growing fainter. "We love you. Remember that."

Summoning every ounce of her willpower, Linda fought against the paralyzing force holding her back. She had to reach him, had to keep him from disappearing again. But her efforts were in vain, and she could only watch helplessly as her son's ethereal form dissolved into the darkness of the ruined amusement park.

7 - 8

Drake reached out to her, his hand glowing with an ethereal light that cast long, flickering shadows across the desolate landscape of the ruined amusement park. "Listen to me, Linda," he said, his voice urgent and tinged with a desperation that sent chills down her spine. "You have to wake up. You're in danger."

Linda's heart raced, her maternal instincts screaming at her to protect her husband, to shield him from whatever unseen threat loomed in this nightmarish realm. She struggled against the invisible force holding her in place, her thoughts a whirlwind of confusion and determination. 'What danger? How can I help you, Drake?' she wanted to cry out, but her voice remained trapped in her throat.

"Lin, please," Drake pleaded, his eyes – so like his son's – filled with a mix of love and fear. "You don't understand what's happening. This place, it's not what you think. It's-"

But before he could finish, a deafening roar tore through the air, drowning out his words. The ground beneath Linda's feet began to tremble, softly at first, then with increasing violence. She stumbled, her arms flailing as she fought to keep her balance in this shifting dreamscape.

"Drake!" Linda finally managed to cry out as she fell, her voice barely audible above the cacophony of destruction around them. The world spun, a dizzying kaleidoscope of twisted metal and crumbling concrete. Through it all, she could see Drake reaching for her, his glowing form a beacon in the chaos.

'I can't lose him again,' Linda thought desperately, stretching out her hand to grasp his. 'I won't let this world tear us apart. Not again.' But as their fingers were about to touch, a blinding flash of light erupted between them, and Linda felt herself falling, falling, falling...

9 - 10

Linda's eyes snapped open, her heart thundering in her chest as she bolted upright in bed. The darkness of her room enveloped her, a stark contrast to the vivid nightmare that still clung to the edges of her consciousness. She drew in a shaky breath, her hands trembling as she pushed sweat-dampened hair from her face.

"Drake," she whispered into the emptiness, her voice hoarse and barely audible. The silence that answered her felt oppressive, a reminder of the void left by her husband's absence. Linda closed her eyes, trying to calm her racing thoughts. 'It was just a dream,' she told herself, 'but it felt so real.'

As the adrenaline began to ebb, Linda swung her legs over the side of the bed. The cool floorboards beneath her feet grounded her, pulling her fully back into reality. She glanced at the clock – 5:47 AM. Too early to start the day, but sleep now seemed impossible.

"Might as well make use of this time," she murmured, pushing herself to her feet. The house needed cleaning, a task she'd been putting off. Perhaps the monotony of housework would help quiet the tumult in her mind.

Hours later, as afternoon sunlight streamed through the windows, Linda found herself on her knees, scrubbing at a stubborn stain on the living room carpet. She paused, wincing as a sharp pain lanced through her left palm. Turning her hand over, she was surprised to see a thin cut across her palm, angry and red.

"That's odd," she said, frowning at the wound. "When did I...?" Her words trailed off as a chill ran down her spine. The dream from last night flashed through her mind – the ruins of the amusement park, Drake's glowing form, the violent shaking. Had she somehow injured herself in her sleep?

Linda shook her head, trying to dispel the unsettling thought. "Don't be ridiculous," she chided herself. "It's probably just from all this cleaning."

As she resumed her scrubbing, a flash of red caught her eye. Linda's breath caught in her throat as she recognized the dark stain on the carpet – blood. Drake's blood. Memories of that terrible night flooded back – the gunshot, Drake's pale face, the frantic rush to the hospital.

"Oh, Drake," Linda whispered, her voice thick with emotion. "What's happening to us?" She reached out to touch the stain, her fingers hovering just above the carpet. In that moment, she could have sworn she saw the blood move, shifting ever so slightly towards her outstretched hand.

11 - 12

Linda blinked hard, convinced her eyes were playing tricks on her. But as she leaned in closer, scrub brush clutched tightly in her trembling hand, the impossible became undeniable. The blood stain rippled and writhed, defying all logic as it began to crawl across the carpet fibers towards her.

"No, no, no," Linda muttered, her voice rising in pitch as panic set in. "This can't be happening."

She tried to pull away, but it was as if an invisible force held her in place. The blood, now a sentient, pulsing mass, surged forward with terrifying speed. Before Linda could even process what was happening, it latched onto her skin, the viscous liquid seeping into the cut on her palm with an audible hiss.

A scream built in Linda's throat as she felt the blood – Drake's blood – being absorbed into her body. It burned like fire, spreading outward from the wound and racing up her arm. Her vision swam, the room tilting and spinning around her.

"What the hell was that?" she gasped, stumbling backward and collapsing against the wall. Linda stared at her hand in horror, watching as the cut sealed itself, leaving behind only a faint, silvery scar. Her mind reeled, unable to comprehend what she had just witnessed.

"Drake," she whispered, her voice barely audible. "What's happening to me? What have you done?"

13 - 13

Exhaustion suddenly hit Linda like a tidal wave, her limbs turning to lead as she struggled to remain upright. She pushed herself away from the wall, her legs wobbling beneath her as she took unsteady steps towards the bedroom.

"I need to lie down," she mumbled, her words slurring slightly. "Just need to... rest my eyes for a moment."

As Linda shuffled past the kitchen, a flicker of movement caught her peripheral vision. She blinked hard, trying to clear the fog from her mind, and turned her head.

There, standing by the counter, was Harrison.

"Harrison?" Linda gasped, her heart leaping into her throat. "But how—"

Her son stood motionless, his curly hair tousled as if he'd just woken up. His bright eyes, usually so full of mischief, stared blankly ahead. Linda reached out, her fingers trembling as she tried to touch him.

"Sweetie, is that really you?" she whispered, tears welling in her eyes.

Just as her hand was about to make contact, a brilliant white light erupted around Harrison's form. Linda recoiled, shielding her eyes from the blinding glare.

"Mom?" Harrison's voice echoed, sounding distant and distorted. "I don't understand what's happening. Where am I?"

Linda lowered her arm, squinting against the fading light. "Harrison, wait! Don't go!"

But it was too late. The light engulfed him completely, growing brighter and brighter until Linda had to look away. When she opened her eyes again, the kitchen was empty.

"No," Linda whimpered, her legs finally giving out as she sank to the floor. "Not again. I can't lose you both."

She pressed her palms against her temples, trying to make sense of what she'd just witnessed. Was it real? A hallucination brought on by stress and exhaustion? Or something far more sinister?

"Drake," she called out weakly, her voice cracking. "If you can hear me, please... I need you. I don't understand what's happening, and I'm scared."

The silence that answered her was deafening.

Vanishing Blood

Blue World – 2024

1 - 1

Dr. Charles Lee leaned over the laboratory bench, his brow furrowed in concentration as he peered through the microscope at Drake's blood sample. The ruby-red liquid swirled lazily in the glass vial, seemingly ordinary yet holding untold secrets. As he adjusted the focus, Dr. Lee's normally calm demeanor was tinged with an edge of excitement.

"Fascinating," he murmured, his soft voice barely audible over the hum of lab equipment. "The cellular structure is unlike anything I've ever seen before."

Dr. Ramirez stood nearby, arms crossed as she observed her colleague's work. "What exactly are we looking at here, Charles?" he asked, his tone sharp with curiosity.

Dr. Lee straightened, rubbing his eyes before turning to face Dr. Ramirez. "It's difficult to say with certainty. The blood cells appear to be in a constant state of flux, almost as if they're... adapting in real-time."

As Dr. Ramirez opened her mouth to reply, a deafening explosion rocked the building, sending tremors through the floor and rattling the delicate lab equipment. Both doctors instinctively ducked, their eyes wide with shock.

In that moment of chaos, Dr. Lee's gaze was drawn back to the vial of blood. To his astonishment, it began to emit a soft, pulsating glow, growing brighter with each passing second. The crimson liquid within transformed, taking on an otherworldly, pearlescent sheen.

"Look!" Dr. Lee exclaimed, his usual composure shattered by the inexplicable sight before him. "The blood... it's changing!"

Dr. Ramirez whirled around, her stern features softening into an expression of awe as she witnessed the phenomenon. "Impossible," she breathed, reaching out a hand as if to touch the vial.

Before either could react further, the glowing vial suddenly vanished in a flash of brilliant white light, leaving behind nothing but an empty space on the lab bench and the lingering scent of ozone.

As the echoes of the explosion faded, replaced by distant sirens and panicked shouts, Dr. Lee found himself grappling with a chilling realization. "My God," he whispered, his kind eyes wide with horror. "What have we unleashed?"

Dr. Ramirez jaw clenched, her analytical mind already racing to process the implications of what they'd just witnessed. "I fear, Charles," she said gravely, "that we may have stumbled upon something far beyond our comprehension. Something that could change everything we thought we knew about the human condition."

As the two doctors stood in stunned silence, the weight of their discovery settled upon them like a heavy shroud, mingling with the acrid smell of smoke and the growing certainty that nothing would ever be the same again.

Back to the Apocalypse

Apocalypse World – 20 A.C

1 - 2

Harrison's eyes fluttered open, immediately assaulted by the harsh glare of a sickly yellow sun hanging low in a hazy sky. The acrid taste of ash coated his tongue as he drew in a ragged breath, his lungs protesting against the gritty air. Sprawled on his back, he felt the rough texture of cracked earth beneath him, jagged bits of debris digging into his skin through tattered clothes.

"What the..." he muttered, voice hoarse and unfamiliar to his own ears. Pushing himself up on trembling arms, Harrison's gaze swept across the nightmarish landscape stretching endlessly before him. Skeletal remnants of skyscrapers loomed in the distance like rotting teeth, their once-gleaming surfaces now dull and pockmarked.

A chill ran down his spine as an eerie sense of déjà vu washed over him. "I've been here before," he whispered, brow furrowing in confusion. "But how? When?"

Memories flickered at the edges of his consciousness, hazy and indistinct like faded photographs. Streets teeming with life, laughter echoing off gleaming glass and steel – a stark contrast to the desolate wasteland surrounding him now. Harrison shook his head, trying to clear the cobwebs from his mind.

"Get it together, Miller," he chided himself, struggling to his feet on unsteady legs. "This isn't real. It can't be real."

But the gritty texture of sand between his fingers felt all too tangible as he brushed himself off. The acrid stench of decay and ruin assaulted his nostrils, making his eyes water. In the distance, a gust of wind stirred up a small dust devil, sending it spinning across the barren plain.

Harrison's cocky teenage bravado faltered as the full weight of his situation began to sink in. "Okay, so maybe it is real," he admitted, voice wavering slightly. "But how did I get here? And more importantly, how do I get back?"

His vivid imagination, usually a source of comfort and endless adventure, now worked against him. Visions of mutant creatures lurking in the shadows of crumbling buildings flashed through his mind. What horrors might be waiting for him in this post-apocalyptic nightmare?

"Focus, Harrison," he muttered, clenching his fists at his sides. "There's got to be a way out of this. There's always a way out in your stories, right?"

But as he stood there, alone and exposed in the vast emptiness, Harrison couldn't shake the feeling that this time, there might not be a happy ending waiting for him.

3 - 4

Harrison's eyes darted across the desolate landscape, searching for any sign of life or movement. Suddenly, a realization struck him with the force of a physical blow. "Dad," he whispered, his voice a mixture of hope and dread. "He's out there somewhere. I can feel it."

The young boy's posture straightened, his trademark mischievous grin replaced by a look of grim determination. "Alright, universe," he declared, raising his voice to the empty sky, "if you're going to throw me into some post-apocalyptic hellscape, the least you could do is give me a clue where to start looking!"

As if in response, a cold wind whipped through the ruins, carrying with it the faint echo of a familiar voice. Harrison's head snapped towards the sound, his curly hair dancing wildly in the breeze. "Dad?" he called out, his heart racing. "Is that you?"

With renewed purpose, Harrison took his first tentative steps into the unknown. His sneakers crunched against the parched earth, kicking up small clouds of dust with each movement. "I don't know where I'm going," he muttered to himself, "but I know I've got to try. Dad needs me."

As he walked, Harrison couldn't help but marvel at the surreal landscape around him. "Man, if the guys at school could see this," he chuckled nervously, his voice tinged with a mix of awe and fear. "They'd never believe it. Heck, I'm not sure I believe it myself."

His eyes scanned the horizon, searching for any landmark or sign that might guide him towards his father. The ruins of skyscrapers loomed in the distance like ancient monoliths, silent sentinels watching over this dead world. Harrison swallowed hard, pushing down the rising tide of fear threatening to overwhelm him. "Just one step at a time," he coached himself. "You've got this, Harrison. Dad's counting on you."

5 - 6

As Harrison trudged forward, the desolate landscape seemed to blur and shift, merging with vivid memories of his childhood. The cracked pavement beneath his feet transformed into lush grass, and for a moment, he could almost feel the warmth of the sun on his face as it had been on countless summer days in the park.

"Remember when we used to play catch here, Dad?" Harrison whispered, his voice thick with emotion. He could almost see his father's proud smile, hear the satisfying thwack of the ball hitting his glove. "You always said I had a killer arm."

The memory faded as quickly as it had appeared, leaving Harrison feeling hollow. He shook his head, trying to dispel the bittersweet thoughts. "Focus, Harrison," he muttered to himself. "You can't get lost in the past. Dad needs you now."

But even as he tried to push the memories away, darker thoughts crept in. The warmth of those happy days gave way to a cold, gnawing feeling in the pit of his stomach. "Why did you leave, Dad?" he found himself asking the empty air. "Was it something I did? Something I didn't do?"

Harrison's steps faltered as the weight of abandonment threatened to crush him. He clenched his fists, nails digging into his palms. "No," he said firmly, his voice echoing in the emptiness. "I can't think like that. There has to be a reason. There has to be."

With a deep breath, Harrison straightened his shoulders and picked up his pace. "I'm coming, Dad," he called out, his voice a mix of determination and desperate hope. "Whatever happened, whatever kept us apart, we'll figure it out together. I promise."

As he marched forward, Harrison's eyes darted from one ruined building to another, searching for any sign of his father. "He has to be here somewhere," he muttered, his teenage bravado masking the fear that threatened to overwhelm him. "And when I find him, I'll... I'll..."

Harrison's voice trailed off as he realized he didn't know how to finish that sentence. What would he say when he finally found his father? What could possibly bridge the years of silence and absence?

"One step at a time," he reminded himself, echoing his earlier words. "Find him first. The rest... the rest we'll figure out together."

7 - 8

The merciless sun bore down on Harrison, its relentless heat sapping his strength with each laborious step. Sweat trickled down his face, stinging his eyes and leaving salty trails on his sunburned cheeks. He stumbled, catching himself on a jagged piece of concrete protruding from the sand.

"Come on, Harrison," he muttered through cracked lips, his cocky facade crumbling under the weight of exhaustion. "You've got this. Just... just keep moving."

His legs trembled as he pushed himself upright, muscles screaming in protest. The vast expanse of sand stretched endlessly before him, a sea of golden misery that seemed to mock his every effort. Harrison's mind wandered, seeking refuge from the physical torment.

"Remember when Dad taught you to swim?" he asked himself, a wry smile twisting his parched lips. "Said you were as stubborn as a mule but twice as determined. Guess some things never change, huh?"

As he trudged onward, Harrison's keen eyes scanned the horizon, searching for any sign of life or shelter. The monotony of the landscape was broken only by the occasional jutting remnant of the world that once was.

"What I wouldn't give for one of those stupid protein bars Mom always packed," he groaned, his stomach twisting with hunger. "Or maybe just a cold Coke. Hell, I'd even settle for a warm one at this point."

Just as despair threatened to overtake him, a silhouette emerged from the shimmering heat waves. Harrison squinted, his heart rate quickening. "No way," he breathed, quickening his pace despite the protestations of his weary body. "It can't be..."

As he drew closer, the outline sharpened into a familiar shape. Half-buried in sand, its once-imposing facade now crumbling and weather-beaten, stood the old courthouse. Harrison's eyes widened in disbelief.

"Holy crap," he whispered, memories flooding back. "Dad used to bring me here. We'd play on the steps, pretend we were lawyers arguing cases." A lump formed in his throat as he approached the dilapidated structure. "This has to mean something. He has to be close."

Harrison placed a trembling hand on the worn stone, feeling a connection to his past and, he hoped, a link to his future. "I'm here, Dad," he called out, his voice echoing off the ruins. "If you can hear me, I'm here. And I'm not giving up until I find you."

9 - 10

Harrison's heart pounded in his chest as he rounded the corner of the courthouse, his eyes scanning frantically for any sign of movement. The anticipation was almost unbearable, his body thrumming with a mixture of hope and fear.

"Dad?" he called out, his voice cracking with emotion. "Dad, are you here?"

And then, like a mirage materializing in the desert, he saw him. Standing alone in the shadow of the courthouse, his father's silhouette was unmistakable. Harrison's breath caught in his throat as he stumbled forward, his exhaustion forgotten in an instant.

"Dad!" he shouted, his voice a mixture of relief and disbelief. "Oh my God, Dad, is that really you?"

As Harrison drew closer, he could make out the details of his father's face. It was worn and haggard, lined with years of hardship, but unmistakably alive. His father's eyes, once so bright and full of life, now held a haunted look that sent a chill down Harrison's spine.

"Harrison?" his father's voice was barely above a whisper, rough with disuse. "Is it... is it really you, son?"

Harrison closed the distance between them in a few quick strides, throwing his arms around his father's frail form. "It's me, Dad. I found you. I can't believe I finally found you."

As they embraced, Harrison couldn't shake the feeling that something was off. His father's body felt too thin, too fragile in his arms. And there was a scent, something he couldn't quite place, that made the hairs on the back of his neck stand up.

"I've been searching for so long," Harrison said, pulling back to look into his father's eyes. "What happened to you? Where have you been all this time?"

His father's gaze seemed to flicker for a moment, a shadow passing across his face. "It's... it's a long story, son. But we're together now. That's all that matters."

Harrison nodded, trying to ignore the nagging feeling in the pit of his stomach. He was so close to answers, so close to understanding what had torn his family apart. But as he stood there in the shadow of the courthouse, with his father's frail form before him, he couldn't shake the sense that he was standing on the edge of something far more terrifying than he could have ever imagined.

11 - 12

As Harrison's eyes adjusted to the shadows, a horrifying realization dawned on him. The face before him, once so familiar and comforting, began to morph and distort. The weathered lines of his father's visage melted away, revealing a grotesque visage of burn scars and twisted flesh. His heart plummeted as recognition set in, and he stumbled backward, his voice catching in his throat.

"No... it can't be... you're supposed to be locked up!" Harrison choked out, his teenage bravado crumbling in the face of this nightmarish apparition.

A chilling smile spread across the disfigured face of Gabriel Angel, his piercing eyes gleaming with malevolent amusement. "Hello, Harrison!" he said, his smooth voice a stark contrast to his horrific appearance. "Did you miss me? I must say, your devotion to finding your father is quite touching. It almost makes me wish I hadn't... well, let's not spoil the surprise, shall we?"

Harrison's mind raced, grappling with the implications of Gabriel's presence. "What have you done with my dad?" he demanded, trying to mask his fear with anger. "Where is he?"

Gabriel tilted his head, regarding Harrison with a mixture of curiosity and condescension. "Now, now, young Harrison. Don't you think that's a rather simplistic question? Your father's whereabouts are but a small piece of a much grander puzzle. One that you've unwittingly stumbled into, I'm afraid."

As Gabriel spoke, Harrison's eyes darted around, searching for an escape route. But the desolate landscape offered no sanctuary, no haven from this nightmare made flesh. His thoughts turned to the last time he'd seen Gabriel, supposedly being led away in chains. How had he escaped? And what twisted game was he playing now?

"I don't understand," Harrison said, his voice cracking. "Why are you here? What do you want from me?"

Gabriel's laugh echoed off the crumbling walls of the courthouse, a sound that sent shivers down Harrison's spine. "What I want, dear boy, is for you to open your eyes. To see the world as it truly is, not as you wish it to be. Your father... well, let's just say he played his part in bringing us to this moment."

Harrison's fists clenched at his sides, a surge of protective anger cutting through his fear. "Don't you dare talk about my dad like that! He's a good man, he would never-"

"Never what?" Gabriel interrupted, his voice sharp. "Never make a deal with forces beyond his understanding? Never sacrifice everything for a chance at power? Oh, Harrison, your naivety is almost endearing. Almost."

As Gabriel's words sank in, Harrison felt the ground beneath him shift, reality itself seeming to warp and bend. He closed his eyes, desperately wishing he could wake up from this nightmare. But when he opened them again, Gabriel was still there, his grotesque visage a stark reminder that some nightmares are all too real.

13 - 13

Gabriel's lips curled into a cruel smile as he took a step closer to Harrison, his limp barely noticeable on the uneven ground. "Welcome back to my world," he said, his voice dripping with a malevolent satisfaction that made Harrison's skin crawl.

Harrison stumbled backward, his heart racing. "Your world? What are you talking about? This isn't real, it can't be!"

Gabriel chuckled, a sound devoid of any warmth. "Oh, but it is, Harrison. More real than you can possibly imagine. The desolation you see around you? The ruins of civilization? This is the future you helped create."

"No," Harrison whispered, shaking his head in denial. "I didn't... I wouldn't..."

"But you did," Gabriel pressed, his piercing gaze never leaving Harrison's face. "Every choice, every decision you've made has led us here. And now, you get to witness the fruits of your labor."

As Gabriel spoke, the landscape seemed to shift and morph, the ruins of the courthouse fading away to reveal a vast, barren wasteland stretching as far as the eye could see. Harrison's mind reeled, trying to make sense of what he was seeing.

"This isn't possible," he muttered, more to himself than to Gabriel. "How can I be responsible for... for all of this?"

Gabriel's smile widened, revealing teeth that seemed unnaturally sharp. "That, my dear boy, is the question you'll have to answer for yourself. But make no mistake, this world - my world - is as much your creation as it is mine."

Harrison's thoughts raced, memories and doubts colliding in a chaotic whirlwind. What had he done? How could his actions have led to this apocalyptic nightmare?

As if reading his thoughts, Gabriel leaned in close, his breath hot against Harrison's ear. "The path to hell is paved with good intentions, Harrison. And you, my boy, have been laying down bricks for years."

The Red World

1 - 2

Drake's eyes fluttered open, the harsh fluorescent lights searing his retinas like white-hot needles. He squinted against the assault, his head pounding with each throb of his pulse. The sterile scent of antiseptic burned his nostrils as he became aware of the tubes and wires snaking across his body, tethering him to the hospital bed like a marionette.

"Linda? Harrison?" he croaked, his throat raw and parched.

No response came, only the steady beep of monitors and the whoosh of oxygen. Drake's gaze darted around the stark white room, searching for any sign of his family. Panic began to claw at his chest, constricting his breathing.

"Where am I? What happened?" he muttered, more to himself than anyone else.

As if triggered by his words, memories crashed over him like a tidal wave. The frantic phone call. The terror in Linda's voice. The mad dash through crowded streets. The ticking clock. The deafening explosion that tore through the air.

Drake's heart raced, the monitor beside him beeping more rapidly. "No, no, no," he whispered, squeezing his eyes shut. "It can't be real. They have to be okay."

He tried to push himself up, but his limbs felt leaden, unresponsive. Frustration and fear battled within him as he struggled against his own body's weakness.

"I have to find them," Drake thought desperately. "I can't lose them. Not after everything."

The weight of his past mistakes pressed down on him - the missed dinners, the broken promises, the cases that always seemed more important than family. Now, faced with the possibility of losing it all, Drake felt a surge of determination.

"I'll make it right," he vowed silently. "Whatever it takes, I'll fix this. I have to."

But as Drake looked down at his arm, searching for the familiar ribbon that had guided him through parallel worlds, his blood ran cold. The skin was bare, unmarked. Something was terribly, horribly wrong.

"No," he breathed, panic rising like bile in his throat. "This can't be happening. Not here. Not now."

The realization hit him with crushing force - he was trapped. Trapped in a timeline he had fought so hard to escape, with no way back to the family he loved. Drake's anguished cry echoed through the empty room, a sound of pure, unadulterated grief.

3 - 4

The cacophony of beeps and whirs from the surrounding machines crescendo as Drake's heart rate spiked, his chest heaving with ragged breaths. He gripped the cold metal rails of the hospital bed, knuckles turning white as he fought against the wave of dizziness threatening to overwhelm him.

Just then, the door swung open with a soft whoosh, and two figures strode in, their faces etched with concern. Dr. Lee, his kind eyes radiating warmth, approached the bed first, clipboard in hand. Behind him loomed Dr. Harmon, his silver hair gleaming under the harsh fluorescent lights, his expression a mix of stern authority and guarded worry.

"Drake, you're awake," Dr. Lee said, his voice gentle and soothing. He placed a reassuring hand on Drake's trembling shoulder. "How are you feeling?"

Drake's mind raced, a torrent of conflicting memories and emotions threatening to drown him. He opened his mouth to speak, but found his throat dry and raw, the words catching painfully.

"I..." he croaked, his eyes darting between the two doctors. "Where am I? What's happening?"

Dr. Harmon stepped forward, his piercing gaze fixed on Drake. "You've been through quite an ordeal, Mr. Miller," he said, his tone measured and clinical. "We need you to remain calm. Can you do that for us?"

Drake nodded weakly, even as his inner turmoil raged. "My family," he thought desperately. "I need to know about my family." But something held him back from voicing the question aloud, a creeping dread that whispered of truths too painful to face.

5 - 6

Drake's chest tightened, his heart hammering against his ribs as the fragmented memories coalesced into a single, terrifying image. The bomb. The frantic search. The deafening explosion. His eyes widened in panic, and he struggled to sit up, ignoring the sharp pain that lanced through his body.

"What happened?" he rasped, his voice barely above a whisper. "There was a bomb. Where's my wife? My son?" The words tumbled out, each one more desperate than the last, as if by sheer force of will he could make his reality align with the vivid recollections swirling in his mind.

Dr. Lee and Dr. Harmon exchanged a loaded glance, their expressions morphing from concern to something darker, more somber. Drake's stomach churned, a cold dread seeping into his bones. Why weren't they answering? Where was Linda's warm smile, Harrison's infectious laughter?

Dr. Harmon stepped closer, his silver hair catching the harsh fluorescent light. His voice, when he spoke, was gentle but firm, each word measured and precise. "Drake, I need you to listen carefully," he began, his eyes never leaving Drake's face. "You've been in a car accident. There was no bomb."

The words hung in the air, heavy and suffocating. Drake blinked, uncomprehending. No bomb? But he remembered it so clearly - the ticking clock, the frantic search, the heat of the explosion. How could it not be real?

"No," Drake mumbled, shaking his head. "No, that's not... I remember..." His voice trailed off as he struggled to reconcile the conflicting realities warring in his mind. Which was true? Which was the nightmare?

7 - 8

Drake's eyes darted frantically between the two doctors, searching for any sign that this was all some cruel joke. His voice, barely above a whisper, trembled with a mixture of confusion and mounting dread. "No... That can't be... Linda, Harrison..." The names of his beloved wife and son felt like shards of glass in his throat, each syllable cutting deeper as the weight of the situation began to sink in like a lead weight in his chest.

Dr. Lee stepped forward, his kind eyes filled with a sorrowful compassion that made Drake's heart race even faster. The doctor's hand, warm and steady, came to rest on Drake's shoulder. "I'm sorry, Drake," he said softly, his voice carrying the heavy burden of the news he was about to deliver. "They didn't make it."

The world seemed to tilt on its axis, the sterile hospital room spinning around Drake as he struggled to process the doctor's words. His mind rebelled against the information, desperately clinging to the memories of Linda's laugh, of Harrison's small hand in his own.

"No," Drake choked out, his fingers digging into the crisp white sheets. "You're wrong. They can't be... They were just..." He trailed off, unable to complete the thought as fragments of what he believed to be reality clashed violently with this new, unbearable truth.

Dr. Lee's grip on his shoulder tightened slightly, an anchor in the storm of emotions threatening to overwhelm Drake. "I know this is difficult to hear," the doctor said, his tone gentle but firm. "But it's important that we talk about what happened, Drake. Can you tell me the last thing you remember before waking up here?"

Drake closed his eyes, trying to focus through the haze of grief and confusion. "I... I remember a bomb," he said, his voice barely audible. "But you're saying that wasn't real? How can that be? It felt so vivid, so..."

He opened his eyes, meeting Dr. Lee's compassionate gaze. "If there was no bomb, then how... how did they...?" The question hung in the air, unfinished, as Drake found himself unable to speak the words that would make this nightmare a reality.

9 - 10

Drake's vision blurred as tears welled up, hot and stinging, in his eyes. He blinked rapidly, trying to clear his sight, but the tears only fell faster, carving silent tracks down his unshaven cheeks. His chest heaved with suppressed sobs as the full weight of the doctors' words crashed over him like a tidal wave of despair.

"Linda... Harrison..." he whispered, their names a prayer and a lament on his lips. His mind conjured vivid images: Linda's radiant smile on their wedding day, Harrison's infectious laughter as they played in the backyard. Gone. All gone.

Dr. Harmon stepped closer, her voice soft but clear. "Drake, I know this is overwhelming. Is there someone we can call for you? Family or friends who can provide support?"

Drake shook his head, a bitter laugh escaping his lips. "No, I... I pushed them all away. Work was always more important, wasn't it?" He clenched his fists, nails digging into his palms. "And now... now I'd give anything to have that time back."

As if driven by an unseen force, Drake's gaze dropped to his wrist, expecting to see the familiar ribbon that had become his lifeline, his connection to hope. But there was nothing there. Just pale, unmarked skin, mocking him with its emptiness.

"The ribbon," he muttered, more to himself than the doctors. "It's gone. How can it be gone?"

Dr. Lee exchanged a concerned glance with his colleague. "Drake, what ribbon are you referring to? There wasn't any medical bracelet or identification band on you when you were brought in."

Drake's eyes widened, panic rising in his throat. "No, you don't understand. The ribbon was... it was everything. My way back, my chance to fix things, to save them!" His voice rose, edged with desperation. "Without it, I'm trapped here. I can't get back to them!"

11 - 12

Drake's words hung in the air, heavy and incomprehensible to the doctors standing before him. The realization crashed over him like a tidal wave, leaving him gasping for air. This was it - the original timeline, the world he had fought so hard to escape, now his inescapable prison.

Dr. Harmon stepped closer, his brow furrowed with concern. "Drake, I understand you're in shock. The trauma of losing your family-"

"You don't understand!" Drake interjected, his voice raw with emotion. "I've seen them alive, in another world, another time. I've held them, talked to them!" He ran his trembling hands through his disheveled hair, his eyes wild. "And now... now I'm back where it all began, alone and..."

His voice trailed off as the weight of his guilt crashed down upon him. Memories flooded his mind - missed dinners, forgotten anniversaries, the constant refrain of "Daddy's working." He had been so focused on winning, on being the best, that he had lost sight of what truly mattered.

"I did this," Drake whispered, his voice barely audible. "My choices, my priorities... they led us here."

The doctors continued to speak, their voices a distant hum as Drake's mind spiraled. He caught fragments of their conversation - "trauma-induced delusions," "grief counseling," "possible sedation" - but none of it mattered. He was adrift in a sea of despair, the anchor of his alternate lives cruelly ripped away.

"Drake," Dr. Lee's voice cut through the fog, "we're here to help you. But we need you to stay calm and-"

"Calm?" Drake's laugh was hollow, devoid of humor. "How can I be calm when everything I've fought for, everything I've lived for, is gone?" His eyes, once sharp and determined, now held a haunted look. "I've lost them twice now. Do you have any idea what that feels like?"

The room fell silent, the weight of Drake's words hanging in the air. In that moment, surrounded by the sterile walls of the hospital room, Drake Miller felt more alone than he ever had before.

13 - 13

As the crushing weight of reality settled over Drake like a suffocating shroud, he felt a strange numbness creeping through his body, dulling the razor-sharp edges of his grief. He closed his eyes, shutting out the harsh fluorescent lights and the concerned faces of the doctors, willing himself to find some semblance of peace in the darkness behind his eyelids.

"I can't... I can't do this," Drake murmured, his voice cracking with the strain of emotions he could no longer fully process. "Not again. Not here."

Dr. Harmon leaned in, her voice gentle but firm. "Drake, I know this is overwhelming, but we're here to help you through this. You're not alone."

A bitter laugh escaped Drake's lips, his eyes still tightly shut. "Alone? I've never been more alone in my life. You don't understand. I've lived through this before, in another world, another time. I fought so hard to change it, to save them..."

His mind raced, memories of his other lives flashing behind his closed eyelids like a twisted slideshow. The feeling of Linda's hand in his, Harrison's laughter echoing through their home, the weight of the ribbon on his wrist - all gone now, leaving only a gaping void.

"Mr. Miller," Dr. Lee interjected, his tone cautious, "these beliefs about other timelines... they're a coping mechanism. Your mind is trying to protect you from the trauma-"

Drake's eyes snapped open, a fierce intensity burning in them. "You think I don't know the difference between reality and delusion? I've lived lifetimes, doctor. I've seen things you couldn't begin to comprehend."

He struggled to sit up, ignoring the protest of his battered body. "I was a different man before. Ruthless, driven... I put everything aside for my career. But I changed. I fought to become better, to be the husband and father they deserved."

Tears welled up in Drake's eyes, his voice dropping to a whisper. "And now... now I'm back where I started. Alone. With nothing but the knowledge of what I've lost."

The room fell silent, the only sound the steady beep of the heart monitor. Drake closed his eyes once more, retreating into the darkness, searching for any shred of comfort in the void that now surrounded him. In that moment, trapped in a reality he had desperately tried to escape, Drake Miller felt the full weight of his choices, his regrets, and the cruel twist of fate that had brought him back to this point of devastating loss.

Epilogue

1 - 2

Linda's eyes snapped open, her pupils dilating frantically in the pitch-black void that enveloped her. The suffocating darkness pressed against her skin, a crushing weight that threatened to steal the breath from her lungs. Her heart thundered in her chest, each beat reverberating through her body as she struggled to make sense of her surroundings. Panic clawed at her throat, threatening to overwhelm her as she tried to move, only to find her limbs trapped, pinned against her sides by an unyielding force.

"What's happening?" she whispered, her voice trembling in the oppressive silence. "Where am I?"

As Linda's fingers brushed against the smooth, cold surface surrounding her, a chilling realization began to dawn. The confined space, the inability to move, the absolute darkness – it could only mean one thing. Terror washed over her in a violent wave, threatening to drag her under as the horrifying truth crystallized in her mind.

"No, no, no," she gasped, her breath coming in short, ragged bursts. "This can't be happening. I can't be… I'm not…"

With a surge of desperate energy, Linda began to pound her fists against the walls of the coffin, her nails scraping against the unyielding wood. The sound of her frantic struggles echoed in the cramped space, amplifying her terror.

"Help!" she screamed, her voice raw with fear. "Someone, please! I'm alive! I'm in here!"

As she thrashed against her confinement, Linda's mind raced, grasping for any shred of hope or explanation. How had she ended up here? The last thing she remembered was… but no, the memories slipped away like wisps of smoke, leaving only confusion and terror in their wake.

"Drake. Harrison," she whispered, tears streaming down her face as she thought of her son. "I'm so sorry. I can't leave you alone. I have to get out of here."

With renewed determination, Linda pushed against the lid of the coffin, her muscles straining with the effort. But the wood refused to budge, trapping her in its suffocating embrace. As the reality of her situation sank in, a sob escaped her lips, echoing in the silent void that had become her tomb.

3 - 4

As Linda's panic reached a fever pitch, fragmented memories began to crystalize in her mind, sharp and vivid as shattered glass. The letter, its edges stained with crimson, flashed before her eyes. She could see the intricate symbol etched upon it, pulsing with an unholy light that seemed to burn into her retinas even now.

"The blood," she whispered, her voice trembling. "There was so much blood."

Then, unbidden, Gabriel's face swam into focus - his piercing eyes boring into her soul, the grotesque burns marring his features contorting as he spoke. His words, cryptic and chilling, echoed in the confines of her wooden prison:

"You've meddled in affairs beyond your comprehension, Linda. The price for such curiosity is steep."

Linda's breath caught in her throat as she recalled his limping gait, the way he'd circled her like a predator toying with its prey. "No," she croaked, "I didn't know. I didn't mean to-"

Her words dissolved into a scream of pure, primal terror. She thrashed wildly, her fists pounding against the unyielding wood until her knuckles split and bled. "Let me out!" she shrieked, her voice cracking. "Please, God, someone help me!"

But as her cries echoed in the oppressive darkness, Linda knew with sickening certainty that no help was coming. Her throat burned raw from screaming, each breath a labored gasp in the dwindling air. Still, she couldn't stop. To stop was to accept the unacceptable, to surrender to the cold embrace of death that pressed in on all sides.

"Drake," she sobbed, thinking of her son. "I'm so sorry. I should have listened. I should have stayed away from all of this." Her nails scraped futilely against the coffin's interior as she whispered, "Please, forgive me."

5 - 6

As Linda's strength ebbed, her frantic struggles slowed to feeble twitches. The fight drained from her body, replaced by a crushing wave of resignation. Tears streamed down her face, mingling with the sweat and blood that stained her cheeks. In the suffocating darkness, she whispered a final, trembling farewell.

"Harrison, my beautiful boy," she murmured, her voice barely audible. "I'm so sorry I won't be there to see you grow up. To see the wonderful man you'll become." A sob caught in her throat. "Remember how much I love you. Always."

Linda's thoughts drifted to the life she was leaving behind, to the moments she'd never experience again. "I wish... I wish I could feel the sun on my face one last time," she whispered, her words choked with emotion. "To hold my son, to tell him everything will be okay."

Her fingers traced the rough wood above her face, a final, futile caress of the world beyond. "I never thought it would end like this," she said softly, her voice thick with regret. "Alone in the dark, buried alive because of a mystery I couldn't leave alone."

As the last vestiges of hope slipped away, Linda closed her eyes, surrendering to the inevitable. Her breathing slowed, each inhale a struggle in the depleting oxygen. "I'm sorry," she whispered to the void. "I'm so sorry for everything."

In the quiet solitude of her tomb, Linda's consciousness began to fade. Her final thoughts were of Drake, of the life she'd lived, of the regrets that weighed heavy on her soul. As darkness claimed her, Linda's spirit drifted into the abyss, forever lost to the world above.

To Be Continued....

Be on the lookout for Drake Millers next adventure in:
Worlds Collide: Book 2 of the Drake Miller Saga – A World So Cold Novel
| Page